Pledge of the Winter Wolf

ISBN-13: 978-0-578-44789-6 (eBook)

ISBN-13: 978-0-578-49371-8

Library of Congress Control Number: 2019900478

This is a work of Fiction. All the characters and events portrayed in this book are fictional, and any resemblance to real people or incidents is purely coincidental.

Cover Painting by Shelby Thomas

Cover Photographed by Lemonwing Photography

THE BACHMAN LETTER

Dearest Descendent or Whom This May Concern,

Today is May 5th, 2109. I have been dwelling in this place, The Bachman Arcology, since we enacted Final Seal Protocol and took refuge from our broken world. Final Seal came on June 21st, 2084. It was only four days after the Wyoming Caldera eruption that we managed to put the last of those on the guest list within these halls and seal the doors against the elements.

I write this not knowing how many days I have left. My doctor assures me that the end is close so I wanted to give you this final capstone to everything you'll find. I fear you'll judge me when you understand the scope of what we did to accomplish this. That you'll understand the basic math of the logistics and wonder why we couldn't do more.

Before you read further I want you to know who I am. I am a man who loved his children and did this for them and others. I sired Marshall, Teck, and Penelope. I have seen the birth of my grandchildren. The foremost who carries my hope is my grandson Azreal. I hope he'll take over for Penelope and guide his people to great things.

Now I shall address the things you might want to know. I loved Elianna for the kindness she showed me. The Queen of Swords, as she was known, had Alexis at her side when I found her again. This is how I would meet the woman who would be my wife after Elianna would leave to go 'out for milk.'

I have told my wife every day since we came down here that we did the right thing in not chasing after her. That Elianna had found her way home and is working from that place to help her now broken world. [See my journals for my side of that story - See Alexis' journal for hers and the essential pieces I was not present for] I do pray for her precious Aardvark to have been well and that Lord Garth stays strong, at her side, and sees to protecting those who were left behind.

I hope that The Janitors found the Seches family and returned to them the necklace with the story of the heroism of Rolf Seches. That Alec would take heart that his brother Rolf did not die in vain. Penelope has seen to it that The Gingerbread Man, that being the aforementioned Rolf, will be remembered for as long as we stand for his deeds are etched into our history now.

I go to the next life hoping you forgive us for giving all of you amnesia. That the words of the Network and your collected understanding of history will guide you to greater days without corrupting you like it corrupted us. I hope you will understand why we had to become who we have already become down here, and who we felt we needed to make you. I hope you go through the past and thank your stars, if you can see them, that things changed. I trust in the truths of the Protocol Document to guide you. We put a lot of work into that just so you know. It's what helped us dodge 'Colony Collapse' thus far. We are not rats, we are well, and I trust the other twelve Arcologies are well because of it.

We tried. The Global Economy [More reading for you] was in shambles when we started this project. We did it because I led it. We did it because Elianna told me one day my umbrella tactics of dodging rain wouldn't work against more than rain. She was right.

She left us, and I went to work. And on the eve of the work being needed The Gingerbread Man came to us. He saved Alexis, Marshall, Teck, and Penelope at the cost of his life. I gave the medallion he showed me, the one I had given to Elianna, to the Janitors [More reading on the Light Switch And Lock The Door Protocol] so they could find Elianna and give it back. If you should see that disc of alloy and etched miracle? Be kind. The person who stands before you is the descendant of Elianna, the woman who gave *everything* for this family. That is worth the plot of land and the house to put on it I promised her. [And so much more.]

As for those that lived to come with, ten thousand in these halls when Final Seal enacted. For each of the twelve others who succeed? Another ten thousand apiece. Forgive us our short guest list compared to the billions we left behind. Forgive us what the survivors will want to do to you. That's why we packed weapons. We saw difficult times ahead when the doors reopened. Find our hidden caches the families left for you to aid in your rebuilding. We created a grand blueprint to aid you, which I hope will still be viable when you need it. Use as much of it as you can as it was drafted by our greatest, that we could afford.

I just wanted to do the right thing. I know the world will survive out there but I don't know what shape it's going to be in when we reopen the door. If by a miracle the ash doesn't trigger an ice age, it could be an ice age in the hearts of those you meet. I fear they won't be pleased to see you. I fear for your people and their future. I fear what you will have to do when you wake from this slumber. I can hope that they will forget us here under the ash.

But that? You'll know better than I. Take heart descendent, I did this for love. Nothing more - Never Less. Never forget it was for love.

- Asmodai Tammerlane Bachman

RISE AND SHINE
Saturday April 17th, 2133

0.0.0 - 11:01

Bachman Arcology - Doorman's Office

☨ William Bachman
☨ Eldest Son of the Bachman Family

Running his finger across the page of the Instruction Manual he took in the words of the easy to read font. *Had to unseal this manual to start the process, and it's getting done today.* Looking at the readouts of what still worked of the electronics and sensors he steeled his conviction for what lay ahead.

I am going to do this today. No more delays. No more excuses to myself. Mother suspects I am ready to enact Rise and Shine and she has told me that it would not be a bad idea. She can't do it, or she will have to be the one to walk out that door first and she is not ready to face the world.

We can't even confirm it's still there. Contemplating one of the still functioning readouts, *you tell me that the world is a pleasant temperature, but I don't know if you're lying. I am going to go into the unknown with only hope in my heart.*

Turning his attention to the calendar he frowned, *it is unfortunate that we didn't make it to the anniversary benchmark but it is a small price to pay for what needs to be done. So on this day, April seventeenth, as far as I know it to be, I will have to open that door. Condemning those who will write the history books to a disjointed set of dates, times, and durations to embellish into the Foundation Myth.*

Looking over the floor plan of the airlock system, ramp, and final outer seal leading to the sky he found himself hoping each piece of machinery would still be working. *To think we almost made the projected fifty years. I regret I do not have a speech for this moment. If I had an idea of how to write one I would. But a speech would just be raising the hopes of others. A cruel thing to do if I dashed them.*

The whispered intonation of his name brought his attention out of the manual before him, "William?"

Looking up he nodded twice and moved his hand to confirm acknowledgement. *And in this moment of facing her, it seems different.* "Sister."

I watched her grow up chasing after my footsteps. I would charge down an avenue of thought and training, and she would be right behind me. When I faced the choice of Textile Expression she advised me based upon her understanding of me. When Cleo found me after the Albatross Dance, she was the one who told me to not be afraid of my heart. With each passing family member she has only held my hand tighter. And this morning she stands before me in her simple slip dress looking far more docile than our legacy would let on.

Cassiopeia is probably not going to enjoy this, but it has to be done. Looking at the projections from his best on the subject he knew without a doubt that he was embarking on the right thing. *The Arcology isn't going to make it much longer in a way that is life affirming. We are running out of everything and the ability to keep this up. Who would have thought we would survive, knowing what we know about what could have gone wrong. We have done so much to try to stay evolving mentally as we have nowhere else to spend our energy. Upkeep and a million games of cards included.*

This sadly goes beyond our psyches and into the realms of technical failure.

A problem I cannot solve. I can only lead our people to somewhere else to begin the rebuilding.

Her tone felt light and carefree as her words found his troubled center, "what vexes you?"

Now we begin the Seven Veils. How much of this am I going to have to reveal before she is satisfied?

Reaching his hand out he waited for her to take it and wrap her hands around it. Keeping his voice down, "everything sister. The least of which is my growing, and, difficult to control anger."

Holding his hand with her hands, still wrapped from the sparring ring, she smiled an embarrassed smile of empathy. Nodding once she kept her tone level, "acknowledged."

We know that our anger is normal for us. No Bachman handles idleness well. Mother handles it better than we do, but she's had more practice. We are who we are though.

Turning back to the picture of the family, taken on the last Beltane, he nodded with a grim feeling of dedication to the future. *Neither Crane nor Sylvester can help me do this. They will be there for advice, as father and grandfather, but when I do this it will have to be on me. They have done so much to show Cleo how to understand me and this. I have hope from their works. My fathers, my strength, my friends. I hope you see the coming days and take them as honor laid at your feet.*

Turning to the proof of life picture of his Great-Grandfather next to the Seal Complete panel he nodded again. *Great-Grandfather Asmodai was next to the door when they closed it, now it falls on me to open it. As a Bachman it is what has been asked of us. I have the things he has given me to make sure I understand how to do this right. The journals, the diaries, the story of a twisted land and twisted people who all needed a hug and a cup of something cool to drink for some and a cup of something hot for others.*

I can't allow that kind of world to come to pass again. Great-Grandmother, feeling the emotions catch in his chest and freeze his lungs, *a woman with a smile so bright. I sat and saw her life through the evidence she left behind. Her adoration of folk lore and silly animal stories. A woman so beautiful and gentle, and people would do that to her?*

And she was just one of so many.

I have to see a world formed which will safeguard the people in it because they matter. Garden variety, rank and file, the lowest common, even they need to be told they are beautiful.

It's how Elianna saved Alexis. Those opening words of amazement that she was so pretty. The gentleness she showed her. If the world was kinder, if people were kinder, then someone like Elianna would be protecting people as the Order the world needs. Alexis would be cared for in the absence of things dying at home. Nothing is perfect, nothing last forever, but we need to raise our children better. We are going to go out that door and we are going to raise the children of the Blue Sky.

Provided it is still there.

"It's time." *I know what I have to do.*

Furrowing her brow, "for? What is it time for?"

She doesn't understand. I will have to enlighten her. Moving to the doorway he raised a hand gently and motioned to be allowed to pass. "Pardon."

Nodding she stepped back with a smile, "will you explain yourself brother?"

"I will show you." Striding toward the walkway leading to the door he felt a boldness in his step. A strange feeling prowling in his heart spurred him closer to the door. *If no one is brave, who will be brave?*

With a panicked lilt in her voice, "are you going to enact Rise and Shine?"

Standing in the spot the manual had dictated, "yes."

"Does mother know?"

"She does."

"Are you scared?"

Taking a deep breath, "dreadfully. I do not know what waits outside. I do not know if we are going to be walking into a world that will want to see us. Our people have been down here for a bit less than forty-nine years. I have lived in this place for nineteen years. That is a long time for a world to change. Or to die. We have a plan from here though. Rise and Shine will guide us. The Protocol will guide us."

Asking her question with a firmness he was not expecting, "what do I do?"

Feeling the emotional stride in the wake of her encouragement, "you need to step back. I need you to seal the airlock over there. If this opens into a nightmare I want those below to get a choice on what to do."

"And you?"

Looking back, "I must be brave. Pascal's Wager. I bid," pushing the words out as the gravity hit him, "my life."

Moving behind the airlock she frowned at him, "you do know the odds are that even if the world outside is still there that you will be rendered a whimpering fool at the sight of the sky."

"Then I will be the whimpering fool who sees the blue sky first. Come get me when I fall down?"

Watching her move her hand on the control panel next to the door with a sad look on her face, "is this why we are the only two Bachman of our generation?"

Stopping short mentally, he nodded in affirmation, "it is no secret our family has a drive to push risks and is often punished for it."

"You know when the time comes I will give this family an heir."

She has a dedication to this family, that goes above and beyond what our guiding principles say she has to have. "You don't have to suffer through something you do not wish. I can provide the heir."

With the hint of a smile, "how long until our great minds just hold you down, take your seed, and bring forth a bevy of Bachman?"

"Never. The plan says that we either do this as loving parents or we do not do this."

Watching her as she spoke the words he watched a smile bloom, "I would love the child."

"And you would not care for your husband as a partner between the sheets. You do not ache as the rest of us do."

"I know. There are a few who I would ask to help me though, when I'm older. I'm still three years off from the opening of the Reproductive Window. I am sure of them I could have a man that would know I would not ache for them. We would paint together to create the children we would raise together. Give me a few years and I will prepare the next branches of this tree."

She is the better of the two of us. "Then you know some good men."

"Good *Citizens*. We are good Citizens. Citizens of Nowhere."

If we are all Citizens then we are ruled by the same rules. No bits and pieces or exemptions for those of higher rank to pardon extreme transgressions. The system must be fair to all and keep all in check. "Well I am going to give us a *Somewhere*."

"If no one is brave, who will be brave then?"

Seeing that she had paused he took a breath before speaking cautiously, "you seek to know my heart before I open this?"

"I do."

"You are my family, I should not expect less."

"Who are these people you would seek to lead through Rise and Shine?"

Measuring his words he set to answer the tested questions she would bring him. "Family and families of families. We are to each other the one thing we have left. Family. We forgive each other every day so that we can survive and one forgives family because family is what matters. As with every breath I have adored you? I know our people love and trust each other in the wake of the lives we have lived down here. We know empathy because we are not alone. If there is a world out there? I want to lead my family to it and give them a new place to rest their heads."

Speaking with the voice of a Gentle Instructor, "what is this union?"

Fighting against the anger of knowing what he knew of the past, he spoke his words with a borderline righteousness, "the one thing we have left! We are without money, no paper, no numbers, no credit scores, no stocks, no bonds, no trusts, no trust funds, no scholarships. We found the emotional currency of ourselves. We are the bonded souls created by those who came from the ten thousand that came to this place. That generation would raise those who raised us! Without the remembered bias of the broken world that had been left behind. We are educated, we are enlightened, we are mindful, and we are going to go out this door today. We are going to step onto the soil of the world we wish to reclaim."

Switching to the tone of the Firm Instructor, "who are *we* brother?"

"We are *Bachman!* We are the ones given this right by the power of our name, as outlined in the Precepts of Responsibility! Our Great-Grandfather placed this plan into motion so that we would have this chance. We are the keepers of the Second Chance! Our name will sit as the one which holds the seat of High Consul. I am going to go out there, and touch the soil that we will never own. It is our lot to sit on the lands of others. No Province granted to our name. But the name which will rest at the head of a great table that will help advise and lead a nation."

Without losing her firm tone, "and our name holds meaning?"

Closing his eyes he reached deep against the emotions rolling in his chest, "it is the duty of a human to make something of themselves. And for that achievement to be offered to the fruit of your loins or the keeper of your heart. What is the point of building something if you have no one to hand it to? Family is the baton pass of destiny! We build things so we can leave them to those we love to remember us by! History! We shall make history for our people because we made this possible! By the Protocol we shall rule and we shall be just in that rule because it is our legacy! We shall be followed because we are not False Prophets!"

Hearing the sound of her coming through the airlock and the door starting to close behind her he knew what her choice was. Her voice was soft and solemn as she came closer, "do you have fear brother?"

"Fear is the emotion we feel because to breed requires seeing tomorrow. Without fear we cannot understand what would stop us from seeing tomorrow. So yes, I have fear. I want to go back to my room and lay down and hope Cleo comes to see me."

Moving closer her tone wavered but did not yield to a fear he could hear in it, "so why do you do this instead?"

"Because if no one is brave, who will be brave? We have a blue sky to face."

Shaking her head and giving him the signal for 'decline.' "No, only you. I will not look. If I hear you screaming I will do my best to come save you. Mother gave me a rope and inflatable donut to throw you."

Looking back with a smile at the rope and inflated donut, "so the tones, cues, and questions?"

"I had to know if you were opening the door for the right reasons."

"I am glad I passed."

Shifting to an urging and insistent tone, "with you to lead us, Rise and Shine will succeed."

We are going to have to secure land, resources, get to our hidden supply depots and set this plan into motion and if someone is in the way they might feel threatened. And if they are the kind of people I don't want touching my people I am not going to hesitate in giving orders. "And if we are hated?"

"Then you will lead us to victory. We did not do this to die quietly. We did this to come back."

Nodding he waited for the airlock to close before he spoke the last words on his tongue, "to a blue sky," taking a breath, "I go to a blue sky morning."

RUMBLING HEARTS

Friday April 29th, 2242

1.0.0 - 23:03

Central Tower - 15th Floor - Adjunct Suite

■Frank Sevilan
■Captain of the Cloak Squadron "Night Terrors"

One more corner and I'll be in position. Get this haphazard plan on track and moving. Grousing internally he checked over the details looking for ideas with a curt efficiency.

Asmodai moved him into the Adjunct Suite as just another guest, in a long line, to ensure that he was taken care of. Some, checking his watch he noted the date, *forty nights ago. Forty days since he arrived, and ten since he killed Asmodai.*

Had him at the crematorium before the body was cold.

Shaking off the useless anger he took inventory. *The Council took the moment to jump into action. To throw Susan on to the Throne and start the demands of their new High Consul.*

I have seen the damage dealt, with my own eyes. I don't like it.

I have nothing to fight.

I have only a bad situation. The not knowing, has become the not doing, and each night erodes my patience with them and their demands.

Stopping next to the security door to the Adjunct Suite he felt the unbidden smile forming, *she smiled. When she came up with this childlike plan to smuggle him up to her office like she's a little girl sneaking cookies in the middle of the night. My not so little girl, who has no idea how to reconcile these moments, much less share them.*

If she wants to see this Wolf who wandered in? I'll bring him to her.

Focusing on the mantra, *I forgive because what was done was the Shadow's Request. I have already dreamt his death. I have been given the sight and knowledge of the end of the man, myth, and legend. I hold no rage. I asked the Divine for this.*

My wish, was granted.

Touching the door he marshaled his resolve, *I don't regret coming here. Saved my life. Now it's my turn to try to help save this man.*

Taking a breath to find his focus Frank went back to the plan. *Susan wants to see her guest, to show him the majesty of the office of the High Consul. I have my orders, best to get to them.*

Moving closer his comm unit relayed his presence to the door which set it to unlocking. Opening the door and stepping inside the room he moved to the wall adjacent to the door as it closed behind him. Looking over to Dhavid Yorklin he asked his question with a soft gruffness, "Status and SitRep?"

Setting a sharp contrast of City patterned camouflage against the backdrop of light wood furniture and pale pink walls he appeared calm. Without looking up from his tablet computer he spoke with a calm tone of discipline, "stable. The cake servers, in all six conference rooms, are getting ready to dish up the celebratory cake. The final mourning moments for Asmodai, and the Celebration of the finalization of the paperwork to place Miss Bachman on the Wolfram Throne will be upon us. Her Honor Guard, are mostly waiting for cake on the twenty-ninth with her core people, meanwhile the hallways are clear from here to Miss Bachman's office."

But what of her more inquisitive men? First one, "what of Northland?"

Nodding with a humored grin of knowing Edward Northland, "to keep him out of the way? He's making sure no one gets left out of cake. He's roaming around in Update Pattern Domino." Looking up with a sad humor on his still youthful face, "he is a good man. It was quite good to share time with him recently. To reflect on growing up in Vancouver, and our shared decision to seek Conflict over Peace."

"It is not an uncommon choice in this field."

"He was able to tell me more about the stories of the things I missed by being born too late to get here in time to see them. The stories that heap together for why Asmodai is remembered the way he is. I still wish I could have seen them in person."

The kind of things that soften the heart. "We mourn his passing. We look to the good times to feel what we know we should feel, the sadness of his passing. We do our best to remember that he was a good friend to the people." *He was my friend too, most of the time.*

Frowning firmly he nodded twice in reply, "if I had not been here to understand the depths of the problems within the Bachman family, I never would have guessed. I grew up under the idea of High Consul Asmodai, the Friend of the Citizen. The man who championed for a better tomorrow, but whom often seemed to forget about today. Coming down here, meeting you, and being drawn into *this*? I learned so much. I just wish I had been born sooner, so I could have been down here, and seen the things that make up the Legacy of the man."

"He was, something else." *We saw him off to the other side. Nothing more to dwell on.*

With a mild rush of the words Dhavid set the moment back on track, "so Northland *is* accounted for. He's nowhere in our path during this."

Wait, come to think of it, "was he meant to be here tonight?"

"He's covering Singleton's shift tonight. Singleton is with his wife at New Hope General. They're running some tests and he wanted to be with her. They estimate that if the tests come back with good news that she'll stay on course for delivery in twelve weeks. Then the big question of signing the Waiver or retiring from Active Duty."

Singleton should go. Then again if he holds his child and isn't moved to stay by the child's side? I'll talk some sense into him. Getting out his comm he spoke conversationally, "I'll leave a reminder for myself for thirteen weeks from now to check on him. If he's a father and not retired, I'll talk some sense into him."

"Noted, and I endorse the idea. Now, as for Miss Bachman's men? Sinclair on the other hand –"

By the Blue Sky, "what's wrong?"

"I just got tossed a note from Guard Justice. Sinclair is *still* on edge. He's been on edge all night. He has something itching at him."

Rusted scrap on a pile of useless chaff. "What has him itching?"

"He said it was nothing, he's being *vague* about what isn't adding up."

Finishing the reminder he put his comm away. *Vague is good, vague means we have time.* "We can hope it's nothing too terrible."

"We can hope."

Looking up at the clock, "ETA to window opening?"

"Soon. Some of the variables aren't on a timer."

Resisting the urge to pace the small room he found himself chiding himself for his emotional state. *My not so little girl wants to protect her new friend, who did something we're still mourning.* "This *has* to work."

Looking up with a thoughtful contemplation, "he's not from Port Refuge, or Port Asylum, or the Freelands. I don't understand why it can't work, but then again I am an Asclepius Cloak, not a Consul." Coughing softly, "not to mention the medallion he brought with him."

I don't see why this can't work either. "Asmodai reacted poorly to his personal space being violated, he put him in here, and it opened up too many questions in his head. The upside is that he was in such sore shape that this has managed to do him some good." Fretting with his knuckles through his gloves, "I am confident that Miss Bachman will find a way to help him. There is no reason for anyone to be hostile about this. With the death of Asmodai though things have been very, *strained,* so she hasn't had a chance to see to him."

Setting the tablet aside he moved to the elbow on knees position, "she holds him with such care when she visits him. Why aren't we allowed to talk to him? I'm not used to being silent around people who want to talk. I figured I'd ask you instead of her."

There is nothing harder than love. Trusting someone is right up there though. "When he did what he did," pausing to collect his words, "she had no words for him because if she stops to think it over? She could find herself not up to scratch. If I spoke to him? I would ask him about the anger he felt as he killed the old man." Pausing on the words he felt the light sting of knowing Asmodai was a year younger than he was, "I would want to know if she was safe. I would become a man of doubts. Considering I was the one who had to make sure that fire extinguisher was never seen again? I know how hard he hit the old man. I don't know what made him this way, and I would worry. Or? He would worry he had wronged her, when she had begged for Asmodai's death in those moments she called *weakness.*" Spitting into the nearby rubbish bin he cleared his mouth, "this is our deliverance. We asked our Gods for an Intervention." Gesturing roughly toward the inner door, "this man, is that answer."

Nodding and giving the signal for 'keeping up.' "We keep the music, and the radio shows on."

"We keep the music on. We don't let him dwell in silence. We smile when we feed him. We do all the things to soften the blow of her not being here. This has to even out."

Looking up with an attempt at a smile, "I hope this works out for her. I read what you gave me, I know that this is the reconciliation of an idea from before the world ended. Elianna gave us Asmodai and Alexis centuries ago. Then she gave us her son. Now she sends us her lost descendant to comfort our leader. She cared for all of us, so deeply, without knowing it."

Our modern myths and legends will gain a new entry when this is over. I know I was floored when I found out the truths behind the lessons we're taught in school. "I hope wherever Miss Seches is? She rests with humor knowing she still changes our fates."

Looking over at the tablet, "it's about time." Taking a deep breath he shook his head gently, "it is almost breathtaking to see the change in people. When I came down here and joined The Night Terrors? I was just a freshly minted Cloak. I was regarded well enough. Then you let people know you trusted me. Watching that statement bloom in a field of trust carrying the pollen of good will? I am still awed when I wake up in the morning and look at the ceiling knowing the life I wake up to. I wanted to let you know that."

He seeks to soothe my savaged mind. "You're going to get me to blush like a school boy Yorklin. I haven't done that in a long time."

Giving him the signal for 'candor.' "It's the truth."

"Understood. Does he know we're going to take him to see her?"

Nodding twice with a small smile on his face, "he does."

"Is he ready to be manacled and moved?"

"He is."

"And the jumpsuit?"

"He likes the newest ones she found him. He's just that much taller than the majority of us. I have to admit I feel daunted when he stands at his full height. The stout comb we found him for his hair has been working for him too. That beard though has proven to be more resistant, he reminds me of someone from the Network."

Nodding and signaling for 'positive emotion,' "his amazingly daunting beard aside? She has fed him, tended to him, and nursed him back to health. He was in poorer shape than he let on when he got here. The sunk has left his eyes."

Taking a breath Yorklin continued, "he has a very distinct face now. There is something that I am still wrestling with, and that is his feelings for Miss Bachman."

The question of tenable romance. She has only had one mutually shared bond with a heart before this. "Something new spoken?"

Moving over to the inner door he looked back at the tablet, "still a moment left." Looking back to Sevilan, "he figured out I could not reply, but I would listen. Which has made playing board games a bit much, but we manage. He was talking about the power of faces to present points of view. He told me he had not seen a heart shaped face like hers in some time. It was odd to hear the things I wouldn't say about her high cheek bones, her open smile, or just the way she is a delight to talk to because she appears to be both honest and mildly majestic at once. I would have just told him she is a pleasing Potentate and left it at that."

The things you take for granted. "She *is* beautiful, but we see her every day. We, as in every male who knows her, know our reality of who she is, and how untenable dreams can only poison the heart."

"Is she tenable for him as a romantic partner? I wouldn't say from the question of if they get along, because they do. But from a social caste issue. It's just so unprecedented. I can't think of a leader who has loved a Ghost, but on the other hand, he *is* who he says he is."

That is an excellent question and point. "I don't foresee her letting him out of her sight for some time. I am not one hundred percent certain if it's her sense of duty and ethics guiding her. Or, if that she finds him handsome, even with his weathered appearance. Charming, even with his overly honest and at points nightmarish anecdotes. Or just generally *appealing*, because he has been so forthright in his honest affection for her. We will know the primary reason she has let her guard down soon enough. I think we can agree we've seen enough to know she likes him as more than a friend or a patient."

"Indeed."

Still more time to burn off, at least I have something else to discuss. "I haven't taken the moment to speak with him on that subject though. When you're not here, he would just ask me questions about the radio shows he would listen to. We are not like the other people out there. He listens with rapt attention to our culture, it makes me hopeful that he sees us as good people." Glancing at the single large wall panel, contrasting with a fresh power cleaning, against the rest of the room, "he told me he didn't know if he should be sorry, yes, he used the word. That he did what he did. Susan opened the door, he came out, and he did the one thing he knew would stop a man. They were fighting for his life. Asmodai was angry at her again, and he did what no Citizen would dare do. I didn't have an answer for him before we were gagged. I still don't."

Speaking the words with a despondent humor to them, "life is certainly simpler in the field."

I don't know if I'll see the field at this rate. I'll be too old to go back out by the time this is over. "It is! I feel cooped up here in Central. The politics, the deals, the bargains. Pacts Pledged almost daily in the wake of the death of Asmodai. Hugh just got home with the Terrors today. I get to see my boys."

Raising a brow with a hopeful lilt in reply, "the Scouts are in town too."

Trying to keep the 'hopeful schoolboy' out of his tone, "Captain Turner is home?"

"I checked the comms, she's got the girls home and tucked in tonight. If both teams are in town, maybe we could see about a meet and greet?"

"Get them thinking of leaving Service in the Fall when the new recruits would be looking to cycle in?"

"Couldn't hurt."

"Truth."

Looking one way and the other with a curious smile, "looking forward to seeing Captain Turner?"

I think we both heard my tone. "Only after her husband gets home. He's headed up to Seattle tonight. It's a quick to and fro."

Rolling his eyes with the sardonic tone to his words, "over enemy territory with flak cannons which could shred that cargo plane of his if he dips too low. Just a simple to and fro." Returning to a more conversational tone, "the man has skills few pilots have."

Nodding in agreement, "he knows what he's doing. I've seen the reports of him courting Blitz Storms to keep his schedule. The man is a genius of the sky and the wind. If it wasn't for his health he would have been a Sky-Dancer."

"You care deeply for him."

"I do. He's a good man."

"Perhaps I could meet with the two of you when you go out for a drink, hear a story?"

"I think it could be good. I'll ask him if he has something to share. If he does? You come, you listen, and then we'll direct you toward the meeting with the Scouts. See what that does for you."

"Oh no, not yet Captain. I was speaking of the humor and joy of them being in town. I'm twenty-six, I have two more years before I'm up for my first marriage review. I'll address that later."

"Good enough."

Looking back to the door Dhavid continued, "he's not too depressed. He's healing. She's healed him with her toil in the fields of his heart. She's taught him new habits he's getting accustomed to. No adverse reactions to all the boosters and immunizations either."

"She takes after her mother."

"She has her own methods but point made. The hypothetical where she is not the High Consul, her empathy would have carried her well as an Intensive Care Manager with The Guild. Looking over her record? She's a bright light that shines like the corona of light around the top of this building. I don't see the Shadow taking Yuri."

If people let her help them. I know she had to help me, twice. "She couldn't heal the old man. She is still raw and bleeding from that. No matter how tempting it is, we cannot mention it." Shaking off the words he coughed and signaled for 'present in the moment.'

"You're right though, I would wager, she'll most likely keep him close."

"I wasn't privy to those details until you told me. It's hard to know it had to be this way. That our systems, our everything, failed to save our leader from himself."

Fighting with the frustration and anger he couldn't put down he moved his hands, 'you asked words of me.' "He could have stepped down. Yuri being here called into question things he hadn't asked himself in a long time. I, had a few heart to hearts with him before the end. You don't sit at a table with the same family for as long as I have and not gain a certain shared emotional space. Our leader, our High Consul, was lost in the woods and he wouldn't trust any more guides. The Shadow, it took him. I followed his calls, his plans, and I have been through quite a bit with him. He didn't want to leave this to his children in the shape it had become. Now, we have this. The by-product of Susan's most lackluster ad-lib. We have a future, that we need to make for ourselves."

"What was on your mind watching the end?"

For the first moment, nothing. Nothing at all. Finding himself thinking about his wife's hand at the end, *it was like feeling the slack in her hand all over again.* "I was sad Dhavid. I knew what moved him to do it. I could see the marks of it."

Speaking softly forcing the words out in accordance to training, "my cousin tells me her flesh is healed from that last attack."

"Speaking of the good doctor -?"

"I spoke with my cousin about that also. The latest tests still show no sign of what felled Maggie."

A ploy within a ploy, and I can still never tell Susan. The only way I can be certain her health stays watched and communication with the Telesphorus Facility remains open was to do this. Upside is Yorklin is a good man and a hard worker. "Is it hard being a false double agent?"

"No harder than being a father to a woman like Miss Bachman. I know I wouldn't stand if the Derecho tried to blow me over."

"She has never tried to blow me over."

"That's good."

"She has *tested* me, for the things she knew she needed to hear from me. The things she would *know* I would say. Hearing them helped her."

"Nothing more than the Gretchenfrages and Blackheart's Motives that keep you near?"

And then some. "Correct."

"Was it as simple as the truth that made it easier to cope with?"

The truth was far from simple. "She doesn't take a compliment easily. I thought I was telling her just the truth, for her? It felt more than she was willing to accept about the good in her."

"If we are selfish, we can be the kind of honest we can all relate to. When we see good in someone, and tell them, they become scared of us seeing the self-centric things."

Now that he mentions it, "even Yuri is touched by it. His stories, all good ones. Solid moral choices. Victories. He hasn't told her the half of it."

"Do you think she would soften if his Blackheart was adoration? If he told her that he liked her, opened up enough to tell her the other stories?"

Tough question. "I don't know. I fear for her it's that she feels *too* soft inside about him already." Reacting to the splash of color from the tablet catching his eye, "I do know we're good to go. Window appears open."

Signaling the 'affirmative,' "understood."

1.0.5 - 23:06

Central Tower - 30th Floor - Office of the High Consul

⁖..Susan Alexis Bachman
⁖..The High Consul

Hard to believe this desk is mine now. Been sitting at it for days and I keep expecting father to walk in and need me to move out of his way. Running her hand over the expansive desk she felt the dark humor of the situation trying to tickle her heart into smiling. *I am just glad that I accept this for what it is. A piece of furniture that cleans off even after things are done on it. It makes an odd sort of sense that Patrick was conceived on this desk. Things were so busy at that time that this is where they spent most of their time together with no one else around.*

Stretching her legs out she leaned back in her chair, tipping her gaze toward the ceiling mural. Lifting her legs slightly she curled and uncurled her toes, *thankfully my lineage favors height so I have plenty of leg room for this.* Rolling her eyes as one of her mother's notes came to her attention in her mind she sighed, *why did mom have to leave me insights like that?* Putting her feet down she looked under the desk and sighed at how much room was still available. *Thanks mom.*

Looking over at her father's portrait on the wall she sighed, *we would always see eye to eye on things even when we didn't want to. I think I wouldn't have discussed this facet of what could be with you though. How what started as a place mom would hide turned into something else.* Blinking in surprise while restraining the urge to laugh at her epiphany. *Neither Yuri or Sasha would fit down there comfortably so I don't have to worry about it! End of Story.*

Why did I think that? Stopping short on the thoughts she shook her head to dismiss them. *I need to focus. The Council has been on me for days for answer after answer and I am running out of ways to question them in return.*

Turning her attention to the ceiling she rose from her chair and moved to under the Grand Mural of the Thirteen Houses. *Why are we at each others throats?*

Fixing her eyes to the first emblem of the wheel she nodded firmly, *House Carnap. Be good, that's what the first Carnap said to his people. Live as good people who do what must be done, when it must be done, and in the best way possible. Sitting on the Eastern Border near the Salt Lake,* watching the logistics of their position dance around her mind's eye, *Consul Carnap is concerned for those who slide past his southern range and ping the sensors. More so for those he knows we're not seeing. How can his people be happy if they can't hold a solid idea of a Green Zone? War and conflict is a place to bravely save that which you hold dear. Not something to create of your own accord.*

I want this to have an ending as much as you do Consul. Just not enough to use the weapons that we can't undo once used, that I pray you don't know I have.

Moving her eyes to the next emblem she reviewed her thoughts, *House Mouse. The Vagabond House. From the first moments of our shared reality, you were unflinching in your decision to divide your people into groups and send them out into the world. A starting place which had been corrupted by the machinations of the survivors and you were left to pick up the pieces. Port Anchor still stands after the sacrifices made to keep it. The local resources were just not enough to support your people, so you gave them as gifts to the rest of us. You sent them throughout our Provinces to aid and assist in the building of the foundations of the settlements. To learn what each Arcology had decided was truth, and bring it to each other. The human touch of telling our shared story. And now your Consul needs to know why I'm holding back when he asks what is going on with this latest chapter of our shared story.*

I just don't have the right words to explain this.

Taking a breath she smiled at the next emblem, *House Deaton. The glory of nothing meaning anything until it means something. That our world is a bastion of knowledge waiting to be explored and reevaluated. Decades spent rebuilding the frameworks of our logical thinking and asking people to be more logical in finding meanings. Knowing that it all means something, your Consul looks at the missing pieces of the puzzle that father hid from her and asks what meaning could be so horrific we would blot the page.*

Considering the depth of things we allow? It seems staggering when looked at from the angle of being worse for why we won't talk about it. When it's far from the worst thing we have. Just a hard situation to plan a way out of it.

Shifting her sight to a far more familiar emblem she smiled, *House Drenner. Consul Amanda, my Aunt. Sister of Mother, Light of the House, Keeper of the weathered office chair of status. Your family serves as partial Custodians of New Hope. Yet, you argue with me about the fate of these people. The question of if we are safe with the renewed sightings of Freelanders on our Eastern Borders to go with the actions of the ones we do not see but we still note the outcome of their actions. You want our people to have the right to live their lives, free of the fear of those that would hound them for it. But I can't tell you the simple truth that Templeton is my problem, not yours. I know he killed Tessa, I know you want vengeance, but he's mine. I owe him for the Grandfather and Uncle I never met and the scars he gave my father.*

Turning her thoughts to the man next to Amanda, *and Micah being from Horizon doesn't make it any easier. We lost Horizon because we underestimated the hatred that waited outside of our lands. Grandfather struck them with such a withering force that Templeton broke rank. He dared empathize with our enemies.*

Rubbing her jaw at the memory she breathed a hard sigh of contempt out her nostrils for the memory. *The cost of not knowing the full truth when I asked what price peace would carry. He disabused me of that notion.*

Getting herself back on task she moved her eyes to the next bright moment, *House Flournoy. Consul Serek, the man who leads those of personal truths. The people who sought to reclaim the Snake River to the north. Your House chose Boise to be there home. Leaving you far enough away that New Hope seems like another world. You worry that we would forget you and your people. Or that one day you would wake and we would not be here. That as much as we assign our own values to things, that we should consider being polite when we decide things on behalf of others. He wants me to act in a fashion befitting one who has to make the decision for all of New Hope. While also waiting for me to find words to explain what it is that I believe.*

What I believe. That's a tough question to answer most days. I believe that our lands need more time to recover, to rebuild, to become whole. We will have threats both foreign and domestic as long as we have what freedoms we have and the concerns for our humanity.

Tilting her gaze slightly she closed her eyes and sighed as the small smile came to her lips, *Holden. Consul Holden. I, really rusted things up between us. Your father is a treasure who advanced your school of thought when he would council my father. We gained a host of unique social tools thanks to your House. I just wish I hadn't tried to burn the bridge between us to ash because I was having a moment of weakness.*

You teach us that to be motivated by worthless and empty things is wrong. Then you remind us that there are beautiful things to value. You remind me that we cannot have sporting events of physical grace and refinement until we have enough peace on our roads to safely travel. Then we can argue the merits of the feelings of localized worship of the arena.

Even in these last days you haven't really spoken to me Alexandria. You send your questions over to Amanda and have her ask them. You might suspect I don't hear the differences in your questions, but I do. To secure the roads we must secure our place with the people who violate the roads. And that is a large scale project of Mice, Rascals, and other forces that wish we hadn't burned Guthrie to ash. Hard to make a good impression when you leave a mass grave.

Turning her attention away from Guthrie before it could overtake her she faltered in her mental steps. *I will find a way, one day, to atone for those days enough to not be struck when I think of it.*

Moving back to her chair she pulled a spare hair pin and set to moving an errant lock of her russet hair back into place. Testing her bangs she adjusted the mane of hair cascading down her shoulders and back. *I am not having a lock fall out of place again. He was far too proficient at putting it back into place.* Pinning another errant lock into place she turned her attention to the pair of monitors on her desk, *and I have so much more to worry about.*

Shrugging off the thoughts she focused on her situation. *Father wanted me to understand his world, over and over he would yell about the concept, and now I'm starting to get a handle on what he was trying to say that I couldn't quite grasp.*

Taking a sip from her cold cup of coffee she tried to remember when she got use to the taste of cold coffee. *One day this stopped being an issue. At least I never need ice for cold coffee, I just wait.* Raising her mug, emblazoned with the single word 'Daughter' to the 'Father' mug on the shelf under her father's portrait, *I hope wherever you are? They have coffee. I loved you more than I hated you. I would like to think if you had been given the help you needed, we could have been lifelong friends. That I could call you. But,* swallowing roughly she took a long sip of coffee to keep the emotions from taking her away from the moment.

Setting her mug down she tried to keep calm in the face of what she was already feeling. *I get to see Yuri. I shouldn't cry before I see him, or he's going to be taking care of me and I can't have that luxury right now. I'm already doing something over the line of feasibly safe just to have a moment away from his suite.* Breathing softly she held in each breath to keep herself from hyperventilating. *I have to stay calm or I'm going to do something extremely reckless, again.* Looking over the project on her right monitor she shook her head in resignation. *I can't find it. I can't find the specific reason why they decided I would be High Consul. There is no certain answer that Jerome or I were able to dig up. Just the words of, it is what it is.*

There is nothing but bias left over from Steven's actions, of which everything he has done that was recorded was within the Protocol. So either this is because of what he did that they're not actually able to cite that he did, or they have had enough of his interpretation of acceptable behavior.

Then again I know a few people who want him dead for what he's done, and those were for actions that were within the Protocol, almost to the letter with how he said them. Thinking it over she sighed, *the Council didn't do this without a reason. They want something from me that they're not going to get from him. They've been pushing me for days on things. They get me to where they think they'll need me and it'll come to light.*

I know I'd do the same thing. Even if I can't stop it, even if I wouldn't like it, I would rather just hear it so I could plan my day accordingly.

And then there's the other problem. Looking to her left monitor she grimaced at the latest reports. Starlight Squadron reports more bizarre sightings and behaviors from the edges of our installations at Bliss. *The reports might be true that we're a part of the Free-lander rituals in that region. I don't envy those who work that region.*

Upside. The Watchmen are finding their new post to be agreeable even if they've only been there a day. At least they had a pleasant train ride.

Downside. They still don't know what's going on out there. Or if it's Ridolfi Junior. They have to find one of the campsites to know that. But given the lack of fatalities it appears to be disqualifying the rise of a new Warlord.

Junior, taking a deep breath she mulled the idea over in her head. *Cousin. Blood of my blood. Family. Raised on the outside of our world looking in.*

Letting the thoughts of her cousin drop she turned her attention back toward the inside of the fence of her world.

Riffling through her other memos she smiled sadly, *and I should be sending Sasha a note before too long. She's this night home and crashed at her place instead of coming to see me.*

I want something for her to wake up to. Even if it's just a cute picture dug out of the Network that she's never seen before. Maybe I could find something before -

Hearing the chime of her notifications she frowned at the newest one. *And they're almost here. I'll have to get her something after I see Yuri.* Touching her face gently, *I'm frowning because I think I love him enough to ponder him under my desk. I'm frowning because father couldn't find him an answer. And I'm going to cry because Steven wants to fight me for if I'm allowed to find Yuri an answer I would like him to hear.* Trying to compose herself she pressed the unlock for the double doors that kept people out of her office. Hearing the massive bolts throw back into their recessed channels she cringed lightly at the sound in the quiet. *I know someone felt they needed doors made to resist breaching charges, but did they have to make the rusted things so loud? They've never seemed this loud before, but then again it has never been this quiet near this office. Everything has been somber since father's death. Hooded mourners and masks to hide the sad faces of workers abound and the usual volume just isn't there.*

I don't think I've hugged as many people in the last few days as I have in the last year. For a half dozen different reasons. After a few moments the doors opening forced her out of her thoughts and into preparing her heart for the worst. After a few deep breaths, Yuri in his soft blue jumpsuit, led in by Cloak Sevilan and followed by Cloak Yorklin, entered her office as she felt her composure already trying to fail her.

I hope he likes that one. It looks like it fits better. A sad place to be in, so beat up that you don't want to be seen without full coverage. Thinking over the recent times of helping nurse him back to health she sighed inside, *I have shown him compassion to the limits of my power. And now I have theoretical power and I'm scared for the future. I have the idea I'm not strong enough to protect him.*

Looking at the messages from Steven she felt her resolve fluttering, *I don't know. My family promised land, and land is something I do not have in my authority to give to a man who is not a Citizen. I have to come up with a plan and I don't know if I have that kind of time without boiling this over.*

I want to show him compassion so badly, centering her gaze on his face, *an almost unfair power dynamic between us. He came to me looking for salvation and instead I've become something closer to his warden playing at being his keeper. I need more time.*

And Steven's words on the subject away from prying eyes and ears haven't helped. Things are barely within tolerance, if I push him trying to protect Yuri I don't know what happens next. He seemed like he'd grown kinder in the last year, but that's a distant daydream when Yuri comes up in conversation.

Walking over with a nonchalant limp, Yuri seemed to be oddly humored as he crossed the room to reach a polite distance from her desk, "two things I want to say. The first is that this jumpsuit is really nice. The first one was nice too, even though it didn't fit I appreciated the gesture of it. Is that two things? If so then the third thing would be more of a question than something said." Pausing he sighed, "I am, yeah." Coughing once he gestured back toward the door, "so where did everybody go?"

"They're eating cake and having refreshments in a nearby conference room. I cleared the path from your cell to here in a way they wouldn't see you. I can't even begin to tell you how difficult moving you around is. I wanted to see you here though."

Still humored he looked around and then past her, "so I could see this *expanse* confused about being office or art gallery? Paintings, statues, sculptures in a wide circle." Looking up at the Great Mural he nodded with understanding, "I see now." Looking around him he sighed, "you even have cardinal directional rugs."

Falling into the practiced habit of explanations with a light hearted tone she set to pointing out the details, "the office is the compass. North, South, East, West, seasonal related, emotions of said seasons related artwork too."

Looking around he reached up to scratch his beard, "so where is your desk on the compass? I don't quite follow the pattern."

More to discuss. "As it's an artistic, and not actual compass, it sits at North. Winter."

Appearing surprised he smiled, "Winter?" Gesturing at the front of her desk, "it looks festive."

It does. "The décor speaks to the theme of warmth, even in the bitter cold."

"I see, I see."

He makes this easy.

"This office is huge, you could raise a family in here."

Truth. "My family does."

Remarking on the idea with a humored grin, "do you put away all the expensive statues when the smalls are around?"

Simple enough. "We do."

"Oh, do I get to gaze out the window too? We must be what, thirty stories up?" Sounding more hopeful after a pause, "and did you say, *cake*?"

"Yes, thirty floors up. More than thirty stories though." Smiling thoughtfully, "and yes, I said cake. A party to celebrate my promotion, however it would normally be a simpler cake to praise those who had worked on the arboretum today."

"Hah. I like it." With a voice of hesitant humor, "you never mentioned you would be the new boss."

"I didn't know."

"Oh, so a surprise. So they are having the surprise party for your new job while we are in here." Mulling it over with a few beard strokes thrown in, "the promotion would certainly explain why you stopped talking to me."

Trying to not sound too apologetic, "I have been quite busy."

Without moving over he seemed to be taking a look out the expansive triangle window, which provided her view of the city below, in earnest, "I see and understand now. You know what else I see? That is a very large window. Some kind of front prow of your office made of glass?"

"The High Consul is the Captain of the ship that is The Rim's destiny. I *think* that was the reasoning. For me? It reminds me of the double edged Sonder I face as High Consul. This city alone has over a hundred thousand stories I will never truly know. I will gaze out this window, and as each small mote of light is another story I will never know? When people look up I am just as unfathomable for truths and understanding. But, we are all connected in our goal of keeping our world running. If I fail? The lights go out. If this office goes dark? Then I don't know what happens after."

Sounding a bit worried, "that's a lot to shoulder. I need to ask though, who cleans it?"

I want to laugh at his attempt to lighten my mood. I can almost feel the buoy he is trying to wedge under my heart to lift it. "Automated system."

"Very nice. No one has to climb out there and hang off the side of it." Looking around the office, "someone likes art. I know we discussed the importance of art to culture, and how the murals and displays of artistic talent I saw on the way through the city are how this is done. But this? It is more like a gallery instead of on office. It's big enough to *be* a gallery."

"It has been a Bachman tradition to commission art. It goes back to before the Eruption. This family has been a patron of the arts since the records of my family begin. Art is a cornerstone of culture," raising a hand she gestured toward her collection, "and these pieces have been chosen to be a lot easier on the eyes and mind. Each one meant to be more soothing to gaze on than other things. Hence the lack of rhyme and reason to the themes of the art overall outside of the theme of seasonal."

"This is really quite the monument. The building, that window, this office," Looking to the side wall he sounded displeased, "you hung his portrait?"

Not the best subject change. Keeping her voice neutral, "I did. It's tradition."

Sounding less than humored, "doesn't make it good."

"I have a few fond memories of him." Holding up her mug, "see this? We got these together. I turned sixteen, underwent the Blessing of the Barista, and we got a matched set. As we were a matched set."

With a tone far more guarded than his usual unapologetically outgoing tones, "I sense something far deeper than you let on in the dark of my cell."

Trying her hand at a reassuring smile, "we'll have time to talk about it."

Holding up his shackled wrists, "speaking of things to talk about? Am I really that dangerous to you and these people?"

Reassuming her neutral tone, "the perception of who you are is dangerous. The whispers are deafening Yuri. The man at the cameras has been told this is a Code Blinkers situation."

"Which means?"

"He sees nothing. The cameras were programmed to respond to Sevilan's presence. As he moved you, the cameras looked elsewhere. The footage isn't going to exist because it was never made."

"Then that man?"

"Loyal to the Protocol. He won't speak of this officially, but the whispers generated by those who know something is different? They deafen with unspoken questions."

Rolling his eyes, "so why these shackles? Goes along with the whole deafening mystery then?"

Trying to keep her tone pitched to a more supportive and informing place, "I can hear your sarcastic disdain for the whole affair. Yuri, if someone did tell, I have to keep up appearances. I don't even know what those are exactly, but I know that if you're shackled it means *I'm* in control. It means Sevilan and Yorklin there have it handled and no one has to touch you."

Cocking his head to the side he nodded his head a few times with the realization, "so *I'm* in danger from *your* people?"

"Ghosts have a bad record here in The Rim. If my brother can get them to suspect you are a Specter? -" trailing off she let her faltering silence speak for the conclusion.

"You explained that to me. That I'm a Ghost. How does a Ghost get his parcel of land and a house to put on it -"

Trying to keep the frustration out of her voice, "I can't."

Bristling with a quiet and subdued anger, "can't or *won't?*"

Trying to plead with him to understand in the wake of her mind suddenly seizing up, "you're not a Citizen." And those two seem upset watching this.

Getting up out of her chair she moved quickly to stand before him cutting off his words with her presence. Meeting him eye to eye she felt her resolve trembling without anger to keep it going. Speaking with a conversational volume instead of something more forceful, "the Quale of Lost Paradise brings him anger. He doesn't understand. Don't judge him too harshly."

Raising his fingertip slowly Yorklin offered, "a pardon begged Miss Bachman?"

"Granted."

"I don't want to judge him, but anger is dangerous when he's that close to you."

Reaching down she took his hands in her hands and held them softly but firmly, "it's *can't* Yuri. There is a lot I have to teach you, but I don't know if the time to do so is a luxury I have. I don't know if I can give you the land you are owed." Squeezing his hands softly, "you are not a Citizen of the Provinces of the Pacific Rim."

"Then what do I get?"

I don't have an ad lib for this. Even though I've had a week since then I've been so busy jumping through hoops that I had no time to come up with a plan. I can't think straight when it comes to him because it's so personal. I have no other ground to stand on. Rubbing his hands gently she heard her voice fall in volume to just above a conversational whisper, "a boat could be arranged if -."

Speaking with a matched volume brimming with exasperated humor, "after *every-*

thing I get a *boat?* Susan! Please?"

Looking up she could see the shock on Frank's face. *This is not what he expected. And there is the signal for Out of the Loop.* Nodding twice to him she frowned at his frown. *Just another reason for him to take his ax to my brother's skull.*

Turning her attention to Yuri, "I can't give you land without Citizenship, it's the rules."

With a deep bass to his words that seemed to reverberate low and sad from his chest, "so you would send me away? After what we shared in the dark? He gestured something, you nodded, there is something I don't understand, I would *like* to. Why are you hiding me? Why is my presence such a bad thing? You sat with me in that cell your father put me in." Raising in pitch and tempo he plowed forward, "you spoke such sweet things to me. You *personally* tended to me. You even let me ramble on about my adventures! And now you're telling me I have to take a boat and *leave?* What if I don't want to leave? What if I want to stay?" Gripping her hands tightly he moved his head to find her gaze, "damn it Susan! *Aardvark!*"

Blinking once she closed her eyes at the sight of the intensity in his amber eyes. Hanging her head she shivered against the implications of what he had said. *He would know as well as I do what that word means. Considering it was his ancestor who spoke it to mine. 'I love you' in a form no one else would know.*

The love that lasts a lifetime.

Flexing her fingers she sighed on the inside when she couldn't bring herself to throw the Decline signal. *I can't lie to him.*

Speaking just above a whisper she didn't raise her head, "I can't."

Letting up on his quest for her eyes, "at least let me stay! I don't want a boat! Aren't you the boss? Don't you run everything now?" Hearing his voice taking on a pleading tone, "how can I be one of those little lights you care for?"

Feeling her mind closing down of any useful thoughts she let go of his hands as the sadness threatened to take her breath, "not now. I can't think now. Back to his room."

"Susan!"

At least he doesn't sound angry.

Watching him testing the distance his cuffs would open he sniffled, "these are not nice right now."

Moving to the side of him she gestured for 'touch.' Waiting a moment for him to nod affirmation she put her arms around him carefully. *This is not what I wanted. Just a few heartbeats into the heart of the matter and I'm already flummoxed.* Repeating herself quietly, "back to his room. I'll visit him next time. *Without* talk of boats."

Speaking softly with a humored candor he seemed to be emotionally at a loss, "Susan? Are you trying to keep me alive?"

Kissing his shoulder she smiled weakly, "yes."

Sighing with a hang of his head he lowered his hands, "I appreciate that. I worried in my cell."

Pushing the words out with a facsimile of vigor, "no boat. I'll come up with something."

With a tone of gutted sadness he appeared to be trying to smile at her, "I get sea sick."

Really? "You never told me."

"It wasn't the kind of story I wanted to tell. The story of," making a mock vomiting noise he sighed, "I'll go back to my cell." Looking up to her as he slid away from her and moved toward Sinclair and Yorklin, "I'm holding you to that. Please, come up with something."

"I will." Raising her head and forcing the words from her throat, "there are things I need to explain. I *will* explain. I will Yuri."

Falling silent after his nod of confirmation she waited until the three of them were gone from her office and the doors closed behind them to move back to her desk. Pushing in the keyboard tray she moved closer and laid her head down on her desk.

How am I going to come up with something? The Council, Steven, the unknown spies, and Ridolfi are all dancing around me keeping me from a decent thought in my head.

Or time spent alone to recuperate in any meaningful way.

Looking over at her father's portrait she felt the moisture forming on her eyes. *They didn't take a second look at the death of the High Consul. I worked so hard to clean it up and they didn't even challenge the clean up job. It was as if he had served his purpose and was no longer needed in their world. Am I just a part they can replace? I'm scared of what I might of missed and I know it. I don't know what to do because no one is giving me a single clue to go on.*

Except Yuri.

And I can't base everything on him. Even if this is partially his fault.

Making a place with her arms for her head to rest she laid her head down with a sigh. *I'll just give this a moment to settle and get something done. Frank will come back and discuss the situation and we'll find a way out of this.*

1.1.0 - 23:10

Arcadia Street - New Hope

⚜Paige Turner
⚜Third Student of Shadows

Standing in the pool of shadow between the street lights she marveled at the Endeavor that Rajan was finishing. *Staying up late, not going home for dinner, and driven to get it done. He might be an Artist yet.*

Moving closer she felt the wash of awe at the details of the work. Moving closer she felt a depth in her spirit in the mix of humidity, quiet, early spring chill, and the majesty of the mural. Finishing her advance she smiled at the street lit illuminated work.

I like it. Rajan's worked so hard for this. Getting better and better and now here we are and he's done good. We told him he would be amazing if he tried. That he could refine it. And now I get to be the first to see it. The Department of Art and City Beautification is going to be pleased. I know I am.

He faced the worry that he could be good at this. That he would do this.

Too serious for the main roads, but this side street was a prime location for him to get his start in getting noticed. I hope his parents approve of their son.

Looking to her and then back to his work he spoke as a man awed that he could create something of such quality, "would you say I lived up to the bargain made?"

Moving her hands she smiled as the words poured out of her lapel speaker, "very good my friend. It was a pleasure to witness. Congratulations on the acknowledgement of your work."

Smiling with a moment of shy modesty, "thank you Miss Turner. Our city was missing a mural encouraging confronting the Five Thieves. I understand that our ways are not even close to universal to this land, but it has been warming to grow up in a new generation of finding our place together."

Moving her hands with a careful vigor to match the smile on her face, "The Five Thieves are reflections of things that we try to avoid by acknowledging them in the things we do. All good things that help deal with being alive are welcome. I am glad you decided it was worth sharing."

"Knowing that this will be seen as keeping the conversation open? I wanted to make sure this could be shared for those who would be interested."

Slowing her hands down without losing her grin of encouragement, "I hope it helps as many as it should."

"I do also."

Hearing a rumbling from the nearby interior road she felt a strange confusion watching the long convoy rolling down the nearby street. *I don't know that emblem, much less why it has visible armor plating on its vehicles. Or why there are so many.*

Moving her hands she blinked when no words came out of her lapel speaker. Pulling out her comm she blinked at the 'No Network Found' which greeted her. *That's impossible.*

Holding her comm up she showed it to Rajan. *I need to go contact Dennis.*

Nodding solemnly Rajan's face echoed her concern, "go then my friend. Go to your teacher and seek his wisdom! I will seek shelter!"

Nodding quickly she pocketed her comm and took off toward her car. *I need to find Dennis!*

1.1.5 - 23:15

1337 Firebrand Lane – New Hope

- ▸Jerome Hope
- ▸"Admin Nobody"
- ▸Network Technician

Glancing from the cards in his hand to the pictures taken from The Private Notions, he relished the smile and the chuckle of humor escaping with his thoughts. "Those dancers really know how to put on a hilarious show. I'm glad we were able to get tickets."

Replying with a humored regret York looked up from his cards, "I just wish we could have had Eve come with us. I think she might have smiled under that mask of hers. I can hear it sometimes," pausing to flounder he sighed, "the smile."

Tossing the words back as a patient affirmation, "as do I."

Looking up from the cribbage board York signaled for 'Subject Broach' with a sheepish grin on his face. Leaning against his chair with a tired grimace he seemed lost in thought.

He wishes to discuss something of import. I wonder what could be more important than discussing the latest show at The Private Notions. Only one way to find out.

Nodding twice Jerome smiled, "it must be something else if you'd ask for a Broach before you speak of it." Putting down his cards he assumed the posture of the Patient Listener, "speak to me friend."

"Are you going to move into the Called Corners? I know this little box of a house is nice, but is there something you didn't tell me about it?"

"This house, is near one of the relay towers, I get amazing signal because of that."

"I see. How's the signal at Called Corners?"

"Not *as* good. Also I'm closer to the CPU for my morning commute. If I moved to Called Corners I'd have to ride with someone instead of taking my bike. Also, I worked hard to get the paint commissioned for my little castle." *I am far too proud of my walls.* "A mid-tone beige, balanced to perfection, with an LRV of fifty four point six. If I moved? I would have to get another run of the paint made."

"Ah, solid reasons. I didn't think I would like beige either when you mentioned it. I, only asked because I saw the invite from The Director on your desk."

"Noted." Reaching out he touched his facedown pile of cards with his right index finger, "so what is the thing that you really want to speak of?"

Stating his words with a confused irritation, "I just don't understand the appeal."

Ah, the romance of Avery and the girl, Tina Morsel. We return to this again. Moving his finger from his cards he nodded once with a solemn air to the gesture, "we covered that physical attraction runs the gamut, -"

"She has nothing to speak of, in so many ways -"

"Then we won't speak of it. Instead? What is the posited thought tonight?"

Putting his cards down he sighed, "I've seen them together and it just seems odd. I *know* The Guild lets people dance outside of age ranges with careful permissions but it just seems odd watching them."

"He still falls well within Guild Standards for autonomy in a Balanced Power Dynamic. Yes, she looks up to him, by everyone's admission, but she still is her own person who has her own ideals. She just happens to be younger. I *know, personally,* what it means to lose one's autonomy in an affair of the heart. I also know, *personally,* what it looks like to be in an Unbalanced Power Dynamic at too young of an age. Personal anecdotes aside? I don't see something to worry about."

"I know. Mea culpa, J-Man, I still worry."

"I know you do. Power corrupts, even the power of the heart. We're far from perfect people and that troubles us because with each layer we peel out of the Network of the 'Things We Did Oh So Wrong,' we worry about doing something like that again. Does he love her?"

"As far as anyone knows."

"Then learn to release the worry for their chronological positions to the other, and just accept the idea that it *could* be as it should be. She's not me, he's not them, and as long as *they* stay good? It can be good. Further on that? They are *just* past the line of recommendation for age gap for their situation. The example using me was a much further distance."

"Noted. But, it's not strange that she stepped in when her older sister stepped out?"

"Love and life are just part of the maelstrom of life. The Guild knows better than we do. Also, if she wishes to secure him for fatherhood later? Is that so bad? He's not an unpleasant man. She is a lively young woman." Holding his hand up for 'Further Notes' he took a moment to breathe.

"Also from my understanding, Avery and Tonya parted on good terms. Not to mention that Mrs. Morsel does adore Avery, so it makes it a more heartening tale of not having to let go of a family you care for. I would like to believe it will be as it should. Leave them to the professionals."

Giving up with a comforted sigh, "I will relent to the logic."

"Good. So how goes the new scent Miss Bachman ordered?"

"The Miss B Happy Toes Anointment?"

The amazing flippancy of their shared endeavors. "Is that how you labeled it?"

Quipping back with relaxed humor, "you know my style. I have the skill, the nose, but none of the gravitas for the field. Which is why I turned down the more formal invite to change professions, again."

"So why Happy Toes?"

"She's ordered it for an experiment as far as I know. You know as well as I do that the work she does is her own ideas. I tried it on my own toes, it felt pleasant. It goes outside of aromatherapy and into the realm of topically therapeutic. I think she might know someone with infected feet that she's going to make a present for. The extra ingredient is a small batch of serum from a Yorklin lab I don't know the emblem for."

"She is a woman of many ideas, most of which we will never learn the initial vector that they entered her thoughts from." *The glory of access to the Network in ways that few people have.* Mulling the moment over, "we should go out for pizza."

"You have a coupon? Otherwise we're splitting the Ration Cost."

"I do! I have a coupon. I have one left from the last time Miss Bachman shared coupons."

"Check the traffic and get me a course. There's some roadwork being done on that end of town and I have no idea. I'm too tired to play navigator. The upside of Called Corners is we would be closer to The Pizza Place. Place is harder to find than it needs to be."

Flipping his laptop computer open he set to finding them a course. *Current traffic conditions are -*

Stopping in midthought as the gravity of the convoy he was witnessing hit him, he felt his stomach knot up at the sight of a vehicle with a matching designation on the access road for his neighborhood. Reaching for a key on the keyboard he watched the window pop up which disconnected him from the system.

Full Lockout Initiated. Sys-Admin Authorization. Pinching his hand to reset his thoughts, *Athens has authorized this without cause.*

We have to get out of here. "York?"

"Yes?"

Trying to keep the panic out of his voice, "get your gear! I'll prep the emergency beacon!"

Nearly jumping into his shoes, "where are we going?"

"Cloak and Dagger, we *might* be safe there. We're Unauthorized Targets of Dire Intent!"

"Rusted scrap! Can you sound an alarm?"

"Negative. Athens is running a Lockout on me. We have to run! Now!"

"To the truck!"

1.2.0 - 23:24

Central Tower - 30th Floor - Office of the High Consul

⁙..Susan Bachman

Staring at the mural on the ceiling of her office again she found a concept to focus her mind on. *Do I know the Consuls as people?*

I know Amanda, and that is about it. I have spoken with many people around each one of them, about so many things, but not the Consuls directly as one would a friend.

I know what I know of them from my attempts to understand them.

I don't know why this transition has had to be so painful though.

I know I searched my soul, their actions, and tried to understand what my father was going through. Now that I am in the thick of it, it makes less sense than it did before.

And now they're treating me like they don't know if I'm going to bite them. They keep making demands. Wanting to know more than they ever asked father about. They ask about every report I don't share from the Freeland Front. Troop movements. Training manifests. What I know about my brother's actions and plans for the future. The exhausting deluge of each one asking me for something.

Even Amanda. Wanting to know why I moved the Watchmen. What the strength of the Honor Guard is really at. When the next call for manpower for them will be as they have too big of a job to do within the new Guild Guidelines of hours served in their line of work.

Or why I don't keep more people around me to protect me. They want everything from me, and now I'm so tired inside that the only person I have who has time to listen is me. I need to see Sasha tomorrow after she wakes up. We can watch a movie I found and spend time together. That should help.

Hearing the chime from her desktop speakers she wasn't sure how much time had passed. Noticing the red flagged Priority Zero message waiting she set to reading it. *What's this?*

Opening the message she felt her mouth go dry in fear as she read through the simple directives outlined in it. *I am to die?* Rereading the instructions she pushed down the nausea and spoke the words aloud to make sure she was reading them right.

"Protocol Amendment False Prophet has been enacted. Miss Bachman will be surrendered for removal from office and execution. No Citizen within Central Tower will be harmed if Miss Bachman is surrendered without a fight. If Commander Bachman is signaled this will be seen as an act of aggression by all parties in Central Tower. When the timer reaches zero all communication options will be closed. Use this time wisely to make your choice."

Well that explains so much.

Sitting in stunned silence at the short amount of time still left on the timer she noticed her comm blinking. Picking it up she found a message from York Benton. *Three over it all adding up, if my words were wine I'd have an overfull cup. And now Jerome is in trouble to the point where he has York sending me one of his watchword phrases.*

Getting up she started to move with weak knees toward the radio he was asking for her to call him on. *Channel seven. It all adds up is four and everything else is a modifier to the base of channel four.* Stopping in midstep as the lights went out she lifted her comm up and used it as a flashlight. *Rusted night for full cloud cover. It's dark in here without the backup lights. I wonder why the backup lights didn't come up? Did the mechanism malfunction for that? Not that it's going to matter soon from the looks of it.*

And now my comm is vibrating. Answering her vibrating comm she held it to her ear and stopped walking, "Susan here."

Sevilan's voice came out of the speaker with something as close to panic as she had ever heard, "lock the doors Susan."

Responding with a voice of gallows humor, "why? False Prophet, I'm done for."

Roaring to life with a voice of paternal protection, "men are coming to kill you! Lock the doors!"

I'm in shock. "And then?"

"Will you order the Honor Guard into the fray to protect these people when they move to protect you?"

"I can't let my people die. You know the answer to that."

"Hurry."

Moving her comm from her ear she navigated to her Directives App. Selecting 'Final Stand' she confirmed her authorization. Watching the indicator turn red she selected the Dominion Override. *I give them Dominion over this battlefield.* Adding a single Caveat she selected the Power Play Override. *I am no longer Priority Zero. My helicopter is out for servicing, I'm not leaving.*

"I don't have enough to spare, I hope they understand that. I'll wait here alone with the doors." Making her choice to stand alone she pressed the last buttons and hit send.

Putting her comm back to her ear, "Dominion Override. I don't have enough to justify someone playing Gate Keeper. I selected Power Play to override. It's Final Stand Frank."

Speaking with a voice which like thunder drawing nearer carrying the promise of lightning, "help is on the way from over the hills then."

The code for en route but unknown ETA. "Thank you Frank."

After a moment of silence she closed the connection and finished her walk to the radio. *Now I have to reach out and signal someone. Thank the Blue Sky for abandoned tech-*

nology. Tuning it to channel seven she held down the transmit button. *At least this still works.*

Jerome's panic stricken voice echoed out of the speaker, "High Consul! Empty air doesn't assure me you're alive!"

Speaking into the microphone, "oh! Mea culpa Jerome. I'm not feeling well."

"Rusted scrap! High Consul! Snap out of it!" After a moment and an audible deep breath his voice came over the radio with an angered anguish, *"Sasha will miss you if you die!"*

Shaking her head roughly she did her best to find her focus, "what's going on Jerome?"

With the sound of an angered truck engine behind his voice, "the Sys-Admin! Athens! *He's gone rogue!* Whoever is out to kill you? They've come for me too but I managed to stay ahead of them! They are being aided by him! False Prophet has been called but not voted on! It's a *lie* Susan! It's *not* authorized! I have my doubts the Consuls could know this is active!"

"That's great, those men still have guns. How are you in a vehicle? Is that York's truck?"

The Day Runner could save him.

"York, he came over to hang out and he's driving. He's driving for our lives. We have a chase vehicle in Hot Pursuit! I had just enough time to get my portable workstation and the radio we're talking on. I borrowed his comm to send you that message!"

Coming from the background the panicked male voice was trying to sound humored, "hey Miss B! Don't die!"

It's a good thing he's trained for this, and that truck was made for this moment. I'm not on task. "Can you take him out?"

"I've thrown countermeasure lockouts on him, the Network is burning, but I can reach The Pale Rider and he won't have authorization to stop me as it is by your will."

The Pale Rider, we've come to this. "Why aren't you doing that?"

The angered sadness of his voice came over the small speaker with a resignation that she found uncomfortable to hear, "I wanted to let you know the stakes. What's waiting for you? I can't save you. There won't be an extraction team. I can't give you a miracle like we gave Sasha. Or the knowledge that the Blue Sky will come again, like you saw for me."

Closing her eyes she found a sad smile for the memories, "thank you anyways."

"I need to go High Consul. I have to go kill the rat who wears the crown. I'll let you know if the men chasing me fail."

"Go with the speed of the Gingerbread Man. Secure your castle Jerome."

"Thank you High Consul."

Turning off the radio she shook from head to toe. *No price too steep to pay for my death?* Walking over to the doors she accessed the manual barring and locking mechanisms. *I can't speak to my people now.* Checking her comm she frowned at the 'No Network Found' displayed. *I am mute, blind, and deaf. I am helpless now.*

Setting to locking the doors, *first the upper bolt.* Opening the panel in the door she pulled down on the manual override lever to drop the bolt into the slide. Gripping the rod firmly she shoved the bolt into place.

That's one.

Reaching for the second lever she dropped the second bolt into the slide. Gripping the rod she shoved the sob down as she shoved the matching bolt into place.

That's two.

I know father left Last Resort in the desk. I get eleven bullets. I know what I have to do if it looks dark. Finding herself shaking again, *if I live through this I have to come up with something. I have to find him an ad lib.*

1.3.6 - 23:29

Central Tower - 15th Floor - Adjunct Suite

☀ Yuri Pastukhov
☀ Descendant of The Queen of Swords
☀ Descendant of The Gingerbread Man

Contemplating the lights, which were trying in vain to come back up, Yuri heard his name spoken softly from behind him.

"Yuri?"

After everything I just heard, what will he ask me? "Yes Sevilan?"

"Are you with us?"

I can only hope this is what I think it could be. "With you?"

"Men are going to storm the building. Security just got knocked out. Workers should be moving to give us a fighting chance with manual overrides of key subsystems. What matters in this moment, between us, is that I'll unshackle you, arm you, and fight shoulder to shoulder with you. If you're with us."

A fighting chance? "You trust me?"

Tapping the security door next to them, "this isn't where you belong tonight. Susan trusts you Yuri. Her embrace? We both know someone is moving against her to keep her from saving you. But *now* is not the time for that. You stay in this room? You may find that whomever opens it? They might like you. Or they'll shoot you. I need every pair of hands I can get though, and I imagine your hands have some skill to them based upon what you said. This building is going to stand up for her. She has been the guiding light for these people for years. She walks with a quiet determination to do good. They won't just give her up without a fight. They give her up? She dies. This *ends*."

Thinking over the stakes he felt the quiet cold settling inside as he turned around to face Sevilan, "but they're just civilians. If this is a coup those will be trained killers outside, no?" Rushing the words as the horrified thought hit him, "are there *children* in the building?"

Speaking quickly with a dismissing gesture, "no. Children aren't allowed to be raised in Central. We're on Night Cycle which means no kids visiting in the building either." Letting out a puff of air, "I know they're not soldiers to your reckoning but they have some surprises though, but I don't know what sort of force is coming up through those doors. I know there are more of them then of us. Which is why they need us."

How can I say no? "I'm with you."

"Good. Let me get those cuffs off and we three shall show these invaders what it means to try to take this castle. Ditch the jumpsuit though, it's far too colorful and paints you as an easy target. For safety those are fitted with colored stripes under optics. If you wear that you'll have a target painted on you."

Holding his wrists out, "at least I have my usual shirt and shorts on under this. As we might not live through this, I wanted to ask something. She mentioned that she was one of your three daughters. And I was not to ask about that subject with you."

Setting to unshackling him, "she's a good daughter. I have walked by her side, when I was not on mission, for a very long time. I lost my girl, I was given the chance to be a dad again. I need you to know Yuri, if I don't make it? Don't mourn me. I'll be with my little girl, and my wife, again. If they get me? Protect her. Even if I don't make it? *Make sure she does.* I was given a chance to live again, I owe a debt. Join me, and I will show you how happy I have been to have had the chance to be in this debt. I want you to know I am honored to have you on my side to help save my girl."

"I, don't have words for that. What's the plan?"

"We'll move up to the seventeenth floor. We counter, fall back, counter, and fall back. We're outnumbered something bad from the sounds of it. We can't make a direct stand or it will be over by sheer dint of bullets. There is something you need to understand."

I hope it helps. "Which is?"

"If those forces are also *part* civilian then they will be staggered with Warriors. Warrior, Civilian, Warrior, Civilian. The one who leads shoots, the one who follows mimics. You shoot every odd man out. If you want to remove them in order of threat? Do not even."

"And if they are all Warriors?"

Answering his question with a grim humor of acceptance, "then we die."

Feeling the explosive reverberation in the floor he looked to Sevilan with what he could feel was panic rising in his chest, "the doors?"

"It feels like there are no longer doors to the lobby."

Getting himself out of his jumpsuit, they will fight until the last breath.

From the wall panel Yorklin appeared to have accessed a manual intercom control. Speaking boldly, into a microphone he had plugged in, he called out with a voice that only hinted at his fear across the speaker system, "people of Central! You do not walk alone this night! Although they come to take from us, we shall take from them! You are not alone this night! All that protects her stands with her! The Honor Guard move to your locations to deny them their treachery! Our High Consul will not live this night if we do nothing! All that are Pledged? Join us! If we fall she will not see the next Blue Sky! If we stand idle and wait for them to come for her? Who is next?" Pausing for a heartbeat, "*if they come for her? If we do not speak? Who speaks for us when they come for us next?*

Speak now for Miss Bachman! I will not lie to you, I cannot promise we will see the next Blue Sky! But I *can promise you* that each one of *them* that does *not?* Will be a victory for our way of life and what we have chosen to protect!"

I am humbled. Taking the gun as he stepped out of his jumpsuit, *I must be better this night than any night I have ever lived. For I too want to see the Blue Sky again.*

1.3.2 - 23:27

Central Tower - 29th Floor - Central Island Kitchen

ˆSinclair Holden
ˆ32nd of the "Honor Guard"

Approaching the High Consul's kitchen with his flashlight firmly in hand Sinclair heard a voice pleading with an emotional force he hadn't expected to hear.

"Miss Augusta! Please!"

What is Miss Augusta doing that has that man so vexed?

Striding quickly into the kitchen he appraised the situation of Heathcliff Riffson standing in the doorframe of the pantry. Motioning toward her with a panicked energy Heathcliff hung his head at the sight of the stoic form of the not quite elderly Miss Augusta.

Pleading with her once more, "*please* Miss Augusta?"

Bathed in the illumination from a battery backup light the silhouette of Miss Augusta filled his vision for what he could see in the room. Garbed in her usual soft red pinafore dress she looked as she always did except for the small sword in her hands. Looking to him he felt the chill watching her quickly cut the knot on her blade with a pair of kitchen shears. Her voice cut through the sounds of workers and panic with the firm lilt of command, "you've come to protect this position Guard Holden?"

"I have. Orders were sent out moments before."

Sliding her blade out of the sheath by a centimeter she slid it back with a grave acceptance to her motions, "I have this location."

She has cut the Peace Knot on her Dauer Blade. She accepts her place in this. "No time to fight about it then. Recommendations?"

"Twenty-eight looks weak. I know she's short handed but there's a partition wall there that if they are aware it exists? They'll punch through the wall with charges and have access to The Director, then this location, and then her. You go there, move forward, and then be ready to protect it to slow them down. If this is what I think it is? Those men will be hunting for the people around her that would be cross with her passing. Men will be looking for me. I will not be left alone tonight."

Signaling past her to Heathcliff, "close and lock the door. If they have breaching charges you'll have to be ready for it. Ear plugs in and guns ready. That door comes off the hinges and you just point and shoot. Understood?"

"Yes sir!"

Moving behind cover near the door Miss Augusta shooed him off, "go! Get going Sinclair!" Looking at him with a note of finality to her demeanor, "if I don't see you again? I go to find Tessa. I'll see if her and the dead old fool made up on the other side."

Don't cry. Saluting quickly he turned and headed off toward the nearest stairs. *Partition wall on twenty-eight. If they know it I'll be fighting for the life of Patrick Bachman. I hope he writes me a really nice obit and eulogy.*

I hope he doesn't have to write one for Miss Augusta.

Putting his helmet on and securing it to his body armor he waited a moment for the tech to catch up with itself. *All lights green.* Switching to local vox channel on his helmet he was pleased to see the local relays had been activated. Calling out his move he tried to keep his voice level, "Sinclair moving to defense! Miss Augusta has cut the Peace Knot and has taken the position of Cook's Guard."

Calling back over the channel Breaker's voice sounded on the verge of losing his composure, "real deal?"

"Final Stand has been called. We have to assume this is going to be to the death. *For all involved.* They've called False Prophet without cause or warning." *I would like to think if Alex knew she would have told me.* "Who here has touched the life of a Consul and yet, we heard nothing?"

"We heard nothing."

"Nothing was said to me."

Taking the first flight of stairs he was thankful for what emergency lighting had managed to engage, "I know the Matron isn't here tonight, but I want you to know that I have faith in us."

Speaking with a solemn tone Northland came over the vox, "we are spread out to rob them of the will to fight. There are too many points that the small staff is going to have to cover. We must each face the nightmare that comes knowing that it is for us, we face it apart from the others. These halls we deemed Hallowed Ground, safe and protected, and are about to taste blood for the first time. Tonight is not the Night of Heroes, tonight we yell our battle cry and hope our ancestors can hear it. If we go to the Heroes Pyre? We should make sure we do everything before then that we can do!"

Running briskly toward the stairs to the twenty-eighth floor he heard the unmistakable sound of breaching charges going off. Taking a breath he paused as the voice of Dagger Yorklin called out of the speakers. As the last words died out in the silence Paulson spoke over the vox, "it's been an honor gentlemen. I advise you to use your combat recorders to speak the last words this world will hear from us. I'm going to the fifteenth, I'll set up an armored shield wall, and when I see my brother? I will say Hello for the rest of you."

"When you see him? Tell him I miss him. If I go too? I'll tell him all the stories he missed."

"Thank you."

Calling out with a fervor Breaker's voice was urgent, "Northland, if you have anything productive to leave behind? You get that recorded for the survivors to find!"

"I will!"

Popping into the conversation Kowalski sounded afraid, "one of the building engineers got a look at the invaders for us. It's a Full Blitz! They're not going to stop for anything! Get those messages recorded gentlemen! We don't have much time!"

Taking the stairs carefully he listened to his friends each call out their goodbyes to each other in turn. Reaching into his pocket he pulled his comm free. *No service.*

Rounding the final flight of stairs he did his best to blink away the tears, *mea culpa Alex. I'm coming home in an urn.*

1.3.4 - 23:28

Kunlow Estate - Consul's Office

♠ Thomas Kunlow
♠ Consul of the Kunlow Family

Taking in the sight of his office, his thoughts turned to the reflection on the life of service leading to the current decisions. *I am here because Maggie was falling ill and I worried for our world with a High Consul who would be compromised by the death of his wife. I finished what my father had started in understanding what the Bachman family had done since the doors had opened. I finished gathering the evidence to convict them by a jury of the Citizens. And with everything in place, I commit to the execution of the last Bachman of any worth.*

The Echo of her father, Miss Susan Bachman.

Kincaid Drexel's voice intoned the words with a low pitched confidence into his ear piece, "the last of the forces are in position at the Doors of Central."

Watching the monitors Thomas listened to the latest round of updates and reports as the doors were fitted with enough charges to break even the best that had been given to the building. *Soon the world shall pay one last price, and the Bachman family and name will be taken from the Wolfram Throne. The puppet will be set into place and there will be nothing left for Patrick or Steven to do but give up or die if they refuse to comply with the new order of things.*

One last piece of the puzzle. "What of Jerome Hope?"

Kincaid's agitation was clear in his terse reply, "my men report he evaded the forces sent for him. They're in pursuit."

Trying to keep the humored disdain from his tone, "he rides a bike."

Breaking into the conversation Athens spoke with a grim emptiness to his words, "his associate, the man known as York was visiting. They used his truck to escape."

"You didn't detect him?"

"The beacon on his truck turns off when the truck turns off by default. The modification on it comes with authorization from Miss Bachman herself."

Say something nice before frustration takes control. "Thank you for aiding me Athens. You also Kincaid."

"I believe in the future. Disconnecting to attend to this."

"Noted."

Speaking after the tone of Kincaid's disconnection Athens echoed the determination, "noted. The future needs to be a brighter place. I have read your manifesto and I'm on board." Adding with a candor of regret, "I regret Hope though."

"There is no telling what kind of trouble he would have caused us."

Hearing Athens' tone belay a panic he didn't factor for, "he's not *done* causing trouble."

"What?"

"He turned the beacon off on that truck shortly after they left the driveway. The vehicle chasing them is closing in on the border of the blackout I put into play. They have not called in that they've stopped him. If he makes that border he can signal for help!"

"Can you do something to stop him?"

"Negative."

"Why didn't the truck stop?"

Reading the words with a hushed horror to his tone, "the arming plating hasn't given out. The Kill-Switch I used to override the vehicle, it said it worked, but it lied to me."

No. No. "The wheels? Did they shoot out the wheels?"

"Run flats from an unknown design. The whole registration sheet for the truck appears to be falsified information. That isn't a truck, it's a Snafu. She gave him a Snafu Prototype!"

Giving into the panic with his tone, "you stop that over important workstation jockey and his burger flipping friend!"

Watching the monitors he witnessed the explosion tear the front off of Central Tower's lobby. *They're out numbered and out gunned.*

Speaking his update with a hollow quality to it Athens' voice betrayed an understanding of what had occurred, "Security reads as detonated. The insider delivered the package."

Reviewing the plan as he spoke the words, "the forces will commit then. Drexel will blitz as far as he can if they resist and the breaching charges will take care of the rest."

With the sound of keystrokes and clicks behind his words, Athens sounded distracted, "keep me appraised. I need to go try to find a way to stop Hope."

We are too close to be stopped now! "Can, and will, do."

1.3.8 - 23:30

Central Tower - Lobby

#Kincaid Drexel
#Leader of "The Fire's Promise"

They locked the doors and ran out of the lobby. So we took the doors out of the equation. Now to step into the field of battle and show them what defiance means for them.

Motioning the last of his forces through the blown out front panels of the entrance to Central Tower, he felt a cold settling in against the fires of his convictions. As the words from the loud speakers faded off he could hear the furious sounds of emergency procedures being enacted. *They don't care if it's real or not. They are going to do it this way.* Swallowing roughly he dug into the pit of his convictions and took solace in the promises he had been given by Thomas Kunlow. *I am leading these Citizens to a brighter future.*

The words were those of the people who stand with her. Looking to his left and right he could see the stunned shock on the faces of those who he had been given to command this night. *Those were not Patrick's words. Those were the words of another. The sounds we hear are workers trying to do whatever it takes to stop us.*

She has built a cocoon of loyalty and the sounds reaching us are the sounds of the loyal readying to fight to the death for her. They have no way to know it's not real. In this moment they are not Citizens, they are Loyalists to another cause.

The idea that the Bachman name, the life of a family, is worth more than they are. She leads because they want to follow. They adore her, because they feel a kinship to her. Even though she stands apart from them.

Rolling his tongue in his mouth he found words for his forces, "the battle will be ruthless. They do not fight to defy Protocol, they fight to save a life, at whatever cost. They will not be consoled if we win. We have to kill them so they can have peace. If it moves against us? End it. Do not leave an enemy today who will be a foe tomorrow. Consider every point of light an equal priority to snuff. Remember that in the future that comes after this, rest assured, the family, the friends, that you have lost?"

Raising his voice he let the full force of his angered sick at the thoughts of what they were fighting to make right pour into his words, "they *will be avenged!* They fight for a peace with *murderers!* They wish to protect those who *take and take and take! Show them! Show them what we have lost!*"

Answering back as a galvanized chorus, "yes sir!"

Renewing his grip on his weapon, *into the Breach. To make a new world for all of us. A world without the name Bachman. A world where our foes are finished instead of given land. First the Bachman Family, then the Ports, then everyone else.*

1.4.0 - 23:32
York's Truck - En route to *Anywhere Else*

▸Jerome Hope

Rusted scrap no! Turning on the camera Jerome sat in horror at the scene which had not changed. Checking the communication line request window he watched the small circle of yellow and red pips flowing with a slow cadence to their blinking. *The Network is rapidly becoming too scrambled to work with.* "The rusted det sucking waste of air! He's burning the Network to stop me."

Listening to the sound of the reactive rims screaming on the pavement, York's white knuckle grip on the steering wheel projected his mood, "we got chased onto the wrong rusted road! We're still fifteen from C and D! Please tell me you have something! *Anything!*"

Keeping quiet as he stared at the closed hanger door he felt his mood sinking further. Catching the flicker of a green light at the corner of his eye he opened the connection window. *I found a line! He didn't find a way to lock out everything I can do as Admin Nobody. The Bachman Relays! Someone turned them on!*

It's text only. Rust. Not enough anything for audio. Typing as the truck swerved slightly he sent his message to Stanley Perkins. *The head of Logistics and Information Processing at Cloak and Dagger. I hope he gets this and gets me what I need.*

Trying to keep the frustration out of his voice, "can you keep the truck on the road?"

Firing back with an angered confidence, "I can! What's the scan?"

"I sent a message into Cloak and Dagger. My permission key to the hardware is being gummed up. I can hardly use the Network."

"Do you have any spare keys?"

"Just one. I have one ace left. The Pale Rider. I still have access to The Pale Rider hanger."

With a voice of a borderline angry scream, "do I *want* to know?"

Yelling back at him over the sound of the screaming rims, "probably not!"

Lowering his voice to a quieter yell, "what happens now?"

"You drive, if the message gets through? The hanger door opens and I," pausing as the words hit him, "kill Athens."

With a tone betraying his panic and stress York's word cut through the cab and over the sound of the still screaming rims, "The Pledge of the Silverback states that each Citizen *must* accept that in their lifetime they could hit a moment that will be kill *or be killed.* I don't want to die J-Man. But I can't take my hands off the wheel. You don't make this choice *just* for you! Think of me you selfish so and so!"

Smiling despite of the tension wracking his body, "I think I am one of the few people who understands you York."

"Shallots understands me. But then again, *he's* a trained professional."

Rust it, why not? "Does he also like large breasts?"

Grinning angrily, "he does! *He does!* And if I live through this I am going to look at more *endowments,* because life is for the enjoyment of those still alive to live it!"

Getting out his handkerchief he reached over and carefully dabbed up the sweat that was threatening York's eyes. *Drive hard my friend.*

1.5.0 - 23:37
Cloak and Dagger HQ - The Commander's Lounge

∩ Steven Bachman
∩ Commander of Cloak and Dagger

"Commander Bachman!"

Opening his eyes and sitting up quickly Steven set to pulling off his breathing mask. Letting it drop to the side he rose to a sitting position as his body screamed in agony at the sudden movement. Gasping out the word he fought the wracking agony, "speak!"

Blinking in shock at the figure of his softly haggard lover, standing in the doorway, holding his coat carefully. *Stanley, you're not supposed to be here. Why do you have my coat ready?*

"Fimbulwinter! It's Central Tower sir! I received a communication from Admin Nobody! It said Fimbulwinter at Central Tower! The Network is on fire, you will need to use the Bachman Relays. They activated mysteriously, but have been a boon."

Rubbing his eyes he rolled his head back and forth taking in the darkness of his small resting room as his body reminded him of the pain it was in, "Authorization Code?" *I'll dwell on Admin Nobody possibly knowing about my relationship with Stanley later. And the idea of magical relays.*

Fighting back the tears and fear as he approached with the coat, "Echo Nautilus Delta Indigo Nautilus Gamma. I have already prepared the system and the forces are moving to position. You say the words and you're in motion."

Feeling the rush of emotion buoy his body against the pain he finished rising from his cot. *The end is nigh.* Pulling out his comm he flipped it to broadcast mode and selected the Bachman Relays, "all hands! Fimbulwinter has been called at Central Tower! *I repeat! Fimbulwinter!*"

All hands, all resources, everything shall be mustered and used. There will be no quarter from here on out. None given, none asked for.

Getting up and sliding into his coat he checked the holsters on weapons he would be hard pressed to draw. Stanley's touch went a small distance in keeping his anger from overtaking him, *The Council betrays her. I will not be consoled! I will have blood! Hold on sister, help is on the way.*

Giving Stanley a small smile he spoke the words before moving toward the door, "thank you Stanley." *He calms the rage like nothing left on this cursed dirtball. I need to get away from him so I can be mad and do what must be done.*

Moving fully out of the way Stanley's hushed words followed Steven out of the small room, "go with the speed of the Gingerbread Man and the strength of Dauer Steel."

Turning back he nodded twice before lurching forward to get away before he slowed down. Pulling out his comm he synced his earpiece and slipped on his Heads-Up Display Glasses. *I cannot fail her. I will accept nothing less from myself. She has to be ready to face this without me as I won't be around nearly long enough now. Don't die on me Sis, this world cannot afford to lose you.*

1.7.0 - 00:01

Central Tower - 29ᵗʰ Floor - The Director's Office

☼ Yuri

And no more sounds of gunfire. We can enter this room that was so important to Sevilan. Screaming this way, that way, and going a strange maze of motions as men kept hounding us. But we appear to be where he wanted to get. Looking at the plaque next to the door it occurred to him why. *Patrick. Not a good night to be working late, I don't like him but I hope he's alive.* Coming in tight around the corner and finding cover Yuri spotted a still moving enemy on the floor. Bringing his weapon to bear he fired off the last two rounds it held. Hearing the click he took a shuddering breath watching the body cease its struggles. *Out of ammo.*

"I'm out, *again.*"

Looking to the other side of their impromptu cover he noticed that Sevilan hadn't bothered taking cover. "Check the room for ammo and for Patrick Bachman. If we fail he can write the eulogy for this night. This is his -"

"What?" Turning his head he spotted the prone figure of Patrick Bachman lying on the floor. *I never forget a face. He looked better last time I saw him. He's still breathing though which is a good sign but his posture looks bad from here.* "How bad is it?"

Dropping to one knee carefully Sevilan started checking Patrick over, "he's wounded. And we're on the way to Susan. This hallway leads to a juncture which will get you closer to her! I just had a hunch he would be here working late."

Dropping to one knee to join him Yorklin readied his med-kit, "I can see to him."

Making his way back toward the door he spotted a shotgun he could grab. Bending down and grabbing it and the ammo pouch he looked up at sudden motion in the doorway. Raising the weapon he focused his eyes to see a beat up member of the Honor Guard who was missing his helmet.

Gasping softly the Guard wheezed out the words, "olly olly oxen free!"

These people and their codes. I need an interpreter.

Without looking over his shoulder Sevilan spoke to the man in the doorframe, "Guard Sinclair Holden, status?"

"Wounded, it's my arm, it's out of commission. The vox is quiet as a tomb. They got the local communication relay. I was running defense on twenty-eight. They sacked me and left me. I took out three after they sacked me." His voice taking on an empty quality,

"I know Kowalski didn't make it. I passed his body on the way here." Using his good arm he offered his carbine to Yuri, "you must be with them. Take this, leave the shotgun. Ammo capacity is too low on that to do you much good. I have two spare magazines left you can take too."

Accepting the weapon, "let me help you to a chair."

Sevilan's firm voice resonated through the office, "Yorklin?"

"Yes?"

"I'll stay here. You take Yuri and get going."

The confusion rang out clearly with Yorklin's one word question, "Sir?"

Without looking away from his ministrations he was offering Patrick he barked his follow-up, *that's an order!*"

I can tell the fighting is dying down, our voices are getting louder. This is not good.

Checking the elbow while moving Guard Sinclair to a chair that looked undamaged, *it's a sprain, could be really bad if he tries to keep going.* Lowering him to a chair, "it's not broken. The elbow is sprained, but it does seem bad enough that you do not want to touch it. You wait here with Sevilan and he'll see to you once Patrick is stable." Taking the two spare magazines he quickly secured them to a tactical sash he had found.

"Thanks. You best get going, you have an order. You're not *that* far behind them!"

Nodding, "we will try to catch up!"

From his new position by the door Yorklin urged him quietly, "Yuri? With me!"

1.9.0 - 00:08

Central Tower - 30th Floor - Office of the High Consul

⟫⟪..Susan Bachman

Listening to the still functional intercom Susan waited as the sounds of activity rang closer and closer. *I've heard fighting, explosions going off, it's a war zone out there. Breaching charges from the sound of it. We lock a door, they break it down. They came ready for the idea that people would fight for me.*

"We're almost there!"

That is not one of mine.

"They told us the Honor Guard were tough, not Dagger tough, but *rust!* Calvin, Will, and Amos are dead! And I can't raise the other squad leaders! *I can't raise Kincaid!* How was this worth it? *Tell me!*"

They have come.

Feeling her blood pressure begin to rise in the response to the anger and the fear she balled up her fists and forced herself to breathe as their words continued.

"It isn't yet. We still have to kill Miss Bachman."

"By the Blue Sky look at that door!"

"The doors to the Wolfram Throne. How many breaching charges do we have?"

"Hopefully enough?"

"Let's get this into place Buchanan."

"Was this the plan?"

With a voice that sped up with rage and sad frustration with each word, "no, the plan was that they would give up. They were going to get the memo, see it wasn't worth it, and let us take her. They could have been spared! They didn't have to die! They just had to be reasonable!"

Fighting with the rage and fear she curled and uncurled her toes as her jaw clenched against the emotions rolling like a storm through her body. Forcing herself to breathe she fought against the tightness in her chest.

"It's fine, it's as it is Hugh. They made their bed, they get to be ash now. We get in there, we kill her, and we're the heroes in this."

"ETA on the Commander?"

"No telling. We're a lot worse off than we were projected to be. Charges ready?"

"Almost."

"Ready yourself brothers, we're almost done. We go into the last bastion of the Bachman family. There's no telling what is going to happen."

"Can we take her?"

Coming out of the speaker with a bold tone of confidant contempt the words struck her with the weight behind them, "there's three of us. *One* of her. She's not a myth, she's not a legend, she's a being of *flesh* and *blood*. She *can* be killed. She's hiding from this because she knows she deserves this. Come on, let's finish this."

"Let's get to cover."

"Affirmative."

Picking up and gripping her father's favorite machine-pistol she moved toward her chosen cover. Moving the safety to off on Last Resort she settled into place, *I am not going to die tonight. I am not going to die tonight. I am not going to die tonight! I shall fight until I have no more enemies before me!* Sliding deeper behind cover, *the last stand of Susan Bachman. A flash bang and eleven bullets. They better remember me as the woman who went down fighting if I lose tonight or I'm coming back from the other side to correct the books.*

At least I'll die with my boots on. And my nicer long skirt. Certainly not the war dress of a High Consul but a wonderful outfit to eat cake in. Focusing on the words she could hear through the intercom, *and they're counting it down.* Sliding the plugs into her ears she wiped the sweat off her palms and renewed the grip on her pistol. Talking herself up to keep the fear at bay, *I refuse to die tonight. Flesh and blood, yes. A legend? Soon enough.*

1.8.0 - 00:05

Central Tower - 29th Floor - The Convergence

☼ Yuri

Taking a moment to review the conference room, having bested another four men with Yorklin, *flush from victory over people who were going to spend a celebratory night eating cake.* "There's so much blood." *I have seen atrocity, and I know its smell. The non-com hid in here behind these breached doors. They came in here to murder.*

Looking around Yorklin blanched, "they're not all dead Yuri! I have a chance to save them! We weren't that far behind!" Moving toward the fallen he called back to him, "can you get to Miss Bachman?"

"I can!"

Moving to the first of the fallen with his medical bag in hand, "pardon me for caring for these people. I have to save them!"

A doctor and a soldier, one then the other. Save those you can for the living are the ones who fight the next war. "I understand. I shall go to her!"

"Ask her, what color is the veil? She will tell you the color of her veil! If she says white you're all right. Any other color? Use your imagination!"

"Understood!"

What color is the veil? The veil is white, the veil is white. Got it.

Turning and throwing himself back into the race to Susan's office he knew they had spent too much time getting to her. *She has to think of something! She has to still be there!*

Hearing the sound of a larger explosion, than he had heard yet since the front doors were breached, roaring through the night he felt the jagged knife of failure tear through him. *No!* Digging deep he pushed his body with one last plead to his muscles to keep working. *No!*

1.9.5 - 00:10
Consul's Office – Kunlow Estate

♠ Thomas Kunlow
♠ Consul of the Kunlow Family

Looking down at his lap he felt the tears coming without mercy. Turning away from the monitor which had kept him up to date on the now failed coup he settled into his chair. In the center of which, the frozen image of Susan Bachman perched over the half overloaded camera, that had been mounted on the side of Buchanan's helmet. *I have failed. The people decided to fight for the Echo. And in her employ killers of men of such skill and audacity I am left fearing for a world that could have created them. They fought with a resolve not promised by accepting the Silverback's Pledge, but something more. And even after everything, just past the doors to the Wolfram Throne she waited for the last of them to come. And then she bested them.*

Looking from window to window on his monitors, *the Sys-Admin is dead. The severed feed proves that. My men and women I sent for her are dead. As it has been, and shall continue to be, the Bachman family creates corpses with its determination to avoid its deserved fate of death.*

We could have had a great future. Bright. Shining. And now? Only death waits.

Turning off the monitor he turned his attention to his walls. Contemplating the moment he took a moment to reflect on the pictures on the walls again. *Asmodai failed to protect us from our enemies. He failed to get justice for the fallen. And now this world is left with whatever is going on behind the darkened eyes of Susan Bachman.*

He made her, the bright child of Drenner empathy, into a Bachman. And now the future gets to deal with her. Ready to kill to protect the lives of our enemies. The wheels of my plan are still turning, but it will be to no avail. I have no loyalty to anything past myself and Octavia now, so I will let them turn without word until they fall off of their tracks.

From the doorway to his study came a sweet soft voice breaking into his thoughts, "Papa?" Looking up at Octavia he found a smile. *She looks so happy. If Miss Bachman is not completely lost then she'll be spared. She did nothing wrong.*

Raising a hand he waved to acknowledge her, my little lady. My sweet girl shall be left to fight her. Even if she isn't quite so little anymore. She's old enough that they'll make her the Consul. She's not the preferred thirty years of age yet, but they'll give her the burden regardless. I cannot bear the burden of telling her though. Of telling any of them of what we have done and lost at. Or that her precious Kincaid is gone. It would be too much to bear.

This shall be our last night together as father and daughter and I don't want it to be the worst night of her life. Spent waiting for the haunting silence of the killers that will come. I will have to take time before morning to write a letter to Yvonne and my boys so they know why I decided to do this. I hope my sons grow up to understand.

Finding an excuse he spoke it, "I was watching a movie. It was very sad. I was just overcome."

"Oh. Do you want to come join us? I know it's late but the Midnight Shift thinks they have something that they would be proud to show you. It's about that project we've been working on for reducing manpower use in Waste Disposal and Recycling. To the end of making the job easier and avoiding unneeded wear and tear of those who toil. If it works we can send the notions down to Seaside. They hope they didn't miss something in logistics, extra eyes and thoughts are always appreciated."

Always working. My tireless Little Lady. To think that when our House survives the judgment coming it will be her voice guiding this family. "Of course Octavia. I would love to. And even if it isn't what they were hoping? I would be honored to hear their fine attempt at greatness."

Clapping her hands together softly, "wonderful!"

Saturday, April 30th, 2242 - Roused From Slumber

2.0.0 - 00:11

Central Tower - 30th Floor - Office of the High Consul

...Susan Bachman

Getting up from the third body she gripped Last Resort tighter with the empty comfort of a magazine without ammunition left to it. *Please don't let there be more. Because I need to throw up. They won't suffer, but that's not remotely –*

Banishing the train of thought she moved away from the fallen. *At least the one died instantly. He didn't suffer.* Whispering the words to herself she tried to take solace in the reality of it, "he didn't suffer."

Looking at the door, now soaked in foam from the fire suppression system, she shook her head as the tears tried to well up. Reaching up to each ear in turn she set to pulling the plugs out, *he said to lock the doors, to wait for him. He said he'd reach me. If they're here then –*

Startling at the sudden shout from outside her office Susan felt a chill at the intensity of the sound. *"Susan? What color is your veil?"*

Yuri. I have not heard anguish like that in some time. Clutching her chest she tried to get her mind to think straight. *If I'm dead in here then he dies too. Where's Sevilan?* Feeling the gut wrenching nausea relax for a moment in the wake of her confusion, *before communications went dark he was being put in his cell. How did he get through a building full of people? Why is he the one who made it? Where's everyone else? Why does he know the veil prompt?*

Screaming the words with an echoing heartache, "what color is the veil?"

Calling out to him, "Yuri? The veil is white!" Hearing her voice barely reach her ears she cleared her throat viciously trying to get her volume back before repeating herself. "The veil is white!"

Coming into the office with a distinct limp Yuri looked at her with something she couldn't identify in the dim lighting of the emergency lights. Looking down into his hands she blanched when she recognized the carbine he was holding as one used by her Honor Guard.

I think this just got a lot worse. I deployed a dozen Guard, where are they? If he's here with that then that means none of them could be. It means Sevilan and Yorklin couldn't be here either. I called Final Stand and it came to pass.

Looking back up at her and following her gaze he nodded gently as his shoulders heaved looking for breath, "heavy losses at the hands of the invaders. I received this one with a direct order to use it to find you."

"What happened out there?" Trying to keep her gun pointed at the floor and something resembling a good posture she heard the scared ache in her voice as the words spilled out, "*where's Frank?*"

Drinking in the air he seemed to be finding a measure of relief, "he's alive, uninjured, last I knew."

Looking at Yuri's torn shirt she could see bloodstains on the edge of the holes in the fabric. "You've been hit?"

Looking down with a moment of surprise he heaved the words out, "I guess I was."

Repeating the question with a more casual intensity, "where's Frank?"

"Patrick's office." After another heave of air, "seeing to Patrick. Who is *also* alive."

Tucking the pistol away she flashed the signal for 'Medical Intervention' out of reflex. Seeing his nod of a reply she set to investigating his chest. *I think it's superficial. Good thing I already know what his chest looks like or I would worry more than I should.* Getting her purse she fished out what supplies she could find and set to cleaning his chest.

After watching her for a few moments he spoke to reignite their conversation, "why are you good at that? Each time you did this before, and now, you know your kit well."

Trying to keep her tone matter of fact, "I'm just doing what little I can."

Frowning slightly his tone reflected a sadness, "are you a politician or a medic?"

Not now, please? Just let me do this. "I am *me* Yuri."

Moving on with a tone of conversational sadness, "Yorklin was seeing to wounded. He hit a group that didn't have a medic."

"Are there more invaders?"

"Invaders? No. We fought them over and over. It is as if they were trying to find Sevilan at points. We would hold still a moment and then they would come. He switched to a faster route and left them struggling to keep up. I believe all of the attackers have fallen."

"Good." Lowering his shirt she sighed at her basic handiwork and emotional paralysis, "I have a med kit in the car."

"None in here?"

Gesturing to a broken up cabinet on the edge of the demolished art gallery, "the blast sent debris into the cabinet it's in. It's no good."

"The art –"

Is the least of my worries, "we can make new art."

"How do we get to the car?"

Shaking her head she sighed at her current state, "not yet. I," pausing for a moment, "if you stay it could get worse."

Rolling his question with an unabashed humor to the words, "can it get better?"

Pointing to the doors to enunciate the answer, "easily."

With an intonation of an oath taken he seemed set in his decision, "aardvark."

All the answer I need.

"I want to apologize Yuri," looking down at the carbine in his hands, "how's Sinclair?"

Asking with a soft concern, "how did you know this was his?"

"Each one has a different logo on it. That's his. He is a son of the Osprey. The emblem of the Seattle Militia."

Nodding in understanding, "he's got a sprained elbow. It's bad. I don't know *how* bad exactly, but it is bad."

Leaning against Yuri for a moment she spoke softly, "I wish I was under the blankets and crying." *The numb is setting in.*

Without touching her he spoke with an upbeat resignation, "I saw a convoy of Cloak and Dagger pulling up as I came down a nearby hall. Forgot to mention that."

Oh no. Spinning the ideas around in her head she found something that held together, "we can't be here."

Looking at her with the slow return of his humor, "*we* can't?"

"Yuri, whomever did this? It's Consul level backing. No one has this kind of a force they can field outside of a Consul. My playbook is a known variable. *We* can't be here."

"Then where can we be?"

"We'll get to my car and go." Looking down at his hands she touched them gently, "leave the carbine."

"You hold and touch me without fear." Moving over to a nearby chair he laid the carbine down, "it is a strange feeling to see a ruler so fearless. Even after everything."

"We had some time in the dimly lit light of your cell when you were on night cycle. I feel like I know you. From the stories, the laughter you tried to give me." Moving to her desk she laid Last Resort down, "and I have more guns in the car."

"Leaving the carbine?"

"It's not *your* gun to leave with. Tracker pin in it. The same with the pistol I just laid down." Laying her hand against the desk she felt the emotional convulsion hit her as the smell snuck past her. "Yuri, I don't want to go out that door."

"What can I do to help?"

I can't think. "Sinclair is alive though?"

"Like I said, sprain of the elbow. Who is he to you? A secret ally?"

"Of a sort." Closing her eyes, "I know my brother is preparing to storm the building, but that takes a moment to set up. He'll be waiting for answers from a force that isn't there to yell at." Breathing softly for three breaths she collected her thoughts, "Yuri, once upon a time? I got in a verbal altercation with someone over the fate of people. I overstepped myself in tone and wordplay, and action. In response when the time came to add to my Honor Guard? This person, she sent Sinclair to me."

"Why?"

"I don't know why *him* exactly. He's a spy, in a sense." Finding a term she liked more she spit it out quickly as a follow-up, "a watcher. He's a good man, his reports he tried to send her were fair approximations of things, but I doctored them. He's *on loan* to me because his presence was viewed as needed. I have this one little light of happiness that he's alive because it means that she won't have to hear that he's dead." Taking a breath, "and I'm having Survivor's Guilt because I have an inkling about how many are dead and how this is about someone's perceptions of what it should be like to kill me."

Sinclair, Frank, Yorklin, Patrick, Yuri, and myself. That leaves a lot of room for people to mourn for. "I'm scared of the emotional implications of what happens next and what I'll hold myself accountable for in ten years when I look back on this night, if I'm still alive." Squeezing the desk with her right hand, "I feel my father's pain."

"If Steven reaches us, what do you fear?"

Looking over to him she felt her sense of self returning, "you might know."

Speaking with a soft awe of the idea, "you're afraid he will kill me."

You took the step no one would take. What no one had it in them to do. "I am."

"And this is *before* he knows I killed the old man?"

That fact might get him to spare you. He'll hate you but he might leave you alive because he wanted it too. "Indeed."

After an audible movement of a tongue trying to create moisture in a dry mouth, "why did you forgive me Susan?"

Moving back to him she leaned in and touched her cheek to his. Speaking softly she tried to keep her lips off of his ear, "love. You acted in a moment of hate because he hurt something you cared for. And, more that we don't have time to cover."

Feeling his arms wrap around her she fought with the sob in her throat. Swallowing the emotion she nodded once, "one minute. I can give us one more minute like this."

Speaking his reply as a whisper, "thank you."

Whispering in return, "noted."

Closing her eyes she touched the watch on her wrist for the one minute timer and surrendered to the moment. Listening to the sound of his breathing she sighed when the tiny chirp brought her back to reality far too soon.

Stepping away from him she felt the desperate smile form, "we won't face him. I'm back to myself to the point where I can lead us out of here."

"No need to worry about Protocol?"

"I need to see something," pulling her comm back out she went over to the nearest dead body. Checking it she smiled at the sight that data service was restored. Taking a picture of the emblem on the shoulder of one of the fallen men, while doing her best to not look at him directly, she ran a recognition scan against the Network. "We file all emblems and iconography with a central database. If this is a registered emblem I'll know more in a moment."

"How long does it take?"

Looking at the results she felt her throat seize up, "it's done."

"And what did it say?"

It says that they're a newly accessible file. Consul level backing, don't know which one though. They have a Clearance rank that's staggering for a martial force. Network appears to be in sad shape though. Which means there is hope for this to work. "It confirms I need to get you and get out of this building."

"Okay."

"All we have to do is get down to the parking garage, get my car, and leave without someone catching up to us. I'm not a medic, I can't do anything for these people." Flinching at the words she spoke she shook her head, "I could hold them as they die but then I'm just a target if there's a secondary attack. I have to hurt all of us, and just go, if I'm going to do this. Protocol states I am to be headed for my secure bunker at this point so they won't be expecting me. Steven will take care of them, I will get to safety, and after I regroup I can unlock the part of my brain that will solve this. I can tell I'm not well." Holding her hand up she gestured at the top of her head, "I can feel a part of my brain not working."

"Noted. I am not a psychiatrist but I know that feeling. With that in mind? Is there a way out we can take he won't notice?"

That sudden look of compassion, I wish I had more time. Getting her mind back on task she wracked it until it spit out the information she needed. "There's a specific express elevator that still works even when on the generators and backup batteries. It was father's backup plan to getting out of here in a hurry."

"And Steven is not going to chase us down and kill me in a fit of pique?"

Trying to muster all her sincerity that she wasn't sure of, "I'll protect you. I have guns in the car."

Taking her hand with a more forceful grip than she expected, "then we shall go. I didn't see this elevator you spoke of on my way to you so it must be the other way around the top of this tower. Which is fine because we need to go around the bloodshed."

I don't want to ask, but I will. "My people are really dead aren't they? I can check what I can in the car, see the full deathtoll, but it's bad isn't it?"

With the softest voice she had heard from him in the time knowing him, "it is not something you should see, yet. The men and women you would see knew the risks, they understood," taking a breath, "or they *should* have understood the meaning of working in a place like this. Many of them have paid the ultimate price, and if you see it? It could change your outlook on your position. If you are shell shocked at this point? It will only get worse. And to be selfish? I need you in good shape if I'm going to live."

Nodding in understanding, *even he can admit to a Blackheart.* Feeling a chill that had nothing to do with the air conditioning, "I'm scared Yuri. I've never been hit like this."

"You are a woman with a kind heart. They wouldn't give up your light without a fight and right now I can see that bastion of light flickering. Don't let the aftermath of this snuff you out. Let me spare you this. And as for Patrick he will need a doctor more than your tears tonight."

I will see those I can see after this. I will get clear, I will put myself back together, and then I will see them. Even if the pieces don't fit together anymore. "I will yield to your experience in this matter."

Intoning his word as a gentle urging, "follow."

Following Yuri out of the office she marveled at the damage the reinforced double doors had taken to force them to give way. *I doubt father ever imagined someone testing them though. Those doors stood through three generations. I get them and they're busted in a week.* Shaking off the self-deprecating humor she followed Yuri through the right turn at the first juncture they came to. Taking care to not look back she trembled against the quiet.

2.0.5 - 00:15

Central Tower - 29th Floor - Office of The Director

■Frank Sevilan

Laying in his supine position next to Patrick's desk, the place of conflict within his head and heart left him in silent contemplation of the pain. *I've been hit, I'll live. I've been hit before, I lived before. I'm just glad medics were able to find Dhavid and let him get back here for me and Patrick. I did what I could for both of us, but he runs his kit better and we both know it.*

Turning his head carefully he flinched at the sight of Patrick's pain strained face. Twinging at the internal strike of pain at the grim sadness of the sight. *You aren't Pledged to the Silverback. I told you that you would be kept safe. That those around you would protect you. And these det sucking trash heaps made me a liar, for the most part.*

Reaching out he took Patrick's hand and waited for him to squeeze in reply. *There it is.* "You in there son?"

Mumbling the words with a panicked grief, "I thought, Frank, rust, this isn't –"

Tipping his head he cast his glance up at Dhavid as he fought to keep his feelings in check, "status update?"

Speaking with a tired efficiency Dhavid seemed focused on the moment, "Director Bachman, you are not *critical*, as far as I can tell. Medical evac to New Hope General *will* be here soon. Help is on the way. Stay calm and give your body rest."

Looking him in the eyes Patrick's face betrayed the misery of the idea before he spoke his question, "was Bonnie here tonight?"

Feeling the frigid specter of doubt crawl over him he laid his head down, "I would assume she was Director."

Pressing him with a pain killer dulled fervor, "is she alive?"

Coughing softly Dhavid sighed, "unknown. I didn't get a chance to check for her."

"She might be gone?"

Bonnie, dead? She took good care of you, and Susan, and many others. Her sons. Rust. Rust. Rust. Feeling the tears welling up he swallowed the sob. *I got here too late to serve in their war. She was there for you because of your father. Caretakers of what Maggie left behind. Loyal to Asmodai to the bitter end.* Trying to keep his thoughts straight he pushed the words past the emotional weight, "she could be."

Whispering the words he gripped his hand firmly, "Frank, you saved me."

Trying to keep it just the facts, "you are Maggie's son."

"Susan, she's –"

Moving to reassure him Yorklin smiled with his words, "she's alive. Yuri made it to her."

"How do you know that?"

Tapping his earpiece, "no one has told us otherwise. Her medics would have broadcast it by now."

Looking back to him Patrick was still forlorn, "why did you waste – "

Cutting him off as gently as he could he spoke with a firm encouragement, "I didn't. Rust it to det Patrick, don't go into the darkness. You don't have to write her eulogy. Yuri made it to her. She's getting clear. She's getting to safety."

Sniffling for a moment he spoke with the cadence of a repentant younger man, "I, wronged, Yuri. I talked with him, Susan wasn't there. He said something to me, it was the truth, and I smacked him. He laughed at me. I left him after that. I, mom wouldn't want me doing that. I, just didn't know what else to do in the moment. I, don't like that I did that. This whole thing, is horrifying to me. Knowing Susan worked so hard to put him back together, but looking at him? I'm scared of him. I don't doubt he'll protect Susan though. He spoke to me how much he appreciated her ministrations. How much being alive meant to him. I, don't know."

Chiming in with a voice of 'trying to help' Dhavid nodded once in affirmation of his words, "Zero Chroma. If you have no idea what the color is, it's Zero Chroma."

"Yes."

Nothing else to do. If it hurts already, the pain goes unnoticed. "What did he say that prompted the slap?"

"He was talking about the past. About the future. I panicked."

"You know he'll protect her?"

Replying with a soft voice of sadness and jumbled emotions, "he loves her. He told me so. The idea that the big scary man who loves my sister is going to be armed and shooting at anyone who wants to hurt her? He can be *their* problem."

I think for the moment he's buoyed.

"You seem aware of life Director."

After a quiet groan, "painfully." Swallowing roughly he plowed on quietly, "if, if, Bonnie is gone? I'll write her a eulogy if her sons let me. If she's gone? I'll call them as soon as I wake up."

Inquiring gently Dhavid asked with a slight urgency, "you were close with them?"

"She was like a mother to me, her sons, it's, complicated. They lead to more discussion."

Amaranth. The younger boy is a friend of Amaranth's. "We will do our best Director."

Speaking with his low tone Patrick managed a few more decibels of volume, "he has to keep her safe. I don't know what her next ad lib is going to be. I don't know what shape she's in."

I don't either. "I don't either Director. I know that is what worries us both."

Giving only a small sad noise in reply Patrick settled back down to continue the wait.

Looking over toward the door Frank could see the shadows of a gurney being set up, "extraction to the hospital is inbound Director. You won't lie on this floor much longer."

Looking between the two of them, "thank you for staying with me."

Replying together in a practiced unison, "noted."

2.1.0 - 00:21

Central Tower - 30th Floor - Halls

⚙..Susan Bachman

Pointing Yuri in the right direction to find their escape elevator her thoughts turned toward the quiet. *It's a stillness that I've never heard. The Bachman Arcology still hums, the Cabin had the sound of the ocean, but this? This is just empty.* Forcing open slammed shut and locked doors she felt the emotional numb of the silence of the halls. *Central has never been this quiet. Even in our Moments of Silence you can hear the sniffling mourning sadness.*

Watching the minutes change on clock, after reset clock, they passed in silence as they neared the elevator doors. *The clocks defaulting to zero means that the infrastructure is busted. They wrecked Central to the degree the clocks don't even know what time it is.*

Leaning against Yuri for a moment she took solace in his rattled comfort. *He's strong, but this is getting to him too. I feel less alone.* Feeling him slow to a stop she stopped with him waiting for him to move. Turning fully he signaled for 'embrace.'

Nodding once she almost yelped as his arms were around her in a blur of motion. "I will be strong again, in just a moment."

Pressing herself against him she felt the comfort of his moment of vulnerability. Speaking with her best reassurance she gripped him firmly, "Yuri, it's, permitted, to not be strong all the time."

Replying with a strange levity to his tone, "we still need to get out of here though."

"Point."

Giving her a squeeze he smiled, "I will be strong aardvark."

"Thank you," taking a breath she let the truth out, "aardvark."

Settling into his embrace she felt time passing without much care for the idea. Startling as the chirp of full service restored came singing out of her comm in the quiet, *Jerome might still be alive.* Looking up she watched a nearby clock snap to the current time. *Twenty and change after already.* Taking a moment of pause to breathe she closed her eyes at the follow-up chirps coming from her pocket. *And that's Steven's chirp.* Pulling her comm out of her pocket she pushed the button as soon as she confirmed Steven's name on the screen.

"Susan!"

He sounds happy I picked up, which makes sense because he has no evidence I lived through that. "Hello Steven."

Firing back with an emotional badgering to his tone, "the rally cry of *Fimbulwinter* is sounded and that is all you give me! Where are you?"

Trying to keep her voice calm, "is Patrick alive?"

Letting out a puff of victory before his words, "yes! Mostly awake too! I found Patrick! My medics took over from Cloak Sevilan and we're getting ready to move him to New Hope General." Lowering his voice his victory faded, "I sent a group to your office but they report you're not there. Just two guns that have no owners in sight. What color is the veil?"

Keeping it matter of fact, "the veil is white. And? I'm going to Safe Housing."

"Protocol -"

Interrupting him gently, "I'm breaking it."

Sounding honestly concerned, "do you think that's wise? What if there are more?"

"I'll handle myself."

Firing back with a fraternal admonishment, "you left your gun in your office!"

Tossing her words back with a casual dismissal, "I have another four in the car."

"Who's with you?" Seeming to catch on with a new harshness to his tone, "where's Yuri?"

Not one millimeter of give. "He's leading me to the garage so I can get away."

Pushing the question firmly, "and who's going to put him back in his room?"

Don't. "No one, he's going to use a guest room."

Hearing the quiet hatred she bristled at the sound of his reply, "no."

Feeling the creeping dread in her stomach she asked anyways, "no?"

Losing his quiet edge he raised his voice, "Susan! That man is an outsider! He can't be trusted! He doesn't know our ways or how to act around you! I come to you under the banner of Fimbulwinter and you walk away like you're going to *tea!*"

Speaking softly but firmly, "the end of us is averted. As for him being an outsider? That ends tonight. As seeing as *my own Citizens did this?* I would rather trust him tonight!"

The retort was almost a shout which was barely held in check by her comm, "Susan!"

He sounds just like father, but I can do a better impression of him. Letting the anger rise to replace the fear she brought her voice into an uncanny resemblance of the one her father used when he needed to end discussions. "*I am the High Consul* and you will know *your* place! I dictate policy! You follow orders! Do you see the differences between us? The *Winter* has been canceled! You have a building filled with people who need you and your forces a lot more than I do! This was Consul level backing! Protocol means nothing to whomever is behind this! I *can't* follow the playbook or I just make it easier for them!"

With a much softer but still insistent voice, "if you can't go to your bunker? I'll send men –"

Without losing an iota of force, "that are needed here!"

"You'll be alone with him?"

Taking a short breath she spoke with a firm conviction, "yes."

His angered reply continued the stress her speaker, "please don't do this! There has to be a better plan!"

"It's too late, I already committed to this course of action."

"Susan!"

Pushing the button she disconnected the call. Reaching for the power button she noticed she had a trio of urgent flagged messages. *I'll get it in the car. I do need to change something though.* Going into the administrative functions of her comm she turned off the Navigation Assistant. *Not going to make it that easy.* Exiting from the administrative tools window she set to turning her comm off. Confirming that it had powered down she slipped it back into her pocket. *He's going to try calling me back, have it go to voice mail, and stop calling. After that I'll have my comm back on and deal with those messages.*

Leaning around Yuri she glanced down the hall, *there it is.* Gesturing to the Evacuation Elevator's door she set to following as Yuri walked with her to the doors. Pressing her thumb on the access pad she was rewarded with the doors opening. *At least that worked.* Getting into the elevator she settled in next to Yuri who reaffirmed his grip on her hand.

Broaching his words carefully with a restrained encouragement, "you stood up to him."

Catching the sight of herself in the mirrored wall she sighed at her appearance before turning her attention to Yuri's face in the mirror. "These men and women tonight? They came from a Consul. Now he'll be so angry that he'll make sure that the Consul behind this will be punished for what they have done. I had to show him that whoever did this? They're not afraid of us."

Cocking an eyebrow he spoke to her reflection, "no half measures eh?"

Nodding once in affirmation of the action, "no half measures."

"Susan, what's the plan? Other than get to the car and get away. Safe Housing you said?"

Not die. "Outside of not dying? We get to the garage, I double check your chest. Then we get my car, and go. We're going to take the long way round to get back to a place I should be safer, that's the Safe Housing I spoke of. I'll have to find out if Jerome is still alive. How many key people died," taking a breath against the feelings, "and understand what I have to work with and how bad this is. Jerome told me that this wasn't authorized. I have to figure out who decided this was a good idea though."

Turning to look at her as he spoke, "is the place we are going a solid building?"

Turning in kind to look him in the eyes, "it's called *Safe Housing* for a reason. It's a former garrison house. Mom," tripping over the word she plowed on, "had it remodeled when she took it over. It looks far more domestic than it used to. It won't hold against something like this, but it has a few surprises in case I need to leave in a hurry."

Furrowing his brow, "how many people know about it?"

Honest answer. "Too many to take it for granted."

Squeezing her hand with his question, "and we have nowhere else to run?"

"Nowhere that would hold out as well as I believe it would if tested. That also will be a place I can feel comfortable while I go off playbook. With no one around we minimize the idea of an assassin blending into the staff, as there is no one else waiting out there."

"Susan?"

"Yes?"

Looking to the ceiling Yuri asked his question with a bright levity to his words, "what did you do to make someone this angry?"

I can tell him. I can also understand the spirit of his question. "First," keeping her tone light and playful, "the local phrasing would be, what did I do to invoke such anger in another. That way I didn't *make* them do it, but they decided this was the best thing to do with that anger."

Nodding with an honest embarrassment, "oh, noted. Apologies."

Hugging his arm with approval, "accepted." Letting go of him she settled her courage for the words, "as for my crime? I wanted peace. The men, before they came through the door? One of them was rallying the others with words about killing me personally. That I *had* to die for their plans to work. The one thing I can think of is that I've done is kept up the peace my father started."

Lowering his head with a thoughtful mien, "in Port Refuge they spoke to me before they gave me directions to get here. They told me of the spooky nature of the peace. That if I did have a token of honor that I would have no fear. No land mines to dodge. I would just need to make sure to not draw my weapons and I would be unharmed."

"All true."

"Then whomever ordered this, they want war?"

They want to win the war that my father opted out of. "They want something worse. They want to do the things my father wouldn't do."

Speaking with a clear but quiet and emotionally fatigued tone, "do they have more soldiers for their cause?"

I wish I knew. "I don't know."

"How many people can we trust?"

Admitting the sad truth, "I don't know exactly."

Brightening for a moment he smiled, "do you trust me?"

Looking into his questioning smile she replied with a smile and affirming nod, "I do."

Assume a proud mien he spoke with conviction, "I am honored."

Squeezing his hand gently she let a smile crack past her neutral mask long enough for him to see it before putting it away. *He's the sort of person I could talk with for hours and not mind the passing of the hours. But now is not the time.*

2.0.2 - 00:12

Cloak and Dagger HQ - Exterior Parking Lot

▸Jerome Hope
▸"Admin Nobody"

Watching the gate close behind them with a rush of relief he tried to not fixate on the visible damage to the glass from his vantage. *I can only imagine what we cannot yet see.* Transfixed by the sight of the armor plated sheet locking back into place he touched his chest and performed the sign of the 'Divine.'

Sitting in the quiet he reached over and took York's hand and held it firmly as he was ravaged by the adrenaline crash. Moving closer he embraced his friend and held him as the gravity and emotional weight of the moment, being over, washed over them. Looking away from the spider webs in the bullet resistant glass he tried not to think about the moment.

Speaking quietly with a voice of hushed awe York seemed coherent, "we, we aren't dead J-Man. The loop around we were sent, it worked, we lost them."

He's better than he gives himself credit for. He did what he was trained to do. And whomever performed the Intercept, they did what they were trained to do. "It did, we're not dead, and we're safe. Now? We have to get inside, I have to secure the Network, and we have to save the dawn."

Hearing his comm chime that he had messages he pulled it out and looked at it, "Miss Bachman made it too. This says her comm requested a file. I don't know what shape she's in, but she's still using her comm."

Without looking up from the steering wheel he nodded twice, "how do I help?"

"You," wracking his brain, "you aren't safe out there for the moment. We don't know how things have gone. I'll bring you inside and you can get me cans of Hatred from the vending machine."

Rolling his head back his voice sounded concerned, "that stuff isn't good for you."

Putting his hand on the release handle for his door, "neither is failure."

Replying with a humored disdain, "point."

"Out of the truck York, we have to go inside."

"Affirmative."

Getting out of the truck he set to moving around the back of it to assess the damage. Looking at the truck he couldn't stop his brain from marveling at the bullet holes which riddled the discretely armored transport truck. *To think, she was afraid this would happen outside the city, not here within the Green Zone.*

Seeming to be honestly angry York fretted at the sight of the damage, "my truck -"

Speaking quickly and quietly to keep him on task, "it will be fixed, you know that."

Hooking his hand around York's right elbow he moved them across the blank parking lot toward the nearby access door. *I cannot have him asking me how his truck took all that damage. Then I would have to tell him. And I do not think he would like to dwell on that right now.*

Hustling toward the door, as a figure stepped free of the doorway proper, he held up his Ration Card, "Pending Sys-Admin Jerome Hope with a Plus One coming through!"

Stanley seemed startled by the sudden outburst in the quiet, "Jerome, did the Pale Rider work then? You *just* missed almost everyone."

Oh, it's Stanley. Good deal. Nodding his head he pulled York over the threshold into Cloak and Dagger Command. "We looped around as to not get in the way of the Commander. As for the Pale Rider? Affirmative. I did, what needed to be done. He was in league with them."

"Clarification?"

Nodding twice he signaled for 'Full Disclosure' before stepping away from the door. Hauling York along he led them down a side hall toward a room he knew well enough from prior visits to perform maintenance, "Athens went full traitor on this one. He was not coerced, he was in it to win it."

"That's horrifying. What is the usual safeguard?"

"Everything he bypassed. Once things are settled I will have a full report for Miss Bachman."

With a tone of honest relief, "she made it?"

Sliding his Ration Card into the door lock he pushed the door open as soon as the door beeped signaling its unlocking. "I believe she did. I received a notification in the parking lot. I'll let her know what he did and ask how she wants it handled as soon as *everything else* is taken care of."

"Good. Excellent really." Looking around the room Stanley smiled with an emotionally lost look on his face, "the backup Router and Switching Control in case Cloak and Dagger has to commandeer the Network. I take it you'll be commandeering it?"

Trying his best to sound confident in the future, "that's the plan."

"How can Information and Logistics help?"

"I need your manpower. I need everyone you can muster for me to go over to the Central Processing Unit facility and hook up with me using our ad hoc line from here to there."

"The usual line is down then? I just process the information, I don't service the tech."

"The Network is doing terribly. It's a localized event though. New Hope is soundly thrashed but I have good news."

"Which is?"

"The carrier lines between Seaside and Respite? They still funnel data through this city without fail. He didn't go that far. He just thrashed the local infrastructure."

"So the plan?"

"I undo what he did."

"Sounds good. And your Plus One?"

"He gets to go into the hall and get me Hatred and Hydration Plus."

"Understood. We do have snacks in case you need something for your stomach. I have an open bag of eggplant jerky I could get you."

Watching the main bank of screens booting up as York slipped back out the door, "I would like that. The snacks, and to start with the eggplant." Reciting the words from his lessons, "when the dawn comes, when we see the Blue Sky, we will see our wounds clearly."

Snapping his fingers Stanley fired out the answer, "Captain Tessa Kane, leader of the first Terror Squad of the Pacific Rim at her appointment after the Night of Lost Hope."

The world could still burn for this. "We cannot fall into old habits."

"I firmly believe from her journal she knew what would be asked of her. The campaign she waged with the Terror Squad might not have been a traditional success, but it did lead to peace. Asmodai returned from the place they traveled with the words of peace. I was just a young man when I saw his speech."

"The Bachman family has a way of changing our reality."

Moving around into Jerome's field of view Stanley had his hands clasped together, "why did you choose me Hope?"

Smiling he laughed for a moment, "good move there changing positions and body language as circumstances and all that."

Replying with a well intentioned sounding humor, "I didn't want you to think it was *ominous.* In a night rife with traitors I wouldn't want to give the wrong impression."

"Thank you for that! It's quite simple really, you were the first line I could raise in the building with what little power I had left to me, that had the Clearance that *could* help me. The power of random chance? I don't know."

"We managed to have a moment of good fortune then?"

"We did." Nodding twice he kept smiling, "I wish I could say there was some deeper reason, but no. Stories need those sorts of things, but I don't have anything for this one."

Falling quiet for a moment Jerome laid his fingertip on the scanner and watched the words play across the screen. Reaching out with his free hand he selected the options to take the position of Sys-Admin in the wake of violent upheaval. Taking his necklace off he uncapped the portable data drive and slid it into one of the free slots on the terminal. Pointing the system to the portable drive he waited for it to scan and confirm his use of the Bachman Permission Key so he could finish the process.

Regarding the drive with an inquisitive humor, "what's on the drive?"

Replying with a 'matter of fact' tone, "Bachman Permission Key authentication file."

Smiling with a hint of admiration to the question, "she gave you such a thing?"

Cracking a smile in return he spoke with the knowledge of the honor, "I am a proven Loyalist."

Nodding once with approval, "noted."

Looking at the monitor at the confirmation he nodded once with a solemn feeling in his chest. *I am the Sys-Admin now. Athens did the impossible for the High Consul and became the Sys-Admin. Now I do the impossible and the crown is mine.* Giving into the dark humor of the moment, *I will need to watch my future apprentice well. I should probably watch my coworkers too.*

Coming back into the room with a pair of cans in his hands York's tone was insistent, "Miss B is going to be, I don't have the word," pausing he pushed the term out, "her sky will be blue again, right?"

"York, I can only hope. Miss B," laughing at the act of speaking the diminutive, "she _"

Appearing as if he was about to break down, "just *lie to me.*"

Rushing the words with a false smile, "she's going to be just fine York and you have nothing to worry about. The sky will be blue, we'll recover from this, and it'll be a happy ending."

Replying with a borderline petulant tone, "you should be a better liar when telling such an important lie!"

Raising a forefinger Stanley hopped on the moment, "Miss Bachman is reported to be one of the worst liars anyone has seen in her age category."

Nodding with a smile Jerome thought back on some choice moments, "she has her ways of compensating, but she *is* an awful liar."

Holding out the can in his right hand, "can of Hatred J-Man?"

Looking at the fully booted up machine he took the can, *ice cold. Only way to drink it.* "Can of Hatred."

2.1.4 - 00:29

Central Tower - 29ᵗʰ Floor - The Director's Office

∩ Steven Bachman

Walking into Patrick's almost empty office with the angered melancholy in his chest he found himself thankful that Hampton and O'Neil would be next to him soon. Sliding his comm into his vest pocket, as he moved over to the supine form of Frank Sevilan, he reflected on the injustice of the moment.

He's injured. Not tagged, but injured. Only reason he would be laying there. The Invincible Captain, and he's laying here in the stink waiting for his private evacuation. Just isn't right.

Trying to keep his tone conversational, "Terrors inbound to get you up off the floor?"

Responding with a quiet 'matter of fact'-ness, "that is correct Commander."

Time to adjust to the only course of action that will work with him. "Injured?"

"Yes."

Matching his quiet 'matter of fact'-ness, "how is Patrick?"

"He's well enough. I made sure he didn't do something unfortunate like swallow his tongue."

I wish I knew what I wanted from this moment. Keeping himself on center he continued, "Cloak Yorklin, he stayed with wounded he found later."

"Did Yuri make it? I know Susan was able to get away, but I didn't know if Yuri made it to her in time."

Trying to keep the majority of the growl out of his words, "he is with her."

Meeting his gaze with a hardness in his eyes, "that doesn't make you happy."

Inquiring within for a half-heartbeat he found the truth of his feelings, "you are her remaining father, I *expected* it to be *you*."

"I thought I could make it," touching his abdomen with a sad look on his face, "I did not. I got tagged with something that got past my armor. The downside of infighting, we have very nice things to hurt each other with."

Relaxing his anger, "point."

Relaxing in kind he looked up to the ceiling, "I don't like being down here."

This helpless feeling, it's terrible. "I don't like you *being* down there."

"Do you like Yuri being with her less?"

Rust. "That's a bit of a personal question."

"I still asked it."

Answering with an off the cuff truth, "Captain, my sister, is reaching into a dark place. Deep into the history of this family with someone who understands just how sickly delicate the reality of things happen to be."

"He knows things you don't want people to know."

Knows things is an understatement of the depth and breadth of his understanding of things. "Correct."

Asking his inquiry with a quiet growl, "why didn't you kill him then?"

That hurts. "Honor. The Virtue which spares life. The Virtue that takes a man to the battlefield to defend something."

Glaring at him with a cold incredulity, "*this,* from *you?*"

We are all prisoners of the past, even me. "I understand you will never forgive me for what I was able to get her to do."

Obviously restraining the snarl, "I won't."

Being mad doesn't undo what was done. My guilt doesn't undo it either. "Instead, I will get you to understand this," taking a breath he clenched his fists for a moment before relaxing them, "Yuri? He is here because of a debt of honor. That's not *my* call on how it was to be handled as father was the head of the family. *Father,* put him into that room while he tried to sort everything out. Now? *Susan,* is the head of the family. It's going to be *her* decision."

"And if it was your decision? Kill him?"

"Your question leads me to believe that she has feelings for him."

"You haven't helped."

I have to make certain things are things. "If she can't stand up to me? She won't survive the Council. Do I like him? No. Do I want him near? No. Would it be easier if he had died and never made it to our world? Yes. Do I want him to stay? No. I would prefer if he left. But that is not my call to make, now is it? *I need her to see that.* She needs to have the resolve to grab the power and use it. To stand with*out* compromise. Without flinching. If she wants to be Potentate? She has to have the will for it. *I have no doubt of her will.* She *does* though. I have to erase those doubts."

Growling at him with no small amount of hostility to his tone, "so it's Guthrie, all over again."

Firing back with the defensive lilt to his words, "I have been testing her since before Guthrie. We are at a turning point for our world. Her decisions are going to be the fate of the future. *This?* Look around! You don't do this to something you are not mortally terrified of. I don't think she knows what her life has turned this city in to. The people who are happy when she walks in. The world that she changes with her will. Father was left in hushed awe of her because she is the product of the union that shook the balance of power. She has to be ready to finish what was started. The future, the Mission Statement, Ridolfi? She has her chance to change things as each generation of Bachman has changed things. I do not take this as a light thing to consider."

Calming in the wake of the quiet and only the sound of their breathing, Frank looked to him, "I understand your logic and reasoning. I don't *like* it. But I *understand* it. Rusted scrap."

He remembers I am also his son, and he was a guardian to me. "As for your question? *I* would have *told* Jerome to make him a Citizen, given him a nice little house, tossed The Codex at his head, sent someone from The Guild to him, and left him be to find a job and be productive while telling as few people as possible about anything outside of our world. Simple." Taking a moment to recover his breath he continued, "also, I do *know* that my plan doesn't work given our suddenly rusted up immigration laws, not to mention our rules on dealings with outsiders. So because Susan chooses to live by the rules? I am left watching her have to shelter this man. Watching her tend to him, and care for him, because no one else can. Every day she bows to the will of the weaker pieces of our world? She keeps him closer."

"Is that so bad?"

Letting the fire into his words he did his best to self-censor any over the line accusations as he spoke, "you were once in darkness Captain. My mother went to you in that place of darkness and she sheltered you. You were not always kind to her in those first two days. You were just one day from the Rangers coming to find you and bring you in for safe keeping. My mother needed you, she picked you, for a specific reason. She used time, precious time she was running out of, for you. She found you new life. You were a *gift* as you were *gifted.* Give and Give. Susan? She has time, but, she is walking wounded, and Yuri? If his damaged self infects those wounds? That's, not something I want to contemplate as a reality."

Reaching a hand up he gestured softly to him, "you are her brother, it's natural to worry. The Codex of Siblings says it's expected."

Lowering himself to the floor carefully he spoke his reply with a softness, "thank you."

"Noted."

Reaching out he took Frank's hand with a careful grip. *I am running out of time.*

After a moment of quiet he cocked his head to the side while looking to him, "would you really break Protocol for Yuri?"

Looking at the extreme contrast in their shades of skin he found comfort in the memories of a life shared. *You were always good to me.* "I would break Protocol to make certain the debt was paid. He is owed. The Debt is authentic and *should* be honored. By obeying the Protocol? She overpays on the debt."

"And if she pays because she likes the man as a man?"

Calming down fully he looked at the floor, "then I would be afraid that she wasn't feeling clearly."

"You fear that while her walls are down for him, he'll find a place in her heart?"

Rust, I have no other truth to speak. "Yes."

"I've spoken to him, many times, I think, feel, that he could be a good match for her. A good addition to her life."

What of her precious aardvark? "And Sasha?"

"I believe they can navigate that." Signaling for 'clarification,' "you support Dagger Herb then?"

"She is loyal." Letting out a single muted chuckle he tilted his head from side to side, "she is also a complex case of people not understanding happiness. Perhaps with Susan being in charge she can get things under control. I understand *some* of the outsiders conjecture about the two of them. I know she can't help Susan with an heir, I just don't want to see her get rejected when they could be happy like they have never had the chance to be."

Stating his words with a hopeful air about them, "you seem confident that we're going to win."

Smiling with a half grin of barred teeth, "I'll kill everyone I must to make sure that we win."

Squeezing his hand with a paternal concern, "you're skilled at that. You are also beeping."

My comm? "Time to find out who's trying to reach me."

2.1.5 - 00:31

Drenner Estate - Consort's Study

≈Micah Drenner
≈Consort of Consul Drenner
≈Lost Son of Horizon

Looking into the mirror while gathering his thoughts he stared intently at his own face. *I am older still.* Tilting his gaze to the picture of the four of them his eyes settled on Asmodai. *You brought me to your side, you showed me how to end a war. You told me that you did not trust Thomas Kunlow, and now, I have all the reason to understand why.* Looking at the framed picture of so many years ago of himself, Asmodai, Maggie, and Amanda he felt himself moved to the center of his core. *Your life ended my friend, my brother from another branch. Now I stand at a distance, watching your children that I stand as Parrain to, suffer. You helped me find this place I call home, this is the least I can do to honor our memories and the nightmare you saved me from.*

Your eldest just needs to see reason and let me in. To trust me one more time. To know that I stood next to you through dark times. That this is another dark time.

Pressing the call request he waited as the Network bounced his request off of the cellular tower backups to reach Steven. Hearing the call connect he was ambushed with the speed of Steven's declaration.

"Commander Bachman here, I am not shocked you called Uncle Micah."

He sounds happy I called. "I want to help."

"I know you do."

Setting to imploring him, "Steven –"

Interrupting him with a soft force, "Micah, you don't have to beg."

His voice is softer than it has been in a long time. The same social move Asmodai used when he didn't want to fight. "Do you have a plan then?"

"Not *much* of one to be honest. I have a hope."

"What is your hope?"

"Overwatch for Susan. She told me I couldn't do it. Circumstances beyond my control. But you, her beloved Parrain, to show that I know her Marraine had nothing to do with this."

He must know something I don't yet to already be willing to trust. "How do you know that already?"

With an almost meandering melancholy to his words, "I know the faces of my family. I did not see my family out there in the halls wearing the uniform of the attacking force."

Sitting up with a boldness in his heart, "I have men I could send, where is she if she is not with you?"

After the sound of a sip of water, "I suspect you know already, but I will speak it for you, Safe Housing."

"I will prepare the men and send you the manifest to Authorize."

"Thank you Parrain Micah."

He sounds honestly thankful. "We haven't spoken in a very long time."

"No, we haven't. I need you to know something," changing to a more familiar timbre of Counsel, "if there is a Second Strike against her? Your men will be hard pressed to survive. The names you pick will be at risk of never being picked again. Weigh your choices well and know what you are fighting for."

He quotes him well. "You quote your father well."

"His words were often apt, if sometimes unpolished."

As I was there with him for many of those declarations? "Truth."

"I need to go. We still have time to change the color of the sky before the dawn."

"May the sky be blue when the sun lights it."

Closing the connection he set his comm on his desk. Reaching down and resetting his Situation Alert anklet he sighed. Taking a seat on his chair he moved his keyboard into place. Calling up a query looked over what forces he had on hand.

The Drenner Explorer bodyguards are about all I have within mustering time. I'll still need a mobile command base, a few extra guns, surveillance equipment, and an Operator with Clearance. I just have to find it.

Opening up the House Manifest he found an answer in short order to what he was seeking. *The Mobile Base and gear left behind with the passing of Captain Kane. I have no recourse, it will have to do. May the fallen forgive me.*

Keying in his orders he nodded with a grim satisfaction, *I'll send this to Steven and then issue a set of orders to the Operator.*

Clicking the last things into play he hung his head before lacing his fingers together in his lap. *He's not stupid. If he looks at faces then he might have seen one he does know. He'll be moving to avenge her. His emotional intensity for his siblings is a terrifying sight to behold. We have no less a terrifying future ahead. But I know the groundwork is being laid to keep us safe.*

2.1.6 - 00:32

Central Tower - 29th Floor - The Director's Office

∩ Steven Bachman

Closing his comm connection he rolled his head around working on the tension he felt. *One less thing to worry about.*

Holding the canteen out to him to return it, "Overwatch for Susan?"

Declining the return of the canteen, "you keep it. And, yes. He agreed."

Relaxing again he moved the canteen to his hip, "House Drenner to protect her then?"

Nodding once with conviction, "yes."

"You mentioned you did not see faces that were familial. Is there more?"

Patting his hand gently, "they didn't do it. This isn't me playing a game. I *know this.* Which is why I told him where she went. He needs to know I know he didn't do it. We have precious little time to waste on games and false treacheries. I'm going to be too busy hunting down the people who arranged this. I need to save all of my hate, my rage, for them. I can't waste a drop." Finding a smile, "they will feel the exuberance I will show them at a job well done."

"How do you know? I am happy you picked your path, but I'm just looking for intel sir."

As you are one of the few I still trust, "I know my relatives. I know the deal that was made. I know the logistics of how this was set up and how it would have had to fall into place. The amount of people out there? They needed to be from one faction. I didn't know a single one of them as Drenner aligned. I may be loathed for what I have done for the good of The Rim, but I know who I'm related to and the lives they are intertwined with."

"Do you trust Amanda?"

Finally looking back at him directly, "this isn't her style. This wasn't her plan. She was prompted into action a year ago which set this whole idea of Susan being the High Consul into effect. She didn't have a single thing to do with it other than acting as the mouthpiece for why it wouldn't be me, or Patrick, in that office. I didn't think that this was the end game solution of those who prompted her though. The funny thing? It doesn't add up. There is something *more* to this. I'll get to the bottom of this though. Heal fast Sevilan, this isn't going to wait for any of us to keep up." After a moment of

pause he sighed, "I trust Amanda to be Amanda. I almost didn't answer your question there."

"She won't be alone at Safe Housing at least."

"Mother wouldn't be happy if she found out that I had left Susan alone like that."

"I would imagine she wouldn't be."

There has to be a Silver Lining. "Susan, if she was left alone? She would ad lib. She would spin another one of her wild plans into being. If I put Overwatch next to her? She *might* feel safer, cozy even. Then the men who watch the house will help me keep eyes on her and her wellbeing. She'll look out her window and see them there, and be comforted that part of the Order of Things is still working."

"Being alone *is* dreadful."

And now to show my cards. "Hampton and O'Neil will be here soon. As will your medical extraction. As this whole sector of the building is unchecked? I am to stay put."

"Noted." Asking his question as a follow-up, "why do you want her to refrain from an ad lib? If she is cozy, and with Yuri? Wouldn't that be worse?"

I am aware of the perceivable flaws in my logic. "Lesser of Two. If she is cozy? She is not trying to rule as the Derecho. Storms run out of energy. She's walking wounded, she's taken life," seeing the wince he nodded, "the man I sent to her office reported the guns. I refrained from asking her about the dead bodies. Last Resort shows signs of being used for William's Kiss."

Firing his words off with an exasperation to them, "you *could* have led with that as for part of why you're so rusted mad."

Feeling like the young lad again, "I was too mad to articulate it."

"Then better she heal, even at the risk of being close to the dangerous outsider, than on the front and burning up what's left of her reserves."

At least we both understand that. "Correct."

"Have you spoken with Yuri?"

"Twice. Once was just wanting to see. To hear his side of the story. The man got within Striking Distance of my father. The second was to ask. The understanding from him of the notions that led me to implore Susan to send him away."

"You fear him."

Losing ground within to the emotional confusion, "I do. But, I want her to fear him less. Risk assessment. The break the Protocol version of it? It would minimize the risk. I just don't know."

Looking at him with a concerned squint, "how have you been sleeping son?"

Opening up with an honesty about his wellbeing, "not well. Blips on the radar. Reports with troubling notes on them. There was *no time* for this."

"Rest. Your boys and my boys will be here soon. There is no shame in a Post-Conflict nap."

Speaking the truth from his core, "thank you dad."

Gripping his wrist he met his gaze with a softness, "you're still a son to me." Easing up he laid his head back down with a groan, "by the stars this is a terrible night."

Moving over with a pocket sized headrest he set to propping up Frank's head, "I concur."

2.1.8 - 00:34

Central Tower - Parking Garage - Sub Floor A

⁛⁙..Susan Bachman

Code Five Seventy Six is active. I should be able to cross the garage and get to my Beast without getting stopped. Adjusting her lapel pin she was thankful for the feeling of security that her bubble was bringing her. Looking up as the light turned green she took a breath as the elevator doors opened.

Stepping out of the elevator into the underground garage Susan brought her chin up as she stepped off the elevator. Blinking and stopping short she swallowed at the sight of the Mobile Yorklin Surgical Triage unit which had been set up.

This is not what I expected.

Flagging her down Medic Talkie moved into her personal space bubble, "discipline me later for the violation of your off-limits code, I need to report."

Signaling quickly she absolved him, "speak your report?"

"Gladly." Holding his hands out to a nurse, who returned to cleaning his hands, he spoke quickly, "somehow someone scheduled all four shifts of your Medical Wagon the night off. I ran into Medic Wingdale with Doctor Yorklin at The Pub, we talked, it shook out." Looking her over, "are you hit?"

Trying to be reassuring and not defensive she spoke with her best upbeat lilt, "I am not hit."

Gesturing to Yuri with more than a modicum of concern, "and him?"

"I will see to him with the kit in The Beast."

"Fair enough." Grimacing at his hands, as the nurse worked quickly, he returned to his words, "as soon as it shook out we activated the Bachman Relays. All four shifts are scattered in the building, along with Doctor Yorklin and her direct assets. We were able to set up triage before the fighting was over. We have two sets of injured, one in a new uniform I've never seen, and no answers. No one in the new uniform will say anything beyond *mea culpa.* The Commander told us to just do what we do and it would be sorted out later. We're working through people, moving them down the reactivated elevators, and then over yonder for pickup and moving. I authorized your Wagon for transport as you had not reported in."

Taking it all in she responding with an affirmation, "good."

"Can I get you to wear the Medical Watch?"

Father wouldn't most of the time, I don't blame him. I wish I could right now, it's not so bad with the new strap for it. "The uniform you don't recognize are insurrectionists. I don't know who sent them, or why. I just know that until tonight they were just Citizens of our world." *Play it safe, no matter how much it hurts.* "Keep the triage running without bias for the uniform. If you can? Peel them out of it and trash those uniforms. We know who is who already, we don't need to belabor it or Out-Group them already. Plenty of time to hate later."

Watching the nurse dry his hands he replied with a somber calm, "I can do this."

"On that note, I *can't* wear the watch. I don't know who might be able to use it to track me."

"Noted."

Give him something, "I will wear it after the dust settles."

Keeping his hands still as the nurse fitted new gloves on him he seemed in a brighter mood, "that means a lot to me."

"To confirm, all four shifts are involved in this?"

"They are. Can we spare one for you?"

"No. Keep the wounded moving. Use your Clearance to enter any domicile or zone to ferret out all the wounded in the building and keep them going."

"Understood."

"I need to get to safety."

"Then get, I have more patients. I will catch up with you after." Looking at her again, "you have no small amount of splatter on you."

Looking down she grimaced at the stains in the harsh lot light, "three that won't be needing your talents."

Closing his eyes and nodding twice, "I understand." Opening his eyes he opened his mouth for the nurse to pop a lozenge in. Rolling it around he tilted his head toward Yuri, "nurse? Lozenge him."

Asking the question with a mild trepidation, "I want one?"

"You do. It's moisture and other good stuff."

"Okay." Opening his mouth the nurse popped one into his mouth before moving on quickly after the departing Medic.

Getting them back on task with her modest decree, "to my car."

Following along behind her Yuri asked his question softly, "what is going on?"

"I'm broadcasting an Off-Limits code, Five Seventy Six. It's meant to keep people at bay. I want to get out of here as quick as I can."

Sounding confused but humored, "he walked past it."

"He's one of the Medics who is in my Medical Wagon detail. If he wanted to kill me?" Trying to keep herself from getting tongue tied at the emotional weight of the moment, "he would have killed me without all this. He needed to report."

"Understood. You, are sparing the invaders?"

I don't have words. "I *can't* Yuri. Not right now."

"Noted."

Wait a minute, "you picked up a new trick to your words."

"I've been listening to those radio shows. I *do try* to understand the people I live with. I have more questions, like," still sounding upbeat while wearing a look of mock horror, "what are the chalk marks next to this scary monster of metal we are standing next to."

Scary monster of metal? "That's my car."

Continuing with a show of theatrics, "that is *no car.* That is a nightmare beast forged in the fires of nightmare and breathed onto the mortal realm to run over those that would get in the way of it."

"It's known as The Beast."

Smiling with a bemused expression, "it's fitting."

Standing still for a moment the temperature finally became something of note to her mind. *It's a bit colder than I expected down here. Must be ten degrees at best.* Looking down she pointed at the chalk markings, "that's the mark of the New Hope Militia Squad which took care of checking for Post-Strike Devices. The line with dashes is their Squad marker, the middle is that they checked the car visually, the third is the quick chem-sniff test."

"Which squad did the check?"

Following the line of chalk marks she pointed to two armored figures and their tall combat shield working on checking another vehicle, "Jaguar Squad. They're trained in shield combat and domestic related counter-terror investigation and tactics."

Losing the theatrics and humor with his reply, "no half measures."

"No." Opening the truck of her car she set to finding her Medical Supply Kit.

"So is it five seventy six for a reason? Not five, seven, six, but seventy six?"

Getting her kit out from under her other supplies she set to removing the things she felt she would need, "history and math are the usual reasons we do anything. It's a reference to a year and historical event which is then extrapolated into a new meaning. We have a master reference file in The Network so we don't double up on meanings. Have to keep things as clear and concise as we can."

"More of the codes you told me of. You said I would learn more when I was free."

Getting her supplies in order, "are you learning?"

Grinning in the wake of realization, "I did. Not enough to know why that number, but I know the why for, and why a number. It's a start."

Smiling at him with her attempt at being jovial as she turned and positioned him in place in a way that minimized his visibility, "your next lesson? Is holding still while I do this right." Snapping on a pair of gloves with a careful alacrity, "you have a larger gash I want to get a patch on and I didn't have any patches upstairs."

"Understood." Looking away as she lifted his shirt, "when you said it was your *car*, I heard it. That lilt your voice gets."

Honesty. "It's a Liar's Lilt. The unsuppressed verbal clue of knowing you are speaking something that isn't quite true, or true at all. Waterlily told me that it could be linked to my feelings of not wanting to be the sort of person who lies, or makes promises they cannot keep."

"Waterlily, the woman you said takes care of your mind."

Working diligently she replied with a small nod, "yes."

Taking a moment to peek into the trunk he laughed softly, "guns, outfits, medical supplies, emergency rations, flares, what isn't in here?"

Letting the humor buoy her and carry her words, "factual or metaphorical answer?"

"Factual, as your metaphors are prone to sadness."

True enough. "A birthday cake. I don't have a birthday cake in the trunk. Not today at least."

"You asked me about the day of my birth, I can get cake then?"

Finding shelter in the simple recitation of facts, "cake, muffins, cupcakes, strudel, marzipan, sweet dipped fruits, or other rare indulgences. We do not eat *treats* as a nation with any regular indulgence. But when we do? We do it as best as we can."

"Do you blow out candles?"

"We light a candle and you write your wish on the paper. It is then burnt and what you believe happens after that? That's personal philosophy and ideology. You do blow out the candle though."

"Oh? Why do you burn the paper?"

"For some? It goes to their God. For others it represents a prayer of added strength to work toward the goal. Others use it as a chance to write something they want to burn and move on from in the coming year. It's a moment between you, the inner self, and the power of fire to move the mind and spirit to an understanding of action and feelings. For me, it changes by the year."

Obviously trying to hold still, "are there simple answers in this land?"

Trying to sound encouraging, "plenty! You find what you believe in, believe in it, simple as that. The depth and breadth of my answers is because I'm the High Consul. I rule over all the expressions and choices. I have to try to understand all of the choice points people can make, so when I encounter them I don't cast doubt on something that is seen as Good by the State. I can speak with at least the amount of understanding of following along. Even if I just finished reading up on it in the car? At least I did try to get it."

"But you've only been the High Consul for a week."

"I was raised by the last one. He taught me quite a bit about the job."

Looking away from her ministrations, "so what is Good then?"

I don't begrudge you the subject change. "That which helps society and those within it to function. A person likes to drink with friends? They go to a tavern or otherwise establishment. They drink a beverage that would impair their driving? The system will provide answers for what to do with them to prevent them from driving while impaired. The upside of being a smaller system, we have more control."

"They can drink to excess though."

"*Impairment.* They can drink, but they are *not* allowed to use that impairment as an excuse to hurt others. Once you put someone else in mortal danger? You lose your right to do the activity without oversight."

With a tone of lessons learned, "what if they become a nuisance?"

"They are removed by the staff. Typically they end up going home. Otherwise they go to the Holding Tank with the City Militia. We process, we correct, we clean up, and another day goes along. We are all asked to learn the grace to accept a punishment and a stern talking to."

"Sounds solid."

"We try to keep it that way." Looking at her work, "I *think* it'll do. If it gets anything that isn't better?" Lowering his shirt carefully, "I'll call my doctor and have her come look at you. I've been getting more practice as of late with these sorts of things."

Lowering his voice his words carried the tone of soft introspective regret, "I wasn't in good shape when I got here."

Trying to keep the frown off her face as she formed her one word reply, "no."

With a turn of a smile at the corners of his mouth his words came as an affirmation, "I'm okay though."

"I am happy to hear that."

Looking to her with a measure of soul searching, "are things square between us?"

"I think so." Taking his hands with a gentle half grasp embrace with her hands, "I had the rations to spare to help you get better. You wanted to get better. That was the price you paid in return."

Nodding with a tone of understanding, "sounds fair."

"Fairness is what we aim for. A measure of equality. With the willingness to give and compromise within the system to respect the needs of the human heart."

Following with a note of inquisitiveness to his voice, "example?"

Losing her anxiety in the simple notion of the moment, "when a child sees a Medical Professional, we give them a single piece of sweetened something. A hard candy, usually a disc or wafer. Something that will last for more than a few seconds. Not unlike the lozenge in your mouth."

Nodding with a smile of approval, "it is quite refreshing."

"A healthy child doesn't know that medical care is the reward, still being healthy and the mindfulness of that. So you have to give them something to convince them to go back next time. To know that their doctor is their ally in being healthy. They are doing something they *should* do, see the doctor. But they don't understand that they need to be doing it. So we give them a reward for it."

"And then when they are older?"

"They get to decide if they wish to ask for the piece of reward. Some find asking for it as a moment of nostalgia worth loitering in. There is no shame in asking for a Child's Reward. It doesn't hinder these moments when the doctor is in the same practice for decades. Many of the primary care provider posts are handed down from parent to child. Talkie, the man who asked me about the watch, he is a fourth generation emergency response physician."

"Amazing."

We need to get moving. "I've been done for a few moments, we should move."

Speaking softly in reply, "you run your kit well enough."

Trying to keep it matter of fact, "I had the training."

Giving the ground with his tone, "I will not press you."

Softening she smiled, "thank you Yuri. I mean it."

Looking at the concern on his face she tried to not think about the sounds of the wounded behind and around them. Checking the exits she spotted one that would work, "I know how we'll get out without getting in the way."

"What do I need to do?"

I am going to get no end of flak and questions for this if he says yes. "Drive?"

Squinting his eyes at her, "The Beast?"

"Yes."

Nodding once he smiled reassuringly, "I will do this for you. I know how to drive a car."

Smiling she dug out her keys and passed them to him, "thank you Yuri."

"Noted."

Quickly putting her things away, "good."

"So how do I get you home?"

Closing the trunk she sighed and took a deep breath. *Mindfulness is key.* Letting the air out she found a smile as she moved to get into the back on the passenger side. Opening the door she paused and gave her instructions, "don't do anything but insert the key, press the green button next to the slot, and then use the panel to select 'Do Not Disturb' and 'Home along the Watch Towers, path four.' There will be five choices for that, use the fourth." Pointing to the West Exit without traffic, "pull out from there. The onboard computer will compensate and navigate you."

Getting in quickly and settling into the drivers seat, "this will do all the things you need it to?"

Lowering herself into her seat she sighed as the soft cushioning embraced her, "it will tell people to leave us alone. And it will give you instructions home to dodge whatever traffic issues have been caused by tonight."

Settling into his seat she watched him find the seat belt with a pleased noise before he set to buckling up, "so I just follow the instructions this screen is going to give me?"

"Just follow the instructions. The whole process is going to take around an hour to get to The Watchtowers, and then the time to go down their road, before getting to the final road to Safe Housing. Don't rush. Take it at the speed recommendations. The goal is to give the rest of the world time to react before we come back down from our flight."

"Amazing."

Reaching into her pocket she pulled her comm back out and turned it on. *One missed call and five urgent messages now. The missed call is Steven,* flipping to the messages she felt a rush of sadness at the name on the first message. *Sasha Herb, my faithful,* feeling her mind trip up for a word she let the sentence drop. *She's going to be worried sick.*

Opening the message, as the cosmetic roar of the engine signaled the start of their journey, she found two words waiting for her.

Status?

Aardvark!

Rolling words around and finding nothing she clicked her front teeth together, *I'll come back to this and do it right.*

Keying to the second message she found it was from Jolene Yorklin. *My doctor is wondering if her patient is still alive. I should reply now.* Setting to it as quickly as she could, and keeping it just to the facts and her endorsement of her presence in the triage efforts, she smiled knowing her doctor wouldn't be worrying about her for the time being.

Feeling a not so gentle pain in her chest thinking about what Jolene would see she flipped to the third message. *It's from York. Jerome is busy securing the Network from C&D Command. The rat is dead. Hope wears the crown. 'Leave A Message' is in effect.* Thinking it over, *that's good to know. Now I have the Sys-Admin in my corner to help slide the scales back into place.* Rolling her thoughts around in her tired mind, *and Jerome is going to be nice enough to divert calls I shouldn't be taking for me. I might get some sleep later when this adrenaline wears off.*

"They let us escape the parking, and we get to go through the pretend forest in the middle of a city someone decided to plant. I like it. Though, I really did think I was hallucinating when I saw this the first time." Adding as an victorious conclusion, "the arboretum you mentioned!"

At least they didn't harm the trees. He listened though, as he does. "It's meant to help provide clean air for the fans. And yes, we celebrate our trees and those who toil to preserve them."

"I understand more now, it is *quite* enchanting though. No Huntsman to chase us though? We get to get away?"

"They have to let us go, it's the Protocol."

Replying with a honest confusion, "that you said you're breaking."

"I *am* breaking Protocol. I am doing so because I feel the need to survive long enough to be held accountable for the notions broken when this is over. The opposite side of this is that they have no grounds to break the Clauses I'm using to break the other ones. Which means I can pull this stunt and no one will stop me because I am not acting *against* the Protocol. I am just failing to comply with the wishes of the document."

With a tone of a slow walk down an unknown path, "so you are using Clauses, -"

"Correct -"

"To do things that you normally wouldn't be doing -"

"Correct -"

"And because it is not a criminal offense -"

Replying with the strange levity of the moment, "they will not stop me because I am not acting *against* the system."

"But you will be facing an accountability review for this when this is over?"

"Most likely. It shouldn't be serious, unless there's a Round Two. In which case we'll have assassins in the living room by dawn and be fighting for our lives again."

Laughing with a grim humor before his reply she thought she heard an honestly amused tone from him, "keep me appraised of our future?"

"I will."

"Thank you."

"Noted."

"So this is quite the scenic route. Over, to the side, and then past the Towers. Seems easy enough. I take it there is the chance we will be followed?"

"Yes, there is a chance we'll be followed. The house I told you about, it is indeed a fair distance outside of town." After a second thought, "and yes, it's a scenic route. It's a road that means a thousand words to me."

"I understand. I shall drive and leave you to your messages."

"Thank you Yuri."

Firing his single word back with a cheerful tone, "noted!"

Watching him learn is so very nice. Turning her attention back to her comm and opening the fourth message she clucked her tongue, *Waterlily. My Counselor is worried for me. I know I would be worried for me if I had the mental power to do so.* Quickly keying in a reply she scheduled a window that she could call her after she returned home. *We can at least touch base, I'm too busy to feel right now.*

Opening the fifth and final message she scowled, *Wallman doesn't have Clearance to get near Central right now?* Accessing her Commands and Authorizations she selected Temporary Clearance Upgrade and moved Wallman up until he was up and over the minimum for getting into Central. *There. Now he can get past the perimeter when he gets there. I'm glad that at least the critical things are still working.*

Flipping back to the first message and pushing the command to call Sasha she waited as it rang once and then connected.

Calling the word out, with the sounds of a hands-free audio pickup almost distorting the sound, Sasha's voice reached her earpiece, "Susan!"

Hearing her name called out with the terror evident behind it she felt a renewed rush of guilt.

Trying to keep a firm neutrality to her voice she spoke the words that she wished she didn't have to, "I have to be stoic because you're driving and we don't have the luxury of time to cry right now."

After a deep huff Sasha fired back with a falsely neutral bravado, "I can be stoic too."

Now to tell her what someone will need to tell me. "Don't lose yourself to what ifs. Don't think about this as if you had come to see me instead of going home to rest. Can you do that?"

Replying with a tone that led her to think that she knew that she didn't know what she was going to learn, "I can try."

"You're going to learn things that aren't going to sit well. It won't be good for your health or your heart."

"What am I going to find at the Staging Area?"

Easy, vague, answer. "What's left of a night that defies logic or explanation."

"Is the Code Clear?"

"Unknown. Medical is on scene and has been on scene. I am *physically unharmed.* I know that I'll get to see you soon. I take comfort in that."

"The Commander said you're en route to a backup plan, a secret plan that isn't on the books because we're compromised. Is he lying?"

Doing her best to keep her tone level and polite, "the plan didn't exist before tonight. So he's telling the truth but giving you the false impression that the plan is older than tonight."

Asking her question without resolve to seeing it answered, "where are you going?"

I will tell her by not telling her. "A place I've never let you see."

"Noted." Pausing for a moment she sounded worried, "you're not on Hands Free. Who's driving? Are you pulled over?"

Time to toss off a reply I've never used. "Mandelbrot is driving."

Replying with an increase in pitch and panic, "why are you giving me a Watch Phrase? Who is it Susan?"

Trying to sound reassuring she made the soothing motion that Sasha wasn't there to see, "you don't know him. Tonight my driver *is* Mandelbrot."

Sighing with a sniffle she sounded oddly hopeful, "do I get to meet him?"

Trying to sound cheerful in turn, "you'll meet him soon enough."

Grousing with a bitter lilt to her words, "we're compromised aren't we?"

Looking out the window as the city flowed past, "I don't know who I can trust that I don't already trust, that means you, much less what tech I can trust. You'll be briefed soon enough."

Speaking with a slightly panicked insistence, "why don't you tell me more?"

Trying to keep the sad humor from taking over her sentiment, "I don't want you crying and crashing your car on accident."

"How bad is this? I wasn't familiar with the code word on all this."

I'll be honest. "I want to go to the cabin."

Replying with a tone on the verge of anguish, "Aardvark –"

Be strong. "I can't quit the field though, not completely."

"Are there enemies still on the field?"

Swallowing once she let out the word with a quiet caution, "unknown."

"Stay safe?"

Conviction. Speak it. Give her this. "I *will* see you soon."

Speaking the words to her with a firm conviction, "I'm holding you to that."

Giving in to the eddies of doubt in her heart she spoke the words without thinking about them, "forgive me for what comes my precious Aardvark."

Sounding far braver than she had a moment ago, "I have forgiven you everything else that needed to be forgiven. I stand with you, always."

Trying to speak with a conviction she felt rustling around in the corners of her heart, "until I see you under the Blue Sky."

"Until then." Taking a shuddering breath she continued on, "I'm almost to the Staging Area."

"I understand." Taking a breath, "Sasha, this is probably going to get a lot worse before it gets better. If I need to, I am going to call you with an unfair request or three if I need you."

Replying with a concerned conviction, "*how* could I refuse you? We've said far too much to each other to turn back from this."

"Thank you Sasha. You know how to reach me."

"I already proved that! And I'm parked now, so I have to go. I look forward to your unfair requests, it's what I'm here for. Because if you're making them, you're still with me."

"Be well and watch out for Steven! And Sasha?"

"Yes?"

Speaking the word softly and clearly without the hint of regret that she thought she heard in herself, "aardvark." *I have to say it one last time, and as firm as I can,* "stay away from the dark places of False Hindsight!"

The reply came to her ear a moment later with the firm conviction she had come to expect. "Aardvark." A moment later words followed with a distinct lack of conviction. "I have to go, I will try to do as you wish me to."

Hearing the click of the call disconnecting she sighed and put her comm away. "Comments?"

"Mandelbrot?"

Another code to teach. "Math. The Mandelbrot Set can be used to create a picture with a depth larger than the universe, from what I understand of it. The Coded Truth I was telling her was that the man driving my car, was a story that would require far more time and detail to explain than we had time for. I have stared into a Mandelbrot Fractal render, we have video on the Network of it, and it as if I was falling into infinity, as it is an infinite idea. The videos follow a single path in the infinite, for a short time. Kind of like us, as people. She knows that she'll get to hear your story soon, that I'm safe, and that I'm not under duress."

With a tone closer to a statement than a question he seemed pleased at the concept, "all with a single word? I get to be all that with just one word?"

"With a single word I gave her all my impassioned pleadings to trust me, to trust you, and to have faith."

"So does aardvark mean the same thing when you say it to her as it does when I," stopping for a half second, "our ancestors said it?"

I - dropping the line of thought she sighed internally. "It does. I have so much to tell you, and I could tell you with simple code words but you don't speak the language."

Returning to a place of hidden anguish with his words, "I would like to learn."

Rushing to reassure him, and herself, with her words, "I would gladly teach you. But I need to rest a moment, to calm down, I have more things I have to do before we get home and I just want to be in better shape when I get there. Mea culpa Yuri."

Speaking his words with a careful cadence and a tone of resigned sadness, "I noticed that early on, that turn of the phrase, and it makes me feel confused for your culture. None of you say *sorry*. It's not a commonly used word in the world at large, but it is nice to hear. I just don't understand yet how a culture tossed it away. The phrase 'mea culpa' is an admission of being responsible for something done wrong but it carries no emotional weight with it unless the user places some in their voice, face, actions, or otherwise." Taking a long breath, "and it hurts me to hear you say it because of what happened. I know it wasn't your fault. You shouldn't take the blame."

"I don't even know what to say right now Yuri. Can we talk more when we're safely inside?"

"Yes. Noted."

Stressing the words with her relief, "thank you."

"Rest well."

Settling into the seat she turned her head and let it rest on the headrest. *I'll think of better places than tonight. I'll think about something else.* Closing her eyes for a moment a burst of inspiration struck her, *I need to file orders with Winifred. If there is a Round Two I need certain things protected that matter to The Rim.*

And if I win? I want there to be a world worth ruling to still be there.

Pulling her head up she opened her comm and set to typing carefully, *I wish that some of these orders were less nebulous, but I lack intel that they can find as they need it from others. This needs to work.*

Finishing up the orders she looked back down at herself. Shaking her head sadly, *I'm going to careen into the end of this ride with messed up hair, bloodied clothes, and this comm in one hand and my cannon in another. But, I will be remembered as the Bachman who went down swinging. Four generations all taken out as passive deaths. I am going to break that legacy.*

And the bodies of every enemy I can who seeks quarrel with me. Keying in another set of she felt the fire within flare for a moment, *I'm not dead yet.*

2.2.0 - 00:35

Holden Tower - Consul's Bedchamber - (Seattle)

▼Alexandria "Alex" Holden
▼Consul of the Holden Family

"Dame Holden?"

Rolling onto her back to look up to see who she thought was talking to her she tried to assess the light levels. *It's dark. Is that James?*

Feeling a moment of shyness at her state of undress under the sheets, she watched the curtain open just far enough for a comm unit.

Is it news from Waldo?

Tensing in a moment of panic she gathered herself up and moved to a sitting position with her chest covered by her hastily rearranged bedding. *He's nowhere near the opening.*

Asking his name with a cautious air to her inquiry, "James?"

Replying with a distraught fear wrapped in professionalism, "yes Miss, it is I."

He's as scared as I am. "Is it an emergency call from Captain Waldo? -"

"It's an emergency call," pushing the words out as a sad blurt, "from Sinclair Holden."

"No." *He's not authorized to call me unless he's seen something too dire to wait.* "From his personal comm?"

"Yes Dame Holden."

"I'm covered."

Why does he look like he's trying to keep from crying? Taking the Consul's Comm from James she moved it to her ear, "Sinclair?"

Hearing his voice ring with an empty anger, "*Fimbulwinter.*"

Sitting still for a moment of panic it occurred to her that she had not asked any of the questions that had crossed her mind. Taking a deep breath she blurted her questions, "what? Where? *How?*"

Still ringing with the empty anger, "Central Tower -"

No, no. "Miss Bachman?"

"She lives."

That's not very descriptive, "is she in one piece?"

"Yes. The rest of us? No." Rushing the words, "we had to save her!"

Curling up in an emotionally defensive ball she spoke the follow-up question, "from what?"

"House Kunlow! I recognized their faces. Dame Holden," hearing his voice ache with pain she cringed at the emotions she heard, "they knew me. They sacked me, my elbow, and left me crumpled in a pile after they sacked me. They tossed me aside to come back to, hoping to, *talk sense* into me so they wouldn't have to kill me. They let me live because they knew me as a friend! I gave my weapon to the Ghost known as Yuri though. I gave it to him hoping he would catch them, and kill them."

What did I get left out of? "Ghost? Yuri?"

"Alex -"

He hasn't called me that in a long time.

"Yes?"

"I saw House forces, this was Consul level, please tell me what I need to know."

By the Ash. "I was not part of it. I would not want, and did not, aid this."

"Thank you Alex. It didn't seem like you but I couldn't say more."

The horrors he must have seen, to doubt like that. "I understand. Noted. Mea culpa."

"Noted." Taking a breath she heard his ragged breathing for a moment, "the man who helped save her, he is known as Yuri. I've already heard the wounded asking about him. He struck like an avenging angel through the halls of Central Tower. Miss Bachman's Ghost, The Winter Wolf, and just *the scary man*, is what I've heard the survivors call him. He was the one who led her out. He was dressed in rags, like a vagabond beggar from an old painting. His beard is wild and resists becoming kempt from the looks of it. And he knew my sprain just by touching it a little. Commander Bachman is furious at him. He's an outsider. The Commander said so himself to confirm it."

He's trying to tell me everything at once. "I will take this all under advisement. What about you Sinclair?"

"I have done two things that I should leave my post for. I was bested by those I should have seen as traitors before this happened. Also. My elbow, if it's no good? I'm done. And I called you and reported in."

The loyalty of those near her. "I understand. Come home?"

His voice almost too faint to hear, "can I?"

He can't Exit Pass, I won't let him! "We'll take you home Sinclair. Get you some Counseling. I can send for you. I have assets I can send down there to help. I can send help for New Hope and a return trip for you!"

"Thank you Dame Holden."

"Did you see Miss Bachman?"

"No. Some of the New Hope Militia, Jaguar Squad, did though. They confirmed she used Code Five Seventy Six and led Yuri out by the hand. They took her car and she's en route to a backup plan that is not her bunker."

"Why not go to her bunker?"

"She opted out."

"Overwatch?"

"No idea."

She doesn't do anything without a reason. I fear for the morning light. "I'll look into it. I'll call Consul Drenner when I have a feeling she's ready to take a call."

"Thank you Dame Holden."

Fighting against the tremors in her voice and the moisture in her eyes, "noted. Call someone else and keep talking. Not about this. About other things. Don't stop talking until you get tired enough to sleep!"

Replying back with a tone of regret, "you are kind Dame Holden."

Trying to keep from pleading too strongly with her words, "come home to your family Sinclair."

Sniffling he spoke with a firm declaration, "I will."

This, is going to be what little I can do from here. "I have to go now."

"I understand. I will close the connection for you."

Hearing the tone of a closed call she set her comm back down on her night stand. "James?"

Speaking with a voice quiet in the wake of the horror of understanding, "yes Dame Holden?"

Replying with the same quiet volume she adjusted her blanket to slide her chilled foot, she was just noticing was cold, back under the warmth, "do what needs to be done for Sinclair. Get him home."

"I shall Dame Holden. And you?"

"I am going to lay here in shock until I can get up and be a Consul that my people deserve."

With a voice that betrayed his professionalism as defense against the reality of the moment, "very well Dame Holden."

Reaching up she grabbed his hand, "James, please, stay away from the dark place. I need everyone I can trust right now."

Giving her a hand a squeeze he coughed against the tears, "I will stay away from it, if you stay away from it, Mutual Pact."

"I agree to this Pact."

"Then I Pact this Pledge."

"I felt no duress from the opened curtain. You were doing as ordered."

Looking to her with an honest smile, "I did my best to make sure if something had been amiss that I wouldn't have seen what I have seen before. I know how you feel on the subject."

The honest mistakes of our past. "You are a good man James. I am glad my father found you."

"I am also." Letting go of her hand he slipped away from her bedside, "a Blue Sky morning to you."

"To you also."

Listening to James leave she hugged herself tightly, *Thomas has betrayed us. Commander Bachman will be out for blood now. And now a Ghost enters the fray? I need to talk with Amanda.*

As soon as I can get out of bed.

2.2.1 - 00:39
Central Tower - 28th Floor - Panfilov's Bench

▲Sinclair Holden
▲32nd of the "Honor Guard"

I am undone.

Looking at his still functioning hand with the sick brewing in his guts he inventoried his moment. *Friends are dead, my not friends are dead, and my one piece of solace is that Yuri reached Susan. My High Consul can see the sunrise, the same one I'll be facing because I survived.*

Hugging himself with his free arm he acknowledged the Survivor's Guilt tearing into him. *Top reason anyone has claimed an Exit Pass since the Arcologies opened.*

I don't want to die.

Blinking away the tears he placed his good hand flat on the bench they had found him to sit on. *Keep him close, keep an eye on him, and get him out as soon as we get the critical cases out. I keep hearing it when they look at me, but, how am I getting home?* Opening the Honor Guard Status App on his comm he felt the guilt redouble at the updates he found. *I am the only one who gets to walk out. Everyone else is getting carried.*

Selecting Singleton from the list he typed out his short message. *Be a good dad.* Rereading the words he pushed the send button. *That's all I have. He wasn't here for this, he was spared this, and now he needs to accept his new life when it comes to that.*

Tipping his head back, he wondered anew how he was going to get to the airport, much less back to Seattle. Closing his eyes he turned off his comm and put it away.

I wonder if she's doing better than the rest of us. Opening his eyes he set to trying to keep his eyes open and just stare at the nearby wall. Staring at the wall it occurred to him that he was looking at a mural to Nickel.

Atomic weight twenty-eight. It's in the place it belongs.

Am I?

Lowering his eyes he felt a presence enter his personal space bubble.

With a voice of quiet gravel and old wounds the words sounded directed at him, "I would like to help you."

Looking up he thought he had heard the voice correctly, "Dennis."

I wonder if I look as awful as he does?

"We don't have long. I know what's freezing in your heart and dying in your belly."

You saw the funeral for Isaac, George, and Asmodai, I can only imagine how your belly feels. "I will trust you."

"I don't want your words, I don't want your confession, I want to get you to safety. I have a vehicle on the perimeter and a driver to get you clear. I'm going to get you to the airport so you can get to Seattle." Holding out his hand, "will you come with me? Will you let me save you as you once saved her?"

Debts and honor. I am saved by a Debt of Honor. Reaching out with his good hand, "I will."

"Good. Not a word until we hit the airport."

Nodding with a humored smile, *I am complying.*

"I did just do that didn't I? Mea culpa. Let's go."

Nodding again he set into pace with him, *I can get home to Alex. I can rest there. Until then, one foot in front of the other. You cannot die if you can still move a foot forward.*

2.2.5 - 00:54

Central Tower - Exterior Expanse - East Lot

† Sasha Herb
† "The Atrial Dagger" of "Samantha's Scouts"

Sitting in her car trying to find her composure in the wake of the delays she did her best to keep her breathing in check. *Dennis found me a parking space in this, don't know why yet, but I'm sure he'll show up and tell me. I'm low on the list of those who need to report in at the Staging Area so this works. I'll speak with him, then cross the checkpoint over there and be in the Staging Area. Should work.*

The Scouts have been informally activated as our condition is listed as Recuperating. Yet here I am. Waiting for Dennis with the power of a nap and a bottle of Liquid Sunshine.

Climbing out of her Duo-Car to look for signs of Dennis she startled at the sudden presence of Dennis Ochenhart and Honor Guard Sinclair Holden. With the quiet voice of command he spoke his whisper, "Sasha, we need to talk. And I need your car."

Not the weirdest or most sudden demand you've asked from me. Nodding twice she moved in close to hand off the key. Looking at his face in the passing pool of light she felt her brow furrow in sympathy, *I can see every night he worked as hard as he could for the good of our world.* Gripping her key softly she moved her hand over to his and laid it gently in his grasp while gesturing toward the nearby base of operations, "I am called."

Taking the key he moved his grip to hold her forearm gently, "delay."

Looking down at the hand she watched his fingers tap out the level of importance to his gesture, "what do you need?"

"You need to know what you did not ask."

"Which is?"

Gripping her arm in an almost comforting manner he spoke the declaration with a sad and somber ache, "Miss Augusta has fallen."

Feeling the numb gain a new level of ache she blanched, "who would go *this far* to do this to us? Why did they kill her of all people?"

His voice raising to something more conversational in volume, to be heard over the activity drawing closer, but no less forceful in command, "our enemies sought the eradication of Miss Bachman and her entire power base. Miss Augusta may have been retired, but her mind was still sharp and she was still loyal. She could have helped rally a counter offensive."

Narrowing her eyes as the wave of anger hit her, "so we are in a blood feud?"

Nodding once with a finality to the declaration, "I believe it to be so."

Fighting with the surge of self-recriminating anger, "I wasted my comm call with her."

Replying with the timbre of the Admonishing Instructor, "by not asking things she might not have the answers to?"

Point. Gripping his arm in their shared grip with frustration, "tell me *something* that I don't know that will convince me this *new* plan they're cooking up is going to be a good idea?"

Giving her forearm a single pulse of gentle pressure, "the Pale Rider is in play."

I do feel better. "Who's at the stick?"

Speaking the words with a softened comfort, "the *new* Sys-Admin."

Wait – "Hope then?"

"He has the Network. I'm going to send him a message as soon as I can get this man clear to start a protected channel for those of us who *need* to stay *in the loop* that might not normally get to be there. It will be on the Bachman Relays, which I know you have access to. I also know that odds are you don't know who Yuri is yet."

"Who is Yuri –" catching on, "Mandelbrot?"

Raising a brow with the surprise in his voice, "she used that reply?"

"She did."

Giving her the gentle tug signal he spoke with reaffirmation, "you *will* be told everything as we can get this in line."

Wait. I have to ask. "The Peace Knot," trying to keep her tone level as she moved in for an embrace, "did she undo the Peace Knot?"

Holding her gently for a moment he spoke with pride, "yes. She went out fighting. They have recovered her blade. It is going to join its brothers and sisters."

Stepping away from him she watched his hand fall away from her arm, "who did this? When will I be told who was behind this?" Stopping in the silence to watch Dennis' face she spotted the guilt and shame on Sinclair's face. "He knows?"

"He fought them." Growling his words with a defensive ferocity, "he has been through enough. Leave him be."

Signaling her acceptance of the idea to Sinclair she paused. Looking at him she softened, "I mean you no harm, or duress. Mea culpa."

Coughing once he spoke with a gravel to his words, "noted. Accepted. The men who fought against me? Died. The men who defeated me? Are dead. The men who ordered this? I do not know."

"Noted. Rest well when you do Guardsman."

"Thank you. I will hopefully be able to comply."

"Noted." Nodding twice she turned back to Dennis, "what do I do now?"

With a voice of grave nerves, "you will be called to do things Sasha, you will be tested, and you must not forget what has been agreed on. Bargains are bargains."

He's playing this for Sinclair. We have never been this serious in our casual understanding of what he wants me to watch for, and be ready to do if I can. If Sinclair is going away he would worry about things being taken care of. This is for him. Putting on a face of stone she raised her jaw defiantly toward Dennis, "you think I would forget? Balk? Shirk my duties?"

Without losing a Newton of force he clucked his tongue at her, "this isn't going to be *easy* pup. Are you in this to win this?"

I told you that her life would be fine without me. I need her a lot more than she needs me. Taking a step back with a biting laugh she wasn't sure she was feeling, "I will win her the Blue Sky! I have duties you're keeping me from."

"A Blue Sky morning to you Dagger Herb."

"A Blue Sky morning to both of you."

Turning around she walked with a practiced cadence, *Miss Augusta is gone, Susan is trying to protect someone, this is a blood feud, and I don't know who is the real enemy. I have never been more afraid.* Looking up to the sky for the sight of a Wanderer Drone's search light she found only the usual bit of lighting in the shadow of Central Tower. *Once more into the breach.*

2.2.3 - 00:50

Comfort Lodge - Parking Lot – Gloaming Boulevard

- ►Winifred Yeoman
- ►"Matron" of the "Honor Guard"

Checking the dial of her encrypted radio on the dash of her Night-Watchman Armored Command Vehicle she felt the fatigue from being roused in the middle of the night hounding her. Taking another large sip from her travel mug of Morning Sunshine she counted herself lucky for those she had left.

I will mourn later. I need to do as willed first. Duty keeps the pain at bay. I hope none of my kids were in the middle of any serious canoodling as it will be some time before they get a chance to return to it.

After a second check of the dial she took hold of the wired microphone and clicked the button on the side. Holding it down she intoned her words carefully, "Matron calling the kids, Matron calling, requesting sound off, over?"

Listening to the sound off she checked each name off the list as she heard them. *All present that I still have left.* "I have our orders. To begin, I asked the *new* Sys-Admin for a SitRep on the Grain Silo. He reports it as reporting as Green. That is not one of our priorities, as with what happened at the funeral, we all know that is *not* something we want to make worse."

I should say something encouraging. "The hearts of the young are fueled by a greater fire. Let the flames die down and they will try again. Amaranth will mend, and we will see her soon."

Looking at her newly healed ink on her forearm she found herself thankful for the little things. *We are betrayed, the dawn sky could be red, but at least my armor won't chafe. Rusted scrap.*

Finding her way back to the moment after another sip, *come on.* "The Twelve who were on shift tonight, will not be joining us in these orders. They're either dead, in medical care, or in the case of Holden, going home for the time being. We're going to be putting one foot in front of the other foot and pressing on. I won't be making any speeches, we have work to do."

Waiting two beats for any dissenters and hearing none she set into the orders. "Kipper? You're taking Gamble and Marlin and going on a rescue mission. There are hundreds involved tonight, which means statistically there are children who are going to wake up asking where mom and dad are. You are going to get whomever else you can get, and find all those kids who are family to those *who attacked*. You'll be moving them to the Cultural Center, to Miss Bachman's room there."

"Yes Matron! I know some good jokes, and some good people, I'll get right on it!"

"Deploy!" Sighing she added with a gruffness to her words, "as I give the orders disconnect and get to it, we're on a time table."

Waiting a moment she chided herself before pressing on, *give them the Matron they know you are.*

"Kelly? You're taking Cage and Rios and going to the Power Production Facility. You're going to make sure that we're not dropped into the dark in the wake of some unforeseen hostiles."

Hearing Kelly's voice ring with a hint of stimulants she sounded confident, "yes Matron!"

Seeing the lights on her radio knock off she moved to the next order, "Greyson! You're taking Cruso and Rea and making sure the Waterworks keeps the water flowing and that no one touches the water supply. There is no line we are to consider that our enemies will not cross at this juncture."

Keeping his naturally boisterous tone in check he woofed his declaration, "yes Matron!"

Seeing another three lights disconnect she moved to the next order, "Porter! You get Polansko and Rattler! You three get over to New Hope General and make sure no one goes vigilante on the idiots who followed this rusted up mess. Hot August Night has been put into effect, and Miss Bachman wants to make sure no other places that are Hollowed Ground see bloodshed."

Yawning with embarrassment he spoke boldly, "yes Matron!"

Nodding in affirmation watching the lights go out she smiled knowing that something was going right, "Draper! You get Haddock and Sutton! Miss Bachman needs you to play it quiet and keep an eye on Jerome Hope. He's the new Sys-Admin and we *all* know how important he is to the plans of Miss Bachman. Do not let him come to harm."

She swore she could hear the smile in his voice as his smooth tenor spoke the words with confidence, "yes Matron!"

Breathing to steady herself she looked at the last lights, "Dorn, I need you, Singleton," taking a moment she paused, "as soon as you're done seeing Northland? You rejoin the fray –"

"Yes Matron."

"– and Mendoza to meet up with Harold Wallman. He's going into the nightmare of untangling this to figure out what we're telling people. I'll be joining you as soon as I take care of a few chores of my own. Do not let him come to harm, the people *need* his voice to be soothed."

Taking an audible breath she spoke with a firm confidence of someone who liked

Wallman, "Yes Matron!"

Seeing the last lights go out she sighed and leaned back in her seat. *Miss Bachman will call me soon enough, I will speak with her, and we will do as she says.*

I don't know who Mandelbrot is, beyond the knowledge that he was the man behind the sealed door. Asmodai was keeping a guest, and we were left Out of the Loop. I hope we can finally get back in that good grace.

Looking through her texts she saw a single picture from Captain Paul Kaufman of Jaguar Squad addressed to her. *What is this?*

Opening the picture she shook her head in shock, *that is someone else getting into the driver's seat of The Beast. He looks like a beast of a man himself. I understand that I do not understand.*

And she looks splattered. Rusted scrap.

Looking at the time, *she won't be calling me soon enough.*

2.2.9 - 00:57

The Beast - En route to Safe Housing

*⁙..*Susan Bachman

Sinclair called home. Looking at her comm while the variables fit together in her mind, *he's wounded. Yuri told me so. He's going to the one place he knows he'll be safe to rest, to heal. Back to one of the few motes of true happiness he had back in Seattle.*

Pondering the idea of him not coming back she frowned, *I'm going to miss him dearly. If she takes him in, if he heals enough she would keep him close? I can see him again if we would visit the other. I could take the Sky-Skipper and fly around the anti-aircraft guns.*

Turning her mind to the variables she found herself in a strange humor looking at his picture. *From the moment I talked Father into letting your name on that roster I Pledged the Pact. I knew you would see things, hear things, and learn things that I didn't really want you to know. But I did it for her. I did it to atone for what I had done. Now you're going to go back to her and tell her what she doesn't think she would get to know.*

Thinking over the words she would say if he was sitting next to her, *you could have been a Counselor, not a Guardsman, but life seldom turns out how you expected. You saved my life Sinclair, now it's your turn to live yours as you choose with what options you find.*

Making a note on her comm she set a reminder for herself, *I'll wait for him to get to Seattle and then send him the warmest words I can muster. He spoke with me with a distinct candor and an empathic heart when we would speak. I'll find out how he's doing before I drop the clue that he can come back and see if he returns to me.*

Rolling through memories of Sinclair a stone cold one moved across her mind's eye. *And now I'm thinking about Guthrie and that has to stop. I need to think about better things. Not that I know what would work to think about right now. Or why poor Sinclair is associated with such sad things in my mind. First Guthrie for having saved my sanity in the moment, and now this for having had to leave me after the last bullet fired.*

Checking the time, *and it's been long enough since I sent out the new orders.* Running down through her contacts on her comm she found The Matron Winifred. Pressing the button she waited for the call to connect. *Have to dig up just a bit more and promise myself rest later. Time to find out if they'll accept this.*

"High Consul!"

She sounds happy to hear from me.

Doing her best to sound as agreeable as possible in the wake of the emotions storming behind her thoughts, "Matron, I hope my orders are agreeable."

Sounding emotionally distracted by the pain, "it's a lot to cover and I have no doubts in our skills. But -"

Setting into her best 'matter of fact' she could muster, "I can hear the question. I have to be honest. I am in pain, quite a bit. I am doing my best to not dwell on what just happened. If I do, I'll freeze up. I'll crawl into a corner and cry like the other nights I've been hit. This is hard enough without giving up already."

Speaking softly with the hurt evident she replied reassuringly, "I never would have doubted your love of those who fell."

Fighting against the tears, "Winnie, you're my Honor Guard and if my Honor is at stake then those places need to be secured during this." Taking on the tone of quoting her father, "we either do this right or not at all."

Using the tone that Susan knew as her comforting tone Winifred set into the moment, "Jerome reports that the Grain Silo is reading as Green."

Good. "Then we can proceed with what manpower we have."

Speaking the words like she was asking her over for tea, "when will we be able to rejoin you in your adventure?"

She's forcing the upbeat tone. "When the storm clears."

"And if you falter?"

She needs this, I can give her this. "I will call Sasha. If I am *in danger?* I will call Captains Mother and Father."

"Do you promise me?"

She sounds like the caring matron I know her to enjoy pretending to be. "You know I don't promise people things I am not one hundred percent sure of."

Laughing the moment off with a grim humor, "your honesty is dreadful."

Joining her in the grim humor moment, "this coming from the leader of the most dishonest bunch I've ever met?"

Firing back with a timbre of pride, "you wouldn't have us any other way."

Far too true. "Truth."

After a moment of the sounds of forced breathing and a tongue fighting for moisture the word came at a lower pitch, "Sinclair -"

Hearing the sad confession in her words as she spoke them, "I'll miss him Winnie." *I never thought he would be leaving like this.*

"Me too."

I can't get our collective hope up that he'll come back. If they message him to come back then that's a different color on things. Taking a breath, "Northland, Canyon, Whiteman, Justice, and Breaker are also still alive for the time being. We'll find out as time ticks on."

With a wavering resolve to her tone she fired her words off, "I'm headed for New Hope General."

"That's a good place to start. When you get done there, get to Harold. From what I understand he's going to inform the public, then head for Central Tower."

"I will see Northland at least, then go protect Wallman."

I wish I had more for her. Something tangible. "Mea culpa."

"Noted, accepted, but felt to be unneeded." Speaking with a warmer candor, "will the Ghost protect you?"

Doing her best to be reassuring, "without me he dies. If my enemies win? I don't think they would take him in. We'll take care of each other through this." Dredging her mind she found an explanation phrase, "Epiphytes and mutually inclined."

With laughter on the edge of her voice, "you want to get him Citizenship before we come back to you. That way we're not tripping over a Ghost and questions."

"I do, and exactly that."

Giving her a few chuckles to listen to before composing herself, "I'll tell the Guard to not worry too much for you, as you're still in there."

Finding a smile of her own, "for the most part."

"We'll still be here when you get done with these chores. As for those who won't be, what of the funerals?"

"Family will be consulted, if they're willing it will be a group outdoor pyre set. I'll," swallowing roughly, "send my warriors to their final rewards at the Rose of Pasadena. We might have to freeze dry them to buy us time though."

"We shall see. As for the living? Let me see them and then? We'll tend to your plan."

One less facet to worry for, "thank you Winifred."

"I look forward to returning to your side."

"I look forward to seeing you there again."

Closing the comm call she rubbed her eyes gently, *home soon enough and things will go on.*

2.2.7 - 00:55

'Network News' - Main Studio – New Hope

- Harold Wallman
- Head Anchor of The Network News

Looking at his tired face in the mirror he felt the deep appreciation for the work he could see covering his face. Nodding to the makeup artists before they set to departing he felt a measure of misplaced irritation. *The world is reeling and I'm worried about how I look. Face of bravery, nothing more.*

Lifting his comm up he looked over the words from The Director. *Proxy Message from Nurse Aligatha, typed on behalf of The Director.*

It has to be killing him that he can't write. I'll see him when he's ready to be seen though.

Reading the words softly, "Harold, I am unable to give you words. You must comfort the people. You must write them something from the heart. I trust you to be you. Please. Give them comfort."

And a full pardon attached for whatever I say. Authorized with his personal seal. No matter what the Infraction would be, I am absolved. Be it breaking down in tears, or telling too much of the truth. Weighing his options he settled on a plan, *I am going to stride out there, speak this in one rusted take, and it will be the words that will give the people the guidance they deserve.*

Looking to the stiff note cards he had prepared what little he could in the short time he had. *This is going to define me in the eyes of others.*

Hearing the sound of shoes clacking gently on the tile he looked over to see it was Anton standing near him.

Taking a breath he spoke with an awed reverence, "Harold, I would like to say something to you, before you go out there."

Keeping his voice neutral but encouraging, "speak it."

Without losing his reverence he spoke with an emotional fire, "you have a full pardon, don't waste it. The Director knows you want to make the News about something more. About the Golden Age of Broadcasting. The idea that we are here to uplift the human spirit with the retelling of stories next to the fire. In your future, in your vision, we are skalds of the broadcasting world. I'm just a man who reads words and makes it sound good. You're a national treasure for a reason. Just, be brave."

Feeling humbled he kept it simple, "thank you Anton." Flapping the note cards he bounced them off the back of his hand with a nervous energy, "I'm worried for Miss Bachman."

Nodding emphatically, "I am also." Looking to the side he tilted his head with the conspiracy of the question, "are you going to mention her Ghost?"

Shaking his head he kept his voice firm, "no. I need to comfort the people, not give them more questions. This is about answers."

Smiling again he took a step back, "good luck Harold."

Nodding once he smiled in return, "thank you."

Moving to walk away he spoke his word with a note of relief, "noted."

Raising his chin he noted the blue light activate in the blink of his eyes. *It's time.* Sliding the door open he felt it taken away by one of the stage hands. Striding into the studio, devoid of an audience, he heard the quiet slide of the door closing behind him.

Just me, the crew, and the cameras.

Moving over to the chair he knew all too well he slid into position as the cameras checked and double checked the moment. Laying his cards on the desk in a spot the cameras could not see them he readied himself. *Only moments now. Network Video, Live Stream, and going out over Province New Hope Radio. The overnight MC for PNHR will be giving me the intro any moment.*

Watching the signal lights flare for a moment he took a breath and readied himself. Waiting for the flag wave he heard the faint sounds of the intro music play.

Leaving his worries behind he set into his words.

"Solemn Greetings to you, Citizens of New Hope, and those of the Provinces who may hear my voice and words."

Letting the beat pass he smiled gently, "I believe that by the cameras, the timing of the hour, and the lack of the aureole on Central Tower that you can safely presume I am not here to talk about the new cranberry salsa slaw at the Grocery Depot."

Moving a card he let the words out without thinking them over too greatly as his smile fell away, "I gave all of you, my words to comfort you in the wake of the loss of The High Consul not even a Fortnight ago. I come to you tonight with the attempt to comfort you. If you find comfort? You honor me more than you might know."

Moving another card he moved his gaze to camera two, "today, the Thirtieth of April, is one of tragedy, but let us not slide further into the Shadow's Embrace. The High Consul is still alive, allow me to stress that."

Turning to camera one he nodded once with a care to his tone, "Fate, has allotted the powers that guide us the test of, and the demands, to be proven. We do not know at this time if something was used to justify this test. I can say for certain, that the Scions of power, The High Consul, and The Director, both survived this test. I cannot speak for those who stand within Striking Distance of them."

Looking to camera three he let his caution enter his tone, "I know this hurts, but I must tell you the uncomfortable truths. If we allow the hate in to our hearts, then the loss of life we have suffered tonight will be compounded by the loss of trust and belief in our people. We cannot allow this to further destroy us."

Keeping his cadence level and his tone of reason, he moved forward, "we do not as of yet know who ordered this, or why. All the forces that are in play around you, many of which you might not see, are seeking answers. For those who have been woke to this, I implore you to try to return to your slumber, and when you wake? There will be more answers."

Moving back to camera one he set to trying to be comforting, "do not allow this to take from you or your neighbors the sense of social hopes and aspired to dreams. If you stay awake? Seek your neighbors, and be of comfort to them."

Looking at his last three cards discretely, "we must stay the people we know ourselves to be. Work, Honor, and Bread to you this morning."

"I know, and understand, you have questions."

Looking at the card with the words 'they capitulated' on it, "the people who did this, that are still alive, survive under the word, the word of capitulation. They will be returned to the Rule of Order. The Rule of Honor and the Protocol. Or they will not be returned to this shared place we call home."

Feeling the energy leaving him, "leave them to The Guild."

I have a full pardon, I've heard the news from the scene. "The family and kin of those who did this, were not there. Without a proven crime committed, there can be no crime."

"Leave them to The Guild."

Laying his hands together before him on the desk, "your thoughts, prayers, hopes, dreams, and emotions are yours. No one can take them from you, or wishes for you to suppress them from being understood in a way that does not violate the Protocol. The Free Speech Preserve on The Network is damaged, our infrastructure is damaged, do not let your hearts and minds join that damage. Unload your ammo, seek those of discussion, and scream until only reason remains."

Finish the moment. Touching the last card he nodded once, "the social furniture of our society is both complicated and fragile. It cannot support the jackboot resting upon it. We cannot set our heels up upon this table. We cannot impose our will upon our reality using armed force when there is no conflict that requires it. If we have not learned that, we have learned nothing."

Smiling with a friendly aura to his being, "a Blue Sky to All."

Seeing the lights go off he swallowed in relief, "clear?"

Stepping behind the shadows of the cameras the stage manager, Claire Mouse, spoke with a civil tone of authority, "clear."

Getting up from the desk he nodded twice, "I have other places I need to get to."

Keeping her tone professional, "Harold?"

Nodding once he didn't move from the desk, "yes Claire?"

Smiling without losing her professionalism, "do your best Harold. You're one of our best."

Nodding again with a smile, "I plan on it."

Waving gently he turned and headed for the door, *to Central. I need answers.*

CONVICTIONS STIRRED

Saturday April 30th, 2242

2.3.0 - 01:15

Sasha's Duo-Car - En Route to New Hope Airport

- Dennis Ochenhart
- Former "Darkest Shadow" (Co-Head of Cloak and Dagger)

Looking at the traffic impact map and finding a route out of Central proper he reveled in the measure of confidence he felt for his plan. *It's a small victory, but I need anything resembling one right now.* Rolling around some old words he polished them with a mote of purpose and spoke them, "I have precious little to tell you, but it is precious. And no games, you should reply with words."

Nodding once he smiled faintly, "tell me."

Laying on the paternal aura he channeled his years into his inflection, "I believe you will be you. Nothing more, nothing less. I believe that you will see you through this to the conclusion you need to draw."

"I hurt Dennis. This hurts more than Guthrie."

This not so young man, "Sinclair, you saved The Rim when you saved her."

His words aching with a guilty frustration, "I couldn't help her enough tonight."

At least you were there. "I feel the same."

"Dennis, how did you know I needed to get back to Seattle?"

Simple cover story. "Your injury was registered. The triage medics on scene put you on a list. I was looking for a way to be useful. Your file says in the case of needing a recovery period, you go home to Seattle if available."

"Then of the building, you picked me?"

Correcting him gently, "of the wounded, who needed special help, I picked you."

"Do you know who Yuri is?"

I wish I did. "Knowing her mother? The things she taught Susan? He is someone who needs help like no one else would need."

Speaking with a borderline manic sadness, "he made it to her though. I had to give him my weapon–"

Get him to focus on it from a different angle. "He needs her to live. Without her to explain? How many of us would try to accept him?"

Coming up short he nodded once with a deliberate slowness to the motion, "I, don't have an answer for that."

Trying to stress the idea of Yuri needing protection he continued, "I don't know who he is. She's left me out of the loop. Who would speak for him? I can't say that we would just shoot him, but in the wake of losing her? I don't know if we would be interested as a people in taking him in."

"I don't have an answer for that either. Does it hurt?"

She's had to keep secrets before. I'm not surprised given what I've seen of this moment. She used my contingency plan and I almost missed it. "No. It does leave me feeling a daunted sensation. Whomever he is? He is such a complicated notion that she couldn't talk to me about it while her father was alive. After she saw him off? She sent me a message, it was written out, on paper. She gave it to Paige to give to me. She promised to tell me what was going on as soon as the Council let up on her. That's how I know his name."

"And now a Consul level force –"

Replying with an empty levity to his tone, "has made this worse."

Looking out the window Sinclair's voice took on a determined edge to it, "what can I do?"

Offering the simple reply he smiled with a quiet encouragement, "heal."

Hearing the sound of a few breaths taken before the words came out with a regretful lilt to them, "and if I don't make it back?"

Tried and true advice is the best advice. "Make a good life, and send her pictures of it."

Still looking out the window the inner conflict was apparent in his tone, "Dennis, the things I have seen –"

Interrupting him with his cautionary advice, "tell no one of them without permission."

Nodding he looked back to him, "when you stand near her, how do you feel?"

Deflection time. "She is the daughter of a woman who was a good friend. When my health faded on me, I did what I could to stay near her. To stay loyal, and of use."

Looking at him with a critical appraisal he sighed before his face went slack, "I want to heal."

Thank you. "Good."

"Dennis, why did she stay near Asmodai?"

The same basic reason I did. "Loyalty."

Looking into his lap with a sadness to him, "I don't know what to say right now."

I can't leave him to rot and rust inside. "Sinclair?"

"Yes?"

I can go and trust him. Give him something to guide him home.

"When George died, I didn't know what to do. I was told to keep going. When Isaac died? Same. When Tessa died? My heart broke. When Bonnie moved from active duty to teach at Cloak and Dagger? I was less broken. Tonight, took Bonnie from me. This is why I want you to heal. To carry on. I'm running out of *carry on.* I know, I know it's a lot to lay at your feet. You want something to guide you out of the dark place? Cling to *that.* Cling to the idea that you must carry on."

Watching Sinclair's face fall as the hidden anguish came bubbling up, "you, were there. The night that no one wanted to talk about."

Not specific enough, oh that hurts. "Which one?"

"Susan, when she came to you, the first time."

And that hurts more. "I put Asmodai on notice. I told him I wouldn't live in a world where he would be able to do something like that again. That if he did it again? One of us wouldn't see the next day."

"Did he?"

"He came close. I had the gun in my hand, and Susan stayed my hand."

Replying with a horrified camaraderie, "it didn't happen often. I didn't know what was going on the first time. I had my gun out, it was almost comical in retrospect. The idea that it was just, *what they do?*"

"The downside of keeping secrets. They gain a perverse life of their own."

Driving in silence he could see the airport coming up in the distance, *soon I will have the next part of my attempt at helping into place.*

Speaking up from the quiet Sinclair seemed a bit lost, "I adore Susan."

Answering back without thinking about it, "quite a few of us do."

Looking out the window with his words, "I feel like I really met her, at Guthrie. A sick turn of events."

Trying to console him, "at least you met her, and didn't go to your grave having known her."

Turning his head back to him, "which Consul did this?"

If I knew I wouldn't be here. "I don't know."

"Is she going to unleash the Bachman Rage?"

The Derecho could still be let loose and that would be the most final answer to the future of those involved. "If they push her? They could see it. Most people don't know that she has it, just a much smaller portion of it. If they give her a target? If someone tells her it would Clear? If Steven tells her it will help her? She might be tempted to obliterate whomever ordered this. If she remembers the Potentate's Puzzle her father left her? She might not order a large scale destruction of whomever is left to take the blame for this."

"The Puzzle?"

One of the few good things he gave her to live with. "He left her the idea that he struggled with the price of peace. That if even one person who was behind the death of his people still lived, was that a just world? Does he honor them with peace? When Asmodai declared peace, he set the idea of blood price for those who had died to be paid. That there would be no more death to rebalance the scales."

"Then if she can do as he did, and find peace without burning the world down?"

"Then the Rage will not be seen."

Nodding with a sigh of relief, "I understand."

"Sinclair?"

"Yes?"

I don't think she's going to want to see you stay gone. "She sees you as a friend. You will be gaining more insight soon."

Sounding more hopeful, "if I keep living, I will learn more?"

Encouraging him with a newfound energy to his words, "yes! Use *that* as guiding light."

"And Yuri?"

Keeping up the wave of energy he kept at it, "give her a chance to help herself to be strong to help him. That man is going to need her full strength, her full sense of who she is if he is going to have a chance now. I don't know what happens next but if she falls, it would be too much for our world to bear."

"Noted. So if there isn't a Round Two?"

"Even if soldiers do not come? The doubt will come. The introspection will come. The fallout from this will come down like radioactive snowflakes poisoning our hearts. She isn't facing *just* more men with guns, she's facing the dawn where we wake up having lived through this and asking ourselves the dreaded question. Now what?"

"I will consider my heart carefully. I will not add to her loss column in this."

"Noted. And also, good."

Driving for a few more minutes he could see the lights coming into view in the distance. Smiling he returned to the encouragement, "I have a friend to leave you with at the airport."

Sounding almost excited with his question, "who do I get?"

"Paige."

"I'm not shocked. She is your student."

Keep him talking, "see if you two have shared something from the Entertainment Network to discuss instead of this."

"I will."

Turning onto the access road, "Susan learned from Maggie. That's why this man is being kept safe."

"You mentioned an *in the loop* channel with Sasha –"

"I can send you what I can as I get my hands on it, and if it is good then I'll share it. *You* need to recover. Bad news is counter recovery."

"Thank you Dennis."

"I know life is hard right now. I know," driving into the parking lot he had arranged the meet in, "that you *feel* lost in a deep dark jungle and you have no lights, no snacks, no water, and are on the verge of catching a jungle virus that is going to leave you hallucinating. But when you talk to me? You are asking for a light. A weapon. *A stick.* Something to fight the darkness both inside and out. I am a long dweller of the dark jungle. I live there now. But you? You want to go home. You want to go back to the civilization you remember that I can only see from the treetops. You want a guide out of the darkness. I will offer you this," bringing the car to a stop in the parking place he had arranged, "you *will* make it back. I know this."

"Thank you for the vote of confidence."

Setting up the quote with a pulse of energy to his tone, "if no one is brave?"

Completing the question with a resolve to it, "who will be brave?"

Looking past him out the window, "and here comes your handler."

Assessing Paige with an honest approximation, "she looks confident."

"With her mother on duty and her father away on a flight she was available. Your bags will be here soon enough."

"How much time did you have to prepare this?"

That's hilarious for all the wrong reasons. "Honest answer?"

"Yes."

The thirty seconds it took to call Paige and get her in motion. "I found out what was going on before you called, so when you called for help I was able to work on this. Word came back to me and I stepped into motion. I was already at Central as Paige had alerted me. I am a man of action using Templates. I don't ad lib the way she does. I don't spin the framework out of nothing while I'm at it. I just fill in the blanks."

Nodding twice and smiling faintly as Paige opened the door. "Thank you."

"Noted."

"A Blue Sky morning to you Dennis."

After helping Sinclair from the car Paige gestured quickly as her speaker elicited a soft female voice, "a Blue Sky morning to you friend."

Waving them off Dennis felt the list of things still pending trying to weigh him down, "a Blue Sky morning to both of you."

Waiting for Paige to close the door he started the car into motion, *what bothers me is none of the variables on the Network, what little I can reach, point to anything that makes sense. This plan has things attached to it I don't understand. I should give this car back and then ready myself for the next bit of someone else's plan.*

I serve The Rim. We have worked miracles before as a people. What is just one more?

2.3.5 - 01:25

222 Anna Rose Street – New Hope

▣Chuck Drenner
▣"Liaison" of House Drenner)

Looking at the readout on his comm for the third time he fought back the nausea. *Micah needs me at the Estate. Full coup attempt at Central Tower. Miss Bachman is alive, Wallman is working on getting into position to help find the rest of the story, and cleanup is in progress. ETA on getting home will be figured out at some point. Can't be helped. And that's all I get.*

Standing next to the door to his modest bedroom he took stock of things, including the sleeping form in his bed. Contemplating the sleeping form with her arm sticking out from under the covers in a sea of pale greens he felt the pang of needing to leave. Reaching for more rational and logical thought to keep the desire to stay at bay, he found solace in the mundane. *I'll need to tell her to eat all of my perishables. I know the sandwich spread needs to be finished off. I'll leave her the run of my modest house, not like my neighbors don't know her by first name at this point.*

Time to wake you up long enough to explain this.

Moving over to the sleeping form of Wendy Whitman he set to banishing his doubts about what they shared. *I moved quietly as to not wake you while I put myself together. Now I get to tell you what I can, and then go to help secure the dawn.*

Sitting down on the edge of his bed Chuck reached out and gently touched Wendy's back in a spot he knew was safe. *Now to give her what I can before I leave her for the front lines of the fallout. I have to give her the hope that this is going to Clear without letting her know that I don't know if that's true.*

Watching her open her eyes he felt the sad unknown creeping up on him as she closed her eyes and counted to three.

Looking up at him she blinked, closed her eyes, counted to three again, and then reopened them before examining his appearance. "You're dressed. Far too dressed for this hour."

Trying to keep it simple, "I have to go. Work."

Narrowing her eyes at him, "you're understating."

I have to be strong or I won't get to work. "I am."

"Do I want to know?"

Forcing his tone to stay level he spoke slowly and measured the words before he let them out. "I have precious little to share. You'll be briefed by Wallman. He has a broadcast up which will explain what is known."

Reacting with a visible panic, "Wallman would only be sharing bad news at this hour."

Keeping to his stoic tone, "I know."

Reaching out and taking his hand, "where are you going? Don't Epsilon lock me out."

Shaking his head he smiled, "I have to be with Consul Drenner. At the Estate. I know you have things to do or I would have mentioned that you could come out to see me during this." Returning to his calm he caressed her hand gently, "it is the truth. It is *very* bad out there. You will be safer here. You will be comfortable here. *I* am just not strong enough to tell you what is going on. Wallman can. And he will tell us more as he learns it."

Hiding her face without letting go of his hand she took a few deep breaths, "what do I do?"

Keeping it simple, "eat my food. I have perishables you could help make sure aren't wasted."

Looking up from the pillow with a frown, "you will be gone for that long?"

Shrugging he felt his shoulders fall, "I don't know when I'm getting back." Touching her gently he tried to be reassuring, "you have your key. The hot tub is there for you to use. My house is still open to you, I just won't be here to share it for the time being."

Looking away and into the pillow she seemed almost shy, "Summer Session is coming up soon, I won't be *around* as much with my new position."

The little things to worry about. "I have to accept that."

Taking his hand firmly she clenched his fingers for a moment, "you will still pay for this though?"

I'm afraid one day I won't because you'll be sharing this. "I have not regretted a single Ration spent on your time or affections."

Replying with a voice which carried a deeper affection, that he had been getting used to hearing here and there, "thank you Chuck."

Squeezing her hand with a more gentle embrace, "I don't regret it."

Looking up at him with a smile, "I am thankful you're not a man of complex needs."

The things we learned couples do, much less the things other Courtesans could be commissioned to share, "I am a simple man with simple needs. Food, warmth, simple pleasures, and kind words."

Nodding with the traumatized humor of the memories, "then I am also thankful *I* am not a woman of complex needs. We *fit together*, don't we?"

Enjoying the turn of the phrase he smiled, "we do. I know. Also, with your new position I imagine I will be hearing some work stories. Which I look forward to."

With a tone of more ephemeral emotions, "always the Silver Lining."

"Always."

Moving her head back under cover, "it's bad out there isn't it?"

I don't want to answer. "It's the worst it's been in a long time."

Retreating back into the bed fully she spoke with a soft and scared honesty, "I'm going to stay in bed."

"You should. I need to go."

"Go with the," after a moment of pause, "I don't even know what you need to wish you well with. I don't know if you need speed, wisdom, strength, foresight, or what. If it is all of them? I don't know that blessing."

Moving to the bedroom door he found the strength to force himself to leave, "I don't either."

"Chuck?"

Stopping a footfall short of the door, "yes?"

With a tone of imploring need, "come back to me."

Reaching for the door knob he opened the door and made sure to commit himself fully to his exit before he spoke, "I will."

2.3.9 - 01:32
The Mental Bastion - Private Office C-37

∂Miss Evelyn White
∂"Waterlily" (Psychiatric Counsel to Miss Bachman)

Rereading her way through the reports, relayed from her comm to her desktop monitor, the information clicked together with a tighter and more horrifying conclusion with the latest round of reports and images.

This is horrifying to look at. The longer I look, the more it makes less sense for why it had to happen. Looking up at the two men she could see through her office door she frowned at their visible body armor, *she's afraid I could be hit for some reason. That whomever is behind this would take it so personally that I would be a target. Those men are armored and armed to the teeth.*

Very polite, but ready to fight to the death.

She didn't mention them, but they seem familiar.

Looking back at the message from Miss Bachman she mulled it over, *she wants to wait until she gets to Safe Housing at the very least. She's taking one of her longer routes back there and I'm left playing the waiting game.*

Calling up the emergency alerts she had Clearance for she felt the cold settling in with a vengeance. *Something went horribly wrong tonight. I'm being left out of anything other than Wallman's broadcast because I have one task, wait for her to call me.*

Moving her thumb to scroll the next barrage of messages she felt her heart sinking at the details. *Miss Bachman was in the center of something like we have never seen tonight. I don't know what the plan is for something like this.*

I'm afraid I will have to write it.

"I need to see Waterlily!"

Looking up as the words registered she spied Heartstrings getting a hug from one of the guards. Unable to hear what they were saying she set to getting up from her desk and moving over to the door.

With the voice of the Welcoming Guard one of them was speaking, "- good to see you Heartstrings, I know you would like to see her, but the orders are clear that *we* can't let you past us. Waterlily *can* though."

Which security protocol is this? Opening the door she spoke softly, "I can?"

Turning to her the other guard nodded in affirmation, "the orders are to protect you, to deny *any* and *all* access to your office, unless you allow it."

Curious. "Protocol designation?"

Looking at his comm and reading the orders, "Full-Block Protocol with Protector's Permissions amendment." Looking up from his comm with a boyish charm to his words, "we don't normally see you, so we don't know who you believe we can trust."

Looking at them Heartstrings seemed confused, "who sent you, I assume, but I would like to know."

Holding up his comm he showed them both the order sheet with the dancing cat in the corner, playing on a slow loop of eighteen poses.

Nodding with a look of understanding Heartstrings seemed taken aback, "Miss Bachman then."

Nodding without losing his boyish charm, "correct."

Back on task. "I can let Heartstrings in?"

Putting his comm away with a smile, "yes ma'am. We're just here to make sure no one causes trouble, or worse."

Holding her hand out she gripped Heartstring's hand firmly when she took it. Bringing her into the office she felt worse seeing the sadness on her face.

Closing the door with her foot Heartstrings spoke just above a whisper, "call me Kaira right now."

Matching her low volume as they moved away from the door, "what happened?"

Pulling out her comm Kaira leaned in close and showed her the screen.

That's her sister's name. Dead. In Central. She doesn't -

Interrupting her thoughts with a grimly resigned tone, "have you seen the House Logistics?"

By the Ash and Dust. "I am starting to get a handle on the names."

Fretting with a sickened demeanor to her, "it was the Kunlow House. The Network distress is clearing up and the health and wellbeing script is firing. Her husband is dead too."

By the Ash. "Same place?"

Nodding with a saddened confirmation, "same place."

I don't know if Miss Bachman is in any shape for this. "Why did you come to me?"

Swallowing roughly she produced a small sheet of individually packaged lozenges. "Miss Bachman can give me a waiver to keep working."

Of all the times to ask for a personal favor. "You want me to get her, to get you, a waiver."

Popping a lozenge she sighed, "yes."

Thinking it over she went with a simple answer, "she's going to need something."

"I don't know what I could say that could exonerate me. I, just, Mack and Millie."

Her sister's kids. Det. Signaling and receiving the reply she hugged Kaira tightly. "Don't give up."

"They, don't have parents. With the Network down I don't know what I don't know."

The deep male bass voice reached her ears without an issue from outside, "I need to see Waterlily!"

Calling quickly toward the door, "let Cloud Watcher in!"

Coming in quickly the older man appeared flush with distress, "Patrick Bachman is being settled in at New Hope General. I need Clearance to see him."

So you come to me?

Sighing in confusion she spit her words out, "why not just -?"

Interrupting with the signal for 'pardon,' "Patrick is unconscious and Miss Bachman is shielded by the Leave a Message Protocol."

"I just contacted her earlier –" *I got past Leave a Message?*

Blinking she noted the look of concern on Cloud Watcher's face as he regarded Heartstrings, "Kaira, what's wrong?"

Replying with a numbed sadness, "my sister was in Central."

"She doesn't work – " raising a single hand gently he stepped back as the thought appeared to occur, "but she's a sweet woman. Why would she be in the attackers?"

Retorting with an overstressed sadness to her tone, "*I don't know.*"

Emoting the leap of logic with a look of revelation he nodded, "then you need a waiver to keep working. And I need a waiver to get to Patrick. His Clearance bar is up too high for me to get past."

I can do this. "On it." Moving back to her desk she called up her messenger client and set to quickly composing the requests. Working the thoughts over she found the reference numbers and hit send.

"Sent."

Noticing an update of note she scrunched up her nose as the words found hold in her mind. "Report here, three of the Honor Guard have grabbed a detachment of Emergency Responders. They're moving from domicile to domicile in search of the children that were orphaned by what just happened."

Sounding concerned with her question, "Mack and Millie?"

Checking the what details she could find, *this is odd.* "The children of the defenders are inbound to the Juvenile Trauma Shelter, that checks out."

Losing the fight with control of her tone, "and the attackers?"

"Unknown." Calling up the files she blinked at the spectacle waiting for her, "each one has a separate movement sheet covered in High Consul Blackout. Dancing cats everywhere."

Offering his words with a hopeful air to them, "Miss Bachman saves children."

Asking with a voice on the verge of panic, "where is she sending Mack and Millie?"

Trying to reassure Kaira, "there all going to the same place. Reference number for the location appears to be randomly generated nonsense. CC-W-17."

With a slightly calmer tone Kaira spoke with a softer volume, "I don't know that location reference."

Tilting his head from left to right Cloud Watcher seemed at a loss too, "I don't either. Although for her to use something random? It seems unlike her."

Running it over in her head she spoke while thinking, "she has nearly been assassinated. Her brother is injured. And she has been seen with a strange man. I don't count or discount anything at this point."

Asking with an almost in unison cadence they both pressed her, "*strange man?*"

It'll be public knowledge soon enough. Turning one of the monitors on her desk she called up the image taken by the Jaguar Squad. "*That* man."

Nodding and giving his simple statement Cloud Watcher offered his words with a lack of direction, "he doesn't look like us."

Explaining it with simple facts, "he's a Ghost, from what the Jaguars could determine. They pinged the two of them for confirmation of presence. Miss Bachman's localized presence responded. This man? Nothing."

Sounding reaffirmed Kaira pressed her gently, "have you spoken with her yet?"

I can only wish. "No. I am scheduled to get to talk to her later this morning."

Pursing her lips and nodding with an idea of the difficult conversation waiting, "good luck."

Blessing her in turn Cloud Water offered his, "a good talk to her when you have it."

Turning back to her comm she smiled with a sigh of relief, "your requests have been processed. She's dumped both of you off on Admin Nobody, who is in the process of approving what you need."

Sounding hopeful Kaira fretted with a shy awe, "she still trusts me?"

Keep it simple. "I have nothing to tell you. She included nothing else."

"Understood."

Moving to the door with his concern evident, "I need to get to New Hope General."

Signaling for 'victory' she smiled, "you're approved. Good speed to you Cloud Watcher."

"Yes, good speed. I, need to go help as I can."

Turning her attention back to Kaira, "Heartstrings?"

"Yes?"

Those kids, no one deserves this. "I'll do my best to exploit my friendship if I need to, for Mack and Millie."

Holding her hands over her mouth with a sad look of thanks, "don't do anything too drastic."

"I'll try to keep it rational, unless it's needed to go over the line."

Lowering her hands she nodded, "good luck, good talk."

Once both of them were gone she thought it over. *What has the significance to her of a place with a seventeen in it?*

Calling up her files on Miss Bachman she hit the find function and typed in seventeen. *Time to try this one way or the other.*

Watching years of data fly by she blinked as the highlight settled on a reference. *Would Room Seventeen at the Cultural Center be big enough for them all?* Calling up the pictures from Susan's birthday party at the Cultural Center she nodded in acceptance of the idea.

I need to wait a few and then head over there. See if I have the Clearance after I talk to her. Those kids are going to need all the help they can get.

2.6.0 - 02:17

North of New Hope @ Safe Housing

☼ Yuri

Pulling the car into the driveway he slowed the car to a careful crawl, *so Mobile Command Base is code for Armored House on Wheels. The panel said I would see it in the front yard, and there it is. Again with the way that they state things. One of these times I am going to meet something with a truly shocking designation and it will be tiny and banal. Calling it now.*

Navigating to make sure he gave it a wide berth he kept the slow pace as his eyes took in the size of the house. Feeling the sense of expectation giving a mixed reaction at the size of the building contrasted with its rustic appearance his thoughts drifted to a comfortable middle place. *Guest room? I think there's more than one guest room within those walls. She told me it had been a garrison house, now I know it to be a manse.*

Can it be a manse if it is not opulent then? I bet if I asked she would tell me.

I'll ask later.

Pulling into place on the far side of the MCB, angling the vehicle so it would have both cover and an easy escape as the screen instructed, he felt a measure of calm. Setting to the process of powering the vehicle down, as directed by the screen, he ended it with the removal of the key. *I did it.*

Using the door release he set to exiting the vehicle and regretting the decision as soon as he reached a standing position. Letting out the long exhale of pain he closed his door gently and took a step toward the house. Looking over to Susan he watched her as she moved past him with a measure of stiffness to her gait.

She has a pair of guns from the car with her. She really did mean the comment about guns in the car.

I shouldn't have had a doubt of that.

Falling into step behind her he found himself no less surprised by the interior of the house once they were inside. "You have a very nice place Susan. Even this mud room is nice."

Sitting down on the bench next to the door she set to removing her boots, "take your shoes off, house rule. I feel like I can pretend I'm remotely normative for a few minutes."

A sound house rule, and I wonder if I'll get slippers with her best at being alright. Nodding he quickly ditched his shoes in the shoe keeper by the door. *No slippers? Odd.* Falling into place behind her he followed her into the living room and tried not to run into her when she stopped at a small bar on the inner wall facing the door.

"We are going to drink?"

Trading two of the guns for bottles from within the cabinet, "I hoped you would join me in a drink."

I get drink with conversation? She is trying to open the door of her house to me. I have no qualms about having a drink. Could use one more than I would care to tell her. Trying to keep the humor in his voice, "haven't had one in awhile, been a bit, detained if you will."

Smiling at him with a reassurance, "well that's over now. I appreciate the humor though."

Giving the position of the bar a thought he smiled, "you can pour drinks for people in the mud room then?"

Getting out two highball glasses she nodded twice, "yes. My mother would greet people as they came in the door with drink requests. While we were going along the Watchtowers I sent the message to the house management system that I was going to be home soon. Ice machine starts up, among other bits of comfort. The perks of power."

That is something else. Watching her quickly putting ice, from a machine mounted in the bar, into the glasses she followed up with free pouring from two bottles, of what he knew was alcohol from the smell.

She pours with a practiced grace. I wonder how many strange training sessions they have put her through? How much she volunteered for?

Putting the bottles aside she rummaged for a moment in the mini refrigeration unit before producing a capped tumbler of a jar and finished mixing the drinks with what he guessed was cranberry juice from the color and smell.

"Hunter's Honor, peach schnapps, and cranberry juice." Picking the highball glasses up she passed him one, "to our continued existence!"

"I'll drink to that." Taking a long sip from the glass he smiled as the warmth lit in his throat as the sweetness of it hit him. "That is very good stuff. I should expect no less from you though, yes?"

Taking a second long sip from her glass she sighed, "we need to talk."

Rolling the words out with a cadence on the verge of babbling he ran through his questions, "is this where you talk and I listen, or do I need to say something? You had me do the talking so often, is it your turn? And does this drink have a name?"

Listen more, speak less, get it right.

Looking into her glass she seemed to be smiling again, "this cocktail is an example of how far we've come. When my people rose out of Nowhere we didn't have nice things like this. The idea of spending over a year on something like *this*? Seemed impractical to a degree no one even brought it up. Now all these years later? Hunter's Honor is my fault."

Her language gives cues, that I am not sure I agree with. "Fault?"

"When the recipe, for Hunters Honor, was found in the Network, I approved research into bringing it back years ago. The Distillers and Brewers managed to get it brought back to us with the aid of working with Agriculture Planning and Enrichment."

Such a strange people working so hard on everything. "Sounds like a lot of work."

"A fair share. When they managed to get it bottled and finished? It needed a flagship cocktail. Thus I suggested," holding her glass up to enunciate the moment, "this."

"What name does it wear?"

Smiling with a shy cast to her tone and demeanor, "it's a Redheaded Smile. They wanted to name it after me, I refused."

Smiling with his shyly spoken words, "close enough."

Looking down at her glass she smiled sadly, "they wanted it to be closer than that. At least this way I share the compliment of a pleasurable drink with every redhead in our lands."

"Where did you get the recipe?"

"The Network. I found a recipe that when tested, I liked, and then we renamed it. The old name had a word in it we don't use anymore. We have a new term that is less pejorative, and more just a matter of the fact of things."

I like it. I wonder what the term is. I will ask. "What is the term?"

"The old one? Slut."

Oh, I know that word.

"But we could not for the life of us figure out what it really meant. The Network has conflicting accounts of the word. This drink was a Redheaded Slut. It could be used as a signal of upcoming trysts, but it seemed pejorative in tone. We begin with toasts, we keep the excess to a minimum, thus it didn't make an iota of sense to leave it like that. Or welcome that word back to our world."

"Understandable. Once words are spoken, they cannot be caught. They are not sparrows, neh, I would agree to keep that word from coming back."

"We do have those who have sex, without attachments, as they please, but they don't do so as a form of bonding. They are *sexually unpledged.* It works regardless of gender."

I will learn something again. "Not unfettered?"

"That would be someone who sexually is looking to try things. Who isn't caught up in a specific set of sexual notions. They flow with you."

Oh, "what of foot loose and fancy free?"

"What if they're actually a more emotionally distraught person? They might not be doing this *because* they are happy. They *seek* happiness. Or recreation. Or fun. Or just want to feel like they're pretty."

"Tramp?"

Shaking her head lightly with a momentary soured expression, "unacceptable. Pejorative in nature." Smiling she touched his shoulder, "sex between consenting adults is just that. Sex between consenting adults. We do have ways to filter our perception of it, but the idea is that if it is *consenting* then the wordplay should not be pejorative."

Ah, she smiles again. "Alright, then, having lots of sex with many partners isn't a bad thing?"

"Not on its own, no. For some it's a life goal. There are those who have an underlying problem and they are cautioned to seek help from The Guild and a Counselor, but for those who are not vexed with a problem? If they're unpledged? They just have to make sure their conquests understand that they're not the pledging type. It makes their lives harder, for certain, but some people are as they are." After a sip, "they do have to be honorable about it. Both parties. But that's more in the Sexual Ethics and Morals Primer."

The radio shows did not fully prepare me for this. "Astounding."

Looking from her glass to his eyes with a mock seriousness, "we're off topic again."

Smiling with a broad grin in reply to her mock seriousness, "we do that."

Without losing eye contact, "to the matter at hand?"

Those sky blue eyes, "of course."

"With that settled? I guess it's a moment for me to talk, you to listen," flashing him another one of her upbeat smiles, "but I would like a reply. And if we end up wandering off, again, I'll understand."

The smile that brightened my cell a dozen times. How a person of such strange circumstances can have such a smile I don't think I could ever guess. "Alright."

"I can't talk about what we just left. I really am not ready to face it. So I'll face us instead!"

But - "you sent out a lot of messages. Did you find out more from them?"

"Some. That *is* part of it, I don't know *exactly* what's going on out there right now. I do know something though." Taking a deep breath, "my gut told me to not offer you the boat. My instincts said that what you want is right and just and should be endeavored to be granted." Reaching over she tapped him gently on the arm with the back of her curled index finger, "sadly I gave into my fears Yuri."

Reviewing her presented notion with an emotional calm, "you offered me the boat, to leave, knowing if you set that idea into motion I would not die."

Rushing to assure him, "that's where I was *then.* This is *now.* No boats."

"You brought guns in the house, are we still in danger then?"

"We could be. I haven't received words of comfort yet. I haven't heard that anything else is still out there to come find us, on the other hand."

"That's, something, I would guess?" Looking around the room he noticed the furniture appeared to be of an odd level of craftsmanship compared to what he expected to see. "Perhaps the furniture has an easier story? Easier than where we just came from. Or the stories of why your brothers do not like me."

Replying with a honest interest, "you have an eye for furniture?"

So many lands, so many nations, so many people trying to make a decent chair. "I have seen many houses in this world. The world has been through much, but it couldn't forbid people from trying to live beautifully, in one way or another. Many hands working many materials to make a good place to stay, a reality. I couldn't help but notice these items are all from the same workbench, but I see different hands, the artistic embellishment and grace with the tools-" letting the phrase hang for a moment he sighed, "you understand?"

"I do actually. And it is the same team of hands which made all of this. When my mother was in Final Year of Secondary School, she commissioned all the furniture in the house from her schoolmates. This is the Final Year project for everyone involved in wood working who wanted in. The loggers found the wood, the laborers who were going to work the mills after school cut the wood, the story goes on like that. It was the capstone to her meteoric presence and the things she changed while she was at the New Hope Secondary School." Beaming with a mix of pride and sadness, "I do have some stories Yuri. I just haven't had a chance to tell you them yet."

Looking into his half full glass, "I would gladly listen."

"I have so much I want to talk to you about because you listen Yuri. You don't wish me harm, I can just talk with you because we don't have a social dynamic, and it's such a nice feeling."

I will ignore the lesson to console the spirit. "You have no one to talk to?"

Taking another long sip of her drink before answering, "I have people I can talk to, but not about what you did. Not about what I did either." Stopping herself she sighed, "I have *one* person who would understand this situation beyond the shadow of a doubt but I hesitated calling him because he's retired. He's given decades to our world and I thought I could solve this without him." Sighing softly she looked at him with eyes that showed a hint of mischief left inside, "that and I figured if I told him what Steven had threatened that he would kill Steven and then I would be left with an even bigger mess. I had to protect my brother from himself, while trying to not lose my resolve, while, -" trailing off with a wave of her hand she lowered her arm to her side.

I do not think I would have handled this as well as she has.

Setting her glass down, "been in a bit of a crisis not of my own making with no clear way out of it." Adding dryly, "don't know if you noticed."

Smiling with relief at her continued humor, "but what about Sevilan though?"

"Frank helped cover up the murder because he couldn't stand who my father had become. To him you did the right thing. No parade, no statue, not that kind of heroic thing. Just the *right* thing to make things better."

I am unsure of my heart. "Then all this care for me? We really could be something."

Watching her hand move he wished he knew what it meant. Looking to her with a gentle inquiry he was rewarded with her look of sad frustration and a smile before she spoke to him.

"That was me, trying to reach the Aardvark within you, with a gesture of mindfulness."

Rubbing the back of his neck with his free hand he sighed, "it is a new thing to be cared about like this." Lowering his hand, "you did a job, that, I have not been tended to like that. Ever. You are, the High Consul, to your people. I'm a bit muddled."

Taking his hand with her free hand, "I am with you. To speak emotional doubt is to acknowledge you *have* emotions. To be *un*certain is to declare that you want to make the right decision. To be vulnerable is to trust."

That is a profound amount of faith. "Who taught you that?"

"The Codex. If I cannot share in your moments, like this, then *I* put *you*, on the pedestal. If I *demand* that you are *always* strong, then I proclaim that I am *always* weak. That is why I said that you don't always have to be strong. You don't have to get on the pedestal, not on my account."

I did not know. Speaking the word softly with a smile, "noted."

With a tone of acceptance and friendship she touched his arm with the air of consolation about her, "the world has damaged you Yuri, I can accept that. I will not let what we have be diminished by your pain. I will hold onto it and keep it nurtured. I can see the ways that you still hear The Shadow."

Such a strange place to have wandered in to.

Intoning the quiet confession, "it was more of a room, than a cell. The lock, it made me think of a cell."

Nodding twice she caresses his arm, "I know. That was why I told you the reasons you had to stay hidden, for the time being."

I will learn, without fear. "The Shadow?"

"The same. The Shadow is not to be run from, but faced. When there is no light, you are not deserted by your Shadow, it is *everywhere*."

Oh, "is that why your tower glows in the dark?"

Smiling with approval, "*yes*. If the tower is a light, and the Citizen knows the light is a continuation of the Pact of Loyalty, then the Citizen is never *truly* lost. They go to where the light leads."

I have made it to the place beyond this world. "Noted."

Speaking with an upbeat candor, "Dennis sent me a message assuring me he would see it back on within the hour." Losing her upbeat tempo with the words, "it went out during the attack."

That's a disturbing distance to go to hate someone. Forcing the word out around the emotional wince, "noted."

Touching his chest with a smile, "you are Yuri. I'm Susan. Sasha is Sasha. The emotional puzzle that Sasha could not solve, was loving me as she does. I have spent ten years trying to convince her that her love is not extraneous. That being irrelevant because she cannot sire my offspring."

I am puzzled now. "Your culture does not mind that women lay with women though."

Nodding she chuffed a sigh, "I am a Bachman, now the High Consul, and will *hopefully* have a brood of children. The Traditional Answer is that I would find a man, and have children. I would prefer to find a man who would not try to drive her away."

"Noted."

Cozying up to him she laid her cheek against his shoulder for a moment before she smiled and tipped her head off of his arm. "You are nice, enjoyable, relaxing, to talk to because we don't have a social dynamic. Who am I to you?"

That's easy. "Susan."

Smiling with an encouragement, "simple enough?"

She is nothing like Lettice. "You do not wish for me to see *The High Consul*."

Closing her eyes she nodded twice with a sad smile, "I am afraid that if you did, you would *not*, choose to stay next to me." Opening her eyes, "if you are a man without a place in this place, but it is granted solely by me choosing you to keep close, what becomes of you?"

I had not thought that far ahead. "That is, *staggering*."

Imploring him with a gentle urgency, "please, keep that in mind, in all of our moments to come."

Now that I know, I can't exactly not. "I will. Noted. All of that."

"Thank you. I, when I found out you had come? I did everything I could to let him push me into helping him. To know, that the Seches line had returned?" Turning her gaze to the floor, "Yuri, your family only shows up when my family is going to die. I was scared that you would not make it. That whatever was coming, would kill you."

Well then. "It tried. It failed."

"Thank you. Don't, don't think I don't appreciate what I did not see. I have names I will never see, faces I will forget with time, and people who will turn to dust in my mind until I no longer contemplate what was shared. Please, don't think I'm not in pain, because I'm not crying my eyes out."

"You are being prudent, and keeping your eyes in their sockets."

Raising her gaze she smiled with a mildly horrified expression, "that is, thank you."

"Noted."

"The Oath that was made," finishing her drink she reached past him and put the glass on the bar, "is a valid debt. I've been afraid because I was afraid I would not be paying it. If I can see my enemies defeated, and you're still alive, I will gladly pay the debt."

If there had been a boat before the attack? "You agreed with the boat, because then I would not be here to die."

"Valid theory. I can't say it was on my mind *directly*, but it holds water."

"Hah, boat, holds water."

"Didn't mean to, but I'll take it."

Finishing his drink he placed his glass next to hers on the bar. Turning back to her he gripped her firmly in a hug. "You brought me food, water, and sheltered me. You kept me locked away, but I did not feel like I was *in prison.* I have been *in prison.* Freedom is just over the threshold, and you cannot have it, and you may never will. You never removed the idea that I would find a way to that freedom when I was well."

"Noted. I am, relieved to hear that."

"The first night, I was too tired to worry about it. Then you arrived the next day and I didn't worry as much. You had a list of things you needed to see happen, a half dozen notes about why the door was locked, and that list was about me getting better and healing from my trip."

"Noted."

"I never saw doubt from Asmodai."

"He trusted that you were indeed you."

Something easier, reaching up he touched her hair gently. Curling his hand he embraced the back of her head gently, "what is the philosophy of power, the reason, the method?"

Speaking into the faltering moment, "noblesse oblige. My mother taught me that if one has power? You use it for the betterment of others and the place where you live. You take that power, you garb yourself in it, and you use it to work your will on the world. It's how you correct for different levels of power in the self and in society."

"Noted."

"I can give you something to better understand why I'm leaning on you. Frank, I love him dearly, as a *Father.* Dennis? *Uncle.* Both of them are familial love. The men in my Guard? Co-conspirators in a game of power to get objectives completed." Taking a breath, "to go back to Frank though, he lost his wife and daughter, and losing his daughter hit him harder. His daughter was the promise he would get home from the wars and battles and be *safe* again."

"You are one of his daughters, yes?"

"Yes. He didn't want to be a lover, or a husband, or a spouse again. He wanted to be a *Father* again. He treats me, Steven, and Patrick with a stance and heart of one who is Paternal. He never disobeyed my father, or ran counter to his wishes. That's the job of an Uncle, by the way."

"Noted."

"Caring for you, felt so good, because I was alone with someone who was not looking for me to be a Bachman. I can't stop being a Bachman, but you don't look at me looking for one."

"The bond between people, outside of occupation. I had a friendship with a Friar in Morocco, that was like that. We were friends, as I was not looking to him for Spiritual Guidance. Just someone to drink beer with after a day of work. He would still speak, act, and live as a Friar, but he was not *my* Friar."

"An approximation which fits, yes."

"I understand more."

"Good."

Time for the big question. "Did you have a hope when you pressed the release on my door?"

Relaxing her hold on him she stepped away with a shake of her head, "I had nothing going through my mind, except panic. I didn't think that it would come to that, but I didn't think of much of anything at the time."

"Noted."

"When you came out, he was already in a worse place than I had seen before. He was the kind of angry this family gets before someone dies. I did not want to die."

I have words. "When he hit me, I saw the look on his face, I have been in fights to the death before. The fire extinguisher was not planned, but noticed, taken, and I only had one thing on my mind. The fight."

"I know. I've seen it. In others. I've felt it myself a time or two, something akin. I hospitalized a trainee once."

"You?"

"I lost control. Watching you, I knew, what you were feeling. I beat her enough that she washed out of the training."

"I understand."

Turning her gaze back to him she held his gaze for a moment before looking away.

My heart hurts when she looks at me like a girl looks at a giant.

"I'm not *scared* of you Yuri, I, I'm saddened because I know how much this hurts. To be seen in a negative regard because of something that you don't have control over."

That changes things.

"Hence the do not shoot at him gesture you gave."

"Yes."

I am understanding, I think. "You are giving me a grief-stricken compassion."

"A fair approximation."

"You did not have words for me."

"No."

"You did all you could, to be compassionate."

"I did. Even telling Yorklin to not talk to for fear you would talk and talk and talk and build a palace made of second guesses and self-recrimination. Or letting Frank step in and he, he would want to be a dad, and you might not accept him, and then you reject him and it just gets worse."

A terrible mind to be cursed with. "Your mind is very powerful Susan. I will keep that in mind."

"Noted."

"Tell me, if you would, if I did have a place at your side, what would be the *worst* case scenario for me?"

"Copper Caste."

"Elaborate?"

Speaking her explanation with a more relaxed tone, "the Copper, Caste, if you will, live in small cubes. Personal space, and solitude, are provided by this."

"Cubes?"

"Personal apartments. You'd get a cube, it's more of a rectangle, and it sits on a base which makes it movable and easily serviced. The cubes are kept next to each other in a larger building, which contains the other services that a Citizen needs. Laundry, Child Care, Community Kitchen, and the like. Then above, the roof is a garden. The perimeter is defensible. A village, of no more than one hundred and fifty, that tends to itself."

"And that is the *worst*?"

"The Copper life is seen as the *simple life*. From there a Citizen gains access to more elaborate housing, services, and the like. The worst case, is that you would join a newly forming village and live as a peasant."

"That's not so bad in the scheme of things."

"Well, by local parlance, it's known as the Baseline, not the *worst*. It's about how one thinks about things."

"Noted. I can handle that."

Watching her move back to him he raised an arm in time for her to slide back to a spot against him. Settling her against his side he smiled when she nuzzled her nose against his.

Trying to ask around his smile, "the nose nuzzle?"

Replying in kind with a smile, "it's a skinship gesture. It's meant to be cute, playful."

Still smiling, "noted. I am not complaining."

"Noted."

Setting his hand on her shoulder their hug deepened, "do you regret sparing the attackers?"

Sighing darkly she leaned on him in reply. "There is a short list of reasons for why those people were there. It leaves me without empathy for them. However, knowing that they had something that could have been solved differently? I feel a deep sympathy for them in knowing that they were in pain. It's something that has to be solved, and not just with more death."

"I do not envy you."

"The Circle, it protects from that which is exterior. This was interior. The principle idea of killing those who betray, is that they betray the interior to the exterior. This was interior on interior. I left them alive, clutching at the idea that I could even say that we don't have a precedent for this."

"Noted."

"There is no small amount of things that we do not know, that killing them all will not bring us enlightenment for."

"I understand that, all too well."

"Noted."

Taking a breath, "there is so much I could say, while I stay here leaning on you, but I would just be tempting the fate of passing out from adrenaline crash." Shaking her head, "I was on Third Shift tonight. For me? The day was just really getting started. Rusted way to start the day."

Trying his best to sound encouraging, "you know, with there not being a boat, I can't leave."

Taking a few moments to breathe she hugged him gently, "I guess not."

"Where do we go from here? The idea of me seeing this through for my plot of land, and house."

Giving him another squeeze she spoke downward from his shoulder, "it won't be easy."

She defaults to the lowered gaze much too readily. "I can survive adversity."

"I can't make you a Citizen with a hand wave. The Protocol is built to prevent that sort of behavior. Also, the unfortunate fact is that there hasn't been a known case of something like this, to my knowledge." Letting go of him she stepped back and addressed him face to face, "I *could* do this for you, but then I would be breaking the Protocol in a way that would make everyone question why I couldn't go through the system. You *can* become a Citizen, *eventually.* A way will be found. It's just not going to be *easy*, given everything that is going on."

The things that would have been easier to understand if I had known to ask what to understand. "Now I feel foolish for not understanding earlier."

Squeezing his hand again, "we all make mistakes."

And that is a haunted tone. "Then what will I be for now?"

With a quiet cluck of her tongue, "a Ghost in the system."

Ghost then? Good enough. "A Ghost then? Makes me seem spooky, I can live with that. Ghost of friendships past."

Squeezing his hand again she nodded. Appearing calm and serious in her demeanor and tone, "and my job demands I walk the moral line between right and wrong."

Trying to keep the sarcastic smile off his face as his thoughts reacted. *I would never have guessed.* "I could walk it with you. And if I am allowed? Try to remind you which side is which if you have doubts."

Taking both of his hands in hers, "will you be my Ghost? Will you walk in the shadows behind me and keep me safe from Specters? Can I count on you to protect me? Can I –"

I need to stop her from saying something she's going to feel foolish for later. Pulling her into a new hug he spoke softly, "yes on all counts."

Her quiet whisper barely reached his ears, "Yuri?"
Lowering his voice to match hers, "yes?"
"Can we cry now?"
I have some tears to shed. "We? Yes."

2.6.5 - 02:20

Central Tower - Interior

■Dennis Ochenhart

Striding into a side room on the third floor of Central Tower, where a clutch of workers were awaiting assignment, he checked the clipboard in his hands. *I have another life to touch and to see if I can make something better for having cast my shadow on it.*

Intoning her name with a confidence, "Tova Morse?"

Watching the eyes turn he could see the looks of recognition spread through the room. *I am the Darkest Shadow, and each one wonders what I want with Tova.*

Stepping out from behind a few of the men, a female figure spoke with confidence, "Sir?"

She takes me back to a simpler time. The color of rich hazelnut, not unlike the neighbors when I was young. "I need your help Technician Morse."

Nodding with a Citizen's Salute, "yes sir!"

Tapping the palm of his hand with the clipboard, "get your tools and follow me."

Stepping back into the hall he smiled when she joined him.

She looks like she's in good state of mind. Good. I will see this task through and keep myself professional.

Asking her question with a conversational lilt, "nature of the task sir?"

Stepping toward the Bachman Elevator, "we, *you*, are going to reignite the Aureole and bring the light back."

From behind him with a tone of unabashed excitement, "understood sir."

Moving down the hall he felt a confidence in his plan he was relieved to be feeling. *Between your supervisor calling me on the way here with a request to check on you, combined with your skills, I have the best way to check on you. Get you to help this moment recover in a definitive way. I have been assured you're familiar enough with the Ivrea boards that you can get this done. And that* familiar, *is a bit of an understatement.*

Stopping at the elevator door he set to opening it, *made sure to get this parked on this floor. One of the few perks left to me from the old days.* "I can get you in with my Clearance, but I need *you* to ignite the Aureole. I've seen the chatter on the comms, the people who are awake *need* to see that light. And *I* do not have the understanding of the system like you would."

The glory of not needing to lie about something.

"Noted."

Opening the elevator fully he stepped inside and waited for her to join him. Nodding to her he pressed the button for the thirtieth floor with a grim authority, "I'll explain in a moment."

"Noted."

Waiting a breath after the doors had closed he explained, "an insider detonated a device within the security hub. The centralized controls for the building are offline because of that."

Deflating with a pensive sigh, "I had wondered. I had heard what I had heard, but the clarification had not yet come."

Moving into his prepared explanation with notes of encouragement, "the Aureole *can* be reignited by accessing the controls directly. I don't know if there is any damage to the components. I *do* know that you have the qualifications, and were within range."

Nodding twice with a softness to the gesture, "I will do what I can."

"I can get the door opened. There is power to the door, and my Clearance is still enough to get it opened. You get it back up and running, I'll see you out, and then you go back to your work and I'll go back to mine."

With a neutral intonation she appeared to be with the moment, "noted."

Now for the big moment questions. "Comments, Questions, Concerns?"

Looking to the ceiling of the elevator, "I saw the invading force, when they came into the lobby. I took the picture that was sent upstairs."

Turning toward her he tilted his head as he regarded her, "are you well?"

Laughing with a certainty to her words, "no. I took a low dose of Tranq I found in the first-aid room on the tenth floor." Drawing out the word with a droll humor to it, "yes," before returning to a more professional tone, "I know it's not good for me, but I could *not* function. I *feel* functional. I put the one foot in front of the other, I can move again, and it feels better than the alternative did."

Replying with a neutrality of his own, "you will be a small hero in the rebuilding."

Furrowing her brow she sighed, "do I need to have words for the moment?"

Shrugging softly, "only if you want."

Looking both ways then up at the floor readout, "is the High Consul alive?"

Smiling with an affirming tone, "yes."

"Is she," taking on a questioning tone that spoke of not wanting to know the answer, "*well?*"

Nodding with a relief granted by his own intel, "I have more than one message that the Derecho is blowing, the winds are picking up again, and we will see a morning with a Blue Sky, not a Red one."

Lowering her head in concern and a voice of somber sadness, "New Hope has never had a Red Sky morning."

Rushing his words he spoke quickly, "if we work as hard as we can, as a people, we will not wake up to one."

Smiling with the question clear on her face, "do you believe that?"

Looking at the readout, *almost there.* "I have no choice that is a choice to make in that."

The thirtieth. Reaching over he set to opening the door by hand. Sliding the door open with her help he moved into the hallway. Getting his orientation he checked the map the medics had released before setting to the task of getting to the Nerve Cluster.

Stopping with him in front of the blank gray slate of a door Tova sounded excited still, "The Nerve Cluster, the High Consul's communications and uplink data center."

"Yes." Swiping his card he waited for the light to turn blue. Hearing the dead bolts throw he smiled when the third clacked. "We can go in."

Opening the door and holding the large auto-closing security door for her he waited for her to go inside. Following her into the room he laughed at her look of disbelief.

Taking in the familiar site of racks and racks of Ivrea unit relays, color coded wires, punchblocks, and the small row of single board computers he smiled at the look of shocked disappointment on her face. *I believe she was expecting something more grandiose.*

"This, is not what I was expecting."

Speaking from a placed of humored condolence, "Asmodai told me that they built this to *function,* then they got busy with other projects that needed more attention than the beautification of this room."

Moving over to the standard issue computers she looked around with a disappointed wonder to her, "I would have thought they could have brought in some fancy cabinets. Or more interesting lighting. Or the stuff you see on the Network from the past." Setting her toolbox down she set her hands to the keys, "the upside is that it will be easy to service if something *is* busted."

Doing his best to make the most of the moment with his tone, "a Silver Lining then?"

Looking around once more, "one at the cost of being awed."

Tossing his words with a playful inquiry, "worth it though?"

Nodding in acceptance of the situation, "worth it."

Waiting a few moments until the sound of the keystrokes quieted, "so what brought you to this career?"

Replying with a conversational humor, "my sister. She's in Coding and Programming. I went Network Technician, I had assumed that I would be able to be her eyes and ears in the field."

Lobbing his words back with a matching conversational humor, "did that work out?"

Nodding once with a distracted smile, "it did. I did end up keeping my hair shorter than she does though." Laughing with a playful jest, "my hair would end up cleaning out the cabinets if I wore it as long as she does."

Joining in on the humor, "I could see that being a hindrance to enjoying one's work."

"It is." Reaching up and tapping her restrained locks with a smile, "so I keep it all under control while I'm at work."

"Then let it out when you're off the clock?"

"Oh yes. The upside is that it plays into Letting the Hair Down."

Pursing his lips and nodding with a smile he watched her laugh before turning back to the screen. *She's in good spirits. Her significant other gets to see the moment, or participate in the moment, of the unleashing of her hair. Good to know she has someone to go home to after this.*

Back on task. "How does it look?"

"There has been damage. I believe I have an answer though."

Watching her move over to a storage cabinet and removing some parts, placing them carefully on a static free platter, with a quiet determination he felt comforted by her confidence. *If she thinks she can do this, then I'm hopeful.*

Watching her move from the cabinet and over to one of the controller stations he waited as she worked quietly on removing, replacing, and rewiring the new pieces into place.

"I'll load the control software onto this, and I should be able to Reignite the Aureole." Nodding twice with a humored awe she sighed, "I can't say I thought I would say that, ever."

Offering the casual wisdom, "one can never truly know the future."

Pausing for a moment she nodded with understanding, "you would know."

Moving the focus back to her, "I am just thankful you were able to help."

Gesturing at a progress bar, "the Ivrea units aren't complicated once you've had the training. They were designed to be approachable. The software is clear as crystal, thanks to all the training courses on the subject."

"Good."

Speaking with a meandering tone and emotional daydream with her words, "Miss Bachman is an inspiration. I know, as a woman, that I am not made something more by the fact that she's the High Consul. However, as a woman? I am happy that I was alive in the generation where a Bachman daughter could be the High Consul. Not that the Bachman family has had many daughters." Appearing to catch herself she sighed, "I'm rambling."

Let me pay you the only currency I have, "I would listen."

Smiling without looking to him she nodded once and continued, "I grew up being told I could do this if I was able and wanted to. I can admit that some of my colleagues lose themselves in this to a much more enthusiastic fashion, but that doesn't diminish me. I have other women to talk to, I have a social structure, so even though there *are* more men in this field I don't feel like an outsider. I like this. I like the work I do. I love that each time the labs come up with something new I get to play with it first because I work at Central Tower."

"Good."

"Dennis," signaling for 'Delicate Broach,' "I have to ask, I can't keep this question locked up. Why did you stop being a Network Archaeologist? You spent your days watching cinema, films, animation, and your essays were spot on. Why did you give that up?"

A fan of my work from my youth, surprising. "I was encouraged. I had watched a long line of military and spy films. Documentaries on war and special forces. I had an idea of what the framework would look like. The Bachman way is to get those who have an idea of how the idea should look, to make it happen. I checked and rechecked against the forbidden histories of humankind to do my best with getting others to understand what we would need."

Nodding she smiled with a wistful humor, "do you miss it, the cinema though?"

Turning away with the question weighing on him, "I don't think I could go back."

"But do you miss it?" Sighing she stopped her hands for a moment, "I read your essays and I saw the passion there. The Silver Screen Appreciation Association in Respite, your essays are part of the cornerstones of how to approach cinema. I, had oft wondered but never had the chance to find out why you walked away and stayed away."

Do not shy away from truth. "I do miss that. I think I would have missed what I did, and what I had, more though. Becoming a tailor let me stay near. I couldn't stay near if I went back to the darkened rooms looking for answers in the dreams of the dead."

Returning to her work in earnest, "you never married."

A regret I have for selfish reasons. "My career became my life."

With a tone of appreciative praise she tossed her words at him, "you raised a daughter though."

Finding himself reflexively downplaying the praise, "I did my best with her. To teach her everything I knew. And to never ask her to become me."

"Did she?"

Smiling with pride he shook his head in decline, "she became herself. She's a vibrant woman, whom I am glad I said yes to when she asked me for help."

Sounding more inquisitive again, "she asked you?"

Thinking back on the post-conflict days in Chihuahua, "she did. She was heartbroken, she did not want to be a burden in an area which was rife with post-conflict burdens. I did what I felt was the most human thing I could do." Running off on the tangent, "she wants to see a better bridge built for our people. Asmodai had the trains expanded from Bliss to Chihuahua on her recommendation."

Looking up with a surprised grin, "he did that for her?"

Nodding once with a rejuvenated happiness, "he told me that she made a convincing case for the need and merit for such a project."

"Amazing." Stepping back from her work with a determined grin, "I think I have it ready for a test. I can move the scripts to the local workstation and get it back to a state of normalcy."

Excellent. "Do it."

Moving back to the workstation she set her fingers to the keys, "the Aureole is a borderline sacred light, if it wasn't just a series of lamps, bulbs, and the like it would seem like magic. We look up, and it's there. It glows, it shines, it radiates in ways that communicate to us the nature of things. What message do you want me to send when it lights up?"

Simple enough. "Testing pattern, full spectrum, and then set it to neutral. If it's stable? Turn on the News Bulletin lights. Then we'll leave."

Nodding with affirmation she set back to the keyboard, "on it."

Waiting in the quiet of the keystrokes and the gentle hum of the fans he mulled over his next move. *I'll go see Stanley next.* Checking to see where in the building he was he blinked at the location beacon, *he's gone to the High Consul's Office? I wonder what he's looking for?*

Clapping her hands she stepped back before taking a bow, "it's done!"

Wonderful. "Already?"

"The hardware was replaced easily enough, and the connections weren't fried. The Aureole was undamaged. It is in the configuration you requested. I set it to go into daylight operations once the light sensors, which are also still functional, detect that the daylight is bright enough."

"Thank you very much Technician Morse."

Giving the Civilian's Salute again, "it was my duty. See me out?"

"Yes."

2.6.2 - 02:37

Safe Housing - Living Room

⁂..Susan Bachman

Drying her eyes she looked up at Yuri's still sad eyes and felt her heart thump with a resonance she was becoming accustomed to. Watching his eyes focus on her she tried to smile, "I needed that."

Matching her still quiet voice he hugged her softly, "I, I did too. I hurt, so much right now, this? I feel a little better."

Hugging him in return, "I have painkillers upstairs."

"I hurt like that too. And a bed?"

I know just the one. "And a bed you can use."

"Susan?"

"Yes Yuri?"

"If good works speak for themselves, and good counsel does not harm, am I good and without harm to you?" Sighing he tilted his head back, "I don't know how close I can be with you in this place and not overstep or appearing to usurp."

He must be concerned about my feelings for Sasha. "I can lead, speaking without malice or deception, to show the way clearly."

Lowering his head he smiled, "would you?"

The Albatross lends me the Wisdom. "I can."

Taking his hand she led him out of the living room and up the stairs to the second floor. "Do you need a shower before bed?"

"I just want a bed right now. I can shower in the morning." From behind her she heard his small laugh, "I smell terrible and yet you asked if I needed one, not that I should have one."

Reaching the top of the stairs she felt her thoughts go in order, "I *also* reek of fear sweat. Our system states no judgments placed unless one is ready to be judged in turn." Turning toward her not so old room, *he needs sleep, I will give him the best bed I can.*

"That is a kind way of doing it."

"It is what we strive for." *The lessons my father taught me on Honor come to mind with a vengeance tonight.* Touching the lone pale red door she tapped it lightly with the fingertips of her left hand, "you can use this room."

Looking up the hallway, "why is it the only red door?"

Smiling in reply, "I like the color red."

Appearing to be in a good humor, "I am confused."

Twisting the door knob she opened the door and stepped inside. Waiting a moment she smiled as the lights came up to a low light scheme timed to the hour of the night. Reaching out she took his hands and pulled him gently inside the room.

Stopping to sniff the air he smiled, "I like the smell. Is that carrot greens?"

"It is meant to smell like it, yes."

Looking past her to the bed, "how firm are those pillows?"

Having another thing in common, it makes me smile. "Like the ones you have been using."

"The ones you picked out?"

"Yes."

Looking around he left her grasp while taking a step toward the bed, "why is there a shirt hanging out of that laundry basket?"

Keep it simple. "This isn't a guest room. I wanted to honor your request for sleep as quickly as possible, so I brought you to my room." Rushing to follow up, "I sleep in the master bedroom usually."

Speaking softly in a language she didn't know he moved the light summer bedding out of the way and set to getting into bed. Stopping as his shirt was about to hit the fabric he sighed, "Susan? My apparel."

Moving quickly to the closet she pulled out a simple pale blue nightshirt. *He can wear this. It's quite long on me, should be more than fine for him.* Turning she brought it to him. "You can wear this. It's neutral in shape."

Taking it from her he nodded, "thank you Susan."

Grabbing the top sheet she held it up like a curtain, "you can get into the shirt, leave the rest, and lay down."

Quickly shucking out of his clothes, "you honor me."

"As soon as I have you tucked in I'll get the pain killers out and see if we can give you a better good morning."

Turning and donning the sheet Yuri slid into bed and covered himself, "will it dull my reactions?"

The knowledge we might not stay alone out here. "No. It's not an opiate. It's not going to do a lot for the pain right now, but it will make the morning far more tolerable."

"I can accept that."

Moving to the edge of the bed she reached into the nightstand and found a bottle of water and the bottle of pills. Shaking a pair of tablets into her hand she capped the bottle and put it back. Reaching over she placed the pills into Yuri's waiting hand and passed him the bottle of water.

Watching him take the pill she nodded twice, "I remembered what you said about how you feel about your body."

With a tone of subdued and hidden need, "can you stay for a moment?"

I can give him time. Sitting down she set to soothing his hair gently with her fingertips, "I can do this until I am certain you are asleep. Then I must go."

"Thank you Susan."

"Noted."

Reaching out from under the sheet he placed his closed hand next to her leg. "Am I alright in your life?"

Never lie to, or lead a man to a conclusion you are not ready to honor. Moving her hand from his hair to his hand, "yes."

"Is it okay that I love you?"

Love is Love, in all of the Facets. I need to get him that Primer. Until then, just the simple answer. "It is. Life is for the living, love is for the giving."

Speaking with a quiet affection he smiled before settling against his pillow, "thank you Susan."

"Noted."

Meeting her eyes he spoke without flinching away, "wishing, is a wasted thing, it has no effect on the world. Doing though, action, deed, those are all things that change the world. I just want to do good. To be seen as good."

I will do what I need to be the good friend you need. "We will teach you what we believe that means. I will tell Steven to leave you be."

"Thank you Susan."

Moving her hand back to his hair she set to a gentle caress in earnest. *His hair is oiled and sweat soaked but that doesn't matter.* Watching his face slowly soften until it became slack with sleep, *I will make sure he showers in the morning though.* Hearing his breathing change she resolved to wait two more minutes worth of ministrations before she would move to get up. *I like this. Mom was right, this is good.*

2.4.0 - 01:42

New Hope General - Observation Ward - Room 1x07

▶ Winifred Yeoman

Standing just inside the door to Northland's recovery room she wrestled with the emotional paralysis from the fear and the regret. Closing her eyes against the cold ache in her heart she wished she had not asked the doctors for their honest opinion.

I need to take the step forward and face it with him. The nightmare for people like us. The idea that we are no longer of use in our Role. I have to wake him, not speak of the grim percentages, and encourage the warm glow in his heart from the upbeat attitude that defines him as a man.

We both know Miss Bachman would never leave him alone in the rubbish bin. I can't forget that. And I certainly cannot contribute to the idea that he would either.

Moving closer she trembled internally at the sight of the amount of equipment she saw hooked to him. Looking down at his catheter bag she felt relief at the color. *No blood. I've lost enough tonight, I'm not losing Northland too. I am going to scream into the universe for a better future and it's going to be one where Northland is alive and well.*

Singleton is going to need the counselor I had sent his way. He can't take on Northland's pain, that'll kill him. He needs to accept that he had no way of knowing what Northland was accepting. That his wife needs him. That his future kid needs him. And that we'll do this right.

At least I won't have to go home to an empty apartment when I need sleep. I have my MCB bunk waiting for me now. Not that rusted apartment which is almost the same sort of empty place Northland goes home to.

Stepping closer to the bed her mind continued down the trail of thought, *were we ashamed to be happy around Miss Bachman? Did we get caught up in the madhouse affairs of the High Consul? Months of work and progress on projects only to have it come to this. I'm just glad Hoover isn't involved anymore. Gutless wonder who spoke in the same sort of dialect as Patrick when he gets writing, with none of the good intentions.*

Now Hoover is gone away, The Old Man of the Office is gone, and only Miss Bachman remains. I will do what I can until I cannot. One foot in front of the other foot.

Finishing her movement over to the side of the bed she cringed at the sight of Northland at closer range, *they really worked you over friend. Maybe they didn't kill you because they were afraid it wouldn't work?*

Adjusting her footing she moved to the spot on the far side of the bed near his elbow. *It should be easy for him to talk face to face without twisting his neck.* Picking up Northland's hand she held it gently for a moment. *And he didn't wake up. Time to push this along.* Tapping him gently on the back of the hand to see if she could wake him, *wake up Northland.* Smiling at his fluttering eyes she singsong spoke without implied malice, "wake-little-Guard, don't-be-afraid, for-on-the-pyre, you-do-not-lay."

Moving his hand out of her grasp he pushed the button for the air going to his nasal cannula before removing it. Setting it on his shoulder he nodded with a moment of satisfaction before speaking with a voice far slower than she'd have liked to hear, "you sound happy. We still have a High Consul to protect then?"

Doing her best to sound encouraging, "you'll be bringing her coffee before you know it."

Looking at his left arm the cadence of his words didn't pick up, "am I out of commission? Is this normal? Why can't I speak very quickly?"

I can't imagine your fear friend. Worse than death, the idea you don't work anymore. I'll tell him the official word on the subject. For both our sakes. "You're a bit damaged. Temporarily. We have five names to replace on our rolls confirmed, six if Sinclair stays gone, or if you bow out. Could get up to seven. The other five on shift are currently being treated. No word yet. If they wash? Then yes, we could go up to twelve."

Taking his hand back and scratching his nose he seemed puzzled, "why doesn't this compute in my head?"

This is less than good. "We need to go slower then."

Nodding once with a lilt of fear, "I like slow. I *sound* slow."

Rushing to assure him, "it's the pharma, and the tired."

"I think I heard the people talking around me, that Miss Bachman is alive."

Still not good. "She lives."

"Is she physically harmed?"

If she was nursing a wound somewhere I think I would come unglued, and I'm not even Dagger Herb. "No. If she was? Dagger Herb would be next to her and giving us a minute by minute update."

Looking at her with the confusion evident in his brown eyes, "why are you here?"

Gesturing at him from head to toe, "to see you."

Appearing to be still confused, "why aren't you with her?"

Time to tell him what I didn't want to admit to myself when I talked to her. "I believe she is preparing for Snowblind. Her enemies have pushed her, and we do not know how many are left unaccounted for. There is a tough moment going on for all of us. A good portion of both sides of the conflict are still alive. Hurt badly, surgery needed for many, and Miss Bachman has signed off on medical treatment for the attackers. The Commander is looking for any of them that he can get cleared to see the Questioners. We're still looking for the mastermind behind this. Until then? Miss Bachman trusts few and the temperature is dropping."

"Wind howling at the door. As for Snowblind, did you tell The Guild?"

Rust. Why would you ask me that? "Why would I do that?"

Smiling at her with a strange candor he seemed at ease, "you're their inside source, don't you think Waterlily should know?"

Miss Bachman needs her freedom to be herself without worry about who is on which team. Keeping her voice level she shook her head softly, "no. Not yet."

Smiling with a far away look on his face he intoned the word with all the meaning in life, "good."

"How did you know?"

"The memory card hand-offs. I caught on. Sunny Day explained everything, that I needed to know, to me, when I asked her."

Silence doesn't seem like you. "Why did you stay silent?"

"It was the thing to do. The Guild, it doesn't always get to be close to the Bachman family. I knew you would be close for Susan. I liked that."

I need a subject change. "Sinclair called home, then went home to Seattle."

With a voice of concern, "is he injured?"

"Yes. It's a rusted up sprain, elbow. He needs to mend for us to find out if he can come back."

Smiling with a knowing grin, "he can mend with Consul Holden. He likes her."

They're family, right? "He does?"

Raising his eyebrows in quick succession a few times he kept the grin, "he likes her likes her."

I guess he's a different sort of relation. Distant hopefully. Though, romantic notions for a Consul put in such a diminutive light? Speaking with a wistful disdain, "mature, really mature there."

Raising his forefinger he appeared to be more serious, "he likes her more than family, but less than lover. He *is* interested in what he never had."

I should ask if only to know. "He open up to you?"

Lowering his hand, "he did."

"Good things?"

Speaking his words with a wistful note of retelling, "he watched cartoons with her. He worked Overnight Patrol with the Seattle Militia. He would go to her at the end of his day, the start of hers. They would share cartoons, a bowl of cereal, and then he would go home. Sometimes she would get him to sleep over in a guest bedroom if he had a long night."

Then his call home policy isn't about family medical care? "I thought his call home was regarding his condition to go home if injured."

"It is." Nodding once before smiling with an attempt at conspiracy, "but it's *also* because those two care about each other. They're good friends."

Touching Northland's hand she tried to stay neutral, "why didn't he say anything?"

Smiling with a mischief she found endearing, "don't you think we would have thought he was a spy?"

Actually? "Yes."

With the simplicity of a child his tone seemed playful, "so he couldn't tell anyone else."

Wait - "does Miss Bachman know? That they're something there?"

"She does. I could see it when she saw him react to her dressing up as Consul Holden. His eyes were sixteen hundred kilos away. She saw it."

I am not shocked. "Learn something new every day."

"And that makes it a good day!"

Reaching out she touched his hand gently again. Moving her hand around she took it with a caring firmness. Watching her pale fingers wrap around his hand, the robust color of his skin gave her hope for his overall health. *Even if he doesn't get to stay with us, he should be able to finally take advantage of his good looks and charm. Finally stop going home alone.*

"Northland," snapping out of the daydream, "I need you to get well, failing that? I need you to help from this bed as you can."

"I can try, and I can do."

"Good enough for me." Adjusting her grip on his hand gently, "how did you figure me out? Was it just the memory cards?"

"Your friends. You were only friends with people who are tight with The Guild. You were *always* there for us with the help we wouldn't ask Susan for. When Singleton needed help clearing his schedule, you made sure he could get to know Constance. When Draper chased his first Silver Mink? You made sure he knew about the classes. When Miss Augusta's sons met Amaranth you knew people to help navigate that space quietly so it didn't get unmanageable." Looking up with a surprised look of revelation, "you know, with Constance so close to term, things so dangerous –"

Rust. "If another bullet gets fired regulations will take him off the field. I'll make sure he stays away from bullets for the time being."

Turning to look her in the eyes with a sad conviction, "he needs to leave us."

Did I miss something? "He does?"

"We are unhappy, if he leaves? We can see the path to happiness and accepting it. He can show us. We're only here, well not you, but the rest of us *weren't good enough.*"

Did he see? "What are you getting at?"

Shaking his head he gestured for 'sad truth,' "you were in the final round of qualifications. Your score was too high, you were going to make the cut. Only a fraction of women have the prowess to make it to Cloak and Dagger and you were going to make it. I watched, the way you moved your body, it was wrong for the weapon you were holding. You picked the wrong stance to lower your overall score until you were *just barely* defeated." Regaining a measure of elation to his tone, "you *wanted* to lead this, so you made sure you were better than the rest of us."

Check the angles. "How do you know I wanted to lead?"

"We didn't know that this was going to happen to us. We went, we *failed*, we rested. Some drank, some fled to Courtesans, and the majority of us showed up to the mustering in sad shape. *You?*" Laughing softly he sighed, "you were fine. You were informed. The time table fits. You knew the day you threw your dreams away that this was waiting for you. You accepted this, and *wanted* this."

My dreams weren't for Cloak and Dagger. It was just for a new home where I would feel where I belonged.

Meeting his gaze she touched his hand gently to find courage.

I will King you as I have nothing else I can say. "And yet you're better at this aspect than me."

"We're not paid to be detectives. Some of us are, but we weren't hired for it."

Northland, please, no. "We were hired because Susan needed protection."

"Do you remember the first time we met her?"

I can do nostalgia. "I do. She told you to get her coffee and it never stopped being a thing."

Smiling with his nostalgia, "I took an Oath. She knew I would leave her coffee alone."

Hold on – "that was on purpose?"

"It was."

Amazing. "She has always been who she is."

"I took the Gourmand's Oath. I vowed I would never meddle with food like that."

I wonder if he knows her worry? "Why would she be concerned about that?"

"She would tell me later. She had read about it on the Network. That forbidden section she delves into it. She read about people who do things to the things others eat and drink, but not for spite, but for obsession. That if they can get you to ingest part of them, they feel closer to you. That if they put part of themselves in the things you touch, that they are closer."

"So she trusted your Oath would protect her if she used you as her shield."

"Yes."

"How do you know this was her motive?"

"She told me one night, years later, over drinks."

"What does it mean when she has someone else do it?"

"She's either trying to get rid of them for a moment, or she has it tested later. She doesn't want to be taken by surprise like that."

She kept something else from me. "Why didn't she tell me?"

"She has her reasons for everything, I was not made privy to that."

I should ask while he's holding still. "Why do you go home alone?"

"I love the job too much. If I find someone like Singleton did? I'll have to go. I don't want to stop yet. This post is my redemption for that week of testing. I didn't have what it took to join Cloak. *This* is my life."

No, how did I not know? "When you stand near the Cloak and Dagger –"

Squeezing her hand with a lilt of sadness, "they remind me of whom we could have been, and the place we ended up instead. We died to protect that place." Turning his gaze back to her he appeared horrified, "when you go? Secure the combat recorders. We all made sure to turn them on. Get them. See the truth of what happened."

My good kids. "I will." Taking his hand with a firmness, *I don't want to leave yet.* "Do you think you're *lesser*?"

Seeing the moisture starting she reached into her pocket and produced a handkerchief. Setting to clearing the tears from his eyes she felt emotionally knocked over.

"At first I did. Then it became a blessing. I just didn't want to leave." Blinking a few times he looked to her with dryer eyes, "why do you go home alone Winnie?"

I want to lie. Rust it to useless scrap I'll tell him the truth. "I was ashamed to be happy. I didn't want to come in, happy from a night of good rutting and a loving breakfast to have to look her in the eyes and be living that contrast. I wanted to reign over her Guard in the heart of the moment. If I was to be a rider on the storm? I would know it as if it was my own life, as it was my life. You can't do that if you have someone to go home to. You can't do that if you're thinking serious loving thoughts. That leads to marriage, children, adoption, and the end of the ride. In a choice between the loving arms of someone who loves me or standing guard on a cold night in the middle of nowhere? I picked nowhere. I picked her life, and the idea of staying in it."

Nodding with a grimly heartened resolution, "we are two of soul."

"We are."

"In Miss Bachman's defense, the hot tea in Port Anchor was nice that night."

Sipping hot tea and watching her and Sasha stargaze. "It was nice."

Snapping his fingers he pointed at her, "stop by antenatal care, see Constance, reassure her having seen me alive. Then go get the combat recorders."

I was gifted with orders that were to find my own orders, so I can do what must be done. "I will."

"Winnie," hearing his voice taking on an almost hoarse quality she cringed internally, "I killed a few before I dropped. I put my foot down and defied their orders. I wasn't helpless, certainly not scared to death, but I did what I was trained to do. I helped move the possible body count to the wounded count by slowing them down. I got to be a hero Winnie. I wasn't at Guthrie, I wasn't a hero yet, I feel like a hero now. Even if this ends me? I went out a Hero."

Taking a moment to breathe he gestured 'one moment' while he nursed air into his body. *I can wait.* Replying with the kindest signaled version of 'I can wait' she could remember she waited for him to speak again.

Hero and Guthrie don't go together. I can't tell you that though. You need to think we did good that day and nothing else.

Recounting the events with a mixture of pride and horror, "they, they screamed at me Winnie. They were horrified. I wouldn't stop fighting. They shot me, I fell down to my knees and kept shooting. They shot me again and I doubled over, they came up on me, they bashed me with a chair. I felt my helmet come off and as I looked up I could hear something frightened, primal, and scared." Taking a breath, "I'm still scared, I'm mourning because I know Kowalski didn't make it, I *know* they got Paulson, I can only guess how my fellows who haven't been confirmed are. I'm sure Sunny Day will tell me. She'll talk me down." Taking a breath, "and because I'm here? I have to accept this next part is on Miss Bachman to design and for you to carry out. Watch her back Winnie. And please, if you look on my combat recorder, or Kowalski's, find the real truth. Get it to Wallman. Tell him to show the fear we *all* felt."

"She'll see us through." Reaching down she stroked his hand gently again, "I'll do as you ask Northland. I'll find the recorders and get them to Wallman. I safeguard him in this. He's my current assignment."

Taking a breath and focusing, "and get Sinclair back."

Keep him useful. "You should call him when you're both feeling better. Help get him back."

Imploring her with his tone, "will you call him?"

Giving the back of his hand a firmer caress, "I will if you will first."

Nodding once with a firmness and a wince of painful regret at the gesture, "I Pact the Pledge."

Removing her hand from his hand she smiled, "I Pact it with you."

"A Blue Sky to you Winnie." Pointing at the window behind him, "I can't see it but I can hope that the upcoming morning sky will be blue. And a gentle breeze to carry the smells of your enemies to your nose before they get close."

The Blessing of the Wind's Favor. "Thank you Northland. May the Wind favor me."

With a lilt of a Warrior's Fire to the words, "the best way you can thank me is to win this."

Speaking with a deepened resolution to win, "then I'll see you when this is done. Trophy in hand."

Encouraging her firmly, "that's the spirit."

Pulling her hand back she shivered against the implications of the future. *I have no more words for this moment.* Nodding, saluting, and walking out of the hospital room, as the sound of the airflow resuming touched the quiet, she couldn't help but wonder what Susan had planned next. *Her enemies are going to get treated to something like they've never seen. She has been honing her craft for a long time and I can't wait to see the looks on their faces. Miss Bachman is going to clear the table of opposing pieces and we'll get back to her side.*

There is no other way this can play out. None that I'll dwell on. None that I'll accept. I sadly have to get back to work. Miss Bachman wants her orders carried out, and Wallman kept safe.

S M Gilbert

As she wills, as it will be.

2.4.5 - 01:46

Base of Central Tower - 5 O'clock Point

† Sasha Herb

Watching the perimeter with an anger seething inside of her she stopped her thoughts to address them.

Address the Issue. Breathe in logic. Confront the Anger. Defang the Tiger Within. Easy as A B C D.

Hammering the thoughts she looked for the source of her anger, *I don't want to be on Perimeter. I want to know who did this. I want to know what is being done. I am the source of my anger.*

Touching her unit patch on her armor she took a deep breath, *I am not Sasha right now. I am Dagger Herb. I am a Scout. I am not alone in this anger. I know she's alive. I know she's uninjured. And it's not enough.*

I want to be inside finding out what they've learned. I want Asmodai to appear from beyond the grave and order the rage into manifest form to smite whomever was behind this. Mulling the idea over she felt a chagrined calm wash over her, *I never thought I would want to see him again, much less see him angry again.*

He never hated me though.

I'm angry because I don't have control. I don't have power. And I want both. Or I want to have Susan to have that power in this moment.

Closing her eyes she felt the final part of the mental puzzle click into place, *I'm wanting to protect my Mate.*

I'm hiding from the death of Bonnie, or that Patrick was hurt. That I might have had to live in a world where he doesn't bring me a drink at the Winter Solstice Party with the joke of 'you have to drink this so I don't. Heartstrings is watching.'

The Tiger wants an easy out. The Tiger wants to claw at the Consul who did this. Taking another deep breath she held it for a three count before letting go. Moving back to her patrol path she resumed her vigilance over the scene.

Stopping short as the Vox chimed in her ear she tapped the wrist control for it. Keeping her voice low she intoned the opening statement, "oolong."

The tired but strong and quite familiar voice of Captain Turner rang over the Vox, "Tea Time."

Group discussion. Keeping her discipline to her tone, "query?"

With tones of forced calm and careful enunciation, "have you spoken with her?"

Shoving her thoughts of self-doubt aside she fired back with Operations Chatter Voice, "affirmative."

"What do you know?"

Looking at the corner of her helmet's HUD she blinked at the amount of people listening in. *This is not normal.*

Speaking with a cautioned intonation of the words, "the channel appears compromised Captain."

Calling back with humor intruding into her voice, "Negative. Proper channels have authorized the current listeners. I repeat, what do you know?"

By the checklist. "She is alive. Uninjured."

Firing back with her question, "is she alone?"

You sound like you already know she is not. "She is with Mandelbrot."

"Who is Mandelbrot?"

What I wouldn't give to know the full truth. "I have a name, Yuri. Outside of that? Unknown to me." Sighing on the inside while trying to keep her mind on the perimeter, "I was left out of the loop. Given an IOU on the loop though. Her trust in me was reaffirmed."

Hearing the familiar sound of Sevilan's voice come over the channel she felt her spirit lift, "welcome to The Loop. Epsilon Code for this Disclosure is Gingerbread Bullets. No one on this channel will speak of what we're going to speak of unless prompted."

Captain Turner's soft acknowledgment followed quickly, "Captain Sevilan."

With the fatigue clear in his tone Sevilan launched into his words, "you will notice the Night Terrors moving into position. I woke my boys. Orders are starting to come in from on high. The Scouts being on perimeter is a temporary situation."

Repeating her question with a cool grace Captain Turner asked without an increase in cadence, "who is Mandelbrot, Sir?"

"His name is Yuri, he's a Ghost, and he is loyal first and foremost to Miss Bachman."

Speaking with a firm but gentle tone of command a male bass voice came across, "entering channel discussion, Captain Paul Kaufman of the Jaguars. My forces can confirm the presence of this man known as Yuri at the side of Miss Bachman. She saw to his wounds with a medical kit in the parking under Central." Pausing for a moment the voice came back with a gentle incredulity, "I have an image file to confirm what I am going to say next. This man known as Yuri was seen getting into the *driver's seat* of Miss Bachman's Beast."

I knew that at least. "What was Yuri doing before this?"

Jumping back in with his Command Voice Sevilan informed the channel, "he was at my side with Cloak Yorklin. We were on scene when the coup started. We were *over the hills.* He reached her."

I was left out of the loop. "Only he did Sir?"

Keeping up his Command Voice he continued, "I need every last one of you to understand something. Our High Consul has a *guest* in her house. This man Yuri, he is the many years removed *direct* descendant of, The Gingerbread Man."

He dodged the question. "The Gingerbread Man died during Final Seal."

Without losing his presence or clarity of speech he seemed unfazed by her words, "when he left his land to come to the side of the Bachman family, he did not know he had left behind a son to be. A goodbye tryst with his best friend according to what is understood of the night shared. She carried to term. Further, he carries with him the writings of Elianna Seches, the Queen of Swords. And around his neck he brought the Medallion given to Elianna before she left Asmodai the First. He is the person he claims to be."

Laughing with a grim humor Kaufman sounded impressed, "if there would be a man who could keep up with the Derecho? It would be the Gingerbread Man. I will inform the New Hope Militia Captains, Yuri will find no quarrel with us unless he starts one."

Explains the Epsilon Code. "He is a Ghost by default then?"

"Yes."

"What happens now?"

After a long sigh Sevilan spoke again, "we don't have Clearance to get in the building. None of *us*. Medical has it, and that's it. The Commander has it under lockdown otherwise. Wallman has Clearance though, granted to him by Miss Bachman herself."

Hearing Captain Turner's voice soothed her nerves, "where is she going?"

"That's too sensitive for this channel Captain Turner, I offer my sorrow for that."

Popping back in Kaufman sounded confused, "if we don't know where she is, how do we know if she's in danger?"

Quipping back with a deadpan humor, "we don't. But there are forces moving to protect her. She's not going to be alone."

What is she getting if we're all here? "Fools to the Front?"

"Close."

I like this less. "What do I do?"

Encouraging her with his paternal tone Frank sounded softer for a moment, "wait for her to call you again and do whatever you can to help."

Easiest order I've had all night. "I can do that."

Kaufman's humor rang in his tone, "I wish us all luck."

Back on task. "ETA on Wallman?"

"Soon. He's going to have Honor Guard with him from the looks of it. Miss Bachman wants him protected."

Sound. "Understood."

"I will have the Jaguars go to her bunker when we're done here, find out if she was right about it by not going to it."

Post Strike in her bed? "Keep us in The Loop?"

With the tone of a Pledged Pact Kaufman replied, "always."

Captain Turner's humored tones left her smiling as the words played over her mind, "then let us go attend to our duties with the Tenacity of William."

Speaking the words with reverence Kaufman sounded determined, "the Ferocity of Kane to you all."

Speaking with a firm paternal grace to his words Sevilan sounded encouraging, "the Bluest Sky to show us the way."

My turn. "The Heart of Cassiopeia to beat in our chests."

Speaking again Sevilan set the closing words into motion, "may we all succeed and come home in time for dinner."

Signaling the closing of the blessing Captain Turner spoke firmly to all on the Vox, "to us."

Joining the final line as a half dozen voices closed the blessing, "to us."

Watching the channel collapse she breathed a sigh of relief, *she's not alone where she's going. She's just there with the new Gingerbread Man. The last one we were given was killed by the end of the world. He saved the Bachman family at the cost of his life.*

I hope this one doesn't have to pay that price.

2.4.7 - 02:01

Central Tower - "The Enchanted Woods"

●Frank Sevilan

Having found a comfortable resting position on the fold-down bunk bench, *two sets of meds in me and I don't know which one is going to win. So far, still awake.*

Taking in the interior of the Nemean Lion Armored Command Vehicle he was thankful for the solitude. *This could be the last moments of my command. I've been gliding along, and I can feel the wind beneath me fading.*

Rotating the meditation orbs in his hand he considered his options, *she'll find me something if I want to stay up and involved. Anything I could want, because that's how she is. I won't get lost, or asked to retire, but I'll have to accept Hugh can take the Squad and lead it.*

I believe in Hugh.

So what in the rusted scrap heap is my problem?

Taking in the smell of the breeze coming in from the trees around him he took the moment to give thanks for his parking spot in The Enchanted Woods. *The tech and resources spent to build a place of magic. Smells nice. Gives clean air to the Tower. Shelter from the sun. And now a place of solace for me again.*

Looking down the mental checklist he sought out the nature of his major malfunction. *The Terrors have their objectives in hand.*

Hugh has the squad in hand.

Susan is alive and in good hands, I believe.

Patrick is recovered and in a place of healing.

Steven is still human.

I –

Growling in frustration with himself he clenched the orbs with a grimace, *I'm disappointed I made it. I didn't want to get hit. I didn't want to lay here like a useless log of meat knowing this is it. My invincible legacy ends here. Det, det, det.*

Taking a breath he touched his face with his free hand, *come on. She's going to find you a way to stay close. To inspire. To lead. You're not so old that you're dead. You're not so old that you're moving to the Sunset House.*

Just old enough to feel old.

Picking up his comm he reread Susan's message for the fourth time. *She just wanted me to see that she was still trying to do it 'right.' That the people get a Second Chance.*

The odd ones out.

Closing his eyes he felt the wash of the emotional crash. *My part in this is done. I did what I had to do to save the moment. You do not fight to win. You fight to avoid further loss.*

Hearing the door opening he opened his eyes. Taking his handkerchief he cleared his eyes, *only a few people can open that door.*

Seeing clearly he smiled at the tired face of Captain Turner.

Addressing her with a practiced formality, "Captain."

Closing the door behind her she moved to him before speaking with a formal tone of her own, "Captain."

Trying to keep his tone upbeat, "does your husband know that you're visiting another man in the middle of the night?"

Nodding with an understanding smile, "he asked me to check on you. He wanted me to see you."

"Is he well?"

"He hasn't flown into any mountains in a moment of worry. Paige is keeping in touch with him as I'm in an Active Theater of Operations." Reaching over she took his hand, "post conflict crash?"

Trying to keep his voice neutral, "affirmative."

Offering him a consolatory tone, "I've never shot at my fellow Citizen before."

Opening up, his tone moved to one of sadness, "most have not. It's terrible. Sam, this is a gross feeling. I was given the baton pass of an idea, that was *never* meant to be turned against the Citizens. Those Citizens, were never meant to face me. Whomever ordered this? They set me against my fellows. With the battle done? I don't want to see anyone else hurt."

Coaxing him with a tone of praise, "I've seen the amount of wounded, which stratagem did you play?"

Replying with the simple fact, "Odd Man Out."

Touching his hand gently with a platonic caress, "solid choice."

Pursing his lips he fought back against the urge to sob, "Sam, this is terrible."

Nodding with understanding she caressed his forehead, "and this is *why* Leif wanted me to check on you."

Feeling stabilized by her touch, "I got hit."

Resting her hand on his shoulder with a caution, "how bad?"

I'm not dead or at General. "I don't have a hematoma, or a hemoperitoneum, as far as Dhavid could tell. It's a mess of lacerations with bruising. I'm scheduled for imaging. I wanted to stay on duty." Going for a cavalier attitude he smiled, "prop me up in a Viper's Nest."

Narrowing her eyes at him she inquired firmly, "did you reach for Last Dance?"

Firing back with a sore humor, "no." Gesturing to it, "that was in my Tactical Harness, hanging up over there. I didn't have my full rig on because the Threat Index was low enough I didn't have to. I was in my lighter duty armor instead of the heavy stuff. Hence how I took the rusted hit. They came with an arsenal worthy of a Shock and Awe Assault. Paulson, he made them work for it. Each one of her boys set up something truly devastating. Her people fought. The best a Consul could bring against the best a High Consul could hide."

Making the sign of the 'Divine' with her words, "the Holy Ground has tasted blood."

Giving in to the gravity of the reality, "blood, death, and fire. It was never meant to be like this."

Laying her hand on his, "The Consul who did this will be found."

They will die when she finds them. "I don't doubt that."

"I," tripping over her words she tried again, "I could have lost Paige tonight."

I was not informed. "What happened?"

Squeezing his hand with a momentary tremble, "Dennis was alerted by Paige. The convoy moved along a set of back streets, under Network Cloak, and she spotted them. She got word to Dennis. If they had known that Paige had seen them, would they have turned?"

Someone else get hit? "Parallel Event?"

Whispering the words with a confused hatred, "these people sent a Strike Team to kill Jerome Hope."

They knew about him? "Hope? The cute boy with the long hair and the friend at The Feedbag?"

Nodding once with a grimace, "affirmative."

Tell me no Sam. "Is he dead?"

Shaking her head she breathed out the sigh of relief, "no. His friend had an armor plated truck, which I don't fully understand. Gossip from an image shared from C&D. His friend got him to safety."

The Day-Runner. Smiling he found a moment of light to bask in, "she gave him the truck because she was afraid he would need it."

Coming up short she frowned with a mild annoyance, "how many Epsilon Codes am I standing on the other side of?"

Trying for humor he tossed her his reply, "a handful." *No go on a smile.* "But, Paige?"

"They drove right past her. They didn't act on being seen by the Student of Shadows. Dennis got word to the Crisis Coordinator, who in turn got word *from* the High Consul Medical, and that's how the triage center we bumped into was forged." Hanging her head she sniffled, "I couldn't imagine my girl as a High Value Target. If they had known?"

Squeezing her hand he tried to reassure her, "Paige is a smart girl. If she had seen them come she would have evaded. She's being honed into another who understands the ways of the Shadows. She is the Third Student, and they say that good things come in threes."

Sounding reassured, "Stephanie, Miss Bachman, and Paige. Paige is in good company. It's done quite a bit for her self-esteem. She's so *vibrant* when I see her."

Keeping up the upbeat line of conversation, "your girl had her car near, yes?"

Smiling again, "yes."

"She knows the layout of the city."

Losing ground to a bigger smile, "she does."

"She had her flares, yes?"

Lowering her gaze she spoke with a maternal concern, "I would *like* to believe she had her flares."

Raising her gaze she looked at him with the narrow eyes of inquiry.

She noticed. "Before you ask? Security got knocked out as an Opening Move. The distress flares were a denied variable. Network Lockout prevented me from using the flares on this," tapping the wall, "and the Bachman Relay able control for them?" Pointing to his tactical harness, "on the same harness with my dose of Last Dance."

Taking a deep breath she emoted her concern and sympathy with her words and stance, "I understand with a richer detail why you want to be alone right now."

Looking back to the ceiling, "it's a rusted sludge between my ears."

Poking his shoulder with two fingertips, "so where's our High Consul?"

I can tell her now. "Safe Housing. She's getting Overwatch from House Drenner." Looking at her disappointment he smiled, "you didn't let me finish. They're hauling out the Sky-Castle, Sundering House-Cleaver Rockets, and the Paladin Battle Armor. Captain Kane's *entire* surviving load-out from Lion's Roar. And with it being Drenner assets? They'll have thermographic drones for extended recon. They're trained to find people that get lost. In this case they'll find the people who try to sneak up on them."

Touching his shoulder again, "you want to have hope."

Unable to reach up and touch her hand with his he settled for touching her hand with his cheek, "I do."

Moving her hand back to his hand she smiled with a sheepish shade to the gesture, "I will join you in that hope."

I don't want her to think it's unfounded. I did learn something about this family being a part of it.

Working his tone to convince her of the truth, "those men she is getting? They are *family.* The Drenner family are a huge network of siblings, cousins, and broods of children. Each one shares blood with Maggie. Miss Bachman is *also* a Drenner by blood, mother to daughter, and they do not take that as a trivial matter. William may have been the most blood soaked Bachman, but he also came to the Drenner's aid when they needed to secure their city. The Drenner family, they don't forget things. Asmodai loved and cherished his wife." Stopping himself he groused, "I'm babbling."

"I understand better now, rest your weary head. I will be hopeful with you without remorse or regret for that hope."

Good. "Sam, I want to believe Yuri is going to be good for her. He's, something else. Both good and bad."

Looking at him with the honest concern, "how *bad?*"

Oversold it. "He's an outsider. He knows, and was raised, in values and ideas which are troubling at best. He's *at heart,* a good person. He's got no small amount of scary stories and a troubling journey he carries with him. Steven is worried about his words getting out and infecting people."

Speaking her question with a clear caution, "he was raised in the Old World?"

"Yes. The scary place that we filter, redefine, and distill before we let people study it. As we learn that everything we have, is just an attempt to suck the poison out of the way life used to be. To quote Steven? His soul is soaked in poison."

Looking to the floor she sighed in response, "is Miss Bachman wearing gloves when she handles him?"

Taking the chance for humor he went with it, "when medically needed? Yes. Otherwise? I would say, no."

Performing the signal for 'hearsay,' "like mother like daughter then?"

"Affirmative."

Lowing her free hand, "Paige is on assignment now."

Might be good. "What did Dennis find for her?"

"Wait with Sinclair Holden of the Honor Guard until his flight comes in."

Sounds good. "Who's the pilot?"

"Who else? My husband has been pressed into service. He will bring down Assets from House Holden in Seattle, then pick up Guard Holden, and a shipment of supplies, and fly them back to Seattle. At least he gets to see Paige while they're refueling him."

Variable. "Is she going with him?"

Shaking her head softly, "Negative. Dennis needs her on standby *if* she'll stay in the city. She's staying to lend her hands to his cause."

Pouncing on the chance to give the compliment of stating fact, "like mother, like daughter."

Rolling her eyes she appeared to surrender to the compliment, "Affirmative."

"Sam," reeling as the second set of medications started to win, "I'm fading out."

"I'll stay with you. When you're fully asleep I'll engage the Lockdown and make sure you're safe."

"Thank you Sam." Finding the strength for the words, "Maggie found me because she needed the Invincible Frank Sevilan. The man who baited the Butcher onto the open field so the Sky-Cleaver could hit him. I don't feel Invincible anymore."

Shrugging with the 'at a loss' evident, "then rest. Accept your limits. Accept the future. Then make that future as beautiful as you can make it."

I don't know what I would have done without your friendship. "Thank you Sam."

Making sure his medical monitor was secure she patted his shoulder again, "rest well my friend."

  Closing his eyes while her fingertips found his temples he let his mind let go of everything and try to relax. *I am going to get some rest. Only thing I can do.*

2.7.0 - 02:45

Central Tower - 30th Floor - Office of the High Consul

■Dennis Ochenhart

Standing before the doors to the Wolfram Throne he felt his curiosity piqued as his hopes fell through the floor. *They tore this thing apart. Precision charges from the looks of it. They had the schematics. I'm not shocked. Intelligence trumps exuberance every time as a strength to a plan.*

Moving closer to the door he felt his courage waning, *I see a boot. They didn't move the bodies yet.*

Moving to the edge of the darkened office he looked into the barely lit expanse. Spotting the small pool of light he called his question to it, "are you there Stanley?"

Coughing softly Stanley responded while clicking off his pocket light, "I am here."

Finding nothing to lean on he stood next to the blasted wreckage, "I know why *I* am here, what brings you here?"

Getting up and coming over to the doors he adjusted his glasses as he spoke with a conversational calm, "I could ask you the same thing. How did you get past the security fence?"

Noting the blood on Stanley's gloves with a grimace, "the same way you did. Bachman granted Clearance."

Nodding with a small smile as he adjusted his glasses again, "we have something in common, more soon enough I bet." Holding up a small evidence bag with memory cards in it, "I am a jackdaw fool looking for shiny things."

Thumbing toward the visible boot, "were they rigged up then? Might be a silly question, but, just being clear."

Moving out of the office he tapped his bloodstained tablet hanging from a shoulder strap, "I need to be more careful with all the gunk on everything." Sighing quickly he focused, "sight and sound. The Guild has the memory cards of the living members of the Honor Guard who made it to New Hope General. Meanwhile, The Matron has made certain the recorders of the Honor Guard who were still here are out of my reach." Moving his hands for 'dearly departed,' "but there is something she missed completely."

The man is not known for his social acumen, he's known for his results and occasional trivia tidbit and pun. Stay relaxed. "Which was, the memory cards of the invaders?"

Smiling with a distracted humor, "correct! Every one of their Captains, and the men in this office. I have their memory cards now. If these yield solid answers, I will know them soon. I have only had time to proof them to make sure they will play."

He saves hole cards. "Anyone else of note in your scavenging?"

Taking a seat on the damaged desk nearby he seemed his usual distracted self, "Kincaid Drexel. I found his body. I found his memory card."

That alone would be worth a small pile of answers. "Keep me appraised?"

"Of course. I know better than to," seeming to be pleased with himself before he spoke, "ruffle feathers."

Crow jokes. "I understand the chain of events which would happen if you said no. I wouldn't have enjoyed them either."

Speaking with a paternal aura of wisdom about him, "if we are a team, we are all winners." Becoming more somber with a sigh, "I just hope what I learn is worth winning."

Nodding in agreement, "true enough."

Swapping to a more conversational feel to his words, "so what brings you back to this place?"

Looking again at the wreckage he sighed, "I wanted to see it."

"It is something else. Ordinance yield puts it as our top tier breaching charge given the way the doors were voided. Platinum level. Then again whomever did this would know that killing a Bachman requires only the most expensive of ordinance. The price of killing a Bachman is the things legends are forged from. From the price of the weapon itself, to the prices paid to use it, and the aftermath of doing such a deed. Whoever ordered this? They are either not a student of history, or, they are such a zealot to their cause that they would be willing to pay that price."

Weapons used to kill a Bachman? Listing them off in his thoughts he mulled over the memories with a forlorn understanding. *The portable thermobaric missile, a Dauer Steel shrapnel bomb, and if I do not miss my guess, a fire extinguisher.* "I hadn't thought that far ahead."

Shrugging with an absentminded charm to the gesture, "perhaps they did not either?"

I don't want to see. "If I go through that door, I heard, there are three bodies."

"Yes. One appears to have been gifted an Adad's Rage to the side of his head –"

Quipping to dull the pain with humor, "that could not have been healthy."

Nodding with a shared pain in his humor, "I would guess that the three bullets he was given afterward, would have been excessive, but one can never be too careful. The second and third men both were gifted three center of mass bursts."

Hear the whole report. You wrote that rule for everyone else. "If she had Last Resort, that's nine bullets."

Grimacing with understanding, "she gave the two survivors William's Kiss." Touching just above his laryngeal prominence, "muzzle to here, high enough caliber to

174

the bullet that they stopped suffering quickly enough."

That confirms her one sleeve and not the other. "Rust."

"That was what I thought looking over it." Looking into the office he pointed to the dimly lit window on the far end, "I assume it was your machinations which got the Aureole back on?"

Something I can be proud of. "Yes."

Looking back to him he pulled out a Clean-Up Kit and started on himself in earnest, "good."

Mulling things over in the quiet he watched Stanley progress quickly through his cleaning. *I need something else to think about.* "Stanley, why do you love Steven?"

Smiling with a relaxed grin that took a few years off of his face Stanley channeled what sounded like the fire of the memories of youth with his declarations. "The romantic reasons aside? For the same reasons you loved George and Isaac, but came to love Asmodai with a greater light than them. They are *Bachman.* The family that defines every generation it leads. They live brighter than the rest of us, they die with a greater cacophony than any other, and each one hangs the promise of this *mattering* with such a reverence that it makes life seem *valid.* When they speak of service on Earth as it leads to the next great reveal with the lessons learned from our times as flesh? They make us *immortal.* They make our lives *mean everything.* It is up to us to find what *that* is, but that makes it all the sweeter. And by saying this?" Sighing with a sad humor he finished his words, "I defy him."

"How is that?"

Taking on an almost droll tone, "he wishes that I do not romanticize him."

Not surprised. Speaking with an unintentional flatness to his words, "it's a family trait."

Smiling with a playful defiance, "I still love him."

I remember that feeling. Hurts to see it in another. "I understand."

Sitting on the desk with a Schoolboy's Grace he kept smiling, "did you love Asmodai as I figure you did?"

I'll confess it and find out. Looking one way and then the other out of habit before speaking, "I did. Storge. It was the most natural feeling in the world. I loved his passion, his tactless grace, and his drive to see the world become better even if he didn't know what that meant some days. I loved him more than George, or Isaac, I mourn him still."

"One day I will mourn Steven." Looking to his shoes he sighed, "I know you know. Or at least," looking up at him, "I would *hope* you would know. Being you after all."

Steven is being cut down early by something not of his own making. Makes me wonder how much of what he does is because he's dying. Or what I'm still afraid he might do if his anger gets away from him. Nodding with a finality to the gesture, "I do."

Getting up to gather his things he sighed, "I am old enough that I appreciated it at first for purely physical reasons. The line blurred between Eros and recaptured Ludus.

Then, it changed. I knew Pragma. And one day? I will be without the Commander and I will have to find the strength to accept the next person to step to his position in Cloak and Dagger as my liege. Even if they are not my love."

Trying to be supportive he heard the awkward tone in his words as he spoke them, "it's not an uncommon feeling. When I stepped down it left many questioning if they could accept Steven."

Reaching over to him with his freshly cleaned hand, he checked it before patting Dennis on the arm, "I know. I lived in that bubble." Settling his gear on his person, "I will endure and move onward."

Trying to return to the moment, "for now, find out what was going on."

Nodding with a casual mood to him, "I shall. A Blue Sky morning to you Ochenhart."

"A Blue Sky morning to you as well."

Saluting crisply Stanley turned from their shared moment and walked away leaving Dennis alone with his thoughts. Sticking his hands in his pockets he turned and started the walk back toward the stairs in the opposite direction, *I will call Stanley later before I go to see Susan and see if he has any further insights. I need something, hope, sunshine,* removing his left hand from his pocket he tossed away the small clump of dryer lint, *something other than dryer lint.*

2.8.0 - 03:11

Safe Housing - Study

⁘...Susan Bachman

Staring at the computer screen, covered in colorful blocks she was moving around, she smiled as the busy work and calm music worked on her savaged mind. *Browne Blocks, the refuge of the unquiet mind. Just keep the blocks moving while waiting for news to come back. How I knew dad needed some time and space to realign himself.*

Hearing a chirp cut through the quiet she closed her eyes in fear of what she would see on the screen of her comm. Picking up the device she flipped it over and had a look at it. *Daisy knows her sister is dead.* Connecting the requested call she double checked her earpiece to make sure it was sitting right.

With a hushed voice the feminine tones ached with loss that was evident even over the comm, "are you alive?"

One can live, without being alive. "I am alive Daisy."

Without gaining a decibel she spoke again, "Bonnie knew the risks of staying near you. I will tell myself that until my dying day." Pausing for a moment, "I did not call to ask for vengeance. I did not call to ask for pity. Nor a reprieve from duty."

Noted. "Then what did you call for?"

"To let you know that I will call her sons. I will call my nephews and break the news to them. But I need to know, did she die as she lived?"

Bonnie was a Warrior first, a Cook second. "She killed two before the blow that felled her came in. Then she killed the one that felled her. He got too close to her and she found a vital spot to cut."

"Three felled by Dauer Steel?"

The small mote of victory. "Yes."

"Noted. We didn't talk much as of late. I have been so busy chasing shadows. I am not Dennis, not by a long shot. Even with the aid of The Farmer's Wife we're having trouble sifting the truths from the lies from the things that we cannot confirm."

I don't like having to say this to her. Not now. Not like this. Pushing out the urging tone, "Starlight Squad needed a leader. That region needed you. Difficulties and all."

Growling the words through grit teeth, "I am going to find Ridolfi. I found you the intel of where to find Wheel Spokes Junction. I may not be who I used to be, but as Captain I will see this through. I will find out if he's still out there or if there is truth to the idea of his son being existent."

I know where the man who dares to answer to Ridolfi can be found when the summer comes, "you *are* the Sharpest Blade. No one can erase that from you. You can cut through his deceptions."

Speaking with a deep seated humor and the undeniable fortitude of her spirit, "only if metaphorical combat would decide this. He got the better of me, Dennis, Kane, Bonnie, and Asmodai once upon a time. Doing this alone? It's daunting."

She has me there. I could try to remind her of her better plans, the way her and Captain Kane changed things. And then we get back to Ridolfi and the good will is gone. "Your sister will be missed."

"She is in good company Miss Bachman. You attract excellence because it knows it can flourish near you. She is one of many tonight. They will add her blade to the Wall of the Fallen. Meanwhile you have the much harder task. You have to keep living."

Nodding she pushed the words out, "I do."

"Turn off the Browne Blocks and get back to work, please."

If I work I can make the hurting stop by stopping the things that bring the hurt. "I will acquiesce."

Speaking with the Military Encouragement, "give it an hour, when you are moving forward again, you will feel better."

"Can I outrun this?"

Speaking with the humor of a Warrior, "if we can use metaphorical combat? Drive."

Fine. Wiping an errant tear out of the way, "I shall out drive this."

"Good." Firing up with a more forceful tone of energy, "see the Dawn Miss Bachman. Long Live the High Consul."

Sitting up she spoke the words with conviction, "greet the Dawn with Honor, Sharpest Blade."

Closing the connection she marshaled her inner self. Moving the pointer she set to saving and closing down her game. *Back to work.*

2.9.0 - 04:04

Central Tower – Door of Lechwe – 12th Floor

† Sasha Herb

Checking her watch she grimaced, *she didn't sleep. I can tell that she hasn't touched the pillow. She would sleep if she felt safe enough to do so. At least she's safer at Safe Housing than she would be anywhere else. She knows the layout of the house and land better than anyone else.*

Contemplating the door where Yorklin had said to meet him at on the twelfth floor, *that looks like a deer like creature with horns. I'm in the right spot.* Noting and reading the placard she confirmed her location, *the Door of Lechwe. Now I just have to wait for Yorklin to bring me the things I'm going to use as my passage to Safe Housing.*

I am going to get back into the Loop with her when I get there.

Thinking over the hypothetical she sighed in resignation, *I'll push like I do, and she'll collapse around me like a typhoon of silk and I'll feel terrible for having pushed again.*

When I could just ask.

Why did I have to go home instead of going to her like a lovelorn romantic? Or would it be lovesick? Rust it to scrap. Checking her comm she found her answer, *lovesick. Lorn is used when the love is unrequited.*

Our love was never unrequited.

Thinking about the possible outcomes of seeing her she wondered what she would smell, *I learned so much about smell. Still haven't learned what to do with my heart.*

Hearing the sound of the heavy door opening she looked up at Yorklin. "Good news?"

"I have all his things." Shuffling out with a large backpack on his back he set to removing it and placing the pack down against the wall next to them.

"Why was I directed to walk a very specific path to get here?"

Speaking with the voice of the Clinician, "going further is sub-optimal to maintaining mental health. To that end, I brought these things down. Also, this keeps us out of the way of the workers. We were on the fifteenth floor, The Junction Box is where a First *and* Final Stand was made, you do *not* want to see it."

The bloodstained wreckage, I didn't see any of it on the way in, and that explains why. "I, don't want to understand."

Replying flatly he shrugged, "then don't."

"How are you Yorklin?"

Dropping the gravitas, Command, and Clinician tones for his usual tones of casual conversation, "this is nothing that doing my duty, getting clear, and drowning myself in comfort food and rented affection can't help clear up. I will tell myself this, do those things, and then deal with if I lied to myself later."

Sizing up the carry case in Yorklin's hands and the backpack against the wall, "that is some backpack, and the carry case too?"

"Yes." Gesturing at the large pack, "this backpack is of no small weight."

Testing the backpack she let out a hiss of air and set it back down, "you are correct. I will pick that up when I am ready to go."

Appearing a shade confused with his tone and facial expression, "staying a moment?"

Trying to sound reassuring, "I would like to."

Lowering his gaze he shook his head, "you don't have the Epsilon Code for the finer details."

Figures. "I figured I wouldn't."

Sighing and nodding his head gently, "you love her."

Nodding once she spoke with the affirmation of the idea, "I do."

Without raising his gaze, "*don't* get sunk in the what ifs of this night."

"Same advice for you?"

"Dagger Herb, I," letting out a shuddering sigh, "I almost reached for my injection, I nearly took the dose of Last Dance. The fighting was hectic before we broke free in the final dashes and rebuffs. I nearly took a chance on still being here for the sake of that battle. I nearly forgot who I am."

I know that feeling. "I, understand."

Looking up at her with a tone and expression bordering on accusation, "you are the Atrial Dagger, are you staying for me?"

I think I am. "I am."

"Don't." Moving his hands for 'unseen kindness,' "*don't.* Let me give you something."

Asking with a hopeful lilt to her voice, "you will recover?"

Shaking his head he replied with a voice rough with a hoarse edge, "not today, maybe tomorrow. But I am going to go see to me. *I* am not your worry. *She* is. You are the Gardener of the Heart of the High Consul. On this night?" Obviously digging deep in his emotions he laid it out with a seriousness she had not heard from him before, "I can tend to me, you can tend to her, and if we are lucky? Then the beings of The Divine will sing in harmony in the coming days. The thing I *need* you to know? The Telesphorus lab results came back negative for Miss Bachman. She is still untouched."

The Telesphorus? That's where Maggie is. "She's still clean?"

"She is. *No* signs. Take those things to her, knowing that she is still there for us to serve and love. The Old Man of the Office, he has done terrible damage to her. But she has healed, time and again. Go to her knowing she is still there to help heal from this."

A night full of traitors, I need to hear something good. "Why do you adore her Yorklin?"

"I answered a call. I came to this place to see to a Princess. A woman with over a dozen hats and a staggering intellect. The kind of person who if she was one thing? She would be the Ten Thousand Hour Master of Reality and nothing else would do. The thing she would become is the Captain of our Destiny. I adore her because she makes the way our world functions visible. Her presence removes the illusions, and the truth is shown. Yuri was," rubbing his face with his left hand, "in terrible shape when he got here. She got him to listen to reason, to allow treatment, and to come back to reality. I saw the woman I knew I was serving give service to another, and it just makes sense."

I'll dare the question. "Does he love her?"

Pursing his lips he moved his hand from his face to signal for 'honest truth.' "So much. So much I fear his heart will burst from it. He shows so many levels and signs of abuse, neglect, and mistreatment that Steven *and* Patrick want him to be handled as carefully as possible."

Oh no, by the Ash. "The Infection, as The Commander calls it."

Nodding with a sad affirmation, "his stories, they would infect the minds of those who hear them. He has seen, and grown normalized, to a nightmare by our standards. He is on one hand the folk hero reborn, on the other, he is a terrible batch of truths of the dark side of humanity."

Trying to sound convinced of the truth of her words, "she'll find a way."

"I hope so. I pray so. We begged for years for an end to what we knew."

Looking back down the hallway she resisted the urge to ask about his wordplay, "is this what we get?"

"This is what we get."

Looking back to the backpack, "I am going to take these things and go."

"How will you get there?"

Reviewing her orders on her comm to make certain she had the order right, "I have a special route I have to go to make certain that I'm not followed. A special vehicle was arranged, which is why this took so rusted long. Once I can confirm a lack of visuals? The Sys-Admin is going to cut my location feeds and I'll double back to her. The mission includes two side objectives of dropping off needed good will supplies to get me clear of suspicion of trying to find her. So vehicle, Package A, Package B, drop out of sight, sneak off to her."

"Sounds like a feasible mission. A Blue Sky to you Dagger Herb."

"You as well Cloak Yorklin."

Exchanging a crisp salute with him she set to picking up the backpack and carry box. *The backpack is braced and counterweighted, that explains why it's so heavy. It's meant to be worn and not carried. I will bear his burden then.* Sliding her arms into the straps she felt the weight settle against her, *walk a kilo with another mans backpack to know his burden.*

2.7.5 - 02:37

Drenner Estate – Northern Parking

◙Chuck Drenner

Getting out of his car he spotted Micah within moments. Cocking his head with his question, "it's dark and we don't have lights out here? Much less meeting me here at the end of the parking row? What changed? I don't have -"

Interrupting his words by raising his hands and gesturing 'clarification' before his words, "I have already roused Amanda. We have a full SitRep for you to review. This is worse than I may have implied."

How does that scan? "How bad is this then? I think an armed coup is bad. The part about ETA of unknown? That's a higher level of bad. What is it?"

With a calm which left Chuck awed at the strength of Micah's will as he spoke, "she's gone completely off playbook, there's a Ghost involved, the Terrors and the Scouts are crawling all over Central Tower. *Both* Captains are physically on scene. The Sys-Admin has changed hands from Athens to Hope. House Drenner is providing the Overwatch on Susan tonight at Safe Housing. Do I need to go on or will you come inside and read the SitRep while we get some breakfast?"

Closing his eyes he set to counting to ten while trying to keep his breathing even. *One, two, three, By the Ash, four, five, I, six, seven, forget it.* Exhaling sharply, "no. No. *This* is what it is?"

Wavering in his composed state, "it is."

Fighting to keep his composure, "I'll go get my things together from the trunk. The House Office then?"

Turning and taking a single step away from him, "set up there. Yes. I'm going to go have breakfast brought in."

"Understood."

Without looking back at him, "Chuck?"

"Yes Micah?"

"Thank you."

Why is he acting like he's leaving something out? "Noted."

Watching him walk away as he retrieved his things from the trunk he found only worries on his mind, *by the Ash. If he's holding something back that's worse than all of that? I'm not sure I want to know.*

Hoisting his gear he layered his belts and straps over his shoulders, *I'm going to find out though.*

2.3.7 - 01:30

Drenner Estate – Master Bedroom

∫ Amanda Drenner
∫ Consul of House Drenner
∫ Sister of Maggie

This has been far too soothing of a wakeup call. It also feels far too early for this sort of romance without provocation. I am afraid he's going to tell me the world is gone.

Finding the clock she noted that it was adjusted in a way that she would not be able to see the time from her vantage laying on her pillow. *I feel every single one of my fifty-one years right now.* Curling and uncurling her toes she looked within for the will to speak, *I will be brave, as you taught me bravery.*

Reflecting on her modest nightgown she wished she didn't have to get up. *I will be strong, as you taught me strength.*

Looking around their shared room she smiled at the private artifacts of their shared life. *I will endure, as you showed me what enduring means.*

Reaching out and touching Micah gently she sighed before letting the words out. "You have sat there next to my bed signaling that I need to hold still. You have told me I am beautiful, to be at peace, to see if I had a smile, and with each platitude you scare me more Micah."

"I wanted to see you as I know you, just one more time, before I have to tell you," obviously fighting back tears, "that our world, had seen another Red Sky Morning."

That is not a thing you would say lightly. "Where do you start?"

Offering the words with a hopeful sadness, "Susan is alive, physically uninjured."

Closing her eyes she wrapped her arms around her chest, "Micah?"

Hearing his sniffle before the question, "yes?"

"On a scale of zero, being a day of light clouds with fresh sun tea -" losing the fight with the implications she quieted. Concentrating on trying to keep from exploding with emotion she felt his hand touch hers, and wrap around it firmly.

Whispering the words with an emotionally hoarse tone, "I cannot say."

Squeezing his hand in return she asked with more than a hint of desperation, "if you had to guess?"

Blurting the number out with a frustration, "Eleven."

Correcting him with a grit of her teeth, "the scale only goes to ten."

Trying to be soothing, "*today* it goes to eleven."

Opening her eyes she looked at the ceiling and pondered the slow motion of the ceiling fan, "the last time we had a Red Sky was Horizon."

Nodding with a factual inflection to his words, "Central Tower from the fifteenth up is in shambles from my understanding. Over a hundred already confirmed dead, between the two factions."

It's a Red Sky Morning.

Finding a concern to anchor her questions from, "is Steven alive?"

Nodding with a smile, "yes. Also physically uninjured."

Asking with a hope in her heart, "Patrick?"

With a voice which had dropped to a loud whisper, "thrashed and listed in stable but serious condition pending review."

Susan and Patrick were at the Tower for this. "If you had to summarize this event that happened that I am waking up to, what would you say?"

Fretting for a moment before responding, "armed attempted coup at Central Tower."

Finding his gaze she looked at him for any signs that she was still asleep and having a nightmare.

Frowning he moved closer, "mea culpa."

I don't want to know. "For?"

Leaning in and hugging her for a moment, "telling the truth."

I will not want this either. Reaching up and caressing his hair, "who was behind it?"

Answering with a confidence to the idea, "the current understanding of it that I have, is Thomas Kunlow."

Closing her eyes she embraced Micah with a greater force as she concentrated on breathing. *Hashem, please keep me strong and true during this trial. Hashem, do not let my eyes grow darkened by the blinders of hate. Hashem, do not let me forget who I am and the faith I place in you.*

Feeling her thoughts slow down with the prayers she reviewed the implications. *The agreement is gone. I don't know what else will be gone within the week.* Feeling her breath catch she coughed out the name, "Cassia?"

Without letting go of her he adjusted his volume to suit the short distance between them, "I do not have an answer. The Network was thrashed and burned with the passing of the Sys-Admin. The new Sys-Admin is working with the ladies in the Coding Cathedral to fix the mess. I have been sent a memo we're getting a Firmware Upgrade because of it."

Blinking with the unexpected information she latched onto the important question, "new Sys-Admin? The rest is fascinating dear, but what happened to Athens?"

"Athens is dead. My sources tell me The Pale Rider flew tonight and sent him off this mortal coil."

He helped secure the peace, now he sides with war? "Athens turned on us?"

"He helped set up the destruction of the Network. Jerome Hope evaded an assassination attempt, the Network burning, and a high speed car chase to do his duty."

He rides a bike, there must be something more there. "Hope was appointed then?"

"He took the appointment when he gained control of the Network. He used a Bachman permission key to use the Pale Rider and take the Network. I have been informed the parent key for it came from Miss Bachman."

History repeats itself with a new twist. "He jumped over the usual system, as Athens did, then?"

"Yes."

Reaching out for a variable, "where is Susan now?"

"She's still on her way to Safe Housing, the current codename for Maggie's house in the middle of the Decommissioned Zone. The men on the Watchtowers sent me a report of her Beast being sighted. She appears to be seeking to take solace there on the edge of our safety. She should be there no later than twenty after the next hour. She's taking a long route, longer than normal, to get there."

Odd that she would go to Safe Housing. "Why didn't she go to her bunker? I know it's drab, but it's safe."

"Consul level backing cast the vote. They know a Consul wants her dead. The chatter on the lines in the Cloak and Dagger forces points to a severe siege mentality building. They're moving forces in and getting ready for something big. My source on the inside says it's Operation Blue Sky Dawn."

They will try to paint the color of the sky before it can be lit. "Was her bunker compromised?"

"Unknown to me. The Jaguars haven't submitted a report yet. The information I have says she was to die in Central though."

A full scale fight for Central itself. Seems foolish. "How did they think they could best her?"

"For one? False Prophet was declared, without authorization, but still sent to their comm units."

That would take a Sys-Admin. "Athens?"

"Correct."

I don't want to ask this. "And for two?"

"They were outnumbered, the defending forces. Consul Kunlow had trained a supplementary body of soldiers for this. He had more than his share of fighters."

"That would do it." *Ask.* "Does she still trust any of us?"

"From what I know, she trusts only her Honor Guard and her Ghost."

Wait - "she has a Ghost?"

Leaning back he looked at her with a smile of surprise at the idea, "The Gingerbread Man? He was a father."

Of all the talks we had, Asmodai never mentioned that. "I did not know that."

Appearing to be lost in the mote of happiness at the concept, "no one did. From what I have been informed, not even the Gingerbread Man himself knew. This new Gingerbread Man is a fierce warrior who has come back to our lands."

Rushing the words as the idea clicked, "so Susan, wait, is alone at Safe Housing with the Gingerbread –"

"Son."

Furrowing her brow in confusion, "- she took him home?"

Moving a small shimmy away from her he sat up and gestured for 'clarification,' "he's driving her home."

I didn't hear that right, did I? "She's never let anyone else drive."

Interlacing his fingers together he seemed unsure of the idea he spoke, "she's never been hunted before. If the sniper round came in through the window of the Beast, if ordinance was arranged for that, even then she lives."

I'm glad I can hear the pain in his voice trying to vocalize that. "Issue with that is if *you* know that he's driving? So would someone else."

Puffing out a breath in relief, "Truth. So then he drove her because she was in no shape to drive, would be my second guess."

It would not be the first time this has happened, "so our High Consul has gone off Protocol?"

"Yes. It appears that with her opponent forgoing it, she's going to forgo it too."

The Bachman way of letting the opponent write the Rules of Engagement and then beating them with their own ideas. "As unprincipled as it is, it's unfortunately a tactic they have used before to great effect. Is she without Guard entirely then?"

"They're moving onto the Operation I told you of. I was able to send the security detail we use for the Drenner Explorers to her."

Those men are just about militia grade, but they're not trained to deal with assassins. "Fools to the Front?"

Speaking the words with a heavy dollop of guilt on them, "I can hope no Second Strike comes."

Reaching out she caressed his arm gently, "what did you give them for a load-out?"

Smiling with a nervousness to the gesture, "as the only family assets for such an Operation are the war surplus? I used that."

Did he? "You put them in Kane's old Mobile Base?"

Regaining some of his confidence, "it was entombed with armor, weapons, and the like. I used what I had on hand."

Those items have seen our darkest hours. "You did right. You are unsure of the decision though."

Nodding with a sheepishness to him, "I had to act in the moment."

Smiling playfully to disarm the words of accusation, "you did not wake me."

Smiling back he sighed, "I did not know how bad it was when I called Steven. Once it was revealed? I moved quickly and decisively. Then I wondered and second guessed myself."

I will not aid him in hurting himself. I will remind him of the King I married. "You learned from Asmodai. You *met* Tessa. Dearest, Light of my Heart, you *were at* The Lion's Roar. You watched it become Broken Spearhead. If you know in your heart that protecting Susan with those things would honor Tessa? I would agree. Tessa loved the Bachman family. She would have adored Susan." Tripping over the concept she felt the aching sadness in the certainty of it, "Tessa would have convinced Asmodai that Amaranth should have been a part of Susan's life. You did so much good, of your own making, that I'm joyous to see you being the man I married."

"I," hanging his head he turned to look at her with a sad smile, "just wanted to do the right thing. Thank you."

Smiling she spoke the word with all the joy she could muster for him, "noted."

Moving on he caressed her hand, "I hope Susan will trust the ones I picked, they all wear the name of Drenner upon them."

I can hope. "She loves her Drenner family."

Reacting quickly to the sound of her beeping comm Micah hopped off the bed and retrieved it from the charging base. Bringing it to her he held it out, "Susan's personal chime?"

"Yes." Taking the comm she brought it to a full wakefulness and opened the communications App. "It's from Susan, personal channel."

Pressing her finger to it she set to reading the message, "Amanda, rough night at the office. Three party crashers I won't be forgetting soon. No complaints regarding the Drenner campout on my lawn. If they get party crashers I'm leaving. When we get a chance I'd like to share the rain with you. When the fog clears and the dark clouds are gone, we will see the Blue Sky again."

She is still alive inside.

Speaking with a humored lilt Micah seemed more at ease with the moment, "I think that spelled it out quite clearly."

"I think it did too."

"Sounded like something Asmodai would write on a good day. I miss him, transgressions aside, I miss him."

Focus. "I miss him too. But you need to stop, no hindsight for you, they call it that because it makes you into an arse. We can't think about what we didn't do right, because then we'll be too busy to do the right thing for the future."

Raising a fingertip, "oh, the three party crashers she mentioned –"

Rust, "what about them? Did I miss a context clue?"

"She didn't give it fully. They would be the three bodies in her office, from what I have been informed."

Closing her eyes she set her comm to the side and took a few deep breaths, "I really do love you, but sometimes when you try to be gentle it leaves something to be desired."

Watching him wring his hands he reminded her of the young man she met after Horizon and less the man she had been married to for twenty-five years. *To think our anniversary was last December.*

Weakening in his convictions he sighed, "I just wanted to go easy on you, and me, it's a lot of ground and problems to go over."

Softening her demeanor she rose to a sitting position next to him before wrapping her arms around him. "I appreciate it, just makes it hard."

Wrapping his arms around her in return, "you'll learn more after you get up and go to the family office. I woke you after I called a friend, Chuck should be here as soon as he can be. It's a bit of a drive."

My protégé was summoned quickly. "You summoned him?"

"I *woke* him and *requested* him. Technically he did *not* have to answer. He is making good time getting here."

"I will get out of bed then, and face this."

Pointing to her comm after it let out a more ominous chime, "you beeped again."

Reaching back and picking her comm up she opened the App to find the message was from The High Consul this time. *I have not changed the Official Decree chime.*

All of us? "It's to all of the Consuls." Setting her tone she read over it, "I won't lose in Round Two. I will go down swinging. As far as I know we do not possess any Thermobaric Rockets. This fact leads me to advise you to seriously think over continued aggression. The next bullet fired will be seen as a summons to a face to face discussion of the situation. A Blue Sky to all of you."

Obviously suppressing his laughter, "now *that* sounds like Asmodai."

Trying to keep her mind from getting lost in the nostalgia, "why are you smiling?"

"I miss the days when he would be tactless and Maggie would help him rephrase. When he would speak to empty air and she would slide up next to him and say what he just said but in a way where no one was afraid of him coming to stab them with a dull knife."

I miss it too now. "I will get up and set to soothing nerves from that. I would imagine that with the False Prophet being unauthorized most of them don't know what's going on. Just that Susan has turned into Asmodai." Getting to a standing position and taking stock of the moment she looked down at the hip on which she wore her tattooed design from a different era in her life, "beloved?"

"Yes?"

I can tell I haven't had any coffee. "Smoke. It's Smoke out the Truth. She knows I had nothing to do with it, but I was on the list. She's putting us all together so we're packed in close with Thomas. We are now all uncomfortably close and able to endanger the other. She's looking for the weak link."

Taking a deep breath he smiled, "she *is* his daughter."

"Also, where is this Gingerbread Ghost from?"

Answering with a lilt of a man lost in dreams, "beyond our world and conflicts."

Sounds like a man to have over for dinner. "I bet he has some stories to tell."

"I bet he does."

Getting up she dressed quickly while sorting her thoughts. Sliding on the last of her Consul apparel she sighed at the chiming of her comm. "It's Consul Holden. I can only imagine what this is doing to her. Wait," *please tell me no,* "was Sinclair on duty tonight?"

Looking back down to the floor he coughed uncomfortably, "to my knowledge, yes. There is chatter on the line about him going home. Alive."

I should find out the rest of it. Moving to her comm she picked it up quickly and put her earpiece on, "Consul Drenner here for you Consul Holden. Morning."

With a voice that spoke of only half of a mug of morning coffee, "can you explain the Bachman logic of beautiful words on a personal channel and then fiery doom on the official channel?"

Sinclair was on duty. "It's Smoke, this is her version of it. I know I was tired, and upset, enough that it took me a moment to figure it out."

Sipping her coffee quietly she sighed and spit the words out, "does she want to know it was Thomas or does she already know?"

Sinclair saw something, he figured it out. "How's Sinclair?"

"You evaded to Cut To It."

Nodding even though it wouldn't be seen, "I did."

Projecting an air of efficiency with her timbre, "he did see it, he told me it was Thomas. To that end I have my people going over everything they can to find out if we somehow helped. You will be gaining a clutch of assets later this morning, direct on Turner Airlines. They have Pledged to be of use to you."

That is a relief and a boon, "thank you."

Softening to a friendlier tone, "noted."

Time to elaborate based upon having helped raise Susan. "She doesn't want to know it was Thomas, she wants a *reaction.* She wants to see what we do with the knowledge. Odds are she already knows it was him."

"Is there a right answer?"

The unfortunate answer. "Not that she'll say."

"Do you know one?"

"Go along with whatever plan comes next for protecting the Citizens from the fall-out from this."

"Sinclair, he wasn't left out of all the planning chatter. He's relayed to me some of what is going on. It's Hot August Night on a larger scale. Some of the people that attacked Central, they were parents. She's sent a few of her Guard on a quest to round up the children by dawn. She's going to move them to a safe place. Among other things in the Operation. It's a rescue mission on a grand scale."

She'll spend the rest of her life atoning for Guthrie if no one stops her. "Her devotion to children is admirable."

"I'm bringing Sinclair back to Seattle. He's the only one who's walked out on his own two feet. Dennis set a girl by the name of Paige Turner to sit with him. I only know that because he told me as much as he could about his situation before I called you. It's why I called."

Makes too much sense. Short notice. "The third apprentice watches him."

"Paige is? This isn't easy being this far away."

It's quite a bit harder to be this close and feel as far away as you are sometimes. "She is. Dennis told me how much he's watched her become something more with her training. Thankfully the codger comes around to keep me informed of things from his point of view."

"I'm, honestly, kind of scared."

I have nothing for the fear. "Keep music on to keep the silence at bay, keep checking for updates from Sinclair, and then updates from your people when they get here later today."

"I found them the fastest flight I could. Pilot Turner is on his way through this morning, as I mentioned, so I was able to get him to agree to bring the helpers with him."

Using her tone that affirmed the double-checking, "the ones you mentioned I could have."

Sighing with self-exasperation, "yes."

Speaking the word to affirm her, "noted."

"I tested, so you know, I was sent to Leave a Message."

Susan isn't taking our calls. "I expected as much."

"I didn't leave a message." After a moment of breath Consul Holden continued, "I have a small office where some of my helpers are down there, today's round are slated to help them, if you can direct them? Let them know. I can also send you a copy of what Sinclair learned."

Smiling she let the feeling into her voice, "first part is a good to know, the second is a good to hear."

"Amanda –"

"Yes?"

Asking with a borderline incredulity at the concept, "The Gingerbread Son?"

Exhaling she smiled with a helpless humor, "from what I understand? He is."

Sounding vexed with her reply, "the last one died trying to help our people. I wonder if Miss Bachman told him about Remembrance Day?"

"I don't know. I *do* know that the Man died saving Penelope, which led to us having this future. The *Son,* has lived through a night which could have ended that future. This one is only in further danger if Thomas has another team on standby."

"And if he does?"

The Sky-Castle was built to survive the impossible. "If the people in the Mobile Command Base in Susan's front yard can use the tools and weapons they have access to? They'll save her."

"What did you give them?"

Smiling with approval at Micah she did her best to keep her words neutral in tone, "Micah opened the Kane Vault. They're using the base from Operation Lion's Roar."

"Dire times."

"If I were Asmodai? I would be in the Command Base, riding over to force a gun point confession out of Thomas."

Through a stifled giggle, "but you're Amanda."

"Which means I play defense and wish Asmodai was here to show what living lightning looks like."

"An odd thing to miss him for."

"Things are going to get darker before the dawn in our hearts. Go and be well Alexandria. Find that connection if it exists between your House and tonight. If you can prove Thomas lied to you? You will save your House."

"I will do so."

Time to wrap this up. "A Blue Sky to you."

"A Blue Sky to you as well."

Closing the connection she sighed, "we shall get breakfast with Chuck when he gets here, odds are he didn't eat. Until then I'll go get fully caught up on what it's going to take to get my share of this done. Which will include finding a way to save Cassia, as with Steven still alive, she very well could be in need of being saved."

"Noted, and thank you."

Turning to look at him with a soft but sad smile, "do you ever regret our marriage?"

Rolling his head from one side to the other he shrugged with a smile, "no. I *do, sometimes,* regret the matching tattoos the four of us got to celebrate our friendship."

To think we spent Rations on these. "My left hip, your left shoulder, Maggie's right hip, and Asmodai's right shoulder. The four to bind, the four seasons of a year. Winter and Spring join with Summer and Fall. We made a complete year. The perils of loving so much."

With a hint of sad nostalgia in his tone, "his love was something else."

The things those two did together that weren't even sexual. "You two made a cute couple when he would dote on you. Fall leads to Winter. You were the harvest festival of his heart."

Looking up with a far off look in his eyes, "we were something else. I spent years with the man. From the moment he picked me up from the front lawn, until the day we made our separate lives. I have not found a man since who made me feel like he did. But

Winter led to Spring and the promise of renewal."

Three children born of Spring. "Spring and Summer sitting as sister seasons. The secrets we kept from the world in the wake of what was too personal to explain."

Focusing her will she found the strength to move forward. "We are not dead yet though. As we are both seasons of toil let us get up and toil."

"Truth. To the office then?"

One foot in front of the other foot. "To the office!"

THE DAWN WITNESSED
Saturday April 30th, 2242

3.0.0 - 05:14

Cloak and Dagger HQ – Routing Control Room

▸ Jerome Hope
▸ "Sys-Admin" of The Network

Hearing the distinct sound that roused his tired mind, his thoughts connected memory to the sound and produced a single conclusion. *Eve.*

Yawning with a savage energy he shifted in his chair until he was sitting up and gazing upon Eve Parsons. Taking in the sight of her familiar body suit he noted the change in the coloration of her respirator mask.

Moving without hesitation into his personal space bubble she pressed the tall travel cup into his hands. Her voice coming out of the speaker on the mask with a supportive urgency, "wake my friend. The fight is not over."

Taking the travel cup he sipped the beverage timidly, *still quite warm. Very sweet though.*

Turning his attention back to her mask, "you changed your mask."

Touching his shoulder she leaned in with a flat incredulity, "you are nearly killed, exhausted, and the first true words to me are on my coloration?"

Smiling with a reckless humor, "apparently, yes."

Taking another sip he set the travel cup into the standard sized cup holder in the desk. *Safety first.*

Getting to his feet he could hear the low rasp of Eve's breathing coming out of her speaker. *She's not in a good place right now. I know I'm not.*

Looking into the opaque lenses of her mask with a gentler humor to his inquiry, "Eve?"

Swallowing roughly she nodded once. Speaking his name as a forced calm inquiry, "Jerome?"

Assuring her with the simple truth of the moment, "we're not dead."

Choking a sob she hugged him with a violent intensity, "*this was not explained.*"

The perils of loving a Questioner, who in turn is learning how to love and be loved.

Attempting to project a measure of stoic endurance, "I am here Eve."

Stepping back for a moment she moved to his side. Moving her arm to below his scapula she established a firm hold on him. "You were almost killed."

Establishing a hold on her with his right arm he did his best to establish a grip on her in return, "I know, it was most unpleasant."

With the anger in her timbre, "those that tried, will they be going to the table?"

I see more. I will pull this taffy apart and hope I don't need her more than she needs me in this moment. "No. They're very dead. We were sent a course correct, and an Interception was performed. The chase car was Obliterated."

Calming with a certainty to her, "The Commander ordered it?"

Reaching up with his left hand he was met by her right hand and the touch of fingertips. "By his will. The Bachman Rules of Engagement."

Leaning her head against his right arm, "those who stand against them, set the rules, and from that mistake, they are dismantled."

Sliding his fingers between hers he gripped her hand with a gentle firmness, "there is no need for Honor in a fight against those who have no Honor. Philosophically it seems dirty, unfortunately it works. They have used it enough times that you would suspect that our enemies would learn."

"One would believe that could come to pass." Squeezing his hand in turn, "what shape is York's truck in?"

I would prefer if he heard it from the techs. "Don't, please don't tell him, but I suspect his truck is very dead."

Holding his hand tighter, "it was not a *chase,* then? York said it was a chase."

Pulling their mutual embrace closer he did his best to hold her still before he spoke the assumption, "he left out the multitude of bullets."

With the return of a sliver of the anger, "*why?*"

Reaching for humor he laid it on thick with a cavalier dismissal, "they did not enter the cab of the truck, why worry?"

Tilting her head up the lenses met his eyes. Imploring him without losing the sliver, "as they were fired, that would be cause to worry."

Smiling with the reassurance of standing before her, "we are uninjured in body."

Moving her left boot behind his right foot, "how did the truck survive such a beating?"

I am not getting away with an explanation, "the truck is not *just* a truck."

Nodding slowly her voice carried the revelation, "it was from Miss Bachman."

She did not belabor the difference between from her, *and having helped found it, at the time. I knew better, but she told me to stay quiet.* "Yes."

Without moving her boot, "how many Epsilon Codes am I standing on the wrong side of?"

Two that you can defeat if you knew their names. "Three."

"*Three?*"

Keep it simple. "The Origins of the Truck, why York has it, and what he does with it."

Moving her boot back to her side, "what do I have clearance for?"

Keep the thoughts in order. "Two. The one you do not is the Origins of the Truck and the code-name it bears. The details, of that. York has the truck because Captain Jefferson Drenner requested an inquiry into the idea that he could get food dropped off on the Border Patrol."

Nodding and keeping up easily, "I remember those discussions."

Keeping it to the easy answer, "Miss Bachman wished York to be safe on those trips. Thus, the truck."

Relaxing against him, "that simple?"

"Yes."

"Where is the Truck from?" Tilting her head to the side a few centimeters she whispered the assumption, "the Snafu?"

Nodding with a smile he confirmed her guess, "correct."

Hugging him for a long moment her words tumbled out as a confession, "if, I was angry you were nearly killed, mad at your Loyalty," hanging her head her tone turned to a dark lilt of self-recrimination, "what do I do knowing that she knew, she knew and did what she could to assure your safety?"

Letting go of her hand he pulled in closer to a one-sided hold, "you forgive. If you would understand, I am not Loyal to Miss Bachman, not as a woman, but as a Leader. She leads, I follow. She shows the way, I walk the path."

"Noted." Sighing with the irritation, "I was scared Jerome."

"I share the feeling."

Clutching him again, "you're, the Sys-Admin now?"

The Penguin's King. "Correct."

"What of Athens?"

Confessions for me. "He died."

"Who's hand?"

Turning his head he found himself unable to look into her lenses, "mine."

Reaching up she touched his cheek with a careful touch, "you have never taken life before."

York had no doubts in me. I did not have doubts in me. Only the ache of knowing what I would need to live though. "I am aware. I am scheduled to speak with my Counselor, the Cloak and Dagger Counselor, and a specialist on the subject of the applications of the lessons of the Silverback."

Pressing herself against him she spoke the word with a helplessness, "noted."

Her suit is distractingly unique. I cannot get swept away by the Shadow as the material is keeping my mind busy. "He had sided with the attackers. He paved the way, secured the moment, and betrayed us all."

Hooking her arms she rested her hands on his biceps, "he secured the Armistice with his actions though. Why did he attack us?"

I wish I knew. "He *agreed* with the course of action. I don't know why yet."

"When you find out, tell me?"

"I will if I can. I don't see you not having Clearance."

"Noted." Rubbing his biceps, "how did you end him?"

Answering before he could reconsider, "The Pale Rider."

Squeezing his arms with a tremble, "then the man who sought your death, the man who ordered your death, and the group that tried directly, are all dead?"

I understand, took me a moment. "The only persons who will come to your table, did not raise a hand toward myself, or York."

With a chuff of relief, "noted."

Pressing the concept, "we are alive, *they* are dead, and the people you will see, are a different *they*."

Echoing her relief, "noted."

"You care."

Firing back to accusation, "I was not meant to, but I do."

Reaching up he laid his hands on her hands, "we can see the other side of this."

"Then I will have to choose."

Change is growth. "If I loved York enough to use the Bigger Bed, I would suggest it. We will stay friends though. We have identified where we *need* the other, and how to not lose that support of the other."

Shaking her head gently, "I do not wish to be *won,* because then someone would be lost. Thank you for not hating the other."

"I am no Warrior. We do not stand on a battlefield. York is like a brother to me. We gain nothing by crossing swords in this. We seek to be good friends even in the lizard brain contest of leaving a genetic legacy."

Lowering her gaze again she giggled, "such bold words."

Truth. "I can't afford to have things go unsaid. I have to sacrifice decorum."

With a more serious tone she looked back to his face, "speaking of such. Cassandra, Athens' apprentice? I would watch her."

"I should?"

"The way she has been looking at you? I would not trust her. It seems, not *right* to me. The way she looked at Athens? I believe her to be his lover."

That says no small amount. "I will avoid my new office then."

"Her children are grown, her husband is a broken bond, and I believe Athens was her Silver Years Romance."

"Noted." *It holds water.* "We can navigate this."

Stepping back from him she took his hands, "you carry on?"

Affirming his grip on her he smiled with the practiced maxim, "one foot in front of the other foot."

Shaking with her words, "Jerome, I didn't believe, I would see a Blue Sky as a Citizen."

Pulling her back to him he held her tightly, "I know how it ends for you and yours."

Replying with a hushed awe, "you loved me regardless."

Pressing the affirmation, "I do."

Intoning the words with a concerned lilt, "York knows what I do, and he loves me regardless."

Chuckling softly he nodded with enthusiasm for the idea, "he does."

"Noted." Pressing both hands onto his back she spoke firmly, "tell me how to aid you when I go to do my work."

"Find the information from the people you will see. Understand they had a *collective* motive, many have children to get home to, and that Miss Bachman has not prepared their Death Warrants."

Asking with a forlorn hope, "she will reforge the Circle?"

I wish I knew for certain. "I don't know for certain, as I cannot see the future, I just know that I've had no small amount of conversations with the woman. The Echo, The Derecho, The High Consul, Miss Bachman, and once or twice, even Susan herself. She refrains from Democide not because she has no taste for it, but because she *must* confirm it is the *only* road worth walking."

"She would give them The Second Chance."

I see a truth, only time will tell if I am correct. "As she has burned those who betray that trust to Ash, it is known to not betray that kindness. There is something *bigger* in play, and it *must* be understood. *Before,* the executions start."

"Noted." Offering the notion a tone of gratitude, "I met Susan. I know this. I wanted to add that."

I wonder when it was? "You did?"

"The day I asked about you. When she told me to meet you and York. It served no purpose, but she thought I might *enjoy* meeting the two of you. I don't believe that many truly meet her."

The power of the Social Arts. The cultivation of self to wear armor made from other selves. "Not many do. She's very guarded."

Speaking the wordplay with a self-congratulatory humor, "Honor Guarded."

"Hah." *Not bad.*

"Advice for my Duties?"

"You can fight dirty with those you do not wish to torment in the traditional sense of Duress. Call Honor Guard Kipper, and have him," *forgive me, whatever rules from the Heavens, please, forgive me,* "take a picture of the children that the individual is connected to. Remind them whom they should be. Frame it directly, and hit them at the Soul's Core."

Standing still for a moment she stepped against him and clutched him tightly, "I wouldn't have to worry about Infracting if they capitulated from that."

She sees through me. "I know."

Whispering the words, "thank you Jerome."

Her speaker makes it easier to hear her. She's very soft spoken without it. "Noted."

Without letting go of him, "I didn't know I would *ever* be this close to a Pair Bond."

"One can only guess at the future one does not know if one will have."

Clutching him firmly, "I, have to get the switch back to where it belongs, for this."

Squeezing her firmly he felt around with his words, "your mask, you're wearing the opaque lenses."

"I've been crying. I feared for you, and York."

"Nothing beyond crying?"

Stepping back she shook her head with a fervent denial, "I have refrained from self harm."

Not that you have, but it's on the Risk List. "Good."

"I have not sentenced myself to the mental prison. I spend my spare Rations on food from The Feedbag, brought to people I know, to help keep me right side up."

Pointing out the other upside of her plan, "you get to see York too."

"Yes."

"He feeds people."

"He feeds me food for thought. I am stuffed."

"Noted."

Speaking the nostalgia of the shared knowledge, "I only know him because he was brave. He came all the way from Boise to dwell in our city."

No one went after his convoy. He rode protected by Divine Providence and overwhelming presence. The Harvest Convoy carried him. "I know."

Speaking with a meandering emotional place, "others who have approached me, they sought the blurring of lines from me. Two men, and one woman, who wanted me to adapt, who assumed I would adapt, my skill as one who causes Duress."

This might be of note. I have not heard these stories. "Adapt?"

Answering with a distracted frustration at the contemplated ideas, "they wanted me to treat them as the masochists they were, are. They, believed, that I *liked* what I do. That in the absence of understanding of who I am, that I do what I do, because I *like* it."

Asking with a conversational inquiry, "how did that strike you?"

Crossing her arms, she shifted her stance to her back foot, with a disdain for the story as she told it, "unpleasantly. Especially when one of them asked me about the details of their fantasies. Jerome," gesticulating with her words, "some people don't know how dangerous what they want is!"

Trying to hide his smile, "oh? Elaborate, but just a little?"

Continuing the gesticulations, "each of them, to be honest, had something they wanted that would take a *skilled* hand to achieve. It was *beyond* what The Guild has on file for training Physically Dominate Partners. The horror I felt, looking over the ideas, knowing that the consequence of failure could be devastating."

Following the story path with her, "did you bring that up?"

Crossing her arms again she chuffed, "I did."

Taking the informed guess, "they didn't care."

"No."

Smiling he refrained from touching her, "did you call The Guild?"

Firing through the words with the timbre of catharsis for having spoken each aspect, "I did! People, are willfully ignorant, and it disgusts me because *I* have a triple checked workspace. Protocols for Safety, Health, Cross-Contamination, Sterilization of Implements, and they're just running around willy-nilly in their minds with the belief that some magical pain fairy can just swoop in and take them someplace beyond where someone else had been with them."

Smiling in triumph, "feel better?"

"You," laying a hand on him as she came down from the moment, "did that on purpose."

Nodding with a restrained Sage Wisdom, "I did. I offered you the Shoulder, the Ear, and the Empathic Heart that Listens."

Rubbing his arm with her thumb, "even as you suffer?"

What is pain? "Eve, life is suffering and pain. If your suffering was reduced enough to return to yourself, your sense of pride in *how* you live, as a professional, even if you don't like *what* you do? Then I can skip over *my* needs, for the moment, and help with your needs."

Looking at the floor with her words, "as you love me?"

Reaching up he gently tapped her chin with his crooked forefinger, "correct."

Tipping her head up her tone carried her courage, "what are your needs?"

Exhaling the long breath toward the ceiling he tipped his chin back down to look into the opaque lenses, "nothing I can have. Well, there is one thing."

Turning her head a tilt to the side, "what?"

Confessing the need, "to touch you, where the back of your hood meets the shoulders."

Nodding she reached up in reply and released the snaps. Adjusting her headgear she nodded with a voice of soft volume and softer heart, "I know the gesture you ask."

Reaching up and around he found the seam and set his hand into place. Rubbing her neck gently he smiled as they relaxed against the other. *Human touch.*

Speaking on the subject her lilt was an attempt at the Clinical, "the power of Human Touch. I do not allow skin to skin contact in the Chamber."

Stay easy on her. "I know."

Stepping back into the shared lean, "what are the other things you want, that you cannot have?"

I will confess with the bold truth, "you, in just a sweater, we are provisioned with hot chocolate and salty pretzels. We are in a cabin to the Far North. There is snow, cold, and we're not going anywhere. Plenty of firewood, and all the time we need."

"Am I *home* to you?"

"You are the Dream of Home." *Fair is fair.* "York, he shares the idea, his dream is different but it is the same intensity. You don't pick a lover, don't pick a weekend, or a year. You're choosing between an offering of a lifetime if it is in the cards."

"Noted." Touching him gently, "I would stay if I choose. New Hope is my Home now. These lands, are my lands, I live here."

"That is heartening to hear. I can imagine that York will have it easier knowing he does not have to imagine a future where you return to the Carnap lands."

With the brave mischief in her tone, "what else does York imagine?"

No harm in this, "York imagines that without the suit, you are to his liking."

With a tremble of uncertainty, "am I?"

Don't get lost Eve. "As I have seen you without it, and the women he desires that are not you? I would infer the answer as *yes*."

"Noted." Audibly changing the subject, "speaking of home, when do you get to go home?"

"That, is a fly in the ointment. They shot a Rocket-Powered Grenade through my front window. I don't *have* a functional domicile right now."

"Does York know?"

"No."

Offering the idea with a childlike timbre, "if you need a place, I have extra room."

If I can find nowhere else, it's good to know I have a place to lay my head. "I will keep that under advisement. I will let you know when I can quit the field."

"Noted."

Offering the Silver Lining, "the tip of the ordinance was not incendiary. The house didn't burn down. It was meant to be lethal concussion, shrapnel, and the like. I know, not helping, however, it means that the things in my bedroom were mostly undamaged."

Jumping to the answer, "your treasures."

"Correct."

"Small favors."

"Yes."

"What are the stakes, of my choice?"

Not a hard answer to give. "Your happiness, one of us walking that road with you, and the other seeking another to find that happiness with. Don't forget that neither of us had thought about being happy again, seriously, until we met you and that was an option we could not ignore. Even in hearing *no,* we have still been changed by the experience of knowing you."

"Noted."

Thumbing toward the travel cup, "what is that?"

"Espresso. Strudel flavoring."

Oh wow. "I rate *Espresso*?"

"You are Gold Two now, as the Sys-Admin. I have some recommendations for what you might enjoy that isn't just caffeine and stimulants."

"Noted. I don't know if I'm staying the Sys-Admin though."

Clucking her tongue at him she ground the words with a gentle admonishment, "Impostor Syndrome is not a good look on you."

Trying to deescalate the moment, "I'm not ready to think about being the Sys-Admin, I'm just thinking about the tasks at hand. They're in a row, I knock them down, and I can make sense of it all."

Easing up on him, "noted."

I don't want to, but that clock isn't stopping. "I should get back to work."

"Jerome, don't forget that you are my friend. Friends, show concern for friends, and they aid them in their battles. I will get you the information you need. I will keep it together, to aid in your tasks."

"Thank you Eve."

"Noted."

"Your mask is very nice though. It's a soothing piece of Art."

"The Primer says that Art, is an Object, that speaks. Then let my mask," reaching up and setting to reattaching the snaps of her headgear, "speak of something more peaceful than my heart and times."

"Of your dreams?"

"Of my dreams."

Lowering her hands she held out her pinkie, "Pact the Pledge?"

Reaching out he took her pinkie in his without hesitation, "I Pact the Pledge, of Friendship, of Mutual Aid, and of being there when the Blue Sky is seen."

Laying her hand over their pinkie-lock, "I Pact the Pledge," taking a deep breath, "of Friendship, of Mutual Aid, and of," sniffling loudly, "being there when the Blue Sky is seen."

"Don't leave yet Eve."

Lowering her hands she trembled with her foot to foot shuffle, "I won't break the Pledge."

"Forgive yourself, and move forward."

"I will try Jerome."

"I need to return to work, the dawn is not yet saved."

"I will not keep you longer."

"Thank you Questioner Parsons. Go with the Insights of The Lily. Speak truth to their fears, get them to confess the missing pieces, and with that grace in your work may the answers flow without rage or application of Advanced Duress."

"Noted. Thank you."

"Noted."

Turning away from her he settled back into his chair as the clacking of her seeing herself out rang over the gentle hum of the electronics. *Fire, pain, and rebirth from Ash. As it has been, as it will be, as we will endure.*

Working his way into the bullet pointed lists of objectives he banged out another missive. *Priority Zero to Priority One, and perhaps being able to touch the Twos in another few hours provided I still exist. Stanley delegated a team into getting as many of the CPU Personnel cleared for duty as able to ensure a team of Loyalists.*

I am not alone in this fight.

The voice from the distance of the doorframe called out to him with a tired yawn around the words, "hey Jerome?"

York?

Turning his chair and looking toward York as he walked in he felt the regret of his eyes refocusing again. "What is it York?"

Waving his comm he sighed, "work is requesting me. They need me as part of the forces to feed people. I have to rally the troops. The gravity of this is setting in and I'm just glad all I have to do is go cook some food." Holding the bridge of his nose for a moment he groaned with his readily apparent fatigue, "I'm going to have to leave you here. I don't get a choice, just informing you."

He looks like I feel, "you are well enough to serve?"

Laughing it off with an irritation, "I can only hope. They're sending a car to get me as my truck is being towed. They're trying to keep the breakfast shift together but they need their leader."

"You go then. Go raise your spatula and serve The Rim in the way you serve it best."

"Will you be fine getting home? Not that I can help with that, the car they're sending should be here in around," checking his watch, "a minute. Hah."

I don't know where Home is right now. "I'll find a way home."

Setting a can of Hatred down next to him, "for when the coffee Miss Parsons brought you wears off. But *not* another can after."

"Thank you York."

Smiling with his words, "she scares me J-Man."

Smiling in reply, "she scares me too, for a different reason in addition to the reason we share."

Losing his smile as he moved toward the door, "neither of us knows her, not really. Seems like a rusted time to start something though."

A gift for you my friend. "It's always a rusted time though. We never see Miss Parsons when it's a Blue Sky day. We need to find an actual one to see her. If you find one? Let me know."

"I'll be on the lookout." Taking a deep breath, "it will have to be good enough, I'm out. See you when I see you. I have to go out to the front parking lot."

"Until then."

Turning back to the screens he continued his work on coordinating the repair efforts. *Sick and twisted plan. Scorched earth on The Network to prevent retaliation in the aftermath of the battle. Key subsystems and hardware locked down with only certain paths and protocols functioning which Athens would be in control of. The kind of thing I would think of if I was a genius of a different color and caliber.*

Losing himself in the work he was jolted to attention by the sound of a boot squeak on the tile behind him.

Gripping himself firmly he set to soothing his ragged breathing and frayed nerves.

Rust. Rust. This is new.

Moving closer to him the figure extended a hand into his line of sight. The masculine tenor reached his mind, "Sys-Admin Hope?"

Steven. Commander Bachman?

Tilting his gaze up he confirmed the presence to be The Commander.

Huffing out the words, "Commander Bachman."

Touching his shoulder with a gloved hand he spoke with a firm resolve, "mea culpa Sys-Admin."

Trying to form an explanation, "this? Is, *new*."

Speaking from a tone of experience, "you were nearly killed tonight. I'm not shocked."

Trying to continue to be cavalier, "it was terrible."

Nodding without giving a hint of humor to his gestures, "it is. Are you fit?"

Taking a deep breath he told the truth, "I, don't know right now."

Expressing the left-side half smile he pitched the idea, "can you fake it?"

Reaching up and touching the gloved hand he nodded, "I can. I have been, I think."

Rolling his hand over he gave his hand a squeeze, "I need a Council Meeting, before lunch. The tech, as you know, is not responding."

Nodding rapidly he stopped when he his head felt off-kilter, "I can run some logistics, get it put together. Do you need to be able to enact anything that they would need to vote on?"

Slowly pulling his hand away, "no. I will be *addressing* them."

Smiling his own reassurance, "that will make it much easier."

"Good."

"The men, who shot at me and York," *I should hear his words to stop guessing,* "why did you terminate them?"

Nodding once he appeared visibly contemplative, "this night, will be known as a night of War. Internal, most likely labeled as Civil, War. During a War of that nature, the Citizen is not the Citizen. They are an enemy combatant. There is *no* taboo against killing an *enemy*. I killed them because they were as I am, in the middle of a War."

I will be braver. "The attackers at Central?"

"Prisoners of that War. Take that as you will."

"Noted."

Raising his hands to praise him, "you did amazing tonight Jerome. From evading what was done to your home, to proving yourself a Hero, to getting here. My sister, she was *so very right* about you. I won't say I had *doubts*, about you. I did however not see the same level of potential and glory to your spirit. I've seen it now."

"Athens?"

"You did no wrong. He was in the middle of the War. You did not kill a Citizen, you vanquished an enemy. You get me the Council Meeting, and I assure you," smiling with a predatorial fervor to the gesture, "this War will be over soon enough. And then, we can return to being Citizens."

The Dark Pact is Pledged. "I can do this."

"Good. Also, you're not going to tell Susan about this." Raising his hands up he presented his palms away from his holstered weapons, "I'm doing my job, let her do her job, and it will all be sorted out in the end."

He offers me peace if I obey him. "Noted."

Moving his hands to a neutral place of thumbs hanging in his jacket pockets, "thank you Sys-Admin."

That was carefully presented. "Understood."

With a voice of cheerful play, "a Blue Sky to you Sys-Admin."

"A Blue Sky Commander."

May the ghost of the ARPANET shelter me in my time of need. For right now I need a shower having seen that smile.

3.1.0 - 06:01

Safe Housing – Kitchen

⁙..Susan Bachman

Nursing another glass of water she took a deep breath of the scented air. *The aroma-therapy diffuser is bringing me relief. Loaded it with dad's favorite. White Fir, Cypress, and Wintergreen.* Laying her hand on the table she flexed her fingertips, *father was a master of self-care and survival. I have every lesson he wrote down to choose from.*

The most important is knowing when The Hammer of The State is needed, and today is not that day.

Opening her comm she found the next message that was pending, *an audio message from York.* Checking the time index she noted that there was no urgency tag on the message.

Pressing Play she waited a moment.

"Hi, Miss B."

Smiling at the diminutive she noted the tired slur in his voice.

"You told me, I would learn to drive. I did not know how well I would drive until now." Sighing with a puff of irritation he continued, "I saw the light was out. Then the light was on. I guess, what I want to say is? I know I don't have Clearance to ask what in the Blue Sky happened tonight. Or what you might have known about what I would need to be able to do to protect J-Man."

Hearing the suppressed emotion York's voice continued, "I got my truck dented. It's being towed. But I'm uninjured, J-Man is uninjured. I don't know what a Pale Rider is, *exactly*, but it sounds effective. The few people in the building are avoiding talking like it's plague. They don't know the Epsilon Code to ask which Epsilon Code is going on out there."

Speaking his answers to the unspoken questions he rolled through his words, "Eve's here. She brought me some Energy Punch. Her hugs are something else. I feel, *human,* for a minute. Yes, yes, I'm scheduled. Shallots said he would even check for whatever Epsilon Codes he would need to discuss what happened."

Laughing with a tired humor she could hear his smile, "I'm leaving the longest audio message because if I call I know I would be putting you on the spot. Not even going to belabor it. If you find a statement you could prepare for me? I would accept that gladly. No rush. I know you have the rest of our world to worry about. I came, I saw, I drove, I did not die. However if you can find a tidbit of thought for me? I'd appreciate it."

After a long moment of pause and a breath his words tumbled out with a tone of apology to them, "even if you don't? That's not a problem."

Snapping his fingers she could hear him working to gain mental traction, "I finished the latest anointment. When, where, whatever, just let me know."

Sighing dejectedly she knew the line as he spoke it, "to think I got good at chemistry to impress a girl. Sitting next to her, the smell of pine and flannel. Rust, time sure flies when you're not looking at it. She's got a husband and kids now. I'm just someone that she used to know, and this will be locked up behind a Code strong enough that she'll never hear of it."

Mea culpa York.

"*However,* I'm still alive. I have work to get to. They're sending a car for me. I will cook, fry, and sauté until all are fed. And perhaps, if I am lucky, someone will explain to me what sort of future I could have with Eve."

Shifting to a tone of wonder, "she touched her hand to where her mouth would be on that respirator mask of hers, then she touched my cheek."

Finishing with a punch-line of bewildered humor, "I think it means something."

She cares. What was once thought impossible.

Closing his words with a tone of more serious intent, "I have more to say, and no words to express the ideas. Good luck Miss B. Sto lat. Sto lat."

Seeing the audio stop she picked up her handkerchief and set to clearing her eyes. *One hundred years. If I'm lucky I'll get half that. If I'm granted a Miracle? I'll see them all.*

Lowering her handkerchief, *Jerome is alone.* Picking up her comm she fired off a communication to Stanley to take good care of Jerome. *Done. And if he cannot, he will find another.*

Reflecting on the veteran of the Intelligence Service, *Stanley. The dad so many of the boys in Command Squad would never have suspected they would get next to them. The cheer you on kind of figure who takes care of his boys with some of the best intel I've ever seen. It's no wonder Steven keeps him near.*

Picking up the last bite of her Meal Supplement Bar she forced it into her mouth and set to chewing it. *I hope Eve lives long enough to give them a concrete answer. The warm non-contest of two men each lost in emotional wilderness who bumped into a woman lost in the same dark forest.*

Calling up the photo of the three of them she smirked at the backdrop, *The Private Notions. Pixies, Nixies, and Brownies night. I wish I could have gone, but that would have been untenable to secure.*

They love each other. It's not unusual for outsiders to love women from the Carnap lands. A certain sort of quality to a woman behind a mask.

Grandfather loved Tessa. The quiet storm of their endless rage. Grandmother's sadly cold confession of knowing Tessa would die on the battlefield. He was just giving ministrations to a

Lost Cause.

Not that Grandmother didn't care about Tessa. She wrote that down. She couldn't imagine losing a sister like that. To have the hole in her heart. Not standing between them was the humanitarian thing to do.

Reviewing what she could remember of the journals and diaries of their affair, *it could work out. They could have peace. They could be just fine.*

Provided Miss Parsons chooses life.

Clenching her hand she fought with the self-recrimination, *I have done all I can. It's not my call anymore.*

Breathing the scents in the air in with a series of deep breaths she searched herself for calm. *To be calm, one must first be calm.*

Smiling with an exasperation with the phrase she found relief with the memories of her father's version of wisdom. *You were a man who insisted you were not the one with the best answers, just a decent question.*

Turning her attention to her own affair of the heart, *do I get to balance Yuri and Sasha? I still need to talk to Sasha about the last piece of the unspoken agreement between us.* Looking at the next round of reports she swallowed the bite she was still chewing roughly, *no more thoughts of me. I'm ringing again.*

Looking down at her chirping comm Susan debated what she'd say as a greeting. *I got it.* Taking a fast gulp of water she connected the comm call from Wallman, "how are the preparations for dawn?"

After a pause, in which she couldn't hear anything from behind him, he spoke with the same voice he used to tell The Rim that Asmodai was dead. "The dawn is only minutes away, I just needed to speak with you Miss Bachman. After this moment, I go to address the people again."

This does not bode well. "Speak to me then."

"I have been granted a full pardon, for this entire day. I just needed to know what you would prefer I leave for another day, another report."

Unfortunately I have such a request. "Guard Kipper has been securing the children of the attackers with his task force. The direct allegiance points to Consul Kunlow with a certainty that makes it almost impossible to refute that he would be the mastermind. I don't need that out there."

"I would agree."

"The Guild has been playing their side of the this almost uncharacteristically loud. They want people looking in one direction, so they don't see him and his forces. I appreciate it dearly."

Keeping his tone professional, "I am going to *attempt* to caution the people to be calm. I spoke with some of the survivors, they tell a piecemeal tail of conversion. Each group, each clutch of them were brought into the idea in a different smaller circle. These cells were played to, talked with, and this was no small time in the making. They understand a single idea, the Bachman Family *lied*. They were told by the High Consul that peace was worth it, that peace could work, and they feel lied to."

Speaking with the sad agreement to the idea, "reduction of suffering is still suffering."

Replying with an insistence to the words, "I will caution those who have no understanding of this moment to stay their hands."

Closing her eyes she sighed, "thank you Wallman."

Asking the question with the cadence cues of an interview question, "do you believe that peace, lasting peace, is a lie?"

Opening her eyes she looked to a piece of artwork hanging on the wall on the far side of the kitchen. *The Last Spoonful.* "Humanity has never found it. I have read of our time underground, we suffered there in our Nowhere. We were not in conflict with each other, but ourselves in a way where our people were their own enemies. We climbed out and have suffered with each generation. Suffering is the natural state of humanity if the past is to believed. The Ash and The Rust tells us that we will *never* escape the pain. The Mission Statement, One Nation, is built on the idea that we will be forced to make every other Nation kneel at our feet, as they will not listen to our words. Only by subjugating them, can we have a chance to lower the shared duress of being alive once they are remade."

Countering her using something she knew her father had said, "the only way to be as One Humanity is to agree to live next to each other."

Echoing her father in return, "we have to exhaust diplomacy, before we extinguish their lives. No matter how tempting it is to kill everyone who gets in the way of the idea of peace."

Keeping to his interview tone and cadence, "that was not an answer Miss Bachman. Although it was good to hear where you stand in that regard."

Sighing in frustration she drummed her fingertips on the table for a moment before words shook out, "I don't know. I do not know if peace is a lie. I don't know if what we think *peace* is, is what peace might be. My father wanted to reduce the suffering when he forged that surrender. He felt that the reduction of suffering and the cessation of that conflict was the preferred outcome."

"Then Consul Kunlow wishes to take us to War."

Speaking the clarification as she understood it, "not exactly. He wishes to gain access to a super weapon which will shatter cities. He will convert the people at sword point. Kneel, or perish. Look upon your world, you may keep your lives if you surrender what you think you are. He does not wish *War,* he wishes *Conquest.*"

Losing his verbal stance of the Interviewer he sighed and spoke with a resigned sadness, "from there we get into the morality of superiority and the weapons of authority."

Joining him in the sadness, "yes."

Sitting in silence for a moment he returned to volume as the Newscaster, "I will caution the people to stay calm."

I need to be honest with myself, and him. "If the future holds the idea that we have to use the weapons we have, and the weapons we can create, then I would be a hypocrite in slaying those who failed to end me. If the people can hold their temper, then we can see the future together. For good, or for ill, or just for rusted truth."

"And Consul Kunlow?"

Replying flatly she spoke the sentence, "he will die."

Coughing once he kept his voice objective, "how would you want them to see it? What is the nuance of the difference between the Mastermind and the Minion?"

Mulling the concept over she bit down mentally on the sour core of the truth she wanted to see. *This is not about me. It cannot be about me.* "Not because he wanted me dead, not because he tried to kill me, but because of those that were killed, on both sides, because of his plan. He killed Citizens with this. He needs to be held accountable for this. He cannot exist in this world, as he is a danger to it."

Making a noise of affirmation and agreement Wallman replied with a well cadenced intonation, "The Citizen loves the Nation –"

The Pledge of Creed, "the Nation must love the Citizen –"

"The Citizen must act with Honor –"

"The Nation must honor the Citizen." Sighing she steeled herself for words she would not be able to take back, "they acted without Honor, led astray in their actions by a member of The State. They were told the future without me, without our attempt at peace, would be the better one. I humbly request the chance to show them the plans for peace. To accept just a few more deaths, a few more attacks, a few more losses before we address the complex nature of society and politics with other nations. To see if we *must* address them with a firestorm of death instead of words and compromise."

"I will do my best to honor that idea in my words. We will see just how ready our Nation is for War with this being laid out on the table. What if the people *are* ready for War?"

Speaking with a pragmatic acceptance of the backup plan, "then they can Enlist. They can help with the feasibility reports. They can help oil the cogs of the war machine and be ready to serve the very storm of death they wish to invoke. If the Citizen provides the forces we would need? I would see it led."

Retorting with a disdain for the idea with his counter-affirmation, "I believe that would stagger many away from the idea though."

Smiling she nodded once, "I would hope so. There is only one way to find out though."

"Beyond this moment, what are your plans? Where do we go from here?"

Looking down at her kitchen table her eyes wandered over the engravings she knew so well. Reaching out she touched the well worn groove of Lana Llama's neck with the memories of childhood floating around the deed. *I have to just come out and say it.* "I don't know, I don't have a plan from here."

Replying after a moment with the hesitant hope in his voice, "do we get an Ad Lib then?"

A world which confronts doubt by asking a Bachman for one more miracle, out of thin air if needed. And in this moment I have none left. "I don't know. I don't know what that would even look like. The question is abstract enough right now that," speaking the confession, "I'm blank."

Pressing her with his tone, "you don't end up *blank* Miss Bachman."

Losing the fight against the empty inside of her, "I do today. I don't have a plan on how to help us get from *now* to *later*. I have to just let my plans run and see what happens. I don't even have an idea of how I am going to see Consul Kunlow put down. Hopefully someone else will come up with something. I have the best team of people a High Consul could ask for."

Calming his tone he spoke softly, "I will go address the people. I will be careful with their hearts and minds and ask them to Inquire Within. The Surprise Inspection of the Inventory of the Heart. Keep me posted if you find a plan to get Consul Kunlow."

"I will. I don't have something in the Bachman Codex or the High Consul Primer for a moment like this. Not that I know of." Feeling her lapel brooch vibrate, "I have a car pulling up I need to go answer the door for."

"Be well Miss Bachman. The sky is still Blue."

Intoning the words with a quiet agreement, "the sky is still Blue."

Closing the connection she shuffled out of the kitchen, through the dining room, and over to the front door. Leaning against the wall she sighed, *I'm just going to lean on this wall until she comes to the door. Then I'll open it and face the next part of this with the empty space between my ears.*

Closing her eyes she tried to find a measure of peace in the darkness behind her eyelids until her comm chimed letting her know Sasha was at the door.

I hear chimes, back to work.

Opening the front door Susan smiled at the lone Dagger standing there with Yuri's backpack and a carry box. "Dagger Herb. Permission to speak with volume."

Speaking with a voice on the verge of tears. "can I be Sasha right now?"

"Request granted." Holding a hand out she snagged Sasha and quickly brought her into the house. Helping her out of the backpack, setting the carry box down, and getting the helmet off of her she assessed the tired face of her Aardvark.

Touching the shaved sides of her head around the temples with both hands she ran her fingertips through the short shag of hair on top for a moment. *The hair of a Dagger. Kept shorter than any civilian woman, with the sides shaved, to mark at a distance the style of one who is Pledged first and foremost to The State.*

Speaking her words slowly with closed eyes Sasha leaned against her, "did you sleep?"

Replying with a simple stroke of words she kept her tone light, "I have not."

Settling in against her with a sad look on her face behind the smile, "did the Overwatch keep you up?"

Reassurances must be given, "they have been quiet."

Raising her hands Sasha found her pose of the possessive left hand on her hip and right hand on her shoulder blade, "Captain Turner, *rust,* I believe most everyone is worried about you."

She knows I like this pose. Letting the levity fuel her words she smiled with a single small nod, "I'm worried about me too."

Burying her face into Susan's shoulder she laughed weakly, "I love you." Opening her eyes she looked down at Susan with a sudden loss of her smile. Watching the frown of anger form she was ready as she gently moved Susan away from her as her finger pointed to a stains on her shirt and arm, "who's blood is that?"

The downside of post conflict anxiety. I didn't clean myself up very well. "The men who reached my office -"

Narrowing her eyes, "that's not in *any* statement I've heard. I called you! You didn't tell me! Don't, don't, don't you use *you didn't ask.*"

Trying to brush off the weight of the memory, "it wasn't important. They failed to injure me. What was done -"

"*Wasn't important?*" Taking a breath and audibly counting to three before continuing, "who was Gatekeeper?"

Trying to keep the smile off of her face, "the doors. I gave my Guard the Dominion over the field on the caveat that they did not come to protect me. I couldn't waste any of them standing next to the doors or just inside." *And there's that look. The I 'went over the line of risk acceptable' look.*

"Susan, you *can't -*"

Gesturing the words 'simple truth' she spoke with her own resignation to the moment, "I did though."

Turning away and slumping against the wall next to her she turned her eyes downward, "so he's the Gingerbread Son?"

Oh dear. "Yes. Yuri is upstairs sleeping."

Asking her question with an emotional mixture that was incomprehensible to interpret, "is he the one I've been wondering about?"

Taking a breath she steadied her tone to try to keep it neutral, "which wonder is that?"

Looking to her with a tired grin, "I have been at your side for a *decade* Susan. I have seen *countless* men get within distance of you, tilt their heads up, and watch you wreck perceptions of reality as the Derecho. It's not just your height, or your name, or how you carry yourself, it's the fact that you blend those together into a *force* that leaves them unable to get close."

I can't say I didn't notice my suitors I kept at bay. Offering with a gesture to her hair, "I do wear the hair tie that declines automatically."

Sighing she shook her head with a laugh, "you don't wear it every single day though. You have left it off on some days because you were wearing a different one. And on those days did *any* of them step toward you? No." Laughing softly she sighed, "and now this Yuri is driving you home in your car."

Holding her hands up in the 'comparison' gesture, "I shouldn't downplay our feelings, but I was in no shape to drive."

Urging her for an answer, "he is the one? The one who can stand near you without being blown over?"

Trying to keep herself level in emotion and tone, "I nursed him back to health Sasha, we have a bond. We don't know if it's romance, or just the bonding chemicals talking. I do know I love him."

Regaining her fire she appeared ready for the truth with her question, "why didn't you tell me about him?"

Rubbing her nose with a crooked forefinger she sighed, "you were away for most of it."

Nodding once with a slow and deliberate motion to the gesture, "now that I'm back?"

"We renegotiate. We get to look at our lives for what we can have now." Rushing to clarify, "as there are only two people who can make that call left. Yourself, and myself."

Looking back at the floor, "I feel selfish discussing this."

Life goes on around you, things spin around and around, and you do not get to control what order things appear in. Make the best of life. Sighing on the inside she pursed her lips, *father's words of wisdom.* "I feel selfish for most of the thoughts I've had since I left Central. I feel the pain too."

"Even now you're using your sympathy and empathy to forgive me for what I feel. I see that way your smile composes when the world is so simple to you and you wonder why people can't see the simple answer for what it is."

"You are my Aardvark. You pulled me from the wreckage."

"You have a talent for finding the worst possible way to nearly die." Holding a hand over her mouth she sighed, "not my best idea of something to say ever."

Wow. Laughing she felt the tension release in her shoulders. Moving in close she hugged Sasha with another laugh, "you are my Aardvark."

"Even though we never, *you know.*"

She's blushing, "you never seemed to want to." Rubbing noses with her, "I didn't worry about it. You never tossed a signal that it was on your mind. You never looked at me with a hushed whisper of come hither and drink from," pausing she sighed with a quiet laugh, "I can't think of a metaphor I like right now."

"You didn't suspect something?"

Time to commit to a notion. "I suspected you did not feel the Lover's Ache."

Looking in her eyes with a light of hope that left her taken aback, "you're familiar?"

I was correct. "I have an ancestor who had the same biological outlook on things."

Retorting back with an apparent confusion, "wait, *how -*"

Waiving a hand in the 'dismissal' gesture, "it's a story not fit for this moment. It's happy for the most part, just not *right now.*"

"Understood."

Moving back in she wrapped her arms around her, "I never pressed because I never wanted to change the tone because it rang just fine in my heart. Even though I know the truth now, it changes nothing but my understanding."

Feeling Sasha's armor gloved hand start petting her hair she smiled as her words came as a happy whisper to her ears, "thank you Susan."

"Noted."

"Why is it you never said no to me?"

Simple answer. "Love. Sitting there in the finger cuff? I saw your love for me and I was at a loss for what it meant. I stayed and found out how wonderful it was."

"Why did you never toss a signal to me?"

Smirking playfully, "you didn't throw it first."

"So suspecting I was unable to feel it like others, you never threw the signal because you knew it wouldn't be good for me."

For so many reasons. "Correct."

"The C&D counselor was thankful you never threw an inquiry at me like that. I told her that I would have tried."

Losing the smirk as the frown formed, "even knowing -"

Smiling at her with a helpless sadness to the gesture, "even knowing. A Lover's Paradox."

Holding her with a firmer embrace, "you don't have to leave me even if I take him."

Looking at her with a confused look, "if?"

Finding a smile for her, "we've been dealing with emotions of a far stranger vintage than most end up dealing with. We don't know if we're lovers or by-products of our situation. It's a little early for wedding bells. But it's far past the point of knowing it's serious."

Nodding twice in reply, "I want to stay, either way."

Offering the words with the honest confidence she felt, "I'll make sure I have the biggest bed I can get."

Stumbling over the words with a shy gait to the wordplay, "you would have me, in your bed, with the two of you?"

"Why not?"

Losing the last of her melancholy as the smile lit up her face, "sometimes I forget whom I'm dealing with. Then you remind me."

Discovering, as she spoke them, it was her turn to stumble as she spoke the words, "to be clear, I wouldn't engage in, *painting*, right next to you. It strikes me as, rude, given the circumstances."

Looking her in the eyes with a wondered smile, "I really do forget whom I'm dealing with."

"The man upstairs came to us looking for nothing more than a plot of land, and a house to put on it. He was in terrible shape, I'll spare the details –"

"Appreciated."

"He had been staying in Central while he recovered and we tried to find a way around Protocol to get him what he's owed. He came to my aid when I was attacked. He fought for us because he was fighting for me. And even now, before he went to rest, he showed concern for the bond I share with you."

Replying with more than a hint of surprise, "he knows of me?"

"I told him. He asked me if with my power, if I had a concubine, or a harem, or a stable of lovers."

Laughing in reply she gestured for 'uninformed,' "he doesn't know you."

"He needed to get to know me, yes." Moving her hands for 'back on track,' "he spoke of the pressure of power, the release of passion, and wondered if I was one to walk that route. So I told him about my precious friend that," licking her lips gently for a moment, "takes good care of my heart. Who tends to the troubled weeds that like to pop up in the garden of my soul."

"I, Susan, why did you never take a lover?"

I had a box of toys and good intentions. "That's a question you've never asked before."

Raising a challenging brow to her, "I'm asking now."

"Father sold me on the idea that when I would find a man, I would marry him, bear children with him, raise those children with him, and that on the other side of my bed should be an ally for life."

Looking at her with the hushed conspiracy of the moment, "that's not what we're taught though. You cannot overstate the need for care and caution in those affairs or you could give rise to purity testing or shame." Touching her gently, "were you ashamed?"

Shaking her head she smiled, "I can explain." *Time to tell a family secret.* "It's what my father was taught, by observation. George, Isaac? They had our traditional values about things. The idea that everything that we teach is permissible, as long as it does no harm in the context of the union, *can* be fine. The downside of them holding to it, as father saw it, was that a Bachman means *too much* in the minds of people. As we are not equals, as we've discussed, a Bachman cannot be as, I don't want to say *cavalier*,-" pausing a for a moment she sighed.

Recovering her train of thought she put the effort in, "he taught me that as a Bachman I can't let it be a biologically motivated moment of hedonism, emotionally trivial, if I bed someone. That once paintbrush meets canvas? That *has* to be for a greater reason than just, *painting.* My father, only knew the canvas of four women in his whole life. Isaac? That was a single month for him."

Nodding with the understanding, "then the man that you would let touch you, would need to be someone you had known and evaluated as the man you would want to have children with. Then no man would face the Denial of the Reproductive Query."

Answering with an exasperation, "I know, I *know*, there are men who have commented that getting to touch my canvas would be fine if it was just a night. That they would tell the glorious story. But, I don't have that emotional connection with it. So I am of no use to their hearts because I don't have the glory of the one night of passion in my heart. I am no Courtesan. If I refrain, then I do not have to face him being over-invested when I am under-invested. I have never had to tell a man that he was unfit to perform his biologic function with me. I wore the hair-tie I did so no man would feel singled out. The hair-tie was true, I had nothing to offer and there was nothing to see."

"I, do understand, so much more now. I have a question though –"

Encouraging her she spoke to the empty moment, "- ask."

"Is he the Fairy-tale Prince you've been waiting for? From what you have learned of him?"

The man who checks enough boxes on the checklist that it would be foolish to reject him out of hand. "He is a beaten up teddy bear of a man with a friendly grin, precision aim, and a warm heart. That is what I truly know of him. Fairy-tale Prince? Perhaps. Do, do I wrestle with the idea of loving him for a lifetime? Yes."

Smiling and with a tone of a Dreaming Schoolgirl she seemed happy at the idea, "he does sound like the sort of man who would be near you."

Nodding once she pursed her lips for a moment, "I'm not sure the Council will allow me to marry him for the time being to get him immigrated. I have to think of something else."

Glowering for a moment she frowned, "the same Council I've heard mutterings that we're going to war with?"

Raising a finger she vocalized a strained noise before her words, "it's a *specific* one, and I would like to *avoid* war. I sent them what I sent them as Smoke."

Nuzzling her fingertip she lost the glower, "I'm not going to go down that avenue of conversation, though I do appreciate the knowledge you give me."

Smiling she nodded again, "thank you."

Returning the smile, "noted." Failing to snap her fingers because of her gloves she sighed before speaking, "then, going to get someone else to marry him?"

Only if he knew someone else. "I'd need someone who would *want* to love him. The marriage can't be a sham. The regulations on the situation won't allow it. Otherwise I would just order Winifred to marry him."

"Noted. To get him married in, you would have to find someone you could trust with loving him?"

"Yes."

Nodding with an air of mocked up wisdom about her, "you do know that if it was Winifred, with her nature and demeanor on things? She might like him *too* much. You would be safer having *me* marry him if we could do a sham marriage. And again, avoiding an avenue of conversation."

Why obey a system that fails me when I need it most?

Because when it doesn't fail me it's actually not that bad of a system. "It would be safer. Then I would have the two of you around all the time."

Nodding once she raised her wrist to check her watch, "give me something I can take back to the Scouts?"

I have just the thing to say, "tell them to get a nap. Time tables are coming closer and I need them rested."

Lowering her wrist back to her side, "live ammo?"

"Quite possibly." Rushing the words with a helpless clarification to the notion, "I *can't* rule out anything remotely plausible until I have more control of the moment."

"When we get through this, can we talk about our nonexistent sex life?"

"We can."

"If we were to lay with each other, and you weren't *feeling the ache* for him, but I –"

I need to stop her before she says something she feels silly for later. "I'd try twice. Three times to be sure."

Raising an eyebrow she glowered with a faint humor, "so you would do it for me, even though you didn't want me to do it for you?"

"Essentially."

Putting her hands to her hips, "how does that scan?"

"I'm a Bachman, we do what we want." Feeling emboldened she smiled, "if I put you between my legs without the ache in your loins driving your ardor? You would be diminished for my benefit. I still feel the ache for people, I just don't act on it. As I have a heart and mind that is ready to experiment and give it a spin. I wouldn't suffer the way you would."

Rolling her eyes with an exasperated exhale, "can you not see the flaws in your Bachman Logic?"

"I can." Touching her on the nose she smiled when Sasha smiled back at her, "I choose to ignore them out of self love for my own logic."

Smiling shyly, "if, if, I felt the ache enough to give it a try, on you, would you let me?"

What's this? Was I seeing what I thought I saw in her body language then? No. I'll sit her down and get to the bottom of this, stopping her thoughts she smiled at her own lackluster joke. "Of course." Dropping the smile she put on an air of seriousness, "I'd want a Watchword though. You speak it and we stop, right there, I am *not* going to hurt you on accident. Either setup actually."

Nodding in earnest, "I can agree with that."

I need to get her to leave. I know she needs to go. "Sasha?"

Looking to her with an expectation in her eyes, "yes?"

I can't do this, not in the mudroom, not with so much to worry about. "You should get back to the Scouts to warn them to get a nap."

Moving onto her she almost tackled her with the force of the hug, "I will."

Meeting her Newton for Newton she moved them toward the door without letting go. Speaking with a strength on par with their embrace, "I am not going quietly into that good night."

"Good." Nuzzling her neck she kissed Susan gently, "as tonight is gone and the coming night is too good to miss?"

Connecting deed to the Holiday she smiled, "yes."

The declaration is made.

Relaxing her hold Sasha smiled as she moved to open the door, "thank you."

Letting go of her Susan watched her open the door, "be well Sasha. A Blue Sky morning to you."

Stepping outside she looked toward the horizon and the dawn, "I don't see clouds. The sky will be blue this morning."

"Let us hope so."

Speaking up as she moved away from the door, "let all be protected –"

Joining her in the intonation, "let all be sheltered."

Smiling with a reverence for the words, "let all be fed."

Intoning the words from well rehearsed memory, "and let all of us live together as Citizens under the Blue Sky."

Nodding at the end of their shared intonation, "thank you Susan."

"Noted."

Watching her turn and head for the armored scout vehicle she said a quiet prayer to her God. *Watch over her you vengeful bastard. You sent her to me, you gave me a miracle, it would be counterproductive to rust it up now.*

Closing the door she turned and leaned against the wall. Looking to the wall across from her at *Bringing Home The Sheep*, she sighed, *my mother and her taste in art.* Finding her center she smiled, *I need to move his things. Backpack to the kitchen, guns to under the sofa.*

3.1.2 - 06:17
'Sky-Castle' Mobile Command Base

#Cernis Drenner
#"Operator" for House Drenner

What is my life?

Sliding the volume control down to the bottom of the row he sighed and set to the act of processing what he had just heard. Removing his headset he set it carefully on the hook-stand on his corner workstation.

I need to find words. Juice and Fuller are staring at me for guidance. And not just lamenting that we're going to miss Beltane. No fire dancers for us tonight.

Turning back to them he went with the most self-centric thing he could think of, "I did not need to hear that."

Thumbing to the monitor speaker Juice shook his head with a lost look on his face, "good call in shutting that off. If it was more than what we thought we heard? I would not want to hear it. We are not privy to those kinds of emotional secrets."

Appearing uncomfortable Fuller gestured at the cabling, "I didn't know that I had hooked and potted that up as I did. Mea culpa."

Waiving off the idea, "we were barely awake, don't worry about it. I adjusted it."

Nodding Fuller appeared relieved, "thank you."

Waiving it off again, "noted."

Sitting on the small couch Juice looked from him to Fuller and back again, "so they're a bonded pair?"

Reflecting on the words he had heard, he picked his reply carefully, "they are a ten year friendship from the sounds of it. I had heard rumors, but the things that were said point to something much more. I can't say for certain what to expect from their future, as they are not sure themselves."

Rolling his eyes Juice gestured around them, "uncertain future? I would say we are *already living in it.* What is on the roof?"

I'll run with him, "a Sundering House-Cleaver Rocket Deployment System."

Tapping his armor he gestured at the vest on Fuller, "and what are we wearing?"

Don't remind me. "The Paladin Protective System, Class Four."

Rubbing his face he nodded once, "and what do we normally wear?"

"Urban Protector Combat Gear, Class Two."

Touching the chest holster he wore he spoke with a hushed awe, "this gun, this is one of Tessa's Teardrops. Each one of us has one of these. We are *not* here to sit and keep Miss Bachman company. Our High Consul has been placed in a situation where a Round Two is expected to come within Striking Distance."

Looking to the two of them Fuller nodded with a look of grim acceptance, "if the Consul who ordered this wants this to continue? We will fight."

Smiling with a sudden look of revelation Juice smiled, "we are not the enemy at least. The fact that we're camped out like this? We know it wasn't us."

True enough. Gesturing to the vital sign readout for the twelve of them he sighed, "we have enough trees that they're asleep still. Strung up in Tactical Hammocks, with sensors planted everywhere. Tremblers, Motion Detectors, and the video leads on the ends of both roads in the event they try a frontal strike. We are ready for whatever happens next."

Looking to the wall Fuller's eyes settled on a framed portrait of the past, "so how is Miss Bachman?"

Finally, some good news. "She's so *alive.*"

Firing back with a 'matter of fact' tone, "she's the Derecho, it's how she is. Tell me something more?"

I have something to give you strength. "The Gingerbread Son gives her strength."

Interjecting from the couch Juice offered, "she's standing next to someone who needs her to be the living legend we know her as. Sure, she's still human, I'm not putting her on a pedestal. However, she's a living legend."

Trying to finish the log file he sighed, "she wants to see him made a Citizen. He has come here looking for land and a house to put on it. Meeting Miss Bachman would be a pleasant surprise."

Pulling out his chiming comm Fuller looked at it, "Cosmo woke up!"

Thank the Divine. "Send him our warm regards."

Waving a finger at the comm Juice laughed, "tell him to not die. That's an order."

Pushing a button on the comm Fuller spoke into it, "Cosmo, don't die buddy. That's an order from Juice. Cernis says you can't leave yet, we still need to play cards and talk about the new neighborhood being built." Letting up on the button he blinked, "he wants to know if Yuri made it to Miss Bachman. What color was the veil."

The Veil Codes. Feeling the momentary high of relief fall away, "tell him the Veil is White."

"Is it?"

Waving his hand Juice echoed the idea with a mild frustration, "tell him the Veil is White. Just tell him that."

Pushing the button he spoke again with a warmth and comfort, "the Veil is White." Letting his finger up he looked at them as his tone shifted to concern, "is it though?"

Nodding with a reassuring smile he felt a confidence to his words, "Miss Bachman wants to keep us from Civil War. She's trying to save people. Not burn them to ash. The Veil is White. The Bachman Rage has not been unleashed. The Derecho is the warm gusts of Fall, the memories of Summer."

Looking at his still holstered sidearm Juice sighed, "so False Prophet was bogus. A Consul sent a small army to stop the wind. And yet, we have heard no word on how Miss Bachman is going to get whomever did this."

Time for the bad news. "She doesn't know. There isn't Protocol for this. She was being so quiet I used the internal surveillance to keep track of her. When I switched to the pickup when Dagger Herb arrived is when the speaker piped up. She talked to Wallman–"

Frowning with a tap of his forehead Fuller sighed, "we missed his update."

"We can catch a replay." Signaling for 'back on track,' "she told him that she does *not* have a plan yet. No Lilt. I can hope seeing her beloved will help recharge her, but gentlemen? Until she pulls an ad lib out of her hat? What we see of her plans? Is what we get."

"Did she say who did it?"

Honest question time, "if I told you, would you wake the rest and demand to go settle up?"

Laughing Juice nodded, "I would be sorely tempted to, yes. So she does know, and it's Consul Kunlow. You gave it away when you asked if we could go settle up. He's the only Consul in range." Sighing he shook his head, "rusted scrap. *We all three,* know for a rusted fact, that we do not know the half of the machinations which keep our world from imploding, falling apart, or otherwise collapsing like a house of cards."

Nodding Fuller chimed in, "correct. We live in the Drenner bubble. A division of House Resources and Loyalty between Respite and New Hope. The Enclave of New Hope, leftovers from the first generation when the attempt to settle near the Broken Gate did not work out."

Replying with a deadpan humor Juice raised an eyebrow, "that's an understatement."

Signaling 'agreement' Fuller continued, "I consider myself a Citizen of New Hope. I grew up here, nothing against Nissim, he handles Respite with a tact and grace, but I like it down here. Then again down here is also where I get to see Miss Bachman distort reality with her presence in only the best way possible."

The things she has championed. "The children she will have will either be painfully boring people in rebellion or the living scions of change."

Laughing Juice asked with a refreshed tone, "she's going to have kids?"

"It came up in her conversation with Dagger Herb. The Gingerbread Son, Yuri, is a possible candidate for that place in her life."

Still smiling Juice appeared pleased, "by the Blue Sky, *that,* is good news. The more Bachman children? The more hope we have for the future."

Raising a hand and moving it for 'no proof' Fuller asked his question, "do you think she's got some rust inside? False Prophet is a heavy accusation."

Trying to be diplomatic he answered before Juice could, "it would depend on if she thinks if we're *truly* astray. If there is something that Consul Kunlow knew about her family that they had done that would be wrong."

Looking at him with a challenging gaze, "you're playing around the truth. You know something."

No Epsilon Code was given, I can share. "Consul Kunlow wants to start the war with the Ports up again. Apparently we have a super weapon that could be used to blow up the Ports."

Appearing sad Fuller sounded frustrated, "so this ideological blood feud, is about if it is the right move to blow up our enemies in a way we have never done before?"

Holding his hands up in the 'comparison' gesture Juice spoke with the Voice of the Advocate, "on one hand, we have no more enemies, on the other, what kind of super weapon?"

I do not know. "I wish, maybe I don't, regardless, I don't know what kind of weapon it is."

Pursing his lips Juice appeared contemplative, "so as a people we are facing the question of war?"

Essentially. Everything else will be resolved for us. "Yes."

"Fuller, get out the Hydration Plus. I'll get the Pork Crackle. If the nation is facing the idea of war? We should be ready to weigh in. Especially when those sleepy so-and-sos wake up and we get to tell them what we've learned."

Moving to the fridge Fuller sounded resolved, "can we send our condolence messages too? Remind people that they are not alone in the dark ocean?"

I love you man. "As that is what we just saw?"

"Yes."

I hope Juice will agree. "We should."

Shrugging with a smile Juice nodded with his words, "it's not a bad idea. We could even inquire as to when Cosmo is going to be well enough to take him out for some fun. See if there are other people in the wounded who need some fun to look forward to."

Coming back with the jug Fuller seemed almost jubilant, "this moment," setting to pouring three cups, "are the last moments of useless discourse. We are going to sit and go over this and do our best to help contribute to the return of the Blue Sky in the hearts of our fellows. Not just *this* morning, but each day after." Closing the jug up and setting to returning it, "each day we have from this moment is a gift from the Creator. We have a chance to be indefeasible in our hopeful future. We will wash the wounds clean, somehow. We will not let them take our High Consul." Closing the door of the fridge, "when these times are spoken of later? We will speak of them with renewed hope for a better tomorrow. For a generation which will not know a pain like what we feel."

Taking his glass and raising it Juice appeared thoughtful, "a toast?"

I know what little to say. Getting up and joining them with his glass raised, "to Miss Bachman. Long live the High Consul, because it beats anything else."

Raising their glasses in agreement, "to Miss Bachman."

3.2.0 - 06:24

Safe Housing – Kitchen

⁙..Susan Bachman

Holding her comm in her hand she looked at the name on the display. *Jerome Hope.* Loitering for a moment in the positive affirmation that he was not dead, *the Day-Runner did what it needed to do. York ended up using his skills not to save himself only, but you. You know what I asked him to learn and why.*

Pressing the request she waited for the call to connect.

Intoning his words with a slight slur to them, "High Consul."

Speaking his name as an intonation of friendship, "Jerome."

Answering back with a matched intonation, "Miss Bachman."

I must say it. "Forgive me."

Playing it off with a Soldier's Humor, "for giving York what he needed to save me? Gladly." Adding with a tone of deliberate understatement, "I don't think the truck made it."

Silver lining affirmation, "the autopsy on the truck will help the Snafu-Works understand how their craftsmanship held up."

Asking with a careful intonation, "how long did it take them to build it?"

It was an exact project, "a year."

Exhaling with a disappointment, "three-hundred and sixty five days of labor, reduced to slag in less than thirty-six minutes."

Agreeing with him, "give or take." Moving her timbre to one of joy, "you're both still alive, so good enough for me."

"Then it will have to be good enough for everyone else."

Cutting to her confession, "I'm blank Jerome."

"What do you need? Reminders? Intel? Radical Thoughts?"

Tough choice. Go with the safe answer. "Intel. See if something shakes out rubbing my brain with information."

Sighing with humor he replied with enthusiasm, "Guard Kipper found a name for the attackers."

This should be good. "What has he dubbed them?"

"The Blackout Bloc. He told the children they were their own faction. The Children of the Blackout Bloc. Thus, they were not the Blackout Bloc. They cannot be given the

226

crimes of their parents as they are not the same."

Trying to keep the stung feeling out of her voice, "I might have used a bit of my High Consul Blackout on the reports."

Rolling the words with a gentle professionalism, "just a few clicks worth." Returning to the intel with a tone of reading notes, "Guard Kipper found two city busses, a small cadre of helpers, and he set to it. Waterlily, she helped him to no small extent once she joined the fray. The VIPs, otherwise known as the people who were in Central who were not in the fighting, have been moved to the Cultural Center with them. Separate rooms of course."

I knew most of that. "Kipper is a juggernaut when pushed into action."

"He has been pushed."

"As for the separate rooms, that's good too."

Sounding almost philosophical in his tone, "I made certain that the building staff all have the time off for mourning. Regardless of it they had any relatives or associates in the Tower proper. This Permission Key is terribly strong combined with the Sys-Admin Permission Key."

The more we learn, the more we need to know. "Keep me informed?"

Chiming back without losing the philosophical tone, "always."

"What else do you know?"

Looking at the window in the quiet she contemplated the rising level of light outside, *I made it to the dawn.*

Checking on him with his name, "Jerome?"

After a noise of forcing wakefulness, "yes Miss Bachman?"

I forgot to ask, "how goes the new position?"

Laughing with a biting honesty to his words, "to be honest? I think dredging my mind and the moment for something I don't know if you know would be an easier question to answer." Sighing as a puff of air, "I am not sure I'm in the best place to do my job. I will understand if I do not hold onto this chair in the long run."

The truth is an unfortunate companion this morning. "From my understanding? Athens said the same thing when he took the chair. My father got him to believe that the impossible was possible. He did the impossible."

Sighing with a deep regret to his words, "and now he's very dead."

That is not the tone of a man who was victorious. "Your heart regrets Athens."

Almost whining with the words, "it does." Stopping with an audible set of deep breaths before continuing Jerome sounded focused on the ideas presented, "but *not* killing him, I *regret,* respecting him. He did this job with a style, aplomb, and gravitas that I felt unworthy of aspiring to. I, trespassed into the Network, I didn't *earn* a place. I didn't gain Certifications. I didn't pass classes. I read everything I could, I took a gamble, and then I met you."

A self-starter though. "You are the sort of person I admire."

"You have said so before. It is *still* a strange notion to wrestle with."

"Be that as it may, you did something that, based upon what little I knew at the time from the files? Struck me as *kind*. They were fools, yes, but you were kind to them. And now? We are moving away from the real problem. Athens."

"He, did this *willingly*. He wasn't coerced, or brainwashed, or indoc-" suppressing a yawn with an almost angry snarl, "-trinated. He looked at this day, and he helped plan this day. I wanted to be as smart as him, know as much as him, to serve in his circle. He never trusted me, because I harbored the unknown. He never liked me, because I was a Loyalist. Am I a good Citizen, being Loyal to you, at the cost of not being Loyal to the Protocol?"

I have to offer him something greater, "give me a moment? It's a small preamble."

Laughing he spoke the word with incredulity, "*granted.*"

Thinking quickly she spun the concept together, "that's something I *also* am wrestling with now. Am I a good High Consul when I walk away from the Protocol like a child and their ball leaving a game they are losing?"

"Not an easier question, or answer."

"Of your question?" *He sounds like he did when we met. When he spent his words defending the right for those who had broken Protocol to be forgiven.* "You have never been a *good* Citizen. You have been a Civil Disobedient, a warm heart, a giving spirit, but you have not been a good Citizen. That was not a luxury for you to gain in this life from the looks of it."

Keeping his tone mostly neutral, "then what am I?"

"A good *human*. As a Citizen? You're dangerous. You're frightening. And to some? Your ability to follow the Penguin's Path? Awe inspiring. The Penguin is the Totemic Representation of our Digital Kingdom, and for some reason you and it get along really well. It doesn't steal your sanity the way he steals the sanity of others." Taking a breath, "Jerome, I didn't save you because I thought you were a good Citizen. I saved you because you said why you did it, and you wanted to forgive them."

Firing back with an almost hopeful neutrality, "what do I do?"

Encouraging him with effort, "what you're trying to do right now. Marshaling the sense of self to survive the revelation that your Gold Standard was a rusted piece of something covered in gilt. You will work harder than anyone else would expect, you will overcome this moment, and you will become someone else's Gold Standard."

"I will?"

I can hear him coming around. Summoning up the effort to keep going without losing the encouragement she plowed into the words, "if you don't give up on you, you will! Ascend the throne of your heart. Rule inside yourself this day. Athens *knew* he had to kill you. He did *not* know that York was there. He sent enough firepower to level your house, *without* the knowledge that you could survive it. He didn't just *want you dead,* he *knew.* He *knew* that you would be a nightmare if you were allowed to run free."

With a lilt of awed candor that bordered on humor, "you truly are a master of King Making."

Reciting the words with a practiced ease, "it is the duty of the woman who accepts men to acknowledge the success and worth of the men around them so that they can see their labors have context and meaning in their world." Taking a quick breath she continued, "even if I am not your partner it is still my objective to express these things. In this case you serve me to repay a life debt. Until you feel it is paid it is the duty of my heart to show you what it was I wanted to save, and my appreciation that you are still here."

Intoning the words with a calmed reverence, "thank you Miss Bachman."

"Noted." Sighing she regarded her half full glass of water, "to think it was Thomas."

"I would not know where to begin in fathoming the depths of that truth."

That makes two of us. "I am not sure I do either."

"I need to ask you something, well, I don't *have* to, but would you authorize moving the City to Crisis Level Five? It removes the prompt on every single person I might move around in the next part of the plans."

Might as well. "Do it."

After a moment of quiet he sighed, "done. I believe I managed to *not* send that as a System-Wide Update."

Checking her comm she smiled, "I do not have an update of that nature. You're good. I have the High Consul Watchdog Update, but not a System-Wide."

"Noted."

Emoting her frustration with the moment with her words, "if I was at my bunker I would have access to the Cloak and Dagger Emergency Action Control Center."

Turning the tables on her with an encouraging tone of his own, "on the other hand? Your orders are being handled by people who have a distance from you right now. They have your will, the orders, and are walking through a moment of soul searching. They have to think over anything they send you. They can't just scream out in anguish and hope you will hold them. You have a moment to hold the compress to *your* wounds and staunch the bleeding."

He knows a few things about me. "Thank you Jerome."

"Noted. You're a good person Miss Bachman."

Keeping her voice thankful, "noted."

"The Yorklins, they have taken the honest inventory on the hour and kept the medical rotated. No one has broken oaths. The medical care continues without a hitch. Your Honor Guard have submitted only a few small notes of people coming to New Hope General looking for answers, not vengeance."

Speaking with an assurance of the idea, "Wallman reached the hearts of the people."

"The people seem to be ready to trust whatever justice will be needed to settle this. And that it will happen."

"That's where I don't have an answer," repeating herself in frustration, "I don't have the answer."

Rolling the question with a timid inquiry, "does The Commander?"

Knowing Steven? Three answers. The one he would want, the one dad would want, and the one I would begrudgingly accept. "I'm sure he does."

"If he said he could get Consul Kunlow -?"

Giving in to the quiet anger, "I'd tell him to bring me the animal in shackles."

Offering the words with the tone of a Subject Change, "there is something else, -"

Please don't be terrible. "What?"

Answering her question with a head-hung defeat, that she couldn't see but could hear with a painful acuity, "the forces that attacked Central, they were heavily augmented by Civilian level fighting forces. Consul Kunlow *could* have enough forces left to mount a Round Two. The Cultural Center does not have enough guards on it to assure that he would disqualify it as a maneuver. If he hit there, *liberated* the children, and used that as a Rally Point if there is a support for war?" Sighing with a guilt to his tone, "he might see that as a viable option."

That's Top Tier Terrible. "Pondering, please wait." Thinking over her variables and ideas she checked what information her comm had. *That's a barely functional plan, but it could work.*

"Move the Holden Crisis Protection and Intervention Operatives from the City Works Office they have, and get them on my VIPs then. Get them sandbags and a few Viper Nests. That should keep them at bay."

Hearing the sound of keystrokes and affirmative noises she felt her hopes rising that the plan would be viable.

Answering with a soft affirmation, "it's in the queue."

"Good."

Trying to stay polite with his question, "how do I ask about your trust of them, without asking it in a way that sounds like I doubt or am ordering? I'm, struggling."

The flaws in your clay. "As you just did?" Smiling she laughed softly to comfort him, "the Diagnostic Question of The Question." Nodding she set to the words of exoneration, "Sinclair was on duty last night. He killed those who came after him. He's not the kind of monster who would abide that sort of plan, much less one which would require him to kill people to cover it up." *Oh, that hurts on accident.* "Consul Holden, she's not that kind of monster either. In *any* of the ways the plan would need to be structured with her *also* knowing. We can *borrow* her assets."

"Thank you Miss Bachman, I needed to hear something good." Adding as an afterthought, "even if you did just injure yourself."

Speaking softly she looked into the water, "you know me too well."

Replying with a forlorn ache, "I am also haunted by the deed."

Forcing herself upright, "we can't do this, not right now. We'll solve that later."

Echoing her tone he fired back, "we will. Later. We'll make a later just so we can be sad in it!"

"Correct!" After a pause she asked the question she knew she didn't want to really know the answer to, "how many of the Consuls knew? I know Kunlow was behind it, but, do you know if any of the others knew and turned a blind eye?"

"I wish I knew how to begin putting that together. The Network is still damaged. Athens torched the code in places and ways that just aren't a simple fix. It's bad enough in some places that we're rolling out a Firmware Update to fix it. I don't know if I told you. We'll be patching the *entire* Network Map, with the Firmware Update to *every* routing and switching device. If the city wasn't already paralyzed? It would be borderline cruelty. The Crisis Management Officer has already setup the process of keeping everyone checked on in the absence of our usual technology."

"Good." Thinking on the subject of Thomas Kunlow, "my heart has a limit Jerome. I think I've hit it. If Steven tells me he can get Thomas, I'll let him."

Returning to his neutrality, "I understand Miss Bachman."

Being honest with herself, "I don't like it either."

Answering with a quiet sadness to the words, "the people have to want peace though, for it to be the biggest concern. Correct?"

A new nuance to the pain, "correct."

After a few heartbeats of quiet Jerome's voice roused again from the speaker, "I look at the updates, and I want to *believe* that the people I see working so hard, from the Orange Ponchos, the Militia Captains, the Network News, and all the people in between? That they would want peace."

"We can only hope." Taking a breath, "Jerome, whatever the future holds? Are you with me?"

Speaking the words of the Pledge, "until the end, no matter how bitter it will be."

Smiling she sniffled, "thank you Jerome."

Audibly changing the subject with an upbeat question, "speaking of Kings? How is he?"

This could be easier territory, "Yuri?"

"Yes! I've heard so much about him, and yet not enough, so I would ask you."

"I believe is handling this without fraying." *I look forward to seeing him.* "I plan on finding that out as soon as he wakes up."

Remarking in an offhanded fashion, "you did not sleep."

Tossing the question back with a casual grin, "did you?"

Responding with a tone that rang with a shrug, "I think I slept for a half hour by claiming I had to use the Necessarium. Then I passed out." Chuckling softly he clarified, "I did get to the Necessarium."

Smiling she nodded, "noted."

Keeping with the offhanded tone, "when will you sleep?"

Thinking it over she considered her options, "I don't know yet. I woke up at twenty-one hundred, not sure when I want to crash."

"Noted."

"Jerome, I should go." Looking at the clock, "I have a call from Waterlily scheduled. I *was* going to admit defeat and go sulk, *but,* I have something to do."

Offering his words with a cautious humor, "you can always sulk later."

Smiling she nodded, "*indeed.* Be well Jerome."

Closing with a greater morale to his words, " be well High Consul."

Closing the connection she set to refreshing her water glass before the scheduled time. *If I know Waterlily and how she knows me, it will be right on the second.*

Watching the seconds tick over to double zero she smiled when her comm lit up with the scheduled call. *I press this and it'll be a five second delay.*

Steady the breathing, and go.

"Miss Bachman, it is good we can speak directly."

She sounds so calm. "Waterlily."

Losing the calm with a rush of emotion, "your, people, persons, personnel –"

Don't rush her, she has something prepared. She always does. She probably has that cute clipboard of hers with her. "What of them?"

Still in a state of reflective awe, "they are a sight to behold. From before the bullets stopped firing, to just the last minute, they have been knocking down this situation with an alacrity that has been breath taking to witness."

Speaking with pride she gushed for a moment, "they're the best for a reason." Reigning it in, "that's not *quite* why you called, is it?"

Easing into the words with an audible concern, "I called because I'm worried about you."

Nodding she agreed with the idea, "I'm worried about me too."

Still concerned but hopeful in tone she asked, "why am I allowed past Leave a Message?"

Firing back with the simple answers, "I never hated you. Admin Nobody knows that. You're my Counselor, we're not meant to shut out The Guild."

Swallowing audibly she rushed the words, "I want to thank you, for Heartstrings."

Making sure her earpiece wasn't going to fall off she started the motion of getting to her feet, "noted."

With a hint of exasperation to the words, "you don't feel that needed thanks."

Reaching her feet she picked up her water glass and moved toward the sink, "no, I don't."

Keeping the exasperation under control, "may I ask why?"

Turning around and leaning against the edge of the sink she looked into the water, "see, any of the polite dodges my father would use in not questioning The Guild."

"I hear the sullen dodge, even in your dodge, I can hear the sullen."

Taking a long drink of water she looked back down at what was left in her glass, "I have some serious doubts that one of the best sexual health therapists and leader of an ambitious project such as she is? Would have time in her busy schedule of making sure people are healthy –" sighing, "do you see the logic train?"

Losing the exasperation she sounded off in agreement, "I do. It leaves the station, it runs the course, and provides you with emotional shelter against it being too personal."

"Yes." Taking a moment to drink she emptied the glass in short order.

"Susan?"

She wants to connect to me as a person. "You used my name, what do you require?"

Hearing the suppressed heartache with the words, "I want to know you're remotely within tolerance."

"I can't give you that, not without risking it being a lie. To clarify I don't have a proper inventory of self. I don't know how I feel yet." Moving away from the sink she placed the glass on a safe spot before leaning against the counter. "What's my status with Doctor Monroe?"

Stifling the laughter, "he wants to know why you're not in his office, or my office, in your own words though."

"Professional Courtesy. I'm afraid of a Round Two. If I go in, that would bring the gunmen into your building, and I know how little you enjoy armed combat in your building."

With an audible fret with her words, "I see."

She's outside, maybe a balcony? "I hear the city behind you. You're not in your office."

"I'm at the Cultural Center."

She's dedicated. "Still?"

"I stepped outside because I'm getting ready to go home and get some sleep. I did all I could. I have other professionals in mind, and I have given them the contact information for your Support Staff. I am a dedicated servant to the cause."

"I will look at your recommendations as soon as we're off the comm. I'll approve them. Get the process expedited."

Speaking softly with a conspiratorial humor, "Guard Kipper said it would work."

Responding with humor in turn, "he knows me well enough. You did good asking him how to succeed in the moment."

"Thank you Susan."

You know how much I adore Kipper's humor. "Noted."

"Again –"

Interrupting her, "you are of The Guild, you are a special caste in our society. It is the best I can do given the moment."

Adding a more urging inflection to her words, "when do I get to see you?"

"I need time Waterlily. I," *this might not work,* "want to make you a deal."

Firing back with a despondent frustration, "you *know* Doctor Monroe doesn't like bargaining, as it makes it seem as if this is punishment."

Trying to sound helpful and hopeful, "I want to offer you Full Disclosure."

Faltering in the moment the intrigued tone was audible, "this is new."

It will work. "I wasn't the High Consul before. Full Disclosure, with option for you to step down if when it's over you don't think we can work together."

Rushing to seal the Pledge, "can I get that in writing?" Huffing in frustration she corrected the moment, "not the step down clause, just the Full Disclosure."

I win by losing. "I'll take care of sending you the Pledge as soon as we're off the comm."

Setting into her with a voice of confidence, "I've known you since you were twelve –"

Stepping over her with her words, "and I never lied to you directly –"

Pushing in return, "- truth, but what does that – "

Failing to keep the sad fear out of her tone, "I don't know if after you hear everything if you'll want to stay with me. It's a lot to take in."

Firing back with a courageous self check, "I would like to think I could handle it."

Smiling she nodded, "me too."

Sighing she asked with a sad 'fact of the matter' lilt, "is there anything else we should be exploiting from the other?"

While we're here, "I have a Ghost, his name is Yuri, I was hoping you could find him someone to be his Counselor when I figure out how to make him a Citizen."

Asking the clarification, "the Gingerbread Son?"

Answering simply, "correct."

"I will see if Ember Glory is up to the task. Otherwise I'll look high and low and we'll find him someone to take on the task. Purple Heart would also be available."

"Good."

Trying to sound hopeful and helpful, "I'll send Doctor Monroe a copy of the agreement after I have it. That will keep him from seeking you out. Or seeing about ordering me to come find you."

Looking at the holstered gun in the center of the kitchen table, "I don't want to be found right now."

"I understand."

"I can do it now, actually." Moving her comm to her hand she pulled out a spare stylus and set to work. Working her way through the windows she set her Seal onto each item. *Nothing like keeping them guessing with something like this. I wonder how long it will take Sasha to remember this cat?*

Broaching the question with caution, "Susan?"

Answering back with an absentminded caution, "yes?"

Keeping to the caution, "why are you alone?"

Smiling she felt puzzled, "I'm not."

Continuing with a caution mixed with inquiry, "is he a friend to you?"

Sighing it was her turn to puff, "he's the Gingerbread Son. His family and mine have a deep history."

Flowing into the tone of inquiry with the lilt of sad reflection, "have you shown him why we revere the Gingerbread Man?"

Closing her eyes she reflected on her decision to not show Yuri the footage, or play him the audio from the moments before Final Seal. *Not yet.* "No." Sniffling against the surge of sadness, which collided with the knowledge of the footage from the hours before being enshrined next to it, "I have told him that he was correct. Rolf died saving Penelope. Penelope would be the one to carry on the line. From that line, that salvation, a Bachman son would open the door and set to reclaiming the world. And when he died, his sister had children of her own, from which the line has remained unbroken. That without Rolf the hope of the Bachman family not faltering in the quest to lead the people would not be a worry, as we would not be as we are."

With a forced neutrality, "I see."

Looking up from her comm the words roared out with emotion, "you don't *just* show a man something like that and tell him, *no big deal.* Hi, I know you just got here, and this might seem unhinged to your perceptions, but if you are whom you claim? You're the descendent of a *living miracle.* He told me, where he is from they have a people not unlike the Ideals, they call them Saints. How do I tell a man of Faith that to *us?* He has the blood of a *Saint* in his veins?"

Admitting with a quiet 'at a loss' tone, "I don't know. That's not in any Primer I know." Trying to sound helpful, "perhaps the Bachman Codex has a Primer on the subject?"

It addresses the Ideals, but not for that. "Penelope was devastated for the rest of her life, having witnessed Rolf's death. Knowing he died, for her. Her words on the subject formed the framework of how a Bachman understands Guilt. She was far too young to have that laid at her feet. She watched the world die, an event too large, too nebulous to wrap her childish mind around. Then she watched a single soul, snuffed out, for her benefit." *I know the feeling.* "I know Paulson is gone. I *know,* he knew, going to the fifteenth would be his last move. I gave him Dominion, he used it, and he died. Rolf had Dominion that day, and he picked his win."

"Do you love Yuri?"

"I adore," catching herself she stopped. Looking back to her comm she finished the pending items she had promised. Swallowing she gasped in the air, while fighting with the surge of emotions, "I was going to deflect."

Trying to not sound too aware of the fact, "I could tell."

Nodding with a firm lilt, "you have your needed things."

Speaking the question again with the easygoing Voice of the Counselor, "do you love him?"

Just tell her. "I love him enough that it makes me whelmed to witness it in myself. I have spoken with Sasha. We're going to use the Bigger Bed."

Losing her Voice to the honest surprise, "no one in your family has used that."

Smiling with her words, "first time for many things."

"Are we at the state of Civil War?"

"Not yet, not to my knowledge."

"What of Thomas Kunlow?"

She's in the loop. "I am marshaling my forces, power, and proof. I have placed the Consuls in the same emotional room together and a few of them can already smell that something is burning."

Laughing with the audacity of the statement, "you're going to use Smoke on the whole Council?"

"Yes. I have already lit the kindling."

"Never let it be said you lack in the Bachman moxie."

Pushing her tone to a deadpan humor, "that would be a lie. So no, let's not say that."

"Be well Miss Bachman. I have duties on behalf of The Guild. As I can not help you further at this juncture? I look forward to the later date when I can sit with you."

Finding herself back at the place of doubt, "don't commit to that idea too freely. You don't know what I've kept from you."

Coaxing her with her words, "will you call me if you need a shoulder?"

Honesty. "If I need professional, educated, and experienced help? I will call you."

Coaxing her with an emotional surge, "you don't have to wait until things are that bad. You *can* call sooner."

Exhaling a slow breath of understanding, "noted."

Speaking the words as a blessing, "be well Susan."

Answering her in kind, "be well Waterlily."

Closing the connection she sighed. *She made many a good point.*

3.3.0 - 06:40

Safe Housing – Susan's Bedroom

☼ Yuri

Opening his eyes in a rush of panic he grabbed the pillow his hand fell on and pulled it close to him. Wrapping both arms around it as his mind raced to remember who or where he was he regained the sense of self to resist the urge to scream.

Inhaling the scent of the pillow the carrot greens smell brought words into his mind, *carrot greens. Susan.*

Inhaling again he felt his breathing slowing slightly as his mind finished waking. Huffing and puffing as the pain hit him he pulled the pillow closer and held it firmly. *I feel less pain.*

Muttering to himself in his native tongue he rolled his eyes in exasperation with himself. Focusing his thoughts he set his mind to the task of the English language, *she will not know what I am saying if I forget to speak in English.*

Reflecting on a life spent hearing other languages, *I haven't heard Russian in so long, much less a syllable of Ukrainian. Years for German. Not as many for French though.*

Taking an inventory of his body, *the pain in my heart is greater than the pain in my body. It hurts less.*

Vocalizing the thought, "less than I expected."

Speaking the words he cemented his wakefulness, "my name is Yuri."

Rubbing his face he looked over at the bedside clock, "not yet seven." Looking to the window, "the sun has risen."

Forcing himself to sit up he looked over at the window, *those are some intense curtains.* Getting up and out of the bed he moved to the curtains to open them enough to look out of.

Bright. Oh, that is bright. Waiting for his eyes to adjust he took a moment of pause to reflect on the beauty of sun lit horizon when one is a free man. *It looks the same as when one is in prison really. It's a star shining on a planet filled with people and it would shine even if they were all dead. It's the confirmation that even without you the world is moving on.*

Rubbing his face again he closed his eyes, *those people are dead though. I didn't get to meet them. I didn't get to share that cake with them.*

Placing his face carefully in his hands he took a deep breath, *I can't turn to such a bleak place of thought. If she leans on me when she mourns them I will be no good to her like this. Start over Yuri. Start over.*

Taking his breaths he tried to form the words again, *the sun will shine as long as it can shine. It doesn't ask the people if they can see it, it just is as it is.* Feeling a moment of victory he smiled, *I am not going to let myself scar tissue scab over. She is going to mourn those people and tell me stories and in me they will live on, just a little bit, in the retelling. I will move forward and be open to the idea of learning who they were. Whom all of them were if she tells me.*

Taking a moment to stretch he winced, *I almost wish I had asked her for something stronger. I can move though, and that is what counts.* Thinking back on the night before, *she handled those kills with an ease that says to me it's not the first time she's killed. She finished the work she started.*

Reflecting as he stretched his sore body further, *she hasn't lost the nausea but then again I haven't lost the awe. The knowledge that for some reason you get to live when everyone else dies. And then you get to the point where sleeping becomes easy again because after everything, you almost hope you go quick and in your sleep.*

Stopping himself he placed his hands over his eyes, *I don't want to be this way. I will not succumb. I will not succumb! I am going to cope, and face her with a smile. I am going to go find her and find out if she is doing well enough to function. Then I will ask her where I can get a shower. I will face her with an open mind, and an open heart.*

Moving his mind to the tranquil place the Monks had shown him was within himself, *she is not my captor. She is my friend.*

Finding the mantras of truth he repeated the words internally to test them for lies. *She is not going to hurt me.* "Truth."

I can trust her like I trusted before and was repaid with kindness. "Truth."

She is not afraid of me. "Not in the traditional sense, as the saying goes."

I need to not be afraid of happiness. "At least enough to get up and go see her."

Feeling the hunger in the pit of his stomach, "and breakfast. I hope we have food. Even those bars she has would do. Or a pouch of emergency food."

Looking to the mirror in the room he moved into view of himself. Running his fingers through his beard he frowned at his unkempt appearance, *I see why she told me to not worry about it. I look terrible.* Turning to the pile of his clothes on the floor he frowned at his things. *That is not going to work.* Looking down at the long shirt he was wearing he felt the uncomfortable knowledge of how little the hem extended past his nether regions, *or this.*

Opening the door to the bedroom he spotted the small bag hanging from the doorknob in an instant. Taking it he looked inside to see a change of clothes within. *She provides for me still. My pride, my ability to feel human.*

I will go see her as a fellow human.

Donning his clothes he turned and looked at himself in the mirror, *I look like a well dressed beggar.*

Touching his stomach, *a hungry one at that. To breakfast!*

Safe Housing – Kitchen

⁚⁚..Susan Bachman

Clearing the almond butter spread from her mouth with a swish of water she gave thanks for the unopened jar she had found. *I may have used too much, but at least I had it to use. Same with the loaf of Breakfast Bread. I did not fail myself.*

Not completely.

Looking to her tablet she continued the task of pouring over the latest round of reports. *This is going to be a Gray Sky in the end. Not Blue, but not Red. Operation Blue Sky Dawn had a lot better ring to it than Operation Not Red Sky.*

Had to think of something though.

Looking at the progress that had been made, *the people have spoken and acted.* Checking the update from The Guild she stifled laughter at the conclusion.

I don't know why I want to laugh, but I do.

The survivors of the Blackout Bloc aren't sure what to say, the ones who are talking. They didn't think they would lose, and if they did lose they thought they would be dead. They set the Rules of Engagement.

Thinking over a reply she typed a clarification to the Coordinator, *the fight was over. The Rules set were considered no longer applicable. I do not wish to harm them if they are willing to work through this. I cannot bring back my dead. I cannot travel back in time. We have to live through this.*

Hopefully that will be good enough.

Looking at the Injured, Incapacitated, and Deceased lists for Central Tower she frowned at the names in the Deceased column. *It's the shortest, but it still hurts. Yuri can say they should have known the risk, but, father had an idea and was working as best he could to make it a safer place to work. When people started sleeping over he started the quiet tinkering with the system.*

Trying to find a positive outlook to cling to she mustered one.

If he was here, he could have seen how much good it had done.

One last gift from father.

I don't think he would have guessed that his neighbors would be the ones to test it though. I don't think any of us did.

Sighing she took another sip of water, *wait a minute.*

I need to not hold Yuri accountable for trying to console me. He's not blaming them for dying, or excusing them dying. He just wants me to be comforted in the idea that they knew the risk and still stood near me. That they made an informed decision when given Dominion over their own Freedoms to express themselves.

Switching windows on the tablet she looked over her discussion questions for when she would be facing a shackled Thomas. *I have more questions for Consul Kunlow now. I don't think he will want to answer them though.*

Going to another window she resisted the snarl at the logistics that had been found and calculated. *This wasn't made in a week, this was long game. That much is evident. Why last night was the perfect moment? I can hazard a guess. We had only a night or two more before I would be ordering the new guards and security that Consul Carnap felt I should be upgrading to. The others supported it, so this would have been the last moments.*

But what was the criteria for this to occur before dad died?

Taking another bite of toast and chewing it roughly, *and I need to get my mind off of that because it's not making sense and that's grinding my gearbox.*

With the aid of another swish of water she swallowed her bite of toast. *Seeing the reports of how much violence occurred I can see why Yuri was rattled.*

He told fun stories of adventure, which always included violence, but he was careful to censor them. He never spoke of the violent parts with detail, only the results of his actions. From the woman whom he had saved who stabbed him not knowing his intent to save her, to the bounty hunting, to the fellow humans he protected. His words in the dark were of a Noble Ideal who did violent things for the best reasons he could have at the time.

The things he saw were not done for the best reasons. They speak to a breakdown in the minds of both sides of the conflict as the desperation escalated.

No wonder he was rattled. But the people he fought with would not have known what to do when fighting against a person of his experience. We train to ready ourselves for the battlefield, when plans fall apart, when forms and stances degrade in precision, and only the fight for survival matters.

To be skilled in surviving.

And Yuri, is quite skilled at surviving. As a Veteran they would have been outclassed. And given the priority in the use of the bullets they had? He was told to take every odd man out.

Looking over the moment she glanced over the analysis of the evening, *Frank being there was a serious change of their plans. Father wanted him near because Yuri responded to him and it was keeping him docile. Kincaid didn't expect Captain Sevilan to be there. It was a secret assignment which was flagged in a way Athens might not have known to even look for it.*

Kincaid would have been faced with the knowledge that the Night Terrors would be howling in if Frank lived too long. He changed his plans, he took the bait Frank made of himself, and he went for Sevilan to keep him from being able to lead them in the first moments of the Counter Offensive that he knew was coming. They used everything they could to stop him. Frank gambled with his life, something he's more than willing to do.

Looking at the time table she frowned, *why he stayed with Patrick, I won't ask. I don't want to know the answer if it is not just because he needed to make certain that Patrick would live. If someone wants to tell me? They will. I just know he sent Yuri to find me. And he did.*

Now I just wish I could expedite the rewriting of the Clause I'll need to get him Citizenship. He can add an emblem of The Rim next to the rest on his keychain bracelet. Names of places I've never heard of, risen up from the ash, and each one gave him a token when he left to remember them by.

Cherishing history for the lessons it can teach you, no idea how that feels. Riding the internal wave of ironic humor, *no idea at all. I'm glad I made sure to include that specifically in my order to Yorklin to hand off to Sasha when he packed his things. He'd probably be sad if it had been misplaced. I would have been sad right with him.*

Looking over at the beat up travelers backpack in the chair next to her she forced another bite of toast into her mouth and started the slow process of chewing it. *When he wakes I hope he finds the bag I left him. If he opens the door he'll see it. I just did not want to wake him.*

He can get a shower, and I can call Dennis over and he can be fitted for new clothes. Most of the things he has are all worn out and just flat out ugly.

Being honest with herself, *and Dennis can see I'm still alive.*

Swallowing roughly she picked up her coffee and sipped it as she tried to finish rereading the report. *Jerome has Stanley proofing these, and making sure to annotate every reference for me to use my Blackout on. I don't need anyone else knowing too much about what happened yet. They haven't given me what I need to know. Until then? They get to look at Thomas and know he's why this is happening.* Using her stylus she quickly edited the notes with the Blackout function until all that remained were the facts she was willing to share. *There. Now if they admit they know more than I am letting on? They will admit it was something learned from their spies they have flock to Steven's side.* Saving the notes with the Blackout on them she sent it back to Stanley to be bundled into the latest report that the Council would have access to.

I don't even know why I'm still following Protocol, but Protocol is Protocol.

Hearing the sound of shuffling feet she waited for Yuri to emerge from around the corner leading to the hall. *The temptation to stay next to him was stronger than I expected. I didn't want to get up and move.* Taking the last draught of her cold coffee she set the mug down as he walked into the kitchen proper.

Standing up from her chair she winced at the sight of Yuri in better light. *He needs more sleep and more care.* "I had your backpack brought over, I see you found the clothes I left for you on the door knob. If you would like that shower? The bathroom here on the main floor has supplies that should smell to your liking. They're in the green basket in the Bathing Room."

Nodding in understanding, "and then I can have breakfast?"

"Of course." Getting up she raised an arm while signaling for 'hug,' "care for one?"

Nodding he shuffled over to her and moved his body against hers.

Wrapping her arms around him she hugged him warmly. "Good morning."

Speaking softly to her shoulder, "I know so little of these lands. The shows helped, but I know there is a cavern of knowledge I have not found."

Hugging him warmly she found an upbeat lilt for him, "I will teach you. I will have others teach you."

Restraining a sob he spoke softly, "I dropped the milk on the way back."

I'm going out for milk. Closing her eyes she gripped him firmly, "you aren't leaving. You made it. I *will* find you a parcel of land and a house *will* be put on it. I *do* run this, and I will see the promise honored."

"Thank you Susan."

Squeezing him again she heard his stomach. *I know just the thing.* Hugging him again to hush him she pulled away gently with a smile. Dashing to a drawer she retrieved one the Breakfast Meal Bars she had found while ransacking the kitchen. Bringing it to him she held it out with a smile, "enjoy your shower. You can eat this as the water preheats."

Taking the bar he smiled, "I will return soon enough. Perhaps later than sooner depending on how good that shower feels."

"I understand."

"It is quick burst, off, lather, then enjoy the hot water, yes?"

"Yes."

Watching him go she wanted to say something more but found herself at a loss for words. *Even after all of our shared words I find myself struggling for something to say. No one has ever said anything like this could happen. And I don't have anything else I know how to say that makes sense to say right now. Rusted scrap.*

He passes the checklist though. Thinking back on being young she sighed, *updated it every year and Yuri passes enough that it would make sense to want him like that. I'm only careful because I'm a Bachman, because I'm the High Consul. A Citizen would be in the shower with him and lathering affection all over him.*

Moving over to her chair she sat down and folded her hands over each other to make a rounded steeple. *Setting her chin on it she contemplated the matter further.*

Even the few times I did help him with bathing in the first few days were a quiet affair. Just a series of wet cloths, a sponge, and a bucket as we compromised a dozen times. I'd gain nothing by confronting his naked form at this time.

Sitting in silence she heard the shower turn on, bringing her mind out of the moment of drift. *At least we have hot water, he mentioned most of the world's showers are cold. And now I'm thinking about him naked and in the shower. That needs to stop, I need to concentrate on things.*

Looking over at her blinking comm she sighed as the custom ring let her know who was calling, *incoming call. Saved from my thoughts by Amanda calling me.*

Picking up her comm and flipping it over, *Consul Amanda Drenner, I wonder what she's going to want to talk about. Much less what prompted Jerome to let her past Leave a Message. Will she want to speak to me as Amanda, or the Consul,* sighing in mild disgust with her meandering thoughts, *just pick up the rusted comm.* Pushing the connect after the fifth chirp she spoke her greeting with a cordial conversational tone, "morning Consul."

Throwing the words at her with a borderline accusation, "you're nearly assassinated and all I get is a *morning Consul?*"

I have to stay calm, or I'm going to emote and I can't have her knowing I'm as scared as she sounds. "It's a greeting one would say when a Consul calls you in the morning hours, thus I said it. I'm surprised that he let your call through."

"I am too. I, I don't know what to tell the other Consuls."

If I knew what to tell them, I would have told them. "Tell them the truth?"

Replying with a flat humor, "that won't help."

Trying to find a philosophical answer of mocked up wisdom she spun words together, "tell them? To have the strength to face questions that they cannot fathom."

"Noted." Her tone shifting to a borderline admiration, "your people are running hard, I haven't seen people this, like this, since the war." Shifting to a mote of curiosity, "I fear some of the Council is confused as to why Thomas still sits in his home."

Keeping herself tranquil she replied with a neutrality of acceptance, "I don't have all of my proof in a row. I *do* have a city in pain, that needs help. So while those who have been tasked with finding a way to do this, do what they need to do? I do my best to ensure that what can be done, is done."

"You reached out and requisitioned Holden assets, did you speak with her?"

I am going to keep myself level, even, and inspire her to be just as calm. "Didn't need to. The City is at Crisis Level Five."

Sounding confused, "I didn't get an update."

"The Admin muzzled it. Didn't want to panic the people."

"But you still called them into play?"

"Sinclair was on duty last night. I will not accept a world where she would let him die as a probable idea of who she is or what she could order."

"Love then?"

"Tammerlane's Tribute, that all of mankind, that our human selves, can be boiled down to love and our relation to it, in all of the Facets. I know she loves him, that he loves her, so the idea that to end me she would slay him? No. Doesn't hold merit as a theory, idea, or even a nightmare because it doesn't make any sense."

"What does?"

Inviting humor into her tone she replied, "she would invite me over for cartoons, hug me, and ask me to give up the Throne. She would offer a lifetime of cereal, cartoons, and I would be the foreman at her ice cream production facility."

Replying with a candid whimsy with the idea, "that sounds *oddly adorable.*"

Always give a second opinion, "you though –"

Replying into the empty air with a bold humor, "this should be enlightening."

My honest approximation of the most effective way you could stop us. "You would ask me to move into the Main Estate, to bring Yuri and Sasha with me, where I would find myself able to marry and have children. You would do something about my brothers to get them someone in their lives and they would have children too. And in the act of losing power, we would finally replenish the tree that fell together and is running out of branches." Adding with a note of humor, "I'd even get to keep the cabin."

Sighing in relief, "thank you for that."

I only speak what I think is the truth. Back on task. "I can't get Thomas until I have something more coherent. The time table, the manifests, the testimony of those from his forces that lived. Not even Asmodai could just point a finger and kill a Consul." Adding with a dry bite, "not that he didn't want to."

Sighing with remorse, "truth."

Feeling the humor pass she sighed, "I hate him though, I hate the idea that he's having breakfast and looking out his window and smugly smiling because he knows I can't touch him under the current system. It's why the Network News and allied media hasn't told our people who did this. I don't want them helping. I want them processing their feelings, working through this, and leave the judgment to the professionals."

"I saw that every backup relay, tower, and communications device this project could find has been activated to take pressure off the Network."

"The Network is in shambles, compared to the day to day processing power it boasts. It's why the Voice of the Morning was broadcasting on FM, and why the AM Channels are filled with the unsecured updates and motions. Only so many options left on the best paths to the people, so we're using the old workhorses."

Forging ahead with her words, "what happens now?"

Returning to the biting humor, "I wish Thomas was dead, so hard, that he actually just dies and solves the problem for us all."

"Susan, I want to ask this carefully, who is Yuri?"

Answering with the 'matter of fact' tone, "he's a Ghost."

Voicing the question with a caution, "how do I ask more without –"

Trying and failing to keep the anger out of her tone, "grinding the inside of my skull with implied slanderous implications that he's a danger to me because he's a Ghost?"

Laughing with an audible regret, "something like that. I take it someone does *not* approve of him?"

Puffing air out to try to release the frustration, "yes. There is someone who doesn't approve of him. Though, he is indeed the Gingerbread Son. He's come here looking for a parcel of land and a house to put on it."

"I can understand that it would be difficult to give him land as you don't own any, Safe Housing aside."

"Right. I need to get him Citizenship, then put his name into every Housing request, and see if I can't find him a spare parcel of land and a house on it."

"You need the Council to approve a change to immigration though."

Rolling her eyes, "and we're on the brink of a political quagmire, bordering on Civil War, so that's not as easy as it sounds."

"When you look at him, you'll be reminded how Thomas is going to keep you from honoring the promise your family made."

She knows my heart well. "Correct."

"And you do not respond well to such feelings."

So well. "I do *not.*"

Returning to the caution, "was he there for the three in your office?"

"No." Swallowing roughly she found solace in her glass of water for a moment. Putting it down, "he tried to be. He was held up saving Patrick, getting Dhavid to a room full of people who needed him, and then the jaunt from the conference room to me was just a bit too long for the three to wait for him." Mulling it over, "not that I've read the report on the conference room yet."

"Cosmo was there, he is," producing an approximation of the Silver Lining Lilt, "still with us."

Closing her eyes her thoughts ran the logistics for her. Clutching herself firmly she let out a choked sob.

"Susan?"

"I, hadn't, thought about it." Lashing out with an angered frustration, "they just wanted to eat cake! To be happy that I was in charge!" Losing the anger to a frustrated sadness the words came unbidden, "share a toast of a cup of tea, or sparkling water. I had been trying to not think about the faces. About those I won't see. I'm not ready to face it."

Rushing to change the subject, "something else then?"

Recovering herself she was thankful for a clean handkerchief, "he, he *is* a good person."

Asking with a parental admonishment, "did you think I would*n't* assume that if you would protect him?"

Bracing her elbow against the table she laid her forehead to rest against her palm, "it was the first thing that came to mind."

Keeping with the parental tone, "is he someone I get to meet at some point?"

Mom isn't here to play mom. You could get to play Mother meeting Courter. Smiling warmly at the thought, "yes."

Asking with an honest inquiry, "does he remind you of anyone?"

"No. He's unique enough that he doesn't cause a full association."

"Is he handsome?"

The Inventory of Honest Appreciation. "No. He's weathered, his jaw is stout, his body is worn by the rigors of what he's been through. He has poorly defined cheekbones. His hands are calloused from years of hard life. But he's in one piece. He doesn't have any melted bits. Or shredded off pieces. As our world becomes easier to live in, we are able to see our more naturally pleasing to behold features shine through. He is not such a beast. But the softness in his demeanor? In his poise? It changes the perception of him inside my mind. He is well toned in his rehabilitation. He needs a new beard though."

"The time is soon to start over and grow it better?"

"Yes. I think when he shaves it, it won't be quite as striking of a face without it. He has a shorter chin, so the beard serves him well."

"You sound like Maggie when she was describing your father the first time after she had laid with him. Not the same details, not at all, but the honest reflections on what made him the person he is and the affection she felt for his imperfections."

The things we could discuss about mom. "I, know we haven't discussed the things she left me."

"When our world is safe? We should."

Affirming the notion, "we will."

Returning to a prior point with her tone of inquiry, "what is going on with your case against Thomas?"

"My dear brother is taking care of that, as the Commander."

"And if he oversteps?"

"I need the Council nervous, you know that."

Retorting with a hint of panic, "why are you doing it this way?"

Feeling the cold tickle of fear caress her thoughts she started in, "because I do not know which of them would have thought this was a good idea. I don't know them like I know you. I don't know them like I *think* I know Holden. I am speaking the most frightening admission that I suspect them. I don't know which of them I can trust or exonerate after the most terrifying night of my life." Swallowing again she took a deep breath to steel herself for the words, "I know that I am saying I don't know which ones of them I can believe had nothing to do with this. I understand the gravity of my implications. I stand by them, needing proof. I don't have *faith,* in this. To that end, I'm cramming all of you into the room with Thomas and demanding that you give me proof before you can let yourself out of the room."

"But that's not," pausing for a moment she made a few helpless noises, "Susan, if they had no idea that this was possible then it will take time to exonerate themselves."

Puffing the air out with an angered frustration she tore into the words, "that's why I told them to not waste time in trying to find me. I have had a rough go of getting into this seat, and to be honest? I don't want to hear face saving words, or promises, I want to hear *facts*. I am out of care for *civility*. The Commander is going to tear into this knowing that he has to have this air tight and unstoppable when he goes before you. If even one of you approved this, and he can prove it but not with conviction? Then we get to look forward to an unending feud in the Council Chambers. This has to be decided, concretely, before we can go forward. So until then? I do what I do best, I spin miracles from dross and make sure every life we can save, is saved. My Citizens, are working harder than they have ever worked, to ensure that our sky can change from red, to the gray it is now, and finally back to blue."

Pleading with her, "why can't you accept that he was working alone?"

Losing control of her temper she settled into the tone and cadence of her father, "a traitorous Consul? False Prophet? The Sys-Admin flipped to his side? By the Ash! You can't tell me that I don't have probable cause for doubt that one of you knew! He didn't want it quiet, he went for loud! He stormed Central Tower and defaced the holy ground of my family! So no, I am not going to *accept* that no one else knew. I want *proof.* The lot of you wanted *proof* of me after changing the rules! You voted to make this happen! You voted to put me on that Throne! And right before, *right rusted before* I would have the security forces to prevent this? A Consul sends a coup into my party! So turn an eye toward your fellows and ask yourself, *where is the proof?"*

Losing her ground in the wake of the verbal outpouring, "I didn't know!"

Losing herself in the anger the words crashed out with a militant cadence, "*you,* don't have to worry. I still hold to the idea that Consul Holden doesn't either. The rest? They *can* worry. Admin Nobody got a promotion to Sys-Admin this morning when one more layer of atrocity was committed! So soon enough? There will be a reckoning and it won't be pretty. It won't be nice at all! And right now? I *don't care.* Let it burn. It is no longer my concern to care for my enemies!"

"Susan -"

"Father told me I couldn't trust you twelve. I couldn't believe in you -"

"Don't -"

Speaking her cold rage to the empty air around her, "so when's their follow-up planned? My next speech? My next trip to the grocery depot? Did you think if you went to them that they would tell you? Let you into their clubhouse?"

Her voice resounding with a devastated sadness, "this isn't you. This isn't you Susan. I called because -"

Slamming her fist into the table hard enough for it to be heard on the other side of the conversation, "they always *made* you do the talking! First for Asmodai, now me! For all I know they're sitting in their little conference call wondering how they're going to get me now that I've cost them more people then they can just throw at a wall and hope they win with! He took those people, he molded them into a fighting force, and he threw them against me in a blood bath because he *could.* Because it was *justified!* Those men outside of my office said they would be *Heroes! Heroes.* Let that sink in."

Breathing heavily in the quiet she heard Amanda's voice come over her earpiece as a sad sob, "that wasn't in any report I had."

I, hate, this anger. Feeling the rage crashing down inside her she hung her head in shame. Taking the moment she could hear her rasping breathing and the pressure of her heartbeat in her skull.

Sniffling Amanda spoke softly, "that is a part of your father I did not miss. The part of Templeton I missed less. Your father could be consoled."

Clutching the table as the fragments of memories played out in her mind's eye, "I know."

"Templeton was worse, he couldn't hold the rage because he had no center. You didn't slander me." Sniffling again she sighed, "your father never slandered me either."

Thinking it over she felt her composure returning, "he never slandered me either. He would apologize, he would lament what he had done, he would feel ashamed because the anger comes too quick and too strong." Daring the question, "did he ever hit you?"

Rushing to reassure her, "no. Your father didn't strike someone he loved in the rage until you."

Feeling the emotional cold taking her energy, "this is such a worthless feeling."

"Maggie kept it in check. She had ways of redirecting his anger. She taught him, guided him, and loved him. He loved her for her faults and through her foibles, and in return she loved him back just as much." Blowing her nose she sighed, "the men at your door wanted to kill you though, to be Heroes?"

Nodding sadly she looked down at the surface of the table, barely able to make out the details through the moisture on her eyes. "Yes. They thought it would make them Heroes. They must have been told about the Mission Statement. About the nature of the peace agreement being a moment of treason if you care to look at it like that. Thomas wants the Fire Maiden. I checked the security on it, its still there. Jerome sent me a report on it. It appears Athens was trying to get the security lax enough that it could be moved under false pretense. I have a few trusted assets shadowing it with Horizon Rifles. If the Hero comment had been let free? People would ask *why*. Those old enough to remember the war are mostly happy it's over."

"So Thomas wants to burn the Ports to ash."

Blinking away the tears she reached for her handkerchief, "yes."

Reaching the conclusion, "and, every Consul has suffered in the wake of the War. So if he had the Fire Maiden –"

Speaking into the empty air as she dried her eyes, "he would blow one up. Build another, blow the other one up. Then build another and blow up The Wheel Spokes Junction, and The Trade Junction Hub."

Asking quickly, "which Junctions are those?"

I'd been meaning to tell you. "The Winter and Summer Freelander power bases."

"We have coordinates on them?"

"We do. Epsilon Code, Seasons of Loathing."

With the awed contemplation evident in her words, "so with a series of bombs, we could end the power bases of every faction that ever fought with us."

Trying to approximate a droll humor with her words, "at the cost of our humanity.

Yes."

"So Thomas doesn't hate you, not exactly."

That would be fair to say. Folding her handkerchief she set it aside as she considered her words, "it's about my name, and the crime we committed when we picked peace as an attempt to keep our humanity."

"Then the Commander is going to do whatever it takes to get Thomas, within the Protocol, so he can show us that we're not untouchable."

"Which is all he can do."

"And you have us in the same room, hoping to Smoke out if anyone else thought the idea of the Fire Maiden's Sisterhood would be the best way out."

This is easier with her knowing what my father did. "Correct."

"If it didn't hurt so much, I would tell you that your father would be proud of your solution as a direct compliment."

Nodding her head she tried to not sound too ashamed, "I would like to think I was listening when he taught me how to survive."

"What about Horse Hair?"

That's tomorrow at the earliest, and that's wishful thinking. "Network isn't there yet. Jerome is working his men with a fervor to get it there. They have to work with the women in the Cathedral first. The plan is a full Firmware Upgrade for the City Network. His note on that says they're very proud of it and they have been waiting to launch it but Athens had been dragging his feet."

"Rust on Horse Hair, a Silver Lining on the Firmware."

"So it's a waiting game on Horse Hair."

"Where is Dagger Herb?"

"She's currently working perimeter on Central. The Scouts drew perimeter detail."

Sounding disappointed, "I understand."

Closing her eyes she felt the agitation of not being able to guess the understood notion. "What?"

"Your father, he would go to Maggie when he needed an anchor. During the time that Micah was around him? He would even go to Micah for an anchor. I worry because I don't know who your anchor is."

"At this moment?" Feeling the awkward sadness of the admission, "I don't have such a person within arms reach."

"Yuri?"

And I return to my fantasy of him in the shower, "I am, whelmed, daunted, and intrigued by the idea. I have been taking care of him. I, don't know what would happen if I turned the tables."

"Worst case scenario?"

I take him to bed and he never gets a choice in the matter. "I use our emotional bond to keep him closer than I had planned."

Sounding underwhelmed, "that's it?"

As he is a gentle beast, and a caring man? "There isn't anything else that has been a possibility that has come up."

"That's, heartening. Would he find you in darkness if you needed to be found?"

I would not be in darkness long. He shines with a radiance when he is near. "I would like to think he would. Is this me, just looking at my parents, and drawing a conclusion as to what happiness looks like?" Sighing she found a question rise to be voiced, "was my mother hard to grow up with? To see her grow, and then meet my father, that sort of idea to my question."

Answering with a quiet reflection, "in the entire time she's been asleep, you never asked."

Replying with a noncommittal tone, "I never wanted to talk about her young life. Or what we lost."

"So now that we've lost so much, it won't hurt as bad."

"Exactly."

"Your mother was a spitfire with a lot on her mind." With humor slowly returning to her voice, "there was a time when we were young that Tim, don't shut me out because of his name, this is almost funny and I'm telling this story for your benefit."

"Go on." Unable to resist a droll delivery of the words, "I'll try to keep my hatred for the dead to a minimum."

"Noted," she continued, "I had been planning Maggie's Sweet Sixteen with Tim. And we had been spending a lot of time together. We were having a good time, without her, and we wouldn't talk about it."

"What did she suspect?"

Sounding both humored and nostalgic, "incest. Straight up told us."

Odd choice, I wasn't there though. "Isn't that listed as prohibited behavior by the Drenner Spiritual Code of Ethics?"

"Correct, and has been since the beginning, listed as prohibited by our Spirit Code."

"Yet she thought you two -?"

"I was already confirmed as unable to bear children. Tim had been supportive during this time. He was without any sort of friend of that type at that juncture. So in her whimsy, and suffering from no small need to deal with her own fire, she had assumed that we were dancing with each other in the flame. Truth be told I didn't have it on my mind with the treatments to try to keep my problems from getting worse."

"So what occurred?"

"She told us of her worries, and how she had interpreted the moments, and even though we had not done anything? It sounded plausible."

Surprised at the humor in her own tone as the words slipped out, "so did you though?"

"See? That's Smoke. Don't think I don't know it when I hear it."

I think I already know this answer, "did Asmodai use it on you?"

Grumbling in reply, "all the time." Restoring her volume and conviction, "there are a lot of things we never spoke of. Things I could tell you about your father now that he's gone."

Putting the idea on the table, "we should schedule that sometime. When the clouds clear."

"When the clouds clear you will come out and we'll make whatever I can find materials for. We'll cook together like we used to."

I could bring Yuri. "And you'll tell me the rest of the story?"

"I will." Taking a breath she sounded somewhat humored as the words came out, "and for the record? Tim never did more with me than easing aches and sickness with liniment. As I in turn never did more with him than applying aloe gel to his sunburns."

"Was it odd to hear the plausibility of your relationship with him and then having to explain that? Watch your world turned upside down and when you right it, it's just never the same? When, mom, when I go through the things she left me? It does that to me."

"Yes. Incredibly odd. Although in retrospect it made it easier to do what we had to do thanks to not being lovers. I think had we been involved like that? What we did to Tim would have been too much to handle."

Wait - "did Maggie? With Tim?"

Laughing softly and then stopping with a far more serious tone, "not to my knowledge."

I will dare the truth, "did she offer?"

"During her explanation? As we sat dumbfounded? She did. Maggie loved us both, and on that day she gave voice to the idea of non-reproductive recreational touch which would land us all in a Guild session to make sure we were all behaving ourselves. Not to mention a House Session to ask why we thought it was a Good Idea. Our Spirit Code is firm on the idea that it is Dishonorable to do so."

"I am aware. As for mom, was she playing?"

With the timbre of nostalgia and longing for the past, "she never said. She did her coy roll of the eyes and 'I understand now.' I know part of why your parents got along is that they both played to win." Taking and releasing a long breath, "now that we're both more like the people we know ourselves to be?"

Keeping it easy on her emotions, "Yuri is my friend. I'm going to tell you to not worry. To trust my judgment on this."

"Will you run Horse Hair when the Network is working again? Will you just leave it on until you stop worrying?"

I do not like feeling this lost. "I'll have to Amanda. I'm scared because I don't know how much I don't know. "

Probing the question with care, "why don't you have your Guard near you?"

I don't trust others to protect our world. "I need them where they are."

"And if people come for Safe Housing?"

Already thought that over. "I hear gunshots on the perimeter? I'll evaluate the moment. If they leave the option? I'll be out in my car and out the emergency road before they can blink. I have enough chaff and smoke charges planted in the front yard they won't see me move."

"You will drive the getaway then?"

"Yes, Yuri drove me home. I was in no shape to drive. I can drive the getaway though. I know the routes better than he would. Also? If I bolt? There is no need for a stand from my kin. They can give chase and have the advantage of battlefield fluidity."

Ceding the point, "good enough."

I wonder, "how are you as calm as you are?"

Replying with a flat admission, "Tranq."

"Oh, I, yeah." *I couldn't.*

"I know you don't enjoy the dose. I, couldn't do it today. I couldn't look at another Red Sky Morning and just *deal* with it."

You have earned your right to Opt Out of Red Skies. "I understand."

"Make some mint tea for yourself and Yuri?"

Good idea. "I think I have some lemon salt in the cupboard."

"Good."

Speaking of drinks, "I, want to see if he'd be comfortable to sit with and have apple tea with."

With a warm encouragement, "then keep him close until winter."

"I will."

"So where is he now?"

Simple enough answer. "In the shower. Something I'm still finding the courage to do."

"I have faith in you."

"I will not be held hostage by fear, I'm going to play this the way I feel it needs to be played. I am going to make whomever is still waiting for Round Two work for it."

"Then we really are in Steven's hands now?"

Even simpler answer. "I have little choice. I don't have recourse to work against this. He does."

"I understand. I don't like it, not at all Susan, but I understand. Don't die on us."

Working to close the moment, "thank you Amanda. I'm going to go. We will speak again when I'm ready to face Consul Drenner."

Replying with a resignation, "Consul Drenner will have to accept that."

Reflecting on the prior moments of anger, *The Bachman Anger, haven't felt that in a while. I feel almost exhausted from it. I need to offer her the best I can.* "Amanda on the other hand can know I don't rightly know a lot of things right now and I'll keep her appraised of things as I can."

Warming back up, "thank you Susan."

"I really need to go now." Pressing the disconnect swiftly she laid the comm down and let the racking sob work its way out of her body. *Maybe I should get some Tranq? No, I can't. I won't do that again. I might be needed to do something I can't do on Tranq. There are nine Consuls left to worry about. Nine. I want to keep Alex off the list. I want to believe in my heart of hearts that she's not in on this. There are missing pieces to this and it's driving me up the wall.*

Picking her comm back up she navigated to 'Communication' and sent a request to Dennis. *I'm certain he'll reply to this. Come make clothes for a Ghost! Get your mind off of everything with me.*

Closing her eyes she listened the sound of the water and the faint male singing voice, *I wish I had a clue as to what he was saying. He would sing in the tub when it was time to bathe him. I got him into the tub in the second week and he would sing songs while he cleaned himself. I know he sings in at least three different languages.*

The strange modesty dance of making sure everything was fine and then stepping outside of the room and around the corner. Sitting in a chair within earshot, and spending more of the time listening to him sing than anything. Even with the light gravel to his tone, he still sounds better than I do. All I could do was listen and appreciate that he didn't hold his situation against us.

Caressing the back of her left hand with her right, her thoughts turned to the two of them, *I told Sasha the truth. I don't know what is which with my feelings for him. Or would it be which is what?* Laughing softly at herself she startled when her forgotten comm chimed.

Picking it up she read the reply from Dennis. Letting out a single chuckle at the speed of his response, *and he'll be here after breakfast. He says work is good for the soul. I'll have to tell Yuri how to handle him. He's a wicked joker when it comes to character judgments and I don't need Yuri getting flustered.*

Laying her head down on the table, then her comm next to her, she let the cold surface try to soothe her savaged nerves. *I'll just stay like this until I hear the water stop.*

3.4.0 - 07:12

Safe Housing – Kitchen

☼ Yuri

Leaning against the wall near the kitchen he reflected on the composure he found himself needing. *The Meal Bar helped. The shower helped more.* Running his fingertips through his hair he curled and uncurled his toes as he regarded the painting on the wall across from him. *Indian Runner Ducks by Rebecca Jelbert. It's very close to what I recall of them.* Looking to the right he took in the sight of the framed picture next to it. Stepping closer he puzzled out what he was looking at.

A young girl with a Khaki Campbell Duck. That looks like the side of a barn behind her. She's pretty. Thinking over his recognition, *I haven't seen a Campbell since Wales. They have ducks.* Smiling at the humor of the idea he felt the bolstering of spirit from the humanity of the notion. *Wonderful.*

Taking a short breath he turned and shuffled into the kitchen with a deliberate shyness, "good morning."

Looking up at him in the same clothes she had been wearing when he fell asleep, the morning light accentuating and highlighting each stain, she replied smoothly, "good morning."

Stepping closer to the table he raised the signal for 'hug,' "if we could share another?"

Nodding with a small smile she rose from the chair and moved around to collide with him. Gripping her firmly he adjusted with her into a more sheltering embrace. *Something has changed.*

Lacing his fingers together across her bicep he leaned and stopped short of kissing the side of her head, "I almost erred."

"It's the side of my head, you can kiss there. It's not the ear, the temple, or the cheek."

Kissing her hair he sighed away from her ear, "what has changed?"

With a hushed sadness, "not enough."

A subject change it shall be, "should I ask about the ducks instead?"

Nodding once she smiled as her vigor returned, "my mother loved ducks. There is a duck colony on the other side of the property, been there since the Second Generation. When she took over the house she made certain that they were not disturbed. She felt it added to the appeal of living out here, to have them over there."

Visitors? "Do they know you are here?"

Shaking her head, "not to my knowledge. Those that work the colony know not to come over. They would invite mother over, and she would bring us, when we were kids."

Tipping his head backwards toward the door, "is Maggie the one in the framed picture in the hall?"

Smiling proudly, "yes. The Drenner Estate has a duck colony of its own. We have a few breeds of ducks we managed to bring with us that respond well enough to being taken care of."

Curious. "She appeared to be next to a barn?"

Speaking the words with a humored reverence, "the Drenner Barns are some of the best barns."

Again I return to items that don't fit together, "estate, barn."

Smiling with a knowing glance at him, "not even those at the highest level are immune to the needs of supplies. Land must be used, supplies must be created, and there is no shame in hard work or the sweat that comes with it."

"Noted." Letting go of her with a gentle regret he looked around, "we are not dead, or invaded."

Without stepping away from him, "Logistics points to an All-In on the Assault, with the Round Two, which has not been ruled out, being reserved for when I make my move. If Consul Kunlow has the forces and drive to continue? *That* is when he will be forced to make his move."

Resisting the urge to embrace her, "so we could be safe?"

Tilting her head to regard him with a smile, "could be, yes." Blinking with a look of recollection she set to moving quickly across the kitchen with a sad laughter, "I *did* prepare something. I found more that you can eat."

Moving to the table he sat down with a relaxed feeling inside of him, "please, don't be so –" gesturing at her, "- everything you are being right now."

Nodding she returned with a mug of something warm and set it down with both hands. "You are a *guest,* in my home, this morning. This is the first time we will sit at a table as equals, friends, and other words of power which mean I am no longer your warden, keeper, or nurse. I'm *enjoying* myself."

Waiving his hand with the palm down and the fingers slack he nodded, "my apologies. I did not know, or understand." Stopping his gesture he moved his hands to the mug, "you do as you wish and express as you will."

Appearing honestly relieved, "thank you."

I did not know she would value this moment. I do now. "Noted."

Looking into the mug he recognized something that had been heavily creamed. *This is going to be indulgent. I could use the comfort.*

I need something to deal with the quiet, "a more personal, about us, question?"

"Ask."

Will this facet change? "Do you always give out hugs so freely?"

Nodding once she appeared contemplative, "I have refused a prompted hug, embrace, or request to be held less than ten times in my whole life. I don't usually prompt others, I *get* prompted. The simple answer would have been yes though. Hugs can be wonderful, therapeutic too."

Offering a supportive counter-point, "though the long form lets me know to prompt as you do not appear to wish to smother me."

Tittering for a moment she moved toward the counter, "mea culpa, smother is for something very specific." Looking back, "do you wish to know either?"

"Smother?"

"As we are romantically inclined adults? That's an intimate term which involves the usage of one body on the face of another. Nothing wrong with that, but it *is* an intimate behavior."

Oh. I think I know what she's talking about. "Then if you hugged me too much? What is that called?"

Removing a plate from a box on the counter he could smell the wafting scent of food as she walked back to him. "As we are romantically inclined adults? If you did not like it? That would be Ceph-a-ling. Named for cephalopod. Aggressive embracing, mate guarding, arms everywhere, and unpleasant." Setting the plate down, "if you did enjoy it? As I am female? I would be Prairie Vole'ing."

Setting the fork down next to the plate her words came as a practiced intonation, "may all be fed."

Replying as Sevilan had taught him, "may all be nourished."

Noting her moving away from him, he turned his attention to the food. Lingering on the bite after the flavors hit him he tried to concentrate on the mash in his mouth to avoid swallowing it out of hand. *Soft bread, light toasting, almond butter, sweet syrup. I need a sip,* picking up the mug he tried the contents, *sweet too. Something dark and robust under the cream and sweetness though.*

Able to speak he smiled, "this is *dessert.*" Looking up he smiled at the glass of water in her hand, "oh, that would be good too."

Setting the glass down she smiled, "coffee doesn't cure thirst when it's creamed and sweetened. So, water too." Reaching into her vest she removed another meal bar and a few more pills that resembled the ones from last night. Setting them down next to the plate she stepped away from him again.

Taking another bite he fought with the surge of hunger. *Reminds me of the bad old days. Keep thinking, slow the chewing,* pushing his discipline he took a deep breath through his nose, *so much to ask. Like, what kind of coffee?*

"I'm steady," holding the fork firmly, "what is the meal?"

Setting to another bite he watched her as she leaned against the counter next to the sink, *she's still wearing the clothes from last night.*

Rattling her way down the ingredients, "Breakfast Bread, almond butter spread, agave syrup, and a small bit of goat butter to thin it."

After clearing another moderate bite he asked, "goat?"

"No cows. We have a lab working on the return of so many things, but it's slow going rebuilding the research of a fallen age."

Swallowing another bite he cleared his mouth with the water, "noted. Also, what is Prairie Vole'ing?"

Blushing slightly she smiled, "it's when a female is very affectionate toward a male. From what we understand of those voles? When they copulate, if the male sticks around for a day? He gets a partner for life. So when a human female is affectionate and sticks like glue to a partner, to inspire them to do the same? She is Prairie Vole'ing."

Taking a long sip from the mug he smiled, "I noticed that, on the radio shows, the stories were often about meeting someone and falling in love with the idea of having a family. At the very least learning more about what it means to love."

Replying with a nonchalant air about the reply, "it's part of The State Initiative in reminding people to find happiness. Have children. The sort of thing a populace needs to continue. There *are* cultural answers for anyone not going the Traditional route and how The State wants them to be happy too."

Dividing the last piece of the bread in two with his fork, "that's good of The State."

"The State gains nothing using oppression. It can find gains using Cultivation, Enrichment, and the like."

Trying to keep his question both light in tone and well mannered, "speaking of Cultivation? Did someone help Cultivate your hugging? Your father gave me an embrace with a caring poise. You have a few different stances to your hugs though."

Shoveling the second to last piece into his mouth he chewed slowly while listening for her reply.

Nodding she opened up with an honesty in her words, "Frank helped, he never turned down my signals. He was there for me when I needed him. He treated me like his own. He was the first person without shared blood who taught me how powerful hanging on to another could be, as he gave me someone to hang on to."

The sad notions of gluing broken people together to keep them from getting lost. "He is a good man from what I have seen. Very fatherly."

"He has been an exemplar of fatherhood. As for children? Which is where most lessons start in some form, as did mine on the ideals of hugging. We teach children to prompt for hugs, and that they *must* be prompted. When they get older we tell them why."

"Which is?" *Last bite.*

"Autonomy. They need to see a world where no one has the intrinsic right to their body or actions in that way. They do not go without hugs, parents aren't told to not care. However, the mutual lesson must be that choices matter, and that they can be made."

Looking at his empty plate, "can people waive the need for a prompt?"

"It happens, as a shared and agreed upon Caveat. Which is not meant to be used as a Leverage Point."

"Example?" Popping the pills he washed them down with a good measure of the water.

Speaking the words with a distancing neutrality, "you give me what I want, and I don't leave."

Setting the glass down with a heavy thud he felt the memories wash over him like a gray tide of sorrow. "You never said anything like that to me, in the whole time I spent in your care, I had forgotten such unfairness was something I have borne witness to."

"I will not dig."

Unwrapping the Meal Bar he nodded once, "thank you."

Switching back to a more upbeat timbre, "you share something in common with Sasha, related to this moment. You do not appear to have a complication regarding hugging or embracing."

Peeling a bite of the bar off he looked to her, "complication? I do not have it about hugging no, but what is it then?"

Elaborating with a cautious lilt, "the nightmares, terrors, that you get. The caution that is recommended when rousing you. That is a *complication*."

Washing done the bite of meal bar with a mild gulp of water he put the words of his question together, "so my issues with being woke up suddenly? Woken? Awoken? How do I put it to another whom is not you?"

Speaking the clarification with a smile, "awoken, which implies someone else is waking you."

Yeah no. "Yes, that, don't enjoy it."

"That is a Complication. If you are afraid someone will wake you and get hurt? You tell them you have a Complication about it. Same with your nightmares."

I can handle that. "Noted." Readying another square of the Meal Bar, "do you have a Complication?"

Regarding him with a slight slumping of her shoulders he could see the sour on her mind as he chewed the bite. *I think I taste peach in this. I like it. Sweeter than her thoughts from the looks of it.*

Dredging up a smile she spoke with candor, "I do. I have a paranoia regarding the thought of food contamination. Not just the thoughts of poison, or sedatives, but the thoughts of something far more intimate than dying." Continuing with a nauseated embarrassment, "the notion that someone might spit in, lick, massage, urinate, ejaculate, or otherwise spill fluid into my food. That in the desire to be closer, or to secretly spite me, they would do such a thing to my food."

Strange. "Odd that you rate that as more disturbing than death."

Returning to her tones of practicality, "if I am dead? I am dead. If I am sedated? I will be rescued. If there is something *else* in my food? I am most likely not going to know until it is consumed. At that point? The other person has provided something my body is going to try to digest, take nourishment from, and bond with my cells."

I missed an opportunity to think of it that way, to share that, and to nourish the hearts of those I have been with. "You just shared an incredibly romantic notion, the other side of that coin."

Smiling with a shy embarrassment, "so you see the validity of my paranoia?"

She needs to be less difficult with herself. "One hundred percent! If *that* is how you feel about it? Then I can see why you would want no one doing such a thing to you." Thinking it over he found words, "you should combine the idea of what passes for being careful with looking at it as a spiritual taboo. Could? I don't want to be too demanding with my helping. I would just caution about using *paranoia,* as you and yours stress clarity of language as so important."

Looking down he could still see her smile, "noted, and thank you."

Tearing off the next square, "wait, you asked me if I could cook, and would cook for you?" Tossing the square into his mouth he waited for her reply.

Looking back up at him, "that's simple, I trust you to *not* do it. You've cooked for many people, in many lands, and I thought it would be a novel experience to taste your dishes and take on food. Meanwhile my complication was not worried as you did not strike me as the type to contaminate my food. And not just because you spoke of how most of the dishes you know are communal pot dishes."

Clearing his mouth with a more disciplined sip he smiled, "I will not fight you on your appraisal of me. I will just be thankful that is the man you see, as that is what I was hoping to show."

Smiling with a confident timbre, "then we stand together."

"We do. Now, I have the nightmares, and the waking, that I know of. Do you have something other than the food?"

"I also have a complication about lying. I have the Liar's Lilt. It's a behavioral issue where the idea of being caught in a lie is so *something* that it's almost impossible for me to pull off a lie."

So is that what that has been? "So the tone when you showed me your *car*?"

Nodding with an embarrassed affirmation, "yes. That's the Lilt."

Big question time, "how do you live as a politician if you cannot lie?"

Straightening up with a firmness to her words and tone, "I don't have to. I am not elected. I am not asked by the people to tell them lies to make them feel better. I am the Strong Leader, the one who knows who can get what done. I tell those people what needs to be done first and foremost. The people know me by my strength."

"Do others get in your way?"

Without losing the firmness she continued, "not normally. The Pyramid of Power is a tight one. At each stage of the life of a Citizen? They will see a limited sized government of those who *rule,* but a larger body of those that *do.* It's the advantage of the system we have. Results and Morale are our top concerns. We have been living hand to mouth for seven generations, the Arcologies were no different, which has left no room for Ruling by Committee."

"I understand more now."

Still firm but with more humor, "I am not here to be pampered, or beloved, because I *exist.* I am here to do what I have spent my life refining my craft of, that I am not as learned in as I would like to be, and that is to make sure that things get done. Even I have to earn my Rations. I am beloved for what I make happen, not because *I* happened."

Intoning the word with a tone of awed appraisal, "impressive."

Lowering her intensity she spoke the words as a quieter afterthought, "I am not ashamed of the quality of the work I give my nation."

Oh, good question time, I hope. "You have not mentioned shame, nor the radio, where is that? Is that a thing?"

"Shame," moving her hands in a gesture he did not know, "is our silent corrective rudder and sinker of esteems. It is the feeling of shortcoming, that one feels a painful revelation regarding. The Social Contract enforces a rule upon people, and some bear the shame of failing that harder than others. If we could help people escape their shame, and just logically accept their misdeeds? Then we could speed up the healing time. Instead we still suffer from it."

I already know the yes or no answer as yes, but I will ask to hear the rest. "Even you?"

Opening up with a quiet tone of confession, "when I am at my private parties, and watching the show, with my glass of alcohol in my fist? I feel a measure of shame at the indulgence. At the spectacle I invoke for my own benefit. Or when I'm alone with a comic book. As much as our culture writes us pardons, we don't always accept them."

I need to find something brighter, "what is something you do not feel shame for?"

Smiling with the return of her pride, "my outfits. I have been shy at points, but never ashamed. Textile Expression is important, and not feeling shame is important when it comes to that."

Understand the roots of the lesson, "what do you teach the children?"

Still smiling, "to cherish their school uniform. To accept that they are all garbed from the same set of ideas and ideals, based upon their bodies and tastes in the issue, because they should be on a level field as Students. They have not joined the Adult World, so they can all sit together as a single faction. They can do a limited set of personalizing modifications, but they must abide by the rules. Then in their own time? They can be as they are."

To be the self is to know the self. "Be as they are?"

Nodding with a mild excitement, "to be as well dressed or overly comfortable as they choose. Wear pajamas all day? Go for it. If it's your time? Then it's your time to spend dressed as you choose. However, even then, when visited by others and they are found to still be in their pajamas? That out of place, out of sync, or intimacy of the moment can catch them in a shame. From there the lesson gets expanded to knowing that dressing for the Endeavor is not an absolute maxim. It's a helpful guideline. It's another lesson to teach people to cope with."

That's a nice lesson. "Noted."

"The home is a Shared Space, as is the School, so when dressing for an Endeavor you end up with people whom are dressed to match the location and the mood. Idea, execution, and variables collide to make moments which can be quite taxing. Examples include, but are not limited to, wanting to spend the day wearing your cutest night-wear, and being found in a *comfortable recline.*"

Feeling the heat on his face he nodded in understanding, "I understand, and will ask no further."

Smiling at him with a hue of red on her face, "thank you."

They've come a long way from fig leafs. "Your society sounds vary caring, again." *She mentioned uniforms and standing as equals,* "so the children, who are students, are they divided into different schools based upon economic standing?"

"No. One standard of education, high, and one educational institution serving a given grouping of studies based upon the age of the student."

"Just one?"

"For each chronological band. They're quite large, to be easier to gather the children in one place, have all the resources they could need, and to be defended in times of trouble."

Practical to a fault. "Noted."

Continuing on her point, "the uniforms are based upon age, body, and seasonal weather. Meant to mute the form, be as comfortable as possible, and lend to the goal of a cleared mind while studying."

"So does The State, of course it does, yes? Sees to the uniforms?"

Responding with an excited pride, "it does! All active Citizen Tailors give a pledge of a number of students they will make uniforms for, and of what type, and then The State matches it up from there. Tailors are compensated by The State with Rations for the work, and the Tailors only make the items they are comfortable with."

They volunteer, and if they fall short? "And if there is a shortfall?"

Replying with the simplicity of the answer, "then The State turns to State, not Citizen, Tailors and orders the rest from them."

Let me see if I remembered the term, "so Citizen Tailors are free associating?"

"To an extent, yes. In the last two decades we have been refining and improving the economic systems that allow for something resembling economic autonomy for those that wish to pursue Art."

Time to toss out a dangerous question, "the people need autonomy?"

"They do. They need it as part of Human Nature. If we stagnate them? They will rot and die. Those that can innovate and stand on their own? Do. Those that wish to be provided for in a deeper way with less freedom? The State takes care of them."

Sounds sensible enough. "Is that in the big book of smarts?"

Pursing her lips in the appearance of denying laughter, "The Protocol? Yes."

I almost got her to laugh. "Then you have a chapter on How to Care and Nurture Tailors?"

"Not in so many words. However, the clothes make the moment. If you look good, you feel good."

"Noted, I follow." *Might as well,* "did you have a uniform growing up?"

Pointing at him with a shy smile her words were delivered with a featherweight force, "I note your grin. However, I will be disappointing you. I did not have a traditional school uniform. I'm a Bachman. I was kept away from the Halls of Academia. I was raised on private lessons, tutors, and the like."

I should clarify, keeping his tone light in reply to her featherweight tone, "I smile because I cannot fathom you as a young miss. Were you always tall? Were you as social then as you are now?"

Nodding with an understanding look she smiled anew, "I have been tall since I was a child, only made far more pronounced when I struggled my way through pubescence. Thankfully as I had an understanding tailor I was not left in a disheveled or mismatched state for long after a growth. Even though I struggled with my body? I still went to where the other youth my age were. Frank would chaperone, or Hugh, his second. I did a great job of wearing wide brimmed hats and serving as a walking landmark so no one could get lost."

Always looking out for others. "I am far more heartened than I thought I would be this morning."

"Good."

Looking at the empty mug with what appeared to be some sort of chicken on the side, "so you mentioned this was coffee?"

"Yes. Thanks to being in my house you get coffea coffee."

I was told coffea was extinct. "I've never had coffea coffee."

Smiling with a simple salute of her mug, "now you have."

Smiling in return at the simplicity of the moment, "okay then."

Moving toward him she picked up his empty glass of water and moved back to the corner of the kitchen. *I will inquire so I understand, as next time I will not be a guest.*

"Tell me of your magical water tower?"

"Cute question, the truth is just what it is though." Gesturing at the edifice, "the drum is mounted on an anchored platform. Ceramic lined water storage with handy spigots. Each spigot is calibrated to the amount of water you need and then it shuts off.

The glasses are measured to State Standards. This house is out far enough that it's just easier this way." Filling the glass briskly she returned to him with a smile. Setting the glass back down next to his hand, "you're in a safe place with clean water."

"Noted, and thank you."

Nodding she set to moving back to the counter, "noted."

"Did you eat?"

"I drank a single serve carafe of Liquid Meal, have had too much coffee, and a slice of Breakfast Bread with the same spread as you did. I did eat to combat the hunger. Even with the stress I could not deny myself eating."

Watching the light highlight the blood droplets in her hair, "no shower then either?"

"Not yet, no." Shaking her head softly she sighed, "anxiety from the attack makes it hard to trust the idea of relaxing like that. I am just declining my own offer of being a stronger person."

Simple question. "What if I offered to sit outside and protect you?"

Pursing her lips together she smiled before shaking her head once, "then I would be afraid of wanting you to be on the inside of the door. To know you were there."

Taking his glass of water firmly in hand he nodded, "I can't say I have been this well liked in some time."

"I was taught by the Albatross to be mature and honest with my feelings. I hope you don't take my declining to chase them as a barb."

Oh, easy answer. "No, that part of the fire went down to embers years ago. Many years ago? I would have asked you the harm, before I learned the harms. It's not a big deal. You will get a shower at some point today though?"

Replying with an affirmation of the idea, "I will get a shower in when my nerves calm down enough to trust that moment to be a good moment."

"I will accept that."

"Noted. As I don't know what it means if you did not."

Words. Thinking over the words he knew he pieced together something he hoped would convey his heart, "I would make a demand. I would stand before you, plead, and push until you did what I wanted because I would feel it was for your own good."

Nodding she smiled to his surprise, "did you hear about the Service Rangers?"

"I heard a jingle on the radio about them, but I do not know what they do, no."

Answering with a matter-of-fact lilt to her words and smile, "they do what you just said."

"So you smile -?"

Without losing the smile she spoke with care, "as you have stated you would abide, but that your demand is from a place of care if it came to that. You're trusting me and not calling the Service Rangers."

A small revelation, but a good one. "I understand more now."

"Even though, I could see you being sorely tempted when I settle up with Thomas, to call them after."

Do I need to be ready for something? "Oh?"

Losing her smile she looked back down at the tile, "he ordered this, he convinced people to follow his heart and do this. We have study upon case study about the power of power. With his power as a high ranking member of The State? He would be covered in credibility in the minds of those listening. We hear what we want to believe. We are haunted by our doubts. And the Shadow whispers what it wants you to *know,* and when those whispers become a speaking volume? The doubts at oh two-hundred become the words of the waking hours."

The things I have been haunted by under the night sky. "I have heard the whispers of the Shadow in my travels. Dhavid, he talked to me about no small amount of the hurt. When you were not around, he was one to talk to me."

Saying the words with an encouraging tact, "men care for men, Brothers Keeper."

Am I not? What did they do with the words? "That is a phrase burdened by an ancient notion."

Looking up with a warmth to her words and demeanor, "we redefined it too. The Conlangers moved keeping to the idea of a Keep. To be Kept is to be protected within the walls of something. So instead of stating that brothers treat brothers as sheep? To be a brotherly Keeper is to protect, shelter, and provide safety for your brother."

"You knew that so readily."

Countering with a quick explanation and an upbeat tone, "I have two brothers. One of which takes looking after his little brother *quite* seriously. I have no doubts in Steven's convictions to get Thomas because he sent forces to hurt his little brother too. I can be the Derecho, Patrick can be the Director, but Steven is still Eldest Son at heart."

That would be heartening if it was not so frightening. "Noted."

Visibly mulling the idea over she offered her words as an explanation, "I am not surprised that Dhavid would see to you. He's an Asclepius Cloak. They do tend to people, almost out of instinct from what I've seen of it."

Nodding he tapped his arm where Dhavid's Asclepius patch had been, "I asked him about the staff with single snake, the patch on his sleeve." Thinking back on his words when he last saw him, "so," trying for a humored turn of the phrase, "it turns out he wears his heart on his sleeve."

Smiling with a quiet sniffling of humor, "he does."

Reflecting on his conversations with Dhavid, "I spent no small amount of time just trying to find my center, get my bearings, and I wish I could have been more active in my conversations with him."

Raising her hand in a gesture she spoke with a thankful tone, "he's not dead."

She's right. "I'll send him a message when we are clear of things, and I have the power to send messages. I will see if he would like to speak at least one more time. Make sure we are a settled idea."

Nodding once with a grin, "good."

Rolling his glass between his palms once, "speaking of settled ideas, I am safe now?"

Answering with a quiet affirmation, "yes."

Setting the glass down he looked up from the water to her, "what changed?"

Other than everything.

Visibly picking her words carefully, "evidence to the contrary was created. My worry, was that Steven would generate evidence that you were not a valid addition to our world. You," gesturing to him softly, "generated a body of work, evidence, and proof of intent strong enough that no one would follow his order now."

They can defy him because I am ally to them? "So he cannot order me dead, even though I am a Ghost?"

Shaking her head she smiled with reassurance again, "he can order it, but no one has a reason to follow it, so they would not. He also cannot do it himself as he has no evidence now."

Wait, "and the family of those I put to rest, would they seek my death?"

Losing her smile she spoke with a humored flatness, "I cannot speak for them."

Tapping the table he narrowed his eyes in confusion, "you just said I was safe though."

Firing back with a cavalier attitude, "safe, within the parlance, is no active threats." Raising a hand to him gently, "we cannot predict that which we do not know."

I follow! "Ah! So the danger of getting killed out of hand is gone, but not the actions of someone whom would want me dead regardless. But that also goes for you?"

Retreating back into her tile gazing, "yes!"

"Noted!" Mulling the matter over, "so your people like me?"

Looking back to him with a grin, "so much. They've already dubbed you The Gingerbread Son, meanwhile there are a few whom are stating that you should not be defined by your ancestor, which means something more appropriate to the man they do not know is needed."

I am a Hero of the Folk perhaps? "Humbling."

Nodding once, "yes."

I should be clear in my understanding of something so important. "So Steven cannot shoot me?"

Shaking her head in decline, "not without evidence now. Otherwise he violates the Intrinsic Human Rights Protocol."

"Is that what stopped your father in the garage?"

"Most likely. You were not presenting as a threat, so even though you were within Striking Distance, you were presenting as someone whom needed care more than a fight."

"How did no one shoot me out of habit?"

"Training. The Training for everyone who has a gun is a series of evaluation and mental short-cut conditions. They are direct responses to the moment, and not a sequence. I will demonstrate a few for example." Touching her hip as if to draw an invisible gun, "the question is posed."

Moving as if she was drawing she rested the figment against her hip, "I accept the escalation."

Adjusting her stance she held the figment gun at a forty-five degree down angle, "you are seeking trouble."

Raising her arms and nearly laying her cheek against her bicep, "I accept your death."

Lowering her arms she sighed, "those are a few of the stances and short-cuts. Even if six people have guns on belts, it's *not* a declaration of war. As we only point when we intend to shoot? Until we are pointing a gun at another person, we have not declared that we are going to, or wish to, open fire with the intent to kill. If we do not intend to kill? Then a less-lethal weapon will be in hand."

Reflecting on the idea, "so the gun is very serious, even if you have so many."

Responding with a small gravity to her conversational timbre, "just laying your hand on your weapon is the question posed of, is this moment going to become a gunfight. *Every* Citizen is taught this. Many Citizen's do not use hip holsters for that reason. We maintain peace, even with all the guns, by assuring that each person knows that a buckled gun in holster is nothing to fear. But instead the declaration of wanting to be ready for the unknown. Anyone who carries a gun, as a professional, is also carrying at least one less-lethal weapon they are also trained with to be ready to fight with."

The best weapon though, "and words?"

Smiling and talking with her hands as the words flowed, "words are the greatest diplomatic weapon. The Militia is trained to be loud with their words, but polite. Speech coaches for how to shout but not yell at, by default. For examples."

This is making more sense now, "so when I appeared, guns still tucked under my arms - ?"

Assuming his stance from that night, "you were a wayward gunslinger. Hands open and in visible sight."

I was not deafened with orders though, "no one yelled at me."

Lowering her hands, "the Watchmen are not trained to yell. They are quiet in their duties. Complex words can be hard to shout, so they do not shout. Also, shouting leads to aggression. Domination. Orders given. They needed you to feel *safe.*"

Looking down at his hands, "he took my hands quickly."

Offering the words quickly with hope, "hand holding is powerful."

I will ask, as I see a lesson she wants to teach me. "It is?"

Coming over to the table she sat down on the chair next to him on the north side of the table. *I have the East side. The door from the bedrooms is to the East. Not just the sun rises in the East I see.*

Tapping his knee with her right hand she smiled, "take my hand."

Following through on the gesture he smiled as the feeling of her hand wrapped around his. "I like this. Meaning?"

Dropping her volume to something still easier to hear at the small distance between them her timbre was solemn but friendly, "I know we both favor our right hands in gunplay, so the hands that take life, affirm life."

Joining her in the friendly but solemn timbre, "so when you do this with Sasha, it is her left to your right?"

"Yes."

"Tell me more?"

"In the Network we know of the concept of Bloodstained Hands. That once you take life the Shadow tells you that your hands are unfit to hold love, children, or goodness. I place my hand in your hand, affirming life."

Again, I sit in a land made more Holy. "You did not tell me my hand did not have blood on it."

Speaking the words with the simplicity of the idea, "human life is human life."

So much that could be taken from that. "Are your enemies human?"

"Persons with personhood? Names we may never learn? Yes, and yes. When you were at Central, no one was going to just *shoot you for fun* –"

Wincing he squeezed her hand gently, *seen it.*

"Yuri? I was worried that my brother would convince someone that you were a *threat* to me. When father stayed the hand of the Watchmen? He was answering their question. When I gave the no shoot order to Frank, I was answering his question."

The depth of this. "I understand more."

"The men outside won't come in, because seeing me next to you? *That,* answers their question."

Endorsed by the Highest with just a simple touch. "I, was worried."

Speaking the words like a Pledge, "I am with you."

Opening up the words tumbled out, "you have been with me, this whole time. You are like an Angel, -"

Squeezing his hand she spoke her words into his faltered moment, "no. That's the Pedestal, and I do not crave the height. I could find wings made of duck feathers, a halo of bent wire, and a drape from fine sheets, but I would not be the being you describe. I am not outside of the potential of woman in these lands. I was just raised with an emphasis on my talents."

A land of such women? "I would like to see that though, you dressed as the Angel."

Smiling with a shared humor, "I would be quite the sight."

"What are your talents called?"

"Sympathy, empathy, social awareness, and enough mindfulness to stay flexible while under duress. From there? Cultivated skills from years of effort to gain the understanding of what I know how to do in regards to martial skill, driving ability, and the ability to blend in with a moment."

They raised her to do this. "So you are an excellent leader."

"I would like to say I am a functional leader. Beyond that? I know who has allied themselves with me that I can call and gain aid from. My father was a stronger fighter, and a far more ruthless tactician, than I may ever be. My goal is to take care with our Nation and our people knowing that they will be in a better place than when I started. Also, to make sure that the next generation has a Bachman to lead them."

"Solid goals."

"I do my best to stay humble in the face of my standing."

As you were humble in my care, I have seen it. "Noted."

"In this moment," squeezing his hand with a disarming smile, "neither of us can draw. It is a gesture, which can be moved to hand on inner forearm, to remind the two involved in a moment that they are not at odds."

Did she mention what I thought I heard? "What are Intrinsic Human Rights?"

"Your life, your freedom, and property. You did not try to take the life of the High Consul, so he did not harm your life. You were sick and in a strange land, so he kept you in a room to recover. Also, your clothes, possessions, and guns are in this house to be returned to you and brought back into your life. To violate those items would be to Violate your Human Rights."

I sit in awe. "Even though I am not a Citizen?"

Meeting his gaze, "you are still a Human."

Without looking away, "are your enemies Human?"

Clucking her tongue she sighed with a small nod, "yes."

Closing his eyes he nodded once, "I sense a deeper set of questions and fears."

"Yes."

Opening his eyes again, "something else then, perhaps, *noted.* What else can I use that for? It seems powerful, but I don't want to understate something by saying noted when I might need something else."

Smiling brightly she nodded twice as her humor returned, "noted *is* powerful. The Conlangers wanted a universal reply that would be modified by a secondary partner term so we could affirm that we had heard someone. From the easy, as you have figured out, someone says something, you reply with *noted.* You can add emotional inflection, if you can, if you want to color the noted. If you don't trust the tone of your voice? Or the person is deaf? Or if they're not very good with tonal cues? You gesture with your noted using our sign language. So from something as playful as flirting to as serious as declaring your hate? You can use *noted* as your foundation stone."

I will ask. "Flirting? I will follow if you will lead, how does this work?"

Appearing to be fighting for an even tone and placid facial expression, "the time you kissed me, on the shoulder, right near my neck –"

You did not admonish me then, don't appear to be doing so now, speaking his words with an honest fondness for the moment, "I remember the moment, yes."

"If two people are unsure of that which is between them, they declare it. So instead of just, kissing my neck, if you had doubts? You would declare it."

Nodding once he smiled. Trying to sound confidant he spoke softly, "I want to kiss your neck."

Tipping her eyes up she met his gaze for a moment and spoke with a breathy encouragement, "*noted.*"

She is fire. Taking a deep breath he closed his eyes with a shudder against the rush of the moment. Hearing her chair move he felt her embrace him. *I do not wish to get burned.*

Leaning into her he felt the calming effect of her gentle ministrations. Concentrating on the feel of her hand he found his calmed center restored. *I haven't felt this in some years.*

Taking a moment to breathe he found a smile, "I can feel why you are careful."

Probing the question with her tone, "as this is the good kind of scary?"

"I agree, concur, and such." Laughing the moment off, "Susan, you are something else."

Lowering the dramatics she smiled still, "I strive to be something more. It's expected."

"Do your people know this side of you?"

Clicking her tongue against her teeth once she shook her head softly, "no."

"Do you want them to?"

"I honestly don't know. I haven't been the High Consul long enough to say for certain."

"Are your people worried?"

Slumping against him she sighed, "I have over five thousand pending messages in a special inbox for Citizens to send me messages, to sort over later, as they do not have Clearance to send me direct messages."

Reaching up with his left hand he dared to minister to her stained hair, "do you have Clearance to send *them* messages?"

"Only if I use the High Consul Messaging Application."

She is back to the usual self I know, good.

Continuing she explained, "it's a specific function on my comm where I send a logged message, contents and all, to them. So anything I message as the High Consul is public knowledge. If I want to keep a secret? I have to go find them, and say it to their face. It's one of the things that controls the power dynamics."

A Tradition of Honest Statesmen? "Easier to just say it in person."

"That's what my father liked about it. No Citizen in New Hope and the outlying area was safe from him and his presence. And if he did not have something nice, which includes being constructive, to say? He would do something else while he processed his response to them. His second would often help him puzzle out the opinions of people so he would understand the context of what was said that had offended him." Taking a moment to lean into his embrace she continued, "so no, the High Consul can't just pull out their comm, type out that someone is a rusted so-and-so, and then send it to them with a smugness of being powerful. That's not part of the position."

"That is good." Reaching over with his left hand he picked up his glass of water and sipped from it, "I will get used to your, *this,* world sooner than later I hope." *Did she say five thousand?* "That's no small amount of messages."

Reaching up with her left hand she placed it on his glass with a questioning flex of her fingers. Surrendering the glass to her, she went about quaffing half of the contents before giving it back. *I would rather share than lose this moment.*

"There was a press release that Wallman put out earlier this morning asking that those who had not sent a message please wait a day or two to give me a chance to go over at least a few of them. Get them sorted. Reduce network traffic. All of the above."

"Do they normally send you messages?"

"Not like this. It's filtered too, so I don't get to see the things I shouldn't. The non-reproductive recreational invitations, if you will, topping the list of things, to be exact. I have a Fan Club, I have people who send me things, including direct messages hoping I will read them. I have a small group which cycle through listening to the messages, sorting them, and then getting things moved along to the people who need to know more than I do, if that's needed. However, if I *do* need to see it? They send it to me. To be fair most Citizens might not know how to send me a message, as it is not something people are taught, it's something people have to find."

Finishing the water he set the glass aside, "I see. Impressive, as usual."

Nudging him gently she spoke with a rush of joy, "if you're wondering, I would give you Clearance if you had a comm unit. To be able to call, message, the works." Stopping she clucked her tongue gently, "I mean that when you *do* get a comm unit, you *will* get Clearance."

Smiling with a short chuckle, "noted."

Looking back down at their shared space, "I would just ask that you don't text me about what happened the other night. I cleaned that up in a way that there's just six people who know, that I know of. You, myself, my doctor, the Sys-Admin, Cloak Yorklin, and Sevilan. I did my best to keep it as small of a pool of people who know."

Trying to keep it as light as he could, "I had wondered."

Without looking up her tone dropped again, "I mopped it up myself. It was part of why I didn't want to talk to you. I didn't know what to say."

She mopped up the murder? "Mea –"

Interrupting him with a voice of authority, "stop."

This needs to be a mutual thing.

Experiencing the fires of anger failure to light, in the wake of her presence against him, he moved his arms. Taking her into a firm barrel hug he sighed. *I do not have the heart to be angry about this.*

Speaking his words as a soft and sad question, "why do you get to take culpability but I do not?"

With a tone that spoke of emotional gravel she spit the words out, "I don't want your *debt.*"

She does not want this? "So *if* I say mea culpa for it?"

Embracing him fully in return, "you give me the debt of doing what you did. We don't actually claim culpability for everything we do wrong. Sometimes we do something, *wrong,* but we don't want to take it back. Or if we do not feel that it was something that we *should* offer our culpability for? We *again,* do not say it."

Touching her hair gently again, "so as you do not wish my debt for what I did –"

Reaching up and taking his hand she sat up and out of their shared slump, "I don't want it. If you give it?" Taking his hand with both of hers, "I get your life. You killed him, if you say mea culpa for killing him? That's the admission that you *owe* me a life. With only your own life to give? You staple yourself to me until the day you feel you've paid it back. I, asked, the heavens for help. Others wanted a way for this to end. For a *resolution.* You, answered, that prayer. I *asked* for this."

I am God's Will? Leaning his left elbow against the table for support he lowered his head, "I was afraid you hated me, for ending him."

Speaking softly she replied after a pair of deep breaths, "Yuri, no one, could save him alone. We were trying to find a way to bring him down without people knowing and having to pull apart the threads of what he did versus the good he did." Looking to her he could see the tears escaping her eyes, "he did things people don't even know created the foundation of our modern times. The extreme side of not wanting a debt, of not wanting to hear it, is that I feel we would be better off if we don't do *this* with him in mind. I don't want you next to me," rushing the word, "*because,*" calming herself she smiled with a benevolence, "you owe me. I would prefer it because you *want* to be here. For the joy of life."

Taking in the sight of her smile he found another small revelation of sense, "noted."

Focusing her attention on him with a softness to her demeanor she smiled with a melancholy, "I have debts I did not want, but I could not refuse. Thank you for accepting that I do not want your debt. We can move from that phase, to the healing process. That's a *much* better place."

I am curious, but should not be. "I should not ask of the secrets of others."

"Yuri, do you regard what you did as something you should give your life for?"

To be truthful, I had not pondered if I felt I should be punished if we were each other. Cocking his head to the side he looked into her eyes as the unfathomed question washed against him, "I had not thought of it as anything other than the way it happened. Not me speaking for me, or roles reversed, just you and me and what occurred."

Still holding his hand, "what was your motive?"

Simple. "To save you."

Lobbing the questions with a gentle intellectualism, "what was the motivation? Your observed evidence?"

That's simple too. "He appeared to be trying to kill you."

Cupping his hand with both of hers, "so why do you owe me a life debt?"

Is this what her forgiveness feels like? Or the idea of not needing to be forgiven? "I, don't know."

Leaning in she nuzzled his hand before settling it in a comfortable two handed embrace, "I don't either." Looking up with a tired smile, "I've had my days to go over it. To pull it apart. To listen to what Frank and Dhavid shared. To come to my conclusion that I did not want to see you dead, or enslaved, for what you did."

Best of intentions collides with grim reality, "I understand more now."

"I will give you this, as empathy, it took me days to understand what I was feeling. It was confusion, repressed and suppressed feelings, and then I found a way to untie the knots. To balance it by looking at the fact of the matter. It did *appear* that he was going to end me. You acted based upon the evidence of defending another. If he was going to take my life, you would take his first, and it was as it was."

No Lilt. "I do feel a bit better now."

"I don't like feeling ignorant, slow, stupid, dumb, or like an idiot, which *yes,* do each carry a different meaning in our dictionary. And as I puzzled it out, and fought for meaning, I felt a measure of all of them in the whispers of the Shadow."

Laughing at her with a morose humor, "you people."

Letting go with her left hand she tapped him on the arm playfully, "of whom you will be one, officially, soon enough."

I feel like I'm dreaming. "Surreal."

Offering as a play on the moment, "with a bowl of cereal, if you wish it."

And we return to the milk. "Do I get milk with it?"

Taking his hand with hers again as her humor shifted to something more somber, "it's included in the Grocery Depot box. You can't forget it, because they make sure you leave the building with it."

"Good." *Perhaps this will restore the good mood,* "you mentioned that you, standing next to me, was a character witness. You vouch for and validate me with your presence. Does *my* presence, next to you, cause others to think things?"

Grinning shyly she rubbed his shoulder with her left hand.

She is holding my hand with a fondness. Squeezing the affirmation he waited patiently.

"There is a picture floating around. Being shown, as part of the character witness of your presence. It's you, and me, and it shows you getting into my car to drive me home.

No one, in the history of The Beast, since I became his designated driver, has driven him. No one has driven me home before. People are going to assume that you are someone incredibly special to me, when they see that picture. And when they ask who you are, and someone says that you are the Gingerbread Son, as there is no Epsilon Code on that bit of information? They could see it as a witness of good things to come."

"I am humbled to be so vaunted, and such."

"One day it won't be the vaunted honor, it will just be the day to day. People will wake up, and not see you as your title, or your implications, but as Yuri."

Sounds nice. "I look forward to that day."

Nodding in agreement, "I do as well."

Oh, wait. "Do they think we could be closer than we are? Is that possible? Probable?"

"Yes, they *could.*" Taking a pause she smiled with the hint of a flush, "you are a man of marriageable age, who fits the criteria of the kind of man I would pursue, who has a freedom to be next to me that no man has ever had."

"Oh?"

"There will be the question of my children. I can't have them with Sasha. She can help me raise them, but she's missing a key thing we would need to have them together."

That's putting it politely, "yes."

"For the roles of governance? We do blood lineage inheritance to the roles of power, *then,* if no children are found that can be used for the roles? The family is queried for applicants. If that fails? Then it goes into a more general pool of talent."

Curious, "so a Citizen could become a Consul?"

"Yes. It's built into the system that if a Consul Family should falter and fall over? That the Citizens would have to be ready for the rise of a new Family. As for mine? The High Consul has been a direct blood Bachman for five iterations now. The idea is that the Bachman's were going to be a larger family to provide insurance and variety in points of view. Then, my family failed to populate a family tree with any notable success."

What would stop them? "What happened?"

"We proved to be unlucky in love, life, or staying alive. The nation has been doing well enough all things considered on the other hand. The General Population is doing well."

"So I would be seen as your kind of guy, alone with you, and you *are* looking for a Husband whom would get along with Sasha." *I -,* "I think I'm blushing."

"You are." Touching her cheek with her free hand, "I think I am too."

Looking to her and seeing it appeared to be true, he nodded, "you are."

"So there will be some who will be pointing out that you are The Gingerbread Son, I am the Derecho, and we are alone."

Swallowing as the idea, long buried, came to light, "oh my."

Reaching out she touched his arm gently, "yes."

I need to change the subject, for both of us. "What is going to happen to those whom are still alive? From the attack. That went with the medical persons."

Looking to him she gestured a series of motions before sighing, "this," holding her hands up toward him in a disarray of fingers, "was me trying to thank you for something we would return to."

"I will endeavor to learn quickly."

Gesturing with the words, "thank you."

Broaching the subject with a hesitance, "so, the people -?"

Nodding once she spoke with her neutral tone, "they are called the Blackout Bloc now."

"Elaborate?"

With a mix of a frown and a smile she answered, "I covered the paperwork about them in so much High Consul Blackout, that they gained the name. I did not want them known as Kunlow, because I did not know the future. I am not on the front line of that Endeavor now." Looking at him with a sad appraisal, "you though, might be called after things are settled if you are needed to help settle things, and would do so."

"In what capacity?"

"You fought against them. They *might* need to see you to broker peace. To state that they are not going to offer further aggression and to know you are not going to offer them any either."

Do we go to this together? "Does that go for you?"

"It *could.*"

"So no Gulag for them?"

"We do not have such a place. We will either find a way to gain peace with them, or they will be removed. The Guild of Psychiatric Care and Psychological Study, they are going to take in as many as will come under their wing. They know that The Commander will not hesitate to *solve this.* He plays the role of the Dark Merchant in a Market of Ideas."

She didn't quite answer. "So if not the Gulag? Where else do you send them?"

"If peace cannot be brokered within the city of the offense? Other cities. Each city has signed and ratified the Accord of New Seasons. In the Accord is the agreement to send our unwanted to each other. The trains and planes which serve as the binding agreement ferry our people around. The condemned are sent elsewhere to live their days trying to put together a new life and become something else."

That would not work for a Consul though. "There is no such place for Thomas Kunlow."

Offering her answer with a flat anger, "the other side."

I am not surprised. "Noted."

"This goes beyond temporary State Custody, or the admonishment of the Drunk Bin, the Long-Term Psychiatric Care Center, this is something we're going to have to write the Protocol for, and hope we never have to use it again."

"Noted." *I wonder,* "I was told half of the forces were Civilian. I did not study them long, I just placed my bullets and stayed in motion. No small amount of cover was taken advantage of in that well furnished castle."

"Confirmed, and noted."

They have spoken of being short on everything. "How many of the soldiers survived?"

"That could see active duty again? The estimate is twenty-six."

That is many that will not serve. "Will they?"

Sounding almost hopeful, "they could."

"Noted."

"We can't build a Gulag, Prison, or the like. If we build shelter? Citizen must be sheltered. Why box up monsters when you can slay them? Why care and maintain those that have attacked your society when you can walk them through a rededication? Prison is an *easy out.* Hot meals, a place to sleep, and for what?" Shaking her head, "no. You set the Inquiry, you find the Truth, and if a Conviction is found? You place the Condemned before their crimes and you run them down with them. You see them get up, and keep walking, because life is not over until it is over."

"You want them to be better people in the end."

Answering quickly with a heartfelt ache, "I do! The State does! It's in the Codex."

Keep your tone light, "that's, quite forgiving."

"Each life we have, is one more light. Snuffing a light should not be a casual thing."

"Noted."

With a resounding conflict in her tone, "The Fire Maiden Sisterhood, the idea that Thomas spun for them to cling to? It denies the personhood and human rights of our enemies."

So rare an idea. "Noted."

"Do I see the the foundation stones of the future needing to be laid during my reign? Yes. Right now, my choices are to mix the mortar with the blood of my Citizens, or their Citizens. Building up the infrastructure that we have, or laying a new claim over the blasted out remains of what they will lose. I have to find a third option."

A different type of foundation perhaps? "Noted."

Holding his hands with audible adoration in her words, "thank you, for letting me Self-Check against you, as the Nation goes through a period of Self-Check this morning."

Puffing up with his assurance, "I am here, as your ally in this."

"The people will be informed as to the *why,* and I will have an answer for them."

"Hopefully they will help you find that third option, or agree to ease up on the notions that would invoke the first. And avoid the second. I am not always good with the encouraging words."

"You manage."

I think I saw a smile, "what did you think of, with the third option?"

Broaching the idea quietly, "there is a *tentative,* third option."

At least she has a future felt out. "Share it with me? This joy? Or smile inducing idea, at the very least. I," trying his words with a placid smile, "I would listen."

"It's oddly adorable when you do that. I feel like I'm in Theatrics again."

"Theatrics?"

"All Citizens are given lessons in Theatrics, as the world is a stage. Theatrics, Dialogue, Dialectic, and the like are considered Basic Educational Ideals." Tapping her forehead with two fingers she smiled, "when you play along with our culture I feel the nostalgia of being in Theatrics and learning how to present ideas."

I will wish for a time machine and the ability to go to school here another time. "Ah. Noted."

"Now, to answer your question, with the item I could celebrate? Consul Mouse. His niece, Miss Harriet Pie Mouse, sent in a For My Consideration document after my father died. It was a repeated request petition for a Logistics Analysis of attempting a social liaison with the Freelander people near Bliss."

So talk to them. "They want to talk to them?"

"They do. Unlike Consul Wing. He wants to test the mettle of those outside of our borders with a more active defense, perhaps an offensive if it would be allowed. The people of the Wing Province provide some of our best guards for Dispatch, among other martial forces. Some of the Provinces embrace more violent ideologies as elevated states. The Yorklin Province is the opposite, for example. They are our spiritual home for the doctors, and those whom are mostly peaceful. We have to send people *to* them to keep them safe."

"But is Dhavid not a Yorklin? He's a Cloak, correct?"

"And is he dwelling in their Province?"

Oh. "Point."

"To that end, I would like my doubts to be cleared up with Mouse, Yorklin, and Wing next."

Oh oh, rushing the question with a feeling of helpfulness, "so if you fell, and the Sisterhood was made, Mouse would not get to talk to the outsiders?"

With a somber tone of clarification, "they would get to talk to whomever was left."

Smiling with the small victory, "doesn't seem like the thing to do, with what you have told me they believe."

Joining him with a smile, "I would agree."

"So, the people who wronged your people, you don't fear them still being alive?"

Correcting him gently with an absentminded fretting, "I fear them being killed without proper investigation more."

I will get the flow of this, - "the Consul, he had proper channels to deal with you?"

Tapping her comm for emphasis, "he is allowed to call me whenever he has a need. It would be logged in the system, but he could call me."

Playing into the moment he heard his own almost glib tone as he spoke, "so if I was a Consul, I could call you whenever I wanted as long as I had it logged?"

"Yes."

"I could ask you to step down?"

Replying with a matter-of-fact simplicity, "you *could*. I would refuse, want to talk it out. Have the other Consuls talk to you about it."

That is not nice, "so he skipped over every proper channel –"

Interrupting with a note of shock, "to see me dead. Yes."

Taking a deep breath he regretted the help he had attempted, "I can understand how this morning? It would be hard to be you." Adding with a helpless sheepishness, "I am kind of sorry I inquired."

Clicking her tongue three times she sighed, "Yuri? If you do not ask? You will never learn. Lessons don't, *just happen*, for everything. If anything?" Swallowing roughly she continued, "it feels good, to be honest with you."

"Wait! If he *skipped over things,* whatever he feels you did, he could have felt that the Council wouldn't support him fully. Thus the lie and surprise attack."

Nodding with affirmation she smiled weakly at him, "that would be safe to assume. This plan was most likely meant for my father, and then given to me because I was standing in the way. The Council, as a whole, has been more *forgiving,* in recent years as the peaceful moments have lasted longer. In my father's youth when the peace was short lived? They all wanted to know when their people would be safe."

Now it could go either way. They could be in on it to forge a lasting peace with the graves, or the dupes would get their dreams of peace fulfilled when Kunlow had won. "This is a lot to take in."

"I know."

"Side question, why does Miss Mouse want to talk to the Freelanders near Bliss?"

"They want to open a door that the Yorklin family can walk through. The idea that if they can help educate those on the other side of the line? Care for them. Teach them to care? That they could be better from the experience."

Outreach? "They would risk their lives, so others could risk their lives, for the sake of your enemies?"

"Yes."

"Are the Freelanders *your* enemy?"

Regarding him with a pensive frown she clarified with an almost gentle sadness, "they have a Threat Index Rating, but I would not commit to the idea of *enemy.* If they were my *enemy?* I would have already burned them to dust."

Oof. "I don't have words."

Gesturing she smiled with a sheepish regret, "see this gesture?"

"Yes."

"This is 'Subject Exhausted.' When you run out of things to say on a subject of conversation, and just don't have a segue? Then use this, wait for an affirmation, and go to a new topic."

Handy. "Oh, thank you."

"Noted."

Trying his best at the gesture he smiled when she smiled and nodded once. *I did it right.*

Trying his hand at another question, "where are your Honor Guard this morning?"

"This, is where it gets a smidge complicated. I don't have a lot of Guards to begin with."

What, a hundred? "Oh? How many?"

"Unknown at this time as the wounded and dead are still being evaluated. The Honor Guard weren't at the same strength as The Watchmen."

Those would be the men from the garage then? "The men I met the night I met Asmodai."

"Correct."

"So how many did you have?"

"That doesn't matter, what matters is how many I have at hand *now.* Which is nineteen."

I have seen leaders need as many as a few hundred. "That is *not* enough."

"I know. That was on the list of things the Council wanted me to attend to as soon as I was able once everything else was done. They want me to get to ninety total. Father went *light* at sixty. This doesn't count non-com personnel."

Turning his head with an exaggerated humor, "where are they now?"

"I have them stationed in key defensive locations to make sure certain people are protected. And then I have three of them attached to the hip of Wallman so he's safe during his working hours."

I will invoke the vocabulary lesson, "why are they called your Honor Guard?"

Remarking with a shrug, "they guard my honor."

Laughing at her simple answer, "details!"

Smiling back she held up her right index finger, "reminder, it's *elaborate.* Details is used when you are outlining the finer points. Elaboration is the continuation of a subject."

"Noted, you and yours with your prescriptive language. I will endeavor to remember though. Question though," taking a breath he smiled warmly, "what is the difference between elaborate and details with them?"

Nodding once she set in, "elaborate? Would cover the ideas that they keep me safe. They assist me in my duties. If I need help doing the right thing? They help me. Honor is strength and dedication to the self and community for the betterment of each day. I go visit sick children in the hospital? They go with me. I go to lunch? They go with me. I go to the gym? They go with me. They help me do everything I do in my life and do it safely. Then *details* would be getting into their status as what level of friend they are to me, what Role each one plays, those details."

Oh, "thank you again. Also, are they going to like me?"

"I think they will. You already have shown that you like something they like."

"Which is?"

Smiling with a forced jubilance, "me being alive."

Faltering he touched her hands gently, "I, yeah."

Relaxing to a more somber tone, "unfair. I am aware."

"No," shaking his head softly, "just a very striking and bold statement. You excel at those."

"I do."

Broaching the subject quietly, "why did they stay quiet?"

Squeezing his hand in reply, "I will explain as best I can." Taking a moment to collect herself, "I had a plan. It was a longer range plan than it needed to be. I was *trying* to get my father to see a way to step down and retire. The problem with my plan was that I thought he wanted Steven to succeed him. Patrick made it clear he did not want the Throne."

Speaking into her pause, "why is it a Throne?"

Appearing somewhat embarrassed, "Theatrics. The idea of holding the power, would be seen as Sitting on the Throne. From there, the Office becomes the place of Court, as it were. Central Tower, a Castle. Then, when the High Consul leaves the Tower, they become a Citizen again. They are not *sitting,* they are standing next to you. In a way, the High Consul has no real power, as all of the power is bequeathed upon the High Consul from the exterior. The Citizen *agrees* to this. The High Consul holds up their part of the Pledge, the Citizen the other, and the Nation is as the Nation is."

I will need time later to adjust to this. "Do continue? Noted though."

"Back to it? Back to it." Taking a breath she fumbled back into it, "Father would just shut down on the subject if I went about it *the wrong way.* And to be honest? I was lost inside the madness of the moment right there with him. I had lost my way in the emotional maze of it all. They knew the stakes of us getting it wrong. So they stayed quiet because the world worked with him at the helm even if his private life was a mess."

"I see." *I wonder.* "So what was it like with your Guard?"

"They kept me busy as I kept them busy. They let me do all the field work I wanted to do. Many of them are more akin to an Instructor or Teacher than a gun toting, martially trained, death dealing Soldier."

Smiling at her words, "stark wordplay."

Smiling in return, "Dramatics and all that."

"Hah."

"Welcome to The Totalitarian Provinces of the Pacific Rim." After a half moment of pause she smiled, "that's the working title of the country."

"Working Title?" *Wait,* "Totalitarian? In the title?"

"We have a Protocol Amendment that we can change the letterhead as the land changes. So if we gain more territory? We can rename it. Also, yes. We're just being honest with ourselves. The State *owns* and *controls* all aspects of life. Freedoms are given as a privilege within those aspects."

And no revolution? Then again I am not sure I have seen anything I would find revolting. "And people don't mind?"

"It's honest expectation of behavior. We have a suggestion box to be kept aware of things."

"Are people punished for using it?"

"No. Protocol Amendments forbid it. Although if you are excessively vulgar in your communications with the State? You are sent a warning letter to use the talents for discourse and presentation of thought that you learned in Primary School."

That's so much nicer than the Gulag. "How long did this take to get into the current shape?"

"Ten years of writing and refining into a working model for the Arcologies. Then the almost fifty years spent in the Arcologies troubleshooting and adding to it. Followed by the Reunification of the Houses after William opened the doors. The establishment of The Network led to the Exchange of Data and Ideas. From doors open to stable interlocking provinces, was two generations. Then three full generational bands, of which I am in the third, of people refining the idea of the Codex and Protocols to best reflect us as a people. Not to mention the adjustments based upon Province and the insights granted based upon environmental and location based needs."

No wonder it seems so massive of a concept. "Impressive."

"Which has led to *this* moment. Defying it to seek safety in the wake of someone not playing by the Protocol."

"I am, glad? I get to share this moment with you."

Losing her poise, "I won't lie Yuri, it hurts. I can see hurt in your eyes too"

"I do hurt. I slept some but I wish I could have slept longer. I couldn't stay down. The atrocity I witnessed is going to chew at me. This house though? It's quite peaceful. That room? Very nice. The colors, the fabrics, the gentle smells? If I wasn't in such pain I would have slept like I haven't in a very long time. I can see why you always looked rested. The Art of War aside, you have also studied the Art of Sleep. This place? Is a house of peace."

Replying with a softly acerbic tone, "even if I'm not always at peace."

"That's what places of peace are for. Quiet bedrooms and gentle beds."

Reaching out to him she touched his shoulder, "will you tell me that story some time?"

Reaching up and patting her hand, "gladly."

Nodding her head twice she sighed, "I don't know quite what happens next out there. So I'm going to worry about in here."

"Tell me more."

Touching his right hand with her right hand, she draped the back of her hand across his. "I just hope that you, like me, find a way to forgive Asmodai enough that we can move past seeing him dead." Swallowing roughly she sighed, "if we can learn to forgive the physical violence? We can heal as people and not look at the other and see the things we don't have to see. I want to see you without the fire extinguisher. For you to know I don't see a monster. For you to look at me and not see his victim, but perhaps see someone who stood too close to a man being consumed by the Shadow." Adding with a rush of half-hearted consolation, "but not deviance at least."

Guessing game time. "Deviance? So no sex stuff?"

"Correct. We never fell into that mess together."

Curious. "You put a special enunciation on that."

"It wasn't who we were Yuri. That's the short answer. This was most poignantly seen by both of us when I was nineteen. We were starting to yell, he grabbed me," watching the smile form on her lips he felt one of his forming despite himself, *I can only imagine where this story is going to go.*

Opening up with a horrified and yet humored candor, "and we hit the wall. My head turned and I could see in a mirror that was nearby, his dressing mirror. And, I scowled at our reflection. He looked and blanched. The pose, it was *so bad.* If someone had come in it would have looked compromising. He let go of me, moved away, and started gesturing for how we needed to go over things. We took deep breaths and the fight was stopped by our mutual awkward feelings on what just happened."

Honest answer. "I don't have words."

"You don't have to have words! That's the great part of stories. You can have one word though."

So it can be this easy? "Noted?"

"Correct."

I needed this word a few hundred times in the past. "Then, noted."

Renewing her firm hold on his hands, "Yuri, I loved him, dearly, as my father. My dad. The overworked paragon of power of my childish youth which lead to a greater and greater understanding of him over time. Not to mention how he was raised. Was our relationship good? It could have been much better. Was it sexual? No. Did too much erode him leaving him turning into a man he never should have been? Yes. So," taking a breath, "I just hope I make sense when I try to fill in the blanks."

Time to see if I can decode the lessons. Good thing I have studied with sages. "You know I have brought up the people I have saved, many of which were women, and no small amount dealt with things of a sexual nature."

Appearing to stay brave, "yes."

"But as you have never been sexually abused, I don't have to worry about grabbing onto you, and getting a handful of scar tissue. Literally or metaphorically."

Without losing the apparent bravery, "correct."

"I think you are too hard on yourself. You want me to see you as you are, not what I might make up. To treat my mental health seriously. Make sure I do something about my anger, as you know *far too well* what that does. I am not a stubborn man of age, I am a formerly stubborn man of youth who is just trying to remember all the good advice he's been given."

"Thank you Yuri."

Leaning in he moved his lips into position to kiss her on the cheek, "I am going to kiss you."

Intoning the words with a nonchalant humor, "just don't slobber."

Holding her hands firmly he leaned against her, holding the laughter in for a moment, before letting it out as a short burst of deep laughter from his chest. Feeling her arms move around him he returned the motion with a playfully savage hug of his own.

Finding his sense of thought he finished the laughter, "slobber? Really?"

"I've had a few! The Albatross covers how to give dry lip kisses so as to not slobber. Your handkerchief can be used as a saliva blotter to give a dry, but warm, cheek kiss."

Nodding with the processing of the idea, "noted. Do not slobber on your face."

"Thank you."

Leaning in he placed the quick peck of a kiss on her cheek before sitting back in his chair, "I did not end the world with the peck."

"No, you did not." Reaching up and touching her cheek she smiled, "I'm going to set you up in the living room. I'll put on some music, turn on the aroma diffuser with a relaxation blend of oils, and give you time to rest until the family Tailor gets here. His name is Dennis, and I am going to compensate him for making sure you are dressed as you choose."

"More of my rights?"

"Yes! You have the right to self-representation in the Textile Expression. You are not my doll, or a toy, and you have not signed a Lover's Contract where you give me that right to dress you as I see fit."

I know I'll get an answer if I ask. "What if a man has no sense of how to dress himself?"

"Then he seeks the Tailor's Wisdom and signs the Advised Waiver. The Tailor then makes and dresses him in the way that is felt to compliment him the most."

Autonomy is more important than I thought. "Noted."

"Please don't worry about the resources used on you, if you can."

The joke is on you, I love presents. "I will endeavor to accept the gifts given."

"Also, I can trust Dennis with you, us, this place, as he has been here before. He's the family Tailor now, as he's retired from his post as the Darkest Shadow of Cloak and Dagger. He has more secrets in his head than most people would dream of. He's an older gentleman. He saw the founding of Cloak and Dagger, the end of the war, the fall of the

Warlord, and a host of other things. I can trust him near you."

Oh odd, "you speak of *the* Shadow, and the Darkest Shadow?"

"*The* Shadow is the term we have discussed, the inner turmoil of self, among other things. Being the head of Cloak, he accept his role as a person whom would walk a darker line. That's why he's the *Darkest Shadow*, and not *The* Shadow."

"Noted! Also, he is quite loyal?"

"He loved Maggie, my mother, as a sister he never had."

"Noted. All brothers for him?"

"Three, all younger, to be exact. He's the eldest."

"Noted." *I can't help myself,* "so what is Cloak and Dagger exactly?"

Visibly mulling it over she offered words, "the secret police, would be *a* term for them, based upon their duties."

That's a terribly kept secret. "But even I know about them now."

Laughing softly she nodded, "we aren't very good at keeping secrets. They recruit at the Secondary Schools. They are an education track to themselves."

So weird. "Noted."

"They have to submit their paperwork just like everyone else. They aren't allowed to just do whatever they want. They're top tier at Investigations, Unusual Combat, and Delicate Matters. If you want to make your life as that sort of person? They're the highest point to shoot for."

"And your Guard?"

"They scored lower than the benchmarks for Cloak and Dagger."

"Then you do not ask for the best?"

"I ask for the ones that would be best for the job. They have one listed role, protecting me. The Cloak and Dagger role list is a daunting checklist of needed abilities that require some of the fastest, toughest, and smartest in their field. People go where they are needed."

"Noted."

"Also Dennis might bring Stephanie, that's his adopted daughter. Be careful around them both. Dennis isn't one to quarrel but in the wake of the losses? He's going to be raw and bleeding. Just, be gentle with him by being quiet. Don't try to use your charms on him like you did on me."

I did not know I qualified as charming. "You found me charming?"

"I did, still do, and look forward to more of your charming perspective on life. Dennis, is a verbally playful man when he's happy. I think if the two of you were left to socialize it would be a hilarious time to witness and be apart of. But right now? Be gentle unless he prompts you to be something else."

I know this type and situation, "I can do this."

"Stephanie is a beautiful woman, she's a few years my senior. Her skin is touched by the sun, kissed with a shade of brown that highlights her features well. Be a gentleman if you meet her, she prefers gentlemen. She's currently unattached, but I would caution against flirtation."

"Oh?"

With an unrestrained irritation, "First Layer? Her marriage was annulled three years ago."

The Layers of Truth. Asmodai told me about them. "Annulled?"

"Yes. Second Layer? Her husband was injured while on patrol four years ago. His physical therapy was intense enough in need that it was putting a strain on the marriage. Against the recommendations of The Guild, he filed for annulment and told her to go."

I am too aware of that idea. "What is the Third Layer?"

"She's trying to get back with him. Their daughter is old enough that she wants to know why mommy and daddy can't be together. He's tried to be a good dad, even if his heart has been broken by being broken. He's not out of her life at least."

"Why did they hurt him like that?"

"Water. He was driving a water tanker from one of our harvesting patches. They broke him to get the water."

Too often a motive. "It is not an uncommon crime."

"I know. But Stephanie, she's a serious person who has spent years learning our ways. She was adopted in at a young age. She, like you, had a lot to learn of how to understand our ways and customs. From what I understand she has been happy here."

"Noted."

"Do you have any questions?"

"He adopted her? Seems nice of him."

"It's how we do things Yuri. If we find children? We adopt them. Even if it's after we killed their parents." Stopping she sighed and spoke quickly with a tone of clarification, "not to say *he* killed her parents, because he didn't, it's just how the endeavor is worded."

Doing his best to reassure her with his tone, "noted." *So he adopted her without a wife?* "Is there anything special he had to do?"

"He had to provide female references. As he knew a small bevy of women at the time who each said they would assist? He cleared the process without a problem."

Heartening. "What kind of life does the child lead?"

Reaching to him she caressed the side of his face before moving her chair to a more comfortable angle to be close to him. *We are doing that thing we do, of not knowing when to stop talking.*

Settling against him with a comforted sigh, "we try to make them equal citizens. We feed them, clothe them, educate them, and try to get them to forgive us and themselves what happened. There are some primitive tribes out there Yuri. When we emerged we came out with some high minded ideals and large caliber guns. Our ancestors wanted to enforce law, rule, and decency. Quality of life, thought, behavior, and moral compass. It got bloody far faster than had been feared. But the children? We try to do our best by them."

"What happened to her folks?"

Rubbing her hands together she spoke the stark idea, "they died. The Warlord's men killed them. When that campaign was over? Dennis was in her city, helping coordinate what we could to make sure they would recover. They have a radically different culture in many ways and we were just trying to be polite."

Continuing her timbre shifted to something akin to a prideful retelling, "Dennis was a mover and shaker in the aftermath of the Butcher's Fall. Stephanie found out her parents did not make it. She needed a shoulder, he was that shoulder, and in the end she asked him to take her home. She was without a caretaker that wasn't pressed for space and time. She did not want to burden her relatives. Children need as much as space and time as they can get. To that end, he took the steps."

"I understand." Looking away he looked at his empty mug, *maybe this will be easier.* "I didn't say noted, as I do understand caring for children that are not your own. But, something easier, that was coffea coffee? It was not what I expected. Do you have much more?"

"Yes. From what I understand the global weather pattern shifts would have destroyed most of the coffee and chocolate in the world. We are correct in that assumption?"

"I have never seen coffea coffee, or what passed as chocolate before the end of the world as it was known. I understand one more thing now." *Wait,* "do you have chocolate?"

"We have a small supply. We smuggled coffea and theobroma into the Arcologies and used them to solid effect to help keep people placid and thoughtful. Did you see the theobroma in your travels?"

The stories of loss I could tell her, if I wanted to scare her into never traveling. "Sadly only stories of loss. The world is very sad in too many places."

"Noted."

Looking up at the half hearted attempt at conversation he nodded at her sad face. "No need Susan. It will be the right time eventually."

"Thank you."

"Accepted, and noted."

Gesturing softly as she rose to her feet, "we usually reply with Noted, then accepted."

Oh fine then, lobbing the word with a mock petulance, "noted."

Smiling she gestured with her hand for him to follow, "follow me to the living room?"

Rising he set to following her. Passing from the kitchen to the hall and then to the living room he did his best to note the layout. *The door to the kitchen is protected by the* staircase. *The dining room has a stout table. The kitchen past that has the escape window. Not too bad.*

Entering the living room again he looked back at the mud room. *There is a discrete door there to the garage I didn't see the first time. Garage, dining room, kitchen. I got this.*

Gesturing wide at the sum of the room, "you can use any of the chairs or the couch."

"Will you be staying with me?"

Fretting for a moment she sighed before nodding once at him, "I can stay. If I doze off? Don't wake me until the perimeter sensor goes off."

I will ask the question that does no harm that I know of, "can we share the couch?"

Looking from him to the couch with an appraising eye, "I *think* it might be big enough. Do you want to have arm over or be under?"

"I am use to being arm over."

"Then you get comfortable, while I load up the diffuser. I will be right over and lay down."

"Sounds good." Sitting down and adjusting to a more comfortable position, "I think I am ready."

Watching her finishing the task, of the preparing and activating the diffuser, his thoughts drifted. *I have never met a woman so tall. It takes a robust diet to be tall and robust, from what I know of things. My children would not go hungry in these lands.*

No lines for bread.

The water is clean.

I am where I was looking for.

Moving away from the not so faint vapor coming out of the small decorative cylinder, she regarded him with a hesitant eye for a moment. Moving closer she committed to the action of sitting down on the couch. Moving his arms he waited and braced himself as they settled into place in a slow flurry of adjustments of body and small pillows.

We did it. We are sharing the couch and she is not going to fall off.

"Let me send a few messages, set up the perimeter update, and I'll put my comm down."

Replying with the languor of the moment, "take your time."

"Noted."

She feels good to hold.

She smells terrible.

Hitting on a conclusion to his worries, *I can't be dead, Heaven doesn't smell bad.*

Feeling her process the things she needed to do he felt her move away long enough to lay her comm down. Leaning back and snuggling backwards onto him, he did his best to get their position just right.

Asking his name as the inquiry, "Yuri?"

This is going to be something. "Yeah?"

With the pitch of hidden laughter to her words, "want to hear something, awful?"

She has a thought she cannot keep bottled. It is an evil genie and I will be punished for wishing for my boredom to end. "Of course."

"To go back to a prior point? Ethically? Father and daughter sexuality is considered objectively not a good thing. For one, it removes a daughter from the breeding pool."

"Noted and agreed with."

"The two, second, is that our Morality is based upon positive life experience. If a daughter lays with her father, then the Parental Role is compromised. This is seen as a negative outcome. Thus, immoral, as the daughter should have a father for life. Not an ex-lover who happens to be her dad."

"Excellent point." *She is leading me to a punch line.*

"A side point to this is we are aware of something called Genetic Sexual Attraction, where distanced family, when reunited, can wish to have sex. To that end we keep families close to each other, and aware of each other to prevent that from victimizing someone."

"Oh, that is again, nice of The State."

"The third, and personal part of this, is I am aware of what my parents got up to in the bedroom. My mother left me essays and writings on the subject, which included anecdotal reflections on sexuality." Taking an audible breath she continue, "I have no common point with how she behaved behind closed doors. Her games are not my games. Her paint is not my paint. To that end, I would have been a lousy partner for my dad."

Trying to keep his laughter restrained he felt his stomach clench so hard that it hurt. Laying his head into the couch pillow he bled off the laughter until he could speak, "oh, my heavens, Susan, I, adore you."

Responding with a humored 'matter-of-fact' tone, "I like being adored."

Firing back with a playfully irritated snap, "good."

Rubbing his arm gently she quieted down, "comfortable?"

Quieting down in turn as the fatigue chewed on him, "yes."

Turning the tables of the moment on him with a humored tone, "I would like that nap now."

Oh, be that way. "I will quiet myself fully then."

Touching his arm gently she spoke a sing-song reply, "thank you."

Snorting back the laughter one more time, "noted."

3.6.0 - 09:12
Drenner Estate – Consul's Office

◙Chuck Drenner

Moving his attention between three tablets, each opened to different sections of the Protocol, he felt his sense of dread growing. *How can it be coming to this? Why does it have to come to this? The fighting has stopped, why are we going into Civil War?*

Looking up to Amanda, sitting with a placid numb behind her desk, he spoke his frustration, "I don't understand. I don't understand why it's coming to this!"

Tilting her head back and looking at the ceiling Amanda seemed to be a hundred kilometers away, "Civil War Protocol will free The Commander to get Thomas Kunlow."

Trying to not sound too hopeful, "is that *all* this is about?"

Rolling her words with an unenthusiastic pace to them as her gaze followed the lines of the design on the ceiling of the office, "it's difficult to kill a Consul. The system is designed to give a certain amount of security to the job. To grant the notion that Endeavors can be ordered, and if it goes *wrong,* that the Consul isn't liable for the outcomes, by default. This goes *far* beyond the measure of what is acceptable. The Commander is going to push for the activation of Civil War Protocol so he will have the freedom to turn Thomas into something we won't soon forget. He will give us something to think about when we consider the idea of betrayal."

"How –" stopping short he rubbed his face, "what is it you know that I don't know?"

Without a smile she replied with a conversational volume, "this is just another tragedy for me Chuck. I have to stay numb so I can think objectively and do my best for the sake of those that are still with us. I know why he wants what he wants, and I fear what he will do once he gets it. I don't know how strong Susan is right now."

Broaching the line of thought with a grimace, "so what's the worst case?"

Sitting up in her chair she appeared more invested, "this, is where it becomes something worth pondering. Once he *has* Civil War activated, how far does he go? What is his plan? Steven was never one for acting without a course set and charted. He *has* a guiding notion. He hasn't asked for anything during this. He's been giving orders, without asking for his own demands."

Let me in the rusted loop Amanda, "what is the note on that you're not telling me?"

Shifting to a more apologetic tone, "I hold out on you too much in the moment. Steven, as Steven, sent me a note to his Marraine. He told me he would be giving Thomas his Honest Reply." Steepling her hands together she seemed almost evasive, "I had to think it over, but I remembered. I once asked Asmodai, many years ago, what he would do if Consul Kunlow asked him a specific question I won't burden you with, yet. He told me he would give him his honest and firm reply." Moving her hands, palms down onto her desk she sighed, "I think Steven knows what that answer is, and that Thomas did indeed ask that question."

That is chilling. "But the Bachman family has a twisted sense of humor when it comes to their dry retorts. Even Miss Bachman is prone to some truly infamous downplays of the truth."

Continuing on with a false calmness to her tone, "I am aware. Meanwhile, the Council, we are fractured because we cannot establish a Council Meeting. We're stuck with small group calls, and exchanging notes. We're," pausing with the 'consideration of words' signal she appeared to be staring at her desk. Looking up she moved forward, "we're boggled, puzzled, and outraged with sadness. Susan's reactions to nearly being killed has laid some wounds in their hearts. They are just as sickened by this as you and I are. They know that Thomas did it, and because of circumstantial evidence they are being lumped in with him. That notion? Pains them deeply. To know that she has let Steven off his leash for the time being? This too causes no small amount of heartache. The comfort the people take when a Bachman is off their leash? It's a saddening reminder of the need to feel comfort in trying times."

I don't have anything of use. "In the last year, your reports said he's become a more mellow, perhaps even docile man."

Sounding almost hopeful with her reply, "he hasn't shot anyone yet. He has agreed to have the survivors interviewed. He has given careful orders in his share of things regarding the Blackout Bloc. He's keeping this close to his chest and under tight wraps. The Voice of Morning is sending out words of caution and compassion. This entire affair has been Hot August Night Protocol to a dotted I and crossed T. The High Consul sends us a dire warning, but she has not sent her people the same measure. Even Steven is smart enough to know the play. The Power of the Public."

"She builds a power play based upon compassion to discredit the idea that she should die." *Well then.* "What does that mean for Steven's part in this?"

"I don't rightly know. I don't know if he's laying in wait for his perfect moment, or if he's going to keep the compassion going."

Not enough, but it will have to do. "Then we wait and see?"

Nodding with a helpless frustration, "we wait and see."

I need to know, "how is the solidarity in the Council?"

Losing some of her hope and neutrality to a timbre of frustration, "we are trying to figure out how we can clear our names. We stand accused. We understand this. We are also carefully weighing our movements as we are being watched by The Commander. It would be reckless to pledge to something that would be *very bad* in the long run. To that end, we exchange messages, and are attempting to keep our people calm. Not to mention we are still trying to make sure our parts of things function."

Pausing for a sip of water and a deep breath she continued with less frustration, "we have Citizens up and down the coast who wish to stay in bed and cry. To mourn. To sit in shock and examine life. Every Chapter of The Guild is out in force making sure people stay healthy in this moment. I am quite glad that I have so many whom I can trust in the Pyramid of Command to oversee these things."

"Staggering. Noted." Mulling the notions over, "if he gets Civil War, and he gets his chance, what might he throw into the mix?"

Clapping her hands together with a minimal sound her tone spoke with an honest trepidation, "he might try to kill them all. Spiritual fibers, mental corruption, the ideas that their minds could be entertaining. Their Consul dreamt of killing the High Consul. They know it. The people have now seen the reality of it. He invoked the idea that our greatest enemy is? Ourselves.

Poising his question with a gentle lilt of being a willing listener, "elaborate?"

"Horizon? The Rifles were saved, the lathes destroyed by air bombing. Our enemies did not manage to get a single rifle or the ability to make them." Taking a short breath she plowed on with a pride in their history, "the long range cannon the Freelanders attempted to use on Holden Tower? Bombed into bits and pieces. The small platoon of men who came for this very house? Routed. The Windmills? Defended. The Warlord? The Sky-Cleaver showed him the error of showing his face. The treaties signed, the accords written, and in one night?" With a voice rising with volume and anger, "in one night our people showed our people what *real* violence and betrayal looks like."

Watching her sit up and fight with the angered sadness he waited patiently without moving. *And now she's going to tell me the thing I need to hear.*

Losing her anger to a moment of emotional collapse, "there is a chance that Steven will order the House burned. But given his family history? That's reality getting off *light*, given the gravity of the crime."

No. No, no, no. "Will Miss Bachman abide at that point?"

Swallowing roughly she shrugged with a deflated unhappiness, "I don't know."

Unable to control the words of angered frustration they came out, "Maggie raised her better than that!"

Rubbing her eyes gently she sighed with an angered dejection, "please don't use her name like that."

Sitting back with the weight of the idea of Cassia gone he felt the selfish stab of his reasoning. "Mea culpa."

Appraising him with an honest forgiveness to the words, "you don't want Cassia dead, none of us do. As far as we know, she had nothing to do with it."

Cassia, Traitorous Mastermind, one or the other. "It doesn't seem like the thing she would want."

Smiling flatly she sighed, "no. It doesn't."

Posing the question with a heavy heart, "do you think Miss Bachman will let them die?"

Waiving a hand with a dismissive gesture, "I can *hope* she won't. I can rally my mind around the idea that she'll come back out of the dark and save the people whom were left out of it."

What a sick idea to have to swallow, the idea of being wrong about her. "I understand."

Reflecting on the idea she walked verbally through the lines of thought, "my sister tried to leave her everything she would need to know to live as a Bachman. Asmodai was not given the gift of a sister, so someone had to leave her the other half of the lesson plan. I think he would have benefited from a sister, as I know I did from having a brother. I, digress." Taking a breath she reached out to her glass of water and finished it off in short order. Setting the glass down she sighed, "there are five children left in this world she asked me to take care of. To check in on. To nurture, to *protect.* If Kunlow burns? I fail them all in one deed. Trust me Chuck, I am going to be doing my best to make sure that there is an unburnt House when this is over."

Nodding he rose from his foldout desk, "I will get us more coffee. And some latkes, I had Jillian make some, we need to eat something."

Looking up at him with eyes betraying her years, "thank you Chuck."

Is this what power looks like? "Noted. Also, mea culpa."

Getting up with her empty glass, "noted, accepted, and," taking a breath, "mea culpa."

Moving to the door he nodded, "noted and accepted."

I want to speak lightly, but I don't have the energy.

Moving toward the counter with the water pitcher on it, her voice sunk with the gravity of the words, "she waits for this in a place darker than Guthrie. We will learn more when we face it."

I do not like this, I have no choice but to abide. "Understood."

3.7.0 - 10:00
Room 3x11 – Observation Ward

*Patrick Bachman
*The Director of the New Hope Media Network
*The Director of the New Hope News

Glancing at the clock on the screen of his portable workstation he clucked his tongue at the time. *He's going to be knocking any second.* Closing his portable workstation as the rapping at the door occurred he smiled at the timing. Wallman is punctual to a fault.

Pressing the button on the bed rail to signal the blue light on the doorframe outside he waited for Wallman to enter. *Freshly washed face and coffee in his veins from the looks of it. I want to look that good without makeup when I'm thirty-one.*

Trying to encourage Wallman to move faster he used the greeting Harold had used on him when they first met. "I won't bite."

Visibly restraining a smile, "do I appear to be *that* hesitant?"

Keeping it simple, "to my perception? Not fully, but I hoped it would help."

Speaking the recollection, "you were, seventeen, when I met you."

"And you were twenty-four and a rising icon in News." Cocking his head to the side he let the humor in fully, "you have seven years on me Harold, it's not normal for you to be acting like I'm the *superior.*"

Broaching the subject carefully he gestured for 'not exactly,' "I was told you had been, *injured.*"

Not going down that road. "Not talking about it." Taking a breath to shift back to the matter of real importance to him he smiled, "however, I would like to clarify that the Pardon was as I was unable to articulate nuance, I used the sledgehammer. It was meant as a gesture of trust."

Straightening up and joining him in the good humor, "noted. Thank you Director."

Recounting the tale without losing his smile, "the poor nurse that helped me, she was trembling around the edges having to help process such a thing. She commented that she knew that the media filter is to prevent emotional and moral outrage. I needed to give you freedom though."

Nodding once he grinned, "for which I thank you."

Now for him to tell me that he wants no part of this. Can't have him knowing I know though. "Noted. I did catch your two addresses so far." Putting on the accent of the youth, "totes worth," dropping the accent with a grin, "as the kids would say."

Gesturing for 'horrified' he spoke with a sarcastic disdain, "please Patrick, don't do that again."

"I won't." Grinning with the moment, "that *hurt* to say. Which is why I know they say it. To drive us up the walls." Sighing with a smile he continued, "I'll stop meandering. I sent you the script, you said you had concerns, now here you are. Tell me your concerns."

Broaching the subject with a greater care, "I'm not sure I can read what you wrote this time."

Trying to keep his tone neutral, "why is that?"

Losing his composure the frustration came out in earnest, "it's not true."

Raising his right hand with palm and fingertips upward, "which part?"

Looking at him with the demeanor of the Frazzled Instructor, "*most of it!* I was *trying* to keep people from *wanting* something like this! This *can't* be from Miss Bachman! This isn't winning *anything,* much less *two* things!"

Taking a breath against his instinctual emotional flare he placed his hands in his lap and did his best to stay focused. Breathing in three times in rhythmic pace he found a softer tone for his words, "Wallman, can you be still?"

I know my Complication, I respond to anger poorly, I just try to keep everyone from being angry around me.

Regarding him with a curious look he moved over and sat down on the edge of the bed. Lowering his voice he pursed his lips with a borderline apology to his demeanor, "I can try sir. If we're not fighting, then tell me what we are doing."

Looking up at the ceiling he leaned heavily on his neck pillow, "Consul Kunlow has stepped over an unforgivable line. Correct?"

Licking his lips he pursed them again, "correct."

Letting more than a hint of encouragement into his tone, "you will not be asked to read this, until *after* it would be needed, if it is indeed needed to be spoken."

Firing back quickly with more than a hint of hope to his question, "Director?"

Wishing he had more than just the lines in the ceiling tiles to look at he sighed, "my brother, The Commander, is preparing this moment. He was given Dominion over this moment by Miss Bachman. My beloved sister is laying down for a nap, with a heavy heart. She bleeds in private."

I don't need to tell him the good news.

Reaching over with his left hand he laid it on Patrick's left hand, "pardon?"

She'll tell him the good news when she's ready. The mote of happiness in the darkness, of feeling found.

Turning his hand over he accepted the grip, "she sent me a small message, familial codes. The translations are that she's taking a nap, she's hurting, and suffering from emotional anxiety and walking wounded emotionally. The Commander still has Dominion over this moment, and he's preparing for an Endgame Solution on Consul Kunlow. I will admit that," weighing his words, "what I sent you isn't my best work. But it's the best I could do on short notice to be ready for the fork in the road of fate."

With a voice of hope, "so this might not be?"

And now for Fresh Air after using Smoke. "Wallman, I don't want you to *have* to read it, but if that future comes? I would like you to."

With the firm ring of regret and excuse he declined, "I, don't think I could sir. I have already told the people what I have told them. I can't be your ally in this."

Squeezing Harold's hand firmly to assure him, "I'll get Anton to read it then."

Spitting the words with a roughness to them, "the old mainstay answer?"

Turning to look at Harold he let the incredulous grin spread over his face, "*he*, at least, does as he's told. He reads what's on the paper. More than I can say about some people I know."

Smiling back with a perplexed lilt to his words, "why do you allow me to be as I am?"

Keeping it to the facts he explained, "the Protocol. No crime committed is no crime that needs to be punished. The people trust you, they believe you, and I was hoping to have that on my side in this."

"I can't. But, how does it not come to this?"

"When Susan wakes up from her nap, and she sees the future The Commander wishes to pen? We'll have an answer in short order. If she weighs them, and turns a blind eye now that we know what we know? Then the Kunlow legacy will be over. A new Family will be found."

"When Thomas dies, who would lead the Kunlow family when Thomas is executed?" Qualifying his statement quickly, "if the family persists."

Keeping it to the facts, "it would fall on Octavia if she is found innocent. Otherwise? A talent query within their family."

Tsk'ing at the concept, "she's a bit younger than most Consuls are. I understand that she knows what's going on within the Pyramid though."

Moving to reassurance out of habit, "it happened to Consul Holden last. It happened to my sister. It's happened before."

After a long exhale he sounded resolute in his tone, "then I have to hope that Miss Bachman has not bled out."

Smiling he nodded once, "correct."

"She *can* stop him?"

Continuing with the reassurance as their grip on each other moved to a mutual clasp of wrists, "she hasn't signed The Reply. He can start the process of Civil War, then enact The Reply. From there? If she disagrees then she can Veto the process." Losing his hope in the wake of the emotional turmoil at the contemplated future he frowned.

"*However,* as he has Dominion and *is* The Commander? If she turns away from the moment? He could sack their House, kill them all, *and* march on Seaside to burn down their Estate there. He has enough evidence gathered he's going to move for the root and branching of their family tree."

Hanging his head with a forlorn slump of his shoulders, "all to get Thomas."

At this point, I don't even know what Steven wants in his heart of hearts. "Yes."

Looking up with a hopeful question, "and if Thomas surrenders?"

Going over what he knew of the options he found an explanation to share, "once he's in custody, it could all be stopped. If The Reply goes into effect, once he's in our hands, she could stop it then. But it would be ugly and bloody getting even that far. Unless he turned himself in."

Sighing with a dejected lilt to his words, "all I have left is hope?"

And perhaps Faith in my sister. "Yes."

"If we get the bitter future, we feed the people the sweet words?"

Moving his hand up Harold's arm he renegotiated the shared grip at around the elbow for both of them. *We have yelled so many times at the other. And we have always come back to this moment.*

Touching on the old wound of a subject they had shared too many times before, "we speak with honey on our tongues because if we do not? They might not find this truth one they can swallow. The Noble Lie –" feeling the tears welling up he closed his eyes and sobbed.

Feeling Harold move closer he didn't resist when he was moved into a more sheltered place in his arms. Unable to think in the storm of helpless emotions he felt the after effects of the attack bring out the tears without mercy.

Clutching at Harold he blew his nose when the handkerchief was provided. Trying to regain a semblance of composure he coughed out the words, "don't call the nurse."

Asking the word with caution, "no?"

I feel terrible, as I am adding to your stress. At least you have practice with the wounded.

Shaking his head he held on with an almost vicious intensity, "if she comes in, we don't get to finish."

With a tone betraying the ache of culpability, "Patrick, mea culpa."

Embracing some of the anger to get the words out, "*no,* it's not you. The men, they told me to *stop lying.* I defended myself with the excuse of the Noble Lie."

Staying calm he tried to soothe him with a firm presence, "hence the tears."

Mirroring his calm to the best of his ability, "yes."

Setting him upright, "can you go on?"

"I shouldn't, however," taking a breath he sighed, "the Death Warrants *are* being prepared as we speak."

Looking at him with a borderline angered incredulity, "*already?* The Network is barely functional though."

He's earned The Loop. Keeping it to the facts, "they were in reserve. My father, he wrote this. He wrote The Reply. It was in *his* Rainy Day Vault."

Inhaling sharply his words echoed his worries, "Thomas Kunlow wanted to kill Asmodai. That's why this seems *too good* of an execution and planning for a short order plan. This was for him."

You already knew, but were unwilling to admit it. "Yes."

Speaking the words with a horrified understanding, "this was meant for him, not Miss Bachman."

I can hope, for the sake of her sanity. "Yes."

"Does she know?" Pausing for a half second he continued, "not my best question."

"She left the Blackout Bloc alive. She knows that she's the stand-in for Asmodai and the notion that was cultivated."

Looking away for a moment he looked back at him before speaking, "so whatever crime Asmodai was on trial for, she knows?"

All too well. "She does."

Gesturing with a fluency for 'the answer is not demanded.' "Is she guilty of it too?"

Guilt is such a strange idea for it. "Yes."

Lowering his hands to his lap he appeared confused, "by the Blue Sky, that tells me so much and *nothing.*"

Keep it upbeat, he likes hope. "When, this is over? We'll figure out what to tell the people."

Cocking an eyebrow at him, "will I be telling them?"

Time to Pact the Pledge. "Harold, if we're both still alive and working for the News? *You,* will tell them."

Dropping the eyebrow he spoke with a candor, "I'm no Trucero Eckels."

Thinking over the contrast, *our last Legend. The man who told us of Broken Spearhead, The Peace, The Cure for the Wasting, and who hosted the final interview with my mother before she left us. He was the last man to hold the trust of the people. The man who retired from the camera to move to the radio on Sundays. The iconic voice of a generation.*

Looking at Harold, *and then there is you. Father said you could be the next Eckels.*

Speaking into the quiet Harold prompted him out of his thoughts, "is the crime something I would hate her for?"

Relaxing his grip on him he worked with Harold as he eased him back against his pillows. Fixing his neck pillow he winced against the pains in his body, "I don't think you would. She wants peace."

Looking at him with an incredulous anger, "her crime is *peace?*"

"She has been attacked, time and again, for wanting peace. For trusting outsiders. For wanting to see the merit in others outside of our lands."

Rushing his words, "I would like to know more."

"We can talk later," moving a hand up, "*however,* I have a peace offering for your mind."

"Something to read until we talk?"

"Yes." Opening his portable workstation he navigated through the windows quickly, "I have just the thing, for you to understand the depths of my father's *crimes*."

"What is that?"

Finding the files he checked the Epsilon Code requirements, *he meets them.* "There is a private server on the Network, one of many, this one is mine. I'm sending you the address and you'll be able to access the entire operation. This is an *example,* of his crimes. Epsilon Code *The Nightingale Flies At Midnight.* I'll link you directly to the folder."

Perking up with an intense interest, "who is the Nightingale?"

Keeping it to the easy answer, "the pilot who flew the cure for The Wasting to Port Asylum and Port Refuge, at my father's orders."

Nodding with gestures for 'wondered but unasked,' "that would explain how they survived something so virulent."

"It does."

Asking as the Interviewer, "who is the pilot though?"

I don't know. I'm not the High Consul. "High Consul Blackout covers the name, vitals, and the like of the pilot. And the plane."

"Your father was careful."

"With vital information? Yes."

Appearing to be honestly pleased, "I can be let In The Loop when this is over?"

That's on her. "You can ask her after this. I'll send her a message when this evens out that she needs to be able to confide in you. The motive being that if you're going to be telling the people that her dream of peace is possible," pressing Send he leaned back for a moment, "you will understand whom you are standing next to."

"Not now though?"

I can confide this too. "Leave a Message has been adjusted. The Commander has closed the majority of communication lines to her. She doesn't know. No one gets to warn her."

Pursing his lips again with a frown, "that seems, dishonest, at best."

It's Steven being Steven. Carrying the most of Father around on his back. "He wants the decision to be her decision. No one else. Not a favor. Not a vote. Not anything other than the Will of the High Consul."

Imploring him with the question, "can *you* call her?"

Only if I want to make this worse. "No."

Speaking with conviction to the idea, "she sounded hopeful. I know she's blank, she said so, but I don't see her letting this happen."

"I have to hope that you're right about her."

Looking at him with a sympathetic horror, "you really are ready to accept the future where she turns a blind eye."

Confiding in him with a candor made easier by the medication, "my family, over our generations, has done no small amount of the wrong in the world we know. We keep trying to do the right thing. To atone for our misdeeds. But if she is handed the final choice, atone via death, or find a way to atone for this later? She will burn them to Ash and atone later. It depends on how much of a No-Win Game that the Council makes this moment. I'm not In The Loop in that regard."

"I understand." Reaching for an idea, "can we call the Council and tell them to lay off?"

That's a non-answer of wasted action. "I don't know what I would tell them to do. They can't call her either. This is going to come down to if Susan, Miss Bachman, The High Consul, or The Derecho makes the final call. We are out of time. We will know before afternoon tea what our future holds."

Returning to his conviction, "I believe Susan will stop this."

"I cannot afford that luxury of wanting to be right like that. I wish I could."

"Do I have the luxury of being wrong?"

I mourn these words before I say them. "No," forcing the moisture to his mouth, "but you, could be replaced. I would *have* to find a new Wallman. Scour our populace to find someone who could be as good as Eckels was."

Looking at him with eyes reflecting their shared sadness at the concept, "and you? Can we find a new you?"

Touching the bandages on his head with his free hand, "I nearly *was* in need of being replaced. It's a heart hardening notion. It leaves me knowing that if I don't live this life, I will lose this life, before the normal expiration date."

Stopping he sighed, *that wasn't the answer he deserves.* "To *actually* answer your question? I have no skill someone else does not have. I *could* be replaced if someone was able to accept themselves as able to fill the shoes I would leave behind. I am just another man. A visionary could rise and transform the Network News into something more. I offer our world my service, but it is not something that is unique to me."

"I understand, all too well." Rising up from the dejection he spoke with mild bravado, "tell Anton that he shouldn't get too comfortable in my chair. I *will* be back."

I hope you're right Wallman. "If they do burn? It was an honor, and a privilege, to get to work with you Harold. I am certain that even if you were no longer a Newsman? You would be someone good for this world, who would be able to take care of his sister. Do not worry for that aspect of your life."

"If they burn? I think my happiness as a Newsman is going to be the least of our collective worries. Though, I *do* appreciate the assurances that I would be around to take care of my sister."

The lessons of the past remind us of what not to be. "We're Totalitarians, not savages Wallman. Without family, what are we? Is she well? I know, rusted time to ask, but I've been a bit Out of The Loop."

Sighing he shook his head with a dejected look, "she's back in Guild Custody. She *went too far,* as she put it."

Service Rangers had to find her again. "Is she well otherwise?"

Fretting with dejection, "she's unharmed, but she needs to find her center, as best she can, again. She gets a bit better with each cycle in Guild Custody."

Embracing what felt insufficient he spoke, "the more they learn, the more people they can have a chance at saving."

"If only we could stop hurting each other."

Another thing you share in common with my sister. "If only."

"I should go." Getting up and moving away from the bed he seemed thoughtful, "why did you give me a choice? When it was time to discuss Guthrie, you didn't give me a choice. You muzzled me and put Anton on every aspect of the two days we spent on it."

Keep it short, keep it simple. "Guthrie was over, done with, and there were too many facets of it I didn't want you to learn about. Those kids would have broken your heart, and I only know what little I know from Steven doing enough shots to talk to me about it before handing it off to Hampton and O'Neil. We spun it as a Win because we blew up the Evil Out-Group. There was far more to it than I wanted discussed or known."

"Noted. Were we looking for peace then?"

The peace of the grave. "No. We were looking to kill a very bad person. In the end we ended up with a flock of kids who all got new, better, parents and families. We didn't leave them to die in the wild."

Sounding lost but vaguely hopeful, "noted."

You should go. "A Blue Sky to you Wallman."

Nodding and stepping back toward the door, "rest well Director. She loves you so much, *people* love you, so for the sake of everyone? Rest well."

Nodding twice he watched Wallman leave his room, leaving him alone with his thoughts.

I hope he's right. I endure being the pessimist in her morality plays because she feels he needs motivation to keep going on his path. Taking a sip of water he looked over at the box of his second favorite treats, "you even made sure to not get my favorites. So I wouldn't taste this room when I would taste them." Setting his cup back on the side tray he settled against his pillow, "a life spent saving lives."

Taking a treat from the box he placed it on his tongue, *strawberry-lime. Not the best flavor but still a solid one. Sister, why? Why do you do this to yourself? To be like mother?* Thinking over the things Steven had told him, *why would you wish that on yourself? She was amazing, no doubt. But the sacrifices she made? Too high a price.*

3.8.0 - 11:55

Safe Housing

■Dennis Ochenhart

Gazing out the windshield of his Duo Car he took in the forgotten and remembered sight of the Sky-Castle. Feeling the numb spreading like an emotional insulation he welcomed the cessation of sadness.

Too many memories to deal with right now. Too many regrets.

Turning away he turned his attention to his tablet with the file Cloak Yorklin had sent him about Yuri. *He collected every iota of data he could, bundled it together, and shared it with me to see him in a better light. Having read it, all I can see is a man that Maggie would have kept close.*

Maggie loved King Making. She loved reminding men of how much she valued the world she saw. He helped save the night, she would be first in line to thank him. To hear his stories and tense up, then laugh because she knows how it ends, because he's telling her the story.

I need to get out of my car. I came to get this done. To see this.

Taking a deep breath he marshaled himself and set into motion. Getting out of his Duo-Car to get away from his thoughts he looked up at the roof and spotted the tell tale markers that the rooftop launcher had at least two rockets loaded. *Sundering House-Cleavers. I can't think of anything Thomas could send this way that wouldn't be stopped by one of those.*

Saluting the MCB with his right hand he said a silent prayer to honor the fallen. *May your sacrifices never be in vain. May your lives be remembered. May your kin tell your story.*

Turning on his heel he moved toward the front door of Maggie's Mansion. *Safe Housing, Maggie's Mansion, close enough.* Checking his comm he furrowed his brow at the lack of a response to him pulling up. Opening the 'Life and Times' application on his comm he navigated to Susan's status.

Asleep. Memo says she's down for a nap. I will enter quietly. Presenting his comm to the door he smiled when he heard the lock open for him. Letting himself in quietly he closed the door without hearing a sound signaling he had been heard. Moving to the edge of the mudroom he looked into the living room.

Sitting down on the mudroom bench he took stock of what he had just seen. *They barely fit on that couch. She hasn't changed clothes though. I'll need to get her to fix that. And I forgot my bag in the car.*

Sighing dejectedly he heard the sound of someone rousing from around the corner. Peeking out he made eye contact with Yuri. Raising his hand to gesture he stopped as it occurred to him Yuri wouldn't know what he was gesturing.

Smiling at him with a foolish intensity Yuri held the expression for a long moment before laying his head back down behind Susan's head. *I will go get my things. At least he's helping her, so that she might take care of herself.*

3.8.1 - 11:59

Safe Housing – Living Room

☼ Yuri

Taking a moment to nuzzle Susan's hair he reflected on the extremes his nose was relaying. *She smells terrible overall but a good sort of terrible.*

Nuzzling the back of her head he felt her shift against him with an approving sound for a moment.

Nuzzling her again he spoke softly, "Susan, wake up."

Speaking the words with a slight slur of sleep, "did the perimeter chime?"

Keeping it simple he explained, "no, someone is outside again. An older man came in, went to gesture at me, stopped with a look of humored annoyance, then went back outside."

Replying with less of a slur to it, "noted. I'm getting up. It is most likely Dennis. He would have Clearance to do that."

Letting go of Susan he felt more than an iota of sadness of losing the moment of touch. Waiting until she was clear he started the slow process of moving himself from the couch.

Looking up he watched as the man, from moments before, endured a collision from Susan as soon as he set down his case. *Her affection is strong.*

Speaking the name with a familial resonance, "Dennis!"

As assumed, it is.

Disengaging her from the hug with a deliberate slowness, "I noticed you were resting. I did my best to be quiet."

Nodding she spoke as a student does to a teacher, "noted. It's, *good,* to see you."

Holding up a hand he gestured with a practiced ease, "do me a favor?"

Appearing more serious with her demeanor and tone, "speak it."

These two have history.

"Go change. Shower, and new vestments." Gesturing something else he smiled as his firmly spoken words carried the paternal timbre, "the vestments of the moment are the vestments of the moment. Go find something more suited to where you are."

Looking down at herself she nodded with a quiet determination, "I shall honor your request." Looking toward him she smiled, "behave yourself."

Holding up his hands with the palms facing outward and upward as she had taught him, "I will."

Watching her leave he was relieved to see the smile on her face as she left the two of them alone. *She trusts this man, and myself, in this moment. I will not betray that trust.*

Turning his attention to Dennis, "where do I stand for this?"

Gesturing to an open corner of the living room, "right there works well enough."

"Noted."

"Let me get my tape and ledger. I'll get you jotted down and reviewing choices before you know it."

"Noted!"

3.7.5 - 11:02

Cloak and Dagger HQ - Commander's Sanctum

∩ Steven Bachman

Leaning back in his massage chair he fought with staying awake in the soothing relief that Stanley's hands were bringing his legs. *He wakes me up, feeds me, and then tries to put me back to sleep.*

Yawning without force he flexed his toes, *it's getting worse. I don't like it. I'll send the Telesphorus my notes. Another wasted set of IV Bags. I can hope the next treatment doesn't hurt like some of them have.*

Posing his question with a lovingly diagnostic tone Stanley sounded supportive, "how's the grip strength?"

Trying not to grumble too hard with his reply, "I can barely hold my gun at points. Maggie had problems not unlike this as she got closer to the end, and I'm starting to see them in earnest. The last treatment helped with the speech issues." Firing the words with a disappointed humor, "it's a rusted up thing to know how wise a person appears when they just stop talking as much."

Reflecting on it with an honest encouragement, "you *have* been a wiser man in this last year though."

I have then. You don't lie to me for my favor.

This hurts to admit. "I will see this through, I will see Winter's Night, and then? I will finish making my peace. This year, I will say as much as I can on the Day of Reflection. As I don't believe I will be seeing another."

Punctuating the word with a caress of his foot, "noted."

Focus. We can play when the work is done. "I need to see my sister next. I have the pieces prepping for checkmate on Thomas."

Broaching the subject with a flawed care, "and the Death Warrants?"

I can hear the humanity in your voice. "If she lets me? She lets me. That House has been led by a thorn in the side of peace for long enough. I have no definitive way of knowing if their *sickness,* goes deeper than I would like to find out it does." Keeping calm he felt Stanley's grip turn far more tender. *Words, no need to be angry right now.* "We can find a new family. We can find a new Consul. What we *cannot* find is a way to undo what they have done."

"And if she stops you?"

Then everyone gets the presents she would give them. The gift of life. "Then those who have doubts in the course of action that Thomas took? They can see her shining light and run toward it *before* something like this happens. Doubt must be erased. Either her enemies must see her forgiveness, or her ability to burn them to dust and ash. No half measures."

Keeping with his careful tone, "I noticed that Cassia Kunlow has a second document next to her name."

Flexing his toes he smiled at the simplicity of the backup plan, "Nullification of Union. If she signs I can make her a Drenner again and save her from the pyre. I can escort her back to my Marraine and tell her to guard her carefully."

Spritzing his legs with a topical medication, "and if she refuses to sign?"

Then she dies a romantic. "Then she can go to the pyre with her husband and die for love. As I said, it has to be one or the other, no half measures."

Setting to rubbing the medication in, "my brain floats in murky water, so I can understand a measure of your feelings. This is not you as the Dark Merchant though. We are at the Crossroads, and either deal we could make, could be seen as a Dark Dealing. Neither option is without *cost*."

The thing my sister asks though, is no less dark. "My sister is asking something more than I am, I would think. We can bury dead, we can wash something clean with blood soaked water, and then endeavor to forget it happened. House Kunlow would be nothing more than something akin to the Foundation Conflict. A crime we know we committed, but that we never speak of, because to do so would cause us to question who we are and what we stood for."

Continuing, "she is asking for what *could* be seen as an elaborate mulligan. To *accept* this. To cleanse the wound in a way that is going to hurt everyone. I need her to know that she's walking the harder road. To never forget that forgiveness is the hardest thing we can do in this life. Hating is easy. Forgiving is hard."

Moving on to his other leg Stanley appeared warmer with his words, "if she knows it, if she can see it, then all will see it. The people will see her taking the hardest road, and she will move forward, and then they will follow her because that is what they do. They follow the leader."

"Yes." *Also,* "it's not like I can take a life in this because I *want to*. Her instructions were quite clear."

Nodding with an affirmation in his tone, "this is true."

Reaching down he touched Stanley gently on the side of his head, "thank you."

Looking up with a paternal grin, "noted."

My peaceful port in the storm. "Do you even know what I'm thanking you for?"

"No, not exactly." Shrugging for a moment of pause he resumed his ministrations, "I just accept it and try not to belabor your love."

"Thank you."

Finishing the other leg his tone turned to one of caution, "I have noticed the way that Dagger Herb looks at you."

It is good to know I am not imagining things. Terrible to be right about it though. "I believe she is playing Watchful Eye. I have set things into motion to test reality, and not all of those tests were well received. I believe, with some certainty, that if I cross a line she has been told to be ready for? She will end me. Then our system will end her. Then Susan will be without her."

"What is feared?"

"That I will, my life running out, cease to be vigilant against the Rage. That I will be pushed to destroy someone. My actions in Bliss were a gray area of morality. I passed a Guild Review for it, but it made an impression."

"Then it is someone who knows you, who also knows that Dagger Herb is willing to sacrifice herself for the good of society."

Solid logic train. "I would agree. Which convinces me beyond the shadow of doubt that it isn't Susan who has set her on me. Someone *else* has taken my sister's Aardvark, and has armed her and set her up to this as a defense against me."

Nodding once with a fouled humor, "I would agree in that assessment."

"It's a sad world we live in." Touching Stanley again he smiled, "cheer up?"

Losing the foul he sighed, "someone wants to kill you."

Flexing his toes again, "*we* both know that more than a few people would like to see me dead. That I have done things I should not have in a better world. Ripples in ponds. My father knew Thomas wanted to kill him, and look how long *that* took to come to pass. Is it *terrible?* Yes. Do I *deserve it?* Perhaps. The *objective* idea though, is that Sasha is being played as a failsafe by someone who doesn't have faith in me to keep myself together. I'll tell O'Neil and Hampton to have shock boxes at the ready."

Getting up from his stool he leaned in and kissed him on the forehead, "you would risk your own life for her?"

I share what happiness I can in this mortal coil with you. She can share the rest of her life, as much of it as can be made, with Susan. "I don't have much of this one left. She has *a lifetime,* in comparison."

"There is no recourse left for you?"

Taking a breath he sighed, "if the new plane being built passes the test flights? I will have to give Susan the file that dad hid. To be specific, the one about the facility to the East. The last medical research center we know of that might have clues to help mom. Well, *me too,* at this point. She doesn't know why I hated him for that. If I die before I get to tell her, you need to tell her."

Running his fingers through his hair gently he smiled with a grimness to the gesture, "it is in your Final Directives list for me."

Reaching up he touched Stanley gently, "I know, I just, sometimes saying things feels good."

"I know, but I wanted to reaffirm you. To let you know that I knew it was part of my tasks." After a moment of pause he returned to his stool to resume his ministrations. "I want to think that if I had the power to order something like that that I would order it for you."

Turning away with the doubt weighing heavy on him. "And, I would tell you I would feel uncomfortable with having an entire team sent on what is essentially a suicide mission. To send them into the unknown where any small thing going wrong with the craft would be the death of all of them? Seems excessive. My life? I lived it, I made my mistakes, this world doesn't *need* me. I just want to give Susan the chance to save Mother if she wants to risk it. Mother didn't do anything wrong."

With the timbre of the Supportive Friend, "the copious files on Maggie show a woman who never did anything *wrong,* she may have made a mistake, but she was never *wrong.*"

Food for thought about the trip. "There was a time when that was space. Man was reaching for the Moon, Mars, and it was the dangerous thing to do. Now? Just going to the other coast is a nightmare of logistics."

"I have faith we will reclaim our glory. I also have faith we will name the Moon something else."

I will dream, larger than my own life. "When we reach it as a people and put our colony on it? We will dub it Selene and the capital will be Luna City."

Snickering with a humor, "did that pass as a measure?"

It feels good to discuss things of no real import. "A Council meeting covered it a month ago. They were going through things that were pending, of far future import, and they decided on that."

"Sounds fine to me."

"It made some people happy to know that we hadn't forgotten about space. It's a distant dream but we'll get there."

Lowering his leg he set to getting back up to a standing position, "so what of you?"

If this was a different day I would have a more pleasing answer. "I get my socks, shoes, and self, back on and go see this through."

Moving over to the nearby table, "let me get your socks."

Chuckling with the humor he didn't want to shove aside, "as you took them from me? That would be helpful."

Picking up a new pair of socks he moved back to him, "I love you."

I would rather stay in and affirm that we're alive. "Noted. I love you also. I might not say it enough, but I do."

"Noted. I know." Holding out the socks to him, "what of Yuri?"

Taking the socks he sighed with a surge of depressed rage, "he killed my father."

Obviously trying to stay noncommittal, "the data points to it, based upon the specific Contingency that was used."

The things you notice my love. Reaching to put the first sock on he sighed at the stiffness still present in his muscles. Holding the socks back out to Stanley he smiled with a helpless feeling as he took them back and set to sitting before him.

Holding his right foot up, "this is part of why I don't want Susan around him. She cares about him in a way that he didn't earn. He is a lost animal, a creature that needs tending, and that creature happens to be a *man* by the same measure."

Pulling the sock onto his foot, "you fear that she'll love him."

Flexing his toes in his snugly fitted sock, "I fear that she already *does*."

Asking with a Diagnostic timbre, "is this a bad thing?"

A man for her to love? No. "To love? No. Because it is her and the circumstances around it? It *could* be. I worry for the unknown."

Setting to the other sock, "you feel he didn't earn her love by measure of his deeds, but by the measure of circumstance?"

I have had some hours to calm myself as best I can. "If we look at his deeds, then he gets the acknowledgement of what he did last night. He *did* make himself useful. He wants to protect her. I just wish she would use the caution of distance to find some perspective on this."

Settling the other sock into place with a conversational ease, "I can see how that would be a valid worry. What with the debt that is owed."

Flexing his toes he lowered his foot. "the debt is valid, for what its worth. How she's having to pay it? Is not."

Getting Steven's boots Stanley's tone was his usual awkwardly chipper self, "does Yuri have anything to fear from you?"

Grumbling at his own conclusion, "*only* if he changes his mind about being loyal."

Smiling lazily with the words, "such is life for all of us."

You're right. "Truth."

"It doesn't ease the moment of seeing him, does it?"

"No. I," forcing his composure in line, "I don't get to know if I could have been friends with my father again. I don't get to know the what might have been. It's, difficult, to want to look at him. I, owe him now though. He was there with Frank when they saved Patrick. He mustered the will to fight when Cloak Yorklin stopped to be a healer first. He, did no small amount of favor for my family."

Tossing the diagnostic question out, "you just wish she didn't love him?"

"Correct." *No.* "No. What I wish is that she would be *careful*. I don't want to wish love out of this world. I just feel she's being reckless. We have so many people whom could have helped her if she just would have flexed her power."

Speaking the mantra with a practiced ease, "Protocol is Protocol."

I am being selfish and hiding it behind concern.

Adjusting his boots with a smile Stanley set to the act of lacing them up, "this is the first time isn't it?"

For Susan? "That she has loved a man? Yes."

Tying the knot in the laces with a firmness, "and she picked the most dangerous of men?"

Fair approximation. "Yes."

Patting the boot, "she is like her mother, from what I know of her."

Rusted scrap. "Makes sense now."

Moving to the other boot he cinched and worked the laces, "we are what we learn."

I feel the care you put into me, and I appreciate it. "What do I do about my feelings?"

"What you always do," giving his boots a pat, "you wrestle with them until you, or they, win."

Feeling humbled by the moment, "I will endeavor to do this right."

Getting to his feet, "as long as you don't shoot anyone you should not? You will be fine."

I will see this through. "I need to go."

Holding out his hand to Steven, "you do."

Taking his hand he accepted the help in being hoisted to his feet. Leaning in he kissed Stanley on the cheek as their mutual scruff chafed. "When this is done? We need to shave."

Stepping away with a smile as he rubbed his cheek, "we do. A Blue Sky to you Steven. Safe Journey Commander."

I need to leave or I won't go. "A Blue Sky to you as well."

Turning on his heel he moved to the door, *I have to turn this Lose-Lose into a Win-Win one way or another.* Clearing the door he set into a practiced stride once he was in the hall. Getting out his comm he signaled Hampton and O'Neil, *we ride.*

3.8.4 - 12:45

Safe Housing – Living Room

☼ Yuri

Looking up to him from his notebook Dennis smiled with an exasperation to the gesture, "you passed."

Furrowing his brow with his reply, "pardon?"

Jotting down the last measurement he smiled up at him, "you passed. She's not in the room so I can speak freely. She obviously gave you instructions on how to handle yourself. I have taken all of your measurements, shown you the things I have on hand, and you've even picked the things we're going to put together for you. And in all of this? You have been nothing but cordial, jovial, polite to a fault. And yet?" Waving his pencil at him playfully, "there is something missing."

Well then. Smiling with the encouragement of the moment, "how did you get her to shower? I wanted her to, but I was unable to get her to go."

Nodding once he tipped his pencil toward him, "I asked her as a favor."

"That simple?"

Answering with a nostalgic and yet conversational timbre, "I was her teacher, once upon a time. She came to me to learn the Art of Shadows. That gives me an emotional leverage with her. I used that leverage, via the request, to get her to do what she wanted."

"Noted."

"I taught her of the Shadows, how to work within the Pyramid, and the cipher to see the information with. The logical sense of understanding the world, with her instincts of how to navigate the social world? Helped create a more expansive toolbox for her sharp mind."

I wonder, "are you still her teacher?"

Shaking his head with a soft sadness, "I wouldn't lay claim to that. I taught her all of the *direct* lessons I did, could, and probably ever will years ago." With an up-tick of happiness he continued, "I am still part of her Personal Tribe."

New learnings? "Personal Tribe?"

"The Network tells us, that each person gets around one hundred and forty-nine people they can be allied with at any one time as a single, personal, tribe. There is a margin for error, but keeping it to one hundred and fifty within a community is seen as prudent. Which means that even when Miss Bachman calls a Convocation of Friendship, she can only invite one hundred and forty-nine. This includes family."

Thinking back to the view from the office window, "but, all the lights."

Gesturing to the nearby chairs, "sit? We have a few minutes at least before she emerges from the office."

"Oh, yes." Moving over to the chair he took a seat and looked over to Dennis, "what is the population of New Hope?"

"Census data put us up and over the one hundred thousand mark last year, of those who are classified as Citizens who call New Hope their home."

"This is such a large city though, the amount of room you have to work with."

"We rebuild as quickly as we can, but we've had," frowning while fighting to smile, "some setbacks."

"How many used to live here? Before the Ash, that is."

"The estimate is no less than four million souls. We make our home in a graveyard."

Focus. "I need to stay on question, she gets one hundred and forty-nine?"

Sitting with a grim neutrality to his demeanor, "yes. She keeps her rolls as light as she can to make sure there is room for someone else to join."

Hold on, if that is this and that is that? "Her Honor Guard, if the get to ninety, does that consume ninety of her allotment?"

Cracking a smile he appeared pleased, "you are well informed. Does she resist it?"

"She seems unhappy, yes." *And I was telling her she needed more.* "I did not know the cultural conventions."

Nodding at him he gave him a pat on the arm with a reassurance, "now you understand why she resisted carrying more. She either gives up space on the rolls, or makes the knowing act of *not* befriending a person as a member of her tribe. This idea has caused a strange fluidity within her sphere of influence. Some would rather *not* befriend her, so that she would have that space for another, content to just be *loyal.* Others? Would *want* that Validation Acceptance of having a place within that select group."

That leads to a new question. "How would she trust someone, not of her tribe, to defend her life?"

"That would be the problem she would have to solve. She solved how to have that many men around her and not end up entangled. She conquered her own ego. She conquered the vulnerability of others. But that question, how to trust with her life those not of her tribe? That was not yet solved."

"Can she compromise and just get sixty?"

"She *could.* That will be for her to navigate."

"When she told me, I would have the power to call her on the comm?"

Smiling with a brotherly air about him, "she was welcoming you to her allotment."

I would be next to her in this in a new way. "I am humbled."

Waggling his pencil with a supportive demeanor, "perhaps a different topic then?

Or knowledge to impart?"

I will get a perspective I have been unable to bring myself to ask about. "On the radio, I heard about the Courtesans, I am still wishing I understood more."

Stopping his pencil he nodded, "I am aware, being as informed as I am, what the original function of such an arrangement was. That's not allowed."

Then what is? "Can a Citizen engage in such a life as their vocation then? Or no?"

Tapping the back of his hand with the pencil eraser he nodded with a look of recollection. "Under a new provision, yes. Sexual Surrogate and Sexual Therapy both have options for a person to enter into such a calling as a vocation. The recreational *play* of the Courtesans is not *as* open to being a vocation, even though it still happens. No one *wants* someone getting hurt. Though, every once in awhile an extroverted and empathic person comes along whom can make it their vocation and that's seen as fine."

I need a dictionary. "Sexual Surrogate?"

"When someone has a flaw in their clay, or a break they've been given? Sometimes more *extreme* measures are called on. In this case it's the specifically trained and cultivated resource of professionals who can combine Behavior Exercise, Role-Play, and Sexual Intimacy into one Endeavor."

Wait, I think I've done that. I will ask the professionals later on that. Though, "your culture made the Courtesans a place of play, joy, and now healing?"

Nodding with a pride showing through, "yes. As per Tammerlane's Tribute."

That makes enough sense that I am content now. "I understand more."

"Anything else I can aid you with?"

Rushing the question he blurted out the words, "can I ask what Code Five Seventy Six is?"

Appearing humored he patted him on the upper arm, "of course you can! It's the history of man rewrote into a turn of the phrase. She wanted out, she wanted to not be stopped, but she showed a hole card. She had a few choices for which code to use Yuri. The one she showed us? In that year the Visigoths set up Toledo, as far as we know. That city is said to have brought us marzipan. Which is a dessert. They have doled out a helping of sorrow and death to her. She will return to them a plate of just dessert."

That's - "and all that meaning was in those four words?"

"Yes. Technically it would have just been the word Code, and the number. Those unfamiliar with it would be able to access the explanation that it's an enhanced personal space bubble."

I have to know. "How do you find time to memorize all these things?"

"The personal answer?" Lapsing into a moment of nostalgic melancholy, "that was one of her father's favorites. He would be feeling down and out and he would use those numbers to escape from the field of battle but vow that he would come back." Snapping his fingers he appeared to snap himself out of it, "Primers though. We have this in the Codex on the Network."

This makes more sense. "I have heard mention of that on the radio."

"Good! The Codex System begins from the moment a child can read. A child will get the first piece of the General Codex as soon as they can read."

"Did Stephanie get the Codex as soon as she had settled in?"

"Yes. She, had a whole new world ahead of her."

I wonder. "What should I expect?"

"For one, we use no small amount of Myth. Based upon what became of us as a people. Myths are the stories that a Civilization tells itself so it can sleep at night. Thus our Myths are not meant to contradict the past, or the truth, but instead ease the pain."

"Noted."

"The children, they get stories. Examples. Lived experiences, of humans, or anthro animals. Talking pigs, goats, and the like to tell the story of us. By removing the human element? Any child can see themselves in the diversity of thought on display."

"Noted. Should I start with that material?"

"I believe you know the important lessons."

"Thank you."

"No thanks needed, but accepted." Continuing, "as the child gets older, in the case of Stephanie she was given a year before she enrolled in the education system. She was given time to independent study, and she made friends with children who were learning Spanish."

"The radio was all in English."

Raising an eyebrow with a humor to the question, "were you listening to an English station?"

"I guess I was."

"The Conlangers see to it that every child learns a second language. Even if it is just Province Sign Language. Stephanie was adept at her dialect of Spanish, which gave her social clout to join a group."

"Neat. Noted."

"Then she got older, and I made certain she was reading more. Bonnie, Daisy, Maggie for a short time, and a few other contemporaries I had at the time were more than willing to aid her in understanding what makes a woman in these lands."

"How much is written?"

"Everything we can find a way to quantify. Each of the Provinces has a unique set to it, complete with flights of fancy and dreams of their people. Thanks to the Network, we can share them and see what sticks to each other. Arming the next generation with all of the wisdom that has come before."

The Library of Being Human? "The goal that nothing is left to chance or slack."

"Correct. Why would we want that? Also, we have Language Primers which cover every turn of the phrase to express and search the mind for what is the truth of the self. Also, those follow a *prescriptive* methodology. So they're easier to use, in theory. Also, the prescriptive methodology is only used on English."

Marveling at the idea, "so every concept, every word, every idea, you are trying to write it all down and have it at the ready?"

"For the most part we have succeeded."

I wonder if this system could have helped me so many years ago? "A story then? A young man finds his fancy turning to thoughts of affectionate touch, and he finds a way to express it in this Codex?"

Tapping Yuri's arm gently and gesturing with his hands, "or he finds he has grown attached to the Levirate in the house and has to find the Primer for that." Adding as an afterthought, "that was the gesture for 'example offered.'"

"Noted. First though, there is the practice of Levirate?"

Smiling with a gentle sigh, "both genders can qualify. I know the Latin means something else but a universal term was needed and it was close enough for the Conlangers. If you're not in a good place and the family of the departed wishes to take you in? You are the Levirate in their house. Still family, still honored as family, even if there are no children. It's voluntary for both parties."

I will ask for the story. "What does this young man say to the Levirate in the house he dwells?"

Meeting his gaze for a moment, "you would hear the story?" Laughing he played with his pencil, "I know that you started this fork in our road, but custom is that I ask for you to confirm before launching into it."

"I would like to hear it. Yes. Also!" Smiling with a boldness, "I *am* slowly getting used to the formal but yet blunt nature of your people."

"Did you ask for stories in your travels?"

It is my turn to sound nostalgic. "In my travels, I would go to other men, and ask them their story. My mentor told me, I must never teach you fear, or you will know even I know fear. My father told me he could not teach me doubt in getting up in the morning, because then he would be seen as doubting his life. It was in short order I learned that the men I would meet would care to speak of fear, of doubt, of feeling vincible. When you are leaned on, being those things scares those around you. I shared my stories, they would share their stories, and with bread, water, and words we would learn of each other. I would give them a safe shoulder and ear."

Asking with an open inquisitiveness, "how well did that go?"

"More often than not? With the aid of a few drinks, I would get a story of survival. The near miss with the grave. Those sorts of tales." *Back to it.* "Tell me though, what is your story of Levirate?"

"My story begins with a declaration. I went to her and said," pausing with a nostalgic grin, "I know your color has turned scarlet, as a new Levirate you are mourning, but I see you as a woman that I wish to know. If you seek comfort? I can be that comfort."

Lead me onto the road of your story, "how did you know?"

"She had spoken of it at the dinner table. She hoped we wouldn't see her as dishonoring his memory."

"So you ran to her?"

"The next night, the night before she was going to go seeking touch, I went to her."

So much to learn. "If she touched you, would it be wrong to do so?"

Speaking of a cherished memory, "no, we had known her for years Yuri, we weren't going to *stop* being who we were with her. My uncle wasn't that much older than her, she was not that much older than myself. Sometimes the ages of children get staggered in unusual ways."

Color codes too, not surprised. "So, what is scarlet? Also, Susan's door upstairs is a pale red, which I don't understand either."

"Red, begins with the ideas of life. Blood. Heart. Heat. When you add orange to it, which does contain warmth, danger, taste, aroma, and fire, you gain scarlet."

"Ah! She was full of life, and fire. Was it wrong for her to want to touch?"

Shaking his head softly, "no. Life is life, the fire burns. My Uncle was gone, she had a friend that was going to tend to the fire within her. Suffering is our natural state, to abate suffering is to ease the pain of life."

That is staggering. "Noted."

"Meanwhile Susan's door is a white mixed red which has rendered it pale but not quite pink. That pale cream red speaks to her softly beating heart. There is no small amount of fire there, but it is washed in an emotional state that lightens the shade but does not change the reality."

I do not know my colors. "Noted."

"Pink, is for the gentle heart. Also, colors are gender neutral. As they have meaning, they are not meant for first names, or a given reality. As a man, there is no shade that is culturally forbidden to you."

I do not look good in pink, but it is strange to know it would be fine. "Oh, that is good to know."

"If you miss bright colors from your travels? You can garb yourself in the colors you choose."

"I will keep that in mind."

"The middle name, as an aside, is where the name of blessings go. You can put the color, emotion, idea, or concept between the given name and the family name."

"I do not have a middle name."

"You could create one for yourself."

Options are good! "I will keep that in mind too!"

"Now, as for her? Her heart had turned scarlet again, because she wanted to embrace life to chase off the lingering doubt of death."

Nodding with an understanding, "you made your intentions known."

"I felt I loved her more than the man she was considering to cling to in that moment. I knew The Guild would get involved in short order. Which means that if I was going to feel like that? If she was going to want something like that? I would volunteer, and would have to volunteer before the day of. I would be brave."

"How did that turn out?"

Still smiling with the retelling, "she took me to her bed and she told me that I would know what I needed to know in the morning."

What will I be told? "Did something happen other than talk?"

"A little. There were no passionate embraces of experienced loves, I was fifteen and had never known the physical love of a woman like that. We touched, we kissed, but I mostly trembled and begged her not to go. She was sleeping nude, so I did get an education of a sorts."

There is no glory *in this retelling, only the warm truth.* "And the morning?"

"She held me close, without reservations, in the morning light. She accepted the idea that I could try to be that man for her."

"What of The Guild?"

"As I said, I was fifteen at the time. After we shared a shower we knew we had to see The Guild about this. I would not be anything less than honest about this. She agreed and we went down there -"

Raising a hand to interrupt, "and your age wasn't an issue?"

"Circumstances. I was the initiator which would color a review before a decision could be made. Being as it was there was no punishment that needed to be leveled at either of us." Looking at his face he nodded once, "we are a people who love to examine the *why* of a moment."

"Was it hard to see them?"

Nodding twice, "yes. They wanted to know what we had done. There's further nuance to sexual conduct reviews. I was sitting there with the checklist, I had a physical clipboard, with the forms and I had written my answers. I had my eyes down in a shy humor for most of it. I was not always shy as a young man, but I was in that moment. No matter how gentle the inquiry into it is when it comes to affairs of the heart they can become comically trying."

Nodding he smiled and waited for Dennis to continue.

"I had to raise objection to the idea of her being punished as I found the words to admit I did feel love."

More to learn. "So what is the distinction there?"

"The Pledge of the Albatross is based upon a layered ideal of love, courtships, and the presence and influence of sex. The young are taught to love themselves, to be at peace with themselves, then to move forward with courtships. By going to her bed, even though I was not inside of her body, she was inside my mind and heart. We take this ideal seriously."

Wait, did he just say what I think he said? "Then, the youth, get to be young?"

"They do. We give everyone the luxury of growing up slowly so they can have more understanding of self and what matters before they think about adding another. I jumped over the starting line and went running as some do."

"Some?"

"Biology is a messy thing Yuri. I speak only as a male in this, but I will tell you what I can. Sometimes when the ardors of youth come calling, it pushes the body forward. Ways of prolonging the process are provided. A culture that doesn't tell growing men that putting themselves inside a woman is what makes them a man, is the first thing. The Primer on Physical Self Love has some interesting lessons in finding the spots of self that feel better than others. In the end? Not everyone is the same. I had seen love, what it meant to love her first hand, and when she spoke of wanting to live that again I felt I could be that person. That's part of circumstances."

Feeling the investment in the moment, "and then?"

After a breath, "we were hand-fasted within the month. Year and a day each time after. She went back into her younger years, just recently left behind, and walked with me through mine. When I was twenty-one I was working for the Network as an Entertainment Archaeologist when the High Consul would read what I suggested."

He leaves the pause for me to fill. "Cloak and Dagger."

"Correct. It was a huge step and Gentle," looking up at him with a heartfelt grin, "it was her middle name which she preferred to hear, knew we were at our conclusion. We parted on excellent terms and I'll never forget her, if I can help it."

I wonder, "so what was your daughter's coming of age like?"

Laughing for a moment he spoke with a humored calm, "far less dramatic. She spent her time enjoying being young. Learning as much as she could cram inside her mind. Then she grew up, found a man, and brought forth a daughter. She was going to try for a son but," glowering with the words, "that didn't work out."

Trying to be optimistic, "if they get back together?"

Losing the majority of the glower for something more friendly, "she told you?"

I will see if this means what I think it does. Raising his hand gently with the index finger extended upward with a slight crook to it, "she told me *some.*"

Smiling at his hesitant gesture Dennis nodded, "that's the 'gentle amendment' gesture."

Lowering his hand with a smile, "noted!"

"As for the hope of them reuniting? Then perhaps she will have a son for her daughter to protect and take care of while he learns how to be a man who could turn around and do the same."

"Is that the role of the men in these lands?"

"The status quo recreated a more concrete Role system, with Caveats for the pieces that don't fit, to make it so that which feels more natural would be easier for people. You are meant to be the person you are. If you are male, or female, or third? You pursue a role that feels *right,* as you are volunteering your life to it. Example, if you want to join the Armed Forces? They're not going to turn you away at first glance from trying to become the person that these lands need. If you don't measure? You won't see duty. But if you do? Then you will."

Life is simpler in some ways. "More to consider, more to learn."

"Always."

"What do I say here? How do I reply in a way that makes sense?"

Speaking his words with a proud smile, "do you feel honored I shared?"

Replying with a soft happiness, "yes."

"Do you want me to know that you felt it was a good story?"

"Yes."

"Do you want to be verbose, or just succinct as you wear your heart on your sleeve? Which, by the way, is probably why she cautioned you to use caution with me," smiling as a well seasoned man of mischief, "because I can get out of hand sometimes."

Simple answer. "Succinct would work for me."

"Then just say *noted.*"

A simple answer again? I'm on a roll. "That works for this too?"

"You are aware of the use of the word otherwise then?"

"I've picked up the gist of things, I just wanted to make sure I didn't miss something."

"Mind you, the tone, the smile, the body language? Show your feelings, is the best advice I can give you if you want to live in this land. I saw the way you look at Susan, it's clear as day. If you fear that you cannot convey your emotions? You give them names. Say it clearly. I am humbled, honored, and touched by your story. And then cap it with *graciously noted.* People in this land? They just want to know someone listened outside of The Guild."

Probing the question, "even you?"

Affirming with a smile, "even me."

"Thank you for the lesson."

"Noted. If you need more? Ask Susan. She will teach you."

"Noted. What's left?"

Swallowing heavily he slumped for a moment, "Asmodai was a shadow of himself when you did what you did."

He knows? "You know? Susan said it was six people who knew."

Cocking his head to the side with an incredulous grin, "*I* wrote the plan for the death of a VIP in Central that would need to be cleaned up. That's why Susan is getting away with it. I wrote her a wonderful plan, I just didn't know when she would need to use it." Shaking his head softly, "I went through more than I would care to review, or have the time for to review, with Asmodai. I was there for him when he buried his father, his brother, and," catching himself, "many others. I was there for the wedding. I was his

Honor Attendant."

Is this a possible question to ask that won't get me into something I do not understand? "You will me no ill?"

Frowning and appearing on the verge of tears, "we all failed him, then he failed himself. None of the children were ready for the Throne if we had to take him off it. Then time just kept slipping away. You ended something that we should have solved a long time ago and you did it in a way that couldn't be taken back. We got what we prayed for. We just didn't know it would hurt so much."

Something - "he was an interesting man to talk to when he would visit me."

"I can't fathom what you must have been doing to him."

Feeling the shared sadness he spoke softly, "he looked at me like I would imagine someone would look at a creature from another world."

"You are."

Fretting with his thumb and forefinger on his left hand he felt at a loss, "what do we do now?"

Closing his eyes and taking a deep breath Dennis hummed a few bars of what sounded like a jaunty tune. Opening his eyes he flashed a resigned smile, "there really isn't much to do. It's not a *perfect* match, but you are the same sort of size and stature as another man I have consulted with before. I know whom I can talk to and get you casual wear in your size in short order. The majority of the things you're looking for are easily made, with just a few of the more interesting pieces to complete your wardrobe, which won't be needed right away. I should be able to have you garbed before you need to look your best."

Feeling the upbeat tone lift him, "neat."

"Indeed!" Smiling again with an honest relief, "it makes my life so much easier."

"Good."

I think I hear Susan in the kitchen. Feeling the humored panic he fought himself for control, *I hope it's Susan.*

It probably is.

3.8.6 - 12:55

Safe Housing - Interior

☽☾..Susan Bachman

Checking the contents of the oven she smiled seeing that the moment was still on time table. *And now to turn this oven off so I can see Dennis out without burning these.*

Turning the oven off her mind wandered as she stared at the baked goodies through the window on the door. *I think Yuri is going to like these. I hope he finds the same joy for the Odds and Ends package as I do. I just hope he doesn't ask what's in them because I honestly don't know. And with no one here to force me to eat I can feed the whole package to him while I feel too torn up to bother with real food.* Checking the time while finishing her can of Liquid Lunch, *Dennis should be just about done with him.*

The reports are in final stage of Action and Reporting. Every door has been knocked on. Every child found. Every last piece of bad news sent.

Turning and leaning against the wall next to the oven she reviewed the polish on her nails as her thoughts lashed the good news together. *Doctor Monroe stepped in on behalf of the Blackout Bloc by offering them a chance to be in a Psychiatric Study.* Rereading the message on her comm she mused at the brick of words, *Observation of the Effects of Extreme Behavior as Result of Group-Think and the Aftermath of Life Post Trauma. An edifice of a title which leaves their detractors with nothing more to say on the subject if they agree to it.*

Putting her comm away she leaned against the wall with a newfound heaviness to her spirit. Unable to suppress the chuckle of defensive laughter she gripped her empty can with both hands. *If I can accept that they are still alive, then perhaps, they can accept a world where I am still alive.*

As I doubt anyone wants to let them run roughshod over reality again, I would suspect they will behave.

I will also make a note to tell Waterlily I will need extra sessions to find a way to stomach it. I want to choke this down, swallow it whole, and just endure it until it becomes normal inside. Those people get a Second Chance. If they squander it, I will send them to their ends myself.

Fair enough? Fair enough.

Taking a breath she moved to the recycling container and gingerly discarded her can into it. *Done.* Looking at the sleeve of her blouse she sighed at the way the fabric had fallen. *Get dressed without paying attention and pay the penalty.* Taking a moment to check her cargo skirt. *It's not like he's going to know what this means, still haven't told him near enough about us. Odds are he'll just see a long skirt with large pockets and a long sleeve blouse and a vest with odd buttons. Dennis will know it's casual courtship in soft greens of travel, and having left my black and white hair tie on my vanity? He'll know where I stand.*

Not that being found on the couch like that wasn't a mostly definitive gesture. At least I can show him how I feel. To have a moment of normal in a whirlpool of the worst day ever.

Inquiring within for answers she found one more for herself. *That and I can't have another woman thinking they should make a play for him as an Unattached. I am just being honest with Yuri, I do want to see what becomes of us.*

Taking a moment to breathe she banished the line of thought and headed for the living room. Crossing into the hall she startled when the front door opened without warning. Reaching for a weapon that wasn't there her hand came up to point at Steven, "what are you doing here?"

Regarding her outstretched hand his face fell to a solemnly sad expression. Moving over to her with a quiet aura of defeat, belied by the slump of his shoulders, he signaled for a hug. Moving in quietly she took him into her arms.

Speaking his words with a tone no less defeated than his expression, "I *refuse* to fight with you. I *can't* use words because they will come out wrong."

Wrapping her arms around his shoulders she kept him close, "mea culpa."

"Noted, accepted, and mea culpa."

"Noted and accepted."

Wrapping his arms around her she felt the nostalgia of their younger years when they were closer wash over her as he spoke. "Susan, I was afraid, that you wouldn't be here to apologize to. The death toll, your people, I can see how Kunlow thought he would win. There may never be a group of people so loyal to you again."

That hurts in ways I didn't know I could still feel today. "I would rather never find out."

Almost leaning into her for support as he spoke, "you sound like mom."

Broaching the words carefully, "where do we begin, as you know the truth -?"

Gaining a measure of upbeat to his tone and demeanor, "I have to meet with the Council to discuss what I have. I might just have the ability to get Thomas' removal signed off on today. Stuff from dad's plans and notes file."

If he got it from dad, it will be the one-shot one-kill bullet. "He had an amazing understanding of Protocol."

Moving away from her a half step, "I have to ask you an unfair question."

Trying to keep the history out of her voice, "it won't be the first time."

Taking his hands off of her he set to clasping his gloved hands together, "I can order the death of Thomas Kunlow, yes?"

Nodding once with certainty she intoned her word knowing she would not be able to take it back, "yes."

Smiling with relief he lowered his hands to his sides, "thank you."

"Noted. I would order it but I don't have the evidence. I trust you will."

Speaking the words as a Pledged Idea, "I will."

"Good."

Looking past her he frowned at Yuri, "you know I don't approve of him."

Trying to stay diplomatic with her tone, "Outsider, was one of the things you called him."

With a solid timbre of grousing, "he doesn't know our customs. If he hurts you?"

Firing back with an upbeat lilt, "I'm teaching him."

Firing back in turn with a flat invocation, "others have more time, and experience with it."

Losing her diplomatic tone and upbeat lilt for something more accusatory, "you said I couldn't trust him."

Closing his eyes with a slump he sighed, "Father told us to reserve *Trust* to a select few. I didn't mean the you can't let him out of your sight trust, I meant the *your life,* kind of trust."

Feeling a moment of deflation to their aggression, "oh, I didn't hear the nuance on the comm."

Moving over and leaning on the opposite wall of the mud room from her. "I might not have given the inflection to it, I was fearing that you were dead, or worse at the time."

Chiming in with a calm but hesitant tone Yuri spoke toward Steven, "if I may ask?"

Pushing off the wall Steven stepped around and to the side to look at Yuri, "of course you can!"

"What is the things you fear?"

With a voice far calmer than she expected her brother's words left her with a sad chill, "I fear that the nightmares you have witnessed will have broken the pillars of goodness inside of you, and that in the end you would hurt her in a moment of madness."

Recoiling visibly for a moment from the accusation, "oof, you hit a man where it hurts." After a moment he sighed, "what specifically? Or is it the nebulous notions? Like a Greek Myth killing his family sort of thing? Or more tangible?"

Taking on a colder demeanor as his words tumbled out, "I fear that something in your moral compass would be damaged. That in your currently disadvantaged state for negotiation? You would prey upon her heart to stay alive, at whatever cost."

Frowning in reply Yuri sounded hurt, "I am sad now."

Without letting up he kept going, "I am also sad, because if you are the man she will invite to stay? The kaleidoscope of worry, concern, and emotion from that idea? It tears me up inside." Moving closer to Yuri he moved his hands away from his body, "this is the signal I am outside of drawing distance."

Watching the moment with a blanked mindscape her emotional state regressed to the moments she had been pinned against the walls of the past.

Croaking the words with a hint of panic Yuri raised his hands in a defensive gesture, "why do you approach?"

Holding his hands up he moved them closer until they rested on Yuri's upper arms. "My family, is one of the last things I have left to me. The tree has been struck by lightning, lit aflame, betrayed, sawed, and what is left?" Speaking faster with a borderline violent fear, "just four. *Four.* And your hands are wrapping around the budded flower of the last living branch. And as I watch, in horror, I am asked to accept that *you, you,* are touching her? You don't know the Codex, not the Primers, not the Gestures, not the cultural lessons. You are a wild beast which has fallen on our doorstep while dying. Look me in the eyes after everything you have done and tell me that I have nothing to worry about!" Raising his voice to a dire crescendo, "*look me in the eyes!*"

Moving quickly Dennis pushed his arm between them and pried Steven off of Yuri. "Susan, hold your brother!"

Moving in with a matched alacrity she took a hold of Steven as the fight went out of him. Gasping in what appeared to be pain he clutched her tightly.

"Steven? Status?"

Spitting the words out between grit teeth, "negative. Tension, headache."

Taking her brother in her arms she moved him over to the small couch to the side and set him down. Looking up she caught the motion of Dennis getting Yuri to sit and the small slap patch of Tranq now resting on Yuri's right hand.

Rounding on Steven with a snarl Dennis' fist clenched for a moment, "you went Over the Line, he's not well, but not how you think! Cloak Yorklin, rust it, just *saying that* feels unnatural. I digress. He took Yuri's symptoms to a Diagnostician. He sent me the notes." Throwing his dominate arm wide he kept his hand painfully visible, "do you think I *didn't* worry too? That *others* didn't worry?"

Raising his head he met Dennis' accusatory stare with a blank look of guilt and confusion. With a disconnected tone his words tumbled out, "I, didn't know what to think. The words. The anger -" letting the words go he hung his head.

Which patch is that? "How much Tranq?"

Snapping his fingers gently with a slow motion near the side of Steven's head Dennis answered her question, "low dose, just enough to bring him a measure of calm."

Staring at the patch on his hand Yuri contemplated it with a frown, "this stuff is very powerful, but it doesn't feel, good?"

Checking Steven's eyes with a pocket flashlight Dennis moved to the timbre of Professionalism, "it's a rusted piece of work we pulled out of the Network. It's not a *nice* drug at heart."

Forming the words with an emotionally empty sound to his tone, "then why do you use it?"

"It has been repurposed to provide calm without joy. It's not psychologically addictive because it doesn't feel good. It saves the day, but you don't want to deal with it."

Gesturing to her for 'handkerchief' and 'tend to him' Dennis took a moment to caress Steven's hair. "He didn't go over the edge, the tension headache cut off the rage."

Nodding in understanding she set to taking out her handkerchief. Folding it quickly she laid it over Steven's eyes. *Recklessly Accepting, Thoughtlessly Open,* the words of her mother's detractors rolling across her mind left her wishing for a handkerchief of her own. *He has succumbed to what those who feared for Maggie feared. That I would get myself lost in the darkness he brings.*

Catching a quick glance of Dennis, she watched as he produced a small soft pouch of a stuffed creature from his tailoring bag. "Yuri, this is Blob Blobberton."

Asking his question with a blank confusion, "what do I do?"

Speaking the words with a straight face, "you hold him, and take comfort."

Watching Yuri take the small creature and squeeze him she felt a heartened warmth as his empty laugh still came, "you people are so weird."

It's a low dose, he still laughed.

Touching him gently on the shoulder Dennis tried to affirm a lack of offense, "I know."

Caressing the back of Steven's head she watched his face show a small smile, "you smile for him?"

Rasping the words without losing the smile, "I smile because he doesn't even begin to know how *weird* we are."

Getting out a lozenge from her vest she popped it in his mouth. "I am overpaying?"

Rolling it around for a moment he nodded his head a few centimeters, "he needs a home, a parcel of land to plant a garden on," sighing, "and all the things I am well aware you know he needs."

Returning to the caring caress on the back of his head, "and you would just break Protocol?"

Clacking the lozenge around on his teeth for a moment he sighed, "what is the point of power if you cannot use it? If you don't use this to rewrite Protocol? Then he suffers while you have to play political games with his life."

Moving closer she hugged him for a moment. "I was going to look into it after Thomas was dead."

Turning his head toward her with an honest smile, "good."

"I didn't have time to look into it in the last bit, the Council had been keeping me too busy to think in a straight line."

"Mom, she told us that behavior like this," gesturing to a vague approximation from her to where Yuri was sitting, "was normal. That compassion is good. I held my ammo and orders over the survivors of those who came to burn your world down. I, wanted to throw up in revulsion, but I wanted to honor your orders and her ideas. If they repent? Then I know that life will become torture for them."

Hearing the guilt in her words as she spoke them, "I had the same feeling."

Holding up a finger straight up to enunciate his words, "*that*, is dad talking, right there, whew. The old man could punish people in the strangest of ways."

Chiming in with a morose nostalgia Dennis affirmed the idea, "your father had a talent for showing people just how much they had hurt him, by sharing the hurt."

Turning her attention back to Steven, "you fear that Yuri will hurt me?"

Settling against the couch with a groan, "I also fear that you would forgive him if he did. I also fear that you will not and it will harden your heart. It's a large glacier, mountain, pile, storm of tumbleweeds, and the like, of worries."

Fighting against the instinct to lay off she pressed forward, "why?"

Taking the handkerchief off of his eyes he met her gaze with an unsettling conviction, "*you*, you, look at him like how mom looked at dad in the videos we have of them. I fear him because I know he has a *valid* place in your heart. But I don't *trust* him because I have no evidence that he can be trusted in the long run. The only way to get that evidence? Is to wait and let time tell." Softening he hung his head, "I can't bring myself to risk you on a hunch. Even if you would."

I am without words. Sitting in a quiet moment she adjusted the handkerchief and set to drying the tears which were coming softly from the corners of Steven's closed eyes.

Moving over to the couch Dennis moved to a single knee kneel before taking his left hand, "Steven?"

"Yes Dennis?"

Reciting the words as he would an Intel Brief, "the assessment of him is that he only kills in anger, never cold detachment. From his testimony he has snuck away from abuse without killing the abuser, on more than one occasion. He's loyal, at points to a fault. Also, he might have a sexual thought or emotional disorder preventing standard arousal and response following the Burned Bridge model."

Choking out a single guff of laughter at the situation, "why was I not given this report?"

Continuing the Briefing tone, "it was prepared in secret. Dhavid felt that it had things that a person wouldn't want to hear about themselves in it, much less having someone else look."

Interjecting without looking up from Blob Blobberton, "oh, you are right about that. That's all mostly true, but, ouch, *hearing* it?"

Nodding she felt the sting of past reports about herself remind her of the concept, "I know the feeling."

Looking up from Blob, "oh, the man, Sinclair. His reports?"

Gesturing for 'Discretion,' "we should commiserate after they leave."

"Can we?"

"We can."

Taking her hand firmly Steven sighed, "I should go get Thomas then."

Squeezing his hand in assurance, "you will get him."

Intoning the words with the calm of the tomb, "I have enough I am certain that I can end him. I won't let them stop me. If he wants a world where you must be dead for him to be at peace? I will grant him the peace of the grave."

Piping up again Yuri gestured, with Blob, at Steven, "for the first time, I think you have said something I wouldn't hesitate to say I one hundred percent agree with."

"You are an oddly learned man."

Putting Blob back in his lap with a look of chagrin before addressing the moment, "I went to school, and learned how to learn. Everywhere I traveled I endeavored to learn all I could."

Speaking his question with an honest curiosity to his tone, "why?"

"Because even if my life means nothing, and there were no gods to find me and mourn me? At least people would have seen me being a man of ethics, good morals, and education. I would then hope they would think that's *good* and want to be more like me."

Tilting his head forward Steven moved until he was able to rise, "then learn our ways, so you don't hurt her."

"I will try."

Getting to his feet, while handing Susan back her kerchief, his grimace dominated his face, "I don't know if I can forgive you anytime soon."

Meeting his gaze Yuri appeared contemplative, "I am understanding more."

Answering with a deflated sadness and resignation, "if he had just used his power, just taken you and actually honored the promise as fast as he could? He would have lived. He could have saved you both. He, was, just walled. Just on the defensive every, single, day." Nodding with a malicious laugh, "thank you for that moment of clarity Yuri. I can now go kill this waste of resources. You have given me back my resolve."

Looking at him with an obviously perplexed smile, "noted?"

Moving away with a resolve, she found almost daunting to witness, Steven set to leaving. Waiting for the door to sound an opening and closing she let out the breath she had been holding. "I, was not expecting that."

Looking at his hand Yuri pointed at the Tranq Patch, "so how long until this wears off?"

Answering him with authority on the subject Dennis' voice carried an apologetic lilt, "based upon time index? I would say five to ten more minutes and then it'll start to weaken in effect. It should be out and fully over in an hour."

"I can endure."

Nodding with a firmness to the gesture, "I am going to get my things together and take my leave."

"I understand."

Flicking his lower earlobe with his index finger Dennis seemed far away, "I have everything I need." Picking up his things and starting to pack his tailors bag, "I'll just get my things and go back to the workshop. I took the liberty of sending a message to Stephanie to bring by casual wear in his size for the time being. Thankfully he's about the same size as Chuck Drenner so we can use his patterns with mild alterations for the custom items. She's going to talk to a shared associate, whom should be able to get the bulk of the day to day wear today. As for the wardrobe you have requested I see created, and he has made his choices for, it will be manufactured as soon as possible."

Progress. "Excellent."

Interjecting gently into the moment Yuri sounded pleased, "I think I will look good."

Nodding to Yuri with a smile, "I'm certain you will." Looking back to her, "I will show myself out."

Holding out Blob Blobberton with an attempt at a smile Yuri spoke with gratitude, "be well Dennis. A Blue Sky to you."

Taking Blob and tossing him on top of everything in his bag, "a Blue Sky to both of you."

Seeing Dennis about to disappear into the mudroom she felt the question form. Getting up she set to catching up to him next to him at the door, "your truth?"

Tipping his chin up he looked her in the eyes to address her, "you are quite a bit like your mother. I think," correcting himself, "*believe*, that outside of a Rehabilitation Suite? He is safest with you. Your heart? It needs this lesson. Do you overpay the debt? No. This? Isn't the debt talking. It's the need to keep him alive long enough to pay it. You like him as a person. You like his stories. You like being near him. That *isn't debt.*" Finishing his words with a tone of Theatric Wisdom, "this is the frightening power of the human heart."

"Is this wise?"

"No. But you should do it regardless. Wisdom is built from doing things, learning, and adapting."

"Thank you Dennis."

"I should go." Opening the door he stepped out into the day, "a Blue Sky Day to you."

Watching the door close she sighed with as the slight wash of defeat struck her.

From behind her, Yuri's question carried a hopeful lilt to it, bringing her back to the moment, "is that food I smell?"

"Yes." Turning back to Yuri, "to the kitchen."

Mustering a grin he rose, "you don't have to tell me twice."

3.9.0 - 13:04

'Sky-Castle' Mobile Command Base

■Dennis Ochenhart

Knocking on the door of the Mobile Command Base he felt the rush of expectation that Tessa or Asmodai would be answering the door.

They're gone. Just a pack of young fools who are hoping to understand inside now. Connecting to the past by sending me a report, and now I have to confront them about this present.

Feeling a thankfulness of still being alive, *it's a gift, that's why it's called the present.*

Watching the door open with a slow caution he was met by a Drenner wearing a suit of Paladin Armor. Looking to the emblem patch he recalled it instantly. *Kit Thompson. He survived the day.*

Regarding him with a puzzled expression, "Sir?"

Snapping himself out of it, "Phantom Memories. Phantom thoughts of the memories of those days."

Replying with a saddened professionalism, "Condolences Sir." Switching up to a crisp delivery of the words, "Authorization and Intent?"

Moving on. "I have come to speak with whomever is sitting on the audio of what was just spoken. Authorization is under the Chanakya Friendship Principle."

Switching to a less formal tone, "do come in."

Stepping over the threshold into the Command Center he smiled at the snack rations and jug of Hydration Plus. "Taking good care of yourselves?"

Gesturing to a tablet next to the snacks and drinks, "we were just finishing up a lengthy discussion on our world. We wanted to be ready to offer insights."

Gazing across the familiar haunt his eyes settled on the figure sitting next to the surveillance equipment, "Operator Cernis Drenner?"

Replying crisply, "Cernis Drenner."

Nodding once, he moved into the moment, "the one who sent me the report."

Nodding in reply with a formal air about him, "yes sir."

Play the demand, "Ash the audio."

Tapping the desk quickly then pointing at him with a smile, "I already did Sir."

Is this because of me, or her? "You did?"

"I didn't want to hear it. *No one* needs to know if that's the tip of the iceberg." Laughing for a moment, "Sir?" Gesturing toward the house he seemed lost, "*that* is the private life of the *High Consul*. I am here *not* to pry into her world, but just to make sure she's safe. I didn't do it for you. I *did* send you a report, but because I wanted your *help,* to make sure you were kept In The Loop. You're not *just* a tailor, no matter what might be said about you."

Smiling at the humbling feeling in his heart, "I thank you."

"Noted. You *are* a great tailor, a good father from what I have heard, but you will always be the Darkest Shadow. As soon as The Commander shut the door on his vehicle I hit the button to Ash the audio."

I wonder how much I'll find out if I just ask. "This level of surveillance isn't normal."

Smiling with a disappointed embarrassment, "our orders aren't normal Sir."

Reaching for the words he tried to give him something to work with, "Micah Drenner has an idea of how to help our world?"

Losing some of the disappointment, *"you, could* say that."

"I won't tell her you heard. I am going to come over and confirm the delete."

"I wouldn't expect less." Moving away from the terminal he stretched, "good to stand at intervals regardless."

Moving over briskly he took a look at the screen. *He did indeed ash it. Advanced delete function at that. Wait, there's a second file he turned to ash?* "The other file?"

"Miss Bachman and Dagger Sasha Herb, the reason we contacted you. The needed notes on the interaction are in the log file though."

Speaking with the affirmation plain in his tone, "you're making the right choice."

"We're making the only choice that can be made. They said things, that," taking a breath and wringing his hands, "I am not in their orbit! I am not to hear those things. Were some really good things spoken? Certainly. But that was not *my* moment. They can remember it, not these files. Although I want to send a Token of Esteem."

Laying a hand on Cernis' shoulder, "motive?"

Holding still with his words, "love is not an easy thing to nurture."

Letting go of the shoulder he smiled, "it is not." Searching for the answer he found it quickly enough, "send Dagger Herb two white cloth flowers, wrap the stems in a scarlet twine or ribbon, and include a single square of Black Powder Crunch. In the note you must write nothing greater than *Noted, Acknowledged, and Heartened.* If you do that? You can honor them. Also, you cannot send it until the day after you leave this post. On the day you leave this post I will speak with Miss Bachman and Dagger Herb, the day after you may send your Token."

"Thank you Sir."

Stepping away from the terminal, "as for your feelings toward me? I am honored. I am humbled that I still carry such weight with people I have never broken bread with."

Gesturing to the open bag on the table, "have a crisp."

Reaching into the bag he smiled at the cartoon fox mascot on the bag, "the yeast seasoning blend known as Faux Cheese. I like this one."

"Glad to hear it."

Feeling the urge for one last question he looked back to Cernis, "the quote we have on friendship from Chanakya states that this is a bitter truth. Is it bitter to your reckoning though?"

Contemplating the moment he shook his head softly, "our self interests are the same, to protect the High Consul and our country. If we are friends under this banner? It is a banner of *honor*. Thank you for the honor of serving next to you in this."

Blinking against the moisture he nodded his head toward the door, "I have to go now. Errands to run."

Nodding he saluted once more, "a Blue Sky and a steady wind to you."

Acknowledging the salute he set to leaving, "a quiet watch to you."

"Noted and appreciated."

Placing the crisp upon his tongue he closed his mouth and quietly made his way out. *Even as we stand on the verge of everything getting worse, we do not falter to be who we are.*

THE LIGHT SHINES
Saturday April 30th, 2242

4.1.0 - 13:20

Drenner Estate – Consul's Office

∫Amanda Drenner

Not wanting to believe what her eyes were showing her, she closed her eyes against the conclusion on the screen. Opening her eyes she was met with the same dread filled words.

We had no recourse.

His knowledge of Protocol and the Caveats was beyond my understanding. This whole thing reads as a monument to Asmodai's Anger on his bad days. Why would you seek to build this? Why?

Screaming at the top of her lungs she let the primal feeling of rage be heard.

Thomas did not budget Steven into his plans.

"You det sucking trash heap!" Slamming her fist onto her desk hard enough it hurt she brought her aching hand close to her and held it tightly.

Thomas has triggered Civil War. The data trails, the evidence, the testimony of those who lived through his orders.

Reconsidering the details coming in she blanched at the depth of the plan. *He's, by the Ash, this will tear the fabric of our world apart if he goes through with this.*

And I have nothing to stop him with.

The deal is over. All the work, the talks, the agreed upon stepping stones to the future. Gone. Wait.

Sifting the data trails she felt her nostrils flaring at the marks of the Sys-Admin on the files. *Jerome had to hide in Cloak and Dagger to avoid getting killed. And now, he is pressed into service. No wonder this was so masterfully put together. Steven stole his father's darkest contingency plan, his sisters best Network Tech, and forged the most forsaken thing he could.*

Looking up at the sound of the door to her study opening she cringed at the sight of Chuck's face. *Chuck. By the Ash.*

Intoning his name with a tone of face saving reassurance, "Chuck -"

Firing back with the adamant demand of his words, "tell me we can save her!"

Coming up short she spoke softer, "I don't have an answer to that."

Raising his voice in frustration, "you said to wait! *You assured me!*"

I could be made a liar in this. "Mea culpa. She said Steven would deal with us, but she didn't say that she knew how!" Finding a thought she spoke it, "she might not know!"

Losing his composure his words came with the echo of an angered pleading, "tell me what I can do to save Cassia!"

Snapping back at him, "if I knew? I would do it *myself!* You're not the only one who's going to lose today!"

Stopping and looking at the floor he retrieved a beaded necklace from his pocket, "mea culpa."

Gazing at the treacherous outline on her tablet she sighed, "it is the way of people to lose control." Gesturing to the necklace, "what's that?"

Speaking softly with a gentle tone of explanation, "a Blessings Necklace, each bead is something positive in my life. Each bead is a flotation device against a mind lost in the dark ocean of thought. I found the chain and the beads on the Open Exchange."

Something to hope for, "which one is Wendy?"

Pointing to a blue bead, "this one," moving his finger to a red one further down, "this one," and then to a green one, "this one is also Wendy."

She has enriched him. "Aspects of Love?"

Smiling softly, "yes." Rolling the necklace up he put it away with a sigh, "what can we do?"

Replying with a tactful neutrality, "we wait for Susan to act. If she really did know? If this really is her doing? We'll know soon enough."

Sitting down in his chair he shook his head roughly, "it can't be this way."

"It won't be. Something will change."

"It has to." Reaching out he grabbed one of the tablets laying around, "let me look this thing over again."

"Please, do so."

I don't think you'll find an answer, but it helps to understand why you can't find one.

4.0.0 - 13:07

Safe Housing – Kitchen

☼ Yuri

Feeling the smile spread across his features as feelings returned to his perception he felt grateful. Emoting the thankfulness into his words, "I can smile."

"And," setting the plate of lunch before him, "you can enjoy your meal."

"It looks good. Still hot. Freshly baked though." Touching his finger to a morsel for a moment, he nodded with a pragmatic honesty, "I will proceed with caution. It feels good to smile though."

Moving to her chair Susan smiled to him with a compassionate empathy, "I don't like that stuff. The Tranq, that is."

Trying to downplay the moment with a humored tone, "it is not the nicest feeling I have ever felt."

Having a seat she seemed almost thankful for the moment, "it is a sad part of our lives, we've had Tranq since the beginning."

I wonder, intentional or curse? "Why?"

"To protect people from behavior that would destroy them. Now? It's used as emergency assistance. With a secondary use of clarity before an Exit Pass."

Setting to opening the ends of the sealed up morsels, *that doesn't sound good.* "What is an Exit Pass?"

Meeting his gaze she appeared to be on the verge of pride with her words, "State Sanctioned Suicide. You petition for the right to die with dignity. If it's the way to handle it? We let you, and help as can be arranged. If you have no other option that you can see, and we have nothing we can give you? We help you go quietly into that good night." Adding with a corrective tone, "Unauthorized Exit Passes are frowned upon."

Curious, "do they try to stop people from wanting it?"

Stopping short she sighed, "I need to clarify. If a person wishes to die because they are under mental duress, The Guild tries to help find them a cure. The idea of life is that the natural state of life, is to be alive. The pride you hear is not for those who are ill in the mind who seek death, and some sort of macabre *going away party.* It's for those for whom we have no cure and for which the future is not one they wish to face."

That is a bizarre mental image. "You take me somewhere unexpected again. *Going away party,* by the stars that's kind of, gross."

Taking his first bite he found it to be pleasing. Looking up as he chewed he set to listening.

Nodding with agreement she spoke with an empathic demeanor to her, "yes! It *would be.* We do have a different sort of party though, for those whom are dying of a physical illness of which there is no cure. In the past? From what we know, the doctors would attempt to prolong life, and you had no right to your own death. Thus the Protocol is that the Citizen should own that decision. Thus an Exit Pass is a filed notion where The State tries to help you settle your affairs in the wake of this world, having failed to preserve your ability to stay alive."

Taking a quick sip and readying his next bite, "so why is The State involved? Other than the whole Totalitarian thing."

Without losing the empathy, "when a person dies, The State has to make sure that the part of society, however small, that the individual held up is accounted for. Be it as simple as a pair of hands on an assembly line, or a garbage man, or a woman providing child-care. That leaves a space, a blank space, where a new name must be written. The State doesn't like seeing people go, but we *cannot* stop you from leaving if you are in sound mind about it. To do so would violate your human right of being alive."

Sipping again and prepping a different colored morsel, "I can't say I've thought about it that way."

Answering with a heartfelt empathy in her tone of explanation, "if a person is sick, be it in the mind, or the body, all options must be exhausted looking for a cure or way to patch the person together. Our science is lacking, and we know it. To that end, each person who is up against the wall is asked to keep going and give the system a chance to find that answer. However, if they wish to Opt Out, then the Exit Pass is there. A dose of Tranq is called upon during the evaluation of their situation so they can speak outside of the emotional duress. It's a complex idea, that is handled by people who spend their days working on the system, and making sure that it is as effective as possible. The alternative to the system is unacceptable."

That one was much nicer than this conversation. Picking up a purple filled morsel, *I'm not going to turn down this moment though,* "which includes?"

"Suicide by attacking the Militia, for one. Or attempting death in the privacy of your own home without a professional. A botched suicide is terrible. Much less the testimonials of the Militia or Service Rangers when they arrive *too late.* To that end, instead of denying that the idea of suicide should be seen as immoral, we shifted the concern to the ethics of the act of self-termination itself."

Spiced beets, kind of good. Taking a long sip he found his question, "are there those who would teach that it is immoral?"

Leaning forward and to the side as if ready to pounce, her tone was playful, "on what grounds?"

She appears to know this is all inquisitive and not critical of her world, "I do not know what someone would say in this hypothetical."

Reaching over and touching his free hand gently, "I do not either. They could attempt the idea that it is murder, as it is the termination of the Citizen. However, if the alternative is *torture* because those around you would rather see you suffer and die slowly than let you go? Then that becomes a majority enforced tyranny."

The irony. Laughing he lowered his hand with the next bite in it back to the edge of his plate. "Totalitarians speaking out against tyranny. Oh, what a day."

Scrunching up her nose at him for a moment she sighed, "tyranny is cruel or oppressive ideas. Duress without concern. If a person is withering from sickness and the doctors have no solution? If they do not wish to face the cruelty of a life cut short? Then who are we to express further cruelty? They are not *forced,* to Exit Pass. The doctors can try to make them *comfortable,* but they can Opt Out. If people force them to stay through emotional blackmail or coercion? Who's the tyrant now?"

I think I understand now. "Prescriptive use of words, means that each term is a set thing. So when you say Totalitarian, as the Protocol is written about *all* aspects of personal, private, and public life? Then The State method is totalitarian as *everything* is governed by The Protocol, then *everything* is governed."

Visibly relaxing, "yes."

Time to test my understanding. "So to your perception, even though you are Totalitarian, you are not cruel."

Smiling with an affirmative nod, "yes."

Have I seen her people oppressed? No Gulag, no forced marches, clean water, food that tastes good. "To be honest at this juncture, I have not seen something I would call cruel either. I'm still looking though."

Watching her smile shift to one of philosophical humor, "as are we."

Nodding slowly he continued on his original thought, "so if The State touches all things, there is Protocol for all things. Including actions and expressions."

Nodding without losing her smile, "correct."

Now to get into the dangerous waters, "you restrict speech then, yes?"

Raising a crooked finger upward, "through the use of Protocol on Social Comport and Social Contract, yes."

Fair enough. Searching his mind for understanding, "you use mass surveillance."

Still holding her crooked finger upward, "we do. We trade our privacy for security. A Citizen knows that The State is watching, because The State will come render aid. Example? When a child wanders into a Blacklisted House? The Militia is alerted."

Finishing his mouthful he looked over at her, *this could hurt.* "Details?"

Lowering her hand she reached over with it and took his free hand gently.

Taking a large bite he put it in his mouth and nodded, *I am ready to listen.*

"The first example I offer, will be the personal. Thomas Kunlow tried to have me killed, thus The State does not want me near his domicile for thirty days. There is a cooling off period while the matter is sorted and steps are taken."

I wish I did not have a full mouth. Looking to her with a furrowing of his brow he gestured for 'continue.'

"That is proof that I am bound by the same rules, for one, and could be seen as prudent as the other point on it. The other is that if two people whom toil for the same aspect of things are in conflict? The State does not punish beyond forcing the aggressor to explain the nature of the offense and working from there. No one loses their occupation over interpersonal conflicts as a default answer. It *could* happen, but it doesn't *start* there."

Sipping his water to prevent speaking with a full mouth he smiled in approval, "noted. Sounds effective."

"There are other stories and anecdotes which go with that? But they can wait for another time."

"Continue though." Getting another one he smiled at the smell, *smells like coriander leaf and lime.*

Rubbing his hand gently as he chewed she continued with an audible tact, "the other example that comes to mind? There are those who are *attracted* to children. If a child gets within distance of a Blacklisted House? The Militia is dispatched to perform a Wellness Check."

I think I understand that. Sipping his water until he was ready he spoke his metaphor, "so the spider says to the fly to come into the parlor, and when the fly does so? Surprise! A group of warrior grasshoppers appears and says, not this time!"

Cracking a smile, "essentially."

You make a secret police watching your every move sound benevolent and worthwhile. "You present a good side. Though, what happens to the spider?"

Reflecting with an honesty she sighed, "that would be decided by the reason *why* the fly is in the parlor. If the spider is looking to feed? Then the spider gets a swat which is on parity with the motive."

Easy enough concept, "as with all crimes."

"Yes."

Running the notions over in his head he found himself lost in short order. "I am reflecting on the concept, and it sounds so much larger than I can quite wrap my mind around."

Nodding with a philosophical timbre with her smile, "I am not a member of the Militia, the Service Rangers, or even an Orange Poncho. Thus, I cannot lay claim to an *advanced* understanding of the scales of justice. Though I can tell you I have seen things I wish I could un-see about people."

Meeting her gaze he felt relief when she rubbed his hand again.

"To clarify, this is over the course of years. We have a murder rate here in New Hope of around one per year on average. Something boils over, and that's that. As for the system? The persons who dreamt up this place worked very hard on it Yuri. They wanted to give us a gift of having a Future."

I will return to my questions about her nation. "Do you seek to control the future?"

Nodding with an earnest affirmation, "yes. To the end of making a better place to live. Rejecting the Repugnant Conclusion that the amount of people is what forms the validity of a place, and embracing the idea that it is the Quality of that place is what comes first."

She mentioned Rations, the radio did too, so I guess a central bank? "Economic Control?"

"What passes for an Economy, we control via a Central Ration System. We do not have a commodity secured currency. The State says the idea of Rations exists, so it does. It's secured by the mutual idea that the Citizen wants to maintain The State. It is secured with labor and effort."

I already know this answer, I think. "Education?"

"Again, State edicts on what is taught, how it is taught, how school life is structured, and the uniforms."

I wonder if boobs on art is allowed? "Art?"

Shifting up to a mild gush of emotion, "we love Art." Reducing the gush she continued, "though the word is used for any profession or skill which creates a physical product or tangible thing. From the idea of the Art of Artistic Expression? The State categorizes those products to reach those who like certain things. Or to be able to open their mind to another type of art or expression."

"Noted." *I need a laugh,* "can Art have boobs?"

Stifling a giggle she caressed his wrist, "yes. The naked form is *not* immoral. If that naked form is doing something that *is* immoral or unethical then it becomes a matter of context. Then it's adjusted further by if it's photography or fiction." Finishing her thought with a sour look, "that falls into the territory of someone else's problem to worry about."

"Bad anecdote?"

"A few sour ones, yes. We are *not* perfect people. I do wish we were. However, we don't fail ourselves as often as the past did. Thus, it's a notable thing when we do."

Perhaps we can escape into humor? "Can you give me a hilarious anecdote?"

Mulling it over she stifled another giggle, "there is an item that some people wear, called a Fur-Suit. We have animal mascots. And as people do love being *affectionate* –"

Speaking to the opening she left him, "you have people who dress up as animals and then are *affectionate.*"

Giggling for a moment before speaking, "yes."

I feel like I have found a rabbit borough. "How does that relate to the photography?"

"They take pictures of it. They trade it to each other. They draw pictures of it and share and trade in those. They have *fantasies.* They're not breaking Protocol, so, it is as it is."

"Noted."

Reflecting on the moment she tapped his hand gently, "as I have said before, I am not above the Protocol. Thought of the term. Queen of an Absolute Monarchy. That's not me. I am held in check by the same rules."

Curious idea. "Why did your forebears consent to such a thing?"

"Absolute power corrupts absolutely. The only way to keep The State in check is to bind The State. *Then* limit the power of The State to slip its leash while teaching all members of the Ruling Party the importance of that equality."

With nothing to lose, they had only the future to gain. "Noted."

"The only power I have, that is not given to me by those who submit to rule? Is force. If I am sitting on my Throne, and life is good, then when the Citizen sees that I support them feeling good? They feel good. They have bread in one hand, a circus before them, and clean water in the other. The flag of my family flies to the side reminding them, I endorse this."

This has been far more than I would have hoped for. "This is no small amount of thought to ruminate on."

Reassuring him, "I understand. I grew up in this, I have spent each day of my life trying to understand this. Seeing the ripples of power, how it replies to power, and deepening my understanding of what it all means. Honing my craft, as it were."

"I will finish my food, chew my cud, as it were."

Smiling with a nod, "I will catch up on work."

Watching her turn her attention to her comm he turned his attention to finishing his lunch in earnest. *This is good stuff.*

I wish I had a dipping sauce for some of it though. A few of these would be strange with dipping sauce though.

Swallowing and washing the bite down a thought occurred to him. Catching her gaze he smiled, "a question?"

"Ask it."

"You speak of your system being this way to make the nation better. Is there a description of that ideal?"

Nodding she poked her comm for a few moments, "here it is."

I should not be surprised. "Read it to me?"

"Certainly." Taking on a quoting air, "the Nation of Humanity will be a place without torture. It will have no laws written with the intention of causing harm to its people. This Nation will seek to remove those who predate on its Citizens, be it Publicly, Privately, or from within the Established Order. This Nation will be one without avoidable waste, which will include a dedication to all technology to bring renewal and new life to the land. This Nation shall have clean water for all of the Citizens to drink, and in that place no Citizen will go hungry. That place will be the True Nation of

Humanity."

No such place exists on this world. "So the Ever-After."

Countering quietly, "but on Earth."

"I have not seen this place." Correcting his tone to something softer in intent, "I have traveled the world and no one has told me of this place you speak of."

Hanging her head with a sigh, "it doesn't exist," raising her head with a hopeful smile, "yet."

I walk along that fine line, not of reprisal, but of sadness. She wants to show me a land to assure me I'd be happy staying in it. I spent a lifetime trying to get here.

I fear she fears I will not love her Nation.

"Which of those things do you need to get rid of still?"

"The torture, for one."

By the Stars. "Details?"

"There is a Program that I'm working on closing. They were a War-Time Necessity, a repurposing of Citizen into something else, to spare others. The Interventionist Ideals prompted The Guild to intervene with children who show signs of advanced Anti-Social Personality Disorder to the point of being a Psychopath or Sociopath. From that program came a group of children which were grown into Questioners."

And this is the thing I understand better. "This would be part of the darker side of life, neh?"

"Yes." Continuing, "ethically speaking, if a Citizen is going to be a liability to other Citizens to that extreme degree? They should be put down. End of discussion. However, at the time, instead of sorting them into the Exterminate or Keep Trying bins? They were given a third bin. Repurpose. Harness the traits. They were able to learn more from them as they were kept around to have a purpose."

And back into the Logical La-La Land. "Noted. Continue?"

"This has been going on for decades. I would like to see the program changed though. No more Questioners."

"What does a Questioner do?"

"When someone won't tell us what we need to know? We give them to the Questioner." Raising a hand gently, "the question is *never,* did you do it? We are *well aware* that people will break and confess to things that they did not do to get the hurting to stop. If we can't *prove* they did something, they don't go to the Questioner. They are used for the *why.*"

"Then why do you want them gone, if they are of use to you?" Stopping he held up his hand gently, "wait, I will be more wise. What is the thing that changed?"

Taking his hand again she replied with a pragmatic grace, "The Guild has reported that they have learned all they can from the program, and then some. I would be willing to trade a weapon, a set of tools, that we have for the loss of the program. It was a trade off, a rationalized breach of ethics and morals for the *greater good.* A concept that does not exist. That rationalization, can no longer be used. *Greater Good* isn't real. When my plan comes to fruition? The bins will be Exterminate, Keep Trying, and Repurposed for Something Gainful."

I ask that which I do not know if I believe in. "The Questioners are not gainful?"

"They don't make it. None of the Questioners has made it to old age. The current group have the chance of making it out alive. If they make it? That's the solid proof I would need. If they do not? I cannot in good conscience order another group trained just to see if that group can live. They have proven that the process is hindered by being Questioners. However, I have been assured that they have a plan for the next group. I have to choose, Questioners, or Citizens. Facing that? I choose Citizens."

Holding her hand with compassion he spoke his word softly, "noted."

"I worry for the people last night. Each minute of distance, each minute I feel a better measure of calm? I spin just a few more strands of hope into a skein of understanding." Looking down at the table she touched an engraving of a turtle gently with her left forefinger, "when I was standing at the target range, with my gun in my hand, looking at the targets I could see a common thread even that first time. Those targets did not look like us."

"Go on?"

Reaching to his hand with her left she hugged his hand with hers. Squeezing gently her words tumbled out in a slow roll, "they were enhanced images of the Freelanders, taken from footage of their attacks. Their dress, profile, the way that they walk, to make a point. Those are the Out-Group. Yes, they are fellow humans, but they want to live. If that means taking your food, water, and security? So be it. You are the same to them. The Threat. Our training techniques try to program in a sense of Empathy for the In-Group. To define the unacceptable idea of harming the fellow Citizen. Last night, those who defended Central had to point at people who looked like *us.* Those people pointing at them looked upon the *other.* I hope for good news in the recovery."

So many hearts to heal. "Noted."

Looking up she caught his gaze, "a different subject?"

Um - "why is your middle name Alexis? I understand that the middle name is for the Blessing of the child. Alexis, she was, *troubled.*"

Pausing he looked down at his half of a morsel and then back to her, *I hope I did not go too far.*

Tipping her head to the side with an incredulous smile she recovered with a quiet laughter, "you pose an excellent question." Laughing with a softness she bobbed her head once before regarding him with a good natured humor, "my parents did not name me in the hopes I would be sleeping in my car. Much less having sex with strangers to stay warm in winter."

That verbal sledgehammer. A weird comfort to know she doesn't flinch from the truth though.

"However," stopping she regarded him with a quieter calm, "you would not know the end of the story. Just where Elianna left off."

She's right. "No, I wouldn't. How did it end? I forgot to ask!"

Talking with her hands her spirit appeared lifted with her words, "Alexis was *healed.* She was a heart that grew warmer and more compassionate with age. She was the first Bachman Mother. The one who knew the streets of her city well enough to guide the Gingerbread Man. She knew people, and she knew reality. She compensated, being just another girl for sale in tough economic times, with being a *better* quality girl for sale. The strength she held? Was the hope for the hearts of others, and the power of knowing other people. I was blessed with the idea of having a heart warm enough to survive betrayal, abuse, and a troubled world of which there was no feasible hope."

The Sledgehammer hits, but blunted with soft foam. "Noted."

"She went on to be there until her dying day as a loving Grandmother."

The idea that I have heard dozens of titles for, all with the same idea. I did not know. "Then you are named for the woman she became, not the woman she was."

"Correct." Touching his hand again, "The State knows things that people do not know. To that end? The Courtesans are never told they are lesser for what they do. They are not educated in a poisoned lesson. Our people are taught about them. From those lessons new Endeavors have been brought forth. We will never, The Divine Willing, see another life harmed like she was."

Oh thank the stars. "Noted."

Explaining with a renewed humored, "my brother, Patrick, he spends no small amount of time with the Courtesans. He's agreeable, and trustworthy. He has an associate within their Endeavor for bringing The Guild and The Courtesans together. Heartstrings, wonderful woman. The liaison from The Guild to The Courtesans. She helped write the role of the Sexual Surrogate with her mentor," reaching for the name, "Allotrope. Allotrope handed down the program to Heartstrings to finish the process of making it a standardized reality."

I will learn more of him. "Why did Patrick get involved?"

"He was curious. She told him," containing a laugh she seemed humored, "you are not a spy in my domain. You are either here to learn, or you can learn to trust."

I like her already. "How did that go?"

Beaming with pride, "he signed up on the spot. He took the classes. He did not sit in as a spectator, he learned by being a student."

Admirable. "Did he pass?"

"In the end? No." Without losing the pride she spoke her words with a gentleness to them, "he wasn't able to be The Director and a student and not have one suffer. He gave it a good show though."

Summoning up a deep bass of encouragement for his declaration, "good enough."

Shaking her head slowly she smiled at him, "how's the food?"

Looking at the remains of his meal, "random. I have enjoyed this journey of knowledge and random food though."

"It is random as it *is* the Odds and Ends."

"Pardon?"

Reaching into her vest she passed him a spoon, "I forgot to give you this."

Taking the spoon, "thank you. I will finish this."

"The Odds and Ends. When they make all of those for the other freezer containers? They make an overage just in case something goes wrong. The weird looking ones, the ones that were under on filling, and the overage from them doing it right? It goes into a final batch known as the Odds and Ends. Sometimes? They put filling in them that isn't normally put in those."

Swallowing with a force he cleared his mouth with a gulp of water, "you are the most powerful person in the land, and you choose this to eat?" Holding up the signal for 'pause' he put together a better question, "teach me how this is not eating a plate of mistakes?"

It is tasty though.

Darting his gaze to her face he caught the smile.

I love her smile. I don't feel dumb when she smiles.

"I can understand why you would term it as a plate of mistakes. The other hand is that it is a plate of forgiveness. For me, and a small group, we find it to be a fun meal. A person can approach it with caution to make sure they don't mix two conflicting flavors. However, they can also enjoy the surprises. It's not for everyone. Some people really enjoy the comfort that comes from knowing what's in the next bite."

Clearing his mouth again he raised a brow, "but you don't?"

Leading her words with a small shrug, "it's novel. I like them. The fresh ones are amazing. Those are *much* harder to get though."

"Fresh ones?"

"To get fresh ones you must first go to The Deli Case. Which is a storefront which deals in previewing and crowd testing the next recipe ideas for the Grocery Depot. On the days they work with those a Citizen can find fresh ones."

"All the trouble and work to design lunches for people? What is the gesture for asking a question I don't agree with?" Rushing an afterthought, "I should have used it a time or two so far."

Holding her hand up she performed a gesture, "this," moving her hand to a resting position, "then rest the hand like this during the question. This will signal your role in the question as counter-advocate. *Or*, you just state that you are the counter-advocate." Reaching over and touching his left hand once more, "I took no offense."

"Noted. So, counter-advocate question, why not just tell the people what they're going to eat?" Scooping up another wayward bite he set it into his mouth.

"Purpose. We train chefs, who work very hard, to make menus and innovation on a large scale. We could just switch to an all liquid diet, stop eating, and be *past that.* The real question for that is, where is the fun in that?"

Chewing slowly he set to thinking the notion over. *What a strange contrast of questions. To be so rich in food, one could forsake food.*

Appearing almost lost in thought she set into an Educational Tone that he recognized immediately, "we do have liquid meal replacement for those who are Post-Food."

Post-Food. Looking at her with a questioning look he smiled at her smile.

"Powders, mixes, and the like made with some of the most exact Nutritional Science available. We cling to meals that are made of food, for the majority, as there is a comfort in that tradition."

Clearing his mouth once more he sighed, "the Totalitarians who believe in fun. Counter-Advocate again, why do you need fun?"

Drumming her fingertips across the table with a spark of energy to the gesture, "we're alive Yuri, *that's* the reason. We even have Lover's Meals."

Oh here I go again. She is leading me somewhere. "Lover's Meals?"

Answering quickly with a more formal tone, "food you eat with, or on, your partner."

I think she's blushing, "really?"

Keeping the formal tone she smiled with a hint of a flush forming, "you sound excited."

Pointing the spoon in his hand at her, "because I know that you're going to tell me something that I wouldn't have expected."

Adopting the timbre of casual conversation, "the Courtesans have a designation for those who like to be the platter for others."

These people, "I am *not, no longer, going to be,* surprised."

Playfully deflating she bumped his hand, "that takes some of the fun out of it."

Restraining his emotions he found a better response, "I shouldn't say things I cannot promise. As for the people platters, how does that work out?"

Replying with a matter-of-fact tone, "you reserve them, like a table at Fancy Tables."

Is that the name of the place? "Fancy Tables?"

"It's a place where you sit at a fancy table and they make you fancy food. Stuff that takes forever to cook, but arguably, tastes better to some."

"I look forward to my Citizenship."

"Those who want to be Platters? They have a Workshop and a Certificate. It's for exhibitionists, primarily. They have food handling training, a specific self-care regimen for that day, and the like. They're not common, and they don't get to work often, but when they do it's memorable."

"You've seen it then."

Flushing with the words, "I have."

I am whelmed by this world. Lowering his head he looked at the empty plate with a bemused smile. *I am humbled because she wants to spend all this time with me.*

Shifting to a more concerned tone, "are you, well enough, Yuri?"

And there goes the fun. "What do you mean?"

"I mean exactly that, you aren't exactly in peak physical health right now and I just wanted to know if I should call the doctor to come look at you."

By the stars. "It does hurt Susan, I won't lie. But I've been in worse pain so I'm not fretting too much."

"Just because it's been worse doesn't mean it should be dismissed."

The Stoic in me is in conflict with the Caretaker in her. Taking the time to center himself he presented his reasons to her, "what it means is that I don't think it feels like something we should drag a doctor in to. My chest feels better already, I'm not leaking blood from any orifice, and I did manage to do a pretty good job of *trying* to save you last night so I must not be on death's door. With all that in mind I should just take it easy, get some rest, plenty of fluids, and let my body take care of itself. Knowing that I *have* stressed my body but it does not feel broken."

Appearing to be relieved, "if that is what you wish, that's how it'll be."

"And later some better clothes will show up and I can hide myself under less telling fabric."

Hanging her head she seemed smaller, "I wish you spoke the language."

"I do too. I do. Then I could know the latest way you're going to be counter to the lessons of the world. To understand, and let you know better, how this place is one I would never have hoped could be real."

"I wish I had come up with a better plan. Not just a reaction in the moment."

Taking on a friendly but forceful tone, "you shouldn't worry about me. You have the rest of those tiny lights to care about. You have the sprawling complexes of people, the legion of those who believe in you still. I am going to be alright. I understand better now. I know there isn't a boat. I was never scared that you would end me. I don't hold it against you."

"I'm still going to make it up to you."

I am not going to live with this. "You *can't* Susan, it isn't *your* fault. No matter what you do it won't change what happened. We agreed, before the sun could rise on the new day, that this new day would be the start of a new future. The past is just that, the past. You have the power to change things for me now, you're using it, it doesn't balance out the past it merely makes the future a much better place to live than the past. I just hope I prove to be worth the aggravation of having me around."

"I –"

Interrupting her, "I'm sure we're going to be just fine Susan." *I am not the smartest man.* "Are you concerned for my body?"

Nodding once she spoke with candor, "some."

Summoning up a smile, "you are a trained problem solver, neh?"

Smiling in return her tone spoke of humility, "I do my best to take care of things as they come along."

Engage the learned student, not the hurting heart. "What lesson is hiding in your Codex on this?"

Speaking the list, "Body Image, Comfort, Self-Esteem, Sacrifice Scars -"

Jumping on the moment, "wait, what is that last one?"

Answering with the simple truth in her tone but a pain around her eyes, "as part of the curriculum on Citizen's Behavior, we have a video series where the idea of battle wounds and scars are covered. It delves into fire fighter burns, gun shot wounds, the works. We take young, impressionable minds, and we smash them into the idea of being without their sense of looking in the mirror and knowing who that is. When they see a person who has been mutilated by their service, they understand the pain they see. It's a terrible thing to be wounded like that."

Keeping his questioning tone to one of seeking knowledge, "why would you do that?"

Responding with warmth, "to make sure they don't shun those who gave on their behalf."

I am getting somewhere. "Do you fear that I am unwell in heart? Not so much head, or body, but in spirit."

Touching his hand again, "yes."

Thinking the care she gave him over he spoke his truth, "you never, balked, when it came to tending me. I thought you were, something I couldn't fathom."

Smiling with a sadness to it, "effectiveness of the teaching varies."

Her pity has been minimal, it even looked like empathy and not pity when I thought about it. Locking the pieces together he saw the hopeful notion, "so, I might be safe with you?"

"I would like to think so."

"I," nodding quickly he turned his attention to his food, "this has been very good. It's a portion size I suspect was meant for two. I just wish I had, a bowl of dipping sauce. Some of those would have benefited from something extra."

"I know the notion."

"It has been worth it though, to experience it."

"I have to spend extra rations to make sure I get a box with my orders."

Not a Queen, not Absolute, so this too? "You do not have infinite rations?"

Smiling with a bemused humor, "that doesn't exist. I have a stipend of High Consul Indulgence Rations, and a stipend of High Consul Friendship Rations. Each Consul gets a stipend based upon how things are going. We have an adaptive structure for the distribution of overages and giving to friends."

"So before you were the High Consul?"

"I used Bachman Family Rations."

"That you share with your brothers?"

"Yes."

"You have three siblings?"

Looking at him with a thoughtful moment of pause she smiled, "I have a half-sister that my dad sired on the side to give his heart a refuge from his life. It's a *long* story. I am just thankful that she's, who she is. She doesn't get to use the Bachman Family Rations. I will explain that when I explain the rest of her."

"Oh, maybe later I will learn more?"

"Certainly. I'll see about introducing you to her mother. She's, hang on, I'm beeping."

Working his way through the rest of the food until nothing remained on the plate he looked up at Susan. Taking a moment to contemplate her new head hung posture he sighed. Looking up at him she sighed in return, "just a lot of bad news. The amount of reports being prepared to properly explain and enumerate our losses, in regards to the future? Staggering."

"I, don't know what to say."

"I don't either."

Looking at the odd sequence of blinks from her comm light, "your comm is blinking."

Turning her attention to it, "it's a message, level is Priority Zero." Picking her comm back up she read it quickly, "the Bachman Reply has been enacted after the session of the Council concluded. There was no need to vote on it. He wasn't calling them together to ask, he was bringing them together to inform them." Appearing to be rereading what was on her comm, her voice came out in a whispered shock, "which means the death warrants for all of them are going to begin processing as we speak."

She couldn't mean - "all those responsible? But they're dead right? Or in custody? He said he would get Thomas, but all of them?"

Still whispering, "no Yuri, every last Kunlow."

"Will they try to run? How does this even work?"

Watching her shaking her head negative Yuri could see a change spread across her features. *I don't think she feels this is the right way of doing things but she's trying to keep from getting too emotional about it. She might not have much left to give before she finds the bottom of whatever wellspring her heart is fed from.*

"They have nowhere to run. They'll be forced back into the family estate would be my guess. I should probably read the details of the Reply." Pushing a few more keys she was soon lost in the battle plans.

Wait a minute, "Susan?"

Without looking up, "yes?"

"What about the children?"

"The children? They're at the Cultural Center. I had the children of the invading force sent there for protection."

"The rest of them though? The Kunlows are a large family I would imagine, I'm sure that little whatever Kunlow who was busy playing with their blocks while this was going on wasn't plotting your death."

Watching the look of horror cross her face Yuri knew for certain before she spoke what it would mean. *She tells me of the adoption and the work they do to save children. And now Steven goes and asks for the death warrants for that same class of people. Her horror tells me that she tells the truth and Steven is trying to make her a liar.*

Reading quickly Susan looked up from her comm with her newfound neutral mask barely in place covering up horror. "He, I don't even know what he's thinking right now. He's not going to kill any of them that are under the age of their Biological Maturation. He *is* going to attempt to replace the family," shaking her head she seemed lost for words.

"And the Council approved it?"

"They didn't have to. It's a Civil War contingency plan. He's plunged us into a state of Civil War because he was able to prove it was Thomas Kunlow who gave the order. We're under a new Protocol set at that point. They had no recourse once he presented his case." Taking a breath, "this is my father's genius wrapped around a plan of such magnitude that, -" trailing off she closed her mouth, her eyes, and hung her head in defeat.

Don't give up. "Talk to me Susan?"

"This *isn't* Steven *just* being Steven. My father wrote this. It was something our father had written because he was looking over his shoulder at Thomas. If he was here? This plan would put Thomas in his place and give him an upper hand."

"But he's not here."

Speaking with a timbre of rationalization, "I know. It means that Steven doesn't have to stop himself. Father would have used this to force the Kunlows to give him Thomas so he could kill him. There would be a new Consul for the House and life could get a second chance."

"But Steven doesn't believe in second chances, does he?"

"Not usually no. If I call for one, a person can get one, but he's not one for them. He," sniffling she pulled out her handkerchief and used it quickly. "He's going to use something which was meant to save lives as a weapon. It's, just how he gets when he gets even."

"Why did your father make this plan?"

Fretting with an emotional distraction to her words, "a simple reason. A belief that Thomas wanted the war to end."

I did not ask then, I should have. "Is this the Sisterhood you spoke of?"

Forcing the word out with the angered sadness that was clear as crystal, "yes!"

So a coup to get the power to blow them all to bits. But they don't even want to fight anymore! "The Ports though, they have no talk of warmongering. There was *plenty* of distrust and bad blood but no wishes to come over the border."

With a lighter tone, "you haven't talked about the Port until now."

Time to give her something she might be able to use. "I didn't want to before. They spoke to me of General Kane and his fall from grace after the Bachman Spear nearly killed him and cost them more than they wanted to pay. Two days later peace was brokered and The Rim has honored that peace."

I don't need to tell her the rest. She would know.

Getting back to it he finished his thought, "if anything it scares them that so few did so much to hurt General Kane and following that moment? The Rim just *gave up.*"

"The Sisterhood is something my father rejected. It would have made the Ports into an ecological disaster, instead of a pair of cities. We could have had all their surrounding lands and moved into *cleanup* in short order. Dad was able to talk to them because Athens, who is now dead, was able to get him a communication line to their leader. Dad decided he wanted to stop the war if he could. He had lost so much, he didn't want to add his humanity to the list."

To be crystal clear, "you mean Thomas wanted to end it by *using the bomb?*"

"Yes. I can safely assume he wants the bomb. This," moving her comm back and forth, "was meant to stop him from getting it."

Then there is only one thing to do! "So how do you stop the Reply?"

4.1.1 - 13:29

Safe Housing – Kitchen

꙰..Susan Bachman

Looking up again at the soft concern in his eyes Susan felt a pang in her heart. *He's got the kind of moxie I admire, and I have no time to spend admiring it. I can't let Steven do this.* Rolling her head to the left then to right and then back to left she watched the idea of how to undo this form in her mind. *He's doing this because he feels House Kunlow is sick. I need to ask for a second opinion.* Flipping through the contacts in her comm she found the name she was looking for. "I stop this with Admin Nobody. I don't know how he can help yet, but I know he can. As his mark is on these files? My brother appears to have ordered him to help him. He's going to know the exact way to undo this, as he helped file it."

Pushing the memories of the last time children had been on the line to the side, she found something better to think about. Waiting for the call to connect she took a few ragged breaths as the memory of her cousin's wedding day came to mind. *I can't let her die. Not her, not the others, not the ones who didn't know.*

Speaking the greeting with a slur to his speech, "High Consul -"

"Jerome, I need -" taking a breath, "I need your help again."

Yawning with a growl he sputtered and growled until words formed, "I knew you would call. The Localized Lockdown Protocol is in play. I'll get Horse Hair up and running as soon as the Network is stable enough to support it, it's *close*. Also, I have kept the message that this thing exists from getting past the top level of protected channels. No one in Respite knows that his second target is to ride into town and serve a blood soaked eviction notice."

"You sound, -"

Interrupting her with the sped up growl still in his voice, "I'm running on my fourth can of Hatred now. Coffee wasn't enough for this."

"That stuff isn't good for you." *I don't know how he got the machine to sell him the third or fourth can.*

Roaring back with a voice like an enraged animal, "neither is failure at a time like this. Say the words High Consul."

Keeping her calm she found a smile to buoy her spirit, *the Warrior growls to stoke the fire and keep the light burning.* Taking a deep breath she set her instinctual worries aside, "I need a motion filed to Veto the Bachman Reply."

"Working on it in just a moment. I'll have the Admin Nobody ready in a moment. I was going to have more prepared but I nodded off. I scripted the protections and then drifted off."

Fighting against the helpless feeling in her spirit, "also? I will need to know what I'm going to tell them for why I don't have much of a plan."

Asking the question with an irritated caution, "did you know what was in the Reply?"

He is trying to hedge his voice but I know this is going to mean a lot to him. "Yes *and* no. Jerome, it's Guthrie all over again the way he's using it! If I knew I would have called you when he told me he was doing this. I would have acted sooner. Please, help me."

His tone betraying a lack of sleep, and personal wellbeing, "you do not need to implore me for help, I just needed to know you are still the woman I call friend. I needed to know he had betrayed you, to know that this had not warped your good nature until it broke and all you would see is the need for fire to burn away the stain."

"Thank you Jerome, for caring in the way you do."

"Noted." After a moment with a softer voice he broached his question, "I have a hole card in this. Will you see a Counselor regarding what happened?"

Considering I'm going to be seeing her for a full weekend, what's another topic? The amount of things I'd want to talk to Waterlily about just grows by the hour. "If that will help? I will. I'm filed to give Waterlily a weekend when this is over, I think. Will that work?"

"Let me double check the wording in the Protocol Document." Hearing the sounds of keys, "mea culpa for my doubts. I should have known, it involves killing on a scale you would never endorse willingly. Forgive me my weakness but I needed to hear your confirmation. I needed to know you were still in there. That they hadn't damaged my friend."

Flexing her fingers she clenched her fist with sad ache at the concept, "I can't make that order. It's just *wrong.*"

"I know Miss Bachman, I know. Grief makes us do terrible things though."

And now that we're walking down memory lane when we need to get back to work instead. "Onward."

"Here it is. Yes!" Taking on a timbre of hope, "the Workplace Trauma Clause would cover it. You had experienced trauma, your brother took over while you were incapacitated, and now that you have regained your senses? You are going to undo what he has done in your stead."

That easy? "I can undo Civil War with that?"

"Not quite -"

Not shocked.

"- the Caveats in this rusted thing are pretty strong. You need to arrest Thomas Kunlow and *after that* you can file the motion to Veto this whole mess out of existence."

That's most of it, "and the no plan after?"

Speaking her name with the lilt of Deep Concern, "Miss Bachman?"

Finding a mantra to cling to she set to invoking it, *one is not a failure if one is emotional. One is not less of a person if one is emotional.* "Yes Jerome?"

Still speaking with Deep Concern, "you are not well."

Face the reality, move toward change. "I'm not. I push the world out of my mind and find a measure of inner peace, then it falls apart when I think again. I'm warm, I'm numb, and then I'm aware of force of the sadness trying to take me away. I have an anchor though." Reaching across the table she took Yuri's free hand. Smiling when he embraced her hand firmly she finished her thought, "I'm not alone, but I'm not well."

Speaking the words as a Pledge, "let me add fuel to your fire. I stand with you. I always have and I always will. You saved me and for that I owe you everything."

The Pledge of the Final Gift. "Thank you Jerome."

"Noted." After a few more keystrokes, "Patrick is injured and with the Veto we won't count as at Civil War. After you have dropped the Veto? The Citizen's Provision for wounded relatives. You can take twelve hours off."

That's, something - "twelve hours to stall?"

"Yes -" after a few keystrokes, "we still have a snag."

"What?"

"You have to do it from Central for one, and you still need Thomas in custody."

The High Consul Council Chamber, "is that room still in one piece?"

After a few clicks, "yes! It's still there."

Think Susan! Think! Running the variables through her head she sifted her mind until she found traces of a plan in the emotional sludge. Rinsing them clean in her desperation she smiled as inspiration hit her.

"I've almost formed a plan that should carry it through."

"You best hurry. I'm glad to hear your mind is working but the Commander is turning toward New Hope. He has a distance to go, but they're preparing the forces to roll when he gets to them. If he gets to them before you get this done? It will be harder to reign it in."

Faltering, "I can't let him win."

Imploring her with a desperation, "then tell me the plan."

Putting the last of the variables together in her head she let go of Yuri's hand. "Get Sinclair and the Night Terrors, full turnout, to the Cultural Center! No need to be a sneak about who else is there. Then," taking a breath she plowed into her plan, "I need Samantha's Scouts sent for Thomas Kunlow. I want rolling authorization for that, and I want it with a Blackout around it. Run full denial and blanket them the way they hit me. Do this to the Kunlow family estate so she can get to Thomas without a word. Those who are in the way? Put my direct message of the incoming veto to them and only them so they let people pass. They want to emotionally blackmail my people? I'll do it right back."

Pausing to catch her breath she set to finishing the plan, "Squad Captain Samantha

Turner isn't due to join the fray until day two of the Reply. I can get her to get this done for me. Also I want Thomas knowing I want to address the Council regarding this so he'll be in his study at his computer when they go for him. I want these two events to happen at the same time. I will Veto the Reply from the Chamber in Central as soon as Thomas is in custody. Once he's brought in? The Questioners will get him and from him should come the needed intel to give Cloak and Dagger what they need to sift the Kunlow family for the truth. I'll use the Clause to buy myself silence while I work on details of the tasks that have to be done!"

Cheering a roar of courage he spoke quick, "wonderful! I'll get this in motion!"

We could still win. Blinking away the errant moisture she thanked him, "thank you Jerome, you truly are a man of your name."

After a few keystrokes, "no time for compliments! You have to go and go now! I diverted Steven down the Watchtower Road, that's how you have as much time as you do. He's still making that turn around though, he's just north of the Drenner Estate. I'll have an updated route sent to The Beast, that should allow you to get to Central Tower *before* he makes it to C&D for the mustering. As soon as I fire this off I'm going to have to find a way out of here so I am not here by the time he gets back this far!"

Rising from her chair, "I'm going! And you should too!"

"Drive! I'll be working hard on finding *anything* else to help you!"

"Thank you Jerome." Closing the connection she looked at Yuri as he rose from his chair, "Yuri?"

I love the way he smiles back.

Speaking her name as a prelude to action, "Susan?"

"Get your shoes! Your guns are in the living room in a box under the couch. I was going to give them back later but you might as well get them now."

"Back to Central then? Why am I going too?"

"*We* are going to Central because together *we* are much safer. *I* am going to act like the High Consul and fix this!" Looking around for a moment she waved her hands emphatically, "shoes Yuri! Shoes!"

4.0.5 - 13:08

'The Hammer' Mobile Command Base - Watchtower Road

∩ Steven Bachman

It's time for The Commander to shake the firmament of the Twelve. Just one more thing I cannot take back. Laughing at the humor of dying before he could be held accountable he felt his courage refresh him. Looking across the Mobile Command Base at O'Neil he smiled with a determination in his heart.

Raising a brow at him, "something amusing sir?"

Smiling with the joy of the absurdity of it all, "they'll never hold me to task for what I've done."

With a discreet roll of his eyes, "and you haven't even done anything *yet.*"

The power of intent. "I'll be placing the plan on the table. I will show them the weapon that I was left with. A Consul wishes to fight dirty? I will fight dirty."

Smiling while reviewing the tablet in his hands O'Neil appeared deeply humored, "the Sys-Admin is sending us back along the Watchtower Road. We won't be taking the curves and rear access back. Communications is still frazzled."

But it's not, is it? "He's lying then?"

Firing back with a laugh, "I would assume. He knows what you will do next."

He's a good asset for what he's worth. "He's loyal to her. We *are* going back via the Watchtowers though, yes?"

Calling from the driver's seat Hampton laughed with his words, "of course sir! We are doing as instructed, *without* confirming the signal strength of the road we were going to use by checking with the Long-Haulers and finding out that he's lied."

Jerome is very tired. "He's tired and not used to lying like this." Looking to O'Neil, "when this shakes out, *after* she stops me? Drop him a note after he's had some sleep and give him some pointers."

Smiling with amusement, "can do sir."

Calling back again with a hope to his words, "she'll stop you Sir?"

"I'm ninety percent certain of it. She's been working so hard on triage and letting her people save the day that I don't see her wavering."

Tapping the tablet O'Neil appeared pensive, "but we're still going through with this part."

It is their role to question and confirm, and my role to lead, one hand washes the other. "I need to say the thing that people will ask her. I need to lay the cards she could play on the table. When I do this, I will watch her take my plans and throw them into a composting shredder with the authority of the High Consul. She will wrest Dominion over this Endeavor from me, and she will show her enemies compassion like they do not deserve. It will not be the quiet cowardice of a leader who's stomach is too sick to say what must be said."

Nodding in affirmation O'Neil spoke loud enough for Hampton to hear him, "she has said she wished to be the Potentate, who ended Hate. Hate between Citizen. The one who would promote love and peace. Tolerance and Compassion. The one whom would let The Guild get more of their dangerous and scary studies into how to show compassion for Friendly Monsters. And importantly, she would be the one to bring the program that creates The Questioners to a close."

Rubbing his neck he tried to relax, "she shall overcome. First though? She must take Dominion over this moment. She must silence her critics. She must show her Citizens that to deny the Kunlow family their rights as Citizens is folly. The only way to do that? Is this quiet threat. Stanley assures me that no one outside of the Twelve, the High Consul, and ourselves will know of this plan. I have all of my documents prepared, my backup plans, the ability to save Cassia if she will forsake Josh and his name when his House burns. I even have a Provision that those too young to fight can be saved by Adoption that can be pointed to. I did everything that the plan stated needed to be done to make it more than just a work of Smoke." Adding as an afterthought, "not that I'm *against* finishing the job. I just have planned on the idea that I will not be moving to that stage."

Calling back to them from the front, "it is a pleasure to serve you Commander."

"Thank you Hampton."

"Noted."

Signaling for 'Orders' he smiled to O'Neil, "patch the Council Address to my prepared audio. Follow-up with the Data Packet with all the details of The Reply. Then cut communications from them." Looking toward the front of the MCB, "keep it to advised speeds. We don't need to be back too quickly."

Tossing the words over his shoulder Hampton seemed in good humor, "and if she lets you burn them?"

Taking on the level tone of Authority, "then we find a new family for that House. My sister will have died in Central, and that Shade of Self back there will be the vessel for my loyalty. I feared I killed her at Guthrie, if *they* finished the job? I finish them."

Looking down to the tablet O'Neil spoke with a graveled hope, "I don't say this lightly Sir, but, I hope she stops you."

Thinking it over he smiled with the simple truth of the moment, "I do as well."

Looking up from his tablet with a firm commitment to the moment, "Orders carried out, Sir."

Nodding firmly he set to laying down on his bench, "I will lay here and wait to see her show our people what this ad lib will bring."

"Good luck to us."

Settling down against the comfortable bench, "we don't need luck. She'll move."

4.1.3 - 13:35

Safe Housing – Exterior - The Beast

༜༜..Susan Bachman

Powering up The Beast, she worked quickly through the list of tasks on the clip-board. Pressing a button on the console she was rewarded with a voice, "Dispatch!"

"I need this," pressing the upload of the route Jerome had sent to her, "flight plan filed from Safe Housing to Central Tower. I'll be using the Eighty-eight kilo, the Leash is coming off, alert my Medical Wagon, and you have no preamble as I'm leaving Safe Housing in under sixty seconds." Syncing the on-board computer with the route Jerome had sent her, "I am transmitting the Flight Plan now."

Firing back with a formal tone, "yes High Consul!"

Closing the connection she finished the process of releasing the Leash. *My Beast is going to get to run like he has not in some time.*

Asking his question with a tone of mild curiosity, "the Leash?"

Keep it simple, "it keeps The Beast from going too fast. Limited Energy Acceleration Safety Harness. The Techs *really* wanted to keep the theme."

Chuckling with a smile, "oh. Makes sense. Anything else to do?"

"I need to record a message for Amanda," adding with a muffled giggle, "and not crash."

Taking on a countenance of wisdom, "good plan."

Pulling out of the driveway she turned left and headed for the interior curves leading down to an arterial access point of the local transportation grid. "The Reply isn't going to be stopped without an extreme measure. I have to take Dominion from Steven."

Nodding quietly he smiled at her, *I feel calm when he smiles at me.*

Reaching to the console she worked the menu of options to get to the voice messaging App, "time to send something to Amanda so she'll understand that this is far from over."

"Noted."

4.1.5 - 13:38

Drenner Estate – Consul's Office

∫ Amanda Drenner

Considering the bullet points of qualifiers for Civil War, she checked them against the Protocol Document. Laying the tablet down she met Chuck's expectant gaze. *I have nothing for you.* Forcing out the words she spoke her resignation to the future, "I think we're going to have to admit that we don't have recourse."

Without looking away his face fell to one of dismal defeat, "and there's nothing you can do?"

I don't know if I told you the truth about this plan, the bomb, or any of it that it would help your heart now. I hope when I do that you forgive the piles of lies of omission I've had to tell you over the years. "He got it past us Chuck. I spoke against it but there really was nothing we could do. Thomas condemned his House when he did this and failed. It didn't have to be this way, this wasn't the only option, but it was the one Steven wanted."

Asking his question with a helplessness hanging from his body language, "what about -"

Trying to console him, "we're back to square zero."

We don't always get to win.

Pacing away from her he sounded rattled, "is this is what Susan wants? We don't get to know do we? Not for certain."

You're not the Consul yet. One day you'll get used to losing. "I just know it's what Commander Bachman wants. He spoke with a furious conviction that we had betrayed her. It's kind of sad Chuck, he loves Susan so much."

Gripping the bridge of his nose with his hand he rested his hand against his fingers. Speaking the question from his pose, "Citation?"

How do I condense a life lived into bullet points? "Nothing I can tell you about specifically. It's just what I know of him, and his history in relating to Susan. It reminds me of the railing anger Asmodai used to have when it came to Maggie's detractors. Maggie would temper his feelings and teach him to forgive people for not understanding. Steven has no such failsafe that I am aware of."

Losing his pose he sighed, "that's fascinating, really. Doesn't really help us, but it's cold comfort to know that he does this because he might just love her and be really upset right now. So upset," taking a breath he let out the name, "Cassia?"

Nodding with a lump in her throat, "and Josh."

"At least," trailing off he slumped his shoulders and hung his head.

He loved her so much. He'll be lost to the What-Ifs soon. We'll be sharing Micah's wisdom and my stash of rum before long.

"My comm is blinking, one moment Chuck." Checking her comm she blinked at the pair of messages waiting for her. *She was spotted on the North Hauler Road, and in motion.* "She's not dead yet Chuck!"

Rounding on her with a hesitant grin, "*what?*"

This isn't over. "Susan has called a Council Session for as soon as she reaches Central."

Furrowing his brow with his question, "isn't that a bit of a drive?"

Checking the details, "her emergency beacon has pinged a warning to get out of the way to a Drenner hauler. She's speeding toward Central now."

Weighing the notion with his tone, "if she uses the beacon won't that reveal Safe Housing?"

Clarifying the move, "she didn't ping it until she hit the North Hauler Road. That's still *vague* for where she may have been resting."

Blurting out his questions, "does Steven have a lead on her? How fast is she going?"

He doesn't want to hope. I know I don't either, it would hurt far too much. Checking the status report, "she's in the lead. As she is going," laughing in shock, "one hundred and seventy. She's let the Beast off the leash."

Asking with a concern for the idea, "isn't that dangerous?"

I haven't seen her let the Beast of its leash without being on the course. Not like this. The roads are dry though, so she's safe. I don't want to tell him of the danger, or to get used to it.

"She's rated for higher. She has more hours behind the wheel of it than most citizens of The Rim have with their vehicles. She wouldn't call this to gloat. She's going to stop it."

Pressing her, "are you *certain?*"

Checking over the details she found an audio message in her inbox. Pressing play she held her comm out confident that she would want to share it.

"Amanda! I *didn't know.* I'm going to fix this! I have an ad lib in motion, hold tight! I'm going to Central Tower, I'll have a Veto *soon.*" The sound of The Beast's engine in the background was loud enough to be heard on the Hands-Free microphone as she continued, "I'm scheduled to see Waterlily when this is over. The Workplace Trauma Clause will get me a few more hours to breathe. I won't let this kill Cassia! I have to go. End Message." After a moment of engine roar, "the prompt didn't work right to end the message. Can you push that button for me? The red blinking one - "

Hearing the message end she set her comm down gently as the questions came to mind. *I wonder when I get to meet him, much less what she has planned?*

Breathing a sigh of relief Chuck appeared to be calming, "the Gingerbread Son at her side?"

Finding a smile, "I would presume."

Asking the question with a tentative air, "Admin Nobody is back on her side?"

Picking up her comm she looked at the latest round of messages, "yes." *The man who is now our new Sys-Admin by Susan's own admission, but I don't need to worry you with that yet either.*

"Do we know anything more that you can tell me?"

"No, but I'll let you know more when this is over. You need to leave the room though, she'll be there soon and this is Consul only business." Waving him off with a newfound smile, "Protocol and all that."

Growling with an almost playfully indignant anger, "you *will* tell me how it goes."

Assuring him as best she could, "I will Chuck, I will."

4.1.7 - 13:43

Cloak and Dagger – Outer Door

▸Jerome Hope

Almost to the door. Holding his bag of gear carefully and fumbling for his card he startled as the sound of shoes on the tile behind him derailed his train of thought.

Hearing the question spoken with the gentleness he was grateful for, "a moment Sys-Admin?"

Stanley. Turning slowly he smiled with a shy trepidation, "I was just leaving."

Smiling in return he adjusted his glasses with a paternal aura about him, "you're a good friend to her Hope. You do such good work for her. It strengthens my heart to know you are the new Sys-Admin."

Replying with a feeling of humbled gratitude, "thank you Stanley, noted."

Folding his hands into the Añjali Mudrā, "I want you to know I'll keep you In The Loop, I have a few reports pending and I'll make sure you see a copy."

Losing the tension of the moment he smiled, "thank you Stanley."

Lowering his hands he smiled warmly, "I did not tell him you were leaving."

"Motive?"

Speaking with a clear tone, "you have done nothing wrong, that I am aware of, and he did not ask me to keep him informed of your well being. Miss Bachman did, but, life is how life is."

Nodding once with a smile, "it is."

"Be well Jerome. Until next time."

"You as well! Until then!"

Watching Stanley move over and open the door he smiled sheepishly as Stanley's humored admonishment was spoken, "and get some sleep as soon as you are able."

"Noted." *One of the many fathers to all of the sons.*

Nodding mutely in reply Stanley waited for Jerome to step out before moving to close the door.

I can only imagine what that report will have in it. Hopefully something I can use.

Looking out he blinked at the harshness of the afternoon sun as the gate to the parking lot opened. Focusing his eyes on the sight of the custom Duo-Car he felt a strange humor at the spectacle of it.

That appears to be the roster of the Cartoon Icons lineup. I called, she said she would get a borrowed car, and I have no idea who she knows.

Waiting a moment she pulled up next to the door and into the Pickup Only space. Moving around as briskly as he could he heard the sound of the door catch pop and the door being left ajar for him.

Getting into the car with a clumsy energy he felt the comfort of the smile on his face. Buckling up he looked into the tired but energetic eyes of Paige Turner, *the student of Shadows, who looks like she needs a nap too.*

Speaking his question with a groan, "standard up-link to speak with Dennis?"

Nodding quickly Paige set to turning the car around. *I should say something.* "Thank you for following your convictions to help Dennis. Even if he doesn't know what he's helping me escape now that things are falling into place."

Breathing out with an excited exhale she appeared to be all smiles for their shared moment. *She isn't the one who saves the world, she just drives the car.*

"Feels better to do something than to sit at home and do nothing?"

Nodding again she smiled and pointed to his tablet. Making the motion for 'hurry up' she turned her attention to the reopened gate.

"Do I want to know whom you borrowed this car from?"

Shaking her head yes and no she shrugged with an exasperated look on her face.

I forget myself. "Mea culpa, you're driving."

Nodding twice she pulled the car onto the main street and into the flow of traffic with a dramatic sigh.

Focusing on his tablet he set to activating his connection as Admin Nobody. Finalizing his login he found the request pending for a Comm Call. Pressing the button with his stylus he questioned the air hoping the microphone was on, "Dennis?"

"It's me. I double checked her perimeter. They already hit Ash on the sensitive files they had. Short list of guests on the party who have an idea of what's going on out there. I'll have a memo on it in your mailbox before you wake up." Pausing for a half second he continued quickly, "I'm glad Paige reached you. I wouldn't want you underfoot of the Commander today either."

One more thing to remember when I wake up. "I'll keep an eye out for the memo. And there's something you should know -"

"Hang on, alert light is blinking." After a moment of pause, "why is Susan going at that speed?" Speaking with a grim finality, "the Beast is off the leash."

The only way to get there fast enough. "She has to save our world."

"I'm not sure she's in the shape to do that. Or what she's actually doing."

"I would agree with you, about the shape and condition, but we don't get a choice. Steven pushed her."

Grousing the question with a graveled anger, "he pushed The Reply into play? *That fast?*"

Trying to keep the guilt in his tone to a minimum, "yes. I had to help him."

Firing back with a aged wisdom to his voice, "you best hide yourself in the secure place she's taking you. Find a Caveat in *something* to keep him from getting near you. He's been a bit softer in the last year but I don't know if that would extend to *this*."

"I planned on it. I get a head start. He doesn't know. I blocked the notifications to his comm from going through. He thinks she's still at home. He *also* thinks that Captain Turner and her Scouts are still at Central and not barreling toward the Kunlow Estate. I gave them my best set of instructions which will get them there as they clear checkpoints. I made certain to plot a very specific course for them."

"Captain Turner is going after Thomas?"

"Her and the Scouts, he's got almost nothing to stop them with from what I've seen. Troubles within the House have kept the remaining forces from coming together on a specific project. Should be an easy hit."

"Good. I might have to watch that footage later. An APC going full tilt is almost comical, *three* of them?" Laughing for a moment he sighed, "I have to go. The Reply is in play, even when she stops it, I'll need to do my part."

Work is the condition of the Worker. "I know."

"Be well Jerome."

"You as well Dennis."

Closing the connection he tipped his head back, "you know a place I could hide from Commander Bachman?"

Nodding enthusiastically she did her wordless happy hiss before nodding twice.

"Your energy is amazing Paige. Hide me?"

Nodding twice again she set to moving to the next turn lane.

I will make sure Susan is secure and then I'll sleep. Not a moment before she's safe.

4.2.0 - 14:05

Crown of Hope (Highway) – Northern New Hope

† Sasha Herb

Keeping a firm grip on the wheel she checked her Heads-Up Display Glasses for the next turn. *She said specific Consul, get a nap, and here we are. There's only one Consul near where we're going.*

Rusted Scrap we're on Extraction.

She warned us.

Breathing with a careful attention to staying calm she readied the APC for another forceful drift around a corner. Checking the relay she said a silent thanks for the two rigs behind her. *I'm on lead. We hit danger and I hit it first.*

They're keeping up though.

Frank and his boys to the Cultural Center means that she's ready for them to get hit. Or for those who would to see the Night Terror Standard flying over the Cultural Center and know to stay away.

She's playing this loud. At least the route is clear of traffic. Admin Nobody managed to make this whole route as eerie as it is helpful. The reinforcement leads me to believe Dispatch is aiding us.

Hearing her vox light up with a voice she knew all too well, "Captain Turner -"

Here we go again Diminuendo.

"- can we *please* have our mission brief now? You called *Scrambled At Negative Five!* You dumped us into this so fast we're *still* waking our sleepers," a moment of respite from her voice later, "come on DiVincenzo! *You can do it!*" Sighing heavily into the vox with her frustrated words, "come on Captain! What is the thing we were warned to be ready for?"

Listening to the roar of the engine, as she continued to push at top speed, she pondered what would be waiting for them. *No one has ever done this to a Consul before. I may have wanted to do it to Asmodai, but I didn't think out the logistics of it.*

Catching the update she slowed slightly to make the next turn. *Service roads now? We're almost to the Kunlow's backyard.*

Hearing Samantha's voice in her ear she smiled at the comforting ease she spoke her words, "we're going to the House of Kunlow."

She wants him alive.

Continuing with a level tone of Command, "we are going to the New Hope Estate of the Kunlow Family. Our orders confirm that he is the Renegade Consul who masterminded the attack on Central last night."

The Commander would burn the House. I don't think they would take seeing Frank lightly. This is a chess move. She's making the only move she has left if she's going to handle this her way.

Speaking into the vox with a tired slosh to her words DiVincenzo asked her question with a daunted timbre to the words, "Collateral Damage Index?"

I'm just glad Divi asks that with the same tone we all do. We all want *to hear zero, or at least I hope we do.*

Without losing the Voice of Command she spoke the word as a promise to be kept, "Zero."

"Opening Salvo?"

She doesn't want it. I think she's in shock that we're getting a peaceful enough resolution. Or still asleep.

Maintaining her control of the Voice, "Nil."

"Brandished Intimidation?"

Adding a lilt of confidence with the Voice, "our orders will speak for themselves, and will be delivered as we close in. We're going in full armor, *if* we're fired upon you will be as good with your weapons as Yorklin surgeons are with their lasers. We're going in the back, the House Steward is taking a chance on us and he's going to let us in. Any and all aggression will be reviewed when this is over. We're there for Thomas and *nothing more.* Cameras on and audio hot, the whole time."

My love is still who she says she is.

Checking her readout she softly barked the ETA, which had just appeared, over the vox, "we are three minutes out from Insertion Point."

Reviewing the orders Captain Turner laid it on the line, "we pull up. Drop gangplank on the quiet. We're under Network Cloak. If we don't make too much noise we can get in fast and quiet. Each one of us is going to be a localized broadcast to those who would come within Striking Distance of what is going on."

Coming onto the vox again Divi voiced her concern, "Striking Distance seems tight."

With the air of digging deep for 'once more into the breach' Captain Turner spoke her demand, "we *can not* have Thomas knowing we're there until it's too late. We *can't* let him Exit Pass either! Understood?"

"Understood."

Calling the update, "ETA is two and a half!"

"Final checks! Suits up, on, and checked! Carbines at Off-Side Drop, Knock-Out Rounds in your Pistols, Shock Boxes at the ready!"

"Yes Captain!"

"Stick to the plan! There is *no* Plan B!"

"Yes Captain!"

Once more with feeling.

4.1.9 - 13:49

The Beast – "88 Kilo Route"

☼ Yuri

Riding in the passenger seat he marveled at the speed and careful efficiency Susan was moving The Beast along.

Her conviction is back with a vengeance. She looks like she could storm the gates of the Ever After and take on whatever Gods got in her way. "I feel like I'm going to be taking off in a moment. Flaps?"

Losing the stern grimace as a grin spread from her clenched lips, "don't make me laugh Yuri! I cannot laugh right now."

Looking out the window he tried to eyeball the scenery, "one hundred sixty? Seventy? It's been awhile since I flew a plane."

Firing back with an almost conversational detachment, "seventy at the moment. We'll be moving to eighty shortly."

Settling in the seat he was thankful for the comfortable cushioning, "why does your *car* not have wings?"

Letting out a puff of a sigh, "because my car has a duality of being. Right now, he's a battlefield vehicle. The original specs were from a project created by the Department of Defense for the old USA. The Snafu-Labs were able to get it to work."

Something new to learn! "What is the Snafu?"

Smiling she returned to the conversational humor, "Scientific Normatives Are Finally Uplifted, it's a place where they do advanced research to try to refine the science which is the backbone of our world. We *are* aware of the past meaning, but we don't have *that* word either."

Trying for comedy, "I have noticed the removal of many words. If I stub my toe, what do I scream?"

Responding in a calm tone she smiled faintly, "gibberish is the cultural norm. You can just emote noise."

Fair enough, "noted."

Speaking with a hint of wonder with the words, "the man on the video we found with the plans for this vehicle? He was very excited about it."

Back on topic. "Why did you have it built? Just for fun?"

"Close. It *was* indeed to see what it would be like. The act of creating this vehicle was years in the doing as they had to make everything to make it, understand it, and then from it? A star-burst of technological innovations. Our military creates things, and then they share it with the general populace if it can be to their benefit. Limited resources, maximum outcome, and maximum need for a better future for all."

Gesturing to the dash, "you kept, him, though."

Beaming with pride she adjusted her grip on the wheel, "the romantic notions of my relationship to my car aside? The armor plating and protective value of The Beast are second to none for a four door vehicle. I was just being prudent."

"Noted."

Speaking with the relief evident in her voice, "the roads are dry."

"They are." *She has a story, I will ask later.*

"I'm going to save Cassia from this, I hope they don't tell her this is happening."

Perhaps an easier story? "So who is Cassia?"

"She is my cousin. My Uncle Tim, maternal side, helped gift this world with a daughter. Her name is Cassia Kunlow now. She's a beautiful woman just three months my junior."

And we are going faster.

"You are close then?" Maybe a happy story?

Taking her time with the words, a gentle pause between each set, "actually no! In the beginning she wanted to be nice to me. She wanted to show me kindness and her rusted father wouldn't let her. I couldn't even confirm I was going to her wedding because of that sack of det!"

She sounds so sad, "did you go?"

Without losing the sad calm she trudged onward, "I did! I went, I stood in the back, and I watched the vows. I watched her settle on Josh because the man she wanted more? He wouldn't, he *couldn't*," after a moment of two deep breaths she continued without the sad, "I should clarify that. I wish to."

"Is Josh good?"

"Josh is a good man, but Chuck was the one she wanted, loved, and they couldn't be together. Josh has been good for her. I'm a romantic, such as we understand it, so Chuck would have been a more ideal partner. However, when I am being reasonable? I will tell you how she has been good for Josh also. How they have forged something good. And how you don't always get what you strive for, no matter how hard you try."

There is some haunt there. "So the man she loved first, that loved her, was not in a place to commit to love?"

"He had an *extreme* Adverse Childhood Experience. Cassia was trying to glue him back together, piece by piece, as a romantic partner. He turned down further ministrations and a shared life. She found a different man, Josh, and set to gluing him back together."

"Is that a healthy place to –" *wait a minute.*

Speaking the words with a forced neutrality, "family tradition."

I don't mind. I should learn more though. "Short answer?"

"Drenner women are from a long standing culture of empathy, sympathy, and observational cultivation. My mother was a Drenner, she brought that idea to the family lessons. Patrick has studied the heart with an emphasis. Even Steven. It's why he's not concerned as much with you having access to my bed, but my heart."

I will side step that, "so Cassia is with Josh?"

"Yes, and we'll cover the rest of this later."

She still wants to win it all, which is nice. "So you can save everyone?"

"I can. The Scouts are moving into place to get Thomas."

Trying his best for a tone of asking a question without questioning, "so why the Scouts on Thomas and the Terrors on defense?" *I will have to ask her for the term for that.*

Answering after a short pause with a more conversational tone again, "people are afraid of the Terror Squad. They are not a *diplomatic* force. The Scouts are made up of women, for one, and they perform a different set of duties. If they saw the Terrors pull up? They would know fear. On the other hand, if they walk toward the Cultural Center and see the flag of the Terror Squad flying above it? They will know fear."

"Why,-" *wait.* Closing his mouth he took a breath, "Counter-Advocate time."

Smiling in anticipation, "not my first choice of venue, but go for it."

Forcing his tone to one of comedy, "why an all female Squad? Why not keep them home, have them make babies and knit?"

Nodding once she kept her eyes on the road. Working the words with a slight hesitation to them, carried with a somber philosophical outlook on them, "because not everyone wants to be happy. Some women want to go where their convictions lead them. That does not promise that a woman will be happy there. Not even remotely. There are women who when faced with the question of grueling physical standards, eating food out of a foil pouch with a spoon, and risking their lives in a direct sense of the idea? They want to chase that life. So they have a place, in all walks of life, a spot at all the tables. Even the armed forces."

"How did it start?"

"Fairly simply really. Five generations ago we went, as a Province, to war with those who dwelled around us. The women who didn't want to sit in the shelters and hope the men could win, thus preventing their life of rape and subjugation as war brides? They wanted to fight too. To answer the original question of, sit and wait or fight and risk dying?"

When you put it like that. "That sounds like a cultural lesson. I am faced with the idea that you're not the only one with stark word-play."

"To be fair, most people use humor to soften it. Telling a joke is a way of coping."

"I see."

"We have two Squads of Cloaks, and two Squads of Daggers, whom are female. One hundred and twenty women."

"Out of?"

"Last I knew we had managed to tip the scale at a million people. Vaguely fifty-fifty spread on that."

Contemplating the math he inflected the scope of the idea, "they are unique women."

Confirming with a firmness, "yes."

"Noted." Looking out the window he watched the buildings fly by, "so which section of the city is this?"

"The Caravanners Row, the place which shipping and receiving is handled. The cities have trade and outreach with each other. We built a fabrication of a Market to give the mind something to strive for. To move past a Scarcity System to one of Honorable Exchange. This road, built for our Long-Haulers is their Domain. I am a Guest in their Domain."

"Do they know you are here?"

"The Emergency Beacon is relaying messages that are preventing traffic from slowing us. They pull over, wait, and watch as I blow past with an apology relayed to their comm units. I move, they move, I pass, they return to their duties."

"Noted."

Exclaiming with an honest joy, "you sound more native already!"

"Even this old dog can be taught new tricks."

With a smile and factual tone of observation she seemed almost playful, "I bet if you shave that beard you'll be a young man again. At least trim it down further than I did. Many men maintain trim beards instead of shaving it off entirely. Or if you start it over you could grow it out to a majestic monument to your masculinity."

Monument to my masculinity, and not just not having a razor for a few years. Explains why she only trimmed the split ends. "I never thought to ask for a razor. You never pressed one on me."

Speaking cautiously she appeared humored, "this is a difficult moment for me, going into this moment."

Curious. "Which is?"

"If I *think* that you *want* to shave, and press the issue? Then you might be influenced by my decision for how you take care of yourself."

I will walk this strange line with you. "Beards are welcome, yes?"

Smiling with encouragement, "yes."

Taking on an air of play acted seriousness, "how do women view beards? From your understanding as the High Consul."

"Most women just ask that you take it seriously. Supplies from the Supply Depot and a regular visit with a Barber who is trained in Beard Care. If you can grow one, and would like to grow one, then that is on the man to decide. If you work with food then you get to wear a hair net for your beard too."

Now for the important question.

"Noted." Looking back out the window he smiled, "do you like a man with a beard?"

Adjusting her grip on the wheel again she smiled, "I will answer. Short answer? It does not play against him. A well kept beard can be a sign of a man who values himself. The Ego, the self, is a part of the mind one must take good care of. A man who has a well kept beard shows signs of a well kept heart. The lessons go hand in hand."

Now to hear the other side. "And a smooth skin man?"

"He either cannot or chooses not to. His face shows the signs of care or lack thereof. Men are not ugly, they are raised to play to their strengths, so a man with an uncared for face is wearing his priorities front and center. I admit, I like the sight of a man who is well kept, at either end of that spectrum."

"Noted. You managed to not give me a true bias to work with."

"As you did not ask for bias based anecdotes, I did not provide one."

I could use the humor. "Would you share one?"

"My father had a beard coming back from the war. Then he met mom and shaved it in short order. From then on? My father was clean shaven because mom had sensitive skin. He could give her beard burn from almost any contact."

That sounds terrible. "Any?"

Stifling a giggle, "especially the good kind. He kept his face polished smooth the whole time he knew her."

Odd. "He was scruffy when we met."

"His second love didn't mind it. Her face could handle the beard. However, no one *liked* his beard. It made him look like someone else. He would polish it away when it would get too long."

"Noted."

"My face is not vexed by beard hair. Even as rough as yours was. When you were recovering and I would speak softly in your ear? Your beard would brush my cheek. I checked afterward. No real burn. The split ends were unpleasant, which is why I cut them and nothing more."

I believe I have my answer then. "I will shave it off, and if I do not like it? I will grow a new one and raise it up right."

"There's shaving supplies in the small leather bag in the basket you would have found everything else in."

"Good to know!"

Going quiet he closed his eyes against the nausea of one last major turn as Central Tower came into view. *We are almost there.*

"So what happens now?"

Gesturing to her left ear, "the beacon and Dispatch have relayed a path for us. We're going around to the East side of the Tower, long circle, and then pulling into place at the front of the Tower on the South side. The garage is a Staging Area for those who are already picking their way through the tasks that come next."

"Noted."

Clarifying with a hint of conspiracy to her tone, "the ear-piece on my left ear is receive only. It doesn't have a microphone on it."

Oh good. "Also, good to know."

Feeling the relief of the loss of speed he spied the large expanse of trees and greenery out Susan's window, "so is that something special that way?"

"That's the Elysian Grounds, with the Elysian Fields."

I know those terms, but do they? "Symbolism?"

"It was a place of refuge in the first generation, they forged and cultivated a place of rest and respite. In the second generation they used it for the weddings of so many. The Guild uses it as a therapeutic visitation spot at night."

"So to find peace, the people lay down in green pastures?"

Nodding once without looking at him she spoke with an intonation of recitation, "The Prophet leads a people who will not lack for the Basic Needs, the people may lay down in green fields and quiet places, to refresh their souls -"

Riding in quiet as she navigated the last turns to bring them onto the Tower Grounds proper he waited as she picked her path around the encamped personnel. *I wonder what the rest is?*

"- The Prophet leads the people along the Path for they are the one who leads. No matter how dark the night, they shall not live in fear of evil, for the Prophet is with them. The Prophet guards them with the Protocol as the Peace-Bringer."

She has been well versed in these words.

"The Bounty of the Land is laid on the table before all who are loyal, and even as their enemies howl outside? In the place of the union they will find refuge at the table. Surely goodness and love will flourish in this place for all of their days, for they dwell in the shared place as Citizens forever."

Unsure of what to say he felt the deceleration complete as they came to a stop before the shattered entrance to Central Tower.

Still holding the wheel with a hunched shoulder posture, "Consul Kunlow leveled the accusation of False Prophet at me. The Failsafe against the system going astray. Not just the idea that I was wrong about something, but that I was leading the world to ruin. His people are afraid of the future because we do not know what will, can, or can be changed. I will see him burn for the methods he has employed. I can sympathize *and* empathize with his people, my shared people, in the fear they have about the future."

"Do you know you can win?"

Raising up in her seat her words came with a greater conviction, "I am the Prophet of the Second Chance, it's what I was born to do. I am a Romantic Nationalist, I believe in these people, that the reason why The State exists is *because* of the people. God, did not appoint me. I was raised to understand this place from the moment I could understand myself." Taking a deep breath she smiled as her posture corrected, "I'm using time that I do not have. We need to go inside."

"Then we go!"

Watching Susan jump from the car and start her run for the front doors he felt a spark of youthful energy rise in him. *That is what I looked like years ago when I was possessed by the fires of youth.* Getting out he set to trying to keep up with her.

Susan waved at the guards standing in front on the doors, "High Consul with an Interconnectivity Code Five coming through!"

"Understood ma'am! Watch for glass!"

Looking over her shoulder, "keep up!"

"Alright, alright!"

Running up to the front doors she stopped in her tracks, "I was not prepared for this."

Looking to the guard to the right side of the door he watched the man salute him. Returning the salute out of reflex he saw the smile spread on the guard's face. Turning to look at Susan with a questioning look he felt a shy moment come over him at how underdressed for the moment he was.

Speaking softly she motioned for him to follow, "watch your step, there could still be glass."

Nodding he set to following her through the sheared path that had been cleared in the broken and twisted wreckage. Clinging to the hope that nothing would go wrong with her plans. *She has spun a truth, and wrapped it with the fragile sugar strands of spun hope and fairy dust.*

4.2.2 - 14:11

Central Tower - The Bachman Elevator

⁘..Susan Bachman

The doors close and we're back in the elevator we left. The circle completed.
Pressing the button for their destination she heard her comm chirping. *Jerome.*
Pulling out her comm she answered quickly, "speak!"
Rushing his words with equal part fatigue and joy, "Miss Bachman! Network minimum stability was achieved! On a hunch I ran Horse Hair on Octavia Kunlow. She came up negative for being in on this! There is no way based upon the logs that she knew what was going on. The Successor to the House wasn't a part of it!"
"Noted. A moment." Watching the numbers on the readout change Susan wracked her brain for a plan. Watching the last of the variables fall into place in her mind's eye she set to expressing them. "Is Sasha on scene yet?"
"They're *inside* already. No shots fired. It's a tense room by room. The House Steward let them in but by the Stars and Sky it's slow going. I called in Guild Assets to *try* to keep violence from exploding into being. My intel is two minutes old."
"Draft up a Proxy Communication from me and get it to her. Secure Octavia! Set up a base camp to prepare for the possible fallout! Give Octavia my best while you're at it! With Thomas dying for this it would be good to know that she knows that she'll be ruling in his stead and I mean her no harm! Make sure the Counselors know that this is the plan. Get it filed, get it official, and try to keep the shooting from starting."
"On it."
Hearing the call close she looked to Yuri, "Octavia didn't know. He hid it from her."
"Oh dear." Nodding with a smile he spoke his hope, "there's something good you can make from this then?"
Taking strength in the moment, "I *believe* so! Now I just have to hope Sasha gets to her before something happens to her."
Looking at the floor his shoulders slumped, "I understand your worry."
Opting for a softer tone she expressed her condolence, "probably too well."
Speaking with a voice of sad understanding without raising his head, "too well. If you request, I would tell you later."
Touching his shoulder she rubbed it gently, "noted."
May this be a much happier ending than our other stories.

4.2.4 - 14:16

Kunlow Estate – Hall

† Sasha Herb

Moving softly with the House Steward at her side she kept a firm but lowered grip on her pistol. *This is not what I expected, any of it.*

Reaching the door to Octavia's bedchamber the Steward fretted audibly without meeting her gaze, "she is inside. Please, I beg, be gentle?"

Regarding the visage of the Steward she quickly reviewed her intel on him as she looked at his weathered face and graying hair. *This man has been here since she got here. This is how he can try to protect her, serve her, and save the House at the same time. This is not the time for aggression.*

Raising her voice above an Operations Whisper she went for a soft conversational volume, "I will be as gentle as I am able. I have been sent orders from the High Consul herself to do this as peacefully as I am able." Checking her wrist display she read the updated words, "her innocence in this changes the tone of the moment. Your home goes from a place of the last hold-outs to those who are angry that they have been painted with the innocent blood of the lost and no one can see that."

Looking back to her with a 'curious' lilt to his question, "did you come up with that, or did someone else?"

Moving her wrist to show the display, "someone else. I'm a Soldier, not a Poet."

Nodding he moved away from the door, "a good moment for you both."

"Thank you Steward."

Waiting for him to get completely out of the way she holstered her weapon and presented her empty palms to him. Nodding he took another full step back. Moving to the side of the door she turned the doorknob gently and set to sneaking into the bedroom of Octavia Kunlow as softly as she could. Stepping inside the door she took in the sight of the low light in the bedroom which was accompanied by the scent of almonds. Spying the slow motion from the bench seat in front of the vanity near the door she met Octavia's gaze.

I am thankful you are not known for your skills with a firearm.

Speaking with a clear volume and conversational cadence she broke the silence, "Lady Kunlow?"

Looking up with the fear evident on her face she blanched, "this is the end?"

"No. Allow me to explain? Check your comm?"

With a slight lurch of her head she seemed to be catching on that something was different, "you're not whispering."

"I am acting as a Proxy for Miss Bachman."

With a rush of newfound emotion she took a breath, "let me get my comm then." Getting up and walking with a less than stable gait she came closer to the door.

Examining Lady Kunlow she noted her attire. *A mourning dirndl? It's surprisingly elegant. That looks like Stephanie's work. I have to be as gentle as possible regardless, but this is a new piece of the puzzle.*

Picking up her comm she brought it out of sleep mode and started reading, "I received the news and put this on the charger. I honestly didn't know what else to do."

"Please let me know when you're done reading."

Nodding and reading the short message she sighed in relief and leaned against the wall. "I am quite whelmed."

Moving in and offering her an arm without touching her she was rewarded with Octavia leaning on her, "let me get you back to bed."

Clutching to her with a lethargic energy she appeared under the influence of something, "this is most unbecoming of a Lady to be so whelmed."

Checklist it. "Are you compromised chemically?"

Nodding she frowned, "it's Lullaby. It was in my lunch smoothie. I did not ask for it. I believe I was meant to sleep through this moment."

"You are to be spared harm." Tumbling over the words she tried again, "not be harmed. We are just here for Consul Kunlow."

Leaning against her with a heaviness to her and her words, "I am safe?"

"By Miss Bachman's will and edict. I am her enforcement of that edict. You shall not be harmed this day."

Tilting her chin up she caught her eyes, "I've heard so much about the friendship between you and her. The roommates turned life-mates." Smiling with a borderline intoxicated humor, "it must be something else to have love like that."

The love she couldn't admit, even if it was in everyone's files. Trying to keep her tone gentle and matter-of-fact, "it is."

Touching her arm she held it gently as her smile fell away, "my love is gone Sasha. He died in Central last night. He believed my father."

Swallowing against the implications she started them moving toward the bed, "thus the mourning dirndl?"

Moving with her she hung her head, "he is not the first I have lost, not my first person I cared for that I wish was still alive. For him? For him I even tied the knot in the back. We were going to be something. And now? Nothing but ashes."

Bracing Octavia against the side of the bed she marveled at the craftsmanship of the short edifice, "I have no words."

Trying to straighten up with her words, "I would hope you didn't." Reaching out Sasha moved her arm as a brace for her to use as the words continued, "cold comfort for both of us." Sighing she set to adjusting her dirndl, "I am desirous of the happiness you have, not so much with Miss Bachman exactly, but the level of happiness you feel. I want to know that again so," finishing her adjustments, "I have been honest. It is what we strive to be."

Unclenching her fist she moved the arm into a more comforting position, "I am not your panacea but I am here."

"My father is going to the Questioners then?"

"Most likely." Nudging her into the bed, "have you spoken with your father today?"

"Not in the last few hours." Getting into the bed with a sigh, "I have nothing to say to him." Rolling onto her back she looked up at her with an overwhelming sadness playing across her usually comforting face, "I would feel very alone right now if you were not here though."

Dig the heel in, in for a millimeter in for a kilometer, "I am going to stay here for you."

Keeping her eyes closed she spoke with a firm presence of mind, "and your mission?"

Without fighting the small smile she spoke her best attempt at a tone which would encourage in its enthusiasm. "I am Miss Bachman's Proxy right now. She has given me my orders, and I will perform them by staying next to you."

Moving a hand close to the edge of the bed, "hold my hand please?"

Sitting down on the edge of the bed she laid her hand down next to Octavia's, "I will, if you place your hand on mine. I don't have the Protocol handy so I would prefer if you could set the tone and timbre of the moment."

Taking Sasha's hand she grasped it firmly in a far more physical grip than she was expecting. "I know you are not for the chasing."

"Thank you."

Opening her eyes she blinked away an errant tear, "is your mic hot?"

Honesty is the only policy. "It is."

Speaking with a firm tone of Request, "may I request that you disengage it?"

"Yes." Tapping the relay on her gear, "Herb to Coordinator? Request authorization to disengage audio. Over."

Looking at her wrist screen she read the words, *authorization granted.* Holding her free hand up she reached over to the connector and removed the plug from the socket. "Authorization was granted."

Smiling with a face of holding back tears, "thank you."

"Noted."

Settling down again she exhaled with a sniffle, "Kincaid left me a message, it explained what he was hoping for, by going into Central. How does a person share their body, their mind, and their dreams but leave out something so important?"

Endeavoring to play it safe with her words, "you were closer than I would know of then?"

"I thought I had a husband, or at least someone to share *home* with. To wake and find him gone, on something so terrible? I feel a mix of sick, sad, and disappointed with myself that I don't have words." Looking to her with a sudden small smile, "a pain you will never know?"

People think so much of me. Known for understanding people to the point that I can read their minds. "Pardon?"

Performing the gesture for 'apology,' "the pain of letting someone into your body, only to be betrayed by them."

I understand more now. "I do not let people inside my body, no."

Smiling with a more familiar visage of comforting, "you have an upside to your condition then."

Keep her engaged, and motivated, "is this the Suzerain I see before me?"

"I believe it is."

"I will admit, I had not thought of that upside. I will add it to my Counted Blessings."

"You have been safe, in the heart, next to Miss Bachman. Others around her might have made it more difficult, from what my files tell me, but did she?"

She was always trying to do it right. "Never on purpose. No."

Broaching the subject carefully, "did she ever unleash the Bachman Rage on you?"

Smiling with the comfort of the answer, "never."

Nodding once she closed her eyes again, "again, I would wish that you never understand this. Not just the touch and betrayal, but the betrayal itself."

Squeezing her hand gently, "thank you Lady Kunlow."

"Noted." Opening her eyes she fixed her gaze on the ceiling with a thoughtful look on her face, "this is one of Miss Bachman's ad libs, correct?"

As she had it kept moving in real time? I would hope so. "Affirmative."

Turning her head she looked at her with a soulful glance, "you are going to stay with me?"

I have nowhere else to go. "Affirmative."

Squeezing her hand gently with the question, "could you, if I can ask of you, tell me what it is like to be as you are?" Letting up on the squeeze she sighed, "if I think of me? I'll break down." With the frustration evident she continued, "if I think of my father? I will break something. And as I am surrounded by my treasures? I do not want to break my treasures." Losing the frustration with a forced pause she implored her, "so if you would, could you tell me of the affair that was kept so secret?"

The sadness at the highest echelon of power. "I could tell you some stories that do no harm in the retelling. Motive?"

Responding with a 'matter of fact' tone, "I am going to be made Consul, with my father shuffling off the mortal coil. I would like to understand the heart beating in the chest of The Derecho. You would be part of that."

The Question must be asked. "Gretchenfrage?"

Smiling with a brightened mood she nodded in approval, "I am thankful you asked. If we establish a rapport, you will tell me of the Winter Wolf. My father saw the footage from last night. He, my father, got into a fight with our Steward earlier, which included telling him that the Winter Wolf was not part of the plan."

The man who let us in then? "Sandor Spratt?"

Nodding with the affirmation, "yes."

Replying with the simple answer, "he's the one who let us in."

Rushing to reassure with her words, "I won't discipline him, he was being a Good Citizen. Trusting in the truths he was told."

I wonder if Steward Spratt is someone special then? "Thank you Lady Kunlow."

Squeezing her hand gently, "who is the Winter Wolf?"

Reciting the mantra internally before finding words, *when you speak of a Warrior, speak with Honor.* "His name is Yuri, and he crossed the whole world, to ask for a debt owed to be repaid. Susan, she told me a very long time ago a woman named Elianna Seches saved the life of Asmodai Bachman. She brought him to the Temple of the Lady of The Unending Magazine."

Nodding once she smiled firmly, "I follow."

"She would go away, having united his heart and fate to the woman known as Alexis Bundkuchen. It would be Elianna's son would return to us, and save the lives of Alexis, and the children she had with Asmodai."

Smiling with a detached wonder, "The Gingerbread Man, this man, is the descendent of the Gingerbread Man?"

Our legends are real again. "Yes."

Sniffling once she nodded as the revelation occurred, "he got here just in time."

"If you stay resting, as you appear comfortable, I will tell you of the docile tribulations of loving the woman I just call Susan. To others her Titles are many. The Echo, The Derecho, Miss Bachman, The Second Student of Shadows, and now? The High Consul. It's a fairly boring love compared to others. It's a love where I have no gropes, no fluids, no sweat, and no passionate moans to give her." Coughing once she smiled, "or to share the tales of."

"And she still asks you to stay." Putting on a playful scowl she scrunched up her nose, "also, when you put it like that? Love is most undignified."

Watching the scrunch relax she laughed softly at the humor of the moment, "I share a flat with a woman who is *all about* the aforementioned notions in her loving of others." Dropping her voice she tried her tone at comedic displeasure, "the things I have seen."

Putting a second pillow under her head, "would you tell me of those things too?"

She needs a reprieve from this as much as anyone else. I know I could use some peace of mind. "I could tell you what I know that would do no harm. I have some anecdotal comedy I could share."

Settling against her pillows with a relaxed body language, "I thank you."

"So where to start – "

4.2.6 - 14:20
The Council Chamber – Central Tower

❄❄..Susan Bachman

Thinking her plan over she looked over her shoulder at Yuri, "I can't have you waiting in the hall so come in with me. Just stand right at the door where the cameras can't see you."

"Understood."

Leading him into the Networked Council Chamber she positioned him by the door and then headed to the center. Configuring the moment quickly she pushed the button which activated the monitors and the cameras. Looking at the bank of monitors she was greeted by twelve faces of varying emotion.

Stopping her gaze at the monitor for Consul Kunlow she smiled at Captain Turner. *Captain Turner already has Thomas? I was a little slower than I expected.*

She's also quite good at what she does.

Adjusting the incoming setting on the Kunlow audio feed she nodded to Captain Turner.

Speaking with a crisp intonation of success Captain Turner shared her relief with her words, "we have the serpent. The Ankylo is pulling up now to bring him to the Questioners. He is alive, and unharmed. The Atrial Dagger has secured the successor."

Please let her be unharmed. "Is Lady Kunlow in any shape to be seen?"

Exhaling sharply she shook her head, "Negative. Steward Spratt has confirmed she was drugged with Lullaby before we arrived."

Close enough to acceptable. "Let her rest then. Get medical on her if she shows signs of anything else."

"Yes High Consul."

Saluting crisply she smiled, "Carry-On. I will not keep you if there is nothing more to report."

Saluting crisply in reply, "Yes High Consul."

Closing the feed she took a moment to steady herself, *was not expecting that of all things.*

Muting her microphone she opened the window she had prepared for the Veto. Contemplating the dancing cat waiting for her, she pressed the Veto into action. *Undo. One of the most amazing functions when it works.*

Reading over the orders she noted pieces of paperwork she had not seen before. *An annulment order for Cassia, and Adoption Choices for the children in the Cultural Center.* Checking the orders she spotted the tags on the files, *none of The Twelve have seen these. He had something prepared to mitigate the inhumanity of his initial idea. But he didn't let them know that.*

Or me.

Feeling her comm vibrate in her pocket she pulled it out and checked to see if was indeed Steven. *It is.* Pressing the button she waited for his voice to reach her earpiece.

With a tone betraying his flabbergasted state, "how?"

Answering without emotional embellishment, "Council Chamber Network Access Point."

Asking his question with a hint of annoyance, "how did you get there so fast?"

Trying her best at keeping the uncomfortably embarrassed feeling in her spirit from being heard, "I got the Beast up to one eighty."

Invoking her name with an admonishment, "Susan –"

Interrupting him she felt the flush rise in her cheeks, "the roads were dry!"

"Noted." Hearing his words she knew the tone of his 'just kidding around' discussions after lessons on debate, "but, why didn't you just call me? Shove a High Consul order down my throat?"

Closing her eyes she put her thoughts in order, *I have to say this right, or he's not going to understand.* Falling into the graveled cadence of their father she spoke the words with the threat they used to carry, "do you have a better plan?"

"Oh." Coughing and taking a deep breath he sounded like he was stalling.

If anyone would know the sting of that question, it would be you dear brother.

Taking a breath Steven's voice lilted into one of confession, "I wanted you to take Dominion over this moment. Father was seen as having granted mercy and sought peace when he was out of Carry-On. I wanted you to show everyone that this wasn't you balking when you asked for peace. The fact that you did as you did, I have to ask," with a voice of honest surprise, "my plan has merit to you?"

Addressing herself inside of her mind she found the counterpoint. *And I have to show myself that I actually want this peace, and that I'm not just doing this because I think it's more Moral and Ethical to do it this way.* "The plan is to kill a Consul, and to judge his House. You offered the end of the House to go with the end of the Consul. Father, he said that the aftermath of things had to be considered. Consul Kunlow, he ordered something that tore our world apart. Many of the people in my Tower, they died because the invaders were ordered to kill everyone to give them the peace of death instead of the lifetime of regret from failure."

Responding with a somber tone, "I have been informed of Kincaid's order to his forces."

Appalled with how easy the words were to speak, "you were offering their House the mirror image of what was done to us. Nothing *more,* just the same treatment. You even gave me the peace offering of the lives of all of those too young to stand on the field of battle by the Protocol."

Replying with a borderline glib humor, "I know of your wish to save the children of your enemies, both boys and girls. I skipped over the argument I knew you would win, because of so many reasons you would give."

"Noted." *I need to know,* "is there something I missed?"

Couching his tone gently he emoted an affirmative noise, "in a *sense.* Being at Civil War, Veto included, does not remove that we were at War when they hit your building. They did not murder, they made War. You are able to arbitrate their crimes using the Wartime Provisions."

Which will make it far easier to keep them alive. "Thank you."

"Noted." Returning to a more formal tone, "did they Veto your Veto?"

Looking up at the green lights she smiled, "they have green lit the Veto. None stand against me."

With a half-hearted humor he spoke quickly, "how else are they going to find out what it means, and what comes next, unless they let you do what you're going to do?"

"How else?"

Assuming his Voice of Command, "what do I do High Consul?"

Issuing her edict with her own Voice, "we shake their House to the foundation stones. You use everyone you have at your command to gain every confession, nuance of thought, and piece of the future. They don't have to be loyal, or even remotely like me, but by the Protocol they are going to agree to internal peace."

Laughing with a distinctly predatory humor, "Noted."

I would be blessed if I woke up to a Blue Sky with Loyal and Loving Citizens, but I do not have that kind of hope right now. "We'll talk more on this later, I have questions, but I have a Council Meeting to finish. I have Dominion."

"Noted. I'll go get to work."

"Good luck, good fortune, and a good hunt."

"Noted. To you as well."

Closing the connection she turned to face the camera. Flipping the switch to open her microphone she smiled with a grim satisfaction, "The Reply is Vetoed. The mirror image of destruction has been deemed to not be the needed answer today. The Commander acted as the Commander acts. A House stands apart, orders are given, and in the aftermath he was reflecting those words back upon the one who issued them. And in that reflection the audacity of the atrocity became *quite* clear."

"Do not mistake this for weakness. Do not," taking a moment to control her temper, "do not think for a single minute that this is weakness. Do not look at my dead and believe I am not seeking justice for them. And for the love of the Blue Sky, do not believe I will forget the words of the men at my office door anytime soon. If my death is what makes a Hero? Then I must prove to any would be *Hero* the fallacy of the idea. If seeking peace is a crime against the fallen? Then I must make a greater peace, a shining place of security, for my people to dwell in. If I am seen as weak enough to replace so casually? Then I must show I am strong enough that I have no fear of a second round of internal strife."

Closing her eyes she mulled over the moment, *I need to build up to it properly, without losing my emotions.*

Opening her eyes she nodded once with a grim determination, "I understand Safe Housing is hiding under a thin veil of secrecy at this point. But I had to move quickly to make sure this could be resolved quickly. I will be moving to The Blackstone Manor soon, that way you'll know where to find me."

Drumming her fingertips across her podium as her father had taught her, "I understand that Drenner forces are parked on my front lawn to protect me. I hold it as a fact of the matter that Consul Drenner had no part in the attack on Central Tower."

Drumming her fingertips again she pointed to Alexandria, "I understand that House Holden has dedicated no small amount of very smart people to help with keeping New Hope in one piece during this. I do not believe Consul Holden to be a part of the idea that my death is what is needed in this world."

Clapping her hands together once to punctuate the shift in her verbal tempo, "what I do *not* know as *fact*, is who is left in this that seeks my death. From the recovering invaders, to my own people, to the men and women in your Houses that helped broker this situation. That worries me."

"The Commander is going to go looking with the Kunlow family first. Each member will be evaluated, lines will be drawn between them, logical conclusions of investigation will be formed. *If* those lines trace back to the other Houses? Questions will be asked. I will settle for no less than a full review of accountability in this. Dark times are coming, and I will not be second guessing the people to my right and left."

Placing her palms flat on the podium she forced herself to keep breathing deeply, *and now to end this.* "Three things remain to be said. The Kunlow family stands as a people and an idea. I do not seek their replacement. The idea that a cultural idea such as a House can be replaced and not change the culture dramatically is a fallacy. I believe that Consuls can be killed, but not the idea of a House, without losing something that we will never find again."

"The second, is that my brother was injured. As Patrick Bachman is still within the walls of New Hope General, I am entitled to use the Citizen's Provision for an Injured Relative to gain a twelve hour reprieve from my duties. I will be invoking this effectively as soon as this session closes."

They do not look like they know what to emote. Family tradition is that the third thing is the worst thing people will not want to hear.

Moving her microphone closer to compensate for the drop in the volume of her words. "The third, is something I *want* to say, for all the wrong reasons. I want to put the twelve of you on notice. To throw down a gauntlet of boisterous rage. To undermine your sense of self, wellbeing, and power because I am afraid I don't understand this moment in the fullest extent of things." Letting the candor flow without shame, "because, I *am* afraid. The questions are many, the worries are a multitude, and the twelve of you are the faces of my fears. The Guild teaches mindfulness in all things, and in this moment? My mind is afraid to the point where I would squander our lives fighting."

"My family teaches the idea of if no one is brave, who will be brave?" Lifting her palms off the podium she set them to her sides, "I will be brave. Brave enough to admit I'm afraid. I've had so much to think about since the attack that my mind is tired. My body aches in places it has not ached in a long time. I am not threatening you because I wouldn't follow through on it. I am not threatening you because, I don't think it will *help*."

Unable to find volume she pushed into the painful words, "our way of life is based upon the idea that still being alive is better than being dead. That we *should* keep living. That being *good* and moving to crawl out of the hole that the world ending put us in was *noble*. Each generation has tried to do it better than the one before. To reconstruct the idea of civilization, culture, and to forge an identity worth sharing in the word Citizen."

"I have my ideas of what this is going to take. Of what painful changes will need to be endured. I am the Prophet of the Second Chance."

Setting up the closing with a recovered surge of energy, "do not try to find me. Do not come to start a war that you won't win. Don't commit to a course of action that will only kill more of your Citizens. Thomas Kunlow is guilty of Treason *against* his House, his people, and The Provinces of the Pacific Rim. The next to follow in his footsteps will be seen as just as guilty of the same crimes."

"A Blue Sky to all of you."

Closing the connection she quickly used the tablet to activate her twelve hour reprieve. *There. Got it in before anyone could call me. I am not dealing with them right now.*

Stepping closer to her Yuri spoke with a forced joviality, "you did not threaten them directly. That is a good thing, yes?"

Shaking her head she looked at the floor, "it's a *passable* thing. I don't know enough yet, but I do know what Waterlily taught me."

Moving to stand at her side he spoke softly to her, "so who is Waterlily?"

Simple answer. "Officially? She's the woman from the Guild of Psychology and Psychiatry who's job is to monitor my mental health."

Touching the back of her hand with the back of his, "I can imagine that is a daunting task."

Taking his hand she sighed, "I think I have sped up the time table of her hair going grayer in the last ten years. She was young in her career when she met me."

"Oh. Oof."

Looking up to meet his gaze, "she knows more about me than most."

Cracking a smile, "does she know about me?"

With a single nod, "she does as of recently."

Emoting his words with a coy humor, "are you going to tell her good things about me?"

You hide your fears behind humor. No idea how that feels. "I'm going to tell her the truth, as I perceive it. If I speak certain things, those could be considered things that are not *net* goods." Letting go of his hand she set to finishing turning off the equipment, "will I tell her that you are the man you are to me? Yes."

Asking his question to her back with the timbre of the School Boy, "what man is that?"

Turning around she signaled for a hug. Seeing his eager nod and affirmative reply signal she set to moving closer to him. Stepping in she wrapped her arms around him, "my second aardvark." Catching her thoughts she laughed and laid her head on his shoulder, "which as it stands is a terrible way to put it. I need to find a way to say which aardvark is which."

"We should," pausing for a heartbeat he spoke with the tone of guessing at wisdom, "sit down with Sasha and figure that out?"

I love you. "That would be the best way. The Codecies of Friendship, Interpersonal Communication, and Romantic Courtship all touch on the importance of shared approval of an alternative name."

Caressing her hair gently as he spoke, "you people. I like it here, but sometimes, the details. I feel less wise in the wake of national mindfulness."

"When you dub someone something based upon character, deed, or notion? If that replacement for their name is negative or detrimental to the perception of character in nature? You are declaring social war upon them. You are declaring, *every time I speak your name I want you to know I think less of you.* That? That's a declaration of aggression."

Switching his touch up for something more soothing, "as I said, I feel less wise."

Enjoying his embrace she sighed, "thank you for this embrace."

Firing back with a lighthearted humor, "just this one?"

"For this one helping me not think about what we're going to face when we step out that door."

Asking with a patience she found admirable, "so what do we do now that we're thinking about it?"

"We?"

Admonishing herself as soon as the word left her lips she buried her face into his shoulder.

Groaning in frustration he didn't let go of her, "rust it? Is that how it goes? If I am upset and need to curse, I say *rust it*?"

Moving her face off of his shoulder, "affirmative. You can use *rust it* as an opening expression of frustration."

Growling the words, "rust it to useless scrap, those were still people out there. I was there."

Touching her gently she heard the slight hitch of a muffled sob as he continued with a depressed tone, "I may not have known their names but I saw their deaths. I saw the sacrifice they gave. It's revolting to know someone thought what happened was a remotely good idea." Swallowing another sob he finished, "I grieve for them too."

Speaking the words softly with a small voice, "thank you Yuri."

Hugging her he swallowed roughly before he continued, "your people and your opinion of the outside world is almost unbelievable. You must have seen some truly sick people in your dealings with the outside world if you would assume I wouldn't grieve with you." Catching himself he sighed, "unless you didn't. Now *I'm* also," lowering his shoulders he clutched her, "I don't know what to do."

Trying to open up, "I'm not very good at sharing burdens. I delegate as much as I can as quickly as I can because once something is on *me,* I don't share that well."

Firing off the conclusion with a horrified conviction, "your mind tells you that they died *because,* not *for,* you."

Closing her eyes against the tears and the truth she nodded, "you are wiser than you think you are."

Asking the question with a borderline desperation, "how do you clear the poison from the well?"

Reciting the words Waterlily had taught her when Paulson and Roberts had died, "you must not accept the water offered by The Shadow. Each concept of the mind is a broken bone which must be set. Align the truth, wrap it in a cast of positive rationalizations, and have it signed by every member of those who still live who care to see it mend."

Pressing the question gently, "what is the first step of that?"

Keeping her eyes closed she felt enough calm wash over her to speak clearly, "accepting the *for,* and Honoring them as per our Warrior Culture. Paulson, he died. He was the one who made the first stand on the fifteenth. His older brother was in the Honor Guard, and he died in the line of service. They both took Dominion over their final moments, and they did what they did. If I martyr myself, and take culpability for their deaths, then I take away the meaning of their sacrifice. If I tell their mother, mea culpa, then I rob her of knowing her boys were heroes who gave the ultimate gift."

"I understand more now."

Feeling a thought click into place she opened her eyes to play Show and Tell again. "My Parrain, he is a man who as a boy escaped from Horizon on the Red Sky Morning. He served next to my father for years. My father loved him. He was one of the far too few who were survivors of Horizon. His writings, recordings, and healing process on the subject are the borrowed words which I'm trying to remember. A person fights The

Shadow using borrowed words, proven ideas, and revered concepts to keep The Shadow at bay."

Smiling with hope he nodded once, "so what *should* you tell their mother?"

"I *should,* and will, thank her and their father for raising a pair of good sons." Nuzzling his shoulder, "thoughts to share?"

Replying with a soft voice of his own, "thank you for never assuming I was a bad person. The more I hear, and learn, the more I am thankful for your kind heart."

Such an easy admission. "You never gave me a reason to doubt you."

Petting her hair he sighed, "you are the nicest –"

Filling the gap with her declaration, "- Potentate –"

"- I've ever met."

Finding a smile she leaned on him, "noted. I do try my best."

"When we go out that door?"

Finding the will to be brave enough to confess she tried the words, "I want to be strong enough to not be overwhelmed. The people, they know I'm a Beacon, a light, like the ones mounted to the side of this very tower. Those are even spectrum tinted to minimize interfere with perception of daylight -"

Interrupting with a soft laughter, "pardon?"

I did it again. "I did that thing where I talk too much because I'm playing Show and Tell."

Bracing his arms around her he shuffle walked them two steps closer to the door, "I did not ask you about it, but I did wonder about the light I saw. It was as a halo."

Settling against him again she found a measure of tranquility in the explanation, "it's spectrum tinted. During the day the light it gives is like the sun. Brighter when the day is grayer. It's a reminder of good light. Meanwhile at night it filters and tints to be less intrusive, softer, and it doesn't convince nature that it's still daylight. It's important not to mess with the animals, they don't know a nightlight from daylight."

"That's nice of you to do it that way."

Embracing the sensation of the comfortably warm and numb she smiled, "it's hard to be dramatic and whine when you hold me like this."

"You're not *whining.* I swear, you are too hard on yourself. Who taught you that?"

Speaking the words as an admission of guilt, "I fear I taught myself."

"Does it make anything better if you hurt yourself?"

Tapping his arms she waited for him to release her. Touching his cheek gently she smiled an assurance before lowering her hand. *I need to step to the side of this feeling.* Moving away from him she leaned against the wall next to the door, "no."

Turning with his words, "what does the Protocol, Codex, Primer, say on this?"

Rolling through the answers, "the Protocol states I have twelve hours to heal without being expected to work. The Codex says that I am Walking Wounded and to attack me socially or verbally is Unethical. The Primer would say I need to sort my sadness into categories, people, places, things, events, and the like. To not see my trauma as a singular thing, which is a hundred times larger than me, but as a series of things tied together. Like beads on a necklace."

"The advantage of writing wisdom down."

"Yes." Reflecting on the words she had spoken to the Council, "is it Heroism to kill me?"

Rushing his words he spoke with caution, "do not take the words of your detractors as gospel. I noticed you stressed that. That needs to be its own category."

Lowering her voice she let the confession out, "I'm glad it's you seeing this and not Sasha."

"Why? Wouldn't she accept this?"

Thankful for the wall behind her to lean on, "she would. She doesn't need to know how hard this is. I did a passable job in presenting that I'm not nearly done for. People need to see that. We understand the emotional weight and appropriateness of the situation based upon the highest ranking person in the room. If I cry? They *all* have that moment to cry. If I stay firm, then it is not a shared grieving time. We still have too much to do for me to start a domino chain of tears. My father was *much* better at this." Repeating the maxim, "if no one is brave, who will be brave?"

Standing before her with the timbre of a man in a struggle, "just because we're afraid, doesn't mean we aren't still brave. You *just* said that, I know, however?" Lowering his pitch and tempo, "I understand the nature of the root statement. The need for someone to put their foot down. The need for strength in a terrible time."

"Correct."

"It has been your family who had to be brave?"

Raising a hand with the declaration, "we're the Bachman House, we have historically *been brave*. Or been *historically* brave, depending on whom you ask."

"I understand more now. I need to ask something."

"Ask."

"You told me once, your father echoed this, that the Gingerbread Man is regarded well. The men at the door, they seemed happy to see me." Shifting slightly he scratched the back of his head absentmindedly, "you had mentioned that people could draw conclusions."

How the moment changes things. "The picture of us is an Open Access file. There's no Epsilon Code on it. Now, you are not a secret and everyone knows how brave you are."

Taking on the demeanor and timbre of shyness she had seen before, "so, everyone knows."

"Yes, everyone who looked."

Looking at her with a puzzled look, "are you worried for something right now?"

Sighing with the exasperation she felt at feeling selfish for being happy about something, "I am worried I'm too happy with the feeling of being in your arms."

Raising a brow he spoke with a downplayed humor, "how is that a worry?"

Taking a sidestep closer to the door with her words, "*we* still have to go home."

Taking a step to mirror hers he smiled cautiously, "is it my home too then?"

Feeling her heart speed up she performed the gestures for 'emotional de-escalation requested.'

Asking with a cautious lilt, "which one is that?"

Frowning she looked at the floor, "emotional de-escalation request."

Sounding confused but intrigued, "what kind of a signal is that?"

Shaking her head she found her composure, "it's a signal for just that, but it's not a *Decline.* Rusted scrap."

Laughing softly he moved to her far side, away from the door, "so which one is the Decline signal? What does it mean though, the request?"

"Decline means I would, as far as I am aware, never wish to pursue that which was offered with you. It's a rejection signal. Depending on how you handle it, is what the other person knows as the extent of the Decline."

"Oh, serious stuff then. So, what needs de-escalation?"

Holding her arm out she presented her wrist to him. "Check the beats."

Reaching out in the quiet he placed his fingertips to her. Waiting in the quiet she took in the sights of the defensive scars on his arm all over again. *The world is a rusted mess.*

After a longer moment of silence he spoke softly with a hint of curious wonder, "it *is* elevated. Proof of condition?"

"Yes."

Removing his fingers from her, "what is the worry?"

Looking to the floor with a blush, "that we end up rushing into something we can't take back."

Seeing, out of the corner of her eye, his gaze look down to his shoes he spoke with a matched tone of uncertainty, "you wish, to make love to me?"

Licking her lips she nodded, "it's been on my mind recently."

Rubbing the back of his left hand against the back of her right hand, "I am flattered. It is a direct moment, I have never been good with those, not like this. To be honest with you?" Losing the small amount of confidence he was emoting, "I was very glad you are such a good person and did not torture, molest, or enslave me when you had the chance."

That sounds as if – "you have been all three?"

Whispering the confirmation, "yes."

Taking his hand she spoke the affirmation, "not again. Never again."

Looking up at her with a shy smile, "that means *quite* a bit to me. You even wish to share a home with me."

"I do." Looking down at her clothes, "to be honest with you? I don't want to lose you to something I can't predict."

With a half-hearted humor, "I am scared out of my mind at trying to cope in this land without you."

Clarify the worry. Pushing herself to be brave she spoke her confession, "I'm scared that some other woman would offer to show you around and you would be smitten."

Tilting his head to her with a look of honest incredulity, "there are women you know that you feel are better looking? More appealing?"

Sniffling she smiled at the severity of his baffled state, "correct."

"Do you have something I could learn from, perhaps not now, but a clarification of why you are not beautiful?"

The things I could tell you. "Yes. I do."

"Fair enough, though, to be fair? I am the beholder." With a tone which spoke of a dare to contradict the idea, "does it still work that way in these lands?"

Smiling with an unreserved grin, "affirmative."

Nodding once his smile returned, "humor me?"

"What is your request?"

Turning away from her he squared his shoulders, "turn around and lay your shoulders against mine."

Moving into place she smiled as they lined up, "I would like to hazard a guess that we have more stories to exchange?"

Reaching back he tapped her at the hip height, "pass me ammo."

Tapping his offside hip she smiled, "pass me the rifle, I'll reload it."

Speaking his words with a humored conclusion, "you believe smaller women are more appealing."

He figured out one thing. "They *are* cute, adorable, and," leaning against him, "easier to cuddle on a couch."

Still facing away from her he leaned into the shared press, "Sasha is almost as tall as you are, yes?"

Firing back without reservation, "yes, my Aardvark is tall."

Asking with a relaxed conversational timbre, "so is it the men who like a shorter woman, or something more?"

Feeling the flush she smiled, "I agree with the men that shorter women are adorable." Fretting for a moment she continued, "I feel *less* cute than other women because I am taller than most men I work with and am around. I am not suited for the role of tiny feminine romantic fantasy."

"Tiny romantic fantasy girls," adding with a tone of clarification, "in my experience, are useless in a gunfight. They are pretty, they smell nice, they are soft and squishy in the right places, but I end up doing all the work." Sighing she could hear the roll of his eyes in his tone, "I bet you have a Primer for that."

Pondering how to tell him the truth she went with the simple answer, "you are correct. Your prize is I'm going to call an associate and have her bring us food."

Turning around he moved his arm around her, "so this is the part where we get into motion? I'll drive?"

Turning into his embrace she hugged him again, "if you would. I'm exhausted, physically, from that drive."

Hugging her firmly he kissed her shoulder, "then I will walk with you back to your car and drive. Is there any notes or things in your mind that need to be spoken?"

You make it hard to keep in motion. "How did you get this good at hugging?"

"I'm a world traveled man who has hugged in every fragment nation he has been in. Compassion is a currency in the world. For me the strongest moment of *receiving*?"

Looking into his eyes she nodded twice, "I'm listening."

With a serious expression juxtaposed by his candid humor, "it was the two minutes one night after I had suffered from a flash grenade. I had been taken and was sitting by a camp fire. While I was thinking of how it would end the small device would land nearby and I would have to be calm. The light was so painful. Falling over I laid there as gunshots followed. It was over so quickly and then a pair of arms would hold me. Just a voice in the fear and confusion. I did not know my savior but they knew me. I would clutch him and make pitiful noises as I waited for my sight to come back. Compassion is a powerful thing."

Nodding softly Susan whispered the only words she could find, "thank you."

"Noted. So what happens now?"

Stepping to the door with her purpose renewed, "we go." Opening the door she led him back into the hall, "and back to the elevator."

Setting to following her Yuri caught up to her in a few steps before offering an arm of escorting, "may I?"

Slipping her arm into place she clasped his arm, "you may."

Broaching the question with an almost glib air about the words, "understanding that you and your people do succession in all things via family first –"

I wonder what the question is? "We do."

"What do you think of children?" Rushing his words, "as an idea."

Suppressing the laugh she took a breath to focus on being serious, "they are what they are. Children. Full of energy, usually, and doing their best to grow and evolve into adults. Because of the length of our childhood educations and maturation ideals, which can end up cut short in many ways, it becomes a layered answer. Childhood, as we know it spans a few terms. Baby, Tiny Human, Juvenile, Adolescent. Then they become adults."

"Do you feel differently for different phases?"

"I," feeling her cheeks flush as she pressed the elevator door control, "I know I should have some offspring at some point. I should honestly be getting started on that sooner than later in all honesty."

Moving with her into the elevator he seemed to be sharing the shy humor of the moment, "do tell?"

"I want to be around for my kids, and their kids. The sooner I have them? The sooner I could retire and leave it to them. I have someone I have to stop though. I have a monster I won't bring them into the world to face."

Speaking as soon as the doors were closed, "that is not Thomas?"

"Correct. The one I seek is a far greater beast."

"So if you slay the dragon?"

Tsk'ing she corrected him grimly, "*Monster*. Dragon is too noble a term. I kill the monster? I would feel safe in having children."

Touching her arm with a reaffirming gesture, "do others know?"

Rusted scrap, I never met him and he lives in my head. "Yes."

"I can imagine they work hard to find this monster, yes?"

They shake Heaven and Earth looking for him. "They do."

"What about other peoples children?"

Finding a fair enough answer, "they border on sacred."

"*Border?*" Relaxing with a cough, "wait, I am not going to start something thinking something isn't what it is. What is sacred?"

We've come a long way. And I forgot to push the button. Reaching over she pressed the button for the lobby before starting her explanation, "Sacred is a term we use to describe that which is connected to The Divine, be it whatever form it takes. Thus, Ritual and Rite which are Sacred, as per veneration, but not we as people. Children, and quite a few other things, fall under Sacrosanct. That which is too valuable to be interfered with."

"Can you use an example of Sacrosanct? Just so I have no doubts."

"The one that my father told me, as per his lessons in being a father, is that a persons sexuality is Sacrosanct. If my vagina was *sacred*? It could be defiled. Because if something is sacred it is dedicated to The Divine. Thus, if I used my vagina for sexual pleasure it would be for my own pleasure and not The Divine. Thus, it would no longer be sacred, or mine. But as a Sacrosanct place, it is not meant to be invaded. But pleasure, asked for, accepted, and enjoyed? Does not stain, tarnish, or dirty her."

Nodding with a profound look of understanding, "that's really nice."

Leaning over she kissed his shoulder with a smile, "so back to your question? As children grow, they show the width and breadth of mistakes made to get it right. Thus, they *border* on sacred as they are looking to connect to The Divine."

"I follow."

"However, they will one day be standing shoulder to shoulder to us. That is always something to remember when dealing with children. What a person shows of themselves in how they act around a child? You are showing them in every deed what is acceptable. Our cultural war against loneliness has children as part of why it is the way it is. Our wisdom from the ash and dust is that children who are neglected are led astray can end up with The Shadow just by looking for care. Thus, children must know where a trusted adult is. They must have guidance from their gender peers. They must be shown what it means to be a good person. They must be kept reminded they are Sacrosanct."

"In that ideal, the Kunlow children? You protect them."

"Yes. They are being held in a place of culture. They are surrounded by men and women, who have guns, but those guns are pointed outward, not inward. The Guild tends to their minds, to keep them from losing themselves in the shuffle of adjustments to what happened. They are not to be bargained with. If they believe that they can bargain *being good,* for *being safe,* when they have done no wrong? That will leave the hallowed halls of their minds defiled."

Exhaling roughly he bobbed his head, "a staggering effort."

"My people are the offspring of generations of effort and toil. This is the sort of day that their parents told them of. This is their Red Sky Morning. When it turns to a Blue Sky? They will know an understanding of the pain their parents endured."

"Noted."

I can be brave. "There are children we have recovered from our enemies over the years. They come from a school of thought which we find disgusting. In their lands? They are given their roles, without being asked whom they want to be. And the girls are found husbands after being raised to understand that being a wife for life will end their strife." Shaking off the notions, "we seek to foster, nurture, and grow our kind of humans. They seek the same, but with a radically different outcome."

"What is the age of marriage in your lands?"

"Year and a day Handfasting as young as sixteen. No children before twenty."

Looking at the floor he grimaced, "and your enemies?"

If I hate I just hurt myself. Taking a breath she sighed, "Marriage at thirteen, children at sixteen, and in some places? Pleasure as soon as she is able."

Speaking softly the echo of haunt surrounded the words, "I am not unfamiliar with the practices. I kept to adult women though. I was raised in a, very protective of children, sort of place."

Nodding she kissed his shoulder again, "life is tough. The world is hard."

"Oh I know."

Riding the last moments in the quiet she felt the creeping embarrassment at the idea of their moment being witnessed. *I have never been this brave in regards to my love life.*

Latching onto the more positive emotion she smiled as she watched the elevator doors open. Setting a foot forward, "shoulder to shoulder."

Echoing the notion with a bold humor, "shoulder to shoulder then."

4.2.8 - 14:45

Drenner Estate – Consul's Office

◙Chuck Drenner

I am without words.
Laying the tablet down on Amanda's desk he walked over to the indoor grow box and set to taking a deep breath of the soothing bouquet provided by the plants.

Speaking from her chair, with the tones of support, Amanda presented as quite whelmed, "I feel the same. Today, I saw Asmodai again. The ten days we dealt with her as High Consul, it was Miss Bachman. Today? I saw Asmodai."

Asmodai was a natural disaster first. "Not the side of him you miss?"

Continuing with a whelmed but conversational account, "half and half. She was her father's fire, his condemnation, and then at the end? She was the man in the mirror. The man her father would talk to on a regular basis. It was striking to see, but heartening to see that she did not lose herself in the anger she's feeling." Setting her stylus down on her desk, "ask me about something else."

I can be selfish now. "Is Cassia safe then?"

Raising a hand in an almost dismissive gesture, "Civil War is over. Her potential death warrant has been canceled."

She's says it so easily. Pinching the bridge of his nose, "how are you calm?"

Setting a small tin on her desk, "I had a Mellow Mint. I was also able to get the rest of the Consuls to agree that we can go have a recess before we speak on this turn. The Council Session was frightfully bad."

I would ask for one but I might be driving later. "The Civil War is over, and that's still frightfully bad?"

"She needs more care taken with her. And more time. We've all had the rug pulled out from under us with this, and it shows. She kept us on mute the whole time. Asmodai only used that trick a time or two. Then again, he never had to execute any of us."

What a precedent. "Point."

"Her Wolf is taking care of her. The notes from Cernis point to that they aren't having problems on that front. To his knowledge. More wait and see." Taking a drink from her glass she leaned back and looked at him with a quiet humor, "I am going to go sit with Micah and see how he's doing. He's working so hard with his people on their share of the burden. I might have to tell him to not worry about me and just go into town."

Perhaps I could intervene. "If I told him I would be here for the duration, would he go?"

Raising her glass to him, "if you can convince him to join the fray without worry? I would welcome it."

Looking back to the tablet he clucked his tongue, "so where do we go from here?"

Looking to the tablet in turn she moved her stylus over the windows, "Octavia Kunlow was not found to be a part of Heart of Darkness. I didn't want to connect her to this, and, Admin Nobody already has his stamp of approval on the idea that she had nothing to do with it. Horse Hair strikes again."

Raising his hand for Counter-Advocate, "is Horse Hair, or Admin Nobody without mistakes?"

With a neutral malaise about her, "no. However, with the absence of evidence? No one is looking for Octavia to be pressed on the issue. Dagger Herb sits with her at this moment."

"That is quite the endorsement. To say she is without culpability, and then set her of all Daggers next to her."

Pointing with her stylus to the Consul's Communication Window on her desktop monitor, "it was not unnoticed."

I will dare the simple and selfish question, "is it acceptable that I'm just happy Cassia is alive?"

Twirling her stylus toward him she spoke without a perceivable judgment to the words, "you still love her."

Responding with candor, "she, was my first. Her emotional fingerprints are all over the inside of me."

Nodding once she waved her stylus at him, "I know."

Rust it, "is Josh going to be safe?"

"That," putting her stylus down, "I don't know. The Commander is launching an Investigation into the Kunlow House. If Josh has done something wrong? The Commander will seek to punish him."

"I hope he is innocent then." *No time to rest.* "I did find a SitRep update while I was waiting outside."

Waiving a hand at him with encouragement, "share."

Moving through the points with an audible optimism, "the city hasn't sunk yet. No one has Exit Passed over this, successfully. The guesstimate for the Effort and Investment Index has hit one hundred and thirty-two percent. No complaints because it's still day one. Also, Turner Airways is on Final Approach, I hope that the assets feel well enough to just get to work after the flight."

Responding to his optimism with a renewal of her energy, "noted."

Review it, then do it. "After I talk to Micah, what's my plan?"

Biting her lip for a moment she made her call, "don't call Cassia. Don't call Susan.

Don't call Octavia directly. Call *any* contacts you have in the Kunlow House though."

Play it quiet. "Noted."

Looking up from a second tablet with a smile of deep relief and humor, "there is a picture I have now. It's from Central Tower. I would like to share it with you."

This could be good. "Is it momentous?"

"I would leave your opinion to you." Sliding the tablet to the edge of the desk she gestured at it with a casual humor. "Enjoy."

Taking the steps he looked down and took in the sight. *Miss Bachman, in Traveler's Green.* Looking at the image of the man he had seen once before, *that is a scary looking man in better lighting.*

Pointing to the man with Susan, "the Wolf?"

Nodding with a hopeful smile, "affirmative."

Furrowing his brow, "no one else with them?"

Offering the humorously downplayed counterpoint, "there was a Medical Wagon outside."

She's not joking is she? "That's it?"

Losing the abundance of humor she continued the downplay, "they were armed."

Might as well find out, "Load-out?"

Returning to a more serious demeanor, "they passed a scanner which was still working. Yuri has a pair of handguns estimated to be forty caliber semi-automatics. Susan had Last Resort and The Shadow's Cannon."

I will evade that. "You mentioned the Medical Wagon, no Motorcade?"

Picking up the third tablet she showed him the missives, "Dispatch routed her a small bubble to work with. She was in quite the hurry as she was racing against time. They did not have time to get anything into position, according to Dispatch."

Reading the data, "does she have a Motorcade now?"

With a mild fret, "not to my knowledge."

No mention of the Honor Guard either. "Is the Honor Guard going to come find her?"

Clucking her tongue she shrugged, "not to my knowledge."

"Is this in her family playbook?"

"Not that I have seen it like this. However the Bachman family has a deep resource of plans, routes, and counter-plays they've never used. To that end, we might not have seen these pages yet. The item that worries me the most? She's carrying The Cannon. We are a people who are not plagued by vampires, werewolves, zombies, or space aliens. That leaves only one monster in the dark. Ridolfi."

I have to ask, I suspect the answer but I have to ask. "Do we know if Thomas was working with Ridolfi?"

Closing her eyes Amanda looked her years for a moment, "that would be impossible. Ridolfi would kill Thomas if he had a chance."

Once again, I am faced with something I feel the need to ask. "What was Ridolfi like?"

Opening her eyes Amanda smiled comfortingly at him, "he was a man who needed to laugh more."

She's trying to comfort me. "Am I overstepping?"

Without losing her smile she nodded twice, "somewhat."

Establish the moment. "Should I withdraw?"

Signaling for 'open discourse' her tone matched her signal, "Chuck, *Ridolfi* was a man who slept in this very house. I know I've told you I knew him, but now I guess I'll tell you too much. I had been waiting for this day for some time."

No other words to say. "I will listen."

Sitting up in her chair she had a sip of water before settling herself and setting in. "Epsilon Code, Son of the Sky-Keeper, and yes there is a hyphen in it, but I don't want you looking for it. You don't have the Clearance to read it of your own accord."

I have a lot of Clearance. I don't hear that line much anymore. "I understand."

"I need you to know these things because Ridolfi is one of our biggest threats because he was one of us. He has a copy of all the Manuals, *all* of them."

A thief? "Did he pilfer the Network?"

Firing her retort with a flat ache of suppressed rage, "no Chuck, he used his Birthright."

No, that would mean, "only a Bachman –"

Emoting the weight being lifted from telling a secret, "Templeton Kane, son of George Bachman and Tessa Kane."

Speaking without thinking, "Tessa's son was killed during the Conflict at Sunrise Cove."

Looking up from her chair at him with eyes wide open and filled with an old pain, "that was his betrayal of us. They listed him as dead and wrote a sad story to cover up his betrayal. Then they set to hunting him. The rest of the war was him spurring the Ports against us."

Ash and Rust! "So Tessa died trying to kill –"

Maintaining eye contact she rolled the words with a hollow ache, "her own son."

Sitting down with a feeling of emptiness he turned his head toward her, "I wish I had known her."

Looking down at her desk her shoulder slumped into a hunch, "I wish you could have known her too. She was like an older sister to me. She was Tim's first Unrequited. He was under the threshold of chasing her and getting away with it, but it was a fires of youth thing, not a serious draw." Looking up as the humor returned with the irritation of lacking the right words, "his first fantasy, if you will. Maggie on the other hand looked up to her because she was never one to let adversity stop her."

Nudging the moment back on track, "so the gun Susan wears –?"

Speaking into the question with a factual intonation, "the five shot cannon was built to kill Ridolfi. The weight of the bullets in it, the velocity of those bullets, we don't have a piece of body armor that can just shrug those off. She will strike, the bullets will find flesh, and he will die. She will kill her Uncle if she gets a chance."

Then if she wears the cannon? "That means Ridolfi is close? It's not just fear about those who might still wish her ill?"

"There is data that was scheduled for day thirteen of the fourteen days of meetings. It was about The Fence. Our tragically porous border could very well have been crossed in a more dynamic way."

"I didn't see that report."

"It wasn't brought to light. I wanted it brought up. It was moved to day thirteen because I have so little to prove it actually happened. I wanted to see if I could provoke The Lilt and get Susan to open up."

Is the Militia ready? "A sensible plan. Do we have the Freelanders or Port forces in our territory?"

"Freelanders."

"Noted." Looking at her Desk Comm, "you're blinking."

"You should go. It's a Consul call. You talk to Micah. If he wants to stay? Tell him to come find me."

"I will do so."

Nodding he turned on his heel and set to leaving. *One more miracle to find.*

4.3.0 - 14:50

Normal Avenue – New Hope

☀ Yuri

And we are here. Pulling The Beast over he found a good place to park. "We appear to be out of the way."

Looking around at the side alley she smiled, "that's the objective."

Not even close to a bottleneck. Three different points to escape from. "So your Citizen will meet us here?"

Checking her comm, "yes. Saffron is en route."

I wonder who she is pulling out of her back pocket this time? "So what is a Saffron like?"

Smiling she tapped his arm gently, "a Saffron? No, she's the individual, known as Saffron. As for what she is like? She would qualify as *easily directed.*"

We have a moment, I'll get another lesson. "Elaborate?"

Nodding she smiled before steepling her fingers, "for a starting point? We have a Scale of Autonomy. She scores in the Absence of it for a desired outcome."

This could get interesting. "Do tell."

"She struggles as one who is in Group Eighteen, and one who wishes an Absence of Autonomy. Once those two things were figured out? Her life was given a new route."

Almost. "Not quite catching it."

"Group Eighteen, in the Periodic Table is where the Noble Gasses are kept. She doesn't react well with social situations. She misses cues, she struggles with heuristics, but she's a Citizen and a talented Artist."

"On one hand she has special needs, on the other hand she is of use and add to the grand scheme of things. Identify the need and unshackle the mind?"

"Correct! Once she was discovered to be, Submissive, as she is. They changed the nature of the approach they were taking with her to ease her pain. They found her a fire-fighter and emergency responder who is classified as a Soft Dominant. He was more than willing to be the partner whom would call the shots, lead her along, and use the framework of Dominance and Submission play to anchor her."

A pleasant stroll into the forest of knowledge. "She doesn't have to guess what he wants then, I would wager?"

"Correct. He tells her the what, where, how, and why. Then he uses his training to lead her down the path of explaining to her the meaning of the what, where, how, and why." Smiling she shook her head, "if she's having a nervous day? He plays the role of the Dominant and does all of her talking for her."

Time to check an angle on this. "Does she have autonomy though?"

Smiling she nodded with affirmation, "all the autonomy she could ask for. With a word? The game is put on hold and they can talk as friends. On the other hand the game gives her a refuge from herself and the world that vexes her. It would just depend on what kind of day they're having."

So many that she speaks of as friends, "you know them well?"

Downplaying the moment with a casual demeanor, "somewhat. I was there for their Handfasting ceremony."

Handfasting, again a word I know. "Details?"

Still smiling, "they were doing so well that they entered into a Handfasting. I was able to go to that ceremony as I had time to go. I was invited as I had met her when she was at work. I met him during an inspection and review."

Flowing with the moment he continued, "what does she do?"

"She sits with persons in the Observation Ward at General. They test how lucid they are by having her read the prompt, which is a question about the Protocol, and then they record their thoughts on it. She sits, listens, does a few sketches in the moment, and learns more about the subjective answer of what people believe the Protocol means to them." Adding as an afterthought, "she's working on her part of an illustrated edition of the Protocol."

Trying to imagine the flowing picture book as large as the sky itself, "The Library of Being Human, Illustrated Edition? How many thousands of kilometers of paper will you need to put pictures on?"

Laughing the question off, "no one knows."

Tough question time. "You trust her with your food?"

Nodding she appeared confident, "I do. Her Mister told her to never violate someone else's food."

How did he earn the trust? "You trust her Mister?"

Rolling through the reasons with a gentle defense, "he has a mostly spotless record, charges into burning buildings, and The Guild finds him to be agreeable. I do not believe him to be a Threat Vector."

No reason to question. "Good enough for me."

Smiling as one reassured, "noted."

I'm going to do it. Pitching his question as a conversational inquiry, "how do you feel about autonomy?"

Smiling she looked away for a moment before a deep breath. Looking back to him she was trying to not laugh, "I'm trying to not laugh because of the mental image I was struck with."

This will be good. "Share?"

"It was myself, wearing an animal ears headband, which is a different story. It was just the idea of me trying to dress up as a more submissive person and be a house pet."

Speak to the worry, "the idea of you trying to be small, and cute, and squishy."

Regarding him with a soulful gaze, "yes."

Find a way through the moment, "I cannot say I have been in this moment before. I don't have some wisdom from another place to guide me through this. This means that we could read the Primer for this together, yes?"

Smiling with relief she touched his shoulder again, "thank you for that."

I like what I see. I wouldn't laugh at you. Speaking his condolence as a warm affirmation, "it's an interesting picture though."

Appearing both relieved and humored, "it is!"

Looking to the third exit he spotted the front end of a decelerated vehicle sticking out. "I see a car."

Returning to the task at hand, "that would be Saffron's ride. For this moment? Just call her, Miss."

Asking the clarification, "Miss?"

Nodding with authority, "correct."

"I shall do so." Taking a second look at the short woman crossing into view with a Take-Away box in hand, "she is adorable, she is what, one-hundred fifty centimeters?"

Firing back with an appreciation, "and that's in her city shoes. We should get out to greet her."

"Noted."

Getting out of the Beast he moved around the back of the vehicle to stand with Susan on her right side. *This tiny woman, no wonder she is known as Saffron.*

Piping up with a quiet almost childlike voice, "High Consul!"

So quiet. She's just too adorable for any words I know in English.

Taking the box from Saffron, which he could smell the faint but delicious aroma emanating from it already, Susan passed the large container to him. Holding it with both hands he watched as the two women signaled and then embraced.

She could carry her on a shoulder, almost.

"Thank you for calling on me."

"You are a good Citizen. I knew I could trust you."

Regarding the tiny woman he took in the sight of her paint and ink smudged vest, the motes of colors on her hands, and the spiral of colored chalk highlighting her dark short haircut. *She looks almost puzzled looking at me.*

Doing his best at a casual greeting, "hello Miss!"

Laying her right hand over her left fist she bowed, "The Winter Wolf." Lowering her hands she looked to Susan, "you have a shoulder to shoulder Miss Bachman?"

I have a new name?

"I do."

Brightening, "glorious." Looking back to him, "I should go. This is not my place and I am feeling the lubricious inclination."

Signaling to her Susan waited a moment before Saffron collided with her. Hugging her with a warm full embrace she laughed, "you are a glorious Citizen Saffron. Go with the Vision of Rache."

Letting go gently she nodded with a hurried energy, "I am going to go. I have more to do."

Intoning her agreement with a softer energy, "as do we. Be well."

Firing back as she moved backwards, "you as well!"

Saying his farewell in turn, "you as well! A Blue Sky!"

Moving backwards she waved to him, "a Blue Sky!"

Watching Saffron depart he passed Susan the box of food, "if I hold this one moment longer I am going to shove it all in my face at once."

Smirking she laughed, "I would almost like to see that."

Moving around the back again, "almost?"

Nodding once she climbed back inside the Beast. Signaling something to him she smiled and assumed a stance of waiting. Quickly getting into The Beast he closed the door. Looking over to her he puffed an exhalation before his single word repetition, "almost?"

Tilting her head with a grin she spoke with an innocent complaint, "then I would have nothing to eat."

Pointing to the box he pushed the question, "you will eat this?"

Setting back in her seat she smiled, "yes."

Taking a firm stance that his smile burst out from behind, "I am going to hold you to that."

Looking to him from the corner of her eyes, "you don't have to, it is too far to get back to Safe Housing before it would be cold. We're going to eat this here." Checking her comm, "and then we go home. Dispatch has alerted me that the Volatility Index around the Recovery Ward is too high to see Patrick. We'll have the safest route home on the Nav by the time we're done eating though."

Picking his words carefully, "unfortunate about Patrick, the rest is good though. Yes?"

"Yes."

Setting to unpacking the food with her, "so what is lubricious in your parlance?"

Snickering with a flush, "the Conlangers moved the two definitions they had together. Single concept of stating that you are having a biological response to a person."

Feeling a flush of embarrassment, "ah."

Escaping into helping Susan unpack the box he smiled at the amount of food packed into the box. *Something easier, and perhaps an easier question,* "I am also the Winter Wolf now?"

Nodding as she flipped down a small shelf from the dash, "the Bachman family is aligned with the Winter. You, after your *performance*, have been dubbed the Winter Wolf. The respect paid to a Warrior who is Loyal to the Bachman family."

Makes sense. "I journeyed a long way. Also, I am not much of a sprinter. More of a marathon runner."

"Thus my Citizens, your soon to be tribe, they give you a name to welcome you, and not the legacy you represent. Seeing the actions of the man, and not just the inheritor of Myth and Legend."

That was very nice of them. "Noted."

Setting the dipping sauce onto the shelf she smiled, "I remembered what you said. We have parsnip chips, sweet potato puffs, and broccoli puffs. Banting Bread toast for buns, quinoa and bean patties, and a sauce made from mayonnaise and fresh mustard greens."

"Do we have drinks?"

Opening her dash compartment she produced two bottles. Setting them into the depressions in the lower dash she smiled, "I am not without resource."

"Truth."

Unwrapping the sandwich he took a large bite and set to chewing. *This is good stuff.* Looking to Susan as she discretely plowed into her sandwich he smiled at the moment. *She eats. Good.*

Pondering the moment he found a question as the sweet sauced sweet potato puff fell apart in his mouth. *I wonder.*

Clearing his mouth with a swig from the bottle of lightly flavored carbonated water he posed his question, "are you close with Saffron?"

Clearing her mouth in turn she shook her head for the negative, "no. I keep notes on my comm. She has what is known as Acknowledgment of Citizen. I know of her, but I do not *know* her. I have a limit I must obey, and I guard it well."

Flow with the moment and hear her version, "limit?"

"There is a number on the Network, the cautionary tale of One Hundred and Fifty. The Network tells us that each person, who themselves are one of the counted, can be a centerpiece of a larger faction of selves. The limit is one-hundred and fifty people within that faction. Meanwhile there is a second number, of which the mind holds upwards of two hundred and ninety people in mind with any real clarity. Saffron knows I *do* see her, and *adore* what she does, but the limits of the mind are the limits of the mind."

I will ponder that further. "When you told me of the Bachman Sonder - ?"

Answering with a romantic wistfulness, "I look out my window, and see one hundred thousand lights within the range and domain of New Hope. I will only truly know two-hundred and fifty with clarity, and then only invite one hundred and forty nine to a Convocation of Friendship. The rest? There is not enough of me, or anyone, to know them all. Our National Creed is defined by the idea that we are all vexed by the same limit. We will never truly know the massive majority of people of whom we share Loyalty with. My Sonder is standing at the top and being powerless to overcome it. The Citizen's Sonder is only knowing those who flow in their circles, but also looking up and knowing that the light is there, and it shines for them."

To look at the Tower and see neither Deity, or Oppressor, but Friend? I am in the Ever After.

After another swallowed bite she appeared saddened, "the Council wants me to change the size of the Honor Guard. I don't know what I'm to do with the idea. My playbook, is admittedly, unfair to them. They work too hard and they've been with me for longer than is recommended, but I won't ask them to leave. On the other hand, the more I get? The more spaces of those within the allotment I get that have to be decided far more carefully."

I am understanding more now.

Giving the 'Subject Change' signal before her words, "my mother, she was not a fan of Autonomy in the bedroom. She wanted to act at the mercy of desire, at the mercy of another, to play with a flame of passion of a different shade. She craved the attention, and she played with a *need* of a stronger pull than Saffron, for example." Working through a few puffs she appeared thoughtful.

I will keep my mouth full of puffs so as to not be called upon, or be tempted to interrupt her.

"My instincts, they don't cry out for the attention. I've read the literature, tested the paints on my canvas, and looked over dozens of scenarios in my mind looking for the *sweet spot.* From all that? I can say for certain I want to keep my Autonomy. I don't have that juxtaposition of care giver by day, and *receiver* by night."

Time to take a risk, "it does make my life easier."

Looking at him with a newfound humor, "it does then?"

Grinning with the aversion of a misstep, "yes."

Nodding in return with a smile, "good to know."

I understand this, time to move it forward. "Well now we get to share the burden, shoulder to shoulder then? Provided I interpreted that term correctly?"

"Shoulder to shoulder, is how we term relationships which have close to equality in them on an emotional level."

"Then I did understand." Giving his words a chance, "is it shoulder to shoulder in the bedroom?"

"You did understand," blinking she smiled with mischief, "if we were shoulder to shoulder, nothing would get done to each other."

Laughing at the mental image, "so what is the bedroom idea then?"

With a slight flush to her cheeks and a puff in her forefingers she stared at the puff with her words, "as with all aspects of a healthy relationship? Give-and-Give. I don't need, I don't think, to be taken care of fully every night. I would give back. Two people, two hearts, one bond of Give-and-Give."

Watching her pop the puff into her mouth he felt the understanding bolster his courage. *I have little to fear.*

Broaching the question without fear, "what does Saffron and her Mister have? If it is not shoulder to shoulder?"

After a fast swig she smiled, *"usually?* Hand in hand. There is shoulder to shoulder, hand in hand for both right and left, on a lead, one step behind for left and right, and two steps behind for right and left."

Curious. "On a lead?"

Answering with a casual demeanor, "for adults? It's what it sounds like. For children, which we do have forearm and wrist based leash bracelets for, it's a whole different scenario."

Blurting the words without thinking on them, "you put children on leashes?" *So very understanding there. Good job.*

Looking at him for a long second she smiled with a reassurance, "not all the time. It's a danger signal mechanism. From heavily crowded areas, to fire drills, to evacuation drills? Children learn that the adults in their lives seek to lead them to shelter and protect them."

I stand reassured, "noted. That sounds, sensible. Like most of the answers you give me."

Smiling with a roll of her eyes, "we try."

Returning to learning, "hand in hand?"

"Saffron, explained to me, that she likes the comfort of it. Her right hand to his left hand. Thus he's got the lead and his dominant hand free."

Deeper details? "What makes shoulder to shoulder good?"

Holding up both hands, "keeps both hands free to protect the other."

I follow. "Are you and Sasha also shoulder to shoulder?"

"Yes. When we started?" Seeming to be fighting with a strange humor, "I don't want to diminish her with this, but, she was bordering on wanting two steps behind to the left. I had to work for years to get her to stand at my shoulder."

Strange. "Why?"

Frowning at the concept, "someone told her the lie that she didn't deserve me. She decided to believe it."

That is terrible. "Oh."

Smiling again she reached over and hooked her finger around the forefinger he had been popping puffs with, "every time you think of her, and her feelings, it reassures me that you want to be a good friend to her."

Curling his finger in return he gave her finger a squeeze, "Sasha and myself? We agree on something, that is very important."

Moving her thumb over to touch his, "which is?"

Wiggling his thumb against hers with an exaggerated humor to the gesture he spoke softly, "you are an amazing person that makes life seem so much more awesome."

Changing up the grip on his hand to something more involved, "I will resist the urge to defame myself."

Speaking from a place of conviction, "is that what false modesty was changed to?"

Meeting his gaze she smiled in approval, "yes! It was ruled to be either false virtue, or self-hate. Either way? It had to go."

Unable to refrain from the smile he nodded, "noted."

Letting go of his hand she reached for one of her last puffs, "the world as it was known, was obliterated. We are the children of ash, stardust, and geothermal rage. We are those who have this last chance to be something more than evolved monkeys. To become the best humans we can be. Which would start with not being afraid of our needs, our wants, or our true beauty."

"Noted."

"Yes, I have been wounded," tapping her right temple, "in the mind. Everyone gets their wounds. Body, mind, spirit? It doesn't make a person *less* for being wounded, or make their pain any less tragic, but it gives them others to be compassionate with."

I return to my humble place of heart. "I am looking forward to my Citizenship."

Intoning her declaration clearly, "I would like you to be one of my one hundred and forty nine."

Matching her intonation with conviction, "I would like to be part of that world."

Smiling with a playful aggression, "then it's settled."

The question that staggers me. "All Citizens are taught about these high minded ideals?"

"Yes." Waving a hand in the 'dismissive' gesture, "*however.* Not everyone lives up to them, not everyone wraps their minds around them fully, and not everyone lives them one hundred percent of the time. Human foibles. It is known though, that they can open the Protocol and find the *easy answer.* Even if they can't live up to the ideals and ideas presented every day and every hour? They are all taught how fragile the human mind can be when the basics get ignored or worked against. Hence why we have such a complex structure to our world. The layers, the Protocol, the careful balance of factors to keep our culture from imploding, exploding, or being found in the corner with a knife trying to feel power over something."

Oof. "Stark."

Clucking her tongue with a faint haunt of guilt in her tone, "I know."

Rounding the corner of the thoughts he moved forward, "noted. Young girls, who are not you, how do they seek power and Autonomy if they desire it?"

Gesturing toward the city past the windshield, "they go out and get it. There is a system of female led peer, mentor, and advisory caretaking for every girl in our land to be able to access. There is a male system too, which is male led, mentors, and all the things that men need from themselves and the lessons of how to be a man. The two systems work together to cross pollinate the encouragement and understanding of the greater system to the young people."

Sounds nice, "an example?"

Pausing for a moment her candor returned, "you make this easier than when I was learning this."

"Well I am glad I provide comfort in some fashion. So will our shared thing be you explaining this world to me until the day I die?"

Smiling still, "considering we are encouraged to never stop learning? I would be right next to you."

"Hah!"

"Your example though, would be Dispatch and Crisis Management. There are more women in the roles of coordination and overseeing in Dispatch and Direction than there are men to women on the front line ground roles. We have found within our culture, that men *like* having a woman's voice on the line, even if it is a boys club in the line of fire and danger. When a group of men are shouting, a woman's tone cuts through that because it's *different* to them. Men and women compliment each other. Not to say it's an absolute of gender to a role, but that there are gender roles which make it easier for our small population to stay on a solid track. People go where they can be of use, have merit, and the talent to succeed at a given task. Just because a boy is a boy, just because a girl is a girl, and just because a third is a third? Doesn't mean they have a destiny ahead just *because*. It's about talent and merit of the pursuit of the job. We can't have someone forced into a role that is a danger to others."

Go with the easy example, "so a woman is only barefoot and pregnant, -"

"If she *wants* to be and doesn't feel like house slippers that day."

As I hope to be a father, I should ask now. "Is motherhood prized in these lands?"

Holding up her hand she paused for a moment, "this is an answer that is faceted, and is integrated with other concepts. From a cultural perspective, it's a larger weaving of notions. The *short* answer? Is that motherhood is a cultural good. From the act of becoming pregnant, to the behaviors during the gestation, to the birth itself, and life beyond. The Full Time Parent, be it the mother, or father, is granted Rations from The State on the promise that they are doing their best as a parent. Each child has a Full Time Parent, or a reasonable amount of hours each week from the adults in their family to ensure the best outcome."

"What will become of your children?"

Letting out a chuffed sigh she rolled her eyes, "as I cannot be the High Consul *and* a Full Time Parent? I will suffer as my father did. I will be given all the leeway I need, certainly, as even the mothers who have served as Consuls would nurse children during meetings."

"Noted."

Snapping her fingers she smiled with a revelation, "Yuri, I forgot to mention something."

I wonder if it is about nursing children? "Which is?"

"As we are going out in public more often? Public nursing of children is a cultural norm. You had mentioned you had been places where topless women were a norm, but I didn't offer that anecdote at the time."

Letting the humor lift him he focused his inquiry, "how do you get women to want to have children, but also careers?"

Pursing her lips she paused before committing to the answer, "a bargain is struck. When a girl comes of age, when she is a Student and learns of reproduction? She is given the knowledge that as men cannot bear children? It falls upon her. When the two halves of the population are moved closer as they reach adulthood, the subject of family and having one is asked in a myriad of ways. Those that respond, are encouraged."

Logical counter-question, "those that do not?"

"Are encouraged to know themselves."

Daring the question with a guarded tone, "what was your answer?"

Rolling her eyes with her energetic reply, "emotionally unable to commit to the endeavor." Regaining herself she smiled, "I am a woman in love with an asexual Seven. Who in turn is estranged from her family. This has put me behind a few different problems."

Enlightenment waits for those who will pull the chain. "Elaborate the details?"

Snickering she smiled, "Sasha doesn't have the biology to facilitate children, as we share a biological reality. Which means, I either find a man to include in our lives, of which I did not have that as I was living a life I didn't want to include anyone else in."

Encouraging her, "noted."

"That would put us needing to use the next method. Brother of Wife. However, Sasha is estranged from her family. I don't know her brothers and they are a fair distance from here."

I follow. "Noted."

"Then the reverse of that is Sasha, being a Dagger, is a subordinate of Steven. Interweave that with her military service meaning what it does to her? That path could only be taken when she retires." Lowering her voice her melancholy rang through, "which, if I am honest with you? And myself? I fear that her plan was to die in service."

That is not good. "Noted."

"Then there is Sasha with Patrick, and my little brother is a bit of emotional mess. If he was to provide the needed ingredient? He would be asked to be a Father to the child. He's *not quite* ready for that."

I have nothing to offer but the assurances I heard and understood all of that. "I will mull this all over."

"Thank you."

"Noted."

"When girls become women, they more often than not have a partner assured. Someone within their professional field, Ration Caste, Field of Interest, or the like. They meet, get married, have children, and when the children are grown? They take on a mantle of a new profession. Full Time Mothers are given education and training on a flex schedule around the child rearing. Which yes, if they start children at twenty, The State gets them for a few children to make sure we continue as a people, then at forty-five they give another fifteen to twenty years of labor? It's not a bad deal."

"What happens after that?"

"The Sunset Years. It's a Citizen's Choice for how they want to spend that last section if they live to see it. Be it working, mentoring, writing on behalf of the Culture, or making products on the Open Exchange. For examples."

Contrast. "A distant concept from the breeding harem."

"Yes. If I had been normal? I would have a five year old child by this point. And more than likely a three and a one, or at least a two year old."

That is a mental image. "I am biased."

Smiling with relief, "I know." Pausing to take a long drink from her bottle she lowered it with a pleased expression, "the whole system evolved from the first generation. When our people rose? Yes, the women were kept safe, but they were not asked to be a breeding harem for a warrior culture. There were no scalps for sex programs. Women, to ease the pain of the men? They made better and better homes to come home to."

I think I know the answer, "is that why Maggie refurbished a garrison house into a manse?"

Nodding she tapped her nose with her left pinkie, "correct. When our cultural paradigm shifted, women became the ones tasked with creating the home that the man would dwell in."

Smiling and nodding along the thought came to him, *a parcel of land, and a house to put on it. I,* catching the thought he let it go, *will ponder that later.*

"Also, when children enter into the equation? The home becomes a place of gently ordered chaos. Toys strewn about, walls that have been vandalized, and the familial notion of *unkempt* is the accepted norm. Children have to be taught to keep their toys safe. They must be taught to value what they have and where to store their things. They must learn the value of stewardship of the home."

"Funny story?"

Taking another drink she constrained the smile enough to not spill. "When I was younger, I would draw on the walls. Oh, that is another thing. Most houses meant for families have a painted divider in the rooms. The lower half is painted with a paint meant to endure the artistic vandals that children can be. Patrick would also draw. We ran out of walls." Pausing to reflect, "mom, she got out a bucket and showed us how to clean the walls. She told us about stewardship. By the time a child is going to the Halls of Academia, they have learned stewardship in the home. Without stewardship, we are callous fools."

I agree. "Noted." *I am trying to imagine Safe Housing covered in toys.* "Thus this is created, and taught to all Citizens?"

Finding a smile after the reflecting, "yes. Tiny Humans don't understand. Until they do? It's a fools battle to punish children. All that will do? Is tell them that the people who made them, who created them from a mashing of bodies or a small miracle of scientific intervention? They would hate them for drawing on a wall. They are given colored wax paraffin to channel their need to see their thoughts put to a wall. Walls will wash clean, but hearts? Not so much."

I am getting a handle on this. "Do you find yourself, *something,* in regards to the differences between you and your mother?"

Nodding with a frown she sighed, "yes. I don't like that either. My mother, was a Mother, Wife, and Inspiration. We cannot survive as a people with quality mothers, and again that touches on the larger integrated answer. I am leaving out so much, but it can't be helped without the chart. Suffice it to say? We wouldn't be human without families. Our system was the only thing we could cling to that would see us through that we could find."

If children are children until they can speak their truths, there is far less to be angry about. "Much to ponder."

Picking up her untouched sandwich, "I'll put on the music, we'll finish eating, and then we can go home."

"Agreeable." Looking at the time, "can you tune it to ninety-nine nine? It's about time for a show I like."

Smiling she reached over and pressed a few buttons on the dash and tuned the radio to ninety-nine nine. *Just in time I believe.*

Hearing the familiar voice of The Big Band Hour come out of the speakers he felt his grin form.

Bopping into the words with an enhanced gregariousness the announcer sounded hopeful, "hello to all of you lovely lovelies out there today! I know it's been a day without words, which leads us to a change in the program. This hour will be provided by something more relaxing than our normal afternoon offerings. We have The Counts Holiday to keep you moving this afternoon, but not too fast. First up, we have a message from The Grocery Depot. The rhubarb is in season, which means you should keep yourself ready for menu updates. Also? The Brewers Bastion has donated a portion of the rhubarb sima to those toiling today who are known to enjoy the brew. They want you to know it's not an error when that bottle pokes out and says hello. And from me, I give you the message of stay lovely lovelies. Enjoy the music."

Smiling to Susan he set to finishing his share of lunch in earnest as the music poured forth from the speakers. *I will become the best Citizen I can be.*

4.3.5 - 14:58

207 Journey's End - Hidden Bedroom

±Arlo Kunlow

Sitting next to the bed, on which Amaranth Dinclair was sleeping, he reviewed his bullet pointed checklist.

I will wake her.

Make peace.

And leave.

Looking at the sleeping face of the girl he wished for a different life. *No one held up their end of the bargain. I was the only one who did what they said they would do and actually got it done.*

The best laid plan. Derailed by the failures of others. First time in my life I did something right and I lose out.

I have nothing to offer her now. She wouldn't come with me if I asked.

Fighting against the conflicting emotions he gripped the clipboard to wait his anger out. *A system rigged to make it possible for men and women to live in peace with the other. I have spent my whole life as part of the margin for error.*

I could have been happy, finally happy.

Speaking softly from her pillow, "Arlo?"

Trying to get a handle on his frustration he watched her tug on the handcuff on her right hand. Looking at him with an accusatory scowl he felt himself withering inside as her hiss of rage came out, "you said –"

Unable to fight the panic he blurted his reply, "it's not what you think! That's a time delay cuff! I mean nothing untoward!"

Moving carefully she pulled the light blanket up to her shoulder with a hurt look on her face.

Trying to reason with her, "don't be mad at me. Don't be mad."

Jerking the cuff gently she closed her mouth for a moment before looking at him coldly, "why do you need a head start?"

Sighing he hung his head, *I feel like useless chaff when she yells at me. I'm thirty. And she can just knock me down like everyone else did.*

Gripping the clipboard hard enough to crinkle the paper he barked at her in frustration, "*calm down!*"

Settling down with a visible fear about her she adjusted herself until she was sitting up and settled down. *That's more like it.* "Just be civil. You don't have to be so rusted up. You're a mean person."

Closing her eyes she sat still as he looked at her. Looking down he set to smoothing out the papers on the clipboard, "if you weren't so mean, I wouldn't get angry."

Speaking with the Voice of the Clinician with only a slight waiver to her cadence, "you perceive me as mean without cause."

Nodding he felt his tension relaxing, "I have been your ally in this. I provided you with shelter, food to your liking, and textiles that you cannot afford."

Firming up her words with the Voice, "the attention was not asked for."

Holding the clipboard he wrestled with the guilt, "you were going to be killed in the original draft of the plan. I would keep you alive by taking your hand in marriage."

Continuing with the Voice, "I was taken by force."

Speaking his rationalization, "desperate times call for desperate measures. Your life was on the line. I had to be certain I could get you, and keep you, with one visit. One motion."

Holding the tempo, "you did not mention this before."

Rolling his eyes, "how could I get you to see reason if I just said, *love me or die.* I needed you to see reason. To see what was offered. To see someone who was not going to wrong you. Not like everyone else."

Losing a measure of the Voice, "this is not wronging me?"

I will have to give her the hard truth. "Your father would not acknowledge you as his daughter. This would be done. You would *be* a Bachman. Consul Kunlow would have you generate permission keys, and then discard you, but I talked him into letting you live."

With a deep breath she whispered the word with an attempt at the Voice, "noted."

Putting his sincerity into the words, "I would have given you *everything.* Safety. Security. Food. Shelter. And every person I knew within the new Pyramid would be on your side. You would have had a wonderful life."

Laying her free hand down on her lap with the palm up, "I would like to thank you for not crossing the line that cannot be uncrossed."

Grumbling at the implications he felt smaller looking at the temptation, *not that it did not cross my mind.* "You were meant to come to me willingly. To see the life I offered, and accept it. I didn't want to see you, eyes gone hollow from the abuse. A broken doll," trailing off he could see the fear on her face.

Reaching a hand up he shook his head violently, "you weren't there! I needed someone like you. But I was down in Seaside. I was born too soon to sit at your table. I could have been sheltered. You would have understood!"

Swallowing audibly in the quiet she looked down at her lap in reply.

Rushing his words, "I had your tailor make the outfits. You could see how pretty you are, not because *I* said so, but because *you* could see it. I'd seen you looking at the displayed outfits. Looked at the dreams you had been having. I could have shared those dreams with you."

Regaining her composure she returned to the Voice, "my sister would have died in the plan."

Trying to be reasonable, "Miss Bachman was not going to step down quietly. The Derecho was not going to be calmed. She was not to be chosen to lead to the future. Thomas Kunlow –"

Watching the snarl form he recoiled from her anger.

Losing her composure she snapped at him, "useless pile of slag!"

Balling up his fist he stood and raised his hand before he regained his composure. Grabbing his brandished fist he became aware of his now lost clipboard. Stepping away from the bed he caught her gaze for a moment. Staring into the fear and anger there he turned away. Nearly tripping over his chair he shook from the force of the moment.

Unable to contain his emotions his pitch shifted to an angry aching whine, "the plan failed. Thomas failed. *Everyone else failed me!* I was going to do something right for once! I was going to be loved! You were going to love me, and the life I was going to give you. I wouldn't take you away from your life." Hunching over he protested against his doubts, "you would have stayed with the Warm Fuzzies. You would have kept helping others! People would *thank me,* for this."

Hearing only the sound of her ragged breathing he took a deep breath to wrestle with the desperate anger, "we could have watched movies together. You would have sat next to me. You would have had the thing that your sister was never going to get. You weren't safe before. *I* would assure you were safe. I wouldn't need to be brave, or a Warrior, or a Scholar, or a Poet, I would be your Savior."

Turning around he felt his spirit shrink at the look of disgust and horror on her face. "I wanted to apologize, and do it right. But *you* prevented that. I didn't want to leave and have you twisted up inside. Then you might end up like Tilly –"

Watching her eyes open and the emotive strength of her bared teeth hate he took a step back. Raising his hands he pleaded with her, "mea culpa, mea culpa! I didn't mean to take her name in vain. What her cousin did to her was terrible. I, just," fighting for words he pushed them out, "the thought of leaving you in a lurch? Seeing you in my mind," gesturing at his head as the sick panic set in, "sitting in a corner with a utility knife, using the pain and blood to stop the Shadow. I didn't want to do that to you."

Sitting in stunned silence she looked at him with a continued rage.

Snarling the words with his newly kindled frustration, "I am not as bad as you think!"

Whispering the word as a hoarse whisper, "noted."

I would have loved you, forever and a day.

Resigning to the moment, "I'm done here. I lost. I lost you. I lost my chance to be happy. I have to leave." Taking out his handkerchief he brushed away the tears with anger, "your help will arrive soon enough. The time delay on the cuff will release you. I have to leave the door locked, but it will unlock before you would run out of supplies. Also, in case of disaster it will open too. I have seen the classic stories, I won't be killing you on accident."

Asking the question as another whisper, "where will you go?"

Shrugging he found no harm in sharing, "I hear Chihuahua is nice."

Speaking the quiet accusation, "bank on our good will and hide with our not quite distant neighbors?"

Speaking the plan knowing he would have to make come true, or die, "I have some papers, trade goods, I would find a way to live there and gain distance."

Finding his gaze, "we would have had a bit of an age difference. As a lifetime partner it would have been overflowing with complexities."

Sighing he cringed again, "I was going to wait for you to come to my bed when you were ready. You aren't *outside of* the age range, not really. And when you turned twenty? I could have been the father for your children. A home, a husband, and a brood. What more could a girl ask for?"

"I don't know what to say to that." Looking down at her lap she asked with a quiet calm, "why would Thomas kill me?"

Trying to be matter of fact to lessen the blow, "with you, *gone*, no one could use you for anything else once he had what he wanted."

Without raising her head or her tone, "what happens if you're caught?"

Feeling the chill go along his spine he shivered, "The Commander has me killed. I just have to evade his men and get to my getaway to avoid death. As he does not know I have you? I will have a head start. And as I did not *touch* you? And I certainly spilled no paint on your canvas? He will not light me on fire. You may not know this of The Commander, but there was a couple, and they did terrible things to a young man about your age. They slipped through the cracks, and they took a Freelander. The Commander was visiting Bliss at the time." Feeling his gut knot at the idea of being in their shoes, "when he confronted them, the man had doused himself with something flammable and was attempting to bargain. Stating that The Guild needed to deal with him."

The video.

Taking a moment to breathe he continued in the quiet, "The Commander disagreed and pulled out his lighter. He lit it, threw it, and reduced the man to a burning torch. If I harmed you? He would harm me so much more. If I shredded your canvas? He would give me a fate worse than death. If you had come to love me? His soul might have found rest knowing that you were cared about, and would live."

Quietly replying she seemed void of emotion, "noted."

"I," sniffling again, "I need you to know something. What I did was wrong, I know that. My death is not something you should feel like you're causing. I'll get a quick one if I'm caught. Or none at all if I hurry."

Raising her head feebly she looked at him from the top of her eyes, "why did you get the tailor you did to make the outfits?"

So you would see your beauty. "His work is amazing. You only have him for your uniform because he offers that service alone to those not of Gold, and normally only to boys. I thought you should have something amazing from someone who knew how to tailor things to you."

Baring her teeth for a moment she composed herself. Asking the question with a gentleness, "then the gifts of pretty clothes, survival, safety, and all it would cost me would be my body?"

Pursing his lips tightly he shook his head, "*no.* Don't take it like that." Wresting with the anger he found himself withering again, "then you're a *subjugated* concubine. I wanted to be your *savior*, not your keeper. I wanted you to *celebrate* your salvation. I wanted to be your *hero* in this. You would see that I saw you as a good woman, and a treasure, and in return for my kindness? You would never leave."

Lowering her eyes again, "that's a tall order."

Finding a moment of calm, "all you would have to do would be to understand and care for me too."

"Why kill Susan?"

Talking with his hands, "you know the stories, she is the Derecho. There was a plan to calm the wind though. Send her and Dagger Herb to the cabin, have them just be Susan and Sasha, and offer them an *out.*"

"And if she didn't accept it?"

Fretting with his knuckles, "they would kill Sasha, *threaten to,* so that way she would behave to save her."

Finding his eyes again, "and if she forced your hand?"

Averting his gaze, "they, they would kill her, and then Susan when she went to fight against the future."

Asking the question with an acerbic bite to the words, "did you offer to take Susan as your wife?"

Recoiling at the idea he clenched his fists for a moment before unclenching them and breathing normally again. "Susan Bachman isn't a normal woman. She was raised as a High Consul, her head filled with the ideas of the legends and stories. The things her people fought and died for. It's a *story, history, just stuff that happened before we existed.* This is the *now* and it's precious. Her people are dead because they valued her future and the power of the past more than their own lives. The only way to calm the wind would be to get it to stop blowing."

Whispering the words with a sad ache to them, "I don't think I need to know anymore."

Looking to his feet with a sickened shame rolling inside of him he gestured at the appliances on the far side of the room. "I stocked the refrigerator, I refilled the beverage case, with things you like!" Lowering his hand he emoted the pain he was feeling, "*please, mea culpa, tell me you understand.*"

Starting the process of laying down, "I will lay here and endeavor to understand," pausing for a moment she looked up, "how do I get home?"

If you can call it that. "Miss Bachman will come get you. This room will stay locked until she comes to get you, or seventy-two hours from now. When Sys-Admin Hope finds what Athens did to the Grain Silo Protocols? She will come."

"She will come save me?"

If only to kill me. "I have no doubt."

Returning to the Voice of the Clinician, "if you fail to escape, you will die?"

That scares me. "I have no doubt."

Pulling the blanket up with her words, "I would wish you a safe journey, but I kind of like the idea of you dead."

That hurts. "A Blue Sky?"

Trembling with her brave words, "may it be the last one you see."

I'm going to go. She's wrong about me! If I go, I'm not a monster!

Trying to put on a face of calm and composed emotion, "I'll leave you to your thoughts. I left the tablet for you to stay entertained. I am going to adjust the cuff to ten minutes and just go now."

"I think that would be good."

Getting closer to her on the far side of the bed, he paused before getting nearer to her. Dropping his volume he spoke with the empty empathy of never having felt love, "you should know, that no man is truly going to see you. They're going to see your name, your rank, your power. Have you ever stopped to ask yourself *why* Susan Bachman, the monument of majesty, her bright dangerous smile, the power to change and shape the world," stopping to breathe, "*why* she is without a man at her side?"

Replying flatly while still looking away from him, "no."

Sitting down on the edge of the bed he finished his explanation, "it is because she has no man that can see her. No one close to her who sees the woman. No one to ask to tryst with her, to share drinks with and then something more, to cuddle on the couch watching a horror movie with her. There is *no one* that has the personal clout to stand near her and see anything or anyone other than *The High Consul* now. And when she looks in the mirror she will see a world where no man will measure up. She will never be *safe*, as all women crave."

"What of Sasha?"

The empty affair. If it meant something, why would they not have acted on it? "Devoted love, friend, but not the kind of love you can continue a legacy with, if you catch my drift."

Trembling with a renewed fear, "I do."

Reaching down he slotted the small key to facilitate changing the time of the cuff,

"I am going to go."

There, it's adjusted.

Brushing his pinkie against her wrist she jerked violently. Jumping away in a matched surprise he scowled. Pointing his empty hand at her he felt his anger rising again, "you look forward to seeing Miss Bachman." Stumbling backwards from the bed, "there was never a safe place for you in the games the Houses play. Your father could only protect you when he was alive."

Reaching up and adjusting the cuff, "your friendship faded with your anger."

I'll just leave. She can have *the key.* Clenching his fists he turned and set to walking away, "I will raise a glass to you from my new life."

Yanking on the cuff she freed her hand, "your last glass will be water before your execution!"

Turning back he regarded her for a moment as she rubbed her wrist. *We could have been something good!* Meeting her gaze he felt the urge to vomit rising with each heartbeat. Moving quickly he fled the room with a slam of the security door. *We could have been something special. I hope she enjoys her life and every moment where she sees how right I was!*

KEEPING THE LIGHT BURNING

Saturday April 30th, 2242

4.5.0 - 16:56

Safe Housing - Rear Hall

☼ Yuri

Sitting on the couch in the back of Safe Housing, with a tablet in his lap, he marveled over the information he had learned and the things he had seen by searching for the words 'Winter Wolf.'

She is a beloved figure, and her people have left me dumbstruck with their words of kindness. The Winter Wolf. Checking the pictures attached to the concept, *they have drawn sketches of an actual wolf, covered in snow, chasing around the figure of Miss Bachman the Derecho.*

These essays on Nationalism, Patriotism, In-Group, Out-Group, and the audio attached is ponderous. They want to find an answer that is not blindly hating. They want to stick to their tenants even in the face of duress. They are unhappy though. The events at Central don't make sense yet. This bothers them deeply.

I have no blame to lay on them.

Hearing his name intoned with a sad lilt, "Yuri?"

Looking up from the tablet he recognized the look on her face as one he had seen before. *She requires my undivided attention.* Setting the tablet down on a nearby shelf he turned back to face her, "I am present."

"I wanted to see Patrick. I sent him a few messages. He has an update, an editorial, and a few other pieces and angles he wants to work to lower the volatility of the locals. It hurts to see them in this shape." Pausing she sighed, "it hurts to *be* in this shape."

Raising an arm he smiled when she slid into his embrace. Feeling her collide with him he nested her against him. Establishing a firm grip on her he found a smile as she smiled. *I have not been this useful in some time.*

Broaching the question carefully, "something else then? This is a large couch. But, it is hiding here in the back. Can I ask about it?"

Nodding twice with an encouragement, "you *can* always, or can *always,*" stopping with a sigh she set her forehead against him, "I failed."

An uncommon sight from you. "Do-over?"

Recovering with a mild grin, "yes. I just wanted to stress that you are able to ask any question which is not inflammatory, by nature, of others. If it is inflammatory by *circumstance,* that you were unaware of? Then it is not on you for having asked. An example would be if I am asked about the boots I was wearing before I get them to the Cordwainer, by someone whom had not seen the shape my boots were in."

Innocent mistakes are seen as without guilt. "Oh. Cordwainer?"

Smiling with the simplicity of her statement, "the person who makes new shoes."

Oh, that's a look before she says something I'm not expecting.

Grinning with a conspiratorial mischief, "sometimes, it has been known for a Cordwainer to be a person who loves feet very much."

I will ask about that later.

Watching her face return to normal she appeared to be lost in thought for a moment.

Prompting her, "what is that look?"

Clucking her tongue she rested against him, "I misplaced your question." Patting the couch gently, "this is the couch that was installed after my father started coming out here. This couch was made extra long so he could stretch out, and even have room for the children."

"Is there, okay," faltering for a moment with an irritated humor, "I *know* there is going to be a reason. I'm silly today. What is the reason it was placed here in the back of the house?"

Caressing his hand with a soothing tempo, "noise and community were the major factors. If it was in his study? We would not come in to see him. If it was the living room? We would lose a room. This place, is both quiet, and a place to come to see him if we were ready to be quiet. To help renew him. Father, could be renewed with care."

I should be certain we are on the same lesson learned. "Is this why I'm here with you, to help renew you?"

"It *is* a lesson I learned. To not be afraid to ask for comfort from others." Leaning against him she smiled with a glimmer of hope to the gesture, "I'm being selfish."

Squinting his eyes at her he emphasized the sarcasm with his tone, "oh yes, because your body in my arms is so untolerable."

Smiling she visibly restrained words before speaking with an offhanded lilt, "you do not mind?"

Rolling his eyes at the cheerful audacity of her question. *Do I mind?* Laughing the word out as a near baritone reverberation, "no."

Patting his hand encouragingly, "I sent my notes to Wallman about what we have done."

Trying for a conspiratorial tone, "what did *we* do?"

Eying him for a moment she smiled and spoke plainly, "the inclusive *we*, was for both what I had done, and that you were there for. He has been well armed with what he needs to know and understand."

I think that she is trying to flirt with me. "Good."

"Wallman is going to tell the people that I had to hurry because we had a solution to solve this today. The solution was found. And a lasting solution is coming and that we will see a better tomorrow in one of the coming days. He accepted that freely."

I think I see it. "Tell me the thing, or if many pick one of them, that you don't want to burden me with."

Settling against him with a sad sigh, "I feel terrible knowing that Miss Augusta is gone."

Adjusting his protective hold on her to accommodate the change in positions, "what of her husband?"

"He faded away about seven years ago. He was a Soldier who served against both The Ports and The Warlord. They met at the Office of Veteran's Affairs. Her sons are now orphans."

"Notes on your comm?"

Shaking her head softly, "she was a friend of the family. Patrick wrote her an obituary already. He loved her so much."

I will seek the lesson. "Did her husband know?"

Speaking with a sad nostalgia for the past, "he did. He even helped mentor Patrick. Steven had moved out, I moved out, and after some mentoring? Patrick moved out and worked diligently to understand so much more."

Asking the question with a careful tone, "if a boy loves another mans wife –"

Correcting him gently, "young man, adores the wife of another man."

Nodding sagely in reply, "nuance of language. I come from a place where the wife is the husband's because she is the light of his world. He does the work, she illuminates the dark, and makes it easier to toil."

Pausing she touched two fingers to his shoulder while visibly working over a reply, "we call that model, if I am understanding it, the Hunter and Caretaker model. The man does the hunting for resources, or the toil, and the woman serves as the Caretaker of the hearth and home."

This sounds almost easier than just winging it. "There are models too?"

"Yes. It makes it easier to find a place if a series of sample places are provided." Nodding once she found a smile, "*now,* your answer. When Patrick was found to be emotionally connected to Miss Augusta, her husband, took him aside. Sat him down. And did his best to keep him from feeling frightened. My father had to have this talk with more than one young man who was smitten by Maggie. There is no honor in violence of one man to another man for sharing the same idea. The idea that man marries woman because she is the other half of his equation. Men, typically, do not want to be unsolved. However, they can mentor the *young* man who falls for their wife. For one? It helps him find his goal, self, objective, that sort of thing."

Pushing aside memories of his youth in Tula, *I need to not dwell in the past.* "How did it go?"

"Patrick missed mom. His need for a mother was bleeding into his first romantic notions. Major Thompson, the husband, he dedicated himself to helping Patrick find his place inside the castle in his mind. After Major Thompson died? Bonnie moved into Called Corners with Ollie and Philip. She had more friends living in Called Corners, and they helped with the grief."

"That is something."

"Patrick Pledged that Bonnie would not be left alone in her grief. He's akin to a brother to the brothers. He's been talking with them. They will still have a place in Called Corners. They might change apartments though. Coming home to a door and knowing that she's not –" losing her voice she closed her eyes and curled up in earnest against him.

I know this pain. Hauling her into a cradled embrace he spoke with a forceful rasp, "I am here."

Whispering the word she hugged him, "noted."

Rocking her gently he stayed quiet. *I do not know your soothing gesture. I do not know more than this.*

I do know I hear a noise.

Groaning in frustration she leaned back and fished out her comm. Looking at it she shook her head and held the comm toward him.

"You wish me to speak?"

Nodding she settled back against him with the comm extended out from her place against him. *I will stand up to this challenge.* Taking the comm he pressed the Connect button. Moving the comm to his ear he spoke a neutral greeting, "hello."

Sounding taken aback the voice asked with an equal neutrality, "who is this?"

Checking the comm he noted the name before quickly putting it back to his ear. *Harold Wallman, the newsman whom is trying to find peace. I can be honest with him.* Relaxing to a more candid tone, "Yuri, the Gingerbread Son, or Winter Wolf, depending on whom you ask."

Taking his free hand he set to running his fingertips through Susan's hair in a mirror of the gesture she used on him before. *I hope this works on you as well as it does on me.*

Asking the question with a professional lilt, "is Miss Bachman available?"

I am not sure what that means in local parlance. "She is right here. Though, she is hurting." Reflecting for a moment he spoke from the heart, "I am in not much better shape. We share a moment of wounded reflection. Were you calling to check on her, or did you have something that you wanted?"

Noting the details on Susan's face he saw no sign that she disagreed with his assessment. *Upbeat but hamstrung.*

Answering after a long pause with the same professionalism, "it is good to know she is being cared for. I do have a request, if you would pass it on. I wish to speak with Octavia Kunlow."

Parroting the tone of professionalism he smiled at the moment, "he wants to know if he can speak with Octavia Kunlow."

Raising an eyebrow of inquiry with her words, "does he *need* my permission?"

Speaking into the moment through the comm the professional timbre echoed with a strong uncertainty, "I don't *need* it, but I wanted to make sure that I was not going to be going over a line."

Trying to keep his laughter at bay at what felt absurd he kept his attempt at professionalism going, "he says he does not, but he wanted to make sure he was not crossing a line."

Nodding with a look of understanding she pitched her voice toward the comm with a firm encouragement, "in case he does not hear me, tell him that he should. I trust him. I believe with her knowing she is not at fault, and with his skill, that it would be a good moment."

Exhaling a sound of relief before his words, "she honors me. I look forward to doing well. I thank her."

Losing the professionalism he let his humor run loose, "ah, he did hear you. He thanks you."

Nodding once she laid her head down before mumbling her reply, "noted."

She needs to rest more.

Hearing the inquiry from the comm spoken with a firm but gentle lilt he was brought back to the moment, "a question for you, did you bring the Bachman Medallion with you?"

Leaning back against the couch he looked upward at the ceiling, "oh, yes. I brought the Medallion. How do you think I proved I was me?"

"Fair point. Another question, did you bring Elianna's Diary?"

"Yes, I did bring Elianna's Diary." Going for the humor, "it is uncensored. Has all sorts of personal details. Scribbles in the margins. I kept it safe as my lineage had kept it safe since she passed on. It's a copy of the original though. It's readable though."

Breathing the word out, "incredible." Recovering himself he returned to the professionalism, "did you know anything about us before you reached us?

Following the design of the upper trim his eyes moved along the engravings with ease, "not really, no. I had no real idea what to expect. I just hoped that a Bachman would be here that still cared."

"I would assure you that she cares if you did not already know. There are many examples and stories of her heartfelt care for this world. I would go over them but she is hurting and I would not want to clutter her thoughts with praise right now."

Caressing her hair he moved his fingertips down the length of her mane, "I know she cares, so much. I would wager right now she's chiding herself for a momentary lapse of strength that you're now aware of."

Speaking with an understanding, "I am aware of her emotional responses. I was there when she lost Paulson and Roberts. That rattled her. Be gentle, firm, but gentle.

This is a much greater magnitude of loss. I can only be thankful that she has you to be there for her."

Answering with the humility in his heart, "noted."

Rushing the words with a timbre of reassurance, "also, giving you the comm is not a test. I know she plays chess, and does moves of strategic social importance, but I would offer you this idea. She wants you to be a part of this world, she doesn't want to bleed on anyone else, meaning that would be her win of two things. Don't misinterpret her way of dealing with this. She does it from a good place."

Much to learn still. "Noted. I had not thought of that though."

"Oh. Noted." Starting over, "I will broach this with you, and her, I would like to do an interview at some point. Just a notion to file away in the back of your mind for down the road."

"Noted. I will consider this."

"I should go. I have more to arrange. Be well Yuri."

"Be well good sir."

Closing the connection he passed her the comm with a sigh. "He wants to talk to me at some point if I would allow it."

Opening one eye she looked up at him, "did he mention anything of note?"

I might as well just tell her. "He warned me to not think that you were testing me. That you have a reputation, that if misinterpreted, would cause me to doubt the sincerity of your pain and reveal I did not understand you."

Closing her eye she spoke with a resigned understanding, "I can understand why he would say that."

Replying with an upbeat realism, "I am glad I did not doubt. You look like someone whom is doing her best to keep herself together." Adjusting his posture carefully he spoke with a matching care, "if you would like? I could stay here, and you could let it fall apart for a few minutes. Let it out. I have seen you cry before, and he does not know that. I can see the intense hurt."

Moving into the moment, "you pick your words well."

Reaching over he picked up her handkerchief and held it next to her hand, "I know I cannot *make* you feel better. I have dealt with no small amount of grief. However, I can offer myself as a wailing wall. You are on a twelve hour rest. Might as well make good use of it."

Taking the handkerchief with a hushed tone, "thank you Yuri."

Retrieving his handkerchief from his shirt pocket, "I will most likely cry too. It's more than fine."

Covering her eyes with the fabric, "thank you though."

Wrapping the cloth around his forefinger he dabbed at the corner of his eyes, "noted. Thank you."

Responding with a mute nod she sniffled as the first motes of sadness came out.

4.5.5 - 17:16

Safe Housing - Rear Hall

⁖⁚..Susan Bachman

Coming back to her center, with Yuri's arm held within both of her arms, she enjoyed the moment of laying on the couch. *I am just this moment.*

Now I'm going to think about what I need to do, because I noticed I'm not thinking about what I need to do.

Looking at Yuri's arm to distract herself from her thoughts, *it is nice to have Yuri like this. I feel like I'm a kid again. He's not unlike Mister Fennel. Laying my head on the pillow in his lap when mom left. Never too old to be a good neighbor.*

I should show them to Yuri. The Tradition of Fennel and Frieda. The ideals and ideas taught by the suits and aspired to by the people who dwell within them. Not a matter of skin color, gender, or the like. Just the idea of the lessons standing on their own wrapped in a costume so anyone can learn from them as a member of the In-Group.

Feeling like herself again she let her thoughts drift, *so much to do.* Letting her thoughts drift away she found something else more pertinent, *I would like to get Sasha and Yuri close to each other sooner than later. I think if they met that they would stop having the worry that they were going to stop the other from loving me. Or that I would stop loving the other because of the other.*

I also need to address Sasha possibly having found that her desires have awoken. If she truly is moving from a place of absence to a place where there is a flame? I will nurture that fire as gently as I can. The writings I have on the subject illustrate that this could be rougher on her heart than I could imagine if she gets twisted up inside.

Especially if it was just a poorly timed moment of thoughts. If she is still as she is, I have to make sure she doesn't feel like she has failed me. Thinking the idea over she found a sufficiently shocking turn of the phrase to prepare, *I don't need your lips on my face to have your name on my lips.* Pursing her lips against the laughter she felt a measure of confidence that the comment would close the matter on a positive note.

Speaking his words after the first notification chime from her comm, "your comm is chiming."

Checking her comm she found notifications from Stephanie, "your clothing is being dropped off. You will have a bag of new things to wear. It will be on the porch."

Removing his arm from her, "I should go get it, yes?"

Back to work soon then. "Yes."

Feeling him carefully move her head out of his lap and onto the couch he smiled. "I will leave you to rest."

"Thank you Yuri."

"Noted."

Taking inventory of the day she followed the design on the wall paneling as her thoughts formed in Yuri's absence. *I know that even with my cooler than normative feelings on the subject that I was warmed by Yuri's presence today. This is what I was told I would have to deal with one day. Loving someone like this.*

Father left me a few things on the subject that still baffle me. Thinking over the audio recordings that her mother had left for Patrick she smiled, *he listened to one of them and just gave them to me. Unwanted knowledge of his parents and their strange love life when they were young. All well founded advice, just nothing he wanted to use in his own life.*

And to think he didn't even get to the story of 'naked except for top hats and canes happy birthday sing song.'

Feeling the quiet sadness of contemplation overtaking her, *I can't imagine what Micah feels in those moments of reflection that come to us at two in the morning.*

Unless he's blissfully asleep.

Embracing the moment of self defeat, *he's probably asleep at that hour.*

4.4.0 - 15:20

Cloak and Dagger HQ - Questioner's Wing

¶Head Questioner Zack Muldaire

Letting up on the manual spigot for the water he stared into the nondescript paper cup. *I have been doing this for a long time. Yes.*

Today? It hurts.

Reaching up and touching his jaw he felt the sad baffling nature of the pain. *I have never been in pain like this. Staring at the condemned, listening to their stories, the details of what drove them to the actions which placed them at my table.*

Today I have someone I look at, and I hate them. I have looked at the Level Five tools with a cold dispassion of boredom at the concept. Now, I would like to use them.

I'm dead regardless, so why should I restrain myself?

Touching his jaw again he snarled at himself, *if I die, I will not know how this ends.*

Looking up from the cup he looked with tired eyes upon his domain. *I am watching my place in things crumbling to dust. The fraying edges of my sanity are consoled with the idea that I have to leave this place.*

And Miss Bachman has the hope that it will not be the funeral pyre.

Would she mourn me? Would she feel I was worth saving?

I need to get back to work. One foot in front of the other foot.

Looking over to his desk and the pile of papers he sighed with the grim feelings in his heart. *I must be more than a living torture device. I could have a new life, with a ticket of a new self to make the trip with. I just have to survive today.*

Taking a step closer to toward the cell of Thomas Kunlow he looked down the hall toward the Questioner's Theater. *My austere domain, remembered by only those who have survived their brush with being condemned.*

Do I want to be remembered?

Have I worked outside of this room long enough that I see it as a cell now?

Do I want Miss Bachman to win and see me saved from this? To see an end to the program by getting all of us to leave of our own accord? We leave without judgment for our actions but a lack of drive to do them again on behalf of The State?

Abandoning the line of thought while striding softly over to the first cell on his right he did his best to keep his hand steady. Reaching out and taking the cool metal handle in his hand he set to opening the door smoothly before stepping inside.

Looking down at the obviously exhausted form of Thomas Kunlow. "I brought you water."

Replying with the hoarse evident in his voice, "why?"

"I believe you just answered me."

Sitting up with a visible lack of strength he took the cup and quaffed the water like a man lost in the desert. Once the cup was empty he held it out without a word.

Taking the cup he fiddled with it a moment. *The Commander wants him to know only pain and torment. The Commander is ignoring the why of our existence. He wants us to be the thing people think we are. Not what we know we should not be. Even though I grieve I have a reason, a function, and if I betray that function then I am corrupted. I am of no use if I am corrupted.*

Unless The Commander ordered what he did as a chess move, as it was an Authorization, not a Direct Order.

Feeling his composure waiver as he looked at the face of Thomas Kunlow, *rust it to useless chaff! You know the problem is if you took him in there you'd go straight to Five and like it. The switch isn't going to hold. Either he talks or you're going to do what you do, and you're going to like it.*

Which is something The Commander would want to know.

Rust.

Setting his tone to a firm quiet, "you still have power Thomas."

With his disbelief evident in his tone, "I do?"

I have to bluff. "You have the power to control perception of you from this moment on. Your choices will dictate your future."

Slumping his shoulders he leaned over and looked at his socked feet, "Miss Bachman said that near me once."

"She taught it to me."

Without looking up his voice was set in his mood of defeat, "what else did she teach you?"

Holding up the fragile notion of his salvation, "the pursuit of Artisan Salads. The various recipes that are a part of the art."

Responding with the simplicity of the statement, "honest answer."

"I am an honest man."

Pitching his voice to a defensive candor, "I did it for The Rim."

I must become a fisher of truths. "Do you claim Patriotism?"

"I," fumbling he finished with a decision made, "I do."

"No small amount of people were killed or injured on behalf of your decision."

Speaking with the tone of a man who firmly believed his truth, "I gave them an out."

Trying to keep the hold on his anger, "why did you need an *in*?"

Looking him in the eyes, "I had to stop her."

Shaking his head without breaking eye contact, "not good enough. Why did Athens want this?"

Recounting the anecdote with his disappointment evident, "when he found the communication line, Athens thought, he felt, that Asmodai should have used it to declare a winning hand. But instead, he surrendered quietly."

Winning hand? "The Lion's Roar gambit had failed."

Plowing into him with an earnestness, "we still had the Fire Maiden!"

What is a Fire Maiden? "Then it was all to get the Fire Maiden?"

Fixing him with a stern glare, "you don't even know what the Fire Maiden is!"

Now you're being rude. "Which Epsilon Code do I need?"

"If you have to ask? You wouldn't know it. Let me tell you – "

Moving his tactical baton to his hand he deployed it quickly and set to restraining Thomas. "No!" Overpowering him he locked the restraints into place roughly before he moved off of him. "*You* do not make that call for me. *I* did not give you the Code. It is forbidden to sway me with information that is not directly related!"

Speaking with an honest shock, "you sound angry."

Letting the anger prowl freely, "I *am* angry!"

Raising his voice in fear, "you're not supposed to feel!"

"I do! But *that* is not important right now! What is important is answers!"

Speaking with a soft voice of a cowering man, "the Fire Maiden *is* related. Miss Bachman has a thing I need. I needed to take control. Stop the Ports, stop the Freelands, and get back to the core values we started with. No more giving away land, no more standing next to people and helping, *conquest.* We need to control all of this, *directly,* so the world will become better."

Regaining control of his anger in the wake of understanding the motive better. *The question must be posed. I don't want to air it, but it must be aired.* "Do you claim Patriotism to the Core Ideals of the Mission Statement?"

Speaking the words as a shield, "I do."

What Asmodai did needs a term. A landmark we can place in our history so it's not a quiet moment. "What if the things our ancestors dreamt under the earth, what if they don't matter now? What if peace, and tolerance, and finding the *best* path we can matter more?"

Screeching his words with rage, "they killed our people! They fight with us! They raid against us!"

"The Ports haven't aggressed on us since the Compromise. The Freelands are dozens of tribes without a unified leader! How can you declare them Monolith?"

"*We should be their leader!* They must be brought to heel and they *will* take the knee before us!"

Raising his voice with the renewed bloodlust ringing clear, "we should take care of ourselves! You lied to those people before you killed them! You sent them a false statement against Miss Bachman! You have poisoned the well! I am not without ears! Your rusted gambit has cost our world more than you will understand!"

Shouting back at him, "I was going to make it right! Had Asmodai not died? This was for him! I was going to give Susan an *out!* Her and that Dagger she covets so much could move to that cabin of theirs and live in peace outside of this! All I need are the Bachman Permission codes!"

Wait.

Clenching his fists as the gravity of what he would do if it was his plan struck him. Locking eyes with Thomas he lowered his voice to an icy whisper, "where is Amaranth? Tell me or –"

Smiling the look of a surprised victory, "you don't know?"

Answering in a blinded moment of confusion, "I was informed that the Grain Silo is reporting as Green."

Reflecting on the idea with a certain quiet pride, "Athens did a good job on that then. She's been," pausing he spoke a careful cadence to the words, "*moved to new housing.*"

Giving into the fantasy he spoke the hate, "e-lab-or-ate. I have authorization for Level Five. Do you *want* to know what that means?"

Meeting his gaze with the look of wonder at something that cannot be comprehended, "you honestly don't know then?"

Tightening his grip on his baton, "no."

Wincing in the wake of the sound of the adjusted grip, "Arlo Kunlow has her."

Seeing the Order of Operations for Level Five teasing him in his mind, "why does he have her?"

Edging away from him as best he could, "in your current condition I am afraid to comment."

Easing up on the baton, "I will not take you to Level Five in a fit of pique. Tell me what I need to know."

Appearing relieved, "I needed the codes, she wouldn't be any use to me otherwise, I was going to get the codes and then make her, disappear."

Will I see Arlo on the table then? "Why does Arlo have her?"

Speaking his reply with a timid cowardice, "he felt he could, get her to, *come around*, and enjoy a life shared with him."

I am going to be sick. Taking a moment to reflect on his feelings, *I don't have time for me.* Barking the demand, "where is he?"

Worming away from his presence, "he didn't say where he was taking her!"

Hardening his heart to regain his professional composure, "I'll get people on it."

With a voice of sad pleading, "you know Miss Bachman will not last."

No. I don't. Correcting him with an audible lack of patience for him, "Miss Bachman is stronger than she looks. She has been through more than you could understand."

Still trying to plead with him, "all the more reason she won't make it. What is your plan if she flips that monster she calls a car on a high speed drive?"

Correcting him again, "if you hadn't pushed her –"

Cutting him off with a whine, "our enemies still exist."

Snapping back at him, "she will deal with that when the time comes."

Rousing with an anger to his whining, "and when they end her as they have ended every other Bachman who found the field of battle?"

Contemplating hitting Thomas he stayed his hand but not his tone, "she'll find a way."

Driving his words home as a contemptuous accusation, "you speak on *faith*!"

I do. Looking down at the baton in his hand he smiled, "I have faith in her." Moving away from Thomas he slid his baton into his pocket and pulled out his comm. Sending a text update to Shadow Ochenhart as quickly as he could type it. *He'll find Arlo, or he'll know someone who can.*

Done.

Wait, rust. Getting his comm back out he checked the Status of Eve Parsons. *On a short rest. Good enough.* Pressing the connection request he waited for her to answer.

Cutting right to it with her greeting, "speak."

Cutting right to it in return, "I need you to go to the Grain Silo. I need an Eyes on Scene report."

Softening the professional edge of her tone, "am I to go alone?"

Rust, det, scrap, "Lemon-Drop. Call Lemon-Drop from The Guild and tell him to meet you there."

Broaching the question with a slight waiver, "it is dire?"

Clenching and unclenching his fist while looking back at Thomas, "I believe it is. I need Eyes on Scene. Can you do this?"

Speaking with a firm conviction, "I can, I will, I shall. Out."

"Out."

Putting his comm away he moved back to Thomas, "Arlo will be found. This is being investigated."

Regarding him with a curious confusion, "why are you hiding your investigation from her?"

Answering with a humor in his words, "Miss Bachman is on a twelve hour rest. If we are too loud she will hear us moving around in the dark and turn on a light. We must do what we can, with what we have."

Regarding him with the continuation of his shock, "you, *care*."

Answering with the confession of faith, "I do."

"I do not have words." Losing the shock his tone moved to one of concern, "I have a question though. What of my daughter?"

Only now do you ask of your daughter. "I have seen the memo on that. She was found to be cleared via the Horse Hair Scan. Admin Nobody vouched for it himself. Although with the things Athens did to violate the Grain Silo –"

Jumping on the moment, "how did you know about the Grain Silo?"

"Miss Bachman is my," taking a deep breath, "friend."

Looking up at him with wide eyes, "I didn't know that happened."

Letting his smirk grow, "I didn't either."

Trying the timbre of the Confidant, "has she played you like a chess piece?"

I would like to find out who infected our parlance with that metaphor for her workings. Marshaling his words he put them in a line, "I think that metaphor is actually substandard for describing her tactics. In chess, you sacrifice pieces to remove other pieces. She does play a strategy with us, but it is not chess."

Still playing the Confidant, "you are fine with that?"

She will not sacrifice me for a Greater Good that does not exist. "I am."

Contemplating the moment with a long pause he spoke with a new question, "why did they fight for her? The False Prophet looked flawless, there was no way they could have known. Why did they disobey?"

Holding up the signal for 'pause' he turned to lean against the cell wall. *Is disobey even the right term for the question? Would it not be better to use Protect?* Rolling his understanding around he decorated it with terms and words borrowed from others until he was ready to share the final notion.

Pushing himself off of the wall he launched into his explanation, "Miss Bachman was granted the night from her father. He gave it to her. She wakes as most people think of evening meals. She watched the sun set instead of rise in her life. Her father would go home, back to Reylai, or to the Blackstone. She would see the people of that moment gather around her for there was always work to be done. That shift, those people, had a *unique* honor among the Citizens of New Hope. They watched their world sleep. Hand picked from people who had trouble sleeping at night for some reason or another. A tailored shift unbothered by the darkness. Your decree could look as flawless as it wanted to, you were trying to take something from them they value more than the word of the Protocol. The name they have Faith in, the name that means that the sun would rise again."

Digging into the idea with his question, "why were they so armed? New Hope is a Green Zone."

For the same reason I have a Room-Broom Shotgun strapped to the underside of my desk. "Asmodai. He gave incentives for people to learn and become better with their weapons. He offered those incentives in person, then would label them as Merit Based Awards within the system. That way he could balance the non-com with those who would carry weapons every night. He loved Susan dearly. He left the doors unlocked during the days of his reign, that people could have a chance to see and know what was going on. He armed as many of the night as he could, because he was afraid of what could go on."

Licking his lips for a moment he exhaled loudly, "and when Ridolfi returns?"

The Monster Incarnate. "She will end him."

Asking the question with a hope to his tone, "can she beat the monster who defeated everyone else?"

I have no doubts. "She will. She is not alone. Ridolfi was a product of his time. She has had her lifetime to prepare for the return of the monster and his legacy."

Looking up to him in a state of sad contemplation, "Faith in her and the rest? Faith, hope, those are the ideals that a man who doesn't care about *truth* clings to. You blind yourself to the *truth* of her matters."

Affirming the idea and himself, "I am not inside of her mind. I cannot know her truth. I do believe in her though. I speak on Faith."

Flexing his arms against his restraints, "what happens now?"

Retrieving his baton and pointing it at him, "now, you tell me *everything* I want to know. Or I'll have to see you put on the table. And when I do? I will tell The Commander what you have done."

Squeaking the words out, "I'll talk."

Moving to untie him, "I felt you would say that."

4.4.2 - 15:27

164 Magdalena – The Shadow's Workroom

■Dennis Ochenhart

Getting his kit in order he waited impatiently for his call to go through, *just like the bad old days. Except this time it's Amaranth on the line. I would kill Athens if he wasn't already dead.*

Regarding the long wall of tools, devices, firearms, and munitions with the honor of having collected all of the items into one place. *My career as a singular monument. Each item tied to a history lesson in modern espionage.*

Hearing the double click of his call being answered, what followed was a professional tumble of words into his earpiece, "Proxy Answer, Cloak Hampton answering on behalf of The Commander, Sir."

Rust it to chaff where is Steven?

Getting to it with a stern clip, "Cloak Hampton, I need help. Sys-Admin Hope is asleep –"

Cutting in, "I'm aware he's asleep. I wanted to talk shop with him but he had already fallen asleep again. Are you looking for the Commander?"

Firing back as he picked out a silencer, "yes."

Keeping it brief, "he's *also* asleep. Early rise has caught up with him. What's the SitRep?"

He's the left hand man. "Epsilon Code for this one hasn't been written yet. Amaranth Dinclair has been abducted by an Arlo Kunlow."

Keeping it professional, "what's the plan?"

I wish I knew. I don't even know how mad to be. "I was going to ask you that. I have an asset working on waking Hope. However I need a Militia Captain I can trust with finding and securing Arlo Kunlow."

After a moment of quiet he sounded confidant, "I would recommend Captain Paul Kaufman and his Jaguars for that. I can bounce you the uplink and a recommendation in just a tic if you like."

Smiling with approval he picked up a balisong and slid it into a sheath on his harness, "I would like."

Following up with another question, "did you get a Guild Asset on the matter? Psych Profile on the target?"

I wish. "I *just* got the intel. The Head Questioner has Consul Kunlow, direct confession."

"I would recommend, here, if you get Captain Kaufman I'll get an asset for you."

"Thank you."

"Noted."

Closing the connection he followed up on the referral. Pressing the Request he set to waiting for a connection. *I will be calm. I will be the tranquil self. I will know no fear as nothing has been confirmed. I am the –*

Leading into the moment with a boisterous tone of camaraderie, "Captain Kaufman here, you have need of me Ochenhart?"

Excellent. "I have a Citizen I need hunted down. He's abducted a VIP of concern to the Platinum, and we need him alive."

After a short chuckle he continued with the boisterous tone, "send me the Citizen Number and I'll start the hunt. How loud can we be?"

Keeping his tone level, "you can have whatever volume you need. All I care is that you get him *alive.*"

"On it. Out?"

"Out."

Closing the connection he sent the relayed ID number. *Thank you Zack. Hold the line against the storm in your heart.* Looking the idea over in his head, *when Hope wakes I'll have him help me hunt down the people who aided this. I need to find them before others do. Keep the skills sharpened.*

Regarding himself in the mirror, "keep a close watch on your shadow, for in darkness, you are one with it."

Catching the sight of a picture of Maggie dressed as a Shadow he laughed at himself. *You were a sister to me. You always giggled when I would be too serious for your liking. The Honor-Bound, the Glory-Hound, the Dedicated Trooper, the Vengeful Ones, all had something in common to you.*

"They all forgot how to laugh."

Reaching up he touched the corner of the photo, "you wouldn't want them dead." Lowering his hand, "you would want them talked to first. Asked about what in the Blue Sky were they thinking, or not thinking. You'd pour the tea, and ask them if they had something they wanted to say. For you? I'll be good. I'll find them, I'll make sure they don't get far, and I'll get someone from Cloak to sit down with them and find out why they would give Amaranth to what might just be an unrepentant monster."

Sliding a fresh power supply into his shock box, "I will give them the benefit of the doubt. If they prove I was wrong to? I'll take care of it like I always do. Provided your son does not do it before I can."

4.6.0 - 18:04

Safe Housing - Interior

☀ Yuri

Turning off the screen he set the remote down and reflected on the moment. Sitting on the comfortable couch he smiled at the memory of being next to Susan. Turning his attention away from the distraction he set his elbow to his knee and leaned on his hand.

Touching his cheek with a gentleness he felt the years mixing around inside of his mind. *Seeing my boyhood face hiding behind the hedge, it struck me deeply. The weight of my journey was mostly lifted by the days I spent in that bedroom. He would visit me and commune with me. She would visit me and tend to my wounds. I feel human again. I was never without my humanity. I am alive.*

And she's far too quiet.

Getting up from the couch in the living room he set to walking softly toward the back end of the house. Touching his cheek again he resolved to grow a new beard. *I look like a child again. A beat up child.*

I feel almost naked.

Poking his head around the corner he smiled when she looked up at him.

Leading into the moment with a humored tone he gestured at her with a slow motion, "you have been very quiet."

Touching the spot next to her on the couch with a smile, "sit with me again?"

Nodding he came around the corner and found a spot next to her, "of course."

Gesturing with her tablet, "I went back to work."

Keeping his tone away from admonishment, "I am not surprised. What is the latest task no one else can do?"

Moving the tablet from hand to hand for a moment, "I, just wanted to know what was in my inbox. I had to face something serious and it's something I had to delegate. I sent it over to the Spiritual Leaders of the city."

Getting comfortable he asked the question, "what would that be?"

Rolling her head from side to side she looked down at the tablet, "Burial Arrangements."

I will listen. "Elaborate, all the way to the details if you can, would, like, whatever I say here."

"Noted." Smiling she held the tablet with both hands, "we have a practice for those who die after crimes which we are not planning to forgive. We use cremation, and then place the remains in an urn which bears their Citizen Number and nothing more. The number is retired forever. The urns are kept in The Traitor's Vault."

Her smile is mostly faded. "Who is to make the call about the attackers?"

Laughing with a slight hollow to the timbre, "The Spiritual Leaders now! They're going to work with the families and find out who would be better served by them going to the Vault, or if they would need to bring them home. I am, sorely tempted to send them all to the Vault."

This might be an important lesson. "Is that your right?"

Closing her eyes she huffed a sigh, "it is."

Reaching over to her he touched her hand gently, "you do not choose to?"

Taking his hand she huffed again, "one? I am not officially working, and even though I am sorely tempted to send all of the fallen attackers to the Vault? I have a word of great power which asks the question it does. The word, Democide. When the governing body kills its own Citizens. If I send them to the Vault? I murder the idea they could be remembered. It would be reaching into the minds of the Citizen and seeking to ask them to forget the offenders."

Her humanity glimmers. "You would not seek this then?"

Squeezing his hand she frowned, "many were parents. They had kids. They had children that I can only assumed they loved enough to fight for a different future for them. I sent this to the Spiritual Leaders so they can do their work. When they come to me with the answer? I can celebrate it. I can look over their victories, understandings, and toil and hold it up and celebrate it."

"Noted." *I wonder,* "so which Primer is the act of Delegation like that in?"

Breaking into a knowing smile she bumped her shoulder against his, "the Bachman High Consul Primer on The Power of Delegation. Dad would cope with the morning SitRep by getting everyone of note on the line, and then he would stress the import of all the things he did not want to do. Mom would speak to him over breakfast, and find out what was on his heart. She would make sure he had things he *wanted* to face. Then he would work the Pyramid until all the tasks were assigned."

"Do you have a funny story for that?"

Nodding twice in affirmation she explained, "there is a weekly SitRep where larger projects are discussed. At that meeting? Thanks to mom being the playful sort? There is a pile of squishy handballs, just the size for the palm of the hand, and they have a number and letter on them. Which labeled them as a given project for the week. Dad would literally hand out the responsibilities."

Speaking the words which sprang to mind, "he would play catch with reality?"

Smiling brightly she nodded once, "yes."

There is a joke about touching balls in there, but the concept of playing catch with reality seems much like the man I met. "That is, something else."

"I know." Following up, "societal ideals would make sure that no one had more than two tasks given to them. Those aiding him would even trade the balls if they felt they would do better. Volunteering makes a person stronger."

"I would agree. That's a," enunciating the word with a questioning tone, "*cute*, system."

Shrugging she smiled, "it is what it is."

A chance to learn. Through the door if it is open! "As for the cremation, I heard Asmodai was cremated."

"Yes." Hearing the pride entering her words as she spoke, "from there, he was divided up, as in life, as in death."

I will be brave. "What became of him?"

Cozying up to him with a tone of recollection she spoke her answer, "close to three kilograms of ash was generated, and then promptly divided. He wanted Amanda and Micah to have a vinyl record with his ashes pressed into it. I don't know what's on the record. For Steven? He was mixed into two hundred shotgun shells. For me? They're going to press his ashes into a glass cover for a light in my office. I'll put it by the window so he can still shine from the window. Patrick is getting a set of pencils. Reylai, his second *wife,* if you will, has already planted a tree with his ashes mixed in with the seed. And for Amaranth a painting with his ashes mixed into the paint. He didn't want to go to the Columbarium."

New word. "Columbarium?"

"Mausoleum for urns. He didn't want to be a useless pile of chaff on a shelf."

Sounds awful. "Well with such options, I would not either. As morbid as that is, the selection of fates for the remains, I think it is somewhat neat. Are their other options?"

"There is the option, for those of New Hope, that the Drenner family maintains and has encouraged. They maintain a large above ground graveyard near Respite. It's a protected place, gates, locks, nice fences. You do not go their casually, and it's a place of deep respect. Not just for the remains, but the idea of the dead. As I have Drenner blood in my veins? I have been informed that the family would prefer if I would be buried there."

To live in the City of the Dead? "Something to consider."

"If a spiritual code or ethic would ask you to be buried in one piece? You go into one of the places like that, none of which have subterranean burials. That being mixed into the soil. There are places like that throughout the Rim, some of which feature underground housing, but not mixed into the soil." Recovering from the meandering moment, "otherwise? The average Citizen is cremated and becomes ashes. The ways my father lives on is available to most Citizens. If you want to become fireworks though, then you have to wait until the next festival, of which we dedicate a section of the fireworks to those of the fallen."

Light up the sky? That would be tempting to request in seventy years. "Noted."

"We have the crematoriums, and, for those honored by The State? There is a large funerary pyre ground for those who wish to go out in a large conflagration. The ashes are typically buried out there in the Heroes Pyre. If that doesn't work for the fallen? Then the body goes where it needs to go and we light a pyre fire in their honor regardless. We place artifacts of their life in the pyre pod. We don't do it to forget them, we do it so they can know it's time to leave. To help the spirits move on."

"Staggering. I am glad that I don't have to worry about it anytime soon."

Touching his leg gently she spoke fondly, "I second that."

Should make sure I hear everything. "Are there any other methods?"

Speaking with a hesitating cadence, "there is one other."

By the Stars I could regret this. "Why the hesitation?"

"The third one is not exactly the most, *traditional,* of methods. Even in our digging in the Network we did not find much mention of it."

Now I'm curious. "What is it?"

Tossing the answer with an almost casual tone, "it's a composting tower."

Ah, I can see with how they like to think how that would be difficult. "Do you throw your enemies in it?"

Stopping in the middle of her inhalation she exhaled sharply. Turning her body she laid backwards over his lap. Looking up at him with a composed expression she smiled when he looked at her.

"No." Reaching up she touched his shoulder with a calmness to her, "our *enemies* are hauled to the border and dumped. Dumped is a bit harsh of a word for it, but it's true that once we leave them we don't go back to check what happened." After a breath, "our composting tower goes to enriching the wild lands outside of our settlements that need help. We don't eat from the lands which have been enriched by our dead. We do not bury those not of our lands as that should fall on their people."

"Noted. I like that last part. I would agree with how your people handle both aspects. As for land fed with the dead? I think the dead people go in the dead people places, and the crops grow in the farm places. That's just me though."

Smiling at him with a simple humor, "noted."

"If you had opted to kill the people, what would have happened?"

Closing her eyes she frowned, "Democide, for one. Which *must* be done in private, as we do kill people who are our Citizens when we have judged the moment to have no other recourse. Which is done in private as to not indulge in the glorification of their deaths. It's *tragic* when people die. It's a *sad* day. No matter how much you want someone dead, you need to remember the reason that this is how it's ending as the important part. Publicly killing someone won't bring the loved ones back. Remembering the fallen well will ease the pain though."

Reaching up he stroked her hair with a comforting firmness to the gesture, "another thing I like, didn't know I would like it, but I do."

"We don't want them to die screaming, as someone has to hear that. We use drugs, strong stuff in unhealthy doses to put someone under and keep them there. The person is settled up with, given their last moments, and then put under. Then they go to the Execution Chamber, are beheaded, and cremated. *Unless* their beliefs and community don't support beheading. In which case they use a different apparatus which causes a fatal wound to the heart. If we could execute without hurting someone, we would."

Keeping his tone as light as he could, "why is that important?"

Speaking softly she spoke with a resonating sadness, "we are The State, and the only tool of enforcement we have, is violence. All other tools are based upon the perception of the validity of the State. Violence is wrong. Killing is wrong. But we are in the place we are in, with what we have left to us. We are hypocrites in that regard."

"Do you have the old fashioned firing squads?"

"That, is an option in extreme cases. If someone has gone over the line into something so heinous we don't have an explanation or emotional rationalization point? We will line them up against a wall and shoot them. They're secured to rigging, and then covered up, before the bullets start. It's not healthy to watch someone get shot, so when people want to do something *that* unhealthy? We get them to mitigate their own suffering by covering the bodies up before the shooting starts."

I will finish my education. "The Exit Pass, how does that end?"

"That is quite gentle. When it's for medical reasons? They find a gentle way out which will go hand in hand with what is killing you. The nudge over the threshold of mortality. The rare times when it is psychological? A shot of something to calm the patient, then a breathing mask, and a shifting mix until you fall asleep and don't wake up. Some Citizens have clay which cannot be fixed. We let them go gently."

Her mother sounds brave then, still being alive. "Your mother, she sleeps?"

Appearing conflicted she regarded him with a curious look before speaking her words, "she had faith that the Yorklin doctors could find her a cure. She opted for a coma and to sleep until they wake her with the good news."

She was then. "She was brave then."

Smiling she nodded with the loss showing, "yes."

Maybe I can find something good again, "so is Cassia safe now?"

Nodding again she brightened, "she is. As far as I know."

"Will her parents worry for her?"

Quieting as quickly as she rallied, "they are, no longer with us."

So many missing. How do they fill the gaps? "Do you have a tradition for older adults to stand in as adult parents?"

"We do. It's deeper than that, in a sense. As you age it is the hope that your peers, friends, will get to know your children and be ready if you fall. There are a few different traditions on that subject. To be off topic? *All* Citizens are reminded they are proxy parents when a young mind looks to them for an answer. To be on topic? She doesn't have a father to lean on, he was taken by Cerebral Apoplexy. I hated him, he hated me, but she was better off with him in her life. I would want to believe that enough that I say it. He did his best when he wasn't lost in his eternal feud with my family name."

Continuing after a few breaths, "her mother, we lost her to violence. The Free-landers, the Mice program, it wasn't far enough to the north yet." Closing her eyes she grit her teeth for a moment, "I'm losing myself again."

Giving her a hand to hold he spoke after she took it in both hands, "take your time."

Relaxing after a moment she frowned as she met his gaze, "we did not know that she would be in danger. She was riding light in an ADR-10, at the time our best hauler in the fleet. One lead, one follow, and a cargo of dangerous materials which needed to go someplace far from ground water or humans. They ended up too close to the Free-landers who were out that night. They went for the truck. She fought hard, knowing what was in the back. The front and rear cars went out shooting."

I know that sort of material. I have seen the signs. The Pancake you do not wish to eat. "Did they open the hauler?"

"No. She managed to get a signal flare up, went out the opposite side, and used her shotgun to get them off of the back. They didn't back down. They wanted the cargo. They stayed too long, and the patrol came by. The aeronautics that swept in with guns blazing, they came back and hunted the attackers until they could find no more of them."

They obliterate their enemies. "Staggering."

Gesturing toward the ceiling, "in my closet upstairs, I have a flannel shirt she gave me. I have been known to visit our northern regions, and it was a boon on those visits. I grew older, taller, and it doesn't fit but it is still in my closet." Adding as a dejected after-thought, "she, when she was around Tim was civil. He wasn't as angry when she would sit with him."

"With her gone, you do not get to talk to Cassia much then, neh?"

"Not as much as I want. She married for love. She found a man who thought the world of her, and she married into his family. She learned the customs of the Kunlow family. And the next thing I knew? Her one year anniversary was going past and I was home, sick."

They are given one life, and they live knowing they only have half of it to live. "Noted."

"I was sad for Chuck."

"You mentioned him."

"He's the man who had," pointing at his shirt, "that pattern for his shirt first. He's almost the same size in the torso, but he has shorter legs."

The strangest details. "Noted."

"The reason he couldn't be with Cassia was that he lost his ability to believe in love. He saw his parents betrayed by the idea. He was taken in by my mom, mentored in key things, and she was going to do the unprecedented for an idea and try to get Amanda to adopt him. Amanda had another relative within the family adopt him. Her cousin Eunice. Charles Hunter became Chuck Drenner and he found his way back out to the main estate."

Nice to hear these things without screaming engines or high speed forces. "Did you see him growing up?"

"He wasn't cleared for Saturdays. That was the day I spent with Amanda after mom left us. That's the Drenner House Day. Each House gets a Day of special note to it. Friday, Saturday, and Sunday are shared between Twelve Houses."

"What day is the Bachman?"

"Tuesday."

Odd choice. "Noted."

"I can hear that moment of question. *That,* is an easy answer. Friday is the day of Humble Splendor. Saturday is the day of Foundation and Family. Sunday is the day of Receptiveness. Tuesday? Restraint."

That was *easy!* "Noted."

"Chuck is a good man, he cared for Cassia, but his idea of their shared life? It would be one where he would be dragging her down. With that in mind, he set her free. She found another."

"Noted."

Brightening again, "Yuri?"

"Yes?"

Speaking the words with praise sprinkled in her tone, "while we're on the subject, you're my first male romantic friend."

Volunteer understanding, "Sasha is the first female, yes?"

Confirming the notion brightly with her tone, "yes."

Are we going in this direction then? "You mentioned *third?*"

"Yes. The Yorklin doctors ask a very simple idea. If you have one set of parts and medical reality? You get male. If you have another set of parts? You get female. If you are born and the parts aren't typical? They leave them alone unless it's a medical emergency and ask you about them when you're older. In that case the base form of male or female gets adjusted with a hyphen and an I. Then we have identity notions. Many people, myself included, wake up and look at our bodies and see the person we see. If that is not true? Then the next box on your identification card has that answer."

"Is it like a lump of idea? Or something else?"

"The third category is a broad spectrum of cataloged notions, beliefs, and emotional adherents. You consult with The Guild, as they cover the state of your head, and then you have the box adjusted. We have limited resources so it's not like we can move the earth and sky for you, but we try what we can to help you feel comfortable in your skin. We just want people to accept what they see in the mirror if they can."

"Do they have a Primer?"

"Many, because of the varied nature of it. Sometimes it can be as simple as not understanding that being a man is as simple as accepting yourself. Or as complex as Gender Dysphoria. The world was still at odds with the answers, so we went for easy solution of acknowledging the complexities of *being human,* by addressing needs and realities, over feelings, as a State. The Citizen must find their path to Inner Peace. The State however will do as it can to help."

What could have been, the question which has hurt me more than most things in the world. "I have a story to tell, at some other time."

"I look forward to hearing it."

"Did you have a friend who was third?"

"I had a friend, Patrick had a friend, and Steven had a friend whom would all qualify as Thirds in one of the facets. However, they were all very different people."

I will start with the one I have the least common ground with, "what sort of friend did Steven have?"

"A waif of a boy who had been weakened by childhood sickness. Instead of trying to be a masculine man, he embraced his features and frame and garbed himself in alluring vestments. He would not be able to achieve the Archetype of Warrior, Soldier, or Strongman. This led him to the dance with the fire of becoming the Peacock, the Dream, and a more Social being in general. Young men, traditionally, establish their sense of self through direct conflict. The Rough and Tumble is the fate of many boys. Steven was his proxy in those battles when the other boys would find the young man contemptible for his physical weakness. Boys have no small amount to learn about what it means to be men. That phase of life is *very* hard on them."

Such a strange thought, "he was the Knight in Shining Armor?"

Answering with a gentle correction, "he was a young man learning the Ethics of life and enforcing them in the way that the minds of his peers understood. It is unethical to attack the boy for being a waif. But those lessons have to be learned by living. Steven gained a reputation as a fierce defender in those circles." Adding as an afterthought, "Shining Armor is only worn once. When it is tested? It becomes Battle Tested."

"Noted." *No pedestals.* "Did your father approve?"

"He did not forbid him. However, Father told him to learn how to use only the amount of force which was needed. That by walking the road, he could not quit that road, or else his friend would be left without an ally. Thus he could walk the road, but he had to be careful."

Is there a twist? "Was he careful?"

Answering with a restrained pride, "for the most part."

So strange a sight, "you're proud of him."

"I am. We've had ups and downs," smiling she held back laughter before the sarcastic inflection entered her tone, "an understatement I know," rubbing his hand in the mo-

444

ment of pause as her tone returned to admiration, "but he's still my family."

Pouncing on the chance for humor, "if the level of intensity I have seen is the *ups and downs,*" laying the back of his wrist against his forehead he feigned being whelmed, "I don't know how well my heart is going to survive this family in the long run."

Firing back with a playful flatness to her tone, "it's not everyday."

Lowering his hand quickly he placed it back in her grasp, "oh, good."

Squeezing his hand for a moment she continued with the timbre of the Storyteller, "then there was Patrick's friend. He's the son of one of the peers of Major Thompson. They were younger men then and the boy had a body which was a host of biological rebellion. From his genitals, to his chest, to his face, the sound of his voice. It was a nonsense puzzle. But Patrick, in a moment of wisdom, told him, in response to why he was not terminated by the State, a simple answer. That he functioned. That the Yorklin doctors could help sculpt him into the figure he wanted, as gently as possible, but that he functioned in his mind. His flesh sack had betrayed the human within, but that did not mean that the human within was not there."

Would not have known him to be such a man, "how did Patrick have such a friend?"

Continuing as The Storyteller, "The Guild, to protect against the savage monsters that youth can be, and the rolling boiling fever of emotions that is growing up, maintains a social circle of young people who are physically off the beaten path. The boy, his choice to be called such, was in treatment, seeking a more stable body, and thus was kept with those who were also in treatments."

Was he different then? "Why would Patrick be near them?"

Squeezing his hand again she continued, "Mom was asleep. He found in her writings that she had challenged herself, when she started what she did and struggled for what she believed. Maggie, mom, she challenged us every day we have been alive. Thus Patrick strove to be stronger, like her."

Speaking his question with a careful inflection to not step on an eggshell, "how did, your father take it?"

Squeezing his hand again she put far more encouragement into her tone, "he told him not to be rude. To be humble. To remind himself that he had *no idea* what these kids were going through. That the only way to even begin to understand would be to ask, but they *owed him nothing.* More often than not? Patrick was good to, around, with, them."

Two for two for happy stories. "Solid. What of your friend?"

Reflecting on the contrast, "Steven's was a man who was openly feminine, Patrick was a man who wanted to overcome biological adversity to become a more manlike man, mine? Was a private matter of the mind spiraling into unquiet territory and raising too many questions."

Is she trying to spare me the truth? "Poetic and yet vague."

"My apologies." Adjusting her hold on him she took his hand and wrist in her grip, "he was playing with emotional and sexual need when he was too young. It's one thing to ask for a waiver when you're fifteen and it's a sole partner within four years of age." Pausing for a moment she moved ahead with a speed, "it's another to be in with a couple." Slowing down she appeared contemplative, "he found in their relationship he felt a greater identity with the female spouse."

I feel the shared daunt. "Was he pretty?"

Smiling with a lilt of guilt to the gesture, "very much so. To the extent I try not to mention it."

"Oh?"

Speaking the words softly, "why would I want to remind him of a time he cannot regain?"

We cannot go back. "Oof. Truth. How does he live now?"

Calming she spoke conversationally, "he keeps his hair long still, but he minds it to keep it from being seen a poetic mane. He wears trouser and button-up, and he doesn't give a single tangible clue that he used to be beautiful."

I should not, but I will. "Something bad happened?"

Picking her words carefully, "something *regrettable* happened. The Guild, they tried," shifting to a more provoked tone, "oh did they try." Using her free hand she covered her eyes for a moment, "he loved the two he had been, *mentored*, by. His parents had been influenced by other things, other moments, and in that loneliness he found companionship." Taking her hand off her eyes, "the very thing we try to prevent, happened."

I will have to tell her of the past at some point. "I do have a story to tell another time then."

Trying to move closer to him and finding herself as close as she could be she sighed, "I will listen when we reach that other time. Judging by your face it's not a casual one."

"No."

Speaking the words with the conflicted regret, "he, he doesn't live like he used to."

"Is it better he lives as he does now?"

"Better?" Closing her eyes the words rang with inadequacy, "that is subjective. People need to be free to be people. I fear he's not free in his own heart anymore."

The Moral and Ethical idea is that Action and Result equals care. If she has no Actions and cannot gain Results then there is no proof of care felt. An intense way to live. "You live a difficult life of supporting others. Do others quibble the right to be people?"

Opening her eyes again she smiled with a slightly eager recollection, "the deeds without harm to self or others are ruled by the Tyranny of the Ethical Precedent. If The State has deemed the behavior or deed to be without harm to self or other? You are forbidden by Protocol from moving against a person for what they choose."

I will make a note of that. It sounds like a treasure trove of funny stories. "If it does harm?"

Ringing with a confidence in the notion, "then the victim of the harm *must* be rescued with the smallest damage amount of damage done to them as possible."

Who rescues you? "One more question?"

"Yes?"

I, catching the scent of tea on the air he felt his bravery leave him, "is that tea?"

"Yes! I made some a bit ago. You'll find it in the kitchen. Help yourself."

Pushing the words out, "I, I will."

Signaling him for a hug her sad smile showed her compassion. Nodding in affirmation he moved his limp hand in an attempt to do the signal. Watching her slide away she adjusted again before draping herself gently against him.

Intoning the words with a casual quiet to them, "we have time Yuri. Time to go over all the weird and unusual questions. The things that pain you, the things that pain me. The things that make us laugh. It *can* be tranquil and good again. You should get tea though, it's good for you."

I don't have wise words. "I noticed there was tea with my meals in Central."

Giggling at the simplicity of the statement, "we like tea."

Turning his head he caught her gaze, "thank you."

Kissing him on the forehead above his right eye she spoke the affirmation softly, "noted."

Waiting for her to move he set to getting up to stretch, "are you keeping in contact with others?"

Leaning back on the couch she laughed with an honesty to the gesture which brought him a renewal of energy. "I don't get much of a choice Yuri! Waterlily, Wallman, Winifred, Sevilan, Dennis, Steven, Patrick, the names go on and on. Each having a different level of priority and amount that needs to be said. I am not alone in this moment, I just am trying to not to spend too much time on one person for fear of losing myself to a shared moment."

You do not deny me your side. "I am humbled that I get to be next to you during this."

Sitting up she gestured something he did not know as she gushed her words in reply, "I am honored that I get a chance to know you and be the one who gets to share her world with you."

I cannot. "I am going to go get that tea."

Toning it down she leaned back, "you should."

"Will you sleep tonight?"

Picking up her tablet again, "I have just a bit more toil, a few more things, and then I can find rest."

The best I can hope for. "I understand. Strength to you."

4.6.2 - 18:35

Safe Housing - Rear Hall

☼...Susan Bachman

Laying on the couch in a haze she looked up at her errant teacup. *Just one more round of work and I'll go to bed. One last check of things and I will go, sleep, and wake up to breakfast before my delay runs out.*

Sitting up she looked at her tablet, *new priority message from Jerome. Rust it, what now?* Opening the message she looked over the notes and reports.

Josh knew.

Reading Steven's orders she scowled, *and he's a wanted man now. Three of the survivors were able to point to Josh. He did not aid but they secured his silence.*

He wanted me to take Dominion and cancel the Reply. Now he holds up Josh and asks me for his trip to the table. Level Four is already authorized.

I can smell the Smoke from here.

Keying in a set of orders of her own she scowled, *he'll go to the Questioners, and they'll start where they believe it should start. He will be treated no differently, and certainly not with a harsher reception than any other.*

I'll send Frank to get him. Have him get some of his boys who need to stretch their legs to go with him. They'll fetch Josh and move him to Cloak and Dagger.

While I'm at it. Arranging for Frank and Sasha to escort Cassia to Chuck she smiled, *odds are Chuck will be at the House. Cassia can sit at home, in secret, and sit out the worst of this.*

Listening to the sound bites included she felt her conviction galvanize. *The Waltz of Power continues, and I will control the tempo of the song.*

Frank will go personally as Steven is going personally. Father and Son of the Covenant, born of a bond thicker than the water of the womb. The only man I can trust to deal with Steven.

I will answer his question. Should Josh live for knowing and doing nothing?

Yes.

We cannot bring back our dead.

We can only make a world where we lose less.

Keying in the last of the orders she took a deep breath, *I will commit to this course of action. I will light the way.* Placing her High Consul Seal into the boxes she looked for a deeper wisdom.

I cannot allow a Double Standard to enter into our system. I cannot allow Moral Outrage to change our system. I cannot allow his fear of people asking the questions they will to drive his actions. I will do what a Strong Leader must always do. I will lead.

Placing the last seal into place, *good luck and a strong tailwind to all of you.*

4.6.5 - 18:57

'Jaguar One' Mobile Command Base - En Route to C&D

⁂Paul Kaufman
⁂Captain of the Militia Squad "The Jaguars"

Gazing out the window at the city, still illuminated by the low slung sun on the horizon, he felt a measure of comfort at the murals he knew by heart.

That was something bordering on fun. The thrill of the hunt and the capture of a force of evil. We get him back to C&D and he'll tell them where to find the VIP.

I would be daunted but he screamed that she's still alive.

Before he urinated down his leg.

Turning his attention to his fellows he could see the shared humor of the moment. *First time getting to do a takedown like that. We trained it, and finally were able to see it in action. Somewhat unfortunate to already being headed back to base.*

Turning his attention to the images that had been processed from the surveillance drones that had witnessed the moment he smiled. Flipping through the gloriously dramatic pictures taken of the Jaguars, as they approached the vehicle of Arlo Kunlow, he couldn't help but feel a measure of pride in his men. *Shields up in a phalanx, captured from a few different angles from both ends of the alleyway we pinned the car in, and they just look great.*

I shouldn't be this proud of them, not for this, but I am and no one can stop me.

Still smiling he heard the chime of his request answered to speak with the Sys-Admin.

"Sys-Admin! A pleasure to speak with you at last."

With a slight slur the voice on the line worked through the words, "Noted. Correct. Captain Kaufman, do you have the target?"

He's still waking up, "affirmative."

"Reason for the requested," fumbling for a moment, "apologies Captain, I am not versed in Militia Jargon to the point of fluency. Request for Casual Discourse."

"Accepted." *I don't speak Network Jargon so we're even.* "You be you."

Broaching the question with a hesitant caution, "why did you call me?"

He knows who Arlo has. "Am I to ask where the VIP is? He swears *she* is alive, but then we followed the gag order and gagged him. To be clear, I am not asking in a *direct inquiry*, as I was cautioned that this was an incredibly sensitive VIP situation."

With an air of false bravado, "Negative Captain. Leave it to the Questioners."

What's the worst that can happen, he tells me no? "Who is the VIP?"

After a hesitated moment he replied firmly, "you don't have the Epsilon Code, from what I know of it."

Not a chance, thinking over the variables he shook his head, "there is only *one* VIP I know of whom, if missing, would be a problem of this caliber."

Answering with a cautiousness, "whom would that be?"

Speaking his answer with conviction, "Amaranth. Girl is a poorly kept secret Sys-Admin. And yes, I am in a secured spot in the APC. No one else heard that."

Opening up with a candor, "we're afraid he's the only one who knows exactly where she is. I'm patching into his comm though, and tracing his motions."

"Then his contact turned the comm back on for you?"

"He did. Made sure he had everything, thought it was odd, and found the comm in a nearby recycling bin. I had him power it up and I should be able to trace it backwards and find his lair."

"Good."

"Please, don't tell anyone about this. We don't have enough data to go forward."

Easy enough. She won't stay missing long. "As you said, I do not have the Epsilon Code. I know the Protocol. I'll take him to the Questioners, keeping him gagged, and move on with my day."

"Thank you Captain."

I may as well ask, "question, opinion solicited to be exact, is it wrong that I'm proud of my men today? I'm looking at the pictures on my tablet taken from our Sky-Drones, and they look great. Fierce. As a Civilian, what would be your opinion?"

Intoning the words with a Fraternal Pride, "if you feel the pride is merited? Enjoy it. No one wants to be on the other side of a phalanx wall, but those who see it will most likely marvel at the sight. I know I do. It is a fact that you don't get to do it that often, you could also see if you want to spend the Rations to get the best snap shots framed."

Good to know his stance. "Thank you Sys-Admin. You're going to make sure Amaranth is rescued?"

"I am."

Maybe a Militia Calendar and this could be our Squad photo. "Thank you. I look forward to working with you in the future."

"A Blue Sky, and a functioning working bond of us," stumbling for a moment, "for you," sighing, "or something."

I know what that tired is like. "Clear your problems and get some rest."

"Yes sir."

"Noted. Be well Sys-Admin. Out."

Putting his comm away he looked over the SitRep.

What a day.

4.6.7 - 19:04

5001 Last Century Blvd. - 'Lounge Lair' – New Hope

▸Jerome Hope

Passing the empty glass back to Paige he accepted the offered lozenge. Placing it into his mouth he set to rolling the hard disc around as he turned his attention to the Network Map. *What could be a needle in a haystack will meet the power of filtered data.* Setting the search parameters of the script he rubbed his eyes with a heaviness in his spirit.

"The Grain Silo was breached. They have the offender in custody, but he has to be processed and Questioned. The Fourth is missing. Her condition is unknown. Athens," looking to Paige he was met with a questioning face of quiet horror and sadness.

Tucking the lozenge in his cheek he closed his eyes for a moment, "Athens was my mentor." Opening them he set to finishing the script, "he had taken the mantle by merit. He kept it by proving himself. He moved through the hurdles of coordinating the Firmware Change seven years ago. We moved up an entire number under his watch. And now? I don't know what to think of him as a mentor now."

Moving her hands her soothing voice with the northern accent played across his senses gently. "To fight is human, to abuse is inhuman. The Shadow took him. Shine your light, and do not be afraid to show how long the shadow falls." Looking at her hands she stopped for a moment, "does Miss Bachman know?"

"She does not. She is on," holding up his hands he moved for 'clarification' at the look of incredulity on her face, "a twelve hour reprieve from duty because of trauma. She is not being *weak,* not in the face of this, or in my subjective opinion. She needs a moment of rest, so we have yet to tell her. *I* do not have an answer to tell her. Her twelve hours is a breath of fresh air for her. For me? It is a chance to be a part of an Endeavor which *must* succeed." Pausing for a moment he found his truth, "how can I show her that I value her leadership if I do not have a task to accomplish to show her?"

"You are in the right. I have not read the Primer on this."

"I don't think there is one." Finishing the commands, "there. This should hunt down the location of the place she is being kept. I have the data from his Comm Unit, I can sift, and find out where he was hiding. My gut tells me that Athens will have rigged up something in regards to *that,* but I'll do my best to defeat him."

"Amaranth is precious. I was told she was away, in mourning. The Warm Fuzzies are without their leader in this dark time."

They're stronger than people understand. "The Fuzzies will find the strength to do as they do. We will return Amaranth to them before the school reopens. We will bring the dawns light, even if we have to haul the sun into place by hand."

"I will go get the winch and pulley."

"Thank you for being here Paige."

"It is good to be of use."

Turning his chair he looked to her with a gentle plea, "while this runs, could you help me back to my cot?"

Nodding affirmatively, "I can, and will. You must rest more. The amount of Hatred you drank was not good for you."

"I," stopping his justification before he could speak it, "would agree."

"You are wise. Let me help the wise man to bed."

Lifting his arms he maneuvered himself as to not lean on her too firmly but still gain the steadying he required. Gaining his feet he spoke the words softly, "just a nap."

Leading him over to the cot she steadied him as he lowered himself into place. Rolling onto his back he turned his attention toward the ceiling.

I will never drink that much Hatred again.

"You will have a nap. If the search finishes before you awaken? I will relay the information to Dennis and Zack."

A boon. "Thank you Paige."

"Sleep until I must wake you."

"I will."

4.4.5 - 15:55

1120 Fairview - The Grain Silo

ΔEve Parsons
ΔCloak and Dagger "Questioner"

Getting out of her Duo-Car she walked with a shy precision to the sidewalk, turning to move the short distance to the car that Lemon-Drop would be waiting in. *I will be composed.* Thankful for her mask she tapped on the passenger window.

Getting out with a hurried energy to the gesture, the clean shaven Counselor known as Lemon-Drop, looked at her from across the top of his car. "Can you tell me now?"

Shaking her head once, "no. We must go inside."

"What is the Epsilon Code for this?"

I don't have one. Turning on her heel she set off toward the door. Hearing the sound of Lemon chasing after her she felt her resolve strengthen as she approached the door of the residence. *If I am to die, I will live my last days with a glorious courage. I will be the person who is remembered well.*

Stepping up onto the porch she startled when the door opened without her touching it. *We are expected?*

Faced with the confused face of Reylai Dinclair she felt a kinship of not being in the expected moment. *Makes two of us.*

Speaking into the moment Lemon-Drop spoke as a man looking for answers, "Miss Dinclair, I don't have the Epsilon Code. I was told that if I came to this meeting I would understand what I did not know I needed to understand."

Gesturing to them both, "come in, both of you."

Stepping carefully into the house she felt the notion of trespassing as her boots connected with the pressed bamboo flooring. *This was the sacred refuge of the High Consul. The place where he recovered. And I am here to find out why this was not reported.*

Closing the door quietly Lemon-Drop visibly calmed himself, "I am here as Lemon-Drop, so I must not implore you with the force that I would prefer to succumb to."

Assuming a place at a respectful distance Reylai spoke the words as a confession, "Arlo Kunlow took my daughter on the threat of her death. I have remained quiet as no word had come that I could speak. I have been informed that Arlo is being hunted."

Pressing the question gently, "did he act alone?"

"No."

Rolling his hand with his words, "do you know the identities –"

"Yes." Pointing to the door, "isolated camera and recording system on that door." Lowing her hand, "they set off the floor panel which relayed the message to an Un-Networked system. There *is* a Network accessible camera system on the door which *was* silenced and suppressed. The backup was not."

We could get those people. "Do you have this on a memory card?"

"I do. However, I wish to know what will happen with the information. I was told my daughter would die if I spoke. They were all armed, and they threatened her and myself." Losing her calm to the suppressed rage and sadness, "I was forced to sign over custody with the forms that are used on parents who have wronged their children when they admit their culpability and are showing they understand they can no longer be parents. What will you do with them?"

Speaking with a reluctant cadence Lemon-Drop offered his solution, "they will be brought before The Guild. Their part in the plan will be evaluated. Then solutions will be found and the healing process will be started. The standard answer."

She's looking at me. I should answer with the truth as I know it. "They will be rounded up, they will see the table, and most likely a firing squad for abduction of a Bachman. The Derecho will howl and they will be destroyed."

With the hope evident in her tone, "you know this to be true?"

I was there for others. Keeping as much of the bristle out of her tone, "the Derecho has dashed many to bits by exposing them and the depths of their monstrous deeds. There is fire, there is rain, and in *this* case? I can assure you it will be fire, and not the soothing rain which is used. Also, The Commander has a vested interest in your daughter. He is a far more likely candidate to rain a nightmare down upon these individuals as he has already ordered the Obliteration of a clutch of the attackers."

Snarling her reply, "the High Consul granted the Pardon of Review to the Blackout Bloc."

She is not the only one who rules over reality. Raising a finger she spoke the correction, "an attack vehicle from the Blackout Bloc was deployed to kill Jerome Hope. He evaded with assistance. They, the attack vehicle, were Obliterated by Order of The Commander." *Calm. Calm.* Taking a breath, "you wish for me to speak to the worry. The worry of them going free. The Darkest Shadow, The Commander, and The Questioners are all aware of Arlo and his scheme. The High Consul is on a Twelve Hour. If this is done before she returns? It will be as is willed."

Answering with a borderline helplessness Lemon offered his words, "I am not to implore you beyond a simple explanation of the terms. I am not forgetting the rules."

Calming she gestured for 'compassion felt,' "what is your professional opinion?"

Holding his hands up he gestured for 'helpless,' "as a member of The Guild, I am to state the options we can offer. As the Counselor who has heard no small amount of confessions from your daughter? She might not like the idea that what happened to her was forgivable on the basis that neither you, nor her, had a way to defend yourselves. We also do not know the condition she is in."

Reaffirming her stance, "if I hand this to Questioner Parsons?"

Moving his hands for 'truth' and 'compassion.' "I would not think less of you, or be concerned for you, beyond either regretting it later or not regretting it later but thinking that you should have." Stopping for a moment he finished his thought, "Social Order has a price to pay. They violated it to an extreme that was also unbalanced. I just hope that she is well. I would say nothing more than to keep track of yourself."

"Thank you Lemon-Drop."

Watching Reylai's careful movement as she stepped near her, she felt a clumsy emotional step looking into the woman's eyes. *She is a Bachman Mother. I feel smaller looking into her eyes.*

Looking directly at her opaque lenses, "may I see your face?"

Squeaking the word out in a moment of emotional surprise, "motive?"

"I would like to see the face of the person I am trusting with this."

She knows what she asks. Reaching behind her head she undid the clasps on her breathing mask. Holding the clasps tightly to keep her hands from shaking she unmasked herself.

Regarding her with a strange humor, "you're not what I was expecting."

Gesturing to her face with a free hand, "this is me."

Holding out the memory card to her, "I give this freely."

Taking the memory card she nodded once, "I will see this to those who will see this to the end."

Touching her hands to Eve's with a tone of gratitude, "*thank you.*"

Looking to her with his concern evident, "are you well Miss Parsons?"

Rolling her hand to work the words out, "I have been seen by so few, it is strange to be on display."

"I could only imagine."

Putting the card into her satchel, "I need to go."

Continuing as the Clinician, "was this hard for you?"

Responding out of reflex to the timbre, "very. I am not usually social."

"What of Hope and Benton?"

Benton. Weird to hear his family name. "York is York. Jerome is Jerome. They are afraid of me, but they still sit with me. They do not turn a blind eye, but they don't belabor it. They're very honest with me."

"Do they pursue you?"

Falling into routine she smiled, "they are very roughed up men. They are comfortable in our romantic friendship. It will be a shame to see it change, but I fear it will, as things do."

"Don't forget to keep your Speed-Dial handy."

"I will endeavor to remember." Taking her mask in hand she set to donning it. "I need to get back. Now is not the time for small talk."

Nodding twice, "Noted. I understand."

Returning to the moment Reylai appeared whelmed, "Noted."

Getting her mask back into place she offered something casual, "it is not that I do not appreciate being observed. I am just unused to this."

Seeing them smile through the lenses of her mask she was struck by the slight differences in the lighting and colors. *I wear this so much I forget it's not what reality looks like.*

Smiling to her Reylai gestured to the door, "good luck."

Nodding to both in turn Lemon-Drop prepared himself to leave, "be well"

Looking to them both Reylai seemed relieved, "a Blue Sky."

I need to go. "To both of you. All three items." Turning toward the door she set to making her exit.

Back to the fray.

4.7.0 - 18:59

Kunlow Estate – Hours Room

† Sasha Herb

Checking the plan one last time she felt the butterflies in her stomach as she followed Octavia Kunlow to the scheduled meeting. *I know Frank knows Steven better than anyone, I just hope this works as hoped.*

Following on the heels of Octavia she kept her eyes on Commander Bachman as they entered the Hours Room. Noting the positions of Hampton and O'Neil she kept her hands where they belonged.

Assuming the flanking position she felt the rising friendship with Octavia giving her a measure of steadfast conviction in the moment. *I made a friend today. Here's to hoping I get to keep her.*

Clearing his throat violently Steven gestured to the sitting form of Josh Kunlow, "he stands accused -"

Without raising her voice Octavia interrupted him, "I request Oversight."

Holding up three fingers to make his point, "I have three accused which point fingers, which means he qualifies for Sinking Ship. The testimony we have points to a dire situation. I am here to follow up on it."

Keeping her voice level, "I demand Oversight."

Raising his brows he laughed, "*you* demand Oversight? If you get your Oversight can I get a Second Look at whatever motivated my dear sister to spare you?"

I am going to get myself killed. Then again I can console myself with that once upon a time this would be considered noble. "The will of the High Consul in this is absolute unless overrode by the Council, or the existence of evidence you do not have. You cannot gain Second Look without a Council vote in this case."

Turning his head toward her with disdain, "Proxy Authority?"

I finally get to say this to his face. Firing off the words with a stern edge to her voice, "Tango Eclipse Nautilus."

Sighing with a taken aback resignation, "noted."

Pursing her lips for a moment Lady Kunlow raised her right index finger, "a question."

Tossing the word out with a borderline friendly timbre, "ask."

Keeping the stern edge of Authority to her words, "why did you seek the end of my

House?"

Firing back with a flare of anger with the reflected question, "why did you seek the end of mine?"

Gesturing to herself with a composed anger, "*I,* did not."

Still in the place of smoldering rage, "then I believe we understand why we are standing here trying to figure out what to do with Josh and his *unique* understanding of the situation. And not at physical odds with the other."

Adjusting her posture to a more defiant puff, "I don't want him harmed."

Gesturing gently for 'bargain' he frowned, "your stance doesn't make this easier. I will adjust mine if you adjust yours."

Shifting to a more relaxed stance he waited for Octavia to follow suit. Nodding once her defiant puff was replaced with a matching Diplomatic Stance he continued, "I need him. I need him to go to the table if he won't tell me what happened. What he knows."

Moving her hands for 'question' 'rage' and 'fire' before speaking her rebuttal, "he is loyal to those that his silence protects. You give him no assurances –"

Interrupting her, "what has he done to deserve an assurance?" Moving his hands for 'longest day' and 'tired heart' he sighed.

The Commander is oddly self-aware today.

Trying a different avenue Octavia lobbed her question, "is he not tied to you by marriage?"

Rust. That was the -

Replying flatly, "point of no consequence."

- wrong thing to say.

Losing the Diplomatic and gaining a flabbergasted air about her, "*no* consequence?"

"In regards to having an assurance -" raising a hand Steven pointed to Lady Kunlow's black string tied around her pinkie, "I refuse to lower myself further than *this*, in this shameful moment in my attempts to be diplomatic with you."

Placing her left hand over her right, "Noted."

Slumping with the weight of the world, "I know, I want to believe, that that he's going to tell me that he wanted to tell Miss Bachman. That he was afraid. That he had no choice he could see. But *I,* do *not,* have my *understanding,* of his plight. If he will not tell me? Then I am to assume that he is hiding things that he would rather perish than explain. *That,* doesn't bode well for my perceptions of him."

"I want assurances that he won't go above Level Two."

Stepping close to her he pitched his voice low, "I cannot give assurances based upon information I do not have."

Taking a step forward she edged past the accepted distance rules for diplomacy as her hand moved within hostile intentions distance of her holstered weapon, "do you seek to harm Lady Kunlow?"

Looking past him she spied Hampton and O'Neil laying their hands on their shock boxes. *Non-lethal takedown for me? What does he have -*

The bark from behind Steven jolted them all in shock, "stand down!"

Sevilan. Looking past Steven she spotted him leaning on a chair at the back of the room. In the quiet of the moment the almost silent footfalls of a half dozen Night Terrors echoed like whispers through the room as they entered from each doorway in matched sets.

Lacing his fingers together and placing them at 'resting' position on his chest Steven smiled to Sevilan, "which side of this are you on?"

Clipping the words out with the Voice of Command, "Moratorium on Pre-Inquiry Executions has been set."

With the casual tone of ordering lunch he fired back, "fine. What else?"

"She will let him go to the table, but it is to clear his name."

"Perfect. Level Four Authorized!"

"That will be up to the Questioner on duty."

Lowering his hands to his sides with a sigh and cluck of his tongue, "I don't see why I have to be the bad guy. He knew. He knew and did *nothing.* He could have helped save all those people! And what do we have? Forgiveness?" Putting his hands into his overcoat pockets with slow and deliberate motion, "burn him to ash now and save the Questioner the trouble."

"She would rather trouble them and do it right."

Clucking his tongue again, "I can see where I am not wanted. I will be taking my leave then. I have other leads to pursue." Nodding his salute to Sevilan, "take care Captain." Nodding at the returned nod, "a Blue Sky morning when it comes."

"A Blue Sky morning to you Commander."

Watching The Commander leave Sasha breathed a sigh of relief when O'Neil and Hampton went with him. *The two most likely to be loyal to him, the fact that they were reaching for shock boxes makes me wonder what he has planned for me.* Looking around the room as the Terrors continued to stand in their defensive formation, *so what happens now?*

4.7.1 - 19:06

Kunlow Estate – Hours Room

■Frank Sevilan

Checking his comm for the confirmation of The Commander's departure he set to it. *Now that the Commander has departed I can finish this in the proper fashion.* Crossing the room he stopped at Octavia Kunlow.

"Additionally I will be removing Cassia Kunlow from the premises."

Bristling at him Octavia seemed unhappy about the plan, "details?"

"Lady Kunlow, this house is not safe as truths are being sifted. Miss Bachman wishes her moved to a different venue to wait out the final act of this power play."

Calming down she smiled softly with a look of questioning realization, "Chuck?"

"Indeed."

Speaking up from his chair Josh croaked out his one word reply, "acceptable."

"Miss Bachman wishes for Josh to clear his name. To do this he will have to go to the table and tell the truth."

Frowning back at him Octavia seemed vexed, "if he is innocent he might suffer Innocent's Remorse."

"Miss Bachman is aware. It has to be this way as he does have accusers which have played Sinking Ship against him. Truths have to be sifted from the ash."

"Will the Level Four stand?"

"It really is the Questioner who has to decide that. It will start at One, *if* they go to the table, and it will go until the accusations are resolved."

Closing her eyes and giving a single nod, "I understand."

I hope for the if. "Thank you for understanding Lady Kunlow."

"I will go and tell Cassia to pack her bags. How long will she be gone?"

"Tell her to pack for at least three days. Also I will be borrowing Dagger Herb for the transport. She will be returned after we have moved Cassia Kunlow."

"Understood regarding Dagger Herb. When will Josh return to us?"

"That depends on the truths. When he is ready to return."

With a slightly befuddled candor muddling her tone, "why did this plan go the way it did?"

"Perception. You cited Protocol and stood up for your House. The Commander is pushing for answers. We will get him answers. He will appreciate this when he has calmed. I would like to get him to take time, to calm himself, but he is still needed, as it were, in the field."

"Understood." Following up, "I have one last question, in this moment."

I have time, "speak it."

"She is protecting Josh, my family, my position as a Consul. The Bachman Rule of Engagement is that the enemy sets the Rules. My father, these moments," gesturing to the empty air, "do you see where I am trying to go?"

Even those Rules state that the engagement is over. "You were found innocent of wrong doing. To that end, all of her interactions with you are governed by a new set of Rules. As you are not her enemy, Miss Bachman does as she chooses to defend you. You, and your family, are her fellows and Citizens."

Nodding with understanding, "I have more to learn about this."

Saluting her as crisply as he could, "you *will* be fine. I need to do my duty now."

"Understood." Taking two steps backwards she responded with a salute of her own. Turning on her right heel she made her way out of the Hours Room and back into the house proper.

Moving to the back of the room he approached Josh Kunlow, "the Night Terrors are taking you into custody to clear up the issue of your innocence of wrong doing. Will you go quietly?"

Sitting back he placed his empty palms facing upwards above each knee, "I will."

Patting him on the left shoulder, "good man."

"Is Chuck at the Main Estate?"

I hope he doesn't go anywhere, it's not a small drive to him. "The last time I checked he was at the Drenner Main Estate. We will be checking again."

"Understood." Taking on a solemn look of understanding he sighed, "how much trouble am I in?"

"Life and death Mister Kunlow. The truth will be known though. No matter how painful it gets? All they want is the truth. You may have to say things you don't want to, but you will. I wish you the best of strength to endure the table if you go to it."

"I understand. Thank you."

An honest moment of thanks from outside of those on the side I stand. Nice to hear. "Now I have to wait for your wife." Gesturing to the Night Terrors who had moved to just behind him, "you will be gone before she comes down."

"When will I see her again?"

"When this is over."

"I understand."

4.9.9 - 23:31

'The Hammer' Mobile Command Base - Journey's End

∩ Steven Bachman

Contemplating the short dead-end known as Journey's End, he felt a measure of dread looking at the tree clogged row. *There are far too many ways this could get someone hurt. If someone has readied a contingency? It will get ugly. I cannot wager anyone on a hunch.*

Rubbing his shoulder he sighed, *everything hurts.*

"Sir?"

Looking over to Hampton he smiled, "yes? Is the comm call ready?"

Nodding the affirmation, "the tablet has moved. We believe that she's awake."

Setting the moment into motion, "time to connect the call."

Connecting the call to his earpiece he adjusted his audio pickup. *Press the rusted button.*

Hearing the cautious voice he knew well enough, "hello?"

Keeping it simple, "Amaranth, it's Steven."

Replying quickly with a concern, "you sound tired."

Giving in to the confession, "it's been a *long* day."

Firing back with a listless tone, "I've just been sitting around."

Her training has kept her in one piece, maybe. "It's good to hear your sense of humor is still intact."

Huffing a few breaths her tone trembled, "I'm going to cry."

Better than I could have hoped. "If you need to? Do so. *However,* I have an update."

Perking up with interest, "what?"

Letting the humor in, "we're down the street. This street is a logistical nightmare. I have people I can call to start the process of getting you out of there."

Volunteering information, "I'm in a bedroom behind a security door."

"Good to understand our objective. We'll get into the domicile, find the door, and get it open."

Striking up the conversation, "how have you been Steven?"

Falling into the simplicity of the moment, "tired. How have you been?"

Losing some of her composure, "scared out of my mind. Arlo was not a nice man."

I'll kill him myself. "We have him."

"Noted."

"Dennis, among others, is looking for his cohorts. It's a race at this point to see who finds the most of them."

Firing back with a prideful snarl, "noted."

Moving to assure her, "this will be over soon."

"He said that Susan would come find me?"

"If that becomes the End Game Solution? I won't stand against it. I know that she does adore you. You would be safe with her. I will not be surprised if she's the one to open the door when we get it clear."

Speaking the Worry, "Arlo said I wouldn't be safe."

"You'll be as safe as any Bachman." Pondering that he let out a short chuckle, "I know, not the best example to use as of late."

"I would agree. Status and SitRep?"

She sounds like a member of this family. "It's been a terrible day. All things considered? I'm alive. What is *your* Status and SitRep?"

Listing off the checklist of items, "I have a bed, food, water, a tablet with Network access, and a Necessarium."

Not the worst list by far. "Noted."

"How long until I'm free?"

"I'll have people out here soon enough. They will clear this layer by layer."

"I can endure. I do not like this, but I will endure."

"Thank you."

"Noted." Inhaling sharply she fired off the question with a rushed push, "did you once light a man on fire?"

Who told? Speaking with a grimly spirited humor, "what prompts the question? I *will* answer, but first, what is the prompt?"

Broaching the words with a jittering air of knowing the answer, "Arlo told me that you had lit a man on fire, once upon a time. He did not, cross the line, as he did not want you to light him on fire."

My past gets me a win in my present. Outcome Bias is a lovely feeling. "Noted. Happy to hear that was the prompt and not something else. As for your answer?" Taking a breath he answered clearly, "yes."

Forging into the answer, "once upon a time, there was a man and a woman, and the psychiatric evaluation of them came back as failure to embrace treatment. They bonded over their mutual frustrations with the system that wanted them to be better humans. They were denied a Marriage License, and with that the denial of a Reproductive Endorsement."

Piping up with a courage, "continue."

Remind her of the Safe Word, "I remind you, that *cease,* will end the story."

Gushing softly, "thank you."

"Noted. They would seek a male for her eggs. They looked outward from Bliss to the Freelands. A scout from a passing tribe would come near Bliss looking to become one of the Mice. The couple were aware of the program, and they intercepted him. They took him home and let him in. From there, the story takes a darker turn."

Piping up with less courage, "continue."

"This part I only know from post incident interviews. Once the fertilization had occurred, the *husband,* if you will, became jealous of the Freelander. This soured things. In an attempt to establish dominance? He turned the *wife* against the man. As she needed the man she had and not the one who had provided the child, she stayed loyal to her future."

Firing off a conclusive statement, "as without him being quiet her deeds would come to light."

She picked correctly. "Correct. She was quickly turned against the man whom was now a threat to her freedom. The mistreatments and madness within the house would grow. I was in Bliss at the time visiting with Captain Augusta. Her sister," *don't do it,* "and the boys wanted to see her, it was a family moment so I went to see The Farmer's Wife. She told me that one of the Mice had reported another one missing. It was looked in to and we found the evidence of him going with them."

Whispering the admission, "you have set a dark stage for a finale."

Putting the theatrics into it, "we went, myself and The Good Sons. The woman came out, and pleaded for mercy, the man? He came out covered in biofuel. He was threatening to light himself aflame. Call the Guild! He called out as a demand. However, his flare in his hand? He had not removed the safety seal. It was one of the flares which have quite a stout safety, so he was nowhere near flammable. While bargaining with him, the Good Sons reappeared with the Mouse in tow. He looked, as one does when one is stripped of humanity."

Whispering the request, "please finish."

Finishing with the dramatics of a story told around a campfire, "I removed my lighter from my pocket, and I tossed it on the man. I denied his opportunity. The Guild was called, and they came for the woman and the Mouse."

Sounding mildly confused, "why did you spare the woman?"

Coming down from the theatrics with a renewed fatigue, "I did not, *spare,* her. She was not doused in biofuel. I could not light her aflame as she was not primed for such a thing. She was also visibly pregnant at this point. The Freelander was already alleged to be the father. The life of the child meant I no longer had Dominion over that moment. I did as I have lived, I turned them over to those for whom Dominion was their right."

"Thank you."

"Noted. I did as you asked and nothing more."

"What am I going to tell my friends?"

Too easy. "You are speaking with the Commander of Cloak and Dagger, we will find you a story if you require one."

Speaking the request, "I require one."

Firing back with the ease of the request, "I'll get those I can trust on it."

"Thank you."

"They will send the draft of the plan to the tablet you have in your hands. Take it with you when you are rescued."

"Noted. Also, could you -" fumbling with her words she quieted.

The girl she looks after, "I will make sure that someone checks on Afghan."

"Noted." Following quickly, "thank you."

"Much like the Coupons I sent you, I will aid you with the service of others. I could not give you presents as she did, but I can continue to aid you."

"I know."

Leaning against the MCB for support, "I was only trying to help, still am."

Speaking with a small voice, "I appreciated it. Still do."

Looking down the street into the dark, "we'll get you out of there."

Offering the notion up, "Arlo, is not well. I don't believe he will do well with the Questioners. They should know to be ready for that."

She still has her wits. "I will pass that along."

Hearing the silence pass she filled it again with her quiet voice, "I found time to mourn dad."

As have I. "Good."

"Do you support me for me?"

Speak to the Worry. "Yes. I didn't do it to spite him. You are my sister. Blood of my blood. Raised within the halls of power and the foot of the throne. You wanted to be an ally of the Citizen, an aid to the City, and were fast tracking to The Guild. I had to do all I could to cultivate that."

With the self-contempt evident, "what if I'm not worth the effort?"

The Poisonous Thoughts have set into her. "The effort was given freely, without regret."

"You didn't try to discredit the question."

I took my classes too. "It's from your heart, an exploratory question, I've answered a few of those in my time. You don't discredit those. You answer those. I head off the price of the effort with the idea it was given freely."

"Thank you."

"Noted."

"No matter how much of a mistake I make, or how much I could fail, or squander all that I was given -?"

Pushing himself off of the MCB he roared to life with the Voice of the Leader, "I gave all I gave freely. It was *not* a bargain. There was no Pact Pledged."

"Thank you." Sniffling loudly she giggled quickly, "I will see Susan soon?"

Intoning the words as a Pact Pledged, "*tomorrow.* Sleep. Eat. Rest. She will be with you tomorrow."

Sniffling again, "I can endure."

Pushing the conviction into his words, "the fighting is over. The Pyramid is putting out the blaze."

Pressing her question in return, "can I stay with her?"

The Honor Guard would be near you then. "I don't see why not."

"Safe Housing is a bit far –"

Doing his best impression of the timbre their father would use when he had a happy outcome to share in a decisive manner, "she's moving to The Blackstone. She mentioned it in Council Session. You will be in the halls of the family House. She will reclaim the sacrosanct halls. You can dwell there if you stay by her side."

Squeaking with excitement, "I don't know how I am going to get back to sleep."

Taking inventory of his body he used the only offer he had left, "I will Pact that if you Pledge to sleep at some point? I will Pledge to sleep tonight. In my own bed no less."

"I will Pact this Pledge to sleep for the sake of sleeping well. When I find calm again, I'll drift off knowing she's going to be here on the day for being open to new ideas."

"She will come find you. The Pact is Pledged."

"The Pact is Pledged. I should go though."

Close with strength and candor, "the Sys-Admin will make sure that you are watched over. I am devastated that the Grain Silo could not protect you."

Whispering the face saving words for him, "our enemies were dedicated and had the intent."

Traditions must be honored. "They were."

"Be well?"

"You as well. A Blue Sky to you."

"To you as well."

Closing the connection he leaned back and sighed.

Offering the words with his arm Hampton spoke first, "I regret we were not there with you at Bliss."

I don't think I share that regret. "I had thought it was going to be a routine visit. I had no idea."

Looking on with a contemplation O'Neil seemed pensive, "you didn't tell her the truth."

No reason to. "That I was livid with rage? That the woman and Mouse are still alive? That the child was carried to birth? That Bonnie is dead?"

"All of the above."

"I wanted to limit her trauma."

Seconding the notion with a camaraderie Hampton was smiling with the words, "it's the right call."

"How are those three in Bliss?"

Moving with Hampton toward the door of the MCB, "the Mouse went home. They couldn't force him to stay in a world he wanted no part of. The mother, she's touch and go. The daughter is doing well enough. No signs of anything. We have diagnosis protocols for illness of the mind as young as *six. Six.* So far she's made it to three without a hitch though."

"Good."

"They're keeping men around who have experience in being fathers to provide her mind with the idea she's in a stable environment. Keeping her socialized with other children." Laughing in self defense he sighed when the ill humor finished, "the terrible burden they face as masters of case studies, human experimentation, and treatment which collide into having to do the best they can with what they have. I do not envy them."

"Good luck and good toil to them."

"Indeed."

Looking up at the lights coming from down the lane, "our helpers have arrived."

"Once you have everything delegated and structured? We're taking you back to your bed. You Pledged, we will see this through."

Standing next to the door of the MCB he sighed at the pain. *Rusted scrap I want a new body.*

Feeling Hampton's touch on his shoulder he looked into a face of concern. Meeting his gaze he seemed to be appraising him. Turning away after the moment had passed Hampton tossed his suggestion to O'Neil, "if you can take care of getting him home? I'll stay here. If you come back you come back. However, I can handle this."

Nodding with an agreement to the idea, "you good?"

"I'm good."

My boys have made their choices. "Sounds good. Let's get this done."

4.8.0 - 20:02

Drenner Estate – South Deck

◧Chuck Drenner

Setting his drink down on the flat top of the tall deck railing, the sigh came as an unbidden exhalation of his tension. *I can remember walking out of Maggie's room like it was yesterday. Looking at the bluest eyes I had ever seen. The haunt I saw that day, I could see in the Council footage.*

But I am not one of her one-hundred and forty-nine.

I wonder if Amanda feels like she still is?

Her people have been as open with sharing the burdens as she has been closed off. Contemplating the memories dredged up with the sight of the barn he grimaced. *I am reminded of something I passed on. And how much I still care about Cassia. A woman for whom I cannot do a single rusted thing. The fence around her as been built and I don't have the tools to get over it.*

Taking out his comm he looked over the messages, *request denied. I filed a request to get over the barricade at the Kunlow Estate and was denied. I have not seen that message in some time.*

Putting his comm away his eyes fell upon the bard. Smiling at the memories he dove into them, *the hustle and bustle of youth. Learning the trade of what it means to care for the day to day. Of making something from labor to never forget that those who toil have it tough too.*

And kisses exchanged behind the barn, or inside in the dark corners.

Moving away from the odyssey he turned back to the tablet he had brought out with him. Touching the screen he brought it back to life with the window of the traffic footage still waiting for him. *This whole thing could have killed her.*

She went as fast as they said she did. She was called and she moved. Wallman spoke such amazing words for her, I don't think I've ever heard him work this hard in my lifetime. I know that not everything he's said is the full truth, but it has been comforting. She pushed Wallman to give his hand at Spin-Doctor for her. Rubbing his eyes with his free hand he felt the creeping ache in his eyes as the tension continued to throb with his thoughts.

It was nice to hear a nicer version of what was going on. If only I could live in those moments and chains of events. I would hope that the Citizens who listened felt that things were not as bad as they could have been. The goal of the Media, to provide News and Hope. To blunt the truth so it does not stab the person who hears it after the fact.

I hope that Wendy listens and trusts that he's telling the truth.

Shaking his head, *Susan is already at least as good as her father at this. No line that can't be crossed if no one gets hurt. People so hurt that they just smile, nod, and accept it when she offers a way out. To be just honest enough that she can lay the cards on the table.* Taking another sip he thought of a new angle on the idea, *at least the world is holding up. At least we're not in a Civil War.*

At least -

Looking into his drink, *stomach it, digest it, and move on. Maggie told me I would have more than a few meals I wouldn't want to eat if I walked this road. I understand now.*

The roads were dry though. We had nothing to fear.

Not even the green she wore. The safety measures that are being waived, she's showing us why she is the Derecho. I wonder if Maggie had lived longer, if Susan would have been my friend and not just my colleague. If I would be on the short list of people she would open up to.

And now I'm just being selfish because I'm caught on the opposite side of the Clearance wall and I want to know what happened to Cassia.

Closing his eyes he chided himself, *I would ask about Josh.*

I would.

Clenching his glass gently, *if I had just said yes. She wouldn't have woke up this morning in the middle of a nightmare. Her comm frozen, her house under lockdown, and the knowledge that someone was filling out an execution form for her.*

And then it would be taken back, like a slight you didn't mean to let slip, and the question of 'can we still be friends?'

Thinking over the footage from the Council Chamber, *she didn't let anyone question her. She took control and she kept things going the way she wanted. They didn't get to say goodbye to Thomas, as he was already gone. To have the authority because of conflict to just sweep in and disappear a Consul.*

Calling up the related files to the removal of Thomas he shook his head softly, *not that anyone has asked for him. Except his wife.*

I wonder what she was told?

Only way to find out would be to ask. Or ask Dagger Herb. Being next to Octavia she might know why his daughter did not ask for him.

She plays her friends like chess pieces because that's the game. Speaking quietly to himself, "because that's how this works right? There is no line that can't be crossed for the good of The Rim. I bet, Amanda is going to call Susan tomorrow and find out what the next step of the dance is. Thomas broke the deal and now she's going to take control over everything and we're going to be left just wishing we had a choice of how this is going to end."

Feeling the sickened anger welling up, "I don't even."

Looking to the sky, "I want to be happy that Cassia is alive but I have no promises about what's going on."

Mea culpa for my weakness. Closing his eyes he held his cup with both hands, "and with my spirit, my body, you are with me, I will not fear."

Standing in the quiet he focused on his breathing. *Each day I struggle with the list of things you ask of me. Each day I do my best to become a better man in your light. Thank you.*

Opening his eyes he took a long drink from his glass, *I will be patient.*

Setting his glass on the rail he sighed as his tablet chimed. Turning his head he gazed at the text notification. *Vehicle inbound, without a beacon.* Activating the application on his tablet which was tied to the perimeter sensors he blinked when he confirmed that it was a heavy vehicle without a beacon. *A vehicle without a beacon? Why is a vehicle without an active identification beacon coming this way?*

Setting his tablet down he set toward the stairs off of the front deck. Hitting the bottom of the stairs he moved into the parking area proper to gain a solid look at the moving edifice as it turned toward the parking area. Getting a good look at it he startled in shock. *That's an Anklyo. Why is there a Cloak and Dagger heavy armored vehicle in our front parking?*

Getting closer he slowed as it stopped without finding a place. Moving to the side where he knew the sliding door was he was rewarded with it opening. Hearing the slight groan of the armor plated door falling into place he witnessed the lone Cloak emerging. *What in the world? What is Susan trying to pull now?* Walking just a bit closer he stopped at a distance that he guessed was about three meters from the Cloak.

The soft male voice, which seemed more than a touch older, came from inside the helmet and reached his ears clearly, "greetings Chuck Drenner."

That isn't Operations Voice. "What is the meaning of this?"

Without losing a decibel the voice seemed somber, "The Rim is going through a tough time right now, and sometimes when people are going through tough times they need a friend, so I have brought someone to her friend."

Turning away from him the Cloak held out his hand and helped a woman out of the Anklyo.

Turning his attention to the woman holding the slightly bulging duffel bag he blinked in shock. Feeling the anger and sick in him fading he blinked again at the sad face looking back at him, "Cassia?"

Squinting in the dim light she smiled with a confused lilt to her voice, "Chuckles?"

"It's me!" Looking to the Cloak getting back into the Anklyo, "you can't go yet. Where's your Operations Orders? Which one are you?"

Keeping a neutral tone, the reply was still somber, "if you missed my name, that isn't my fault. As for operations paperwork? You don't have the Clearance to see it."

"Wait! I have Clearance for -"

Answering firmly and without humor, "I do not answer to you Chuck Drenner. Your Clearance is not enough to question this. You lack the Epsilon Code." Sliding the door closed briskly the figure disappeared from his sight.

Watching in helpless wonder as the Anklyo started turning around he turned his attention back to Cassia, "what happened?"

Stepping closer she threw caution to the wind and dropped the duffel. Moving in quickly she put her arms around him. "Chuckles! It was horrible! All I did this morning was cry. Josh told me that the family had been committed to something and it didn't work out. And then he told me what had happened." Burying her face in his shoulder, "they wanted to kill Susan! Then Steven was going to kill me! And then I'm not dead, just under suspicion of being in league with the coup. My comm hasn't worked all day, I couldn't log into the Network, I felt so alone. Josh was strangely distant all day, he wouldn't talk to me and I didn't know why. There's been a Dagger squad in the house all day and they've kept Lady Kunlow under strict watch. And then," appearing to be on the verge of a hysterical fit, "the Commander himself came to the house to get Josh. The Night Terrors moved him instead."

Trying to not lose his own nerves in the wake of what he was hearing, "how did you get in that Anklyo?"

"When the Night Terrors showed up Cloak Sevilan overrode the Commander when it came to Josh. Then they took Josh away and came to find me. Cloak Sevilan would borrow Dagger Herb from Octavia and they put me in that, Anklyo?" Looking back to see that the Anklyo was already gone, "they had a tablet and said they had an update to the operation." Taking a breath, "I'm out of order. I was also told to pack for no less than three days and be quick about it. So I packed my duffel and they led me out of there. From there I was brought all the way from New Hope to here. I didn't get to see Josh before they took him away."

Get the information before it's lost. "Did you see anything else that we could know?"

"Two things. One is that they picked their destination via something they appeared to be tracking. They didn't say where we were going, they just turned on the dash tablet and it had a blinking star. And two? The tablet, I did see something on it. It was a strange little logo of a cartoon cat, and I think it was dancing."

Susan's High Consul seal, had to have been. "Those orders came from the High Consul. It's her personal seal that comes into play when she gives a direct order from the top of the chain of command."

Looking to him with a hint of wonder behind the perplexed question, "how do you know that?"

Adjusting his hold on her to something more diplomatic he took refuge in the factual answers, "Amanda. When Susan took the Throne, she showed me the Protocol Agreement Susan had signed. It had a dancing cat on it. That cat has been the emblem that was next to all the things she has signed since then. I asked her about it and all she would say is that Susan is as Susan is, and as the High Consul if her personal logo is a dancing cartoon cat? Then that is how it is."

Sliding out of his arms she took his hands without breaking the connection of touch, "Susan wanted me here then?"

Susan wanted me to see she was unharmed. An offering for me? I don't even know. "Apparently."

Squeezing his hands, "Cloak Sevilan just said I needed to be with a friend –"

This makes all the sense in the world. Rushing to reassure her, "I'm not surprised."

Switching her grip on his hands to something more needful, "why is that?"

Chess moves on chess moves and the lightness in my chest makes me not want to care about what my mind is screaming at me. I am going to just enjoy this because I would rather laugh than cry. "It's a long story. What matters is that you're here, with Chuckles, and Susan wanted you out of the way of the Inquiry."

Letting go of his hands she walked over to her duffel and picked it up, "so if I'm here, that means she thinks I'm innocent?"

It means she knows you didn't do it. I don't know how but I know she knows that she didn't have a part in it. I wish I could tell her that I can only base this on intuition from having communicated with her so many times. "I don't think it's a question of innocence, it's a question of her sparing you either way. She's risking faith in you."

Rounding on him with a swing of the duffel, "even after everything? I haven't seen her in person since the last time she came over to see Amanda."

I should confess on her behalf. "She's seen you since then."

"When?"

I hope she smiles, I want to see her smile at this. "The wedding."

Appearing to be quite confused but smiling from ear to ear, "she was at the wedding?"

Nodding, *that's the confused smile I love for no good reason.* "I saw her in the back, doing her best to not be noticed. She left after the kiss and didn't come to the reception."

"I never knew." Stepping close to him, "Chuck? Why were you out here today? You don't live here."

Trying to keep his tone conversational, "since you married Josh I've been picking up my duties for the family and I took over your duties on an administrative level. When I received word this morning I drove out here, established an impromptu base of operations, and watched the fallout of today unfold. I was here to help Amanda, I gave her someone to lean on today."

"I'm glad someone was here for her." Glancing to him with a thoughtful smile, "and as for the extra work? Mea culpa."

Giving a playfully dismissive gesture, "you married for love, what greater goal is there in this life? And? Noted."

"I don't know. And is that Amanda on the deck?"

Looking back, "it is. Let's go."

Leading Cassia onto the deck he heard Amanda start in before he reached the top of the stairs, "Chuck? Where did you get off to? Your drink is still here on the rail."

Pitching his voice to an approximation of cavalier humor, "I was welcoming a house guest for the weekend."

Turning to face them Amanda's jaw dropped, "*Cassia?*"

Lifting her hand for a small wave and wonderstruck greeting, "hi Auntie."

Looking over the rail toward the parking area, "how did you get here?"

Butting in, "a pair from Cloak and Dagger in an Anklyo with its beacon turned off just dropped her off. They had orders from a certain dancing cat. A dancing cat who is sparing her the ugliest part of the fallout."

Her words ringing with the timbre of concern, "and Josh?"

Keep it professional. "He's still in the thick of it. Odds are none of the Kunlow family will face a *physical* inquiry into what happened without a really good reason given. However I would hazard he's going to be sweating bullets if he knew even a hint of what happened. As for Cassia? With the Anklyo lacking a beacon and with the Kunlows on lockdown? No one except for Cloak Sevilan, Dagger Herb, the High Consul, and the people there and here this weekend will know where she is."

Glancing between the two of them, "what strikes me as *odd,* is that she didn't tell me that she was sending Cassia this way."

With a sheepish grin Cassia nudged Chuck with her duffel, "from what I could guess the dancing cat ordered them to take me to Chuckles. He just happened to be out here."

"I would have to agree given her description of how they picked the destination. A pair from Cloak and Dagger wouldn't need directions to this estate. They were looking for me."

Speaking with an enigmatically friendly tone, "her powers of observation were always spot on."

Not dwelling on that thought. Rushing to change the subject, "I think we should get Cassia inside, let her unpack, and then perhaps a toast to good faith?"

Piping up with relief Cassia welcomed the idea, "I could use a drink."

Nodding once Amanda echoed the sentiment, "me too."

Ushering both ladies back into the house his mind turned back to Susan, *the moment I think I have some idea of who I'm dealing with when it comes to you? You change the nature of your power play. The morphing logic chains in your mind are truly terrifying to behold first hand. Perhaps this is nothing more than a power play. Or perhaps this is you, giving me, something I would never ask for.*

No telling.

4.8.5 - 20:22

Safe Housing - Den

⁖⁖..Susan Bachman

Sitting at her desk, with a years old scrap book, she endeavored to get a hold of her thoughts. *To think Sasha doesn't know this exists. I wanted her to be authentic, and never told her that those around us took pictures for me to keep in this book. The story of us, told in pictures, to make certain I could never forget.*

Tilting her head up her eyes caught the sight of the current flowchart of meaning behind the moments. *The SitRep Chart, still too many blanks on it for my liking.*

Too many notions in my own mind I don't know.

Reaching into a desk drawer she produced a small pad of paper and a pen. Setting to drawing a chart of what was on her mind she hit on a concept fairly quickly. *If I don't mourn them I may forget them. If I mourn them too much I won't want to let them go. If I don't mourn them I could forget the thing I could see done for each to honor their sacrifices.*

Setting the pad down with the pen on it she frowned at the page for a moment. *At least I think I know what I'm thinking.* Returning her attention the scrapbook she was thankful for the artifacts to keep her memories in order.

Turning the page of the scrapbook she dwelled a moment in the memory the picture presented. Checking the faces for anyone that she might have lost she felt a sickened glimmer of recognition. *Did I lose someone who was at my party?* Checking the casualty list search returns she felt the emotional hit at the name. *Mrs. Cross.*

She played a cello. They killed a woman who played a cello and was good with a comm unit. Gripping the pen and reclaiming the pad she set into a new diagram.

If I have them lined up and shot, I lose my humanity.

If I stay this course of not killing them out of hand, pausing to dwell on the thoughts, *I can see steps taken so that this does not happen again.*

Honor The Loss. Hanging her head gently the concept from William's Diatribes haunted the inside of her mind. *The Loss is the only constant in life. Happiness is fleeting, life is a one time Endeavor, the world cannot be experienced twice, thus if you Honor The Loss you can find your way through.* Setting the pad and paper down she felt a resigned sort of defeat.

I need something more than this.

Opening the heavy bottom left drawer of the desk she retrieved the hand written copy of the Diatribes. Turning to the bookmarked page she took a deep breath, *guide me William.*

Laying the notebook down she looked to the desk-lamp illuminated words.

Do not lament The Loss, it did not ask to happen. Inventory the Loss. Find every aspect of the pain. Clean the wound to ensure you do not seal a single microbe of poison within it.

Turning the page of the scrapbook she found the picture she was looking for. Sasha, and herself, posed near Mrs. Cross and her cello. *She wanted proof to show her husband where she had been. She helped arrange the music for the dancers.*

Jotting the note down to herself, *I will Honor the Loss by having her name etched into the Phare Rouge when it is complete.*

She laughed at the idea that I would accept the words of the past that society has facets which cannot be removed. Thus, they must be given a place to be safe. The Phare Rouge would join The Private Notions as a place for adults to be adults about adult things.

Turning her attention to a picture she was in she felt the self-doubt of how tired she looked. *Father could see my dedication and need for approval manifesting. He told me to honor myself in the most outrageous way I could tolerate giving myself.* Turning to the next picture of the two of them posed with the dancers from that evening. *They were a constellation of beauty in motion. Pole dancing, to combine the athletic with the artistic beauty of the human form.*

The look on Sasha's face was priceless. Snickering at the memories, *she teased me for throwing such a party but being unable to invite Patrick.* Thinking back on the night, *we went into the Necessarium together and I told her how much the moment meant in confidence.*

The teasing stopped.

Making a note she frowned, *I hope Mr. Cross understands, one day, that if I cannot find which bullet killed his wife that I cannot condemn all of the Bloc to death even if I would care to.*

Mass executions are not the answer.

They're a question, but not the answer.

Making another note, *I need to appoint a Cultural Advisor for the Phare. Give them the building plans, the contact list, the budget, and watch someone have the will to aid me in washing the blood off of our culture so we might entertain another place of peace.*

Hearing her comm beep pulled her from the task. *Two messages.* Bracing herself to not smile, she opened the first one and found herself smiling despite herself. *Dagger Sasha Herb strikes again with a picture of her smiling face, Objective Complete, and a thinking of you.* Opening the second she found a message from Sevilan, *your wishes have been made real. I serve to see the beauty of another tomorrow knowing you'll be the one painting the Blue Sky.* Saving the picture from Sasha she deleted both messages with a sigh. *Cassia has been brought to Chuck and placed in his care. Frank, he always knows how to touch a person's heart. He never fails to remind me why he serves. His daughter would draw him Blue Sky pictures to put on the refrigerator. Now I paint him Blue Sky realities.*

And now here we are. Checking the timer she groaned, *twelve hours is just not enough time to get everything in order and do everything else I need to do. At least I won't be bothered unless it's an emergency when that timer hits zero, because I should be sleeping.*

Opening her eyes the green blinking light on her comm caught her attention. Picking it up she checked to see who was calling. *An emergency so great it overrides my twelve hours? Or is it because Chuck is there?*

Pushing the accept call button she put her comm to her ear, "Consul Drenner, what has you calling me before the clock hits zero?"

Speaking the words softly the tone was every bit the loving Marraine, "I wanted to thank you for tonight."

Is it needed to thank me? "I had nowhere else to put her."

Sliding the edge of humor into the loving timbre, "going to play gruff with me?"

I didn't say noted. "I'm not playing. I had to keep her safe. You and Chuck are shoulder to shoulder as Drenners do. I figured you could take turns keeping her well while the other worked."

Asking the question with a familial warmth, "then it was for me too then?"

I am too tired to cozy up to this moment. Trying to keep her tone matter of fact, "Cassia is one of the last of the core family left. She is where she should be in a moment of crisis."

Nudging at her verbally with a tone of humor and introspection, "you also fit that criteria."

Sighing she moved to close the thought, "I just wanted her kept safe."

Still sounding humored, "deflections?"

Sighing again she rubbed her face with her free hand, "long day."

Broaching the question with a pragmatism in her tone, "what are you going to do with Thomas now that you have him?"

"From what I understand?" Feeling the decided lack of sadness she let the words out with the quiet finality of truth, "he dies tomorrow."

Replying with a distracted yet somber tone, "I, understand."

I don't know what I heard in that. "Do you want him spared?"

Snapping back with a sharp-edged irate grief, "how could you ask me that?"

Firing back with her confusion, "you sounded –"

Interrupting her with the concern far more evident, "- it's about *you*, not him. These are going to be your first ordered executions as the High Consul. I had hoped it would be more than a fortnight before you would be saying the words."

I can agree with that. "I had hoped for the same thing."

Tsk'ing before the words, "you can't spare him regardless."

Contemplating a world without Thomas Kunlow she felt the relief at the idea, "I don't think I want to."

Sitting in silence a conclusion reached her active thoughts, *I suspect she also called regarding Wallman's broadcasts.*

Waiting in the silence she took a breath and committed the words, "say it. Say the thing you don't want to say."

Opening up with a sad candor, "you compromised Wallman."

Known him for years, never asked, or prompted him to do anything other than consider which order he presented his facts in. "I know I did. He did so willingly. He lied to give the people a happier idea of what was going on."

"He doesn't normally lie, does he?"

Sighing she admitted the reality, "that's why people love him, he doesn't lie to them."

"A question," laughing for a moment before the sound of a quiet drink, "why are we all working together? That wasn't *quite* the meeting I thought I was at."

Easy answer. "That would be insurance against The Council acting against me. The Council cannot act against me now without the people being angered as Wallman told them the truth he did." Taking a moment to sigh, "as it is accepted that you, the Council, The Director, and The Commander tell Noble Lies, among other lies. Wallman is on his personal channel. Presenting facts of the matter with minimal conjecture and doing nothing more than seeking truth. He has more credibility than we do."

Taking another sip, "I understand."

I forgot to ask. "Is Cassia better than expected?"

Sighing her timbre was one of hope, "she is as well as could be expected. She is draped on Chuck with the shameless need for safety I suspected I would see from her. He sits with her, in his arms, with the quiet calm of a man who loves someone that needs him for something so simple."

Perhaps it was not my kindest decision, but I have to make unkind decisions. "I understand."

Turning the question on her with a return of the timbre of the Marraine, "are you well?"

Intoning the correction, "I am *functional.*"

With a light lilt of teasing, "taking on his turn of the phrase?"

Faltering for a moment internally she uttered the truth, "it's apt."

After the sound of another long sip, "noted. Also? I saw the green you wore, I know your mother left you advice, so I am going to leave it at that."

Small favors. "Unless I have need. Thank you."

The smile evident in her reply, "unless, of course. Noted." Sighing she continued with a moment of reflection and contrast, "your battle plans aren't as orderly as his."

He had more practice, but I won't whine. "I know."

Continuing the reflections, "you remind me of, Maggie. Easier to just say her name than say my sister, or your mother, we both knew her as closely as we could. You remind me of her when you spin something from nothing. She could spin whole realities out of observed ideas. She was very kind to Tim in her dreams of him."

Too bad she was wrong about him. "Oh?"

"I can hear the strain in your voice."

Trying to restrain the flare of indignation, "it was *never enough* with Tim. He wanted things his way with a stubborn determination that was beyond comprehension."

Responding with a gentle defense, "he wasn't always like that."

Offering the acceptance of the idea, "my father wasn't always the person I lost. Concept holds."

Breathing for a moment her words carried the weight of the past, "I don't know if you're looking to share empathy or contempt."

Suffering under the emotional truth she emoted the feeling with a reckless honestly, "*both!* I shared the power plant! I built him a monument to Bailey! It wasn't *enough*. She died saving the day, she died following her convictions, and I made sure she was remembered. But it wasn't *enough*. I still have the flannel shirt she gave me, I haven't worn it since her death, it sits in my closet as proof of life that I had an Aunt named Bailey who drove trucks and liked the open road." Taking a breath, "and at your estate is the not so little girl that came from Bailey. Proof of life lived."

Acknowledging the shared sadness, "we mourn our dead."

Touching the edge of the Diatribes with a meandering heart, "we mourn and in mourning we look over those we have mourned and find the ways things connect. I send you Cassia, you hold her close and make sure you don't have to mourn her too."

Placing a paused cadence emphasis on each word, "I don't want to mourn you either."

I may as well ask her. "Is peace wrong?"

Waiting in silence she heard the sound of Amanda refilling her glass from a bottle. *Only the best poisons for the highest of the Rank and File.*

Hearing the bottle touch desk her words returned with a strain, "no Susan. No. Asmodai asked me the same thing. He was mourning his dead. I told him it was better to seek peace with life than seek it through mass graves. History can sit and rust. People, a Nation, could rise that could survive its neighbors without killing them. I don't believe I would be the person to see it come to pass. However, I told him I had faith in his ability to help it become a reality."

Which meeting was this? "When was this?"

"The Saturday after your mother went to sleep. He brought me before the Fire Maiden and asked me if peace was wrong."

He did not write that one down where I could see. "What happened?"

Speaking softly with a lost conviction, "we embraced. I told him that *if* he needed me that I would go with him."

The Choice was revisited. "What happened after that?"

Rolling the words with a pleased sadness, "he told me that Micah needed me more.

That he would find another."

Why would she face The Choice again? "Why did you offer?"

"I loved him. Always had."

That is the truth as I know it to be. "Noted."

Wandering away from the thought, "I think Cassia will always love Chuck, it won't die. She'll go home to Josh when this is over though."

Rushing to reassure her, "I told them to use care with Josh. He knows quite a bit and I want him able to give details, not just tears."

Asking with the Voice of the Consul, "you have Final Authorization?"

Pledging the words with her conviction, "I won't kill Josh."

With an audible sigh of relief, "noted."

I don't know if I can handle more, "is there more?"

Taking a deep breath she sighed, "I don't believe so. I believe we have done enough good and ill to the other at this juncture."

Trying to be helpful, "you should get back to them. Give her a different pair of arms to calm the pain. Get her something from your blender to soothe her."

"I will." After a second of pause, "sleep well and be well."

"Sleep well and be well Amanda."

Pushing the disconnect button she laid the comm down on her desk and stared at the rapidly diminishing clock. "The morning will come and the testimony of Thomas Kunlow will have been measured and I will know my next move."

Touching the Diatribes again she looked over the well worn pages, *you led a bloody crusade against a people that you would not accept. My Citizens rose up against me, they killed Mrs. Cross, but even you would want to know what they would do had they won. Or if they could be like us again, to Square the Circle once more.*

The people you fought refused to change to what we considered normal.

Can things be normal again?

Wandering down the meandering thoughts of William and the reflections provoked by his conversational writing style. *You warned your men about the Thrill of the Massacre. They only lost control the one time, and it was that unit which was sacrificed on the Victory of Broken Gate. You left behind the Edicts of Veterans Rights.*

Our Nation lost you on the Beach of Glass. You had secured Fort Glass, and with it the Coastal Garden. You chased them to their boats and sent them North to Port Refuge.

You wrote down your advice, confessions, observations, and thoughts as one having a conversation with a friend. When I read from your works, we are connected even though you are dead. You are an angry friend who reminds me I have not found the center of self to start my own chronicles of self. I spend all of my spare time reading those who came before and applying it. I should find the day when I will put pen to paper and fearlessly tell my children, their children, and those who come after the truth.

Just as you did.

Moving her hands away from the tome she sighed. Bracing herself to rise from her chair, "I should just go to bed. Tomorrow is another day and I have to get up to make coffee. I need to ask Yuri if he would like to learn how to use the machine tomorrow." Getting up she groaned softly in protest, "I have too much to do."

4.9.0 - 21:00

Mobile News Center – Rally Point 'Xan'

► Winifred Yeoman

We are back to where we started. I don't know if Wallman has more Carry-On but I'm out of Carry-On. I want to be done with today.

Dorn, Singleton, and Mendoza are off shift already to go home and sleep. I have City Militia coming to finish this baton pass.

Hearing her comm beep she pulled it out and took a gander at the latest updates. *Priority Zero for The Matron.* Stopping short the emotional vortex opened up inside of her mind. *Am I still The Matron?*

Reflecting on the updates on her comm she felt her perception of her world slipping through her fingertips. *I am lost. How can I be a Matron to a group that isn't a union like it used to be?* Putting her comm down she met the troubled face of Harold Wallman. Speaking with a hoarse softness, "I beg for mercy from this day. The doctors, they tell me that the shift was a loss. If Sinclair does not return? None will have survived as Guard."

Speaking the soft acknowledgment of loss, "Final Stand is called that for a reason."

Losing control of her tone as the words tumbled out, "my boys, my beautiful, ugly, boys. They haven't told her." Trying to get her tone in check, "they *have not* told her."

Moving over to the seat next to her his tone was as soothing as ever, "The Guild needs her stronger than she would be if she knew they were gone."

Caving in under the weight of the sadness, "they're dead Wallman," hanging her head she laced her fingertips together on the back of her skull. "They were *so brave*. I watched, I listened, I did my best to sort through the wreckage of what Northland told me to look for. They did everything I could have hoped they could do given the odds. I have *two* left that *might* be able to come back to the fold. Northland, I don't think he's going to get to come back. Sinclair, rust, Harold his arm is an unknown. I can't imagine what his heart looks like."

Sitting down next to her he touched her shoulder gently, "I have to say what I must say. I am not someone who understands your microcosm, or the weight of what you are feeling, so I *must,* do nothing more than speak the words of Compassion, Encouragement, and Resolve. I can only hope you forgive me."

Lowering her hands to her lap she sighed, "I can forgive you."

Imploring her to see his agreement, "your men *were* brave. I watched it too. They saved lives with their bravery."

The ache in her back heralding the emotional constriction of the pain, "I need to mourn."

Laying a hand on her hands he spoke his directive, "go. See Northland."

Is that fair? "I can't lay this on him."

Shaking his head he spoke with a theatrical firmness and hurried cadence, "go to him, not to lay it on him. Go to sit in his small light which is trying to illuminate the dark as he does what he can from that bed of his. The day is gone, the night is upon us. Go sit with his light and let him know you have not forgotten him."

Protesting in the wake of the flush of weakness, "he'll know I'm in mourning."

Squeezing her hands, "if he's *half* as good as what I have been told of him? He already knows that his fellows are dead, and those that are fallen and they will need new lives are as they are. His brothers are dead. If you are correct that he can't make it back? You can open up to him emotionally without risking having to work with him."

Asking the question that formed in her emotional haze, "and if he talks me into staying on?"

With a greater gravitas, "then he talks you into the thing you want. In the end? There can always be another to shoulder the burden. I will pass, you will pass, we all pass on. Humans have passed the burden to the next humans for as long as we have been humans. If you want to carry the standard, to bear the colors? Then you will do so. There is no taking that from you. Only you can choose to surrender it."

Finding her resolve in the emotional couch cushions of her heart, "I will go see him."

"He could probably use the company. If I understand the attitude of those who are close to our High Consul, a measure of selflessness comes to mind. I am sure he's on the bottom of the list of those who seek the company of company."

"Most likely. He even has a few people he could be seen by, that he likes, and almost enjoys opening up to. But he would say something about someone else needing them more." Turning her gaze toward him, "will you be well?"

"I still have the Militia to protect me. The Commander is ready to dispatch a work crew to give me a Hadrian Wall if the Threat Index doesn't come down. When Dorn, Singleton, and Mendoza get some rest they will be back on rotations. Also? I am not un-armed. I have Headline News with me."

Tilting her head to the side to gaze upon Wallman's fully automatic rifle with high capacity magazine, *may you never have to star in your own news piece.* "Good enough. I go to Northland's light."

Squeezing her hands one more time he stood and stepped clear of her, "fair enough."

Regarding the man with a flare of adoration, "be well Wallman. A Blue Sky tomor-

S M Gilbert

row morning to you."

"A Blue Sky to greet you Matron."

Getting up with a nod she made her brisk exit, *Northland is a night owl, he'll be awake.*

4.9.5 - 22:27

Kunlow Estate – Lair of the Guardian

† Sasha Herb

Standing before the door to Octavia's bedroom she paused at the sign above the door. *Lair of the Guardian. This is new.*

Perhaps this bag of Take-Away which Spratt said she would eat will help keep the lines of communication open, and include this. I know I enjoyed what we ordered from this shop.

Was nice to spend time with dad too.

Back to work.

Tapping on the door twice she turned the knob and let herself into the room. Moving in at a casual pace she spotted Octavia moving over to her with a hurried pace.

"Did you?" Moving in quickly she snagged the bag with a bright smile, "you *did.* Sandor told me you were bringing me something to eat I would like." Moving toward her desk she appeared to be in bright spirits.

Is this more than I could hope for? "You are well?"

Sitting down with a sigh her hands fell into her lap. Looking to her with a fainter smile, "I am trying to accept the present, forgive the past, and move toward the future."

Thumbing toward the door behind her, "you are a Guardian?"

Unpacking a pair of chopsticks from a desk drawer she nodded, "I am not a Ruler, I am a Guardian. I prefer the term over the use of Servant."

Sitting down on her campaign chair, "you sound like someone I know."

Steepling her hands horizontally over the meal with her chopsticks across both hands she spoke with a humble conviction, "I am kept humble by acknowledging reality. I choose the Ideal of Suzerain as it sets the tone that I do not believe that I know a persons life, or role, better than they do. That those who do the tasks can tell me how they know best. I, like a certain someone, am a rudder of which society is aided by. I am added onto that with the Pledged Idea that I am a Guardian. If this piece of reality has been given to me by the fall of my father? Then I will guard it well."

Nodding she mulled over the notion as Octavia set into her meal with an earnest energy. *I did good.* "Noted."

Sitting in the quiet she noticed the piano music on low which was covering the sound of Octavia's chewing. "The music, it sounds very happy."

Turning away from her meal she nodded, "correct. It is a piece known as the Goldberg Variations. It is a saccharine work of G major. I listen to it, for the specific idea of ignoring it. I had been informed you were returning with food. I set it to play before you arrived to make sure you would not hear me chew."

Another careful planner. "Noted."

Playing with her food for a moment she appeared contemplative, "I do mourn him. He was there for me. He even agreed that I could move to New Hope to be closer to him."

Her father then. "I would listen."

"I will get to the past and the future in a moment. I would like to ask a question about earlier. I saw your hand move, is there something in this I am not seeing?"

She is a Consul, I should not lie. "Affirmative."

Asking the question with care, "were you afraid for me?"

I will not lie. "The Commander, he wrestles with the Bachman Rage. He has lost his father. His sister was nearly killed. His brother was put into the hospital. After all that? What does he have to vent his Rage on? I do not know. I did not want him to choose you."

Without losing the care, "if he had chosen you instead?"

Continuing with only the facts, "I would have done as ordered."

"Which was?"

"Protect you."

Contemplating her for a moment. "I don't hear bravery."

Just the best foot forward, "what you hear is me knowing just how unreasonable these moments get. The reflection on just how tenuous of a thread reality is stitched back together with."

Asking with a greater measure of curiosity, "is he a Strong Man?"

I'm going to sound like a love-struck schoolgirl with the truth of my esteem for him. "The Commander? From what I know of him? Nothing has defeated him. I was informed, with proof, that at the battle for Guthrie he hefted one of our Ballistic Shields and lead the charge. From there they moved a Sundering House-Cleaver rocket vehicle into position to get the right angle on the helipad."

Gesturing her inquiry with the chopsticks, "who was at Guthrie that he wanted that badly?"

It's not as if she lacks the Clearance to know. "Ridolfi. The man who laid the Governess of Sunrise Cove to rest, among other things. The monster who haunts the dark."

Picking up another bite, "does he lead the men well?"

"He *inspires* them. No matter how vitriolic he gets, they follow because he shows them the way. His Wolves are fed with the dead bodies of monsters."

"Does he inspire you?"

Thinking the question over, "the night that Miss Bachman stormed into C and D Command, he was sick. He was at the hospital in the grips of the flu. When I returned from danger? I was met not with his anger, but a relief. He was *so happy* to see we were not dead. There were no words of admonishment. He took our intel, he gave us Rations, he mourned our fallen, and then he mobilized a Reply for the people we had met. He saw a group in the dark, he judged them, and with fire and fury he cleansed them."

Answering calmly, "noted."

Continuing her elucidation, "the men follow him because he does what they agree is *right*. I am a fail-safe against his Rage not because he is a bad man, but because he cannot be allowed to lose control."

"Do you hate him?"

"No." Feeling the helpless feeling of the question and answer prod her tired mind, "what I hate is the idea that the Bachman has something that can beat them. I want him to be the best man he can be, for the sake of Cloak and Dagger. I get angry with him because he shows me a weakness I don't want to see."

"Noted."

Changing the subject with a casual deflection, "how's the food?"

Making a noise of approval she swallowed a sip of water to clear her mouth, "very good."

I assume she has an answer, I should practice the question. "What does it mean to be a Guardian?"

Picking her way slowly through the pieces of her answer, "to protect Reality. Culture, people, way of life, the day to day. It's all a piece of our Reality. I have a new document, it is a glorious collection of notions. The Three Nines and Companion Precepts. The Nine Noble Virtues, The Nine Betters, The Nine Charges, and a collection of pieces to that puzzle. I want to rise from the Ash with those of my House who survived this. I have been following this project as those behind it locked the pieces together from that which was found in the Data Archives."

She's working on perfecting that answer, "new territory of your heart then?"

Nodding with a poise to the gesture, "correct. This House will learn the way together. If I am to be trusted with this? I will have something worth trusting to guide me."

I need to be careful or I'll end up in her fan club, "again, you sound like someone I know."

Pointing to her softly with the chopsticks, "I have an unrelated question. You would agree that you are romantically in love with Susan, yes?"

Smiling emphatically, "yes."

Turning back toward her meal with the question, "have you ever felt romantically inclined toward a man?"

I have seen a few inclined toward me, but I never felt what I was told it meant to feel it back. Not the way that Susan makes me feel. "No. I can't say that I have. It's why I refer to myself as a Seven. The notion that I would need to call the Conlangers for the correct term for?" Running her fingers through her short hair, "I present in a more masculine fashion. I don't wear skirts. I don't wear dresses. The only items I use on my face and body are care products. I sit with men and feel a kinship as a soldier. We all buy into the Soldier's Kinship. Then, I sit with Susan."

"What happens then?"

Smiling with the notion, "I feel softer. I don't feel like a soldier. I lay down my Dauer, hang up the guns, and with her? I feel softer. I feel as the Protector, the Defender, and when she touches me? I feel vulnerable. I feel cherished."

"No man has given you that?"

"No man. I don't feel the attraction to men like that. I don't see men other than the extended family of brothers, cousins, uncles, and the like. The men see me as a compliment to them on the battlefield. I do not serve to one up them, or to outshine them, or to believe I will. They see that kinship of someone who would *choose* to do what we do. I have not felt the spark, much less *warmth* from my fellows."

"Noted."

Rubbing her hands together, "I am thankful to still be alive."

Replying with a loud whisper, "as am I."

Anything. Grasping at a notion she spun the words together and shared it with a recklessness befitting friendship, "I wish, even though you said it was a blessing, I wish I could let Susan inside of myself and enjoy it."

"You would not enjoy it if you did let her in?"

Sad truth. "No. I have felt *broken,* for so many years. She, I feel far less broken when I'm with her. She gives me this dream I had, that is real with her, that I don't have to be able to pleasure her to please her."

"What do you get, have, that sort of thing?" Turning back to her food with cheeks fully flushed, "if you would share it?"

The glory of being emotionally shy. "The Guild, they told me they counsel some who are repulsed by the idea of it. I, couldn't imagine. Only because to live with people who can't understand neutral from a personal perspective, I couldn't imagine them trying to understand *repulsed.* I have been neutral my whole life. I had, learned to enjoy the freedom from the emotions and things I didn't understand. I could reach down, find peace, and stimulate the body to earnest passion and release it to find a measure of joy. A place of sound, color, but not faces. Not people. Not penetration or licking or what –" touching her cheek she laughed, "I'm blushing."

Testing her own cheek with the back of her hand Octavia's tone spoke of acknowledgement, "you are."

"I have witnessed the act, seen it up close. Smelled the after scene of it. And whenever *people* enter the moment? Regardless of what it is? My brain just shuts down. It cannot pursue the thoughts. It refuses to bond with the idea. She makes me feel less broken. I can lay there, and she's comfortable. Soft to the touch in all the best places. No jutting bones, no harder knobs, and she never asks me for a passionate sheet soaking."

Pointing her chopsticks at her, "as I have said, love is *most* undignified when you put it like that."

Turning her attention to her face, "you're still smiling."

Appearing to be in high spirits, "I am. I am smiling because I know the things that you do not know, and it *is* most undignified. I would never say it like that, but I understand. I am quite happy to hear that the two of you have each other. It's a good thing to know something good exists in the world."

"Noted."

"She's never pawed at you though?"

"No. She's cooler than many on the idea."

Firing back quickly with a tone of piqued interest, "she is?"

"It's not much of a secret for those that know Susan. Susan doesn't act on lust and need like some do. She has her toys, she has her fantasies, and she has the need to be just and good with the power she has to Validate others." Taking a moment of pause she gestured for 'juxtaposition,' "the other side is someone I know who treats the risks of being dead with the affirmations of life whenever she gets home from a Mission." Sighing she laughed, "I have a fellow Dagger that I share my domicile with. She, oh, by the Blue Sky does she have needs. I could *not* imagine needing that much physical upkeep."

Setting her chopsticks down, "I miss it already."

I tread on to sacrosanct ground. "Kincaid was one for it?"

"Correct. He would," giggling for a moment she looked to her with a flushed face of her own, "we had an agreement. It was as ugly as it was beautiful. He was enamored with me, he made it clear, so we came to an agreement."

Sitting in the moment of wonder as the last layers between propriety and candor peeled away, "which was?"

"I play piano, and if while I was practicing I would shift to a specific song? He would be free to make his intent known if he was feeling so enchanted. I would give him the option, if he accepted? He had until the end of the song to see if he could get me to stop playing before the song ended. I set the question, he would answer with his level of need, or absence of it. I, just didn't, want to put it so bluntly to him with words."

"He couldn't ask you?"

Fidgeting with her chopsticks she rolled her eyes, "I found any which way he could ask, to be undignified, to the point of my embarrassment. Also, I have, usually, a set schedule for my day. The system I devised was for *both* of us. He knew that the time we had would not be rushed, and that I was open to the idea. I would proclaim myself to be the feminine conquest up for grabs, and then he could swoop in and conquer me if he was so inclined. We would both win."

Acknowledge the loss. "You have my condolences."

Exhaling sharply with a bitter edge to the words, "I need a new subject."

"Then lead us somewhere else."

Returning to a sweeter tone, "our first Companions?"

"Deal."

Vocalizing the nostalgia with a good humor, "I remember her fondly. She felt like K Orbit with lips flavored with citrus balm."

Was not expecting that. "Quite the kisser?"

Rolling her eyes in an undignified fashion, "I learned that I had far more to learn from those kisses."

Volunteering the nostalgia of her own, "I was the cuddling type with mine. She was my boon companion. She smelled of the temple. Incense of unique blends and her hands smelled of sodium bicarbonate."

Nodding to her with a smile, "she sounds memorable."

"She was," coming down from the ethereal nature of the feelings with the grounded follow-up, "I would hope she still is."

Offering the question as a gentle suggestion, "if you did not desire her -?"

Feeling a renewal of the flush to her cheeks, "I never leant her a helping hand. Although, I was her headrest a time or two. I could still feel the joy of our friendship. I just never wanted to, *help.* I still get the emotional affirmation of being cared about."

Reflecting with a saddened lilt to her words, "noted. I only lent a helping hand with my *second* boon companion. Sometimes I look back and wish I had been a better friend to her."

"How did you meet yours? Either?"

Giggling for a moment Octavia seemed to be blushing, "the first? She was the daughter of the nanny my mother had brought into the house because of my brothers. We were just starting something like that when I would leave. Kids games. We were not old enough for anything more than just kisses and games of make believe." Pausing for a moment, "the second? A young girl of equal age, who at the time was also learning the piano."

"I sense a story?"

Pushing the counter-inquiry, "tell me how you met yours?"

Simple enough facts. "She was the sister, of the boy, who was the boon companion, of my second eldest brother."

"I sense a story."

The things we never speak of. "You do."

"How about we set a date to swap them? I will throw in the story of my *second* boon companion to fill in the time to make an equal exchange."

Her smile makes me braver. "When?"

"I'll ask you after you no longer dwell in this house."

Easy deal to make. "I agree to your terms."

"Good."

Although I could ask this, "do you miss her? Your boon companion that is. Either of them."

"I do. My first? I look into her life and make sure things turned out right for her. She grew up, got married, has a child with another on the way. I sent them a wedding present and a baby shower present. We shared hundreds of kisses and the childish dreams of growing up together and taking on the world together. We may have had to become adults, but that didn't mean I couldn't thank her for the beautiful memories. I felt it should mean something, I acted on what I believe. Do you feel the same?"

"I do. I parted ways with mine, her, after I joined Cloak and Dagger. Not because it was a requirement, but because we were just so different in occupation it was easier to wish her well."

Setting to packing up the empty Take-Away containers, "I can imagine being in Cloak and Dagger gets in the way of dating."

Shaking her head she smiled, "it doesn't *have* to. It's just what it means in the end. If you fall in love, and wish to make a family, you have to leave."

Walking past her with the bag of trash, "do they explain that rule from the inside?"

"They do. The main reason is that children should not be deprived parents. Cloak and Dagger is a hazardous job. You have a child? You get moved off the front."

Pausing she appeared puzzled before setting to the task of placing her bag out in the hall. Closing the door she rounded on her with a smooth pivot, "how is it Captain Turner serves then?"

The dread question. "She signed a waiver, which was cosigned by her husband." Feeling her mouth go dry she pulled out her canteen and took a long sip. Lowering her canteen she tried to keep her face neutral, "as a union they authorized her right to die in battle."

Taking a step closer, "if he had not signed?"

Keeping the explanation to the facts as she understood them, "Couples Counseling would have followed. The Guild would have had to look into it. Paige is a special case of a youth with a parent who serves in a violent profession, while the other serves in a dangerous profession."

Taking a place next to her she leaned her shoulders against the wall, "if I ask about Forks, would I find a story?"

Feeling the dread settling around her she shook her head softly, "I can't. I would rather talk about most anything else."

Holding her left hand out, palm inward, her tone was one of care, "I don't understand directly, so I retract the question."

Raising her right hand she placed the back of her hand to Octavia's offered hand, "thank you."

Moving her hand in a gentle circle, "noted."

Lowering her hand she closed her canteen. *She is a gentle soul.* "I'm scheduled to be relieved by an exterior guard with Captain Turner on deck after you have me vacate so you can sleep in peace."

Without moving from the spot she lowered her hand in turn, "why is Susan having it be only you, Cloak Sevilan, or Captain Turner who would sit in this room?"

The best excuse of an answer, "you'd have to ask her. I just do what I'm told."

Pressing her inquiry again, "do you know why this means so much to her?"

Deflecting the notion again, "she is as she is. You'd have to ask her."

Quieting down she shifted the inquiry, "do you support her decisions in this?"

It is not as if I enjoy the thought of firing squads to solve problems. "Whatever it takes to make sure this isn't like the last time innocent blood was part of the equation."

"Do I sense a terrible story?"

Turning her head she bent her neck at an odd angle to look at her, "with your new found Clearance?" Pausing as Octavia moved into her field of view, "when it finalizes? Look up 'Guthrie Incident' in the Consul section of the Network. There's another side and angle to that story that isn't common knowledge."

Slowing down to a cadence bordering on trepidation, "is that all I get to know?"

Taking a breath she steadied her nerves, "the report will clarify that we only saved a handful in a battle of vengeance and ideology. Not an apples to apples comparison but close enough for emotional resonance. For now. I don't technically have the Clearance to discuss what I know on that one. I have Proxy Clearance. Also, use the Epsilon code of Tranq when prompted to leverage your Consul level Clearance to open the details."

Holding her hand out again with fingertips splayed, "I see. Then those words you spoke in the Hours Room?"

Reaching her hand up she touched fingertips with her, "High Consul Proxy. It wasn't an Epsilon Code though. It was just a statement that even if she is not here, I am, and I can speak for her."

Regarding her with a calm detachment, "she trusts you that much?"

Cringing slightly she clucked her tongue to signal a self annoyance, "that's a bit of a secret you should know about. As you know I said what I said. I am *technically* authorized to speak with *her* voice in an issue. If I use that improperly? I can get myself in *serious* trouble."

Sliding her fingers between and assuming a firm grip on her hand, "Miss Bachman has loaned you her voice. It must be something to be that close to her." Settling into the moment with a markedly relaxed body language she smiled wistfully at her, "to think after everything you told me that she's Pastel."

Reflecting on the idea the musing slipped out, "I hope that Yuri likes Pastels."

Pursing her lips as a smile she spoke the gossip, "she wore green for him."

Smiling brightly, "I know!"

Appraising her with a mild confusion, "you sound excited."

Relieved.

Contemplating their enmeshed hands she met Octavia eye to eye, "do you wish to sit?"

Flushing she nodded, "your lap, and arms, would be a safe space for me. I do not wish to fear you. I am not one for standing apart from others."

Nodding she brought Octavia into her lap and settled her in as one would a child. Feeling Octavia slide from the outside lap side-saddle to the full lap side-saddle she swapped the bracing arm. *She's no small factor of smaller than Susan.*

One hundred and sixty centimeters in her socked feet from the looks of her. It's good that it's me and not Susan doing this. I could imagine that gossip, the High Consul having a fling with a Consul in the wake of what happened.

Not impossible. Diagnostic and Upkeep touch gone into the realms of the extreme.

Broaching the question with a careful timbre, "you are unvexed by my presence?"

Taking inventory of her feelings, *I do not believe I am.* "There is nothing immoral about this. Neither of us is a man, or woman, looking to erode defenses and kiss away tears."

Smiling in agreement, "this is true as far as I know." Snickering she leaned against her, "your uniform is very tough."

She has such nice hair. A long and dark cascade. "It is. The exterior is made to survive as much as possible. The inner liner and garments are softer."

"Textiles aside? As to my observation, you sound excited for Miss Bachman?"

Too easy an answer. "That's an easy answer of just being honest with myself. I wouldn't say it's compersion, as I don't know if the idea and feelings will be the same after witnessing the reality, but I can hope for it."

"Noted."

I hear the sniffle. "Have you mourned?"

Squeaking the word, "no."

Mourning cannot be done alone. At least one must hold another as the mourn.

Clutching Sasha's uniform with her left hand, Octavia asked her question with a poorly composed bravery, "have *you* mourned?"

Taking stock of the question she found her answer. "No. I was horrified of what I saw, ran away, and resolved to deal with it later."

"It, it can be later."

Tilting her head to get a look at her she noted the pair of handkerchiefs. "You first, I will follow when you have made the journey."

"Noted."

Assuming the sheltering arms pose she closed her eyes as the grief, held back, was given free reign. *One foot in front of the other foot, until you can walk no further. Then rest.*

It is time to rest.

Wincing as her quiet keening began she drew the parallel, *The Derecho and The Guardian share something soon enough.*

Dead fathers.

Counting the blessing of Frank in her life she felt the stab of empathy of the place of being emotionally orphaned. Contemplating the sobbing Consul to be in her lap, she closed her eyes as her own tears became too much to see through.

She's on her own train ride of the soul. A journey to a new place, a new life, and I can only hope she finds a new constellation to be a part of when she gets there.

4.9.9 - 23:01

New Hope General - Observation Ward - Room 1x07

►Winifred Yeoman

Opening the door to Northland's room she felt her emotionally timid state fade as she committed to the deed. Closing the door behind her she stepped further into the room to take in the sight of Edward, sitting up and working at a lap desk, with a welcoming smile brightening the color which had returned to his earthen face.

The handful of women in our support staff who would love a mug of your coffee colored love might surprise you Northland. Now is not the time to distract from the moment though. At least I know that there are more options for you ahead.

"Status and SitRep Edward?"

Looking up with the grin he tilted his head to the side after a moment, "you called me Edward."

Edward is what passes for your Civilian name. "I did."

Watching the smile shrink until it was a more thoughtful look. His words came out at only a slightly slower tempo than expected, "you know two things. The fate of our shift, and the confirmation I am not coming back to you."

You're still you. "Correct."

Gesturing to the chair next to the bed, "you are welcome to sit."

Nodding with a solemn air she moved to the offered chair, "I wanted to see you."

Brightening with a sudden humor, "I wanted to be seen, or I would not have told you to come visit."

He knows something I have not been told? "Continue?"

Working through the words with the same almost normative cadence, "I can speak at a slow conversational pace already. My math skills are not what they used to be. I am thankful I am not on a Horizon Rifle Duo. I wouldn't be able to do the math anymore."

Did the doctors tell him? "Brain damage?"

Nodding with a shrug, "could be. I know my brain needs to heal. I already have a waiver regarding my fate as it is pending my Full Recovery."

No need to rush. "Good."

Moving his camera over to the edge of the desk he called up a picture. Setting it down where she could see it clearly, "Sunny Day stopped by. She was kind to me. She told me such nice things I had to shoo her away."

I wonder. "Motive?"

"That energy, is needed on those who have less energy left within them. I feel a strange peace today. I'm working, I'm finding out how I will cope with the broken cogs in my gearbox, but I don't feel the screaming screech of grinding pieces. Maybe it's emotional shock and I'll break down later?"

Puzzling it out she found words, "we can hope not."

Smiling again, "we can!"

Time to lay it out, as many cards as I can bring myself to be honest about, "Edward, what do I do about the Guard?"

Firing back with the simple statement, "find more hopefuls."

"Planned on it."

Assuming a solemn air about him, "take the combat recorder audio, play the meaning of Final Stand. Don't let them take the Oath until they hear it."

We already do that with the Night of Lost Hope. "Is that before or *after* we play them the audio from Lost Hope?"

Scratching at his chin for a moment he snapped his fingers. Pointing to her he smiled with the revelation, "play Lost Hope when they start training with Miss Bachman. Help them understand what it means to lose a Bachman." Losing the smile, "I could not fathom the pain they must have felt at Asmodai's side."

Intoning the Order of the Last Line, "Protect this Bachman with your life, he's the last one we have."

"The same Order has been given before in our history. It was a heavy weight they carried. They must not see Miss Bachman as anything other than Miss Bachman as they train. Once they believe themselves to be ready to take the Oath? That would be the time to play the Final Stand."

"Last chance to change their minds."

Nodding with a deadpan humor to his tone, "or else someone else won't give you a choice about leaving." Blinking a few times he snapped his fingers again, "I need to tell you!"

He is slower, but he's still thinking deeply. Encouraging him, "tell me what?"

Moving his tablet into place he showed her a set of reports, "the helicopter! Both of them, to be exact. They were *not* compromised. It is correct to state neither were present when it was needed, *however,* the events around them being loaned out, then sent in for service? There is no evidence of preplanned malevolence."

Good to know. "Data Trail?"

"Came from the New Hope Crisis Coordinator's office. The Bachman Williwaw was loaned out to aid them, when it was done with the missions it was sent in for service and maintenance. Unless the people behind this used weather control to cause the flooding and a need for rescue? Then a Blitz Storm can take that blame."

"That explains the Williwaw, what about the Mistral?"

Producing the report on his tablet, "Medical Emergency from the night before. Miss Bachman had loaned it out for them to move a sick child to a specialist. It had not been returned as it ended up in Respite and was being used to aid them after a boating accident."

Leave it to Miss Bachman to be everywhere else at once. "To be of aid, but not be of aid."

"I have sent condolence cards. Support is working with the pilots and those involved to make sure no one gets rusted up over this."

"Good."

Setting the tablet down he turned his attention back to her, "what were we discussing again?"

Straight to the Heart of it. "What becomes of you and me."

Shrugging with a glib humor, "I have already been offered a post within our Support Staff. I do not know if I'll take it. I'm still finding myself in this. I am no longer good with math. However, I still have the ability to plan. I also have a calculator now I keep with me."

"Sound."

"As for you? Will you stay as the Matron?"

Speaking the sad confession, "I don't know what I would do if I wasn't doing this."

Moving his attention through the data on his desk he tapped an item, "I know she does not know, about our Status and SitRep, but that authorization came from Doctor Monroe though."

Diplomacy first. "Doctor Monroe is Doctor Monroe."

Musing to the open air, "Asmodai always liked him."

New data still? "He did?"

Speaking slowly through the recollection, "he once remarked to me that Doctor Monroe tried, he tried so hard. He used to be closer to the Bachman family. He was Mind Keeper once upon a time."

He used to help keep track of the mental health of George, Isaac, and Asmodai directly. "I know his history. I just didn't know Asmodai still held him in esteem."

"You overhear things sometimes. I overheard Asmodai caring about something the good Doctor said in the wake of the Forks Incident."

The thing we never ask about. "Which was?"

"To calm down about trying to keep Susan and Sasha apart. It was from that moment that Asmodai gave Susan the Final Word on the subject. He never brought it up again. He would ask about Sasha, certainly, but he *stopped* saying things that could be seen as *un*supportive. It was a good day."

The joke of 'un' even now. Returning to the moment, *learn something new everyday that you can learn.* "I knew that things had changed, I just didn't hear the tidbit that Doctor Monroe had encouraged it."

"He did. I'm going to hold my tongue and not tell Susan the Status and SitRep unless asked."

"Speaking of things to tell Susan, Miss Bachman," *stay the course,* "I want to stay on as Matron."

Meeting her gaze with an aura of soul searching about him, "you will not give up on this, us, or the future with your place in it?"

Marshaling her resolve in the light of the passion in his eyes, "I'll keep going. One foot in front of the other foot."

Folding his hands together he did his best bow toward her, "Stay Level and Aspire to a Higher."

Licking her lips she broached the question with less courage, "can I stay here, by your side, for a few?"

Gesturing toward the door, "will you go home after?"

Lowering her head she sighed, "I can't face that empty box."

Warbling his tongue quickly to get her to look up he smiled and spoke with encouragement, "get the nurse to get you a Watch-Cot. Pull up some floor-space on the other side of the bed. I'll be quiet and maybe even sleep if you do."

Civilian or not, he's still Northland. Performing the salute of the Honor Guard, "I'll take it."

Saluting her in return, "thank you Matron."

"Thank you Northland."

For a moment, things are as they could be.

Turning his head toward the window, "Winnie?"

What's he looking at, "yeah?"

Turning back to her his smile carried a deep sadness, "I know it's not quite the first, but, Happy Beltane."

Nothing else for it. "I'll get the tea, and we can tell our fallen brothers to step through the Veil and go to their just rewards."

Mourning on Beltane, what a rusted mess. But I have Northland to bear the burden with me.

Speaking with conviction, "I am not dead Winnie, I can still be of use. I will get the recorder ready, in the event we are moved by the passion of the day."

"Noted. I will get the cot, set up my place next to you, get the tea, and we will do this."

"Noted."

STANDING IN THE LIGHT

Sunday May 1st, 2242

5.0.0 - 00:42

Cloak and Dagger HQ - Questioner's Wing - Kitchen

ΔEve Parsons

Pacing the floor with an irritated contempt Questioner Jonas growled out the words, "we are going to die."

Following him with her eyes she grimaced, "I don't plan on dying here."

From his countertop perch Zack offered his agreement, "I would also enjoy getting out of this alive." Looking into his mug he sighed with the follow-up, "meanwhile neither Questioners Chart or Fava are getting out of this."

I missed something while I was out. "They are not?"

Scowling with a deeper irritation Jonas' shoulders fell, "they infracted today, *hard*."

Nodding Zack appeared guilty, "I called the Guild. They were both removed at gunpoint escort."

What broke them? "We have been working round the clock. Stress?"

Fidgeting with irritation in his tone Zack fired back, "at what? We're not meant to feel anything more than *boredom*." Taking off his glasses he set to cleaning them again, "I'm fraying. The empathy, sympathy, this rusted switch is a nightmare to cope with. Chart was dealing with Ardent Kunlow, the man who brokered all of this. He lost his temper and used the electrical prod at a high enough setting it would daunt a much tougher creature."

That's not healthy. "And Fava?"

"One of the persons that Dennis brought to us, she was there when Arlo took Amaranth. Fava, he couldn't handle it. Once upon a time he had tried to light his sister on fire, in her bed, and he wrestled with the grief of knowing what he had done. To attempt to mangle someone who was defenseless. He looked upon someone who reminded him of his crime, whom would take a girl and set her into a different blaze. He snapped and set to attack the reflection of his own deeds."

I am thankful I only tortured animals. Catching the thought she hung her head with a sigh, *I am not well.*

Gesturing to the door Jonas asked softly, "do you want me to handle Mister Kunlow?" Clarifying, "the other other other one. Josh."

Shaking his head Zack pushed out the order, "don't take him to the chamber.

They're all being cleaned. We'll work together. We'll get him to talk without having to take him in into the chamber."

Snapping at him Jonas' anger showed clearly, "he knew."

Nodding sagely Zack affirmed the idea, "he did."

Frothing spittle with his words, "he knew and did *nothing*?"

Dropping his voice low and cold Zack pushed back verbally, "do you hear your own voice?"

Stopping with a look of horror he stepped back and clutched at himself, "why did she do this to us?"

Volunteering the idea that gave her strength to fall asleep at night, "to give us a chance to get out of this alive. Questioners don't get out alive."

Turning to her Jonas spoke softly, "you know this for a fact?"

Turning to face him she grimaced, "I do."

Putting his glasses back on Zack sounded calmer, "she's correct though."

Keeping her voice firm, "I want to get out alive. I want to have a life past these moments."

Asking with a biting curiosity, "for you or for one of those two you care for?"

Putting an icy bite to her words, "I don't know. I have already walked down *that* road. What it would be like to escape this, choose one, and then lose the person I picked as a life preserver to escape this with. I do not know if I would survive *that*."

Settling down Jonas' grief showed through, "we are running on borrowed time?"

Setting the terms on the table, "we have to find something that makes sense to the self to escape. The very thing we remind people to focus on, who they are, and why their words matter. They have the advantage that they know what that is. We just have the survival instinct."

Sitting down at the table Jonas sighed, "at least we still have that."

Folding his hands and looking to them Zack's resignation was clear, "I have salads. I know how to make sauces. I have a recipe book of things that are *mine*. If I fall? Don't let that book get lost."

Looking to him Jonas signaled for 'brother,' "if I do not fall first? I Pact this Pledge."

My turn, "if both of you should fall, but I remain, I will endeavor to see the recipe book saved. I Pact this Pledge."

Nodding Zack gestured to her, "what is your anchor?"

Shrugging softly, "you know it."

Shaking his head he pressed the question, "what is your anchor? Speak it for yourself, in your own words, facing this."

Laying her right palm flat on the table she ran her fingertips through her hair with her other hand. "They, inspired *romance* within my heart. The emotional bravery to fearlessly look past Ludus and into Pragma, to blend them, temper them with the Ten Offerings of Love, and to remember that each day is another chance to show that love."

"Even with all you have done?"

I worry for them for that reason. "Even then."

Grinning with an ill humor Jonas pointed at her, "they are strange men."

Agreeing wholeheartedly she smiled, "they are! I scare each one differently." Gesturing to Jonas, "I believe this is your turn."

Taking a moment Jonas drummed his fingertips on the table, "I have nothing which I managed to cultivate other than this restless feeling."

Offering the words as a consolation, "perhaps she will have an answer with that in mind."

Sitting back in his chair Jonas sighed, "she will, of that I have no doubt. If I told her? She would spin me a half dozen choices and send me to be advised in how to try them all." Hearing his humor fall away in the face of truth, "I am a man of contemptible character, heinous deeds, and macabre spirit. I just want to live."

Offering his words at low volume Zack's timbre was hopeful, "then prove it by getting Josh Kunlow to talk without having to hurt him."

Looking to the ceiling he sighed, "the sick irony of not being able to touch the very work we have done for years because we would enjoy it."

The truth I had to come to peace with. Returning to the central thought of their moment, "she wants to pardon us."

Scowling at her with an incredulity, "The Shadow screams for my painful death. To hear and reflect on the things I have done and the Shadow wails at me to suffer. I punished those who failed at what they were asked to not do. Just *don't do it.* Then they *did.* Then I punished them to get them to tell me what they did and why. Why he hit her, why she tortured him, why they hurt that person, and on and on and on. I sat here, safe, in my empty place. Dispassionate and bored as they told me the next *sick, sad, twisted,* thing they had done for their own pleasure."

Nodding in acknowledgement Zack waved his hand in a flowing motion, "I believe Miss Bachman wanted us to learn to care so we would be able to stop doing this and do something else."

Calming in the wake of Zack's calm, "how do I put all of this away? How do I rationalize all this?"

Assuming a calmer state Zack answered him, "admit you're jealous of the people who had the chance to be normative Citizens and you had to deal with being the Outsider."

Touching his forehead gently with his fingertips, "is that what this is?"

Reaching over she laid her hand down near Jonas' "it could be. Finding out if that is the truth, would buy us more time. We have heard that cry before, *it's not my fault.* We were born with a flaw in our clay that was beyond normative flaws. We were never going to be normative. However, we could learn to survive ourselves."

Touching her hand with the back of his Jonas appeared resolved, "I have become the thing I find contemptible?"

Pressing her skin against his, "the only way to find out is to investigate the idea. Otherwise you silence the Shadow with a bullet to the brain."

Picking up his mug Zack looked into it, "we exist as a last line of defense against the sickness within the cracks of flawed clay. We are weaponized sickness. It is time for us to get well."

Looking to him Jonas appeared cautiously hopeful, "can she save us?"

Shaking his head softly Zack spoke with a humored calm, "no *one* can save us, only we can save ourselves. Our lives are in our hands. We deal with Josh Kunlow. We try to deal with Arlo without breaking under the duress of looking at his rusted face. We will have answers by the dawn."

Intoning the hope Jonas smiled, "the Dawn is not yet Denied to us."

Nodding in reply, "correct."

Moving her hand away she set to collecting her gloves and mask, "let us get to this."

"Let's."

Draining his mug Zack set it down in the sink next to him, "I'll take point. If I falter, I'll signal and we'll rotate."

Rising from his chair Jonas smiled, "good plan."

Once more with feeling.

5.2.0 - 02:12

Safe Housing - Bedrooms

☼ Yuri

"Yuri?"

The sound of his name brought him out of his semi-sound slumber. Looking around he heard it again from near him. Looking on the bedside table he spotted the small box which was asking for him.

Turning on the bedside lamp to get a better look at it, "ah!"

Pushing the button on the intercom box he spoke slowly as to not slur his speech, "kakój?"

Letting go he waited a full five count before he heard a reply, "could you come down here?"

English. Speak English.

Pushing the button he spoke softly, "I am, en route."

Getting up and out of bed he fished into the large cargo net bundle Stephanie had brought by earlier. *I need a shirt before I see her.* Tossing it on he made his way out of his room and down to her door. *She has freed me, housed me, fed me, clothed me, and now she wants to speak to me in the middle of the night. Perhaps she wants a lullaby? It's not like I don't know enough of those. I could sing to her. Put her savaged mind to sleep.*

Knocking on the door with a double tap of his knuckle he opened the door slowly and let himself in. *Even after everything I get nervous in these situations.* "You requested me Susan?"

Answering from the pillow her voice was quiet, but at ease, in the nearly silent room, "I did."

Taking a step forward he noticed the lack of dynamic embellishments. *A simple room. Lighter shades of stain on the all wood furniture.* Closing the door with his foot his eyes caught the sight of a darker changing screen, covered with more etchings and engravings, *more stories. I wonder where they file that? Stories on changing screens?*

Raising her head from her pillow, "come over and sit with me?"

"Can do." Leaving thoughts of the screen behind, his eyes finished focusing on the pale green walls curiously devoid of paintings of ducks. Moving to Susan's side of the bed he waited as she edged away from him to make room. Carefully lowering himself onto the bed in his lethargic state he found a firm place to sit. *This room smells very nice.*

Then again she smells nice all the time so I'm not surprised. Reaching out and touching her shoulder he was rewarded with a smile. *I find it heartening to see a room so rustic in its charm without lavish embellishment or waste. This isn't a palace for a ruler, it was a home.*

Meeting his gaze for a moment she smiled reassuringly, "you want to ask about something?"

I might as well. "How old is this house?"

"This house use to be a Garrison House, hence all the bedrooms. It was built when this region needed it. This land was the sight of more than a few battles. This was shortly after our nation rose from its slumber. So first generation after the Rise."

More to look up. "Which generation are you?"

"Fifth of those who have risen."

I wonder if she has some meaning for that too. "It looks nice for its age."

Reaching up she caressed his hand for a moment before retracting her hand back under the casual spring drape of a blanket. "Thank you for coming down here Yuri."

Oh yes, sleep. How to get her to sleep so I can sleep. "What keeps you from sleep tonight?"

"Everything. I closed my eyes, and it was hours later in a blink. I don't feel rested, but I can't get back to sleep." Hearing the ache in her tone, "I want to close them and keep them closed until the sun rises."

I know that feeling far too well. "Everything is, a lot of things."

Offering her words with a meandering tone of loss, "Father used to have problems sleeping when he wasn't at Reylai's. By that point I would be living in the dorms over at Cloak and Dagger so it's not like I could help him with that. No glass of warm almond milk from me. I'm worried my sleep cure is going to be something I can't get. Or that I'm rambling too much."

Focus. "How did you use to get to sleep before?"

Licking her lips before speaking her tone betrayed a confession, "I would get Sasha to get in my bed in the dorms and soothe me to sleep." Sliding into a humored clarification with ease, "which is actually a bit of a misnomer."

Asking his words out of reflex, "how so?"

"She would fall asleep first, then I could sleep. I could match her breathing, match her calm, and I could find rest then."

"How did that come to pass?"

Rolling onto her back she looked up to him with a long resolved pain, "we were sharing a room, and, I had a rough day of it. I was visiting the recovery wing at General, and found out that one of the kids, Moose, he wasn't going to make it. I was facing the moment of having been in the room when the doctor had come to talk to the family. They were out of options. Not even something I could buy him with my Rations would do it. They had, *nothing.* I was crushed." Wiping the tears away with thumb and forefinger she continued, "I was recovering from that when Sasha would suggest that we could do what people who care for each other do. This is after our declared feelings were known to the other. I laid down with her. That started a routine for me, us."

Only one thing to say. "Noted."

Reaching to his hand he relented and worked with her to lace their fingers together as she spoke her declaration, "I've never loved a man before."

Smiling he tried to reassure her, "I want to say something like, it's easy, but I know that you would tell me that it isn't true."

Squeezing his hand she smiled, "I would. I would *also* clarify that I have never loved a man with these feelings in my heart. Love is a many faceted thing, and this would be a Pragmatic Desire."

I will look that up later. "What is the easiest way to get through *this* moment?"

Holding his hand firmly, "I use terms and words that you don't know, which result in you laying down next to me, to help me sleep."

Cuddles? No problem. "That sounds easy enough. I was afraid I would have to wake enough to sing you a lullaby."

"Yuri, -"

"Yes?"

Reaffirming her grip on him her tone was jagged with sadness, "the reason I didn't want your debt, was that I was afraid I couldn't love you if I had your debt. He never went for my throat before, it was never quite like that before, I *was* afraid in that moment. I had to wear make-up over the bruises, and be careful, afterward."

The break point became the broken point. "I understand."

Sniffling she adjusted her grip on his hand, "I, am troubled."

"Why?"

Reaching out she found his arm with her hand in the dark, "because every time we have spoken, where a sad notion, or awful thing, gets expressed. You, *understand*."

The things I did not tell you. "The world is a troubled place."

With the familiar tone of offering him a compromise, "if you hold me tonight, I will hold you in the morning. We can see the Beltane Sun together."

It's Beltane already. The days got away from me. Focus. Thinking back over his time recovering, her words came to mind, "if you let me help you this much, I will help you help you the rest of the way."

Caressing his arm gently, "there are things we're going to have to figure out. Not just me giving you my comm number so you can call me."

Touching her hand gently with his reply, "oh?"

"I have, had," squeezing his arm gently she sighed, "I have a bedroom in Central I haven't had checked on. It's where I take time with Sasha when she's in town."

Taking a guess at the question, "do I get to come visit you there?"

"See?" Laughing softly in the dark, "that's something we have to figure out."

What did she make for herself? "What is this bedroom in Central like?"

Meandering her way through the explanation, "It was an unused supply room. We used all the supplies in it, and then moved the storage space for things like them. I had it remodeled into a bedroom for me. I gave Sasha clearance for the door, so she would be waiting for me."

Embracing the humor, "oh, here we go, some of those sweet perks of leadership."

Feeling her fingertip draw the question mark on his forearm before her words, "why does that make you happy?"

It's not like you wanted a gold plated toilet. "If a leader will take care of themselves? They show understanding of self care. When one cares for the self, you know what others want for themselves. Empathy through experience. You weren't striving for an indulgence, but *care*, for you. Keeps you on the ground."

Speaking quietly she drew an exclamation point on his arm, "I am happy you are you."

Smiling in the wake of the affirmation, "I am happy to be me, most days."

Giving him another squeeze, "you are very forthright with your feelings. Sasha, she pined in quiet for me in a way I didn't understand until Sevilan took me aside and gave me *the talk* about things. I was emboldened, I sat with her to build that bridge. You're bold enough to not let a moment fester. You'll be able to talk to her because you'll be brave and face down the awkwardness and not run from it. She shouldn't think she should leave."

"I will tell her as much." *Oh, oh!* "The lie she was told, I will not entertain it."

"Thank you. Noted."

I wonder, "did your father tell her the lie?"

Answering with a thankful candor, "no. He never told her the *lie*. His doubt was based upon her dying, *not* about her being lovable or loving me."

More to learn. "I understand more."

Hearing her breathing gently in the dark her words came as an upbeat admission, "I look forward to waking up in the morning."

Squeezing her with a lightness in his heart, "good."

Settling down against her pillows she looked up at him from under the edge of the blanket, "why do I feel like this when I'm with you?"

"What is, *this*? I can hardly see you, so I don't have much to go on."

Replying with a half smile she exhaled softly, "vulnerable, I would hazard would be a good word for it."

Do I have wisdom for this moment? "Good or bad vulnerable?"

Caressing his arm with a light tone to her word, "good." Touching him gently with a care with her question, "do you feel like I have an unfair place in your heart?"

Firing his mirror question in return, "do you feel the reverse of the question?"

With a gentle sound akin to the smack of lips she whispered, "a little."

Confessing the truth with a humor, "I would agree then." Laughing he squeezed her hand, "Susan, this is what dealing with people can be like. Awful. You need an emotional ice pack, not self doubt. Being in love is terrible. Did not our ancestors face these same moments?"

Reaching up she caressed his bicep with a timbre of emotional confusion, "Elianna left though."

Swinging for an upbeat reply, "she loved Lord Garth, he needed someone to look after him." Rolling his eyes with a playful humor, "I don't have a Lady Garth."

Whispering her reply with an uncomfortable trepidation, "only because I haven't let you near another woman."

I am not awake and present enough to navigate this. Offering the alternative, "how about I get comfortable and we leave this moment to blow away?"

Sitting up she hugged him with a warmth to the gesture, "that sounds agreeable."

Moving awkwardly with the embrace he nearly fell over trying to follow her into the bed. Laughing he put his hand down for balance, "I did not train in bedroom gymnastics."

Joining the humor she slid away from him, "there, I made room."

Turning he reclined backwards until he was laying in the spot she vacated. Moving an arm over as he rolled onto his left side he felt her welcome his presence. *She is fearless.*

Settling against her he felt her settle quickly. *A practiced bedmate when it comes to the act of sharing a place to sleep. I could have used her company on many a cold night with less understanding warmth buddies. I wonder if she'd like to hear those unfortunate stories?*

I bet she would.

Whispering with a comforted tone, "you're good at this Yuri."

Whispering his explanation, "many cold nights in the world. You can be shy and miserable or fearless and sleep in comfort."

Touching him gently on the bicep, "I bet there's some stories there."

"There are, and they're for another time." Seeing what he could of her attire he processed what he was feeling in his arms, *it seems rustic.* "Is this a dress of sorts?"

Answering quickly with humor, "more of a drape with straps to it."

Touching her socked foot gently with his bare foot, "I like it."

"It's a story for another time." Touching his hand with her hand he heard a smile in her tone, "in the morning I will hold you in return. Then I'm going to get up and get a shower. I would prefer to go without words in the morning. Just quiet."

Not a problem. "I can be quiet."

"Thank you Yuri."

"Sleep well."

Feeling his heart slow and his breathing relax, *I feel peace. I like this.*

Whispering his name with conviction, "Yuri?"

"Yes Susan?"

Feeling her hand find his he held still as she squeezed it, "aardvark."

Choking up he sniffled and hugged her gently. *I have no words, only happiness.*

Soothing him with her gentle timbre, "we are in a good place Yuri, just get some sleep."

Kissing her gently on the temple he did his best to settle down to get some sleep. *My blessings feel as numerous as the stars in the sky.*

5.4.0 - 05:30

5001 Last Century Blvd. - 'Lounge Lair' – New Hope

▸Jerome Hope

Leaning back in his chair he took in the feeling of having finally found some personal equilibrium in his mindscape. *I have managed to trip or bust through a half dozen failsafes. I get to see my Doctor, my Counselor, my Spiritual Guide, an Oversight Counselor, and a Cloak and Dagger Advisor when this is over. And until I see them? I get to stack up my infractions against reasonable behavior and mortar them together into a solid wall of resolve to keep going.*

Turning his head up he smiled at Paige as she set the tray of food next to him. Smiling she moved her hands, "more food and drink to stoke the fire of the body. I wish to wish you the greeting of this day, but circumstances, leave me daunted and shy."

Checking the calendar he felt the rush of shared shyness at the date. "Happy Beltane, from the place of Platonic Adoration for," tapping his forehead, "one whom I would describe as a Blooming Philia."

Hissing laughter she tapped his shoulder, "we understand the other then."

Taking a deep breath he sighed, "we do. This is a day that *is, what it is*."

"To Decline, not out of disinterest but instead of shock. Two souls, who know of the other, but having not met before, now alone together on a day of passion and life."

Turning the chair he took in the frustrated humor which was visible in her expression. "The Codex on this, I do believe, it exonerates us of Negative Judgment of the other. This moment is not one where we are assessing the other in any way, just stating, this is no good time. We must be stronger than the tone of the day and the message carried in the Dawn."

Rubbing her face she revealed a smile far less frustrated, "I would like to become friends, as we do run in the same circles."

"I would be all for that!" Turning his chair back to the keyboards, "question? I am scheduled to see no small host of professionals based upon what I have done. Are you scheduled?"

Hearing her hissing chuffs of laughter the words came a moment after, "I am pending review as the circumstances were revealed. For getting me involved in this? Dennis is also pending a review."

I can understand that. "Do I need to worry about the Service Rangers coming to take

510

you away?"

Turning his head to the side his neck protested but he kept the post as she smiled with a dismissive shake of her head.

"No. As I am on assignment, being registered as an asset, they cannot intervene. However when you return to your regular location in life? I will be expected to comply or they will come get me."

Raising his glass of Cold Morning Beverage as a humored toast to her, "welcome to adulthood."

Taking a bow she set into her words, "happy to be here. It is a place of tired people, but I am happy to be of use."

Turning back to the monitors he took a long swig from the glass. *Not bad.* Putting down his glass he smiled at her assessment, "noted."

"I will step away so you may eat and find your bearings."

"Thank you Paige, noted."

Picking up his breakfast pita he looked at the information he had gathered and set to drawing conclusions.

The movement was in plain sight. They covered everything up though. They knew about Horse-Hair. They knew what it could see, and they moved around it. They tied it up in pretty ribbons and frills to hide the truth.

Athens beat me. He outsmarted, outwitted, and got past every last thing I could think of. Chewing an angry bite he closed his eyes against the frustration prowling inside of him. *But he's dead.* Swallowing with the hunger he felt awakening, he opened his eyes and snatched his cup of water. Gulping the water he chewed his way through the pita with the aid of the water until he felt a measure of sated.

Setting the glass down with a heavy heart he picked up the glass of Cold Morning Beverage before moving the tray away and, the rest of his breakfast, from his direct concern.

Moving into his line of sight Paige smiled with her words, "I talked with Amaranth until she could sleep."

What a rusted state, so good you're here to help. "Thank you Paige."

With a questioning expression, "the next move?"

"Must be made for it to be the next move." Tapping the commands he brought up the request for communication. Engaging the request he leaned back and adjusted his headset. Looking to Paige he gestured the thumbs up before looking back to the monitor without asking her to leave.

Noting that all the parties had answered he engaged the call, "are we all present?"

Speaking softly Zack affirmed his presence, "present and more than mindful of this moment."

Coughing softly and letting out a single chuckle Hampton seemed to be in good spirit, "present and kind of surprised I get to be here. Everyone else is asleep though."

With a voice that carried no fewer clues of fatigue Zack kibitzed, "you sound tired."

Grousing back with a borderline playfulness to his fatigue, "I have been up *all night*, working on the Journey's End debacle. Which, as a note, we did find *two* sniper nests. No one in them, but we found two nests. On that note? I feel vindicated to the Nth power that I stayed up all night making sure we could do this safely."

Answering him with a neutral inflection, "noted."

Tossing something resembling praise together he offered it, "today? You are a good man Hampton. As I cannot speak of you otherwise."

Laughing with a yawn he replied, "noted."

Rubbing his eyes he smiled, "status on Arlo Kunlow?"

Chipping in Hampton sounded still humored, "found and brought in by the Jaguars. Correct?"

Affirming the answer Zack yawned, "correct. I have not taken him to the table though."

Fighting the yawn of his own, "motive?"

"This is going to be a noteworthy move?"

Laying it out with his tone Zack's voice carried the strength of a man still living, "I can *hope* that you *both* appreciate the scheme. The plan is that we are going to wait until Miss Bachman is almost here. Then we will move Arlo to the table, as he has been in no shape to put on it, and then she will go in and get to yell at him in person for the information. Last I was aware we still needed the password for his door, correct?"

Unfortunately. "Correct. I was able to use the Network to gain access to the door, but the rusted thing is set in a manual override. I can't open it via the Network."

Adding to the moment Hampton's humored disposition eased the moment, "I have authorization to use whatever The Commander has as an option. I have the Quad Busters, all four of them, scheduled to come in after breakfast to do an evaluation on the door and how to open it without hurting Amaranth. I *just* got a look at the door. She's a beautiful door, would be a shame to wreck her. I would *like* to see a salvage team haul the whole door out."

Sounds good, both pieces. "Solid planning. We either get the code or we take it down if able."

Asking with an offhanded neutrality Zack's tone bordered on curious, "the domicile was in difficult terrain?"

Laughing with another yawn, "that, is an understatement. Not to mention it's a Second Generation Terror Shelter. The door *is* counting down, so if we can't find a way to open it? It'll open *tomorrow,* but that's a day away. Why put off to tomorrow what we can do today?"

I have nothing to say. "Truly."

Remarking with a timbre of acceptance, "that is an impressive cage for a Bachman."

Laughing again Hampton sounded as the man of jovial spirit that Jerome had heard stories of, "I have been at the side of The Commander for a few years now." Pausing to yawn again, "and I can tell you this much, if it *wasn't?* She would be free already. That girl was raised to understand that the only limit to her achievements and life lived would be finding her limits as a person. And, unlike some girls? She did believe the message wholeheartedly. Not knowing that she couldn't escape? She would have found a way if she doubted in the strength of her cage."

Answering back with a lilt of approval Zack's neutral mask fully slipped away, "noted."

I wonder, "do you know her well?"

Sighing for a moment Hampton launched into it, "*well?* No. Seriously? I'm the guy next to her bigger brother. It's not like I get a mass of insight or time into the reality of Amaranth. I get to be the guy who sees it from the first person vantage, however, I don't really comment or interact with their moments. Did I feel the awkward haze in the room when Steven found out she had been asked to pose semi-nude for a painting? You know I did." Adding as a quick follow-up, "it is as being family without being a part of the family."

I did not know that anecdote, "how did that moment turn out?"

Reflecting on the outcome with a warm spirit, "she declined. Even with no obvious bits showing she didn't have it in her to go through with it. She sent the invitation over to an associate of hers who was more open to the idea."

We need to get back on track. "That's amazing. However, we do have details to finish exchanging."

"True. Tell us Sys-Admin, did you figure out what Athens did on his end?"

"I did. He prepped the needed sorcery to move the idea of her being a Dinclair to a Bachman into a time-delayed server task. I found the task, I removed it, but I kept all the data. It's legitimate. She *is* a Bachman. There is a genetic test, documents, and the rest of the proof needed to change her reality with a keystroke."

"To what end?"

The sort of Nightmare Fuel that will not shake easily. "This is the thing that has left me daunted, spooked, and the like. He wanted her to generate a Full-Access Permission Key. In the event of hardware or software problem a Bachman can get a new key to the kingdom. He was going to get her to make a new key, and then give it to him. At that point Kunlow would have a Consul Key and a Bachman Key."

Chiming in Zack sounded honestly curious, "what's so special about a Full-Access Permission Key?"

The Fate of the Penguin Kingdom. "The check and balance is that when Miss Bachman uses her High Consul presence, it's logged. She's using the High Consul Key. It *does* have limits. There is one key *higher* than that. The Full-Access. It is *also* logged, but it does *not* have a limit. I have a Key on a necklace around my neck that is made from that Key. It's an Authorization Key. It lets me pretend that she said *yes* to something. It is not the Key in question, but my powers as Admin Nobody are all sourced from that Full-Access Key."

Snapping his fingers audibly Hampton pounced on the conclusion, "thus enabling Thomas to see all of our nude pictures we have stashed away! He would have seen my paintbrush and paint-bag." Stopping for a moment he returned with a serious tone, "no, I follow. Game, Set, Match, sort of win over the Network. Why did Asmodai never use it to just take over the world?"

This is where we go into the dark territory of the plan, "the Sys-Admin is to power off the CPU Unit using the Network Compromised Protocols."

Firing back with a mildly horrified revelation, "what if the Sys-Admin thinks it's the best idea for someone to control the Network in that fashion?"

Adding to the moment Zack's voice carried his awe at the stakes, "then you have a problem."

Rolling into a mockup of a dangerous tone Hampton posed his Inquiry, "question, Sys-Admin Hope, would you turn off the CPU?"

The truth, the whole truth, and nothing but the truth. "That's my job. If Miss Bachman tried to take over the world, I would turn off the CPU and ask her to calm down."

Laughing Hampton seemed humored, "this sounds like a Network Upgrade in the making!"

"Yes."

"I concur."

Prompting him with his question Hampton's tone carried a more modest curiosity, "why is the Network like that?"

The honest answer? "Mistakes made when they were building it. The truth about the Network is that it's made from a patchwork quilt of hardware, software, and dreams. Each year something gets better about it, and other things just get replaced. Are we a *stable* society?"

"No."

"I would say not."

I am the Sys-Admin, I get to say the declarations over my Kingdom now. "You can have your Network Upgrade, where all of the Permission Keys and the mistakes are mended, when we're a stable society."

"Noted."

"Understood." Continuing Zack sounded concerned, "is Amaranth well? Clarification, I *know* she's in the mess she's in, but I don't have a way to talk to her. I don't quite know what I would say. I don't have a direct connection to her, but she is part of the Bachman Constellation, thus, I worry."

The stars we make our wishes on. "Paige stayed up with her, kept her up talking, and saw to it that she would sleep again. She knows the rescue is on the way. That we are doing the best we can. She even read the Protocol to be ready to forgive us for following it to make sure we all stay safe."

"Excellent."

Confess the variables that you do not like, "I have no small amount of data to sift. The sort of thing that will have to wait for me to claim my office. I will keep *everyone* who needs to know what they need to know. I'm not going to quit or slam the door of communication shut."

"Good."

"Good man."

Time to move this along, "what happens next?"

Interjecting with a renewed calm Zack spoke his words with a careful diction, "I have prepared the morning that waits for Miss Bachman well. The injectors are primed, the guillotine is ready to usher the sleeping dreamers to their final rest, and the Execution Orders are waiting. There are four. I expect her to remove one from the equation."

"Which one is that?"

"Josh Kunlow. After hours of trying to get him to avoid going to the table, we were able to pry the truth from him. There were others who did not go with the Blackout Bloc whom were aware of the situation. The Guild has sent further Inquiry into the subject. Mister Kunlow has proof, saved back on memory cards, which shows he was coerced into silence. He was unsure that others had made the same decisions, or to what degree they were involved. The Commander has placed his Execution Order in the pile."

Answering with a lackluster attempt at apologetics, "about that. The Commander *is* really unhappy with this, whole situation. He's been placing some *strongly worded* recommendations into play. Good job not taking him to the table though."

"Do you know why he sent him to me as he did?"

Chuffing out a sigh Hampton groaned quietly, "I will not whine." Taking a deep breath he set to it, "watching him and listening to him? My hazarded assumption is that he wants him to be forgiven. He doesn't *want* Josh dead from a man to man perspective. However, from a duty unto death perspective? Mister Kunlow dropped the ball. Thus? If Miss Bachman spares him? She'll most likely spare all the people he told you about provided they too were in the same situation. *Those* people will be willing to take the risk of trusting, and not shoot their way out of the moment. I know it's not a great time to be pushing things like this, *but,* it's something that he felt was worth the risk."

Answering with his own conclusion Zack spoke with a tired vigor, "he seeks to quell the bloodlust by showing people asking for blood that they have a valid question. He asks for them, The State will respond with death for some, life for others, and an unflinching stance on the moment."

"Correct."

In these moments I am reminded the stakes we play with. "Has Josh been told of the request for his death?"

Answering him with an almost clinical detachment, "he has not been told that anyone wants to kill him in a direct fashion, outside of The Commander saying he should die for his acceptance of his failure. We have taken care to look over his data and show him why we do not believe he could have succeeded. Thus, he is not a failure, as he would have failed and he knew that. To that end, he was being careful and ran out of time. Asking him to apply the principle idea that ones life is worth living, and has meaning, so if the meaning of this pain is to save others? Then he suffers for others."

Offering his words Hampton's timbre was one of regret and embarrassment, "for what it's worth, mea culpa."

"I appreciate that Hampton."

Back on task, "everything is ready for her?"

"I do not wish for her to use that cannon of hers in my domain. Precious little is unfazed by the munitions within, and none of those things are in my domain. She has dealt with those whom have exhausted the Second Chance before. I would like to continue the idea that the number that she has dealt with *personally* to stay as low as possible."

"I appreciate it."

"Wrapping this up with a little bow? Josh will be spared, the others done the right way, Arlo will confess to her, -" making audible thinking noises Hampton jumped back into his words. "Then Miss Bachman will take Amaranth home. Provided the plan holds."

Asking his question with a firmness to his words Zack sounded frightfully present, "sitting as far back from that situation as I have, why are they not sisters?"

"That's simple. Asmodai didn't want to burden Amaranth with the idea of being a Bachman. It's a pretty miserable life from what I've seen of it. She would have a life of her own choosing. To grow up and become whomever she wanted to be."

Leaning back in his chair he set to listening to the two men have their moment. *Go where others fear to tread Zack.*

Following up on the idea Hampton's timbre carried an openness to it he recognized as the same familial tone of the Bachman family, "if you love someone, set them free. If they return? Make a good place with them."

Countering with a flatness to his tone, "that seems, almost irrational."

Firing back with an Orator's Grace, "by the time Amaranth was born? Miss Bachman was a part of Miss Bachman. Susan is not an easy woman for most people to cope with. By keeping them apart she wouldn't be in her shadow, or have to listen to The Shadow about her place in her father's life. Sure, it's a rusted up idea, but he did his best to keep the two of them knowing about the other. I saw the dynamics of it."

"Example?"

"Steven would slip her Service Coupons. She would get to learn the ropes of having power and the Pyramid without being a Bachman. She still needed something to bargain with. Meanwhile Patrick would get her what aid he could get her. Steven got her a plus one status for many meet ups and gatherings. She loves people, Amaranth, and she wanted to see how the city worked. She built herself into a person of her own making. She didn't *have* to be a Bachman, she made that *choice*."

"Again, this seems almost irrational and illogical."

"Look, the old man of the office wasn't always the best planner when it came to social or family affairs. I've seen it. I *know*, about the time with the beating and the fight and the leaving."

"Do you know the *why?*"

"Gents, there's this guy we all know from our lessons on history. Ridolfi. The Kin Slayer, the Betrayer, and so on. She wanted to know why they couldn't make peace. She wanted to know the details of what went *so* wrong that he won't be happy until every Bachman is dead. *That* question? Is what changed our future."

Pressing him, "you know this for certain?"

"Patrick told me himself. He came across them, and he yelled from the stairs. Asmodai went up the stairs to get him, Susan went out the door into the night."

Returning from his silence he spoke his question into their interchange, "did he say what happened when Asmodai made it up the stairs?"

Dropping the Orator's Grace he returned to the timbre of casual defeat, "his version is that the old man got up on him, he told the old man that he heard the front door and the car pulling away, and that he could do what he wanted as he had already won. The old man broke down crying." Adding as an afterthought, "I couldn't imagine being *that* angry. I mean, I saw the footage from Susan's, *outburst,* in the training circle. Ouch."

Caught a Cloak and Dagger Cadet from behind and put her in the Medical Center. "I am aware."

Asking quietly Zack's conflicted state was apparent, "was he that angry while Maggie was with us?"

"Not to my knowledge."

"Or mine."

Putting his foot down with his tone Hampton put his declaration forward, "what I care about? As a soldier in this mess? Is that she *wants* Peace. I've heard her talk. I've heard her words on the subject. She's *no* coward. She has a big heart, a caring spirit, and if she can find a way to reason with those rusted up maniacs? Or find someone who *can*? I'm all for it."

I haven't seen her act the coward, no. "You are correct, she is not a coward."

"She does not flinch from the truth."

"Then Gents, what's left to say? My bed is calling me."

I have that answer at least. "Frank Sevilan goes to the House of Kunlow to fetch Dagger Herb. It's approaching oh six-hundred now, we want him there around seven. They have breakfast scheduled for seven thirty. It depends on how his morning goes. He's resting at the Cultural Center with the Terrors, so as soon as he's awake and cleared he'll go to her. Then she is to go to Miss Bachman and tell her that the day awaits."

"I can sleep soundly then? I'll drop an update in The Commander's Inbox and then hit the pillow."

"Yes. Sleep soundly."

Zack added his status to the moment, "I had a few hours, I will attempt a small nap before she gets here."

"Prudent."

"Be well Gents."

"You as well."

"A Blue Sky to us all."

Closing the call he picked up his fork and looked to Paige, "does your mother worry about you doing this?"

Moving her hands with a smile, "mother does not worry beyond Mother's Worry. I am Non-combatant. I only work in Green Zones. I am a Student of Shadows."

"And the future?"

"I have taken the Pledge of the Silverback. I know how to defend myself. I am not one who seeks quarrels or to fight for causes with martial prowess though. I am a child of peacetime. I will not be Cloak or Dagger. I *will* be of use though."

"I understand. It is what all Good Citizen's seek, to be of good use to our society."

"I have overheard, by sitting near, so much I do not see on the Network. I fear the Director is overzealous in guarding our truth because we do have a more beautiful world than I think he knows. Then again the Codex says I speak with a loud and emotive heart because I am young and burn brighter at this age. I am expected to be aflame with emotion."

She is very emotive. "Truth."

"I hope to still see a beautiful world under a Blue Sky when I get older."

Nodding the affirmation, "I do too."

"Is your world beautiful?"

Looking at the latest data reports he nodded twice, "it is beautiful."

"Good. I will stop so you can eat the rest of what I brought you. Silent meals, mindful of the taste and flavor, are the best meals when only one is eating. Also, your tea is ready."

"Thank you."

"Noted."

Tossing the word back as he adjusted his fork and prepared to finish what was on his tray, "noted."

5.6.0 - 07:04

Kunlow Estate – 'The Feasting Hall'

●Frank Sevilan

Reaching a hand out he touched the engraving he recognized on the large double doors leading into the Kunlow Feasting Hall. *Panels carved by the wood workers of the South. I know this image. Chicomecoatl. Been a long time since I saw her.*

I wonder if Susan is going to have something beautiful like this put into Central now that it needs new doors. Can the bastion of our power put on some makeup to hide the bruises? Chiding himself, *that was unneeded, no way to be. I need to lighten up. Execution orders are pending and there's only one person who will make it easier to tell Susan she needs to come into work.*

Lowering his hand he chuffed softly, *I have been told that she just has to send them away to the automated chamber. Free Josh, authorize the other three, and talk to Zack in person. Routine. Simple.*

I need to get to it.

Opening the right door he slipped inside quietly, *and they're about to say a blessing on the breaking of bread. This can wait.*

From the head of the table, an obviously tired Octavia Kunlow, spoke softly but firmly in the quiet of the morning meal being set before those at the table. "This morning raise your horns and give thanks for we have this day to act with High-Mindedness, to seek the freedom we desire, and honor this Kindred we have formed. Break this bread and pass around a measure to all at this table for we are here to share it and live by the Nine Noble Virtues. Take heart and be heartened for we stand together." Rubbing her eyes she smiled at them, "let's eat."

Moving over to the chair Sasha was sitting at, he looked at the faces that were looking his way, "good morning Mistress Kunlow, and all assembled. I have an order I have to pass on to Dagger Herb. I wanted to see her in person to make sure she was fit to drive."

Raising her glass to each in turn with a smile, "I made her rest hours before I realized I would be sleeping after breakfast. She has a good six hours of rest to her credit."

"Then she's fit." Leaning in, "I'll put the orders on your comm. Eat breakfast and then go to Susan with your orders. Her comm is in voice mail mode and her day is calling for her."

Keeping it professional with her acknowledgement, "understood."

Raising her cup toward him Octavia spoke her question without apparent guile, "will you be staying for breakfast?"

Reaching for an excuse he used it, "I don't know what the Nine Noble Virtues are -"

Speaking into his pause, "we can explain them. This is the first breakfast of those who value this Kindred. I take my father's place at the head of the table and lend voice to the hearts of those assembled."

Sounds like if I stay I might just learn something. Taking a breath he smiled, "I will stay. It's always a good day if you learn something good."

Raising her glass to him Octavia smiled, "sit, eat, learn."

Moving to the nearest empty chair he nodded, "I'll do just that."

5.7.0 - 07:59

Safe Housing – Master Bedroom

☼..Susan Bachman

Laying on her back she looked up at the ceiling. Glancing at the pale glow of the LED lights in the ceiling she smiled at the tranquility she was feeling. *I'm awake. I didn't set an alarm. I canceled all of my notifications.*

Not sure what time it is. Looking at the curtains, *I can see the glow of sunlight. Sun is up.*

Turning her attention to Yuri she took a moment to check herself over. *I'm not unaccustomed to an arm over me.* Taking a moment to be honest with herself, *the warmth on my hip though, that's another story.*

Taking a deliberate breath to keep from giggling, *I don't want to rust this up. It's not like I haven't seen it.*

Feeling it though? Different story. Glancing at Yuri's sleep slack face she smiled, *I am in no danger. Mom warned me it was a novel sensation. She was right.*

Moving the blanket with her left hand she let some of the cooler air in to the space under the cover. *My night dress is a little thick for a bed as warm as he makes it.* Looking at the pale gray undershirt he was wearing, *that can't be comfortable.*

Moving her leg slightly she found a source of cool breeze. *I'm glad I wore this and not my night band, I'd be drunk on skin-ship and not want to get up. Warm and safe. Like watching Sasha sleep and knowing nothing was pending.*

No one would be against me being happy. As of last night the people were happy about the idea of the Winter Wolf being next to me.

I would want to marry Sasha though.

Rolling the idea around she felt a measure of conflict with the unknown pieces to that puzzle. *I will have to talk to them both about the future.*

Feeling Yuri adjust in his sleep he pulled her into a more possessive embrace. *This isn't bad.* Reaching up and touching Yuri's back gently she grimaced at how warm his shirt felt. *I need to wake him just to cool him off.*

Reaching up she set her fingers to his temple and started a gentle circle of touch against the spot.

Speaking her name with a lethargic pace, "Susan?"

Touching his shoulder for emphasis, "Yuri, you feel like an inferno."

Meeting her gaze he closed his eyes in a long blink, "what?"

Hugging him gently with her free arm she nuzzled his nose, "you feel overheated."

Looking at her with a look of comprehension, "yes. Oof, this is warm."

Reaching out she touched his shirt, "please?"

Nodding with a sad look he moved away from her and set to removing his shirt. Pulling it over his head he laid down on the bed with a sigh of relief. Reaching over to the bedside table she pressed the control on the ceiling fan. Rolling back toward him she laid her arm over his waist.

Laying on his back he looked up at the fan with a smile, "oh, that is nice. I was not expecting the bed to be so warm."

Confessing the oversight, "I was not either. It was our first night sharing."

Tilting his head toward her, "was I untoward? I couldn't tell."

Squeezing him firmly with her arm she smiled with her best reassurances, "it was fine. I have never had a paintbrush laid on me before, it was, novel."

Looking to her face, "you are turning red."

Pursing her lips she nodded her head, "I am."

Turning his gaze back to the fan, "I am uncertain in moments like this."

Laying her head down she nuzzled his shoulder, "you have mentioned this."

Asking with a tone of concern, "are you overheated too?"

Falling into the moment with a smile, "a bit. I should have worn my night-band. It's a wrap around the chest sort of covering."

Speaking his quiet declaration, "we learned today."

Agreeing with a quiet humor, "we did."

Raising his right hand he gestured with a curious lilt, "did you have this problem with Sasha?"

"No. We slept with different clothing on. Also, as we are both girls? The bed was never as warm as it would be otherwise. During the winter? Depending on where we were and how hard the winter had been? Socks, gloves, and then whatever modesty drape."

"Your night dress then?"

"Yes. I put this on before you came in here."

Raising a brow at her, "what were you wearing?"

Answering with an embarrassed smile, "nothing."

Nodding he smiled and spoke with practical wisdom, "okay, I can see why that would be cause to get dressed."

Kissing his shoulder, "I did not want to cause you duress."

"You mentioned that before. I appreciate it." Stopping for a moment, "did you say *paintbrush?*"

"It's erotic parlance." Setting to caressing his hair, "the paintbrush designation is part of the uniform sexual education we all get. When you take the Oath of the Albatross, thank you for not laughing, you learn the social aspects of mating and dating.

With that, in time, comes the Codex of Sexual Art. And that teaches that it may be a," finding herself daunted to keep a straight face, "penis, but it's also your paintbrush. Penis for medical or technical, paintbrush for other reasons." Taking a breath she moved her thoughts forward gently, "we're taught that even if there's no greater plan beyond the moment? It's still painting. And as myriad as art is? So is sexual activity."

Without moving his head he spoke with a humored but still sleep touched cadence to his words, "I see. That's a very nice way of putting it, phrasing and all that. The metaphor is nice, elevates it to a different level than other ways. I take it that sexuality is kinder overall in these lands? I would *assume* so, I just never thought to ask."

Doing her best to slide into the light hearted feeling in her heart, "it is."

"Is there something you can tell me that will help me?"

We could lay here for hours. "Hearts are fragile, but strong, and we skipped so much of what we would normally do in me just calling you to me."

"You had to trust in me without knowing how to talk to me as you speak to others then?"

Affirming the idea with her tone, "yes. I had to just trust in you." Pitching her timbre to one of casual conversation, "you aren't like us, in some ways." Keeping her hand moving slowly, "for starters I would have asked you if you wanted to engage in the Sleepers Waltz."

Musing the word with a humor, "elaborate?"

"In the form of the checklist? Share my bed, but not my body. Learn to navigate the perilous dance floor that is the bed. Find ways to be close without cutting off blood flow, choking on hair, or overheating the bed."

"Then you also have dance codes?"

"Yes, *however,* we do swap the front of the term to indicate what is going on. That way you know if it's an invitation to an evening out or an evening in."

Letting out an overdramatic sigh, "I have more to learn."

Prodding him with her tone, "it will be good."

Smiling brightly at her, "with you leading me? I have no doubt of that."

You make me a better person in these moments. "You challenge me to be a better person by being close to me."

"How is that?"

"You need someone who can not only live their culture and experiences, but *explain it* in a way that makes sense. I have the honor of translating who we are, who I am, to a more universal and less jargoned version of English."

"I should confess, I like the jargon."

This should be good. "My turn, elaborate?"

"It means that someone took the time to think it over. To tell all of your people that things could have order and meaning in specific ways. Dennis told me a few things that helped me see that it's meant as comfort."

"With clarity and communication people can find a measure of honesty and comfort there. The ills of our world have answers and counters for a reason. To ease in the act of being alive."

Inquiring with a gentleness, "is this a new dance for you? I am not sure what I might have just asked, I think I know, but," grinning broadly, "it's too late now."

Feeling the internal smile that matched his grin, *you make this easy.* "With a man? Yes. I do this fairly often with Sasha."

"Did you treat me, as you treat her?"

"Well," rolling the words with humor, "I didn't put my leg in a specific spot as you have something there that she does not."

"Hah." Laughing for a moment he stopped, "but does she put her leg there on you?"

I should clarify, "she is not one for rubbing on me, and in turn I do not rub on her as that's not part of what she enjoys. Legs do end up there, as we like to be close, but there is no, *added friction." The stories.* Forcing down the laughter she nodded twice, "there are some stories I could tell you about us. Which include how having had the, now confirmed, suspicions I did? I did not trespass upon her. We did share no small amount of random chaos which provided us humor though."

"Did you want to rub on her though?"

I will confess. "The trait that Ozzy was plagued by? –"

"The cooler libido which flared once or twice a week, she wrote of it."

"It never stopped, and in some ways continued with a greater intensity, in the family. I have never been one for rushes of *need.* Opinion Offered, I believe that many other women I know would already have painted with you. The romance of the recovery, our quiet nights, the closeness, I do believe that you would be in a different place with a different woman. *That,* is the root of the care I'm using to let you know I'm not saying no. I don't want to be seen as cold to you, in that regard."

Talking with his free hand as his amiable tone played the words out, "you should know this, I am unduressed, not caused duress, help me out here?"

Clarifying with a smile, "not under duress. Free of duress. As there are layers and levels for that too. For example if you did not want to push the issue, thus causing *my* duress, but did want to admit to a driving sexual need? Then ways of mitigating biological need could be balanced with your emotional needs."

Jumping on the idea with a shy smile, "as when you brought me the *lotion* and soft fabric when I was recovering."

Pouncing on the moment she smiled with an embarrassed energy to the openness of the moment, "yes. Exactly. You had safety, privacy, and a way to doodle."

Laughing for a moment he touched her hair gently with a soft caress, "Susan, Elianna wrote that she loved Asmodai because he made her feel like she was more than a distraction from thinking about death. That he was able to see the beauty in things, even watching the two women he loved *spend time* when they invited him to sit by the bed. Did something from that endure?"

Caressing his hand she did not move it, "I do not know if I could bring myself to watch you without being too loud. Either with a giggle, or wanting to communicate. I am not a polite voyeur in that regard."

"Experience?"

No harm in telling. "The time I tried to be a voyeur, story for another time, I wore a face masking hood which prevented speech for that very reason. I was a *silenced* observer."

Nodding with an officious humor, "noted."

Back to the complete answer. "Having the rest of the writings? Watching them, was about connection with them. He wasn't doodling out his desires, or anxiously waiting for permission to jump in with them. He was a man without enough meaning, or beauty, in his life. Watching them brought him a measure of solace. They showed themselves, he acknowledged that, and asked them with his acceptance why they had trouble accepting themselves."

"That makes more sense."

"Normally, self-love is seen as a private affair. Cultural normative to prevent the expectation of getting to watch someone else. Create a soft taboo to make something more special. I acknowledged your need for self-love without words, just deed, because it is a soft taboo. It cannot be made banal if it is shrouded."

"Someone thought about the cultural need to touch themselves at night."

"Yes. In the Kiosk of the Divine, where one orders their Introduction to Faith, we have a host of choices that all have in them a shared message." Tapping her head gently, "as above," gesturing toward her feet she pursed her lips to control the embarrassed smile, "so is below."

"Sex is important to you and your people."

"It is. But not just *the act,* but the meanings and power around it. The drive to pursue it, the relationship with it, the words around it. The rituals. The circumstances. We teach a robust course on that leaves many of us shy about it, not because it is filthy, but the emotional strength of it is mighty."

Smiling after a moment, "you are not ashamed."

That which is positive should bring no shame. "No Yuri. I'm not."

Catching her eyes with his for a moment, his face softened in contemplation, "I like it here."

Affirming him with conviction, "good."

Resting against him in the pause she reveled in the comfort of his presence. Relaxing she set herself to caressing his right shoulder gently instead of thinking about getting out of bed.

That was more energy than I was ready to expend.

Looking at her with a soft intensity, "you look a distance away."

Honesty, "I'm whelmed."

"No wish to rise and face the day?"

Speaking the truth without stopping it, "if I don't look at my comm? No one else is dead."

Nodding with a pained compassion, "a story, a blessing, something else then?"

I have something. "I will tie the two notions together. Painting, and people who aren't dead. Speaking of the painting, our culture is a bit *more than happy* to engage in sexual activity. I have seen some *amazing,* just flat out *awe* inspiring moments of sexuality as Need, Art, Music, and Energy that set a moment on fire and took my breath away."

"I look forward to that."

Taking a breath she broached the idea, "the story –"

Hugging her with his words, "I like your tangents, stories, and the like. Do continue?"

Waiting for him to ease up and settle she started in on the confession, "I have seen no small amount of sexuality. We do not have pornography as it was known, but we do have art. In that art they have tried to capture the power of the naked form, the emotions, the want and desire of life. The passion so strong that it fills the senses and sets lovers grinding against each other while leaning on my garden shed."

Blinking he smiled with a confusion, "the garden shed?"

"Yes."

"That's, funny." Watching the realization spread his shock was apparent, "the garden shed on *this* property?"

Trying to keep the laughter in check, "yes."

Putting on the air of mock horror to go with his surprise, "no!"

"Yes! It was funny then too! Not one of those moments that is gross, or trying, then funny later when you look back. It was, borderline giggle inducing. I waited patiently. I'll tell you the details another time, but suffice it to say? The two were not on shift. They're still alive. They can still be alive, and love, and –"

Retreating for a moment into the hug he offered she sighed, *not quite ready to get out of bed.*

Whispering his words to her, "I have seen needs that would break a heart, effort that would break bodies, and vengeance that knew only victory or death for the sake of those feelings. I know what it means to stand in awe. I empathize."

Rubbing his bicep with a curled grip she kissed his scratchy cheek, "right now? I feel the purr in my chest. Warmth. I feel a low roar and I could only imagine that someone else would be giving you a sheet drenched tsunami."

Clenching his jaw and pursing his lips with a look of humored frustration he buried his face in the pillow to release the laugher. After a few moments he looked up at her, "I *get it.* You did it. You can stop trying to make me feel amazing. I feel *great.* Just stop, the purple prose is killing me. I am a simple man who is just happy he's alive and well. You don't have to orgasm natural disasters or a monsoon season on my face for me to feel encouraged."

Stopping in the wake of his words she smiled with the pride of the magnitude of his words. *That was wonderful.* Nodding with a sage wisdom, "just now? That was an excellent bit of forceful wordplay."

"You approve?"

I love you another iota more. "I do. *Orgasm a natural disaster.* I'm keeping that one."

Quipping back at her with a renewed humor, "hopefully not to yourself."

"Hopefully." *Now for something less humorous.* "Now, I am not saying this to be self-deprecating. I just want you to know we have a term for it. I am not Completely Inside Specifications."

"Another thing to look up?"

"Yes. The gist is that there's a parameter set that is accepted, scientifically backed, and we wouldn't use the term *ideal,* -" taking a breath she continued, "but it's the hoped for life we try to provide. Once you encounter life outside of this narrow band? You become someone who understands something that we hoped wouldn't be, but is bound to happen, because we're humans. There is no *perfect.*"

"How close to the goal are you?"

Now to count my blessings. "Closer than many. Others have lost parents, others have fought with a parent, others have buried their dead. I can still walk on my two feet. Not everyone has two feet, or can walk. The list goes on. Each? A blessing to count. However with each thing that is *outside* of the lofty idea of perfection is an acknowledgement of what isn't perfect and how to live with it."

"What do the people without two feet do?"

"Crutches, braces, and the like. Or a chair and are shown to the wheelchair access points to everywhere. The whole city was designed with a full sized wheelchair in mind. No doorway less than eighty-two centimeters. Unless it's a double door."

"Noted. And here I was going to ask if your libido counted as different. I got distracted by the feet though."

"No harm. Noted. Also, it would, my libido that is. For one, the majority of women self report as only being interested in men. I'm interested in women, as you know."

Nodding with a smile, "yes."

"The other notion is that it is low. The upside was that during my formative years when other girls were being, driven a bit daft with lust? I was just uncomfortably warm. I didn't have, half, of the problems they did. Thankfully we don't have notions of purity based upon having had or have not. I was seen as untouched, but not, pure, if you will."

Appearing to be mulling the information over, "noted."

He doesn't know the rules, you don't have to obey them. "The reason I mention this is because I like you, I love you too, and yes we have those as separate things. They're not terms which build on each other as evolutions of feelings." Taking a breath she quieted looking within for words.

Laughing softly he hugged her, "good to hear."

Kissing his cheek she found a few to string together, "I, don't need to be swept off my feet. Not because I don't believe in it, I," stringing the idea together, "I offer that disclaimer because I do not want you to expend effort only to have it be in vain. The Codex warns about many things, and that is one of them." Stopping her hand she cuddled him for a moment before continuing, "I *don't* know what your ideal courtship is. I just know, that I feel, a warmth with you that I like."

"I like it here too." Pondering her with a quizzical look, "what else does the Codex warn you about?"

Something that helps makes a happy marriage, "your emotional vulnerability. That as a man you are held to a paradigm of strength, but you *must* be allowed time to rest. That the act of resting is sacrosanct too. From not being consumed by fear when you are in a state of weakness, to knowing that you need male friends to socialize with without censure."

"Do I get a Primer for that?"

Nodding with a smile she was thankful for an easy answer, "the Primer on Adult Male Socialization in Male Spaces."

Relaxing into the moment of conversation he seemed nostalgic with his tone, "are there Female Spaces?"

Easy again. "Yes."

"Shared Spaces?"

Brightening with the turn of the moment, "those too."

Touching her gently on the cheek with his question, "does your libido trouble you?"

Smiling with his touch she nodded, "yes, or I wouldn't have said what I said. I'm still learning how to court you in turn. I don't want to throw a signal that will read as a Stop or a Decline."

"I won't be dissuaded easily then. I will endeavor to not just *give up* because it seems like the thing to do."

"Thank you Yuri."

"This culture, is very honest then, yes?"

"When we can be. An example would be myself and Frank."

"Do tell?"

"Frank was never openly doubted as my second father, the sincerity he brought to the moments coupled with my demeanor and reactions to him created a clear picture of care. He did wear a body camera at all times, as part of the regulations on being on duty, which prompted us to get the highest quality one we could for when he was around. He spent no small amount of time with my father, as a friend and co-parent."

"You had two fathers then?"

I don't think I had time to explain this. "A child can end up with multiple fathers and mothers as per the Pact of the Covenant and the Pledge of the Tree. Frank was another father to me."

"Your father did not mind?"

The words are only truth, not slander. "My father was trying to help Frank by sharing not only his family but himself with him. On a certain level of truth, I was Frank's daughter because he had lost his and needed someone to put that identity toward. My father was helping him heal by accepting him. I did, in learning how to grow up, make a few odd moves though."

"Oh?"

"When Frank stayed over, he had a duty cot. Standard issue. If I was tired I would nap in it. I've never been afraid of the beds of others in that regard. I had to learn to not sleep wherever there was open territory. There is a military limitation in that there are more soldiers than beds in many places. They learn to use a special duty cover and rotate the use of the mattress. We are what we learn. I had learned of the custom, and thought it was universal." Closing her thought with humor, "the things we believe as children."

"Hah."

"Even if I was unsure of what to say about my dad, I was never shy about talking about things with myself and Frank. I learned that people see you based upon what you present. Thus even as I told lies of omission about my father, I was able to tell the truth of being thankful for both of them."

"Noted. If we are what we present and learn from that? What did I teach you of me?"

The big question. "I see you as a good man, with a gentle heart, a fire stoked temper, and a breadth of experience which helps him hang on in this strange place he has found himself."

Visibly mulling it over he smiled, "I like that description."

"I learned, from my parents, that social monogamy is a mutual pact of trust and assurance. You are what you present. They presented as a couple, with children, whom were only engaging with each other in the bedroom. By the time that Steven was born? This was true. They were transformed by being parents into an exclusive partnership."

"In the plan where you are with Sasha, but I sire the children, what happens there?"

"Sasha and myself would present as a life-bonded pair that did not want to lose the other. Meanwhile I would present a sire for my brood that was loyal to staying within the family group. The tradition there is that if we were having relations beyond *just* the conception? That you would just have relations with me and I would endeavor to maintain my end of a relationship bargain."

"Noted."

"However if our relationship, which I don't want to cast doubt, but I need to be clear in expectations –"

Sounding cautiously optimistic, "it's fine, say what you need to say."

"If we do not maintain a partnership that is sexual in nature? I have to accept the idea that you are seeing someone else, but you have to accept that you are still the father to the children, something I would hopefully never forget. Unless there is a direct transgression? Parental Rights *must* be maintained for all parents involved. Which can include non-biologic parents in the cases where it applies."

"Noted."

"We endeavor to maximize the good, there is no *greater good,* but there are ways to maximize good."

"Noted." Laying back he looked up at the ceiling, "I feel amazing right now. I don't feel guilty, or scared, or duress."

"I trust you," *he doesn't know, time to tell him,* "and have communicated this through King Making."

"King Making?"

The Art of Appreciation. "Men, are Kings in the Castle of their own Hearts. Men are not taught to shy away from their feelings. How can they live otherwise?"

"I, don't know."

"As a woman, I have been taught the layers and ideals of King Making. The Codex of King Making and To Be A King work together to provide a picture of how to handle the concept. If a man does something you respect, appreciate, or benefit from that was asked for or appropriate? A woman does her best to pick the right thing to say or give in return." *May as well,* "an example would be my comments about not wanting to dissuade you."

Chuckling with a shy demeanor, "is this where you tell me that painting, which I suspected was not going to happen, is not going to happen?"

"Well yes. Though, not in a way that makes you think it could never happen. As, to be honest with you, I can't say it's not going to happen."

Looking at her closely, "what is the other part of this that troubles you?"

He reads me well. "Is it wrong that I'm moving on you? Risking your heart, being this kind, sharing the Waltz? You came here looking for a parcel of land, a house, a new home. Is it, good, for me to be the first who does this as I have an unfair advantage?"

Looking to her with a mild incredulity, "hey, I'm a bit scared too. You mentioned I could be vulnerable, so I will. Is it going to be just fine and good? You are The High Consul, and I'm going to be bounding about in your life when the dust settles and people are just going to have to *deal with it?* That's quite a bit of *could go wrong.*"

I believe Winifred is going to like you.

Asking with a tentative air about her words, "is there more?"

Adjusting them until he had her in an arm up and around cradle, "no. However, I noticed you and yours like a word, so I will adopt it too. I am not under duress. Love is a process, a journey, yes?"

I agree. "Yes."

"I won't give up on us. I'm not so scared I would bow out. I will journey with you in good faith."

I make the Pact, freely and with love. "I Pact this Pledge of Good Faith."

"I Pact this Pledge with you."

Touching his chest near the dressings he was still wearing she contemplated the smell of him mixing with the scent of the medical tape. *I'm Seven for Seven.*

Prodding her with a tone of encouragement, "I saw that look. What epiphany did you see?"

"The Seven Reasons."

Chuckling with an at-a-loss humor, "to do what?"

Touching him with fingertips to count off each point, "to touch, love, be with someone."

"What are they?"

Reciting them with the ease of rote knowledge, "Recreation, Desire, Reconciliation, Sadness, Failure, Diagnostic, and Upkeep."

Musing the moment over, "that is no small amount of import."

"We are a people who value life."

Touching her with a gentle accusation, "you are a romantic then."

Countering with an honesty, "I just try to tell the truth."

Holding her with a quiet gravity, "will Steven try to harm me?"

Kissing his scratchy cheek again, "no."

"Am I a danger to you?"

"He spoke the words in fear and anger without knowing you. You ask the question because you have self-doubt. I will speak to your worry. You are no more a danger to me than anyone else is."

"Thank you." Touching her cheek gently, "you are afraid of hurting me. This whole time I have been afraid of hurting you, you were afraid of hurting me."

Going over the recollections of the lessons on the subject she found words for him. "Yes. I understand, as best I can, that when a man *loves*, it's a deep in his soul and guts kind of thing. If you loved me, and I hurt you? I would be tearing out the flowered plant, bush, tree, metaphor of life from your soul and guts. From the day that I met you, I never wanted to be the person to do that to you."

Nodding his head gently with a humbled smolder about him, "noted."

Kissing his cheek she wrinkled her nose at the scratch of his new growth. "Aardvark?"

Tossing his word quickly with an upbeat lilt, "yes?"

Reveling in the joy of the sentiment, "I am with you. New beard to grow and all."

Answering with his turn at sage wisdom, "I am where I should be then."

Moving to a higher seated position she kissed the top of his head, "if you want to take some time out to Doodle before breakfast, you should."

"Doodle?"

Feeling the giggle escape before she could stop it, "pleasure yourself."

Laughing with a renewed rush of energy, "I am still getting used to the word. I had heard you, but I wasn't quite sure."

Trying to keep her laughter at bay, "when those with a paintbrush do it, yes."

Waggling his eyebrows, "what is it called when you do it?"

Closing her eyes for the words, "Testing The Paint."

Furrowing his brow with the question, "Paint then?"

"Yes. The colors of passion, desire, the heart."

Raising a finger with a hesitance to the gesture, "what color is the paint? Is that a thing? A code question then?"

"It is. The hues and shades." Rushing the confession, "mine are pastel."

"Pastel? Sounds pretty." Laughing again, "you have turned me upside down with such few words."

Nudging him slyly, "I meant it though."

Asking with a humored resignation to the unknown, "what color are my Doodles then?"

Tapping his shoulder with her hand she smiled, "that would be in the Codex of Self Pleasure, the Primer on Doodles. You read the Primer, you answer the question yourself."

Sighing while laughing he covered his face with his free hand. When the laughter subsided he set to moving out of her embrace and sitting up, "this will confound, amuse, and leave me inspired until the day I die. I can see this, and believe this, now."

"It is good to see you in good spirits again."

"You have never had to try hard to bring sunshine to my heart, you make it *easy*, to just accept the joy of life. Though," pitching a thoughtful tone over his words, "you didn't mention the Doodle term when you brought me lotion in my cell and left it."

"It wasn't the best of times to say anything on the subject."

"True." Nodding in agreement he took a deep breath. Exhaling heavily he picked up his shirt, "noted, before I go, as I need to use the Necessarium. Could you, would you, share with me one more thing? Something of note, perhaps an oddity, that will send me on my way with one more laugh before the day awaits?"

Most odd thing I can think of right now – "consumption of urine in sexual play is rare in our lands because of phosphorus extraction."

"You mentioned that, the phosphorus extraction," tugging his shirt on he laughed with a whelmed but humored tone, "I just, had not thought about what it did to the whole sexual play aspect of it."

"It limits it. I have an associate I work with, and its one of her favorite things to include in the bedroom." *The anecdotal descriptions of that,* looking up to him she noticed his knowing look. "You're aware of the act in a matter more intimate than my morbid curiosity on the subject." Catching herself, "also, I called it morbid when that's far too strong of a word compared to cultural norms."

"It is?"

Nodding she propped herself up in the bed, "it is. No one gets hurt if you do it right. Safety goggles when in doubt. Which *most* women already own by the time they're adults."

"If you ever dabbled in it? Don't take it directly into the mouth without an understanding of what's going on. It can become *quite* the mess."

Pondering the interconnections and implications she laughed softly, "that is what is known as an Express Route Train of Thought. I provide words, you provide words, but I should not infer a Full Route."

"Oh?"

Asking the loaded question with all of the casual humor she could muster, "who else would I *dabble* with?"

Stopping for a moment he braced himself against the footboard of the bed as the laughter erupted from him. Basking in the moment she tossed her follow-up at him, "what is so funny?"

Ceasing the laughter he straightened himself back upright, "I had nothing else I could emote. You were sparing me again." Wiping an errant drop of moisture from his eye, "oh. Seriously though, I had too much to drink, she tickled me too earnestly, and we had a mess on our hands."

That sounds like the anecdotes I've been told.

Assuming a more serious posture, "though I will admit I would never ask you to ingest it as I have never ingested it and it would seem, hyporudical to lay such a demand on your palate."

What in the what? "Hyporudical?"

"To be both hypocritical and rude at the same time. The opposite of that is to do what is asked, that would normally *not* do, but you do it because the person is so insistent. I *did* pee in a man's canteen, *when he asked me to,* as he was so desperate for the sensation of drink he broke under the strain of the sun."

I will ask and I will regret this, but I can't leave it be. "How did that turn out?"

"He kind of liked it. He told me so. Then," assuming the timbre of a scary story, "he drank another gulp."

Not as strange as I thought. Fighting with the giggles that demanded emoting, "Yuri?"

"Yes Susan?"

"Do you ever worry that you're boring person in the bedroom and everyone else is far more exciting?"

"With what I have seen? Yes." Taking another breath he let out a sigh and tone of apologetics, "I am going to go now, as while we're on the subject –"

"Go. I'm going to get my things together and then be along to use the shower. There is an unopened toothbrush in the bathroom in this hall. You can get your new brush and head downstairs to get the coffee, breakfast, that sort of routine."

"Oh, neat. I had forgotten to ask." Gesturing to his mouth, "did I offend?"

"No. I am just trying to be a good host."

"Thank you."

"Noted. Thank you Yuri. You're a wonderful man."

"I am blushing, and I'm going." Moving to the bedroom door, "I'll get the brush, then head down for morning coffee.

"I'll meet you there after my shower."

"Noted!"

Watching his back disappear through the bedroom doorway and into the hall she found herself reflecting on her mother's writings and recordings. *I think I want him to be the person I hope he is because it just makes sense. Mom went out on the deck to talk to Asmodai and fell in love with him out there just watching his hands wave as he spoke. She woke the man hiding under the emotional scar tissue and she never wanted to leave him.*

Never perfect, but never worth undoing or regretting.

When the dust settles and the smoke clears I'm going to do this right. I suspect my heart is already made up.

Setting to getting out of bed with a spring in her motion she smiled at herself in the bedroom mirror. *I look terrible but so did he. All is well.*

5.8.0 - 08:36

Safe Housing - Interior

☀ Yuri

Walking down the stairs with a lightness of spirit he noticed the front door was opening slowly. *She did not mention visitors, but no sounds of violence.*

Calling out the hunch toward the opening door, "Steven?"

Opening the door the rest of the way and stepping inside the woman looked at him with a perplexed grin, "not quite."

Watching her close the door he noted the Dagger patch on her armor. "You are a Dagger?"

Replying with a matter of fact pride, "Dagger Herb."

Oh. "I am Yuri."

Regarding him with an expression of being lost in contemplation, "you are he."

The moment I had wondered of. Moving down the stairs with a slow but steady gait, "you are her."

Posing the question with a tentative grace, "a parcel of land and a house to put on it?"

Nodding twice he smiled, "that's all I came here to ask for. What I was told I could ask for according to the legend."

Speaking with a tone wrapped in compassion, "she cared for you?"

Nodding again, "she kept me in a safe, cool, dark, dry place. A root cellar of the heart, if you will. I was not in good shape when I arrived."

Stepping closer with a hushed awe, "you survived the place beyond the horizon."

I am not surprised to hear horror. "I did. I needed healing, she gave me healing. I, did what men do, I have grown, attached, to the happiness I feel at her side."

"Do you fear her?"

"No." Musing on the notion he branched the question, "do I fear *for* her? Yes."

I will speak the truth.

"I do not seek to diminish her, but I have seen the tornado, the hurricane, the monsoon, the typhoon, and the volcano. I have witnessed the stampede. I have learned to fly and barely kept my full tank of fuel with wings aloft until the tank ran dry and I landed a part of a world away. I don't see chaos, or destruction, in her eyes. I see *home.*"

Touching her hands to his with a quieter presence about her, "I see the hiraeth in her eyes when I look for meaning in them."

I have not heard that word in a long time. "Your home is no home?"

Cocking her head at him with a smile, "you know the word?"

Rolling into the friendlier moment without hesitation, "I have seen Wales. I learned it there." Pausing he slowed himself down, "the question stands though."

"Yuri," stepping close to him she spoke calmly, "I had the best upbringing I could get, but I didn't belong there. I didn't *belong* somewhere until I found Susan. When I look in her eyes I wish for things that can never be and I have to learn to cherish what I have."

"Noted."

"I don't know what to say, looking at you, as I didn't think to prepare anything. I couldn't find a place to start the thoughts."

If she does not know, I will speak. "I don't know if I should say mea culpa or speak of a shared good taste in love."

Firing back with an assuring tone, "there is no crime in your love for her. I have waited the whole time I have known her for you to arrive."

"If you have waited for me, I would ask, what do you know of me?"

"For one, the thought that I don't want to go to."

"Which is?"

"May I preamble?"

I don't know why not. "Please do."

Holding her own hands she spoke with a daunted bravado, "the men in her office, they were wired. Dennis provided me with a snippet of that audio."

Oh dear. "What was it?"

Sniffling she turned and leaned against a blank section of wall with a shake of her head, "you screaming her name and asking for the color of her veil."

Stepping to her he staggered as she collided with him. Moving his arms around her he braced her and himself against her shaking form.

They did not tell her how close it was.

"I *knew*, I *saw*, the blood on her clothes, on her sleeve. I understood that she had to fight for her life. But, but, I didn't think about her being *dead*."

"Has she been this close before?"

"Twice."

"*Twice?*"

By the stars.

"When she was young, she was visiting the North. She fell through ice, and they nearly lost her then. The other, I saw. She was training, driving, on the East End of New Hope at a course the Cloak and Dagger maintains. A Blitz Storm had soaked the thing, but she was scheduled and she was going to drive."

"What happened?"

"She flipped the practice car. I ran faster than the medics to get to her and help get her out."

That explains that.

"In the moment, it was simple, get her out of the car. She would be alive if she was removed from the wreck. I haven't seen her as close to being *dead,* as you did."

I understand more.

Stammering his name for a moment she recovered, "Yuri, I *understand* that you love her. I heard it. She's not your Derecho, or your High Consul, not like she is to us."

"I would hazard an agreement with that."

"I, I don't get to walk next to her today. You do though."

"I will walk with her, as I do, is there something special about this day?"

Stepping back from him she nodded with suppressed anger in her voice, "Thomas Kunlow waits in custody for her judgment."

The mastermind. "The man who spoke this into motion?"

"Yes."

"What must she do?"

Grimacing with the words, "confirm his execution or see him spared."

Oof. "I will be by her side."

"I don't know who else is with him, I just know that Frank told me that I would come out here, tell her to go in, and she just has to place her Seal on a few boxes. Nothing to worry about."

"Noted."

Reaching up she touched the shadow of the beard that was returning, "the Winter Wolf. The legend they are writing for you? It is no small set of words."

Feeling the humbling implications, "they write a legend for me?"

"Your snarled battle condemnation, it set a memory in those who witnessed it and lived."

Taking a moment to assess her eyes, "are you afraid of me?"

Closing them she shook her head softly, "no." Opening them she elaborated, "you are the sort of man I had wondered of. It is not fear, it is the honest admiration of someone who is strong."

"What is strong, in local parlance?"

"It is not how many times you fall down, it is if you can lift the burden and get back to your feet again. Strength is found in defeat. In setback. When the dynamic energy of victory and youth is spent? Is when you find out if you are strong."

I can wrap my mind around that. "Noted."

"It's been, no small amount of turmoil."

"Truth."

Tipping her head back against the wall she looked him in the eyes, "I have the," stopping for a moment, "without code this is harder to say."

"What is the code?"

"The Whole Pie of Factors. We have pie charts, circle, lines, different colors. When used as the fullness of an idea it's offered as a Whole. Goes into the metaphors about food for thought."

I think I understand. "I believe, that I follow you. Speak the statements?"

"I believe the three of us would be better off if you did not leave her side."

Smiling he nodded, "thank you, noted. I don't believe you should leave either."

Nodding with a smile of her own, "I believe that if we were allies in this, that we could keep her safer."

Yes. "A few good pairs of hands makes a load lighter."

With a reduced smile, "however, as I am still human, and prone to folly, I am jealous of you."

"Eh?"

Sighing she straightened up, "Yuri, I *am* jealous, and conflicted, and not in a good place right now. But those *aren't* cancellation statements against the validity of your place. That's why I have to offer the Whole Pie."

I will rescue us both from this. "Sasha?"

"Yes?"

"We can, from my understanding, just search the Codex for answers as we come to them. If you can stay honest with me, I can stay honest with you." Taking a breath he picked his path, "we didn't paint last night. She didn't clean my brush. And I certainly did not go," fumbling for a moment, "the downside of the paint metaphor. When it is water I could use bobbing for orgasms."

Stopping in her tracks with a titter of laughter she hung her head, "you are also someone who uses words as she does."

"I have spent a lifetime studying language."

Raising her head with a bewildered smile, "you are a Conlanger?"

"What is a Conlanger?"

"Those who study language and who tend our dictionary."

"Isn't that just a linguist?"

Rolling her hands she shrugged, "I was taught that linguists study foreign language. To the human mind, any language is native if it is learned first. As our version of English is Prescriptive, it means different things than the Descriptive English of the past, also it is not ashamed of other languages and their words that don't translate well into English. Secondly, with our treasure trove of knowledge and materials from before the Ash, other languages are still needed to translate and communicate ideas."

"You know more than English then?"

"Quebec French and Southern Spanish, to a fairly healthy extent."

"Neighbors?"

"Yes."

Back on track, "as for the three of us, you are staying, yes?"

Brightening with a resigned courage, "I am going to ask her if we can schedule a time to discuss our future."

"Good."

Inquiring with a caring candor, "when do I get to meet you?"

The first step must be taken to have a journey. "When the dust settles? I will be here, hopefully, and will be able to communicate with you. Honestly and openly."

"Good."

I should make certain, "there is a Primer for this, yes?"

"Not *exactly,* but there are many which I believe will be close enough to advise us."

I am not without experience, "I may have learned a few things in my travels to aid me."

Reaching to him and touching his hand with her hand for a moment, "what is the foundation of what you know?"

Taking a moment to marshal his truth he tapped his chin with a crooked finger. "My God. He gave me the capacity to be good. To learn the lessons from those who speak on his behalf. To gain strength by being good. I have spoken with men who had told me that there is no God in the Heavens. That there is no Ever After. That this is a cosmic joke. I still pressed on because I could be *happy* if I was good. It was who I am. Even if I had to pay a price to be as I would choose to model myself in my framework of madness. If the shark is the shark, the lion is the lion, then the Yuri is the Yuri. Even if this is all a delusional fantasy of hoping for my life to have meant a single thing? *I would enjoy living it.*"

Catching his gaze with sad eyes, "you met an Anti-theist?"

This is new. "Anti-theist?"

"You've seen that we're attached to our Gods."

Truth. "You are, it's kind of nice to see people with different Faiths not fighting over them."

Lapsing into an Academic timbre with a airy look on her face, "the bedrock message of Faith is searching for a way to wrap our minds around the concept of The Watchmaker. The Universe came from something, so theism, Faith, is trying to wrap our minds around that idea. We have atheists, who are people who do not believe in the theism and that system. They have Faith in people, in our minds, in our ability to create a better world without the thought of Thor, Odin, Zeus, Amaterasu, and the like. When you said *delusion,* that falls into the purview of the Anti-theist. The person whom by their words seeks to harm those who believe in theism by speaking against them and their beliefs."

They allow even that then? "You have people who do not believe in God?"

"We have some, yes. The atheist is encouraged to not be rude, as the theist is told that we all find out the truth on the other side. Someone is most likely wrong about something, at least we all made an effort."

"Are you?"

"No. The Captain takes us to temple when we have time to go. We worship in a house of wisdom and examine the ideas of Nanė and Anahit. The long story short? It helps us to make the decision to stay in the military or retire to become mothers. Either way, we have meaning and beauty in our lives and service."

"Noted." *I will try what I have heard,* "share a worry?"

Tapping her thumbs together, "just one?"

"I have delayed you long enough for her to finish her shower up. I believe I have time for one."

"Noted." Visibly pondering for a moment, "I worry that she will experience sex, love it, and then try to console me in ways I will doubt because I'm still not ready to be loved as she loves."

I will be brave, "would you rather I console you?"

"Not so much a rather," shaking her head she puffed up to her full height and off the wall, "however, maintaining a friendship with you? Is something that cannot be shirked. The moment we become, and stay, in opposition? Is the day we tear the whole thing down."

A heart divided cannot stand. "Then we shall be at the side of the other. I Pact this Pledge."

Reaching a hand out to him, "take my hand."

Taking her hand he smiled, "I Pact this Pledge."

Nodding the affirmation, "we walk toward unknowns, we need to find a map, but I will walk with you as ally in this. I Pact this Pledge."

Squeezing her hand he lowered his hand as soon as her grip relaxed, "I will guard her this day."

"Thank you."

"I need to go get the coffee. I saw Travel Mugs? I can also try to find us food."

Fishing out her keys, "I forgot the food. I brought breakfast for the two of you."

Taking the keys, "where do I leave them?"

"Just leave them in the car. It can't lock if the keys are inside and no one is sitting in the driver's seat."

Good to know. "Noted."

5.8.1 - 08:47

Safe Housing – Bathing Room

⁘..Susan Bachman

Washing the last of the soap off of her neck she paused a moment to caress herself gently from the top of her left shoulder to her left wrist. *I should finish and face my day.*

Looking down at her legs she smiled at the freshly shaved state of them. *Did manage a bit of self care.*

Hearing the door opening she moved her hand over to the press and release plate. Readying herself to retrieve her shotgun she paused, waiting for the person in the door-way to speak.

With a firm timbre of reassurance, the voice from the door, rang out over the sound of the shower, "olly olly oxen free."

Sasha.

Moving her hand away from the plate she didn't try to keep the relief out of her voice, "what brings you to me?"

Without moving from the door she called out again, "the Commander wanted me to see you in person to drop off the SitRep."

Moving over to the curtain she pulled it open slightly and spoke with less volume, "why are you standing next to the door? You haven't been shy in some time."

Lowering her voice she answered, "I'm *whelmed.*"

Rinsing the last of the soap off, "good whelmed or bad whelmed?"

"*Both?* I wasn't ready for how well that went."

Turning the water off she opened the shower curtain, "can you be less vague?"

Turning her attention to her and then away with a 'put upon' expression, "no."

No use fighting with her. "Fair enough."

Turning back to her with a lost smile, "I knew, what you had said, but *hearing it,* from him? I," licking her lips she smiled at her with a dumbfounded look on her face, "get to be happy?"

Taking a moment to look Sasha over she ordered the concerns in her mind. *I'll get the SitRep and then deal with my Aardvark.* "Give me the SitRep."

Holding up her comm she waived it for a moment before setting to reading, "Former Consul Thomas Kunlow has been exhausted for information. Execution order is pending. Former House Kunlow Head Supply Agent Ardent Kunlow, who knowingly brokered the arms, armaments, armor, and supplies has also been exhausted. Execution order is pending. Marissa Kunlow has been confirmed as the Delivery Agent for the Terror Strike Device which cost the lives of three equipment operators in the Security Nerve Center and causing the Aureole of Central to be temporarily extinguished. Her execution order is also pending."

Reaching over to her towel she plucked it from the hook, "is there something else?"

Laughing with a bitter bite to the emoting, "always. It's not *the worst thing* though. The Commander put Josh Kunlow before the Questioners. I have a report from Head Questioner Muldaire that Josh did not see the table. He would like you to deal with Josh first, then move on to the Execution Orders."

The Dark Merchant strikes again.

"What do you know about Josh's situation?"

"On or off the record?"

I need to know if my first hurdle is your heart. "Off."

Grimacing she clucked her tongue, "he knew. He didn't like it. He wasn't supporting the endeavor. He was put into a puzzle box prison he couldn't solve. The Questioners, the three you still have, have submitted the recommendation that he be spared."

Three is better than zero. Taking a breath she steadied herself, *I will free Josh and then move forward with the day.* "Noted."

Nodding she stepped out of the shower alcove and set to drying off. Watching Sasha moving over to the storage cabinet, "do you need something?"

"I'm getting the coconut oil for your hair. I need to make sure you get into motion. Yuri is getting the breakfast I brought for the two of you, making the coffee, and prepping the travel mugs."

Teamwork gets it done. "I'll need the body butter next to it."

"I know. I *do know* your routine." Grabbing the two containers, "there is no small amount of chatter about some extra project that went down last night. The Commander is digging something out. Hampton took over when he went to get some sleep. O'Neil had to drag him off the field this morning."

"Is that in my SitRep?"

"No. Word is that The Commander will explain when it's time." Setting the containers down near her she looked past her at her robe. "Is that the," looking at her with a flare of shock, "did you *seriously* make the hem of your bathrobe your High Consul Seal?"

Finally noticed? Grinning with an unabashed humor, "you commissioned the robe for me. I had a new one made when I wore the last one out. I liked the symbolism of it. Also? Jerome assured me that the one I use has security features that will make it harder to compromise. Each cat is a different passkey." Reaching out and touching Sasha's cheek, "security that's hard to compromise? Sounds like someone I know."

"You know just the things to say. I'll get the oil in your hair while you moisturize."

"Deal." Taking the container she set to work on herself, "how many others does The Commander want dead?"

"None." Moving behind her with the coconut oil and hairbrush, "he's been giving ground to those with Dominion with an alacrity which is not typical, but it's appreciated by those dealing with him."

I can't leave Jerome out in the cold, "is he angered with Jerome?"

"Not to my knowledge." Setting to the gentle brushing, "Jerome is still holed up somewhere secret. Dennis, before he quit the field this morning, relayed to me that Jerome is somewhere Paige found for him in her social network. She's running in a borrowed vehicle and has him stashed somewhere he normally isn't found. Even if The Commander isn't mad? If there were any Assets left in the wild? It's prudent."

Dennis and Jerome getting to work together is going to be a security fiesta. "It is."

With a tone of offhanded friendliness to it, "I'm surprised you're this far behind your timetable."

The inconceivable. "I slept in."

"*You?*"

"Yes." *Really get her with these words,* "then? I stayed in bed for some extra time."

Chuckling with the humor of her words, "*that,* I know all too fondly."

Speaking to console her, "we'll get a bed big enough for all three, and if you both have need? I'll lay in the middle and try to be enough for both of you."

With a mock rise to the occasion, "this is the part where I joke it would be *me* in the middle. But I'm not very good at Smoke."

Countering with a cool grace, "you do love hugs. I wouldn't be shocked."

Chuffing a sigh, "I need more inner peace."

Agreeing with a light tone, "you do."

"If I had the inner peace I crave? I would be able to joke about threesomes, flirtations, and the like. You're fun, he seems to be a fun person, and I'm just standing here wishing I had the peace to have that kind of fun."

"It's something you could work on. Assuring yourself that he doesn't bite, that he won't misunderstand, and then you could practice having fun."

"Noted. Truth."

Turning around she met Sasha's gaze, "I know you have a thorn in your mind. Yuri does not know about the depth of the thorn. The kindness he showed you was without the full context of how much pain you have in the back of your skull." Reaching up she placed her lotion slick hands on Sasha's jaw and neck, "I will lay you between us, it will be friendly and uplifting, without a threesome, and you will see truth. I will garb you in truth and you will be armored against the Shadow's Thorn."

Watching her relax and relent to the touch she watched a matching smile form, "you are good to me Susan."

"Noted."

Opening her eyes she appeared present, "we need to finish so you can get going."

Nodding she let go of her and turned back around. Setting to finish the moisturizing, "what's left unsaid?"

"The Commander has an appointment to speak with me when this is over. We don't have a specific Time Index, just that the appointment exists."

I can clear any Smoke before he sets it. "I'll ask him about it."

"Thank you." Continuing as she ministered to Susan's hair, "*dad* is at the Kunlow Estate. He's learning about their new book of Faith. It's a newly restored piece of work. What I learned before I left? It sounds well structured and ambitious. The sort of Faith which makes Good Citizens."

"Good."

"When you go and I go, do you want me to stop by the Grain Silo? With this wrapping up, it might be good to have the next item on the table."

That would be good. "As you were the one she saw drop off the presents? That would be good. Reylai already knows you from the interview with Captain Turner."

"Susan?"

Taking a quiet deep breath, *that's her serious tone.* "Yes?"

"When the weather calms, I would like to discuss becoming your Consort."

No answer but one. "Deal."

"I have wanted to ask you about that for a very long time."

Smiling brightly to her in the mirror on the wall ahead of them she caught her glance for a moment, "I am glad we finally got to deal with the question."

Ducking her head back behind her, "you're almost someone else."

That's a new one to hear. "Do you still recognize me?"

"I do. I can still hear the howling wind of the Derecho but it's different now. *You're* finally *you.* Not an *Echo,* not a construct of thought, not a game, but *you.*"

Picking up a hand towel she set to patting the excess off, "I am glad you see it that way. It feels heartening to hear."

"Have I told you how majestic you are?"

Thinking it over she smiled, "yes. The first time we showered in the same locker room. I came out and you took a look at me and spoke the term under your breath. It was so quiet that I barely managed to hear it."

Watching Sasha step out from around her with the whisper of, "your hair is done," she regarded her as she came closer. Holding still as she moved forward she smiled when she reached mere centimeters from her.

I wonder what she's going to do. "Aardvark?"

Smiling suddenly Sasha leaned in and kissed her on the cheek, "the world didn't explode."

Taking the other container from her she spoke using her sweetest syrup voice, "my heart did."

Smiling with a look of unburdened humor to her Sasha stepped back laughing, "Susan, I love you."

Setting both containers on the nearby shelf, "I love you too."

Going over to the wall she snagged the robe and held it out to Susan with a thoughtful grin, "to think, I commissioned the original *nine* years ago. It's a long time to forget about something. Especially when you haven't worn it around me since the dorms."

Offering the simple answer, "it is what it is."

Answering with an honored humor, "you made your High Consul seal, *that*, of all things though."

Tying the knot with a smile, "I did."

"It's not the same color, is it?"

Standing in the moment she felt her heart lifted, "they were able to get *close* with the shade. The downside of our handcrafted reality."

Reaching out and touching her gently she sniffled, "you knew, this whole time, how much you loved me. From kept mementos, to the patience you showed, from never pushing me like we discussed."

Kissing her on the cheek she moved over toward the door to assuming a leaning place against the wall next to the frame. *The depths of things I left unsaid,* "to the fights I had with father until he gave up on the subject."

"Did you make him a Deal?"

As many as the stars in the sky, and one for us too. "I did. I told him when the time was right I would bring forth a child to show the women of our lands that even I would embrace the renewal of the generation. That it was so safe that even *I* would do it. Then I would bring forth at least one more so the child would not be alone."

"I won't leave your side."

"We'll talk more about Consort when I have my world back in order. Not from a yes or no angle, but the logistics of it."

"Noted. As for Yuri at your side? I believe that the people will accept him. The Potentate, The Gardener, and the Winter Wolf."

Thinking the image over she felt the need to ask an artist to bring it forth. *I look forward to seeing the reality of it,* "that sounds like a future worth being in."

"The Legend, the Myth, and the Gardener in the middle. This time the story gets to see an ending that isn't someone leaving or the sacrifice of a life."

That audio. The price of power. Of life. "I am heartened." *Don't cry,* "the first time his line met mine, was saving the life of Asmodai The Reborn. The second was saving the life of Alexis and the children, specifically Penelope. This time, I think I get to help save him in return."

Offering the idea as an upbeat hope, "third time is a charm?"

Nodding in affirmation, "I hope so."

"Me too."

I can confide in you, "I do have something I have to see put to rest, or we can't have a happy ending to our lives."

"Which is?"

"Admin Nobody has done a trace and profile on the supplies used by the attacking force at Central. The munitions, firearms, and supplies for that night came from various places. They were brokered for, traded for, and arranged to make sure that the Kunlow House had enough to do this. Proxies were used, hidden under identities and acquisitions, all to fool the system into not sending up an alert via the watchdog scripts. This was no flash in the pan operation."

"Based upon what I saw, I would agree."

Grousing about the truth, "this was for my father, and they just handed it down to me."

"How many stand against you still?"

"That's the thing, the crux of my issue, I don't know. I don't know if Thomas duped them all and they are just as scared of me as I am of them. I will go deal with Thomas and find out the roots of his betrayal. I have Consuls that I am praying it would not be. In the end I want it to be none of them. I want Thomas to have played them for fools."

"I do not know what Ardent told the Questioners. Perhaps you will know more sooner than later?"

If Ardent knows, I will know. "Truth. Noted." Taking in the sight of her smile, "thank you for the smile. I didn't want to ruin our Spirits and Sweets moment with talk of the cry of the Whippoorwill sounding."

"What becomes of your plans in the wake of this?"

"I know that my father, he wouldn't hide if he saw an answer. He would lead a charge with his carbine and *show* his people what glorious foolish anger, drunk with courage, would have looked like. I don't know if that's what this is going to become. If it does? I will practice my riding into battle waving my sword."

Laughing with a desperate humor, "I love you."

"I love you also."

"Aardvark?"

"Yes?"

Moving to the spot next to her she bumped her hip with hers, "you need to get back to work."

"I do." Moving away from her to the other side of the door, "grab a shower, freshen up, then go see Reylai."

"I will."

Reaching back and taking Sasha's hand she squeezed it gently, "if I falter and use the wrong words? Do not feel diminished."

Raising her chin in a playful defiance, "I don't recall being taught that you loving us both was bad."

I am going to risk her wrath, "I love both of you with a recklessness not befitting a High Consul, it fits that of an Irish Wizard."

Eyeing her with the hint of humored vengeance, "one of the sadder shows in the Network. Which I *wouldn't* know about if you hadn't *subjected* me to it while you watched it."

Letting go of Sasha's hand she stepped away from her to face the door, "it is what it is. I won't stop loving though."

Shaking her head negatively, "no one should ask you that. Not even you."

Placing her hand on the knob, "thank you Sasha."

Waving her off, "go do your work."

Moving a step away she looked to her with sweet syrup in her voice, "be well Sasha."

Rolling her eyes with a put upon expression and a tone bordering on melancholy. "you said that already."

I really don't want to leave. I don't. "I did. Meant it both times." Opening the door she let herself out into the hall, "I will see you when I see you again."

Calling after her with the loving tone ringing clearly, "until then."

She doesn't want to see me leave either. It's not our choice to make though. Closing the door she turned on her heel and headed for her room, *time to put on the Vestments of the Enforcer.*

5.7.5 - 08:08

164 Magdalena – Ochenhart Residence

■Dennis Ochenhart

Reading the clock with a disdain for the truth that it was still morning he sighed. *Only a few hours and I'm awake again.* Flexing his hands he felt a measure of weakness of his fingers and grip. *How terrible a sadness that trounces a body without a single drop drank.*

Hearing the inquisitive tone from his doorway, "Father?"

Looking to the doorway he smiled weakly at Stephanie, "come in."

Moving closer she examined him with a frown, "what plagues you?"

Gesturing to his tablet covered in funeral notices, "everything. I was up late hunting and am debating if I want to be awake so soon."

"You have not gone," pausing on the word her voice was filled with questions, "*hunting*, in some time."

Trying to play it glib, "I had something I wanted," correcting himself, "*needed*, to attend to."

Finishing the movement to him she sat on the edge of his bed, "the wicked?"

"Thieves. A VIP was stolen. The ringleader was found. The VIP is being found and removed from the box they were put in. But the *helpers?* I wanted to feel useful. I wanted to be *young* again. I tracked them. I hunted them. I gave them a choice to make."

"Did you find your quarry?"

Nodding with an empty smile, "I found them. All five of them. One was already dead. Unauthorized Exit Pass." Rubbing his face for a moment he sighed, "I was able to alert the correct people, and warn them of what they would find. The other four are in custody."

Caressing his cheek with the back of her fingertips she moved his bangs around with an idle playfulness, "my father the stalker of the wicked. The races you used to have with others in pursuing quarry."

Defending his actions with his words, "I endeavored to bring them in alive, when I can."

Touching his shoulder with a tone of comfort, "I know. I know that sometimes that you don't want to. Did you feel better when your hunt was over?"

Making a strange face at her he relaxed his muscles into a smile, "I did."

Affirming the notion, "then it was a good hunt."

Gesturing to his tablet, "I couldn't face the list there, knowing who had fallen, and do nothing in the wake of it. I atoned for my self imposed ideals."

Urging him with her tone, "you do not mourn them alone."

"I know. I will stand while others sing the requiem."

Finding his gaze, "will there be fireworks?"

Next Sunday. "The Day of Laughter is next weekend, first Sunday after Beltane. The arrangements are being made to see if there can be a display that night of those who would wish to be celebrated for having lived, and not for having died."

Averting her gaze, "I don't know if I will be home to see it."

New developments? "You are going somewhere?"

"I had received a communication, a letter, from my family in Chihuahua the day before the attack. They wish for me to come visit. It was from my Cousin Iago. He was there the day I said goodbye. He was just a boy, the one in the green shirt."

I remember. "He said he would find a way to see you again. I brought you back for your quinceañera, the same honor you share with Miss Kunlow," pausing to reflect on the memories, "seems like yesterday and a forever ago."

"He did see me again. He was there when we went. He was the handsome one in the festive poncho. He wants to know if I would bring Juniper and see the family that could not afford to keep me."

Never miss a chance to maximize the good in your life. "You should take Fritz with you."

Speaking his name as a single stumbled intonation, "Fritz –"

Pressing the issue, "is *still* her father. You want him back, yes?"

Nodding she kept her mouth closed.

"Then give him a *mission* to do, that only he can do. Tell him to escort you and Juniper to Bliss, to see Miss Augusta, and then to escort the two of you to your destination."

"What changed?"

She knows his name as well as anyone who didn't know him, "Ridolfi's agents are near. Take Sharp-Shot Sally to Fritz, and tell him that the Fence is Breached. You need to be somewhere safer than here."

Confirming her plans, "I leave today, at fourteen-hundred."

Enough time to find a husband, pack a child, and get to the train station. "There is still enough time to make all the arrangements you need to make."

Regarding him with a sad understanding of the plan, "is it safer to be at your side, or to leave it?"

"I am not alone. There are others who will wish to speak with these agents. I just have to be careful to not be taken unaware."

"Noted."

Looking to the ceiling he reflected on the thoughts he didn't want, "I cannot fathom the depravity of spirit it would take to snuff out Miss Augusta."

Grasping his hand firmly she squeezed it, sharing the grief with her timbre, "I miss her as well, and I too am without words. She was one of the more gloriously bright lights in the pantheon you found me to understand the life I was given here."

"I have a question, it is unfair, but I am hopeful."

"Speak it."

Always seek the Light in the Darkness. "What will you do if you convince Fritz to come home?"

"I will convince him to grant me the place at his side again, and siblings for Juniper. I never asked him to leave me. I was too willing to give up on him when he gave up on himself. I didn't understand then, as I do now. Fritz no longer looks like a melted candle, which leaves me hoping that he would let love back in."

"He did not find another. Neither did you. I would hope that he could see that for what it is."

"I hope as well."

This pain is the sort that makes life coming to a close seem like a promise of rest. "This hurts like it hurt then."

Taking his hand with both of hers, "you healed from that. You have survived the dangers, the snares, and traps placed before you by your enemies. You carried me, behind an armor plated sheet in the back of your vehicle, through the storm. You found the moment of Grace granted, and helped see a bolt of justice set upon the Warlord. You were there to bring an end to the conflict. I *know you,* you are strong. You *will* mend."

I can Pact the Pledge, even if I don't say it. "I will endeavor to heal from this."

Tilting her head to the side she nodded twice at him, "what is the thing you aren't telling me about this? You get a look about you when you are hiding a facet from me."

You know me as well as family can. "Miss Bachman is going to go reclaim her sister."

Gasping in shock she covered her mouth with both hands, "*Amaranth,* is the missing VIP."

Nodding as best he could from his supine position he scowled, "yes."

Lowering her hands with a look of surprise, "you didn't tell her yet. It's *pending,* isn't it?"

"Correct. We took steps to make sure her sister was safe and going to stay that way so we could leave it to her to do."

"You cannot be by her side in this?"

"No. Her sister, she is going to be in rough shape, at the very least emotionally. We are not to pry into her condition. She deserves, and has the right, to privacy."

"I understand. Have you spoken with Daisy?"

"I sent her a memo. I told her I didn't have enough room in a memo to mourn Bonnie. I told her, in code of course, that Ridolfi had touched the fence. She has a backup plan where she can get the Starlight Squad on our fastest troop hauling plane and get them back to New Hope."

"Are you afraid of invasion?"

"I don't know what I'm afraid of. Invasion? We could call the Sky-Cleaver to service, and that would be the end of an invading force."

Doing an approximation of an upbeat tone, "it broke the Warlord and his forces."

Enough talk of the dead. "If you have need? Speak to Daisy, she could convince Fritz to come see her."

"I will keep that in my playable cards."

One of my better students.

Touching his hand gently, "I have a question–"

"Speak it."

"The man I saw take the bundle I left on the porch of Safe Housing, that is Yuri?"

Smiling with a vacant humor, "I would *assume* so."

Assuming a tone of praise, "he was taller than I thought he would be."

The man is a beast, "he is a very large man."

Without losing her tone of praise, "he sees to her?"

Affirming her with the truth, "he does."

"I can accept him."

Looking to her face he reached up and touched her cheek gently, "how are you?"

"Unwell." Holding her hands in her lap she sniffled softly, "Susan makes our world brighter. When I looked up and saw Central dark? I was horrified. What must you do to stop Ridolfi?"

"I have to trust the people I have watching for those who came looking for her. No one really knows who they are. The Network has no answers right now. Thomas picked the absolutely worst moment for this."

Pantomiming a clipboard and checklist, "tell me once more how I can be certain Fritz will agree?"

Running over the plan to make sure he couldn't see any holes in it, "first? Get Sharp-Shot Sally. Have Daisy prepared to call him either way. Then give her back to him, tell him of the danger. If he agrees? Signal her to encourage him and ask him to stop by to see her. If he does not? Signal her to ask him down as a personal favor to look over the situation. One way or another combine Juniper, the rifle, and Daisy until he agrees."

Checking the last thing off she dropped the act with a firm resolve, "I can do this."

One more thing to see done before I die of exhaustion. "When you get him out? Catch him by the toe, do not let him go."

"I will not let him go back into darkness."

Sitting in the quiet he closed his eyes for a moment only to be roused by her question.

"What is your end game?"

Opening his eyes with a grimace, "I get Ridolfi. He's been poking at Bliss, he's learned to stop poking at the Carnap lands, but now he's made it across a lot of distance to get this close to us. I will find his assets, I will trace it back to him, and I will *beg her* to let me see this to the end."

"I will go finishing packing my things." Leaning down she kissed him gently on the temple, "you have my blessing father. Hunt your enemy until he troubles you no longer."

"Thank you Stephanie. Thank you so much."

Getting up and setting to leaving him, "send for me when you have defeated the monster."

"I will."

Looking back at him from the doorway, "I believe in you."

"Thank you."

Nodding once she spoke her reply, "noted."

Watching her disappear he closed his eyes, *either I win and she hears from me. Or I lose and she hears it from someone else.*

I told her it would be good again, that where she was going was a good place.

I'm not going to let Templeton make a liar out of me.

5.8.8 - 09:50

The Beast – En Route to C&D

☼..Susan Bachman

Setting her travel mug of morning coffee into the cup holder she took a moment to mull the moment over. *Sinclair is alive and doing better with each message I send him. Exonerated of all wrong doing with the truth of the matter.* Looking over the diagram of the Pyramid she grimaced at the state of things.

Opening herself to the emotional pain she went over the words from the Bachman Codex. *Close Ranks. Regroup. Tend to the wounded. Reinforce Ranks. Hold the Line. Surrender not even a millimeter to your enemies and their machinations.*

I'm not the only one who is going through this process.

Hearing the music lower she looked up at Yuri, "yes?"

"You look troubled."

"I, am. With Thomas dying today, his daughter is going to be the head of the House. She'll be going through a process which is no small amount of hurt. I don't want to lose her as an ally before I have the chance to gain her as one."

With a timbre of assessment, "that is the woman that the Sys-Admin said was not involved, yes?"

He seeks to understand the Pyramid. "Yes. Lady Octavia Kunlow."

"Noted. Just doing my best to keep up." Pausing for a moment he laughed, "is there diagram of this? There *is* one, yes?"

Smiling in the sudden humor, "yes!"

"Can I see it?"

No harm in it. Public knowledge is public knowledge. "Yes. Longer Answer? I can go over it with you, orientation of it, and then make certain that your borrowed tablet can view it."

Sighing dramatically in relief, "that would be *wonderful.*"

I have the moment, "I have another example of wonderful."

Putting on a sing song tone with his curiosity ringing, "you do?"

"You cleaned up well. You look very nice today." Gesturing to him, "Casual Yuri."

Nodding with a smile he pursed his lips for a moment before his hesitant words came out, "you King me again. How do I Queen you?"

How to keep this from taking days to explain?

"Yuri, I King you, because when I did it the first time, it worked as intended. If it did not, there would be other ways to praise you. The internal archetypes of the male mind being what they are. Being as *I* am, you don't King, or Queen, me. To praise, adore, appreciate, or the like? That's Gardening."

"Gardening then?"

Relaxing with the words, "yes. I don't rule from the center of my heart, I just *exist*, as nature. My ad libs are the wind. My pain and heartache are weeds. The metaphor goes on from there. You, as the man you are, are a King in your own heart. Your Castle, and land, is the world as you view it from within. The first step in praise is to King you. The second is to make sure that you tend to your lands within you. In contrast, I, am the land itself within."

Speaking casually of the understood notion, "tread softly then."

Tilting her tone toward appreciative, "I do appreciate the softer footfalls on the land of my heart. Though, as the *land* and what grows forth from it? I do have a more, earthy, sense of humor."

Reflecting on the idea, "you have laughed at some of my musings, jokes, and the like that many women I have met did not."

Echoing her notion with a smile, "the earthy sense of humor."

Seeming satisfied with the idea, "noted, you are as the earth," gesturing to her quickly before returning his hand to the wheel, "what is the nature of the tarp you place over the soil to protect it?"

Looking down at her Vestments she nodded once, "this outfit is the Vestments of the Enforcer. I want to show I am on official business, and I would prefer if people stayed out of my way as the business is not peaceful."

Raising his brows for a moment he appeared taken aback, "Enforcer today?"

Hunting for strength she found the notion to lean on, "there are three people waiting for me to sign the order on them being executed. I don't have to do it personally though. I am cautioned to *not* do so. Also, one that I need to send home to his wife. Wearing this? I show people I don't have time to socialize."

Smiling again with relief, "ah! Noted."

Keeping it simple, "I am to go in, review the moment, sign off on it, and move along. I wear this so I don't balk or shirk my duties."

"Fair enough, neh?"

"I can hope."

"I do appreciate new clothes though. The shoes are nice too."

"Noted."

"Question," pitching his tone to a humored fear, "does anyone have to wear burlap clothing?"

Laughing at the sad reality of the idea she shook her head, "no. The burlap is needed for the bags, gardening, and crafts. We create fabrics and materials, and then use them where they need to go. The Ration difference in the outfits is typically complexity of outfit, dyes, embellishments, and craftsmanship level. The State subsidizes all school uniforms for this reason."

"The State does?"

"The State doesn't have unlimited hours or resources, we're on a budget, so a student only gets *one* uniform at a time from The State though. Parents can arrange more than one uniform, but it has to be to uniform specifications. Otherwise? That would defeat the purpose. The goal is to prevent economic differences from showing in the classrooms. After the students leave the school? What they wear is on them."

"They cannot wear what they wish?"

The darkness of the past. "Deep in the Network we found case upon case of how the idea of the return to the schools in the fall, it caused a social phenomenon that was jaw dropping in the abuses and emotional madness which stemmed from it. Which included recalled tales of selling bodies as young people for money to afford to be *normal.* To get a new round of clothes for the year in exchange for such things."

Grimacing with his sadness evident, "I am familiar with the concept, economic prostitution, yes."

"Our system built a system to side step the idea. To use the give-and-give to strike a bargain with the youth. When a youth chafes under the authoritarian enforced uniforms, they are taken to a more comfortable, and personal, viewing room and shown a presentation on why we do it that way. We ask them to not speak of this presentation as it is troubling to some. From there they are given a day to think it over and then they are approached again to find out their thoughts."

"Reeducation?"

"Yes, for us. To find out how they absorbed, digested, and understood our message. If you tell a young person that things are how they are, and never tell them why? That solves *nothing.*"

With a humored tone of reflection, "I know that one *far too well.* I had to rotate adults to find all my answers, so I did not wear out my welcome with their ears and shoulders."

I know that moment all too well. "I as well."

"Do they decorate the uniform?"

"Yes! How else can you tell them apart? Club Badge, Association Badge, School Merit and Honor Badges. Custom frills, pins, ribbons, and the like. They are not blank slates, they are developing minds who need to be connected to meaning."

Smiling with a renewed vigor, "I like that."

"It also prepares people for our Culture of Uniforms. When at work, you wear the Vestments of Work. As a student, you wear the Vestments of the Student. Then when at Play? You wear the Vestments of Play."

"Solid logic."

"Also, that goes for the bedroom. We have Vestments for that too."

Laughing he spoke his reply with a playful sing song, "I did not doubt it."

This is what mom spoke of. Turning her eyes from him she looked down at the subject lines which reminded her that her work was far from resolved. "I, need a moment."

Reaching over with his hand he held it over the outside of her left thigh. Speaking with a tone of concern, "take the time."

Clasping his hand for a moment she set to the stress exercise she had taught him. Mouthing the words as she spoke them silently, *I am not alone, I am not forsaken, I am not lost. I am safe, I am kept close, I am found.* Flexing her hands against the apprehension of what was coming she went back to her tablet. *I'm not sure I can work in this condition.*

Dealing with the messages she delegated tasks as well as she could before taking a moment to retreat from her tablet. Raising her head she turned to regard Yuri, *I wonder what he's thinking.*

Easy way to find out. "Ration for your thoughts?"

Taking in the sight of the deep consideration for something crossing his features as he maneuvered them around a corner she felt a moment of ease. *I'm thankful I am not alone in this.*

Gesturing to the tablet on the dash with his right pinkie, "as a note, I am making sure that I follow the instructions. I do not want your Medical Wagon to worry."

Watching the buildings go by, "they're within the recommended distance?"

"Yes. The two Si-roc," trying again, "Sir-oc?" Grunting he laughed, "whatever they are called? They are also listened in their proper relative position."

"Noted." Tossing out the pronunciation with a casual air to the gesture, "Siroc."

"Ah! I hear it now! Sirocco?"

"Yes! Those are fast moving vehicles which will blow in and cause hurt if we are attacked."

"Noted. That is a fitting name. As for my thoughts?" Taking on a timbre of restrained enthusiasm, "do I need to be presented to a parent to ask for a Blessing? We are serious about the possibility of me being the sire, so I will be serious about learning the cultural ideals."

That is a different topic, much easier to worry about.

Smiling shyly at the boldness of the moment she went over her answers. "Yes, we do have a ritual for that. However, we did change the meaning around."

Laughing his boisterous words filled the moment, "of course you did! I expect no less." Dropping the volume to something more controlled, "apologies."

"Theatrics has a place, also, my ears are unharmed. No harm done."

"Tell me of the new meaning?"

"Within our culture, we have the idea of Closing Ranks. If tragedy strikes, we Close Ranks. When children are going to join this world, the parents of the child go to their parents and family to prepare the emotional landscape. When a man stands before a woman, and knows he will Sire? He goes through the process of preparing his half of the emotional labor and support. The woman, who will carry the child, must do the same labor."

Intoning the conclusion with a stark realization, "you ready for death before you create the life."

Washing into the moment with a life preserver of hopeful tone, "the children at the Cultural Center, they have lost parents. When they leave there? They will have to go somewhere that adults who will care for them will be. I've seen the reports already, that have been shared with me, that give credit to the lives of the children as the water which has cooled the fires."

Nodding once his courage returned to his tone, "who do I meet with, to prepare the future?"

"Frank and Dennis," trying for humor she laughed knowingly, "I believe you have met them."

"I have! Fancy that!"

Hearing her humor deflate, "Steven and Patrick."

Nodding with a gentle sarcasm, "I have met them," pitching to something more hopeful, "I would like to meet them again for the first time though."

I would like to see that. "Noted."

Encouraging the moment, "who else?"

"My Marraine and Parrain. Then you'll get to meet Waterlily."

"Noted."

He sounds happy to see our shared future, as awkward as it could be. "As you already know Sasha."

"I look forward to sharing a Blue Sky with her."

Nodding with a gush, "I do as well."

Tapping the wheel he worked the thought out, "does Sasha know all of these people already?"

Come to think of it, "she does."

"Do they all believe in her?"

Not one agrees with the lie, "to various degrees, yes."

"I will endeavor to be the me I want to be, and wish to be seen as."

Peace can be found. "I can ask no more than that of you."

"Noted." Musing the matter over, "do I change my family name?"

As I don't even know it? "No. You would be Yuri –"

Speaking into her pause, "Pastukhov."

"Sire of the Bachman Children."

Smiling with a hint of pride, "noted."

"That is your identity as a named person. By giving you a name, you are proven to exist. You are," gesturing to him, "right there."

"Noted."

"A way to make you a Citizen will be found. The Citizens are aware that this is a Work In Progress."

Bouncing the question to her, "how do outsiders normally get to be Citizens?"

"One way, is the Pledge of Nonviolence, which requires surrendering your weapons. From there you get worked into society."

Grimacing with a put upon demeanor, "I could not do that."

Shaking her head she vetoed the idea, "I would not ask you to."

"Thank you."

I might as well mention it, and why it doesn't work, "the next is adoption, but you are beyond the age of adoption."

"Noted."

Civil War doesn't qualify for this one, "the next is the Pledge of the Covenant of Blood, but we are not in conflict or in a conflict of that nature. Civil War wasn't cited under that Clause, or we could use that and you could be welcomed in."

"I will live, noted though."

This one won't either, "the last is Marriage."

Answering with a humored tone with hint of gallows, "which we cannot do as you are going to marry Sasha, yes?"

I wish we could. "Yes."

Snapping his fingers he offered his question, "does she feel guilt over that?"

His heart shows like sunlight through clouds, "not to my knowledge. Excellent note though, I will make a note of that and make sure that she doesn't stumble into that without a rebuttal."

"Good!" Laughing for a moment he continued, "so you have no real immigration policies then?"

"No. We started as an isolationist country, as we were too intent on taking care of ourselves. This includes the tradition of closed borders. The systems I mentioned have allowed the outliers of the other societies a place within our nation, however, we never established an office to allow people in. No one knows anyone actively seeking to immigrate, but in case we meet someone? Or if the option of coming over that border did appeal to others? We should be prepared with the best system we can have."

"Noted. I am Yuri, The Citizen. What then?"

Returning to the facts of the matter for stability, "that would be depend on the circumstances of your choices. We have need for help, for an extra pair of hands, in almost every field you could be considered qualified for. Your talents will be evaluated, the roles will be opened to you, and you will find a place."

Responding with humored pride, "then I am Yuri Pastukhov, the Citizen, who does a thing, who dwells within New Hope."

"Yes."

"Where does my Copper, Silver, Gold, Platinum fit into that?"

Time for care with the concept. "That's an economic reality, not an identity facet. For one, you are not the Ration Bracket of your job, which is also not you. Rations are compensation, not identity. I can give an actual example though."

"Please do."

"In Recycling and Repurposing there are some very brilliant Citizens who have changed up or otherwise made the system kinder to the Worker, more efficient, or increased the output without an undue cost. They're Copper level because Recycling and Repurposing as an idea is no small amount of grunt work. Labor of the body without labor of the mind. However? They have been given extra Perks because of the gains they have made for the system. Which fits into the quest for deed and recognition. You do something of note? You get a reward. There are persons within the economic classes who have nothing more than the Basic Needs and Perks of that class, and others whom are sitting on a small pile of Rewards."

"The Citizen can build wealth then."

"And expand their wealth in a system which we evaluate and try to keep balanced in the idea of Opportunity. You would be entering into a System which divides people into groups, but then gives them the safety to just be, and also the incentives to leave us awed that we were graced by their minds."

"Can The State take stuff from the Citizen?"

I wonder if he'll feel as our neighbors do? "On a limited basis, yes. The State Agriculture has hydroponics, aquaponics, the warehouses, and the like. People toil there as Workers. The fruit of that labor? Belongs to The State directly. It is sent to processing centers and kitchens which are also owned by The State. Then those items are served up at The Grocery Depot. Put into the boxes. Provided to the people in exchange for their labor. This is a *forced* association. Our neighbors to the south feel we're not nice people for that."

"Why is that?"

"They have volunteerism and free association. They have outlets where you bring currency and exchange it for goods and services, without forced association beyond logistics of locations for sale, production, and the like." *I can admit the worst part.* "To them? We have enslaved our populace to meet our demands and needs. We do not try to enslave them, that being our neighbors though, which keeps them from being too obstinate about how we live."

"Do your people go hungry though?"

"Not to my knowledge. Now mind you, The State is *not* the only source for food. That came up in the earliest moments of spare land. You mentioned you would want chickens for your parcel of land."

"Yes."

"You can have those chickens, or ducks, or a private crop of lettuce, or whatever else you might require and have time for. You have the same Opportunity as anyone else! It's up to *you* to decide the Outcome."

Asking his question with an upbeat tone, "can The State take my lettuce?"

That would be unapologetic theft. "No. The lettuce is on your land, in this case, and you toiled to get the lettuce planted and growing without use of State resources. That would be *theft*. How could you be at ease if you thought The State could come in at any moment and end your lawful existence as you knew it?"

"I would endeavor to not think about it."

"Also, that is in the second level of the Pyramid of Needs. Safety of Property, and Resources. We have a document for what passes as Human Rights which explains it further."

"Noted." Faltering and picking back up, "what is the, I guess, *a*, fear of The State?"

"Failure. To lead people astray. To not cultivate the people properly and see them wither on the vine. You would be joining a people for whom our backs are against the wall and we know it. We don't have *another* backup plan. We don't have another Plan B option."

"I will stay. By your side. I won't leave."

"Thank you Yuri."

"Noted." Musing for a moment he popped up with another question, "speaking of people staying by your side? With your mother gone, and your father as the High Consul, did you have a nanny?"

The odd story that was. "Two. One male, one female. Frank's younger cousin, Thando, came to work at our house with a high recommendation. He was already a caretaker of children, when, yeah. He had lost no small amount of the kids he helped take care of. The opposite side of the moment was Lia, who was just starting out as a caretaker. She was going into Adolescent Psychology with The Guild and said the," reaching up and making air quotes with her free hand, "*wrong*, thing to my father. He hired her on the spot."

"Do you still talk to them?"

With a timbre of nostalgia, "no. Thando ended up getting married and moved to Seaside. Meanwhile Lia ended up overwhelmed by the intensity of our family and resigned from the position." Adding with the notes of dark humor, "that was before any of the truly shocking things happened."

"Noted."

"I did send them birthday cards, a few Rations or Coupons for something in there. The maintenance and thanks for the service they gave equal to half of the time they spent in service. I did have lunch with Lia when she finished all of her Certifications. She thanked me, for what it was worth, for the experience. She doesn't hold any negative feelings, and appreciates that I do not either."

"Good. Noted. Yay."

I'm not afraid right now.

Gesturing toward the city with his chin, "I look out this window to the world, and I wonder. How do I ask what the current situation out there is?"

"SitRep. That's the magic word. The SitRep answer I would give is? *Controlled.* The people are being shown each aspect which is functioning within parameters, to show that we have control over the moment. The helpers and teams are delegating the tasks to those who can do those tasks. The people have an outlet for the helplessness, which keeps another facet under control. The Guild is moving quickly still to staunch the bleeding in hearts. Meanwhile the Courtesans Collective is moving in as living bandages. Wallman is on his private channel working hard to spin the truth into something people can understand, juxtaposed by the calm dignity of the smooth concepts that Anton is giving them on the official news channel."

"Living bandages, very to the point then?"

Shared sorrow cauterized with an analeptic of flesh. "People need touch."

"Noted." Taking another corner he gave a pleased noise, "you mention that the people are hoping for your decision about immigration. Do they vote on things?"

"No. The first aspect is the logistics of getting one hundred percent of the populace to vote. Also, to make certain they understand the issues and the tyranny of the majority they would be invoking either way. Instead? We teach them Civics, Politics, Ethics, and why it matters to be informed. If a person feels a drive to join the Pyramid of Power? Then they pursue that goal of joining The System. We have accountability and accountancy of actions available to each Citizen whom might request it though. Voting is a Tyranny of the Majority. To open the Commons up to that kind of power is to usher in tragedy."

"Democracy is bad then?"

The things I know of the crimes of people under the system. "Very. We have a Totalitarian System, which we know has its flaws, but Democracy as we understand it? Has so many more."

"Example?"

"I have two. Your immigration is one. If the popular idea was to just *let you in,* then you get in and we have a popularity contest as how we judge people. That's no way to manage a system. We need to build an *actual* system."

"Noted."

"The other is the opening of Moral Outrage. In the Protocol we have a Clause about evaluating any addition to the Protocol for if it is nothing more than a function of Moral Outrage. Thomas Kunlow did a great wrong, but he will be executed with dignity in a quiet and careful fashion if all goes as planned. If Moral Outrage called for him to be stripped naked, flogged, tarred, feathered, and then hung in the town square? Would it be *Just* to do? If the only qualifier was because fifty-one percent of those who let their opinion be known are angry?"

"When you put it like that Democracy doesn't sound nice at all."

The Path of Corruption is paved with those stones. "If The State does something? It is acting as the rudder of Civilization on an Administrative level. With the spending limits on Rations? The people do not have to worry that I have commissioned a hundred pairs of shoes. Or that I am walking around dangling Rations before people and asking them to debase themselves for gain. Or that Patrick is waking up in a flesh pile of women who suckle at him for the wealth they cannot have otherwise."

"Can he afford a flesh pile?"

"Not really, no. Unless they sold themselves cheaper than Market Guidelines. The Courtesans Collective, they set a price on bargained touch. Thus if he wanted a flesh pile, they would need to be women that were going around the systems. Or Volunteers. However the Sexual Ethics taught by the Albatross caution against that behavior on the basis that it is not typically a Net Positive for those who do it. Also, a *pile* is the inclusion of four or more into the same act."

"Noted."

I can open up, "we, The State, we have all read the history of power. We know academically how sick, sad, twisted, and perverted the call of power could make us if we do not stay shored up against the lure of power. Which is part of why we strive to be seen as accountable and transparent in our movements when we can. Even the people who will die this day, a Public Record will be made, with the needed information to explain why they died."

"Today will be Public Record then?"

"Yes. The system also helps us find out those who are suffering from paranoia and the like. Or that might think that Anton is a lizard person."

"I like the system still, of everything I've heard."

I wonder if he heard me right. "We do our best to upgrade and uplift ideas."

"Wait –" pausing with an incredulous grin, "you said someone thought he was a lizard person. No Lilt. No joke."

What a strange moment that was. "Yes. They were afraid he was a lizard person who had been sent to lie to them. It was cleaned up before they got near him. As far as I know? He was never made aware of the situation."

Broaching his question carefully, "cleaned up?"

He's still looking for the dark secret or unforgivable moment. I'd be afraid of finding it too. "The Guild maintains a series of *dormitories.* They sort, catalog, and work with those whom are either a danger to themselves or others. They have a fairly robust budget for beds and those who sleep in them. It keeps us from having to make the hard decision if someone whom can no longer function, and will possibly kill, loses their bed."

"Because of a danger to society?"

"Yes. Living animals get put down. No one has met someone who was slated to be put down, and then complained they were put down, yet."

"Solid system."

"We endeavor to make all of our systems as logical, practical, and within our means as we can get and keep them."

"Interesting. You accept that humans are as they are. The joke is on you though."

What joke? "How's that?"

"My soul isn't worth what you've already paid for it."

Can't leave that there. "Emotional Protocol," smiling with a shy candor, "I won't bother reciting the chapter and verse as I would probably misquote the numbers." Going over the section in her head, "I don't have the exact wording on my mind, but, one is to refrain from demeaning the self in the light of affection or gifts given that are enjoyed. One is to accept and note that the other party feels the gifts and affections are merited and even if they do not feel worthy they are encouraged to respect it. To disagree with them in the light of wanting said affections is wrong."

Setting up his moment with a humored irritation, "*so you have a law -*"

Correcting him gently, "a Protocol Amendment -"

Obviously trying to keep from losing himself to laugher, "- that says people are not allowed to say *you shouldn't have.*"

I wonder if he knows how easy his humor makes this. "Yes. I'm familiar with it as I've had to cite it many times before. It also covers what you just said. It goes on to nuance what the Citizen can do in the wake of not feeling worth what is given. The caveats about what to do about unwanted affection follow right after."

Quieting down with a thoughtful look on his face, "if I sell you my soul -"

"You have to take the payment, all subsequent payments, and at the very least say *noted* to acknowledge my judgment call. But, you are *not* allowed to say I am in the wrong. Unless of course you feel I have become mentally maladjusted in the wake of my affections and then you should recommend counseling. Or seek protection from the local Militia House. We have shelters for that. You would be housed at the Y."

"The *why*? Or *the Y*? Single letter?"

"Single letter. It's a shelter for men of all ages when their domicile is compromised and the Militia has to step in with Investigations and figure out how to safely get them home."

Pausing he smiled with a relieved candor, "that's something else Susan. What else did your land make illegal?"

Can't help myself. "Mistreating masochists, persecution of monsters attempting to live in society, -"

Holding up his hand for a moment, "wait," placing it back on the wheel, "why did those two things come to mind first?"

Keeping her voice steady and humored, "I'm trying to shock you, that's why."

Making a noise like a snort and growl tackled a guff of laughter he took a breath before reply, "I see."

It's still a true notion. "Those really are covered though."

"The more, I think your society is, *odd,* the more I have to remember what Elianna said about Ozzy. I know Ozzy, allegedly, and his feelings about the world, so I'm not, *shocked. However,* it is still something else to confront head-on. Hug, embrace? Head-on?" Pausing for a moment he clucked his tongue with a deliberate motion to it, "I believe, that I should use *this* and not *your* for the wordplay too now."

He's getting the hang of this. "It would be *this* for your wordplay if you wanted to show you were one with this society. Stating it is mine would infer that you are not part of it."

Bopping the wheel gently to punctuate his words, "*this* it is then!"

Firing back with the moment of elation, "noted!"

Checking the dash tablet, "one more question? This says we are almost there."

"Of course. Provided I have time to answer it."

"Will your wedding to Sasha be a spectacle or modest?"

Answering with a humored introspection, "it will be modest in intention, but perhaps a spectacle in emotional weight. I will invite those who need to be invited, Sasha will invite those who need to invited, and they will witness something everyone has waited a long time for. Even as the High Consul I am *not* expected to use every spare ration on the moment."

"Noted. I will go quiet with this. I appreciate everything you do. I also appreciate all of the people who worked very hard on your world so it would be here, for me to find, and to meet you."

"You're a wonderful man Yuri. I look forward to the future when you're around."

"And I look forward to having a future, here, with you."

I am just going to nod and go back to my tablet. I am not going to cry.

Or complain about wishing I was the one driving.

I'll live.

5.8.6 - 09:31

5001 Last Century Blvd. - 'Lounge Lair' – New Hope

▸Jerome Hope

Reviewing the progress bars from across the Network he smiled in relief at the relentless effort being brought forth. "The firmware upgrade continues. We'll see an end of a half dozen bugs, two glitches, and the foundation in the code for new security features. Once its live the Code Cathedral will handle the bug reports while the Digital Monastery will set the time table for the next two cycles."

From behind him at the edge of the desk Paige laughed a soft hiss as her speaker carried her words, "good news of the bad news?"

"Something like that." Pointing to a window on the monitor on the far end of the desk, "that? Is the manifest of everyone I've been loaned. The Protocol is very clear on what we're doing, and how we're to do it. I just get to lead it. It feels," taking a breath he found a simple idea, "as if I am no longer an impostor in my own life."

"Good."

Leaning back in his chair he gestured to the displayed map across the two monitors on the wall, "that's the network map, at highest elevation. If you look into it long enough? The Penguins come and take your sanity."

"I will avert my gaze." Setting a capped bottle of water down near him, "you have Miss Bachman on your side, from what I know? You always have had her on your side."

I did what I had to do, told her what had to be said. "Truth."

Moving to a face to face position, "what bothers you?"

Dennis has stated she is his student, I can share this lesson. "In the data I have sent her, are the initial logistics findings. There is a facet of this that bothered me," bringing up the window of data, "this is the load-out report. Someone, decided that it was more than fine that this would go wrong. The strike force? Trained. The equipment? The best you could expect. The load-out included a Breacher for each team. The amount of Demolitions issued would leave a Dagger Squad envious."

Scrunching up her face in revulsion, "the Breacher is the heavy lifter with the crowbar, shotgun, and breaching charge satchel kit. Yes?"

Looking away to his monitors, "yes."

Chuffing a hard sigh with her single gesture, "disgusting."

Hearing the plea in his tone as the words rushed out, "I had to tell her."

Looking to the feeling of fingertips on his shoulder he turned his gaze to Paige. Taking in the look of compassion he nodded in ascent. Waiting a moment for her to release her touch he watched her hands move.

"Miss Bachman is the woman whose footprints I walk in as a Student of Shadows. I know you had to tell her. She will need everything she can know to make the right choices. Life is painful. But that pain can be beautiful."

Wrestling with the dread his tone was quiet, "they told her that killing her would make them Heroes."

Puffing up with bravery, "we idolize Heroism. She is a Hero of our people. If she was the Villain to someone, then her death would be Heroism. The Principles of Flipped Perspective."

Nodding with his timbre of thankfulness, "thank for helping me not judge myself for telling her."

"Noted." Appearing embarrassed with the emotional weight of the moment, "I will go get more food for you. And then you will continue to save our Network. The people need their Network to know they are all still there."

A goal should be spoken of, "The Exultation of Reunification. The day the first conference call between the Thirteen Houses took place. We will see a new Exultation before this is over."

Nodding in affirmation with a look of determined hope, "everyone will work hard. And when this is over? They will see each other and we will be at peace again. The Exultation will see to that."

"Thank you."

"Noted."

5.9.0 - 10:25

1120 Fairview - The Grain Silo

† Sasha Herb

Standing at the door to the pleasantly bright house in a row of different modeled houses she pushed the doorbell again. *Her car is in the driveway.*

The Grain Silo, only known to a select few as what it was. Now I just need the door to open so I can make sure the SitRep is Clear.

Reaching for the bell again she stopped when the deadbolt in the door threw back with an audible clack. Moving her hand back she watched the door open swiftly, leaving her face to face with a tired looking Reylai Dinclair.

"Come in."

Moving in as she moved back Sasha voiced her questions, "no watch word? Pass phrase?"

"You are Dagger Sasha Herb, the one whom Miss Bachman favors. You have come to see if this place is secure even though the Network says it is."

Moving her back to the wall of the entry room, "is it?"

Hanging her head softly with a sigh, "no."

Rusted scrap! "What happened?"

"There is something you need to know, that I feel you need to know at least, and that is I stayed silent out of fear for Amaranth's safety. I have been visited by The Guild and Questioner Parsons. I have given my evidence and testimony."

Reeling herself in, "did she have news of Amaranth?"

"Not enough. I understand my daughter is alive. I have been given the information to bring me close enough to In The Loop that I did not regret the choice I made."

Walking slag heaps, "what were they going to do to her?"

"Arlo told me that if I signed, he would keep her alive. I was pacified with this. It would buy time, buy time for it to be undone, if I just went along with it."

This - "why didn't you speak up when they took her?"

"They told me to speak would get me killed. I stayed silent to stay alive. They took her before the attack on Central."

Trying to keep the pressure to a minimum, "did you know?"

Nodding with a grim resignation, "I *suspected* something terrible was going to happen. They told me to call in vacation time and stay home." Closing her eyes with a guilt-stricken frown, "I did."

Thumbing behind her to the door, "where is she now?"

"At the hidden house of Arlo Kunlow."

The Quad Busters - "two oh seven, -"

Confirming the notion, "as I understand it? Yes."

Appraising Reylai with a more forgiving feeling in her heart, "I would ask if you were well, but I know you are not. I'm just in shock. I didn't understand her to be a T.o.O. in this. Will you be pursuing help for yourself after I depart?"

Moving her arms around herself she hung her head, "I will be calling The Guild after. I am ready to communicate with them."

Reaching for a hopeful promise, "we'll get her home – "

Shaking her head sadly, "don't. Don't bother."

This doesn't scan. "I don't understand."

"I signed the forms, I told her that I would rather see her alive than dead, and I stayed silent for one last reason. Something we don't try to talk about. Something we had to talk about when her father died."

Where the Emissaries of The Divine fear to tread, "which was?"

Wringing her hands firmly, "I don't really love her."

Reaching for meaning in the wake of the wash of numb at the concept, "Clarification?"

Turning and leaning against the wall she signaled for 'confession.'

"When a mother bears a child into the world, nature tries really hard to make sure they love the child. That they forgive the child for being a tiny bundle of needs and screaming. Ozzy, he gave me so many *outs* when it came to Amaranth. He hired a nanny, he hired a stage hand for me, he did everything he could to tell me that it would be better than it was. I grew to *befriend* my daughter, to be able to see the good in her, but I never felt like Ozzy did. Ozzy *loved* her on that instinctual level."

Keep it simple. "What do you request?"

"Anywhere else, within reason, than here. She knows. She knows, that I don't really love her like I was told I could. She *forgave me.* She forgave me so I could live. When they walked her out, she called back to our conversation, and I knew it would be the last time. Just take good care of her. I have her things packed and ready to move. One last thing to attend to before her rescue."

To know this pain from another, still helpless. "I don't blame you, or judge you, I have an associate who feels the same for her sons. It troubles her that she leaves them with their aunts and uncles, but she just *doesn't* have that gut instinct you spoke of."

"It's not unheard of, The Guild takes good care of me. I have decided that when this settles? I am leaving. I'm going to go on a longer assignment."

Leaving? "Amaranth no longer needs you?"

"I can't be the thing she is seeking. It falls to someone else."

Nothing else to do with that. "I understand."

"Be well Dagger Herb. I know our visit was short, but we have nothing else to say. Do we?"

Rusted dreams of dust, "no, I guess not."

"Be well."

"You as well."

Opening the door and letting herself out into the day she felt her stomach clench in sickened sadness. *To never love your own child. My mother and I don't get along for long when I see her, but I know she still loves me. I still love her. But to never love? I couldn't imagine.*

I'll get back to my car, I'll send my report to Susan, and that will be that until she calls. Getting into her car she startled when her comm chimed. Answering it without looking at it, "hello!"

Hearing the lightly distorted voice she knew the timbre and disturbance as he spoke, "Dagger Herb, it's Admin Nobody."

What else could have gone so wrong? "Why did you call?"

"Don't tell her."

Stopping in place she vented the frustration at the idea, "why *wouldn't I?*"

"She is going now to see Arlo. She has a trial before her of this moment. She needs to overcome the trial with as clear of a head as we can give her. Then she will call you and Sevilan to her side for the rescue mission."

I'm in the Loop. I'm in the Loop. Jumping onto the idea of moving forward, "what do I do?"

"Go get Sevilan, and whatever vehicle you want. You can use anything you deem appropriate. I can Authorize *anything* right now."

Noted. Good question time. "SitRep on Amaranth?"

"She's napping, hopefully sleeping. She's been keeping busy, reading, watching movies, and trying to keep herself together. We've given her people to talk to when she needs a fresh human voice. The mote of note? She's consulting with the Russian Language Primer."

"Yuri is a foreigner, did she find a clue?"

"Already looked. He had a battle cry during the defense. Which, is somewhat of a misnomer. Outside of the *urrah* he was exclaiming? He was saying something that sounded to me like he didn't know if he was saying spat or spite. I asked the Conlangers and they believe it to be Russian, and *sleep.* This is in the documentation that Amaranth has access to, which is why I believe she wants to be ready."

Going over it, "she knows Susan is coming, and she *is* a Bachman. I'm, relieved to hear that she's still doing what her family does."

"Indeed, and truth."

Nothing else to it then. "I will go find Sevilan and make sure I am available."

"Noted, and thank you."

"Noted. Be well Admin Nobody."

"You as well Dagger Herb."

I will go and be ready. Pressing the ignition switch, *duty calls.*

5.9.5 - 10:37

Cloak and Dagger HQ - The Questioner's Lounge

⚞...Susan Bachman

Feeling the weight of the holstered cannon on her hip she took a last moment of mental preparation before the called upon moment. Leaning against the wall next to the pale green trimmed door she reflected on the minimalist décor around her.

Gray-blue tiled floor, cool blue plaster walls, and the playful graffiti of cartoon sketches to capture their history. Pictographs of the people who worked here and the trials of being in C&D.

Gesturing around them at the cartoons Yuri seemed humored, "why did someone draw on the walls?"

Smiling at his smile, "history lessons. As I had said about Art being a part of Culture, even the cartoon sketches you see here are part of that. Each sketch is authorized, logged, the story is written, and the answers are available on request."

"The foundations of such a practice? What brought this to being?"

The answers we'll never know, "as we scoured for resources, we opened building after building, and we found no small amount of unanswered questions. At least with these," gesturing to the sprawling iconography, "we don't have to live without the answer."

"You are people who informed their culture from ruins?"

Intoning the stark cultural truth, "from graveyards."

Chuffing before his word, "noted."

Taking a breath she moved away from the wall and moved to the pale green trimmed door, *the lounge of the Questioners. The backstage of their macabre production.*

Opening the door to the Questioner's Lounge she waved Yuri in with her before closing the door.

"Is this where we are going?"

"Yes, for the moment."

Entering from the kitchen attached to the lounge Questioner Zack appeared tired. From his gait to the dark circles under his eyes she took in the image of a man worked to the edge of endurance.

Speaking the truth as she witnessed it, "you do not appear well."

"I have finished my work." Raising his cup of tea he swallowed roughly, "we are but three now. Myself, Parsons, and Jonas. Fava and Chart infracted. The Guild does not have an ETA for their return." Sipping his tea with a grim humor, "I do not believe I will see them again."

I will not mourn them as failures. The mortality rate has been one hundred percent. You cannot fail to save someone that cannot be saved.

Moving his gaze to her from his tea, "you *are* trying to save us."

Truth. "I am."

Testing the notion, "do you mourn?"

Yes, and more. "I do mourn, that they are most likely gone. I *regret* that I could not see all five of you saved. Not everything I unleash is a win. Not every Endeavor ends in success. Not every hope and dream is something that can be real."

"Thank you for the attempt."

"Noted."

Looking past her to Yuri his timbre rang with a ragged thanks, "thank you for your part in this. I appreciate having a High Consul. You did your part. I thank you for this."

Give him something, "I regret I did not get a chance to try the latest salad."

"I could make it again."

Stepping back into the verbal dance Yuri affected a friendly demeanor, "noted, the thanks. If it is not too much to ask, could I also try the salad?"

"If I have the time to make it again in the near future, I will make it and share it with both of you." Lowering the teacup with a sigh, "I called you here, not to complain, not to mourn, but to ask you to forgive me for assuming what you would want."

Raising an eyebrow she tried to embrace humor, "I don't know if I should be overjoyed or afraid."

Turning his eyes back to hers, "you *are* aware we have Josh Kunlow?"

I hope for good news. "Yes. SitRep?"

Yawning for a moment he smiled with a dark humor, "we kept him from the table." Closing his eyes he spoke the checklist, "he had damaging information, he had dangerous information, and a few anecdotes which skirt the line of acceptable." Smoothing to a more casual cadence, "in the end he found it in his own self-interest to tell us what we needed to know. The appropriate authorities have the information. He is still alive. The Commander has a pending Death Warrant for him, that Mister Kunlow does not know is waiting for him. I would like to know if I did this as you would wish?"

They did as I would have hoped and more. "I can pardon him and send him home without him knowing how dire it was?"

Nodding once, "you can."

It shall be done. "I will do so."

"The tablet on the table works."

"Noted." Having a seat on the small couch she set to the task. "When we leave, are you going home?"

"I am."

Keeping her tone professional, "will you still be around tomorrow?"

Laughing with a dark contemplation, "I believe I could be. I am not there, *yet*."

Checking the tangential SitReps, *Rain-Dancer is waiting outside. I need to weave an answer to this that solves all of the loose ends.*

Speaking into the moment Yuri's voice was soft, "I do not understand. Enlighten me as she works?"

Replying with a flat humor, "I am a Questioner."

Hearing the careful broach with his words, "Asmodai, he mentioned that I would not meet you."

"Had you committed a crime?"

I might have enough wits about me to get this put together.

Laughing for a moment she heard his shrug, "not to my knowledge."

Pressing the inquiry with a borderline monotone, "are you a Citizen?"

"Not, to my knowledge."

Putting his teacup back on his saucer with an audible clink his tone lightened, "then we would not have met, for that reason."

"Continue?"

Hearing the lilt of self-recrimination, "I am a threat of harm. I harm people until they tell me the details."

"Why would you not be around tomorrow?"

"Oh! You meant that you did not understand why I wouldn't be here." Laughing with a dry bite to the sound and shaking his head he had another audible sip of tea. "I would end myself. I have become painfully aware of myself. Of my deeds. I struggle."

Looking up to Zack she spoke the words softly, "mea culpa."

"The High Consul," gesturing to her with his teacup, "authorized something back when she was coming into an understanding of power. It was a reckless idea, bordering on the ethics of emotional care and not hard logic. Even now as The High Consul she keeps the project afloat with her direct will and signature. She set before us the question of being saved. Did we wish to be saved? Or did we wish to die when this was over. Further? To see an end to this project. And as much as I appreciate being alive?" Deflating to a low pitch, "understanding the pain of others, and knowing what I have done? I struggle."

Looking up she caught the sight of Yuri moving closer to Zack with a serious bearing to his demeanor. *Peer to peer?*

"You know that what you did causes you pain –"

"Yes."

"If you leave this mortal coil before you mend that dissonance? How will you find peace with the divine? You *should* stay, calm the storm, and become the more pious you. That person you know you wish to be." Stopping he sighed, "does pious mean what I *think* it means?"

I need to get him a travel tablet with the dictionary and lexicon loaded on it.

Smiling with a relief Zack looked down at his shoes, "pious is to be good for the sake of being good. Sanctimonious, however, that is the use of moral superiority over others. I have strapped a few failed spiritualists to my table and had to find out what was going on in their groupings."

"What are the moments you regret?"

"The painful exonerations. Or the uncovered plots. We are flawed clay, and in those flaws? The unfortunate happens."

Rain-Dancer answered my text. He's willing to work with me.

Gesturing toward the inner door Yuri pressed the pointed question, "is this all that is to your life?"

Laughing he shook his head with a heartbroken smile, "I have lived my life as a repurposed disaster. I, have engaged in painting. I have friends. I have people who smile at me when I walk into the room. My survival instinct waivers, but it is still asking me to let me live."

Touching Zack on the shoulder his press appeared gentle, "you feel the dissonance of what you are?"

Nodding twice, "I do."

Sitting in an emotionally silence watching the two men she felt a deep gratitude for Yuri's support of her idea. *He loves without thinking about it. He just loves.*

Rubbing his fingers together on his free hand he stumbled through the words, "can you become saved, tranquil, to walk in the path of the Divine?"

"How do I forgive myself?"

Reaching with his freehand to steady the cup and saucer, "trust in yourself. Believe. Have faith. Look in the mirror daily." Taking on a timbre of personal truth, "tell yourself that you know, but you forgive. You don't let up on yourself in the idea of being the person you want to be. When you have a chance to be the good you want to see? You take it. Be bold. The dissonance is like a vibration, and it seeks to sever the cord between you and your happiness. You have her endorsement, yes?"

Looking to her with a few tears on his face, "I do."

Feeling the emotional gut punch she removed a handkerchief with a trembling hand. *Good to know he hasn't lost sight of reality.* Holding it up she waited a moment.

Taking it from her Yuri pressed it on Zack, "then hold on to that too. Walk the road of the ideal you wish to be until the day comes when the change from one who wishes, becomes one who *is*, with but a single step."

Regarding the two men she forced the words out past the emotional paralysis, "I wish I could give him more, but it's all I can give him at this point. If I say more, I set an expectation. It is no longer at his will that he would live, but mine. Then he lives not for him, but for me."

Seeing to his tears, "I do care for Miss Bachman as my liege, however, I do appreciate that she is leaving the decision to me."

He's almost here. "We are being joined. Zack, if you would please retrieve Josh for us?"

Nodding twice he returned to duty with his poise, "on it."

Moving quickly to put the saucer and cup on the lounge breakfast bar Yuri's question rang with hope, "you are spinning an Ad Lib?"

Finding poetic words for the moment, "from the filament thin threads of hope I weave a net to catch happiness."

Coming back to her with a smile, "I will get to see the power of miracles?"

Not quite that much power, "the power of people on the same team."

Looking to the exterior door she nodded at Rain-Dancer as he walked into the room, "Counselor. You agree to my terms?"

Raising an empty hand with an attempt at a smile, "I do not have an alternative that is a choice worth making."

"Does this cause you duress?"

Lowering his hand, "no. It does not."

Turning her attention to the interior door she smiled at Josh as Zack prodded him into the room. "Josh, it is good to see you, circumstances of your arrival aside."

Raising his hands he gestured for 'helpless' before laughing with an audible relief. "I did not know that Level Zero existed. I also did not know how much this would hurt."

Speak the truth, "the Second Chance is rarely pleasant."

"The, weight, of it all was beyond my understanding." Turning his head, "Rain-Dancer –"

"I brought your medication. I have also, been informed, that I will be taking you to a Secure Location to recuperate."

"I need to recuperate?"

Interjecting between the two men, "refrain from being too glib, if you would. No one is asking you to be stoic today Josh. You can go unburden this moment from your shoulders. Let off the weight of the last long while. Meet my gaze?"

Waiting a moment for him to turn to her she focused on him, "the Questioners Report on you states that you were imprisoned inside of the situation. Boxed in emotionally. I *need* you to understand that I *understand* that. This is not something that can be taken back once you walk out the door. The issue will be designated as *settled.* No one will come looking for you for it, not legally. You can go, have your grief, and then return to your wife."

Nodding with a relief about him, "noted. I do not have sufficient words at this juncture."

I may as well, "do you have other words?"

Nodding with a furrow of his brow, "well, as I have you here? You didn't come to the anniversary party."

I told you then, "I was sick."

Scratching his temple with a crooked finger, "not a dodge? It was in text only, I had wondered."

Signaling for 'embarrassment' and 'confession,' "I was oozing from my nose, was mouth breathing, and my intestines were rebelling. I was *gross* level sick. I was not going to a happy moment like that."

"Noted." Shuffling from foot to foot for a moment he looked over to Rain-Dancer, "are you in a rush?"

Shaking his head in reply, "no. I may be where I do not belong though."

Gesturing to him with a welcoming timbre Zack set to retrieving his tea, "stay Rain-Dancer, you are of The Guild, our trusted allies, correct?"

Nodding with a look of experience on his face which betrayed his years, "correct."

I shall see this through, "Josh, do continue?"

"In the early going," fumbling he recovered the thought, "you did not come to either Last Night of Wandering."

Cards on the table, "Tim wasn't dead yet. He went to your party. Did he not?"

Nodding with a hiss of failed diplomacy, "he did. I tried to befriend him."

Why leave it unsaid? "He was why I was in the back at the wedding."

Seeing his brows rise with his tone of surprise, "you were there?"

Speaking her testimony to reassure, "you stumbled for a moment on the vows, you were so happy. After you kissed her? I had to leave in the revelry that followed. I couldn't have Tim seeing me."

Lobbing the question with a friendly air about it, "will I see you at the next anniversary party?"

Nodding once she affirmed the idea, "I'll endeavor to make a space in my schedule for you."

"Can I schedule that with your assistant?"

Taking the moment to gently hiss, "I don't have one yet."

Signaling for 'noted' his hand flowed into the 'wait' gesture, "why didn't you go with Cassia to her party?"

I don't have to hide it, I never did, but I certainly don't now. "The Scouts were back in town, I was, preoccupied with stripping layers of mission filth off of Dagger Herb."

"Oh!"

"Not as exciting as you think." *Time to move forward into the breach.* "Rain-Dancer, take him away?"

"Vehicle waiting?"

Tapping the tablet for emphasis, "of course."

"You paint –" stopping he looked to the fold of the fabric at her hip, "you have work."

He saw the Cannon. "I do."

"You paint the Blue Sky High Consul. Be well."

"You as well."

He's going to report what he saw. Suppressing her sigh she waited for them to leave. *At least one thing is going right. Josh is secure and out of this moment.* Feeling the anger starting the prowl inside of her heart she rose from the couch. *The Tiger within knows I wish to keep her tamed. I will see if I get what I want.*

Gesturing to Yuri for 'follow' she moved with Zack into the main room which contained the cells waiting for her decisions. *Steven wants them dead, and Zack only spoke for Josh. Time to find out if Steven gets his way.*

Stopping before the first cell of the line Zack gestured to the security door with a large sheet of shatter resistant glass in the middle of it, "within this room we have Ardent Kunlow. The Arms-Master of the Kunlow House. His actions were the knowing acquisition of each item used, with full knowledge of the road ahead. He is one of the three you are to see."

Trying to keep the knowledge of the manifest from eroding her control she took a long deep breath. *Calm.*

"My brother kept it to three?"

"The Commander stated that he was willing to trust you. But these three? He will not trust. The others? He dismissed the whole affair with a wave of the hand. This is the first of the three to review. He is also the last person that Questioner Chart will have placed on the table. He, *infracted,* on this man."

I knew the time was ending.

"Open the cell."

Intoning the words with a grave foreboding to them as he moved into place, "his crimes are the gathering, obfuscation of the truth of why they were gathered, and stockpiling of the weaponry used by the invading forces. Every bullet fired came from this man. He knew full well it was a coup, he supported the end of the Bachman family, and his exact words to justify it were," pausing as he turned the bolt on the door, "if they didn't want to get out of the way of progress they would be run over by the wheels of progress." Stepping away with a gesture to her, "as for you? One must break some eggs if one is going to make an omelet."

Closing her eyes she could see the faces of the dead from the Cloak and Dagger reports. *The downside of having to read the reports is that I know what Yuri tried to shield me from. I could call Steven and say this is approved, or I could do this myself.* "Open the cell."

Without showing emotional markers, that she could make out, he replied with a slow and simple intonation of his words, "yes High Consul."

Restraining the urge to look at the cameras in the room she kept her eyes focused forward. Trying to keep the Rage in check she waited as patiently as she could. Hearing the click of the door lock moving to the open position she emoted the growl to direct the energy somewhere. Waiting with grit teeth as Zack moved inside, and restrained him with zip ties, she dug her nails into her palms.

Hearing the click of the zip ties finish she rushed inside and grabbed the listless figure by the collar. Bringing him around she looked into his eyes, "look at me!"

Waiting for his eyes to make contact she plowed onward, "those were people! People you sick, rusted out, pitted, worthless, not even fit for scrap, det heap!"

Mumbling quietly, "they should have just given up, then they could still be people."

Shaking him fiercely she leaned in and whispered hotly, "did the others know?"

"What others?"

Bringing her voice down to the softest whisper she could manage she leaned into Ardent's ear, "the other Consuls. Did the others know why you wanted what you ordered and what it was really for?"

Speaking with no more volume than her, "those that bothered to question me? Yes. It was meant for your father. When you lowered the security levels of Central it actually made this easier. You made those choice other places safer when you moved those assets, but you left yourself a target."

Reeling from the implications she blurted the question, "why did it have to happen to me?"

Looking toward her hip he nodded toward her hand cannon, "because we both know what happens next. We both know what he trained you to do. You aren't a High Consul, you're an attack dog when angered and a chess master otherwise. You Miss Bachman, are nothing more than his Echo."

Looking back to Zack and raising her voice back to normal levels, "what's the next one guilty of?"

"She befriended the security officers on duty in the control room to be able to gain access to it. She was in the habit of making regular deliveries for Miss Augusta to the control room," lowering his voice, "may her soul find peace." Swallowing roughly he raised his voice again, "she was the one who put Central Security in the dark. I lack the Epsilon Code to understand the soft demolition device used, but I do know it's from the Snafu-Works. I have been getting stonewalled by the technicians about what it was. Perhaps you will have better luck."

Thomas knew. Looking at Ardent she gave into the anger, *if he feels this is what he's going to get? Then I shall oblige him!* Dragging Ardent with her she went to the next cell. Shoving him against the clear wall of the cell she waited for the woman to look up when the sound of Ardent's weeping came through the cell wall to her. "I know you can hear this," looking past Ardent she found a name for the face, "Marissa!" Without looking back, "what did she do after she knocked out Central?"

"She escaped in the confusion."

Pulling The Shadow's Cannon from its hip holster she placed it to the back of Ardent's head in her two handed grip. Steadying herself she heard the soft bark of Zack's voice behind her, "*cease!*"

Regaining a measure of composure, as the word she knew well from training, helped her find control over the Rage. Forcing her finger off the trigger she kept the gun to the back of Ardent's head. She could hear the hoarse anger in her voice as she tried to keep herself remotely level, "one must never leave a living enemy behind them. The trail blazed down the road to the future will have footprints on it. Those prints will be formed from the footfalls of giants treading through the blood of the battles that rage around them."

"You quote him beautifully Miss Bachman, but I command you to cease because the walls of my domain cannot handle the munitions in that cannon!"

Rusted scrap. "Then what do I do? How can I kill him Zack? He *helped.* He looked at what this was going to do and he *made his call.*"

From inside the cell Marissa croaked out her words, "am I next?"

Looking past Ardent she called her words to her, "yes! By the Blue Sky yes! I cannot think of a single reason *either* of you should live past this moment we're sharing!"

"I have a solution prepared Miss Bachman."

"Speak it."

"I have the injectors and the guillotine prepared."

Feeling the anger calming, "I can endorse that."

After a moment a pair of larger members of Internal Security entered the room with them with a quiet air of duty about them. "You had this prepared then?"

"I know you Miss Bachman."

Holding the gun to Ardent's head, "I want to hold him like this. Inject him but let me hold him like this. I need to know the last thing his soul knew was me."

"I understand." Moving closer he pulled the injector from his coat, "I would expect nothing else."

Leaning in she whispered to Ardent, "as you feel the needle, I want you to know that wherever it is you are going? I hope it is where you need to be as you were so quick to reject this mortal coil."

Ardent's words were solemn as the needle touched him, "thank you for listening to reason Miss Bachman. I did not relish finding out how long I would survive a wound from your cannon."

"Farewell Ardent."

Waiting in the silence for the drugs to do their duty to his system she endured the silence. Watching his eyes close she surrendered his body to the two men from Internal Security. Catching the names on their identification cards she knew why Zack had picked them. *Staunch defenders of the Bachman family in their personal time. Keep the loyalties thick in times of trouble.*

"Open the cell."

Nodding twice Zack unlocked and opened the cell. Turning his attention to the baton in his hand he readied the zip ties as Marissa screamed and launched herself right

S M Gilbert

at her.

5.9.6 - 10:50

Cloak and Dagger HQ - Questioner's Wing

☀ Yuri

Standing still he looked into the cell where Susan had followed Marissa after the initial crashing altercation. Shuffling to the side a step he tried to focus as the pain in his ears, from the echoed rapports of the cannon, distracted him from thinking straight.

Turning his attention to the three other men, *why is no one else moving?*

From next to him the man who had Ardent's ankles, rushing to urge the other man to get him loaded onto a stretcher they had brought in, asked with a fear in his voice, "High Consul?"

Standing next to the fallen body of Marissa, splattered in blood from the two point blank discharges of her weapon, Susan called back, "I'm alive." After a breath her voice called out with a slight emotional crack to it, "Zack?"

Moving into the cell Zack set a pair of fingers on Susan's right wrist, "I am here High Consul."

Nodding at him she held still until he took a firm grip on her wrist. Moving her out of the cell he placed her against the wall to the right side of the door. Turning to the men, "get Ardent out of here! Those sedatives don't last forever."

"Understood sir."

"Away with us."

Lifting her chin she looked at Yuri, "I will continue with this shortly. I was not expecting her to do that."

Moving toward the desk in the room Zack appeared emotionally frazzled with his motions and his timbre, "we can get you cleaned up first."

Moving closer Yuri took in the sight of the damage he could see that had been done to Marissa. Turning his attention to Susan he touched her cheek gently. Seeing a hint of a smile he tried to rationalize the moment. *That cannon is not meant for this earth. What did they tell her she would face that she would take that of all things as her weapon once upon a time? I was told I would be a killer of men. I learned the nine millimeter, the 7.62 rifle, the knife. And here she stands before me with a gun of such magnitude. What did they tell her?*

Returning to them with supplies in both hands Zack pressed a bundle on him, "take this and get to work."

Unpacking the supplies he started by touching Susan's cheek with a wet napkin,

"Susan?"

Looking up to his eyes for moment she blinked twice with an intensity, "I'll live Yuri, I'll live."

"She will recover Yuri, she has killed before. It is still a thing which sickens her when she does it, but she will live."

Turning back to Susan, Zack seemed softer, "Miss Bachman? I am going to get your face, hands, and other exposed skin clean. You are going to have to address this later. This is *not* the worst news we have for you today."

Cocking her head at him with new light in her eyes, "this *isn't* the bad part?"

Answering quietly, "no."

Nodding twice she relaxed against the wall, "then I will abide and regroup as I am now curious as to what could be worse than this."

5.9.7 - 10:53

Cloak and Dagger HQ - Questioner's Wing

᠅᠅..Susan Bachman

Closing her eyes she let Zack wipe the area around her eyes as she listened to his words, "there is an upside of this."

This should be good. "Which is?"

"After Thomas Kunlow, who is next, I will introduce you to the last pieces of the puzzle. By the time this day is over? You will have the moment secured."

"Good."

Prompting with his question Yuri seemed displeased, "did you think Marissa would attack?"

Hearing Zack's angered apologetics clearly, "no. She is the one that Fava infracted against. She had built up a friendship, only to use it to slide the knife into the backs of those who trusted her. Fava was jealous. To not only have made friends, but then to be so sick as to throw it all away? His mind buckled under the strain. I would have assumed that what he did was going to leave her more docile."

Opening her eyes she caught Zack's eyes, "mea culpa."

"I will only accept yours if you accept mine."

Fair is fair. "Noted. Accepted."

"Noted in turn, and accepted in turn."

I shall end this. "I get to see Thomas now?"

"His was an enlightening interrogation, which has helped us in prioritizing this whole affair. I have a full report made up, but he is here if you wish to say anything to him." After a moment, "I have an injector ready for you to do it yourself."

Agreeable. "I would like that."

From the side Yuri raised a finger, "elaborate?"

I can tell him. "Do you remember what I said about ending him?"

"Yes."

Speaking without anger she looked for the calm within her heart, "I am going to end him myself. He crafted a nightmare for me, and he hurt so many in the process." Taking a moment to steady herself she continued, "the Pyramid of Needs is built on a foundation of being alive, and quality of life. The spirit of it is the notion that we have to have the ability to find a measure of security. Thomas living, would not be a part of that goal."

Touching her forehead with the back of her first two fingers, "I am far from the only victim in Central. However, in this moment I act as proxy for *all* of his victims. If I leave him alive? I address them all with a singular statement. When he ceases to be? I give them my honest hope that knowing he does not have this life to live will help ease the suffering."

Lowering her hand, "don't think too highly of me, in this moment. I *do* want him dead for personal reasons. I want him to die never having seen the sun again. Never feeling loved again. Never being held again in this mortal shell. He will never taste his favorite dishes again. We don't do last meals. He won't have his last supper to savor this world. He dies hungry."

"Noted." Gesturing a rolling motion with an open hand, "this isn't capital punishment, not by what I understand of do wrong and be snuffed, is it?"

Taking the injector from Zack, "this is making it so people can sleep again at night. I'm not going to go inject him *just* because of what he has done. It is because I firmly believe there can *never* be peace between us. The people who knew, that are not here? My brother decided to let the professionals ask if there can be peace. Ardent's words to me was that when this was brokered? It wasn't for me. It was for my father." Chuffing quickly, "I can't claim ownership of the idea, of being for which it was started. But, in this moment? I am the one who is called to decide how this *ends.* I do this so the people of my world can know that the one who would choose *this* route to change, is gone."

"Then the reason you said monsters who try to live in society -"

Speaking into the opening, "is because sometimes something bad happens but it isn't the absolute of a person. Or they have not yet done something and are afraid they would do something to hurt another. Either way? If they shouldn't be dead for it? If bridges can be rebuilt, if wounds can be healed? They live. We move them to another city and have them carefully handled from there if we have to. We are, who we are."

"I understand now."

Turning to look at Zack, "what was the motive?"

"I think he should answer that himself. As he answered us without going to the table. He didn't face duress in the wake of the width and breadth of his confession."

"Level Zero in protest of my brother's orders?"

"Correct. I won't disguise the truth." Signaling for 'Denied Joy' he seemed to carry an air of guilt about him.

The camera wouldn't have seen that, but it just goes along with wanting to stay alive. Moving to the cell door she looked through it at him, "tell me Kunlow, what brought this on?"

Turning his attention to her the remaining strength still evident in his poise, "your father failed to understand history and the costs of an Empire."

The Mission Statement returns. "Elaborate?"

Rising to his feet he assumed a strong stance as his words poured forth with the conviction of a Consul, "we erupted on to this land a scant century and change ago. The purpose of our return was to establish this Nation. To move forward. To make the best of our small time we would have before inner struggle would claim us. Your father? He brought us to our knees with his wretched excuse for an answer."

The Deadline. The Time Index point at which a Nation ceases to be as it was, and rots into something else. Flexing her hands she worked her mind for the answers to defend herself.

Speaking further into the silence Thomas pressed his words on, "I was asked, without a choice to make in the issue, to bow to your father. To kneel and deal with him on his policies and agendas in the wake of the peace he brokered." Stepping closer he stopped and turned his attention to Yuri, "the Winter Wolf."

Nodding in reply, "I believe that is me, yes."

Gazing at her with a unmasked contempt, "trading Citizenship for semen? Looking to tie the knot -"

Stepping to the door she snarled the word in contempt, "*silence.*"

Contemplating the humorous look of shock on his face she let the words form themselves on emotional instinct. Falling into the cadence and force of her father she spoke without emotional hesitation, "your contempt and cheap emotional trickery will get you no more than *this.* He is going to be a Citizen. A system will be created, which he will champion, to find the things that will be needed of a person whom wishes to stay with us. Have I made myself clear?"

Nodding quietly in reply he stood still for a moment.

Moving her points forward she reveled in the fearless anger, "we're not the *only ones* facing The Deadline! The Ports were too tough a fortress to crack without doing things that could not be taken back and moving into a campaign of extermination. My father, *yes,* he was *done* with the war. He wanted *out.* He took it. *However,* I have been asking for logistics, querying every informant and source of information we have, and I counter with this simple question." Taking a deep breath for effect she let it out slowly, "how are the Ports *really* doing?"

Placing her palm on the door she forced her chin up to get her gaze steady, "if all Nations burn down, if all are conquered, if all must die, then can we not live as we choose? We get two and one half of a century to be borne, live as an Empire, and then fade away. The Ports were fashioned after the Eruption, what is their late stage plan? Invade the Freelands? Try to beat us in a second War? Or will we find a way to open the doors of diplomacy, pave the roads, and absorb their attempt at City-State Empire."

Roaring back with unabashed shock, "you would *forgive* them?"

"War requires two factions, and no one is *right* in war. War is the greatest atrocity that the human species is able to perform as it suspends the taboo on murder. Both sides did things in that war, and if they would also forgive us? Perhaps they would be reborn as new parts of the greater *us.* Without another bullet fired."

Sighing with a dramatic irritation he turned to pace his cell, "you would expand The State? The framework is as it is for a reason! If The State grows unchecked it will be as the cancer of human sickness and eat the country alive!"

"There would be only *two* new seats on the Council. Still an odd number to allow for balance."

Rounding on her, "face saving promises! How many more would you spare the truth that we expand and conquer as a species through *violence?* You cannot tell me that you sit blind and deaf to the fears of the South."

He would know them, being connected to them. "That would be the one where we wish to conquer them for their resources, yes?"

"Yes! We are humans, we eat, we take, we rape, we kill. Work, creation, refinement, are the only way to escape our inherent violence. They sit, *right there,* waiting for us to fall back on the ancient habit. We could just oblige them. Take the Ports, take the South, and put it all under a single banner, moving outward, and then take the Freelanders. We are meant to create the Empire of the Second Chance. The chance to be made whole. One world, one state, one human species. Become one with us, or die."

Keeping her voice level she answered back, "this was meant to be the Second Chance, we could do it a different way."

Smacking the door with a palm he continued to seethe, "you want to coddle them! Teach them the lesson of this world! Their beliefs are garbage. *Absolute walking atrocity.*"

Stay level. Keep the bubble within the lines. Be as the level. "We are what we learn. *We,* change *them.*"

"It is futile to work *against* human nature. We are by nature the animals that we are. Do you believe that they will just stand on the sinking wreckage of their world and hold a hand out to you and ask for salvation?"

Correcting him, "it won't be me, not personally."

Without losing the seethe, "you are still asking them to surrender!"

"You're asking them to just *die.*"

Raising his hands in anger, "I am giving them the most honest measurement of themselves. I have the bigger bombs, the will to power, and the honest interest in all of them dead. I will give them the peace and compassion of making the war quick and efficient so they will suffer the least amount of time!"

"You don't have the Fire Maiden!"

Amaranth.

Laughing at her he chuffed with victory, "you figured it out? I took her so she would give me her permission keys. I –"

"*Open this rusted door!*"

Moving quickly to open the door Zack appeared calm, "this was the worst part. We have a full plan and Amaranth is alive and physically unharmed. You will be seeing her later today."

"Noted!" Getting out her canister of Howling from her vest she started shaking the can unable to quell the hate, "I will drench you in Howling!"

Screaming at her with the timbre of self-defense, "*I did it for the future!*"

Raising the can as Zack opened the door she waited the blink of an eye as Thomas took to his knees. "The Pyramid –"

Spitting in contempt, "you *shattered it.*"

Raising his hands in protest, "don't."

Holding the canister in place she screamed her words at him, "*spare you?*"

Crying he sniffled, "I wanted you to see reason. That our enemies are our enemies. Your family is meant to be that which would destroy all of our enemies. I hated your father because he would let his Citizens be harmed. Your care based morality is going to be the end of us before we even begin."

Without lowering the canister she spoke softly, "I am aware that I have the capacity to care for my enemies. To want to know them. To scoop up their children and try to give them better lives. However, my loyalty is still first and foremost to my tribe. If my tribe can bring their tribe to their knees and gain their loyalty without using any more bullets or lives? I'd take that win. I know that the moment I choose them, over us, I would be the False Prophet."

"You would risk growing The State for them?"

"If they would have us? Yes. They would be a springboard into the Pacific Theater."

Spitting the question with a lilt of contempt, "would you also spare Toronto? Montreal?"

That's not the same! "At this time? No. They shot first."

"Did the Ports not shoot Cleo first?"

The lost love. "Cleo entered a situation she did not understand, hoping to save a life, and she lost her own. Did she reveal something that was not going to stand? Yes. She made her choice, they made their choice, William made *his* choice, and the rest was a blood soaked war. It's a *mutual* question."

"And the Maple?"

"They didn't like us *talking* to people. They killed scouting and assessment operatives. We lost," wracking her brain she found the name, "Captain Jacques Waldo and his Wanderers were lost to a man because of them. I have been informed his brother Captain, -" reaching for the name she tried to recall the report from Seattle.

Meeting her gaze Thomas intoned the name, "Wyatt."

"That sounds right."

Nodding twice, "he put out an all call for supplies and help for Saskatoon. Things haven't been going well for them, I authorized some extra biofuel we had in reserve to be shipped up there. Warned them they only had a month to use it, they didn't mind."

"Noted."

Looking up to her with a solemn sadness, "I didn't want you on the Throne."

The things you learn too late. "I'm aware, now."

"Your brothers would have made more sense. Far more loyal to the Protocol. Far more loyal to the future we should see."

Will he know the exact reason? "Why did they want me?"

Chuffing with a firm discontent, "for the very reason I did not want you. You have a much tighter bond with the web of politics in this city, and the Network? You, border on being an Ideal." Gesturing to his pose, "even this, there are men who would envy me. They would seek to kneel before you, for, *other* reasons."

Feeling a rush of embarrassment she gestured to the cot, "you can sit. Your pose has proven its point and stayed my hand."

Nodding with a relief he moved onto the cot, "my knees hurt."

"You took Amaranth."

With his head hung and shoulders slumped, "I ordered it, yes. Zack has assured me that she has been found, that she was physically unharmed. Your supporters have moved the earth and sky for her and all aspects of this."

Touching her gently on the wrist Zack's eyes were filled with regret, "you needed rest. We had to take the time we had to find her, assess all of this, and prepare this for you. You would have been unable to rest otherwise."

Rust it. "Solid logic."

Tossing the idea into the moment with an almost casual air, "you spared my people."

Chuffing she spoke the truth she had to swallow, "they aren't *your* people. They're *Citizens.*"

Regarding her with confusion, "even after they betrayed you?"

"*That,*" putting the canister of Howling away she gestured for 'false paradigm' with her free hand, "is you framing this in a way that asks the wrong questions."

"Then what is the right question?"

Shoving the hate down she took the high road once more, "why did they do it? And? Can they live with their failure?"

"Noted." Taking a deep breath he tried to gesture only to set his shaking hand down. "What becomes of my daughter?"

Keeping it to the facts, "Exonerated via Horse Hair. She'll be the Consul. The future is hers to make for her House."

Lifting his chin he turned his eyes to hers. Intoning his words with a hopeful sadness, "you seek no quarrel with her?"

Shaking her head gently, "none to my knowledge."

Nodding with a burst of tears he hung his head, "noted."

I am no Ideal, as the Ideals wouldn't fear these questions. "Why did I have to die?"

Without lifting his head, "you are in pain Miss Bachman. The suffering, all too apparent. When you lose yourself? You will burn reality around you. You touch, and have touched, so many lives in a relentless quest of understanding our world. Would I call you his Echo? Only when you're angry."

"To end my misery?"

Replying with a fatherly correction to his words, "I would kill you to end the suffering that was all too apparent. Your father was a monster to you and there is no way that you have come out of it without damage. The High Consul is a person who must give up their life to live for The Rim. I just wanted to make sure it would be someone who would last more than a generation. And to be honest? I hoped you would rest in peace."

"Why did they follow you? To end me?"

Shaking his head gently without lifting it, "no. I showed them the Fire Maiden, the proof I have of it. I laid the stakes on the table. Them, or Us. They picked *Us*."

That makes it easier. "Noted."

"The Pyramid of Needs, the continued aggression and threat from the Ports violates the majority of the Pyramid. Thus by supporting the peace, they supported the pain. They accepted this idea."

Chiming in Zack spoke softly to her, "this is confirmed by Guild Interview. The new crux issue question is what to do with the ethical ideas of this now that they have been pardoned. The quest for answers to preserve life, and avoid executions, continues."

"Noted."

Raising a hand gently Thomas spoke with a philosophical sadness, "if we became *one nation,* of the world, could we not have world peace? Sort all cultures and ways, test each with logic and reason, and burn out all the aspects which no longer give us strength. No more infection by primitive times, only the bright shining future."

Holstering her cannon she answered him, "the questions of world domination were not given to me in my lesson packet. I was taught how to deal with the problems of *this* generation so as to not leave them for the next."

Lowering his hand he rested roughly on his clutched fingers against the edge of the cot. "We don't have forever. Not in this life, or the life of our nation. The Deadline will come for us. We will sink into the abyss and we will be forgotten as this world will not rise again. We had a taste of the moon, Mars, and now? We die in the dust."

"We will deal with the Ports in this generation."

"Will it be as your father did when he helped them grow? When he betrayed the chance he had to watch them wither and die when he employed the Nightingale?"

Looking between them Yuri scratched his chin, "I hate to interject, but, who or what is a Nightingale?"

No need for Codes until he's a Citizen. "The plague known as The Wasting, it made it to The Ports. When the Yorklin Doctors finished the cure and vaccine for it? My father sent the means and formula to both cities. He used a classified pilot, locked it behind High Consul Blackout and Rank H-8, and hid the file."

Offering the question with a shy air about it, "why would he cure his enemies?"

Shaking her head she clarified the idea, "they weren't his enemies at that point. They were the people who knew the people who had been at our throats. It was years past the end of the war. His humanity wasn't gone. He was taking a chance on them."

Looking toward Yuri with fear on his face Thomas glowered, "better to let them rot."

Shrugging with a cavalier humor, "I was there, they didn't seem *so bad* to me."

Pointing at Yuri with an accusation, "don't step closer. Not one step. I saw what you did. You stay away from me. It does not matter to me that you come from the Gingerbread Man. *You,* are the Winter Wolf, I have seen the way you move. Called to the side of the Derecho to be no less of a walking disaster zone."

Appearing hurt he grimaced at Thomas, "I had not planned on coming closer."

"Good."

Hold on, "you watched it?"

Kibitzing into the fray Zack offered his words with a hopeful lilt, "Commander Bachman has the video from the general forces, Stanley Perkins has the footage of the men in your office and Kincaid Drexel, and Matron Winifred has the memory cards of your Honor Guard. No one has put any of that information in any open report though."

"I watched the helmet cameras, the body cameras, I, was left sickened and awestruck by the raw violence of it."

Looking contemplative Yuri tossed his question at Thomas, "did you serve in the war I hear spoken of?"

"No."

"Why not?"

"I was the Consul's son, I was to be ready to lead."

Pointing his hands in opposite directions, "Asmodai was to be the High Consul, but he fought. He is The Leader of Lions to those of Port Refuge."

"It is not traditional for leaders to be on the frontline of battle."

Lowering his hands, "Susan –"

Interrupting with disdain, "is *not* typical. Dominion is granted to those who have the training to take it. Like her father she has passed enough courses, certifications, and Trials that she can walk almost freely into a place of violence with Dominion."

"Noted."

Turning to face her again, "you scare me Miss Bachman. From the fact that you've been Miss Bachman since Maggie went to sleep, to the training levels you aspired to, and the fact that no one who had the authority to tell you to stop would tell you so. You lived a life which scared me. I looked at my own daughter and felt sick at the thought of her suffering the way you must have. The idea that she would be Lady Kunlow and not Octavia again? It chills me to ponder. You traded your name for a title that means nothing and yet everything. You traded your standing as a person to become an idea. A rusted idea at that."

This attitude of his, "do you believe I am going to spare you if you best me in debate?"

Firing back with a petulance, "I believe that if I am to die I am going to say my piece and have it haunt you so when I am proven right? You will regret that you did not listen!"

Contemplating the concept, "I have already thought over regretting executions. That's why your people live. Why Josh lives. Why I did not just see you, wave, and send you to the next life."

Deflating, "I had not considered that."

Taking the initiative, "you saw me rise, you know my skills, my worries, and when you could have taken your time to deal with me leader to leader? You would not share your worries with me. You did not think I could understand. You crashed your myopic sunk cost fallacy right into Central and killed more people for the sake of the old wound. The damage from this will resonate for *years,* but I believe we can see healing." Taking a breath she finished her thought, "without you."

"I, -" deflating fully he hunched over and sniffled. Raising a hand he begged his question, "you would forgive them for being themselves?"

"I would hope we could help them change and evolve."

"They subjugate women."

Good thing I already addressed their transgressions to avoid moral tunnel vision. "I am aware that the woman's role in their society is confined to the Hearth and Home. That what we offer as an *option,* is their status quo."

Offering the side comment Zack sounded helpful, "from a population growth perspective, it is beneficial in that regard."

"I would rather have a smaller society with higher quality of living for all. The number of people in a society does not make it better by default."

Nodding in reply Zack held up the 'cede' gesture, "I cede the point, but we are still at under our target number so a few more women being happy to have happy homes and Dominion there would be nice."

Turning to Yuri she smiled, "give me time and I'll lead a birth rate spike."

Regarding each of them Zack seemed pleased, "you will lay down with your Wolf?"

Clarifying the point, "we're in negotiation."

Grousing back into the moment Thomas sounded angered, "The Ports, they *cane* people. They haul them out in public and they cane them!"

"We can ask them to consider alternatives. Show them what we know about how to maintain order and see if they would be interested. Exhaust the roads to peace, by learning what it means to build them. *No one,* has, *ever,* managed a lasting peace between Nations which doesn't involve some sort of dominance game. If we could ask them to play the ultimate challenge with us, perhaps they would be interested?"

"What is your long game? If you will not use Scorched Earth, what is your alternative?"

"We rebuild Horizon," taking a moment to breathe she forced the words, "and we move all from Port Refuge that wish to come that will accept our way of life to Horizon if they wish a different life. We follow this up with a city at Olympus for those of Port Asylum. We *create* Citizens instead of *enslaving* them."

"You would force their government to see its people slide through their fingertips like sand? The poison pen of just *walking away* from their society?"

"Yes."

"What if they embrace Democide to stop you?"

"Then we intervene if asked."

"You would ask our military to intercede to save strangers? To risk their lives for outsiders?"

Not without reason or cause. "That they could join our tribe? Yes."

Pleading with her, "you will lose more of your Citizens with your plan. More will die. More lives will be lost."

Firing back, "your plan requires a greater loss of life."

With an angry ache he launched back, "yours is a greater loss of *Citizens*. The theoretical Citizens are just that, a theory. We bleed, they bleed us, and now you wish to ask them to bleed again?"

"If they will go, I will send them, and we will start a campaign that will end with the rebirth of the Ports. When the time is right. There are still things that must be tended to."

"You are not strong enough to save our world, as small as it is."

"I am not alone! This world is not on my shoulders alone! I have The Commander, The Director, the Consuls, the Captains, and each person in the Pyramid who has spent their lifetime training and honing their crafts." Meeting his gaze she snarled the words, "I walk this path because I believe in them! I believe that my people can get through this! I do not need a series of bombs to change the Endeavor! I am *not* afraid of the future. Not like you!"

Getting up from the cot, "you are not the girl I met those years ago."

"I am a Bachman, this is who we are."

"If you go rogue –"

"My connection to the system is born of Stanislavski Empathy. I have walked a distance in the shoes of many to understand this world. Telling each I do not believe I *can* or am remotely *better* or able to do their job. I just wanted to *understand* from the inside of it. To see their pain. I have touched as many lives as I was able to understand my world. If I step off of my path? I would hope there would be a hand to catch me and pull me back."

"Noted." Rubbing his face roughly, "I don't know if Octavia is ready."

"There is only one way to find out."

"Not my wife then?"

"She is busy with her Diplomatic Endeavors with the Estados Unidos Mexicanos," *I hope I said that right.*

"Why, with the Mission Statement being what it is, did the Bachman family never seek to conquer them?"

"Logic. Reason. They are a Nation, as strange as they are about it, and when we came to the table with them? They Acknowledged that we were one as well. They set the conditions when they approached us with a warmth after the time apart from the first generation. Your wife, she is the outcome of that warmth in their hearts."

"She is."

"The Mission Statement, the idea of one world, one set of flags, one banner, it proved to be *much* harder than expected. It's not gone and forgotten, it's just not our primary concern."

"I am, defeated."

Turning her attention to Zack, "he stole Amaranth, but, what's the other part of that?"

Interjecting with an ill humor, "I needed her Permission Key."

Turning her attention back to Thomas, "she can't grant them."

Waving his hand with a sigh, "DNA tests. All of the legwork is done. With a simple authorization she's a Bachman. With you out of the way? It would have been easy."

Is there more to me being out of the way? "Why did I have to die? The misery aside. Or was that the sole reason?"

Holding her gaze for two blinks he spoke with something bordering on praise, "do you believe for a moment I could quiet the Derecho without silencing you permanently?"

Nodding with a sad revelation, "I believe we understand each other."

Laughing for a moment he hung his head deeply, "I believe we do."

Gathering her resolve, "I have a sister to save."

Pacing away from the door, "the *world* needs to be saved. I don't have faith."

Calling to his back, "I am not alone Thomas. I do not walk alone."

Rounding on her with the pain and fear evident, "your father was not alone!"

Clenching her left fist as her right hand moved with a controlled alacrity, "he drowned out the voices. He withdrew from the light. The sun set in his heart and it never came back up. Reylai, Amaranth, they were a set of twin moons in his night sky, trying to reflect the light to him. I was no longer his daughter, I was his Echo. I can freely admit that which is truth. I have so many of his bad habits, his anger, his speech patterns," swallowing she forced a breath, "and I have his strength."

Taking on a quoting tone and timbre she spoke of his strength, "you wake up in pain, hurting, and not a single thought comes to mind to get you out of bed. So you find one. You force the body to comply and you rise from the dark. When the light hits you?

You remember all the reasons why you rose. You count your blessings. Then? One foot in front of the other foot."

Sitting back down with a whimper, "I don't want to die."

"Few people do."

Feeling something pressed into her hand she looked to Zack as he pressed the handle of the injector into her palm. *It's time to finish this.*

"I have a sister to save."

"Do I go to the Vault?"

"You go to a Surgical Execution. The machine with the scalpels and targeted severing of key parts of your body. You will fall asleep, and wake up on the other side. Then your body will be dealt with as per your family's wishes."

"What if there is no other side?"

Spitting out the cruel words of callous design, "then we are a cosmic joke. The rudest of humor from a universe that cannot be called callous because there is nothing at the helm."

"It is my turn to take the Wager?"

"Yes."

Meeting her gaze with eyes filled with panic and sadness, "I'll be good."

Clenching her teeth she shook her head and spoke her denial, "no."

Stepping through the doorway she caught the sight of Zack's stern face echoing the moment and the Pacification Baton in his hands.

No one wants to die, but not everyone gets to live.

Taking a step forward she was mindful of any last moment movements as Thomas curled up on his cot.

"I don't want to die. Will Octavia miss me?"

"I don't know."

"You don't think I'm a traitor?"

The truth hurts us both. "I think you wanted your people safe, and were willing to cross *any* line to do it."

"I don't want to leave."

"Say hello to my father when you see him."

Setting the injector to his neck she pulled the trigger. Moving the injector away she spoke softly, "goodbye Thomas."

Speaking from the cell door Yuri addressed Thomas, "you go to God, the Divine, the force that created all of this. The Watchmaker, the World Builder, the source of all that is visible and invisible. There is a Divine which is the force that turns the universe and the majesty of all in it. The Divine which moves in our lives, who has been flesh, who sends Agents and Provocations to nudge our Destinies. Never in absentia, but giving us the Absolute Dominion over this Earth. Our lives are *not* jokes. The Universe is not cruel by design or indifferent lacking a master. Sleep now, wake on the other side, and may this dream end in Paradise."

Gasping the words with a look of profound sadness and wonder, "thank you."

Taking a step back she felt the bile rising as she swallowed and forced it down. Leaning heavily against the wall she felt Yuri's hands leading her from the cell as Zack gave orders for the removal of Thomas' body. *It is done.*

Moving with Yuri as he led her over to a wall for her to lean on, she clutched him while she waited for the moment to pass. *I still need to save Amaranth.*

Waiting with a sickened patience, as the men who took Marissa and Ardent returned and wheeled Thomas out on a gurney, she focused on the feeling of Yuri's presence to ease the pain. *A pair of twin moons.*

Hearing the door close she embraced Yuri firmly for a moment before letting go of him. Turning to Zack once more, "how did he keep her contained?"

"A Pact with Athens. And, a man we have on the table."

"SitRep?"

"We have the address, a cleared path to a door, and a door with a lock we can't get open. Arlo, the man on the table has the code as it is his door. Your brother has asked the Quad Busters to evaluate the door. If you gain the code then you can get them to leave the moment and handle it without having to blow the door off its hinges."

I don't fully follow. "Why did you not get the code from him yet?"

Leaning against a wall in turn with a defeated exhalation, "we are all compromised."

"I'm clouded Zack."

Nodding in understanding he ran through the checklist, "we have the location, the man, the plan. We have secured Reylai, spoken with Amaranth, confirmed every variable but the rescue itself. If you can get the code from Arlo? You can go to the domicile, and rescue her."

And the no plan after? "I get to keep her?"

Shaking his head with a sad smile, "I cannot answer that. Only *you* can."

Simple answer. "Then I get to keep her."

Clapping his hands once with a smile, "joyous day."

"It will be."

"One more thing?" Pulling a remote out of his pocket Zack pressed the button on it quickly, "the cameras are off."

"Speak your piece freely friend."

"I have spoken with many about the why and why for. It is true that the attackers, they wanted the finality of peace through obliteration, to calm the loss in their hearts. They feared you because you were trying to walk the road of peace, but you have also been through much. The strength of your family, the small tree which bears the weight well, would mean that the war could die. The Mission Statement could be changed. The very foundation stones of our world could be laid anew with new words chiseled upon them. You know your world from the inside, you wake up to it. They wake up and they know the fear of your name."

Taking a moment to pause and breathe he signaled for 'more' and then continued, "to wake up and know that the *Bachman* lives and breathes at the heart of our body. Thomas knew your father as the ruler of his world. Thomas did not rule his world, or his destiny, it was your father who commanded everything he surveyed. Even if you do not have land? You have the hearts and destiny of the people of this land."

This makes more sense now. "So I was wrong. I didn't fail them by being *too weak*. I failed them by presenting myself as just as strong as my father, but my father was not seen as strong in the hearts of his detractors. He was seen as *uncaring*. He was a Tyrant to them. I? I wish to be the Potentate to them."

Speaking with the tones of compassion, "I can hear the anger there."

He's changed so much, I hope he makes it. "I can hear it too Zack."

"I needed you to understand. I knew you would come in here with your cannon and I wanted you to have an out to be who you are. We both know your cannon ends life quickly, but precious little can stand up to its bullets without being damaged. I was trying to spare you a blood misted shower."

"I appreciate that. I get where you were coming from today." Nodding with a sad smile, "you were just trying to help."

"That is all we can truly hope to achieve in our communications. That someone else gets it. Even if we can't put it into words. Even if I was daunted until the moment your gun touched his scalp. I had to do what I did because you had told me it was possible. You create this world with your will Miss Bachman. You *have* to understand you are not *his daughter.* Not anymore. You *are* Potentate."

"I need to see Arlo. My sister," growling in frustration, "I *should* have seen it."

"No one can see everything Miss Bachman. Not even you."

Ridolfi's timing couldn't have been any worse. He has me jumping at shadows, moving my pieces around the table, and in that moment I'm not looking another player moves and claims a piece. "I know. I know."

"I am going to turn the cameras back on."

"You do that."

"Now go." Pushing the button, "we're back on the clock." Gesturing down the hall, "you know the way."

"I do."

Walking toward the inner hall she found herself feeling worse than she had felt in a long time despite everything. *The dawn will come. The sky will be blue. I will walk the Path of Peace around the Elysian Fields soon. The next day will come and it will be a Holy Day.*

Reaching the door to the chamber which was in use she quickly ran her card to open the door and ushered Yuri inside. *This is where the truth comes out. One of the three chambers used for this purpose.*

Walking over to the table she nodded to the Questioner on duty. "What do we have here Questioner Jonas?"

Looking up with an open disdain on his face and in his words, "Arlo Kunlow. So far he has proven to be resistant to Level One Duress. I was getting ready to upgrade to Level Two when you entered."

Looking down at the man strapped to the table she couldn't help but note how average he looked. "this is the man who is my enemy?"

"This is your enemy High Consul. He has not denied that he has Amaranth in custody."

My half sister waits behind a door that is strong enough that Steven is calling out a demolitions team to blow off its hinges because he can't think of a better way to get it open. Someone did no small amount of work to shut this door in my face.

"There is only one answer for this though."

"What is that High Consul?"

I have to get this done. The only way to save Jonas from an infraction is to scare Arlo into thinking that he's going to Five. He'll talk, and Jonas can be saved. Moving to a spot where Arlo would be unable to see her she relayed the variables of the plan with a fluency of unspoken speech. *This is the last man you take to the table. Your career ends here. He spooks, he gives, and you go home alive.*

Nodding slowly he pulled out a handkerchief and set to his eyes while gesturing for 'Pledge is Pact.' "I am your willing helper High Consul."

"He goes to Five."

Trying to find her with the limited mobility granted to his head his voice rang with panic, *"Five? What is Five?"*

Now to sell this better than I've sold anything before. And his crime is going to make it all too easy. Clearing her throat she tried to bring out her best sugary sweet voice. "Arlo, there are five levels of duress. We don't talk about this so I'm not surprised you don't know. Level One? Is stimuli from the classifications of audio, visual, and taste in the most negative way possible. This is what you have just undergone. When you move to Level Two you will know the first level of pain. This is essentially a very well placed set of pins, needles, and nerve stimulation to make you wonder why you're not talking. This can get *quite* unpleasant. Level Three is when it really starts to hurt. The Questioner gets out the electroshock kit and straps it to wherever he thinks will get you to talk the fastest. A kit which uses a current which is not going to be good for you. If that doesn't work they move to Level Four, which is a practice from a long time ago called water boarding. From what I understand you'll feel just like you're dying. It also has been shown to be the cause an unfair share of psychological trauma in the few people who've been subjected to it. I guess there is just no way to sugar coat that one. It's going to stick with you for a long time."

Waiting for him to reply she was rewarded with his look of horror and timbre of fear, "what's Level Five?"

Trying to keep her sweet voice, "Level Five is when he gets out the blades, hooks, and creative devices from bygone eras and mutilates you so even after you do talk? You'll wish he'd killed you."

Thrashing against his bonds Arlo's voice betrayed his fear. "The combination is eight-A, seven-C, one-D, six-E. Please don't hurt me! Please! Please! Mea culpa! Mea culpa!"

Switching to a tone fitting the anger she felt rushing back, "what have you done with her?"

Looking up to her with the fear in his eyes, "Amaranth?"

Resisting the urge to strike him she fired back, "yes Amaranth!"

Nearly shrieking out his apology, "*mea culpa!*"

I'm going to be ill. "Tell me!"

Repeating his words with no less intensity, "*mea culpa!*"

"How did you get her? What did you tell her mother? Who helped you? *Why did you do this?*"

"I was trying to keep her alive! Thomas was going to kill her when it was over! I thought if she lived and had a happy life it would be better than her being dead! I could give her that happy life!"

Reaching for her weapon she heard Jonas' rushed voice from the other side of the table, "High Consul! As his lips have yet to render a full confession there may be things he could tell us that could be of use. He could still be a boon to us if we spend some time with him at this juncture of our understanding."

Feeling the cold realization she gripped the table, "a word Questioner?"

"Agreed."

Moving over to Arlo with a pair of sound canceling ear-cups Jonas secured them into place. "He cannot hear us."

"If you stay with him," trying to keep her voice level, "you could infract."

Nodding three times his frown was deep as the words came forth with the tone of revelation, "your brother wants to know if we're *safe* to release into the wild." Gesturing toward the door with an irritated growl, "Zack has those salads, and the people he's met, and *friends.* Rust it, even Parsons, *tied up a snared deer and was elbow deep in it's guts* Parsons? Has not one, but *two* men who both think she's the shiniest thing since indoor plumbing. I have? *Boredom.* I have no joy, no hobbies, no point of interaction with the world. I wake up and it's too much of a hassle to live and too much paperwork to die. If I infract? So what? I'm dead *anyways.* This sad sack of det can be one last test. I get the information with a confessed time table, motive, and information for The Guild to use without an infraction and it'll be a *good sign.*"

I yield. "I see your wisdom."

Raising his hands to a self-soothing gesture of caressing his scalp for a moment the emotional duress was evident. Dropping his hands roughly he sighed, "you cared. You cared so much about this idea, and us, and don't think I didn't notice all the things you dangled in front of me to see if I responded. When they were dragging Fava out? He cried out *mea culpa.* The man who was caught as a child ready to burn his sister to death in her bed for drinking his milk, was able to feel sorrow for something he had done." Hanging his head with a sigh, "I don't want to die, I don't want to live, I might as well do something to prove something to myself."

He has Dominion. "You have Dominion, a good journey toward what comes next."

Straightening up he gave her a smile, "if I take the Wager over this? I just want to say *thank you.* It's been an honor."

"Noted."

Removing the ear-cups he moved over to a pad of paper and set to writing with a practiced alacrity in contrast to the neutral and controlled tone of his voice, "there is no room for mistakes in our fields. I am well aware of your passionate heart when it comes to your compassion being attacked by inhumanity. If it's anything it's the reason this entire division supports you. I will do as you ask, even if he takes this to Level Five, I will do what is needed of me."

"Thank you Questioner Jonas."

Calling to her from his place on the table, Arlo's whimpering voice was surprisingly clear, "Miss Bachman! Please! Thomas was going to kill her when this was over! I was going to keep her alive!"

"How?"

"I was going to be her husband! I was going to protect her!"

Roaring her words at him, "*after* she was a slave?"

Whimpering his words back, "she would be taken care of! Well kept! Not a *slave.*"

Trying to keep her hand off of her cannon, "did you hurt her?"

"That's unfair! She was very cross with me, so I have to assume the experience hurt her!" Whimpering loudly, "it's not fair to ask vague questions."

"How much did you hurt her?"

Pleading with his words, "I caused the emotional duress of forced capture. I didn't use physical violence, or sexual violence, on her!"

"That makes it okay?"

"I did my best!"

Stepping into the moment with a verbal force Jonas gestured for her to leave, "get going High Consul. I'll upload the combination from the local recording so you have a hard copy and proof of what he said. Then I will get him to tell me everything else."

"Noted."

Shooing her off, "off with you, I have Dominion. Go to where *you* must take Dominion."

Nodding she moved to the door and led Yuri back out into the hall.

Speaking from a place of not knowing Yuri's tone was empty of clues, "I do not have words."

That makes two of us. "I don't either. I *do* have someone to call."

One must clean a wound before you can treat it. Getting out her comm she pressed the speed dial for Steven with a shaking hand. Taking a few jagged breaths, as they moved down the hallway, she was rewarded with him connecting the call.

"Susan, I can hear your angry breathing."

"Amaranth is behind the door, I have the combination, you don't need to spook her with a bomb."

Replying with a surprisingly neutral tone, "it is why all four of the Quad were called to help me get the door open in case Arlo did not share. I will send the Quad Buster Squad home."

Still angry she spit the words out, "I didn't kill Josh. I made sure he didn't know you wanted him dead."

Continuing with his neutral tone, "I didn't think you would, on either count."

Don't play. "Are you testing me?"

"Test? No." She could hear his gently malicious grin in his tone shift, "it was an *either way I win.* Also, by accusing him? I asked the question some might ask in the dark of their hearts. Now it's out there, asked, and rebuffed. I am the Unloved Merchant in the Marketplace of Ideas."

Rust it to scrap. Feeling the anger falling apart she sighed, "noted."

Switching to a far more casual tone of conversation, "I'm going to get everyone out of here, and then I'll be waiting when you get here."

Feeling emotionally winded she sighed the words, "I don't know if I want to see you right now."

Asking the question with the same level of import of if she would want ice in her water, "or is it, that you are afraid of what I would say in the presence of your followers?"

He's something else today. "That too."

"I will be on the back porch, it's covered, and private. You will come out here if you believe you can see me in private. Understood?"

"Understood."

"I will see you then." After a half second of silence, "have you eaten recently?"

"Sasha brought us breakfast but I'm still hungry. It worked but it didn't go far enough."

"I need time to get everything out and clear. Go find something to eat and then come here when you can have this to your liking."

"Consider me en route after I find something to eat."

Disconnecting the call she pulled out the keys to her car. Passing them to Yuri, "I need you to drive again. I have orders to issue and calls to make."

"Understood."

Leaning in close, "we're going to go get my sister and make this right. And when we get home? I'm going to need a hug like the one you gave me next to the mini-bar."

"I will hug you until you tell me to stop."

Choking back the emotions she was feeling, "thank you Yuri. We have to go now."

"Lead on."

Taking the fork in the hallway to get back to the lounge without going to the main room she checked her comm, *it's a message from Jerome. The Prophet Leads the way to the Promised Land. The Path is clearing, only you can walk it though. Show us, without doubt or fear, what the future will look like when it is made from your hands.*

He has been working on his wordplay. I appreciate it.

FULL SPECTRUM BULBS
Sunday May 1st, 2242

6.0.0 - 11:00

Drenner Estate – Consul's Office

∫ Amanda Drenner

Reflecting on the hastily cobbled together SitRep she felt her doubts moving to the side as her desk comm chirped. Checking the name on the readout she felt the smile form, *Josh.* Transferring the call to her ear piece she set her lapel switch to 'Do Not Disturb.'

Opening the conversation with a simple question, "Josh?"

Speaking with a moist hoarseness to his voice, "hi."

"Free?"

"Yes. Moving to Protective Housing to exhale. Rain-Dancer is here too."

I must tread lightly. "What can you tell me?"

Speaking his confession, "I figured it out, what would be, and was muzzled."

Emoting an acknowledging noise she waited.

Continuing with no less guilt and pain, "I failed. I got to the bottom of it, and I had no recourse I could see. My emotional flares, were blamed on my symptoms, my medication. I was given new duties, that I *volunteered* for. I threw myself into that with a flurry, to escape the pain."

"Noted."

"I called you," fumbling for a moment he pressed on, "you told me after the wedding that you *understood,* the sick in the pit of self moment when a man falls over and can no longer. Micah, he gave me the assurance that you had aided him. I called because you told me, that in this moment, I would be comforted. If I emote this to you, and Rain-Dancer hears, then I did not have to look him in the face and tell him all of this."

Speaking to ease him, "I am with you."

Recalling the recent time with a tone of fumbled recollection, "I did not, *not,* face the table. They took me to a strange lounge of a room. I was set in a padded armchair, and they brought me tea. I was given a Blob Blobberton. I drank tea, I stared into the faces, as they rotated, of the three of them. I had only heard of them, until now."

"You do not run in their circle."

Continuing without heed, "the man, Jonas, he had a Sweet-Ration Bar. He broke off pieces with a pair of tweezers and would pass them to me. He told me the blood on his hands was too thick, it would smudge the honey. They kept me talking. They told me I had power."

A sad truth, "no one who goes to table *has* to go to the table. They don't tell them they can avoid it if they talk. If the condemned, finds that answer and gambit to try? They can save themselves."

"I did not know."

"That's the point. If you are ready to emote, to tell the truth, the truth comes before they make it flow. They made a point to spare you."

"That," taking a deep breath his tone fell through the floor, "was a favor to me."

Affirming the truth, "yes."

"They, got a Wipe-Board and pens. They wracked my brain. I must have thrown Blob, a half dozen times. They would go, get him, brush him off with an apology and return him to the chair. I felt like a child again."

"They had to try to let you save yourself, by your own decision."

Laughing with a bitter self-defeat, "if only I had understood the power of my own decisions. I didn't think to pass a memory card, or how to send a secret communique, or the half dozen other methods of bypassing a surveil that *they* knew of." Taking a long breath, *"why are there so many ways to keep secrets?"*

He might not like this answer. "The longer Cloak and Dagger has existed the more ideas they have tested and played with. It's how they *have fun.* The Consuls have spies, Mice, Rascals, and other Agents and Actors to keep an idea of what's going on. With no margin for error? We do what we feel we must."

"Noted."

"What happened when she saw you?"

Whimpering for a moment, "she, *forgave,* me."

"Good."

Sniffling he blew his nose away from the comm before continuing, "Rain-Dancer, he caught sight of something near her hip. There was a large bulge. I suspect a firearm. I don't know anything in the EDC catalog that would be that large."

The side holster for the Cannon.

I have to nudge him for answers. "Josh, I don't have Clearance right now for what's going on in there."

Tripping over the name, "Issa, Marissa Kunlow, Ard-ent Kunlow, and T-homas, they were still in there."

I hear the pain.

"What do I not know?"

Answering with a tactful defensiveness, "I knew them, to some degree, or another."

Backing down, "I will not press."

"Thank you. I know, I know you're trying to know all the angles. I don't hold it against you."

Checking through the cameras near Cloak and Dagger HQ she found the image she realized she didn't want to find. *The Enforcer.*

"How was Miss Bachman dressed?"

Laughing it off, "in that scary outfit she likes to wear when things are not good."

"Noted."

Sighing, "I know they're dead. I know that she wears the scary clothes when she has to do the tough things. It's a Uniform. We all wear them. That *one,* is just a bit more severe. As her brother, something fashionably distinct to cut right to it."

I worry that she's going to pull the trigger. "Are you pardoned?"

"I am a settled matter. She let me go. I'm to heal, go home, and regain my wife."

"You can, and will."

"I will endeavor."

Trying something more conversational, "what did she get to carry you away with?"

"It's a Juvenile League Van. Comfy seats. Plenty of room here in the back for me and Rain-Dancer. Miss Bachman weaved this together on no notice for me with what was on hand. I can't complain."

"You were removed from the moment before she addressed it?"

"Yes." Adding with an ill-humor, "it's as if people feel I shouldn't see or experience things they don't think would be good for me."

"Noted. And you should not experience things that are not good for you."

Broaching the subject with a trepidation, "Consul?"

I will be without fear. "Yes?"

"A *city* destroying weapon?"

All will know soon. "Yes."

"You know of it?"

"I do. Say no more about it. I will call Admin Nobody and check on it."

Dropping the subject with a relief, "as long as you know."

The late night confession, soaked with wine and regret sees the light of day. "I loved Asmodai, I was part of a different level of Inner Circle once upon a time. I am aware of her, the weapon that carries a female identity."

"I will speak no more on it."

I will confront him as I confronted other men. With the gentle plea. "Don't Exit Pass Josh."

Sitting in a long silence he roused with a modicum of energy and hale humor, "if I do that, how will I see my wife again? How will I hold Cassia in my arms again?"

"Thank you Josh."

"Noted." With the lilt of a man prompted for action, "is there more?"

"You know we're doing this backwards, you called me, so I should be asking you. However? If I could ask a favor?"

"What?"

"Don't worry about what you heard, saw, or could imply happened today. Worry about you. Worry about Josh. Because if Josh gets better, Josh comes home. I'll have you and Cassia out to the main estate and we can make that strange dish you love so much."

"Bounty of the Forest?"

Feeling far less helpless she flowed her confidence into her words, "that's the one. I'll put in the order for an Elk from the border region."

"On my behalf?"

"For you and Cassia? Yes."

"Thank you Amanda."

"I need to go and place that call. You will be well?"

"As best as I can be."

"Good." Closing the connection she quickly found the listing for Sys-Admin Jerome Hope. Activating the call she waited for him to pick up.

This is going to be interesting. I hope he's going to go along with it.

"Consul Drenner."

He sounds like he knew I would call. "I want the footage from the Questioner's Wing when they're done in there."

"Authorization Request motive?"

"I already know about the device. It has a design on the side. It's a young woman, cartoon design, she's dressed in red. Her hair is fire, in her hand is fire, and she is asking *do you like it hot?*"

Whispering something she couldn't make out he coughed and spoke with a hushed awe, "I was not expecting this when you called."

"Can I have the footage?"

"As soon as it's ready I'll send it. It will be a few minutes."

"Is Thomas Kunlow dead?"

"Soon. He's being sent to the Surgical Execution. A stone will be thrown into the pond with his passing. He wanted something of a magnitude I am not trained to speak on."

"Do you understand the Fire Maiden?"

"No. It was a High Consul secret and as Miss Bachman has not needed to confront it directly, I do not know of it even from the second vantage." Following up with a conversationally tempered trepidation, "if I ask, will I be enlightened?"

He has the will to ask, I have the will to answer the question with an answer. "Yes."

"Then I ask."

"It was a year after Asmodai started his courtship with Maggie. He was smiling more than he ever had. He had a question for me, because I knew Tessa Kane better than he did, he alleged. She had been a friend of the family. He brought me to the device and asked me, without warning, if he had honored her by not using it."

"I would hope the answer was yes."

"I told him I felt from what I knew of Tessa, that it was yes. For as much as she hated, the thought of slaughter was not chief in her goals."

"Did he know that? Or just need to hear it?"

I want to believe what I believe. "He just needed to hear it. I was not there, but I have reviewed that day, thanks to Micah having been there. I wanted to understand his pains. He walked me through it, we gained access to the recordings, the audio, the chain of events. We had figurines made and we worked out the entire chain of events. We gathered the survivors, and those who had interest, and ran through the entire campaign and recorded it. Now when people find the interest to understand the need to know? They have a way to understand." Sighing she tried to focus, "I digress."

Going back to the night of confession she closed her eyes and could almost taste the champagne in her glass again, "he needed me to know who he was. To know the choice he had made. He would be joining our two families together. Tim would never love him, but I did."

"I am honored." After a moment of pause, "what facet, the why, I guess? He was a man of deeper meanings and I feel like I missed part of the story by not knowing him."

And the reason that she loved him, was the reason I loved him too. "I loved him too. He wanted me to know why it had to be Maggie and not me. We cleaned up the story after that. We erased the doubt in the retelling. Focused the gaze on what was important."

With an audible timbre of questioning the unknown but unsurprising, "you loved him?"

I doubt he would tell Susan. If she knows? She knows from what Maggie would have told her. Or Maggie stayed quiet and has left our feelings alone. "Once upon a time it was almost the three of us in a Bigger Bed. He would have had love from both Drenner sisters and children from Maggie."

Offering the question as nothing more than a prompt, "why didn't you?"

"I love, loved, and still love, Micah. We both knew it would be difficult to juggle three, much less *four*. I was happy, still am, and hopefully will be even as we get older and weathered, with him. Asmodai wanted things to end happily. For him to tear his heart out and show it to me as proof that Maggie's heart would be safe with his. He showed me his heart and I was humbled."

"Humbled?"

The knowledge that keeps me from being the Consul the future, or Susan, truly needs. "I still hate them Hope. I still remember the feeling of my sweaty hand holding my gun in the hall waiting for them to crash into my estate. Of my parents fighting over ammunition levels in the house, or how many Horizon Rifles needed to be primed at once. I was humbled because they killed his family, they shot his friends, and he had somehow recovered to the point where he could stay his hand. His decision brought us peace, which let me finish growing up in a more peaceful world."

"Chess move?"

You spend too much time near Susan. "Somewhat. The other part is the act of confession of life lived, of holding it up, of pulling it out of the rubbish bin where it would die otherwise, and showing it someone? It's a good thing. Now you know. You can know that day happened. The more you know about Tessa, and Bonnie, the better. They can be kept alive for just a little while longer."

Speaking softly with a reverence for the fallen, "we must honor the honored dead so they can be the honored dead."

"Thank you -" leaving the moment hanging she wondered what he would say.

Speaking his name firmly he seemed present in the moment, "Jerome."

"Thank you Jerome."

"Noted." Adding with a more reverent tone, "I am humbled that you shared this with me."

"Until I leave my seat? I will be dealing with you. I needed us to get off on the right foot."

"We got off on the right foot years ago Amanda Drenner. Thank you for honoring me. I understand a bit more where Susan gets her lessons in King-Making. I will slip in some notes on what you are going to watch. There are most likely going to be some things you will need insights into which she would have not spoken of."

"Noted. A Blue Sky to you."

"A Blue Sky to you also."

Closing the connection she laid back in her chair, *I will regroup, watch what I get to see, and make a decision. And perhaps a drink.*

6.0.2 - 11:09

Cloak and Dagger HQ - Rear Parking Hanger

⁙...Susan Bachman

Rifling through the clothes in the trunk Susan found the outfit she was looking for. "No one is watching?"

Checking both ways Yuri seemed confident in his assessment, "no one is around."

Checking her hands, "and no blood in my hair?"

Stepping behind her, "none. I think we got it all."

Taking off the locked clasp hair tie she looked at it in her hand. Watching Yuri as he moved back into her field of vision she could see the question clearly on his face. "You want to know which one this is."

"Yes." Frowning softly, "as anything else we could talk about would be too much for this moment."

"You are correct." Finding her center she put her thoughts on the right rails, *he has found enough comfort that he seeks every answer he can get. I like this side to him though.* "Now to tell you more to make your mind a little sharper to our details."

"I welcome it." Visibly placing himself on task, "so that one? Metal, plated, and a spring lock to keep your hair in place? Armor?"

"This is the outfit of war. The holsters, the two guns, the boots, the bullet resistant long skirt, the armor laced leggings, and it just goes on. This outfit is dyed as dark as possible with the tones of skeletonized blood. To that end, the hair tie is armor. I am not the woman doing her job in this. I am closer to an Enforcer in this. This outfit was born from the tasks I helped my father with. People aren't always very nice Yuri."

"You've worn it a few times before." Hearing his voice betray a note of sadness, "Susan, you are a woman of a thousand surprises."

"I will take that compliment even though you didn't mean it." Moving quickly to getting her new top on, "I can't go find my sister covered in blood. Much less that outfit I was wearing. If I swap the top and skirt it will become a new outfit and not send anywhere close to the same message."

"Good to know. Is she unharmed?"

"I don't know how optimistic I can be. Unharmed? I can pray. You heard him. Jerome sent me an update that she is alive though. Listening to music, sleeping, and just past a very tough door that if we don't open? It opens itself later. I want her out of there as soon as possible though." Quickly setting to swapping her skirt, "I have filed some outlandish motions as we were coming down the elevator. I am going to get her back. Steven is moving his men out, and I have a few things that are being moved into place to make sure this stays quiet and Amaranth can have some dignity in this. Sevilan and Sasha are going to meet us there to make sure that this stays in the family."

"It's nice to see you doing this personally."

Seeing the Protocol Amendments, Caveats, and Stipulations, which would normally bind her from her course of action play across her mind's eye, she grit her teeth with a smile, "I'm doing this personally because she's my family. Protocol can sit off to the side of the Rank and File and watch the game play out. I think I'm in the clear about a reprimand but I can only hope that as has been said, I have Dominion for Conflict."

"I am happy to hear family means so much in these lands."

Adjusting herself one last time while getting into her newly chosen shoes she looked at him, "do I look functional? I'll be fixing my makeup on the way to lunch." Seeing him nod she continued, "to respond to your point? Family is all we have some days. Be it born of blood or bonds of words and deed. We gather brothers and sisters, fathers and mothers, and establish a network of care far more intricate than tree branches. To be honest, without family what are we?"

"She'd never guess how your day has been going. And that is a lot of food for thought. I would say we are just alone in a desert."

"I would have to agree. Thank you Yuri. The one downside of all the things I want for today? They take time. We need to go to The Feedbag and feed us while this plays out."

"Why there?"

It is the place I know the truth. "I'm safe there."

"Extra measures?"

Nodding with the comfort of the truth, "yes."

"Did Cassia get the news yet?"

"I am going to voice record that message once we're in the car and in motion." Bagging up her bloody clothes, "not that Amanda won't tell her from her spies sending her messages but this way she can have an *official* word on the subject."

"You know I'm trying to be delicate about how I'm going to get my insight into who Amaranth is as a person."

Sealing the bag and closing the trunk, "she's someone else I'm charged to protect, and I failed her Yuri. I thought our paths wouldn't cross again anytime soon but I still put in what I thought would be watchdog during the fallout from my father's death. And yet somehow it was bypassed, which if I'm not mistaken I can pin on Sys-Admin Athens and his assistance rendered to Thomas. I used to have a few from the Honor Guard check on her because of things I would rather not go into. But since father's death? I've been running a gambit that took more hands. I had to leave her alone for a few days." Repeating herself with a helpless tone she didn't want to emote, "it was just a few more days."

Taking a moment to compose herself she looked over to the concern on Yuri's face. *All that time in the darkness and now he walks through the shadows of truth with me.* Shaking her head with a sigh, "it still means that I failed to watch over his second love and I failed to keep tabs on my sister." After a second of breath, "half-sister technically but what is *half* when dealing with family? You either are or you aren't. Unfortunately for us father didn't want his two families blurring so I guess you could say we're not sisters in any sense other than my sentimental notion that sharing the same father makes us something."

Speaking his words with a certainty and a softness she found comforting, "it's okay to be sentimental."

"Noted. Thank you." Taking a breath, "we get in, you use the dash screen and just press Waypoints. You'll find The Feedbag listed there. Easy to use."

Getting in to drive his voice seemed lighter, "I want to make a joke about me being easy but I don't know how to do that in this culture."

Grinning despite herself as she climbed into the back seat, "we'll figure out something later. As I am unsure if you mean overly agreeable or willing to paint or something else."

Smiling, his broad smile, at her for the first time since leaving the Questioner's Chambers, "I look forward to the lesson!"

6.0.4 - 11:22

Drenner Estate – Consul's Office

∫ Amanda Drenner

Standing before her wall of personal artifacts she looked to the framed photo of herself, Thomas Kunlow, and Asmodai. *The Custodians of New Hope.*

I hope Chuck looks forward to a picture with Susan and Octavia. Miss Bachman, Lady Kunlow, Chuck. He might need to find himself an honorific.

I can just imagine Lady Kunlow, nose plugs and gloves, perched over the Garbage Center watching the toil. The Drenner family attracted some of the better minds in waste reclamation in their fights with The Garbage Shelf.

The Alchemists of Dross.

Bringing her comm back to her attention she shook her head at the better picture that had been sent to her. *That outfit. The promise of violence. And a missing section of footage. To be so bold as to just shut the cameras off? The words spoken must have been something.*

Three more dead. But Josh lives.

I can stomach that.

Stepping to the side she stood before the framed portal to the past. Taking in the sight of her younger self, garbed in the jagged fashion of her time before being Consul, standing proudly next to Bailey to the side of her ADR-10. *You were one of the few women who had the temerity to look at the logistics of being a long hauler and decide it would be just fine.*

You father had been a hauler. His father had been a hauler. Your brothers became a mechanic and a machinist respectively. You would choose to drive the engine of thunder. We were two of body and soul after Cassia was born. Your body buckled under the strain of childbirth and didn't recover.

Touching the frame she set her focus to the framed portrait next to it, *Nissim and Dale, we sent them the bulk of the children we were promised support for. The swath of a brood they brought forth for the family with the aid of our pain.*

Dross and Chaff to Glory and Family.

You loved, honored, and cherished Tim with a light that he needed.

Lights go out.

Clay breaks.

Even in the shadow you stayed and found one more dawn.

612

Then they took you away from us.

My branch, I give my pride to see the torn cutting from another tree to grow.

Your daughter strengthens another tree.

Maggie's brood works to heft the weight of the world onto their shoulders.

I give my place, I resign, so that one with a light as you brought the light, can guide this House through the next darkness.

Closing her eyes she squeezed the tears out. Taking her handkerchief she wiped her eyes clear. Dabbing at the tears she was roused from her reverie by the gentle knocking on her door.

Turning away from the pictures, "do come in Cassia."

Opening the door she poked her head in, "news?"

Opening her arms she smiled as she extended her hands, "Josh lives, and will continue to live. The order was just filed that he's not at fault for anything."

Coming in quickly she closed the door gently, "I could have told them that!"

Holding her hands out patiently as she approached, "he knew Cassia, for some time before the attack."

Deflating slowly she seemed shocked as she gripped her hands, "I have no words."

"He, knew that the Kunlow House was going to make a play for Susan. He knew enough that he could have warned her. But he was quiet because he wasn't going to trade everything for that building and those in it. Thomas was going to kill him, and you, to make sure his shot at the throne was protected. He had Athens on his side. The Questioners had him walk them through all of the angles, it was checked with Admin Nobody, and they concluded he had no answer that could be seen from within the puzzle."

Slumping her shoulders she sniffled, "he didn't tell me."

Moving closer she caught sight of the signal to go further with the comfort. Wrapping her arms around Cassia she held her with a sheltering hug, "they would have killed you had you known. Thomas wanted to end Susan with every fiber of his being. He sacrificed a lot of good men and women for this. He's hurt everyone with his act."

Speaking quietly from within the embrace, "Miss Bachman forgave Josh though?"

I believe I know the answer. "I don't think she sees it as something that *she* has to forgive. I don't think she sees him as in the wrong. Not right or wrong, more of a *it could have been,* but it wasn't. You don't get him back yet though."

Tilting her chin up with a confused frustration, "why not?"

"He's going to a protected place for an exit chat about what happened. And they're going to see him sit with a student counselor to give him a chance to come down off of what happened. The stakes were set at his life, no warrants that he saw, but his life was on the line. He lives, but it came at the cost of having to be honest about it all. Accepting defeat. For some it's a worse fate in the light of what he couldn't do. Another thing to consider is that he had to confess who did what, he had to tell the truth about who he knew was in on it. That is no small amount to unpack."

"I'm not sure I follow."

"She did it, I believe, because she is as she is. She doesn't want him to suffer, or have a secondary psychiatric wound from complications of the event. He could have been a hero, had things been different. The sooner he knows that she doesn't hold him accountable? The sooner he can let go of his own guilt. He has to have some space from the events, from the storm, to find his inner calm. To check to see if he's bleeding internally."

"I follow now. I can endure."

"Good."

"And Thomas?"

Truth is easier to tell when it's the only real option. "Dead. She put him to sleep and sent him to his execution. She put him down herself."

Hanging her head, "did she have that cannon of hers?"

Well that answers that. "You're perceptive."

Stepping out of the embrace with a wringing of her hands she shook her head sadly. Waffling her fingers together and held her own hands as the words tumbled out, "it's hard to not notice that when she does all the dark work she carries the same gun. It's a huge gun." Taking a breath her question came with a tentative air, "did she fire today?"

"She did."

"By the Ash. Tell me, how was she dressed?"

No heart harder to care for than a Bachman heart. "She was as the Enforcer."

Retorting her question with a flare of her nostrils, the pain at the thoughts evident in her tone, "the locking clasp hair tie?"

"She was called into another dark moment."

"Did Josh see her dressed in those vestments?"

"He did. But she brought him out of the moment. She separated him from the moments of judgment and pain."

"Who was not spared?"

Left to right. "Ardent Kunlow, he managed to broker this in a way that *all* of the Houses *appear* guilty of collusion."

Raising a hand she shook it with her confusion, "he seemed just, *confident* in his abilities."

Pushing forward, "the other was Marissa Kunlow."

Clenching her hand into a fist the implication was evident, "she worked with Miss Augusta –"

Pushing the truth along, "to the end of being able to leave a device which crippled the Tower. It was what turned of the light. She escaped, they found her, and she was ended."

"Susan?" Eying her, "personally."

"Yes." Nodding she fought with her composure, "she attacked Susan. That was the end of her."

Taking a half step back toward her, "when can I call her?"

Inflecting a gentle plead, "tonight."

"Not sooner?"

"She is in the middle of an Endeavor."

Stepping away, "how many saw her?"

"Everyone who was in the building at Cloak and Dagger. They would have all seen the moment unfolding."

Grumbling the resentment, "unable to comment."

"Unable."

Rounding back toward her with palms open and presented, "can I get a Second Chance with knowing her?"

Reaching out she set her hands onto Cassia's palms, "she is the Prophet of the Second Chance, you are both still alive, so I do not see why not."

"I would like to." Cupping her hands against Amanda's her tone dropped to something inflected with humor, "and not just because I wonder what is going on with her and the Winter Wolf."

Pressing her hands against hers to emphasize the idea, "the greens of Courtship point to the idea that our prayers could be answered."

Presenting a smile she took a deep breath, "on that note? I have been opening that line of discussion with Josh. That it was time to begin that chapter of our lives."

"Good."

"What's the SitRep out there?"

"Things are calming."

"What of Octavia?"

"She's been briefed. They've given her the Consul's Consultation. She's been given everything, good and bad, from this hand-me-down coup. I can only hope that she is well. If anything? She's a hole card we have for the future being good."

"How is that?"

"Susan has no quarrel with her. She's a reminder that she doesn't hate *The Council* as a whole. It's something we need."

"Should she hate the Council?"

"No. She knows she shouldn't. Another hand-me-down from her father. We have not so much a bridge to rebuild, but a city of two way streets to repave."

"Hope yet?"

"Yes. Not to mention that Dagger Herb has been watching out for Lady Kunlow. *That* alone sends a daunting message to any who would go for Lady Kunlow."

"As the understanding is that to hurt Herb is to hurt Miss Bachman?"

"Correct."

"I didn't even put two and two together when they put me in their rig. That it was

Captain Dad and the Atrial Dagger. Instead it was just two helmets and the fearful confusion. I knew the roads in nothing flat, the idea of coming home. Back to where I once lived with the man I was so happy to see."

Adjusting her grip she implored her, "don't fall into a pit trap of guilt."

Hanging her head, "I will endeavor to avoid such a folly."

"Then it is settled?"

"If she saw Thomas off, what were his parting words?"

Whispering the words with the sick tragedy they held, "I'll be good."

Whipping her head up, her horror was evident, "after all of this? He –"

"Yes."

Holding her hands for a moment she shook her head and trembled for a moment. Finding a measure of calm she returned to her questions, "was her Wolf with her?"

"He was. He has no other place in things than at her side. He's cleaned up since his first showing." *Share the food.* "He said a Last Rite over Thomas before he lost consciousness."

Stopping she turned her eyes back to her, "what is his faith?"

I have only theories. "I don't know. Whatever it is? He has compassion for the fallen, even the enemies. His battle epitaph? Sleep. I believe I can have faith that a good heart beats in his chest. If he is the Sire of the Bachman Children? He appears to be someone to have faith in."

Blinking a few times she nodded in comprehension, "amazing."

"I have something good in all of this." Nodding once she rolled the hand grip to one of holding gently, "there is one more thing. Where Susan is going."

Tossing out her guesses, "Home? The Blackstone?"

"The moment with Thomas, it has wounded her, which makes it easier to see where the blood trail is going to lead. Amaranth was taken as part of the End Game to this plot. She goes to rescue her."

Furrowing her brow, "wouldn't that be dangerous?"

"Before becoming The High Consul, Miss Bachman was trained and certified in the Art of War. She has enough certification that she, like her father, can claim Dominion over the battlefield up to a certain Threat Index. As the field she heads to does not exceed her Rating? She can go, and there is precious little that can be done to stop her."

"Assurances?"

"Her Medical Wagon, The Matron, Captain Dad, The Atrial Dagger, The Commander, Cloak O'Neil, Dagger Hampton, and her Wolf will all be near. All to find the missing Fourth of the Quartet."

Smirking with the old joke, "the girl named for military cereal."

Offering as a rebuttal, "I like the popped seeds, however," pausing to regain her serious demeanor, "I know from Asmodai he named her for the enduring nature of the red color. And *not* for the bowls of cereal he ate while on the front. I *still* keep it in the house for Micah because he misses it and needs a bowl here and there before a day of yard work or other labor."

Or at one in the morning when he can't sleep.

"We digress."

"We do!"

"Will Susan recover and leave the woods?"

"I would like to think so. I would like to believe that this is not going to be the tone for the next twenty years for her."

"I should hope not. I mean, I *do* hope not."

Letting go of her hands, *I need to get her focused on something productive.* "You could go to Chuck and ask him for help in preparing Josh's homecoming."

"It will not do him harm?"

"It would be good for the two of you to work together again. You were once quite good at it."

"You didn't say –"

"It shouldn't harm him. He said no. He has moved into another direction with that energy in his life. You have moved in yours. *However,* the two of you forgot that you were also K, or at least L orbit to the other. I look at the two of you and you seem like you didn't notice you're coming back from Q orbit. Solve the orbital?"

"I will endeavor to do my part in solving it before I go home."

"Noted and *good.*"

"Thank you Auntie."

"Noted. Accepted."

"I will leave you to solving your troubles."

"Thank you."

"Noted."

6.1.0 - 11:42

The Holden Spire – Guest Bedroom - Seattle

▼Alexandria "Alex" Holden

Working her hair with a comb she regarded herself in the mirror. *I haven't seen him yet. He was cleared by Medical to see me, brought to me, and place beyond these doors. I shouldn't keep him waiting.*

Putting the comb away she touched her stomach as the nervous nausea wracked her resolve. *I need insight into Susan and to get it I am going to have to pick at the wound in Sinclair's heart.* Rereading the message from Amanda on her comm, *Susan knew far more than I could have suspected. The inadvertent cruelty to all of this is not lost on her either. But I feel the need to ask, so I shall ask, and be careful with this moment as if it was made of spun sugar.*

Knocking on the door she was rewarded with a voice from the other side, "I left it unlocked so I wouldn't have to get up."

Pursing her lips she opened the door and let herself in. Closing the door behind her she leaned against the wall with a sigh. "So formal."

Looking up from his chair, garbed in the casual around the house attire she had only seen on him a time or two, he seemed wistfully at a loss. "I have to be careful with my wishes."

Vague, so helpful. "What did you wish for?"

"To stop missing Susan. She sent me a small missive as the plane was landing. It," stumbling verbally for a moment he recovered, "went quite far in making this hurt less. She sent me a message this morning. It was quite a bit longer."

Did I miss something? "What did it say?"

"She said that she cherished our time together. And that," looking away from her, "there are others who are going to miss me."

Oh, not what I thought. "Details?"

"I had friends outside of work. Three sets of friends." Counting them off on his good hand, "the ones I knew through Miss Bachman, the ones I knew through Susan, and the ones I knew after shift."

How did I let you get so far away from me? "Tell me of those who will miss you?"

"For one? My workout partner at Sweat Generators."

"You didn't work out in house?"

618

Laughing softly, "no. I heard that the rolls at Sweat Generators were a bit low so I joined. Someone had the bright idea, pardon the wordplay, of taking all of our advances in manual locomotion power generation and building a gym around it. As life comes in seasons it was one where fewer people were going. I joined and helped get the music back on. From there I convinced others to join. We were advancing research while we advanced our self-care. My main workout partner, Borvon, he reached out to me while I was in transit when he figured out I was not going to be coming in. I let him know I did not know what the future held."

Someone outside of your bubble reached into your bubble to find you. "Noted."

Tapping the arm of the chair twice with the tips of two fingers, "Alex?"

Now we get serious. "Sinclair?"

"She told me she doctored the reports I sent to Ajax. That the majority of the things I think you know, you don't know, and she's leaving me to navigate the space. She told me about the message she sent to your comm. The things I sent in the moment, in that space, it was one thing. Now? I feel," pausing to breathe, "conflicted."

Moving over to him she pushed a stool over to his undamaged side. Sitting down she leaned in laid her cheek on his arm for a moment, "conversational dodge affirmed. I missed you."

Relaxing back to a conversational state, "I missed you too."

Sitting upright she smiled encouragingly, "you seem less bereft of happiness."

Touching his hand to hers, "I made it to a place I know as a home. I was able to get back to you. I didn't expect to see you at the airport when I landed, but it was nice to see James again."

Tell the truth, don't try to save face. "I was in meetings. Our logistics teams are trying to figure out how we can prove we didn't know the logistics of what went into this."

Tapping her hand with a crooked forefinger, "mea culpa."

Helpful as always with the vague apologies. "For? It helps if you say what you did."

Speaking the apology with an embarrassment to it, "I didn't record a message for you. I checked my weapons and listened to everyone else without recording anything myself. I said a prayer, but I did not speak what I could have said."

That is so you. Touching his hand gently, "outcome bias, I will lay my thanks on the outcome bias. I accept the apology that is unneeded now."

Hooking his finger around hers, "the end was not good. We were short handed, the logistics of that moment, it was Final Stand. The reason I'm apologizing is because there is something I never said, that I didn't say then."

The thing I wouldn't say either? "Speak it?"

Straightening up his voice spoke of grace and tact, "I do care, and adore you, in a way that cousins, albeit distant, should not."

How romantic.

I feel the grateful knowledge that mind reading isn't something anyone can actually do.

Caressing his hand with a gentle tease to her lilt, "outcome bias, again, as I suspected that you felt as I did."

Smiling in return, "you do?"

The Soft Taboo we cuddled against for a few years. "I do. That is important because I will walk with you, through this moment." Wrapping two fingers around his good wrist she tried to muster a smile, "I will listen and hear you."

Settling back against his chair he nodded, "I didn't want to trouble you with a death's door confession. I thought of you, how if you knew this was going to happen that you would have told me. It gave me the strength to fight as I needed to."

Pulsing the touch on his wrist she waited.

"The others, we have all met Consuls, at least one or two, which made it seem easier to fight the lie. Not one of us would be dropped a warning? It seemed, impossible."

"The Honor Guard regard us well?"

Furrowing his brow he nodded, "I would say we do. We were treated fairly in each Province, we were fed, housed, and shown the glory of their lands. The Consuls, their adult children, and their allies in their Pyramids were various degrees of kind and helpful. It seemed *unreal* to see the words. My, identity, was on the line. Paulson, his brother was brave, died to save others. He made the choice to be brave."

Pulsing the touch again she offered a mote of understanding, "bravery is not an essential quality of a man. It is the choice he makes. It is not metaphysically given, it is a gift from within."

"He traded his life, to set up the Shooting Gallery Defense. They were on Full Blitz, the counter is some way of forcing them to slow down or take heavier losses to maintain time table. He knew," sniffling for a moment, "he knew what he was going to do. No chance of living through it. We had to buy time. No matter what we did, it had to buy more time."

Pulsing the touch she weathered standing in the emotional gravity of his confession.

"They had a mission. Miss Bachman was stashed away. The Wolfram Gate would have to protect her. See a Breacher Bag? End the one who carries it. If no bags can make it to the top floor? She'll live. I heard it Alex, the screams of war and battle over the vox. There was nothing we had left to give that night, just our lives. Asmodai warned us, he *warned us,* in private, swore us to secrecy. That we would die at her side."

The Oath of Duty Unto Death.

"We didn't *have* lives, or *homes,* or a *place.* We had a view, from the top of the Pyramid. Grow old, endure, survive, and muster out having seen that which only a fraction of a percentile of our people *would ever, remotely, understand.* To be saluted in the streets by Citizens who know the price we have agreed to paid."

Forgive me.

"Alex, I lived a life that few men would ever know. I thought, I thought I had an idea of what it meant to live as a Steward of Humanity, to serve in the City Militia, and to walk next to the Citizen as a *needed* element in the Alchemy of Civilization. Then I did as you asked, and I went to her side. I am no longer the same man, but I am still me."

Trying to fight back the tears she succumbed to the grief. Lowering her head she let the tears out. *Mea culpa.*

Feeling his hand gently petting her hair, "I know, I know you wanted to console me. But just as Paulson made his choice, I made mine when I agreed and went down there. I made mine every day I woke up and put the uniform on. I paid a price, but I paid it of my own accord. Every six months we were asked if we wanted to leave. Go home. Quit. Admit that you can go no further. I Pledged to stay, each time."

Feeling marginally better she laid her cheek on the arm of the chair as his hand kept up the ministration.

Mea culpa.

"Men, who were my friends, they stopped me on the Twenty-eighth floor. They wanted to talk. I talked to buy time. If I shot? It would be seconds, perhaps thirty at best, I could buy. If I talked? I could buy minutes. I bought minutes."

I cannot fathom. "You knew them?"

"They were men I knew as friends, from the Pub. They were a social group of men that *didn't mind* that I was busy most of the time. We would sit, and talk, and, I believe that if they needed intel? I provided no small amount of it."

"They broke the Circle."

"They did. I helped. Then, as they stood before me, they told me their truth. They didn't do it, not to kill us. We were in the way of their quest. They didn't want to kill us, we were Loyal until that night. To them, to stay with Miss Bachman was to be disloyal to the Citizen."

"Did you relay this?"

"I did, some, in return Stanley, from Information Processing, he gave me more insights into the moment. To try to heal my heart. To absolve me. I was not the only vector of information, I was not the only person that had been befriended. I sent him more and he sent me more. He showed me just how many pieces the Circle was in. He gave me the understanding he has of the Winter Wolf, and how much Miss Bachman means to him."

Time for the question I have not heard answered yet. "What did they want?"

"The Fire Maiden."

This does not sound good. "Can you tell me more?"

"Of course I can, you're a Consul." Recovering a measure of stability to himself, "during the war, we lost Isaac, to a Thermobaric Rocket."

Wait - "why does this matter in regards to the Maiden?"

"The Ports, got the Rocket with the aid of Ridolfi. From what I came to understand? We created the Rocket. It is known as The Fire Maiden's Kiss."

If that was a kiss - "then what is a *Fire Maiden*?"

With an almost casual tone he replied, "the full sized bomb."

"*Full* sized?"

"The Kiss, was apparently a prototype that the Snafu had created to test the technology on a portable scale and to establish the math of scalability. From there they created the Fire Maiden herself."

But we've never used something like that. I didn't see that in my files. "I did not see this."

Continuing to sound calm he soothed her with his good hand, "it was before the end of the war with the Ports. A history lesson for me."

I'm confused. "It was unused? I don't remember learning that we used it, or had it."

"Unused. The destructive yield is estimated to be sufficient to destroy the core of Port Refuge or Asylum as a single strike. The secondary effects would turn the surrounding areas into an Ecological Disaster Zone. The history lesson I have, in the recorded words of Asmodai Bachman himself, is that to use it would be to forsake humanity. The peace we have, such as it is," taking on an air of contemplation with his words, "was forged from the decision to be more humane."

What did Thomas want with that?

Smiling with an attempt at a more dramatic intonation, "to own the Fire Maiden, is to control the fate of the future."

Unable to keep the smile from her face, *him and the movie trailer voice.* "Why didn't he just steal the Fire Maiden?"

Appearing uncomfortable, "he needed The Sisterhood. As only by becoming the High Consul could he order more."

That explains that. I feel slow today. "That's why they're called The Fire's Promise."

Correcting her gently, "The Blackout Bloc."

"Why change it?"

"To separate the individual from the group. Each survivor must evaluate the future as an individual, without a group to lean on. The Promise was broken. Now they are the individual, standing on their own, being asked what becomes of the future." Adding with a smile, "you like that? I didn't write it. I found it as a memo on my comm. I liked it."

Hanging her head, *he can bring me cheer out of a Blitz Storm.* "You try and succeed at your endeavor."

Replying with an upbeat timbre, "good."

Raising her head again she felt the pensive frown on her face, "she ordered Thomas executed."

"Good."

I need to know then, "who is Amaranth?"

Watching his eyes widen in fear he spoke slowly, "motive for asking?"

He knows. "She's a VIP, -"

"Yes."

"That was taken."

Taking a deep breath he appeared to be steadying himself. Speak his words as a focus for calm, "she was held safe in the idea that she was an obscure variable. To protect her with Shannon's Maxim would be to alert others of how strong a presence she had become."

Not a real answer, but closer. "Who is she?"

"The Fourth of the Bachman Quartet. The poorly kept secret, but a secret regardless."

Thomas took her. "Then Thomas could use her to leverage for the Throne, if Miss Bachman was not in his way?"

Appearing mildly horrified with his word, "yes."

"Miss Bachman, she goes to save Amaranth Dinclair from her captivity."

Smiling with a grim humor, "people will die for this. The Commander will have blood."

Now I am not sure I want to know more. "What happens when Miss Bachman finds her?"

"My approximation of the future? She will bring her to her side, and we will see the Quartet united. Asmodai, he," pausing he mused darkly, "he's *dead.* And I'm glad." Sniffling hard he grumbled, "he can no longer trouble us. He helped pour the mortar for the bricks of *Miss Bachman.* I've met Susan, she's, almost harmless."

I don't believe I heard him correctly. "Say again?"

Softening his demeanor his words flowed with a sad humor, "Susan, the delightfully forgiving and understanding woman, no less an emotional ball of fluff and joy than her mother, as per my history lesson understanding of the woman. She *garbs herself* in the identity of Miss Bachman. The outfits, when I met her I thought she was playing dress-up. I was wrong. Each outfit was a focus, a meditative tool to focus the Will and Rational Mind to the task. Just like the School Uniforms, but a deeper paved road of the mind. I did not see the layering."

Stay calm. "I will listen."

Trying to clarify his statement, "she is not The Derecho, but The Derecho is a part of her."

"She isn't acting quite like The Derecho. She's being very quiet, and it has taken every asset I have, and allies I can call on, to stay informed."

Pondering he nodded with conviction, "Snow Blind."

Again with the not quite helping. "Elaborate the Details?"

"The Derecho Wind, is a storm of authority and proclamation. The trail of destruction is clear from kilometers away. Absolute Darkness is the term for late night Operations when no one bears witness to the changes made. No light. Few to no records. The hour before the attack? She used Code Blinkers to move a VIP through Central Tower.

She moved us all away from her side. There, in Absolute Darkness, she would bring the Winter Wolf to her office."

I follow. "I understand and follow."

"When she walks plain and tall, showing her movements, that's Sunshine Stride. To walk in the light."

He doesn't want to say it. "You can say it."

"Snow Blind, is when you know she's out there, but you can't get a solid visual. There is no color beyond the oppressive blizzard. It's getting dark. There is no warmth there. And when the storm clears? Lives, truth, villains, whatever she was looking for? It will be lost to the blizzard and you will see no trace."

"The people who took Amaranth, they have already been removed from their positions and their lives are being closed out."

"They will be consumed by the Blizzard. You will be blind to see it. Where is she now?"

"Reportedly on the way to The Feedbag to get Lunch."

"Who is with her?"

"The Winter Wolf."

"What are publicly seen assets around her?"

"None."

"Search Party Formation."

"What are the Quad Busters for? I have a snippet that they were roused. There is a domicile that The Commander is attempting to raid. Why do they need something blown up?"

"If Amaranth was abducted? You'd need a prison to hold her."

"Why is that?"

Beaming with a small amount of pride, "she took the Escape and Counter-Abduction Training."

That is not a casual course. "How did she do at the e-CAT?"

Nodding with a hesitant demeanor, "poor at physical escape, moderate marks at the technical aspects at escaping the prison, and top ten percent marks on interaction and threat avoidance for her age group." Looking at his hand as he flexed it, "how that will translate to the real world? I don't know." Looking back to her, "I can *hope* she remembers her training and picks her way through the moment."

"I can hope that her captor was not pressed or motivated into harming her then."

"Correct. We can have an educated hope that Miss Bachman will find her unharmed in that regard."

"A lighter question?"

"Set the new course."

"Does she think of all of these things herself? The presentation of things is very Theatrical, I was just wondering if she gets help."

"Help? Yes. Once you're in her inner circle? You get access to the suggestion box about how to improve her presentation of herself and her way of governing. From what to name things, to the art, to the iconography, to the terms used and the meaning behind it. It's almost a game."

"Disturbing."

"It is the culture of the village of Susan Bachman."

I have cartoons and ice cream. "I feel smaller."

"You walk with your people. Cheer them up. Battle against the lower amounts of sun, not as low as north of here, but you battle it. She? Has the weight of the Provinces to consider. Cloak and Dagger has a Mustering Clause where they will make for any front that the Twelve get conflict on if they are needed. She is, in a sense, next to you always and needs to know what is going on, everywhere."

"Noted." *A question to pose.* "She's very militant, forceful, and the majority of her ways and means are violent or conflict based on the outer face –" losing the train of thought she sighed, "I lost the question."

"I can still give an answer." Adjusting his sitting pose he touched her cheek with a smile, "she was raised to think this way. Her core? Is Maggie, from what I understand. Maggie left her a pathway to womanhood covered and paved with the understanding of the feminine power of softness, agreeable motes of giggles, and the beauty of an open heart. From there? She learned how to armor herself from her father in the brutal side of meeting the world iota for iota. Rounded off by Dennis, and the Augusta Sisters who taught her the power of mystery. It's all armor around a caring heart."

"Underneath it all, we're not that different?"

"If you take it down to the idea of warm hearts and an interest in beauty and art? You are kin. Not to say that she doesn't like cartoons too though. I don't even know what I'm trying to say."

"Does she know me then? As I don't know if I know her."

"She knows you from anecdotes. From cartoons watched, to a bowl of Breakfast Boomers, to an understanding of the Inox Crescent."

She - feeling flustered she set to breathing to find her center.

"Do you want to know about the cartoons, the cereal, or the Crescent first?"

What a choice.

"That order."

"I believe she finds you to be a good person. She sees you as a student of your father and his philosophy. A worthy successor to the seat of Consul. Whom she regrets attacking in a moment of inability to cope with the fear of loss. Attachment causes fear, which is expressed in anger, when that which one would lose is going to be lost."

"I know. I have spent no small amount of time trying to understand that night. The Gardener of her Heart, a secret too well kept."

"She went to the Network, and requested to understand the cartoons, and animation, that you love so much. Through Stanislavski Empathy she would walk in your shoes and know you. I witnessed her watching Teenage Samurai Super Chipmunks on more than one occasion. She would dress up in an approximation of a Cartoon Comrade, I gave her insights into the attire of a Sleep-Over, and she would use the moment to relax."

One of the easier questions of the day, "what else did she watch?"

"Time for Adventure."

I'll risk knowing the truth. "Did she like it?"

Patting her shoulder with a smile, "she found it to be more enjoyable when she consulted the notes and translation key on it. To see the idea of a surface level story, then the subtext, and then the layer of the shown but not spoken ideas that bordered on subversive? She found a respect for animation as a medium with that."

Almost too good to be hoped for. "Is there more there?"

"She did try The Business of Survival. It hit a bit too close to home. The realities they face, come too close to things she understands."

Truth. "Noted."

"She wore pajama pants and a strap secured top which bordered on ethereal. Opaque, but ethereal. The air smelled of cotton candy."

All to understand me. "She really went all out."

"She did."

I need to ask. "The Boomers?"

"Captain Leif Turner bought her a box while he was up here."

Marveling at the length and breadth of the endeavor, "she went that far."

"She did."

I wonder, "did she like them?"

"For breakfast? No. They were too sweet. I pointed out that you live differently than she does in that regard. You eat them around nine, then go into the more physically demanding part of your day. She did like them as a cold dessert though. However, Sasha, she loved them so much that box was not long for this world."

That, is adorable. "Thank you."

"Noted."

Oh, now it's time. "Why did she get the Crescent?"

Shrugging his good shoulder, "she wanted to know. To understand. You were, and have primarily been with*out* a partner at your side. To know you found succor with such an object? She wanted to see it, heft it, feel it. The story goes that Dagger Herb hefted it, and wondered what sort of weapon it was. I wasn't on shift, but I was assured that it was as it was."

Feeling her cheeks flush she hid her face, "did she *like* it?"

Petting her head gently he laughed softly, "she said it was an experience that was as healing as it was strange."

"Did she keep it?"

"She did. I've seen her use it as an after caress post leg roller treatment. From the luster of it? I believe she only used it, *once,* as it might be said to be intended to use." Taking on a quoting tone which reminded her of herself years ago, "some women like feathers, I like Inox Steel."

I found another fan of Inox. "Then she enjoys the caress of the Inox?"

"From what I saw, yes."

"I feel less strange."

"Good."

I did this backwards. "I came in here to ask you for truth, and to console you. I feel as if you are consoling me."

Smiling with all of the luster and charm of their times from before, "I feel as if I have some sort of power in my words. It helps my ravaged mind."

My Night Watchman. Under the stars you protected my city. "If you can't go back to her?"

"I can go back, it would be a matter of staying. I *do* need to heal first. Take the exam. To see if this arm of mine can be whole again."

I must be brave. "Do you want to stay with her?"

Fumbling over his words his conviction was evident, "Alex, when I'm on the Horizon Rifle, I don't feel like a God, or a Valkyrie, I am the Protector of something bigger than myself. I have a first person vantage to the future. I don't know if I'm ready to muster out. If my arm is no good?" Pausing to sigh, "then I don't have to worry about making the choice. That choice becomes metaphysical, that which is. I can surrender to the weakness of the flesh and let my elbow decide."

Trying to get the question out, "if you don't, don't stay, come home?"

"To you?"

Feeling the flush in her cheeks, "yes."

Swallowing audibly she could hear two deep breaths before he broached his question, "why did you ask me to go?"

Casting her eyes down she found enough courage to be honest with him. "Sinclair, you're no ordinary man. You won the lottery of body, mind, and strength. You rose to a greater level of achievement. This city was too small to hold your spirit, the call within you. I needed someone at her side, and you were the only one I had who could hit those benchmarks. I saw you train, striving, and breaking the marks that were set before you. I had to choose, take you as my husband, or send you to the frontline of something I did not understand, but I knew would need you."

Touching her shoulder gently he spoke softly, "Alex, I, need you to know something. On that note, I want to ask about me, but I need to tell you what I did."

Raising her head she met his gaze, "what did you do?"

With the emotional pain visible in a way that left her feeling uncomfortable hearing the words, "I saved her life."

I didn't hear about this. "Where's your medal?"

Closing his eyes for a long pause he reopened them with the guilt showing, "I didn't get one for it. It was after Guthrie."

The mass grave without answers and only the testimony of salvaged children which scream a warning to not try to understand. "The *Incident* so strong that I *still* can't read it?"

Nodding he kept his pace low and level, "the Epsilon Code, password, is Tranq. I have a personal report I can dig up for you. I saved her life there. Before, we address us, I need you to know that there was a Net Good in me going to her. That, you didn't reject me, but, confirmation bias, I was where I needed to be."

Nodding she thought it over, *our sacrifice becomes his unanswerable question which leaves him a secret Hero. I will share the burden.* "How did you save her?"

"Guthrie, was not a good day. Our enemies there, were no less monsters, albeit a different type, than Forks."

Giving him the honest truth, "I avoided reading the reports. My father read them and told me to not read them. To just let it pass into dust."

"That was for the best, I think, I want to say. It was," making a disgusted noise he sighed. "The battle had been fierce to get them back inside their power base proper. The Commander had laid siege to it. We were not far behind, we were waiting for something the Snafu was still finishing and it was too late for The Commander to take it with him. We brought the device that would open the door and give us a chance to get at Ridolfi."

The Dragon of Chaos himself. "Ridolfi, the Denier of Dawn?"

"Yes."

Why would he be there? "Why was he there?"

"To find more allies to attack us. The people of Guthrie had already massacred the Homesteaders around Spoke Can. He wanted to move them against the agriculture community of the Apple Valley."

The Apple Valley, that's not a place we can afford to lose. "Why was I not told?"

"The people of Guthrie, they ceased to be, by the time we had left. They were no longer a threat to the Apple Valley. Your father was worried about the Valley people. The confirming intel was found in the building."

Then how was Miss Bachman in danger? "What got close enough to Miss Bachman?"

"Miss Bachman."

I don't follow. "How? Why?"

Turning his head away she could see the shame that she had seen twice before when a raid failed. "They used, they used the Homesteaders children as human shields. We had a breach point, and they clustered the children on the other side of it. She was not privy to the intel. The thing that Snafu had built was going to knock the door down. A primary charge directional EMP with a secondary armor piercing and high pressure warhead. Miss Bachman used it on what passed for the great gate of their city. It made a door, and it ended the lives of every man, woman, and child on the other side."

Staring at him as her mind reeled she braced herself for more.

"She ordered us in, to recover what was left of the children, which we did get. We found them, got them out, and when I went to her to ask her what to do next? She had, her Cannon, to the underside of her chin. She was going to give herself a William's Kiss to escape. Thankfully, she had not cocked the hammer. I startled her, moved quickly, disarmed her, and talked her down."

Sitting in stunned silence she forced something out, "that's, *horrific*."

Fighting with the old wound in his spirit he visible contorted to keep the sadness at bay. "We found her, we found her a silver lining. We found her the last boy of Spoke Can. He was, at that point, all that remained of them. I don't know where he lives now, or how he lives, I just know we loaded him up. She knew something, they exchanged words, and he stared at her in wonder. Some bit of ancient history of the surface world we left behind."

The reports he told me to stay away from. The quietly handled salvaged children. They were sent to the Olep for a time. "I don't have words."

Affecting an 'at a loss' demeanor, "I don't know how much she redacted from my reports."

"I would assume *most* of it at this point."

"Then you may not have the answer to why the Honor Guard was formed."

The things she has kept from me. "The reports were all light, fluffy, I wondered if something was wrong, but I had no way to reach you."

Speaking the confession, "the old man of the office, he, unleashed the Rage on her one night. When she was sixteen."

Feeling a rise of nausea at the idea, "his own kid?"

"I was shocked too. Then I looked deeper. I examined more. Alex, I believe they have an anger disorder. Flaw in the clay level disorder."

"I had not considered that."

"I looked, they battle with anger as a family. Each child of the line, they pass down a gradually decreasing anger and capacity for Rage. Susan, she asked her father about Ridolfi, and if they could find peace. If, some sort of accord could be forged to stop him."

"Then he hit her."

"He beat her, and she fled. The Honor Guard became the way he would see her safe, even if she wouldn't stand next to him for years. They, mended what they could, of the bridge between them. Neither *wanted* to hate the other. But, having hated once, it could not be undone. The scar they had left on the other, would never fully heal."

"Noted." Committing to the question, "do you know of a time when the Rage got the best of her?"

"I do." Taking a breath she watched him visibly wrestle with the words. "Winifred showed me the first time Miss Bachman was seen afflicted by the Rage in training. One of the other female recruits to Cloak and Dagger had been humiliating Susan in the practice ring. Tripping her, knocking her over, and otherwise just taking her to task. *However,* she was not using the Inner Peace Instructor method."

The understanding instructions, calling for the student to know peace. Where each failure is learned to be loved because it educates you on what you did not know in the moment. "If not Inner Peace, then which Instructor was she?"

"She was not the Instructor. She was the Mocking Judge. Then when it appeared to be over, Susan grabbed one of the practice swords from the edge of the arena and attacked her from behind. It was quick. The swords were out as the next to have the spot would be working with them. There was no reason for that moment. The woman, she took a sound thrashing. Winifred jumped in to save her, and having seen it? I don't believe they get a choice. Our Foundation Myth states that William was so angry that no one could stand within five meters of his directed Rage and live. I fear there is no small truth to the Myth."

That would mean, "a flaw in the clay."

Nodding with a somber appraisal, "a weaponization of the flaw, yes."

That is one way to play the cards dealt, but still. "Sobering."

"He's dead now. He's dead, he can rest, and leave this world to us. To her."

Never meet your Heroes. "You sound glad."

"If he's dead, she can move forward. No longer spending her energy trying to keep him afloat. Watching her sink in the dark water of his spirit, it killed me Alex. I just wanted to scream at her, *let him drown.*" Lowering his voice, "let him sink. If we have no recourse, we have no recourse. Learn to let go."

"Noted."

"I, can't drown us, I need something lighter. I will tell you of a lighter moment. I remember the first time she changed in front of me."

I need to know more before I have an opinion. "Pardon?"

"She was at New Hope General, visiting patients, and someone threw up on her. She was in a casual medical outfit, a colorful pant and shirt combo, and after helping clean up she went to the next room and just started changing. It only took her a few moments and then she was right back at it, but the ease she let her convictions guide her? I was taken aback."

"That sounds endearing."

"It was."

"Tell me of you?"

"I'm, *I'm still alive.* I laid awake last night, thinking about my brothers in arms, those for whom this was the end. To know each one, *each one,* left behind jagged and frayed ropes that used to tie everything together. She can't kill the killers because it just makes more frayed ropes. She can't tie it all back together if she keeps cutting the ropes while screaming *look what you made me do.* The old man, I'll give him that, he never told her it was her fault. He told her, from what I know, the very next day it was his fault for being cold, and angry, and weak. He gave her a dozen culpas."

"Staggering."

"I don't know what I need right now Alex."

"Stay here, in the Tower?"

"I can do this."

"Good."

"I, am thankful I returned to you."

"I have left a stone unturned."

Breathing to recover himself he smiled at her, "The Winter Wolf?"

"Yes."

"He is who he says he is. Our Myth, has gained another installment. I am not worried for Miss Bachman, as the Wolf is by her side. I don't need to belabor what is known, as it is truth."

I feel better now. "Thank you."

"Noted."

"With the Traveler's Greens, and the trust, does she love him?"

"I believe so, yes. I saw how happy she was to visit him while he was staying in Central. It's why I didn't push, why none of us were interested in pressing the issue. She was *happy.* Good enough."

Leaning in she nuzzled his cheek above his facial stubble, *I missed you.*

"I cannot die if you keep doing that."

"Then I will do it again if I need to."

"Thank you Alex."

"Noted."

Hearing the wrapping on the door she looked up, "James?"

Poking his head in with a smile James appeared pleased and vexed at the same time, "there is someone looking for Sinclair."

"Who?"

A male voice, ringing as a deep baritone, announced himself from beyond James, "Pointman Vastaro Vineyard! I have come for the Osprey known as Sinclair Holden!"

Sinclair looks happy, "let him in." Sitting back down she waited a moment as the guest came into the room.

Appearing out of place with his signed cast on his left arm, empty holsters, and tactical points bereft of equipment Vastaro smiled with the broad humor of the unapologetic. "When word hit the Precinct Command? I was dispatched."

Tilting his head with a laugh, "what in the Blue Sky happened to you Vineyard?"

"Stray dog. The end of the world couldn't kill them all. Was hunting a mean one with a taste for blood. It had friends. It only took a few moments, but it got the best of me. I put two in the brainpan of the monster. It was the biggest and meanest of them, but it's why I'm the Pointman. The other Ospreys mopped up the rest. At the Medical Center I was able to share my pain with the victims. To give them closure that the menace was gone."

Clarify the moment, "the Ospreys wish to see Sinclair?"

"We do!" Turning back to Sinclair, "you went from Scout to Valkyrie. Normally I would tease you for taking on a woman's work, but I've seen that rifle you held."

"I have a steady hand. The Matron needed someone who could tote that monster all shift and not complain."

"*You,* not complain?"

I will see him rejoice, then we will speak again, "Gentlemen? I believe you can continue this at the pub."

Laughing the moment off Vineyard smiled sheepishly, "she knows us well."

"I have missed you."

"We are denied a greeting of Warriors." Nodding his head to Sinclair, "rise. Your brothers and sisters wish to see you again."

Without rising he spoke cautiously, "I do not know if I'm staying."

Laughing with an encouraging humor, "you would return to the eye of the storm?"

Eying him with a dry humor, "the howl of the Derecho Winds makes it easier to sleep at this point."

"You sir, are an absolute madman." Moving in he held out his hand, "come with me?"

Taking the hand he was hauled to his feet, "I will return Consul."

"I'm counting on it."

Watching the two of them leave she was left alone with her thoughts. *He has another facet of his choice and life to consider. I will know when he knows. Waldo is still some time from getting to come home on leave from the Snow-Front. I'll have until he returns to get this figured out.*

Then I get to find out how he'll feel about what he does not know.

Checking the time, *I need to go to my study and open the SitRep Window. The Coordinating Captain is going to want to get me a Daily Update. The more I find out, the less I know.*

But, consoling herself with the truth, *the more I learn.*

Standing in the doorway James looked to her with an inquisitive glance, "did it go well?"

Shaking her head sadly, "I still love him James."

Steepling his fingers, "so not well at all."

Pursing her lips she shook her head, "no. Not well at all."

"Worst case?"

Adopting a cavalier humor, "I take him to my bed, just to know, and then watch him slip away."

Standing patiently, "noted."

Losing the humor she spoke the hardest truth she knew, "which is tied with the other worst case. I take him to my bed, he stays, and then we find out that was not the choice that needed to be made."

Lowering his hands with an empathetic frown, "noted."

I can deal with these emotions later. "I need to go check the SitRep. I informed the Coordinator that I would not be there, but I would speak with his Second later. Now I can make amends."

"Very good Consul."

"Yes."

A SitRep a day keeps the men feeling less far away.

6.1.3 - 11:55

Mobile News Center – Rally Point 'Yosh'

▶ Winifred Yeoman

Checking her comm for updates she nodded with a smile, "it's working."

Looking up from his comm Wallman flashed a hesitant smile, "the last ditch line to keep our High Consul safe?"

Nodding the affirmative, "she's gone full Snow Blind, diverted forces in a blizzard, the snow flurry is keeping media updated and everything off balance in a way that makes everything appear to be normal. The Citizen knows that when Derecho Winds howl that something amazing is about to happen."

Watching the data points connect, "by the Blue Sky Holden was right on the money for how to handle this moment." Casting the map of updates to Wallman's tablet she smiled, "Snowshoes and Parkas Gambit is in play."

Reading the details he seemed almost unimpressed, "so you have a band of do-goods all using Personal Day Leave to keep an eye on her?"

Railing in the reflexive flare from the sting of her pride, "hand picked using only the most corrupt of methods. No one else knows who else is in on the Gambit. We have an address of where she's headed, and an idea of how she will get there. I staggered them from Cloak and Dagger along the route. Each one is going to update through a Protected Guild Channel and I can keep an eye on her. She doesn't checkpoint and we'll scramble."

Nodding in understanding he sounded more interested and impressed, "and she won't spot them?"

Calming herself fully she spoke with esteem of the idea, "not at first, hopefully not at all. It's enough to buy us time. I was given a status update of her leaving Cloak and Dagger so I moved the pieces into play. I have never been able to use this before, as I do not want to spook her with it, but I wanted assurances this day."

Taking on a demeanor of engagement with the moment, "why is it you don't want her to see them? Does she not love her Citizens?"

She does, however, "right now, I don't know how much of her own threat narrative she has written. Much less if she's feeling open to the notion of strangers inside of this moment. I want to keep her safe, but I can't let people know what she's doing or why. If I can maximize her safety without compromising her personal liberty? Then I will go as far as I can with this plan."

Nodding he signaled for 'better grasp,' "the old saying of trading liberty for security returns to us."

"Yes. This is a nudge toward risking the compromise of her liberty and privacy, but, it is my career to walk that line."

"Truth."

Opening up on the stakes, "she's going to find her sister, the fourth of a Quartet. The Citizen, doesn't really understand that even remotely. What these moments mean or what is going on with them as a family. I have to protect that. However, I have blips on the radar which state that there could be Freelanders in the City proper. As much as I want to trust all of our people, I cannot trust the unknown variable."

"Two things. One, I was not allowed into The Loop about Amaranth, not fully, not even until you told me just now."

Quickly speaking her earnest apology, "oh! Mea culpa."

"Accepted, but unneeded. That does change the nature of the day and the plan. I understand more. I respect your work in making sure that The Circle remains unbroken."

Can't keep a secret if you tell the newsman. I didn't think of that aspect of it. "We Square the Circle, we Call the Corners, we align diagrams of loyalty and faith. Today, I can't show the people what the Endeavor is about, just that it is important. The plan moves into effect, the snow covers the scene, and I give the right people a parka and the shoes to walk into the mess and just make sure we don't lose sight of her in the flurry."

Intoning his words with a liberal wash of self-recrimination, "the advantage of a State Media which does as its told."

I don't know if he's being sarcastic. Calling the moment to task, "don't think I didn't hear that Wallman."

Holding up his hands he signaled for 'clarification' and 'honest introspection.' "I gyrate against the system, against the Protocol, and I remain unharmed. I do love the freedom I have, but I often ponder the why of it. Is it just to give people the illusion of rebellion? Just to entertain them?"

I will thank Admin Nobody and whomever he had write the words he sent me later. "I'm not much of a Philosopher, so it's Borrowed Words time. People, are not singular in identity or axiomatic in application. From our Taboos to our Protocol there is give and give from two sides. Positive, Negative, Up, Down, Left, and Right. Forces have opposites. You dear Wallman, represent the stake that the people who want to know what was left unsaid have. The Director Writes it, you or Anton read it, and then they get to hear the rest of the story from you in private. I want to believe it's about the heart and soul of the issues."

Smiling with a humbled timbre, "who said all that?"

Keeping it conversational, "it was part of a Data Packet that Admin Nobody sent to explain why you were so precious that I would be sitting here, next to you, and not next to Miss Bachman."

Tapping his desk with his fingertips, "I had wondered."

Gushing the honesty, "I did too! Then I asked, and was rewarded."

Picking up his clipboard his words carried a humbled candor, "I am without words, and a bit humbled at my value." Pausing for a moment he checked his clipboard, "I need to send off a few missives and then I'll be clear to move this operation to the next stop."

The classic question of life, "where do we go from here?"

"Next stop is the New Hope Holding Tank. I have some dissidents I want to talk to about their behavior."

Nodding twice, "Hot August Night saves them."

"The Compassion of the High Consul saves them from themselves. I want some perspective from them though."

"Can do." Firing off a small string of orders via text she smiled at the progress being made, "there is hope for us yet."

"Good." Sitting down next to her, "how was your visit with Northland?"

I would rather be somewhere else but this discussion. "It was, what it was."

Lobbing the question with an Interviewer's timbre, "how's his situation looking?"

"Grim. The doctors are unsure if they were too generous in their initial prognosis. His body should mend, but that hit to the head is going to lower his abilities and our standards are high." Faltering in her thoughts, "that hit to his head is going to leave him knocked down a peg, and that is going to separate him from success if it doesn't get better."

Keeping up his Interviewer's timbre, "the Cloak and Dagger standards are an unflinching reminder of the lack of compromise in the art of war. Even the Honor Guard standards are what they are for a reason."

Focus on the Silver Lining. "He'll live, that's what counts."

"Perhaps find a wife?"

Nodding once, "perhaps."

"Will you seek a husband?"

Running her fingers through her short hair with a chuff of laughter, "when I find a successor to my place in the Guard? I would consider it. I trained for years for this, to channel what I felt into action, and here I am. I have a few years left to this stage in my life, then I can step down and be the mother I did not understand being when I started this journey."

"If I may, what sort of husband would you be seeking?"

Laughing at the notion, "I don't know. I look over the Archetypes and honestly can't make up my mind. From there it becomes the husband for whom all of this," gesturing to herself with a dismissive gesture, "is what he was drawn to. I think it's something best dwelled on during a time of peace."

"Fair enough."

Turning the question back on him, "why is there no Mrs. Wallman?"

"I have a sister," holding up his hand to stall her, "it relates, pardon both the word-play and the poor segue. She rotates between Guild Custody and Probationary Autonomy. When she's not in treatment? She takes no small sum of my time. With how I throw myself into my work? I do not have the time to spare to find the other half of the Heart's Equation. If *she* found *me*? I would find a way."

Accepting his reply with a nod, "fair enough."

Nodding in turn he offered, "I *am* Registered with the Registry of Hearts. I spent the Rations which gives me the Assisted Matchmaking. When they think they have some-one whom I match, and who matches me? They will call. I will answer."

I should consider it. "Noted."

Turning his attention with a long sweeping gesture to their tablets and map, "what happens now?"

We wait. "We watch the updates, I have forces ready to speed toward her in case. Also, her Medical Wagon is at a discretionary distance from her. If Amaranth is injured? She can have medical in nothing flat."

"Good that she can have it, let us hope she does not need it."

Hope springs eternal. "Truth."

6.0.8 - 11:30

The Feedbag – 'Bad Vantage' Table

☀ Yuri

Having a seat at the modest table for four he couldn't help but notice the friendly décor. *This is The Feedbag. A nice enough place from the looks of it.* "York is going to be making our food then?"

Sitting down across from him Susan nodded, "he's already been appraised I'm here and what I want. I used my comm to set this up."

Assessing the room he noticed they were being left alone, "and your people don't seem to notice you are here?"

Nodding she reached up and touched the charm on her hair band. "See this one?"

"It's quite distinct. An orb of metal, painted with a metal sheen."

"An ironclad personal space bubble, tempered with the color of gunmetal. This is the signal they see and acknowledge. In case they miss it? My comm also pinged the notification to them when I came in the door."

"What happens if you take it off?"

Without pitching her voice low, "then if they wish, they would come over, and perhaps even converse. I might get a hug, a word of condolence."

She is going to do something, "why did you pitch your voice like that?"

"Yuri," reaching up she started to untie her charm, "I have already seen a half dozen signals that ask if I really mean the charm as truth."

"You have a signal for that?"

"It's a clarification signal. Not a direct challenge to my hair charm, but a general question."

Be ready for anything, "what becomes of this moment?"

Taking the charm and laying it on the table, "now my people have the chance to come and check in with me. I don't normally keep such distance. I think I'm worrying them."

"How do you know you can trust them? Most leaders I met were afraid of their people."

"The same way I ask them to trust me. We have all joined under the same banner. With a word? I change their world. They have spent a lifetime learning the Protocol. There is only one thing we can do at this juncture. We have to trust each other."

"I understand."

Turning she pulled the chair next to her out and worked through a series of hand gestures. Lowering her hands she placed them on the table and looked over at Yuri, "they know what they need to know."

I must learn another language, "which is?"

"That there is a time limit, you're off limits, and that I'm having a low QoL day."

"QoL?"

"Quality of Life." Taking a sip of water she looked past him, "and here comes my first supplicant."

"What do I do?"

"Stay friendly if you can."

Easiest thing I have been asked all day. "Can do."

6.2.0 - 12:09

'Lion of Restraint' Parked @ 207 Journey's End

●Frank Sevilan

Casting a glance over at Sasha from the passenger seat he contemplated the signals in her body language. Intoning the question with his practiced paramilitary timbre, "you have something you want to discuss Dagger Herb?"

Twitching with a visible sting of frustration showing, "no. Sasha does though."

Relaxing his timbre he took a breath to clear his head, "what's going on?"

"Is it going to be, good, if I'm the third, second, *second,* person in her bed? With her being the first, I don't know if that works as a way to explain it."

The day is nearing for my girls. "You're going to be her Consort?"

"It, it's on the table now. It appears that Yuri will be the other person in the equation. Offered the place of Sire of the children. Her children, not mine, I don't think."

The upside down day. "Well for one, you would have to leave the Scouts."

Nodding with a firm conviction, "I can live with that. We are all told it does not lost forever, one way, or another."

Speaking as the paternal presence, "for two, you would have to accept the idea you could be happy."

Intoning the agreement with less conviction, "I *think* I can live with that."

Always check the corners and closets, "is there more?"

"It's daunting. I feel like if I was her Consort, I should do something along the lines of bringing forth an heir with one of her brothers with the aid of science."

Well that's no small declaration. "I don't have words of recommendation on that one."

Gazing at her hands her voice spoke the fear with the plan to fix it, "it would be an answer to give her family more heirs."

The worry of the Budget of Bachman hits even you. It's not a stupid plan. "Problem. It would be against the rules if you *did it for her.* The Guild would catch your devotion and take you aside to try to help you stomach the idea that you could just be a loving partner and parent to the heir she would bring."

Turning her attention to him, "and the stories of the myriad of rules the Bachman family breaks in the wake of wanting to serve our world better?"

Reaching out he took her hand to quell the moment, "you could pull it off if you got her permission and help with the Polite Fiction that you would be writing. Or if there is something I don't know, and it's an honest feeling."

Laying her other hand on his, "is that along the lines of the gravity of the Polite Fiction you helped her with the night her father died?"

Don't ask what you don't want to know girl, "I did help with Polite Fiction that night. The door closed. We repainted the door."

Pausing with a daunted intonation, "no one seems to care it was Polite Fiction."

The price we pay to put one foot in front of the other foot. "They care more for the future, they agree to pay prices for that future. Even if they smell the paint they know they should just nod and smile. Walk away."

Dropping the subject she retracted her hands with a renewed focus, "if I wanted to help her like that, we'd just need to paint the door that I would walk through?"

How to word this?

Meeting her gaze he tried to be reassuring, "yes. If you said that you were doing it for her? That's your life, changed, and a life made not for the glory of being alive, but from fear. If you *wanted* to be a mother, next to her, belly to belly, they would see that if that was on your heart. A solution born of *becoming*. The problem is that it would have to be Steven, as Patrick? I know for a rusted fact they're set on getting him married."

Nodding with understanding she intoned the practiced words, "address the logistics of the plan, the paths to victory, and the costs to get there."

If it applies, it applies, "Basic Training applies again."

Folding her hands in her lap she appeared in better spirits, "I will examine my idea in better light and get back to you."

"Good."

"I also, won't ask about that night again. I just, I just wondered if I was seeing something where there was nothing or if I was just feeling smart about something I didn't understand."

"There *is* something that was left unsaid. You did see the truth of it. No evidence, but there is a truth left unsaid. Best to leave it alone."

"I will."

Taking a moment to discretely check for seepage he caught Sasha looking at him.

Throwing the question with an unabashed concern, "what is it?"

I won't lie to my children, "when we finish here I need to go back to Samantha and get my dressings changed."

Flaring with a deeper concern, "your *dressings?*"

Hearing the verge of a gruff whine in his voice with his frown, "I'm wounded."

With a distraught glance, "are you still functional?"

Trying to laugh it off, "I'm fit for light duty. No combat."

With the concern evident in her tone, "did you tell Susan?"

Losing his attempt at humor, "no."

"Did you tell the Commander?"

Nodding once he spoke with his Captain's Voice, "he's been advised. He respects my wishes to remain on duty."

"Frank?"

Softening he sighed gently, "yes?"

"Is she, Susan, really as strong as she seems?"

I can hope. "She might be. You know how she gets when she has an ad lib."

Speaking with a smile an unrestrained adoration, "they make her strong. Her convictions toward a plan, no matter how strange it seems to us, she comes crashing over the finish line with everything tied together."

The simple truth. "She is Bachman, the ties that bind our world together are her birthright."

Fidgeting for a moment her question carried a lilt of confusion, "what happened to the other eighteen men and women on her Honor Guard?"

Sighing he spoke the word with a grim intonation, "reassigned."

"What is she doing with them?"

What isn't *she stretching her ranks thin doing?* Smiling he tried to work through the Objective Checklist he had seen on the subject, "between the Honor Guard and her other assets? Protecting Wallman, Guarding the Cultural Center filled with VIPs with the aid of the Night Terrors, finding the last evidence of Ridolfi tongue kissing the Green Zone fence. Also, placing a surveil on Jerome Hope, another surveil on Dennis, one for Patrick too. Are they spread thin? Yes. Will they see relief? Only when this is settled. But, this is what they signed on for."

"This has to get better."

It will, and that's what gives me strength. "She'll turn it around. This is the third on the Worst Turns in my life. When she rallies? It will be the Best Rebound I've ever seen. This will be the beginning of her looking in the mirror and seeing another person, another light, that she needs to protect."

"What else is pending?"

"You mention bringing forth an heir, will you accept it when she's with child?"

Asking with a tentative squeak, "is she -?"

"No. Not to my knowledge. I was just checking in with you on the subject."

Painting the picture with a bold courage, "when that day comes? I'll move her to the outside of the bed, closer to the door, so she can run to the bathroom at oh two hundred."

I miss even that. "It gets better."

Quieting down, "I know you know."

"Live, no matter how hard it is."

"I will Frank." Taking a moment to steady herself, "is this really what it is?"

Something that we shouldn't have had to do, but here we are? "A rescue Op to save her sister? Yes."

"I know far more about her than I should."

Get away from those thoughts. "*Should,* only by the definition of those who sought to keep a secret. You know about her because Susan needed you to know." Shifting to a sound of relief with every word, "my good girls watch out for each other."

"We were kept safe and guided by a wonderful father."

Smiling with a humbled humor he turned his attention to the ping on the dash tablet, "update, they're en-route, should be here soon enough. When they get here, not a word about me being injured."

"Understood."

6.1.8 - 12:00

The Feedbag – 'Bad Vantage' Table

☼ Yuri

Dipping his last round of fried parsnip into the small cup of dipping sauce he paused and looked at the young child next to him. *His parents waited in line for this moment and now he's sitting here while they give their words of encouragement and condolence to Susan.* Seeing the discrete gesture and the hand under the table he met the boy's eyes for a moment before making his choice.

Setting his bite down on the edge of the dipping sauce bowl he set to wiping his fingertips off on his napkin. Reaching down low he held his hand out to the young boy, "hello. My name is Yuri."

Nodding twice with a somewhat practiced measure, the boy took his hand, "I am Feagan."

Letting go he spoke softly, "it has been, something else."

With a slight tremble he spoke softly with a courage in his spirit, "a kid I know at school, his dad was at Central. He's still alive. They told me you helped. So, thank you."

Nodding once with the solemnness he felt settling on him, "noted."

Visibly relaxing, "how far into the Silverback's Lessons are you?"

I wish I knew. Playing the moment for a laugh, "I'm not sure how to answer that."

Looking down he spoke shyly, "I retract the question."

Sitting in quiet awe of the moment he followed the motions of the Darwins as they finished hugging Susan before moving to collect their son. Feeling a poke on his arm he looked to see Feagan prompting for a hug.

Why not? Leaning in he hugged the boy and was rewarded with a firm squeeze before he let go and was moved away by his parents. Looking back to Susan he caught her sighing.

Is something wrong? "What is it?"

Intoning her words with a solemnness echoing his own, "Exceptions to Terms. I heard what he said."

I am relieved. "That simple?"

Letting the moment go with a casual dismissal, "that simple."

What is the lesson? "Did you want him to not do it?"

Gesturing to his orphaned bite, "I wanted people to not overwhelm you, I had to

644

set a fence around the idea."

Picking the bite up he set to finishing it as he listened.

"The fence had a Zero level weight to it, no one was going to get hurt if they did nothing wrong."

Mulling it over he cleared his mouth with a long sip of water. Setting his glass down he stated his lesson learned, "you told him to not do it, but there would be no punishment if he did."

"Correct." Taking a sip of water she set gestured for 'follow-up,' "the idea lends weight to the hearts of people. He was told not to, he did regardless, and when the door was opened he acted on the strength of his convictions to thank you. Sometimes people are told not to do something because it would be easier, but if they want to take the risk? It's there for them."

Does this also apply? "Example, when your Medic stepped over your bubble line?"

Nodding with a pleased smile, "Zero, again. I just wanted some space. He needed to report."

Wait, "why did he say to punish him later?"

"It's the polite way of saying you know that you're overstepping."

"Ah, understood." Mulling it over he found a question, "what is a level one punishment?"

"Rank One for Social Interaction Punishments? Removal from the moment. He would have been asked to leave you alone, refusal would have prompted him to be moved by his parents, in this case, back to his seat."

"If a person is going along and they need to go places but they don't want to talk to people?"

Answering swiftly with an understanding of duress to her tone, "they would set their presence using their comm to Rank One Avoidance. If you are having a terrible day but still have to get your groceries from the Depot? You set to Rank One and they'll serve you without a word."

Might as well learn more while I am here, "I noticed that the staff here are all wearing masks."

Assuming her 'Show and Tell' demeanor fully, "it's to keep their faces softened. With the masks, they can frown, they can be sad right now, because the masks can stand in for their faces. If you smile? The world smiles with you. If you frown? People wonder. This way the smiles keep going even if they are unable. As soon as one masks up? They all do. They work as a team."

"Then no one knows which one is actually not feeling well."

"Exactly."

"Do they have a Codex, *Primer*, on that too?"

Nodding with a smile, "yes. They have a access point with a larger screen in the back room. They can go to it as a reference document and guide when they have questions."

"Who makes the masks?"

Answering the question with a simple answer, "the mask maker who made the masks."

Ask a simple question, get a simple answer. "That is a profession?"

"It is a Craft, and then they would be purchased on the Open Exchange. Depending on which land you're in is which kind of mask you can expect to have made. Also that determines the level of use of the masks."

"Who started the tradition?"

With an appreciation he could hear clearly, "those of the Carnap lands. They all wear masks outside, at all times, which all match. From that first moment of meeting our Masked Tribe? Our forbearers took the lessons from their tradition and found the part of it that worked for each of us and brought it our homes. It was as this for most of the major traditions."

"Thus, thirteen sets of traditions?"

"Yes."

"So which is Bachman?"

"Corporate Technocrat. The Arcology we hailed from embraced technology and developed a good portion of the tech that is used for social interaction in our day to day lives. Our family keeps those close who keep the Network functioning."

"Is Amar-, she going to be happy and hale?"

Smiling at his recovery, "I'm being kept up to date. She is still currently sleeping. Jerome can hear her breathing through the microphone on her tablet."

Speaking the conclusion, "the reason we have the time we do."

"Is because she's asleep. I'll let her sleep and then we'll be there."

Hearing the slow shuffle behind him, "I believe we have more people approaching."

"We do. Last supplicants. We'll visit with them, quickly, and then we'll go."

"Understood."

6.2.1 - 12:20

207 Journey's End

☀ Yuri

Pulling the car over in front of the house he wasn't surprised to see that Sevilan and Sasha were there already. Looking past them at the vehicle they had arrived in he shook his head in wonder.

The malice their craftsmen can put into their creations is staggering. An odd juxtaposition after that meal we just shared. Her people came, sat with her and offered her words of encouragement. They did not complain, they did not cry, they told her the kinds of things you would expect to hear from a friend on a bad day.

They offered her succor for her troubled heart in remembering that it would be the Blue Sky again. I learned and have confirmed the greatest thing. The Blue Sky.

The gentleness she exchanged with her people was staggering after everything I've seen. And all it took was taking the bubble from her hair. I will find that Primer next and get to understand it. Even though from the looks of it the men wear armbands as the women wear hair ties. I'll have to ask Susan about it. Or just look for an armband primer. Getting out of The Beast he nodded to the two of them. "And we meet again."

Sevilan nodded briskly, "good to see you." Giving a nod to Susan, "duty is our calling, we meet because we have work to do. You have the combination?"

"I do. Let's get this door open."

Closing the driver's door he stepped toward them and managed to find a place to fall into formation with them. Slowing as they reached the front porch he paused for a moment watching the outer door open without a problem. Smiling at the thought that Steven left the door unlocked when he left, *well that's convenient.* Walking through the torn up house he found himself marveling at the ruthless efficiency someone had used in taking the place apart. *I wonder what they thought they were looking for.*

And that is a hell of a door. "I'm not sure anyone would have been able to knock that door down without taking the wall too."

Sevilan appraised the door quietly, "I would have to agree with you. That's not a normal door." Nodding to Susan, "you do the combination and then we'll go in first."

Sasha nodded in agreement, "there's no telling what's on the other side of that door. We'll go in, review the scene, and then let you know if it's safe."

"I appreciate the sentiment but the only reason you two get to go first is because it goes against Operational Procedure for me to go into the unknown. I don't have Dominion over this." Keying the combination while looking at her comm she smiled when the lock audibly disengaged. Stepping back and gesturing for them to go on ahead, "good luck."

6.2.3 - 12:23

207 Journey's End - Interior

⁙..Susan Bachman

No one told me to bring Medical. She doesn't need Medical.
I can hope she forgives my failure in vigilance.

Hearing the softly spoken mumble from behind her she turned to see Steven waving her toward the kitchen. Nodding she signaled the 'affirmative' before turning to Yuri. Touching his arm gently she nodded toward the kitchen and whispered to him, "I'll return shortly."

Waiting for his silent nod she stepped into the kitchen and into the arms of Steven's hug.

No signal. Moving with him around the corner she felt the odd comfort of his apparent humor.

Opening with the casual humor she was feeling, "hi, you said you were going to wait outside."

Without losing his brotherly grin, "something signaled for my attention, I couldn't wait *and* also make sure I saw you."

Squeezing him gently, "Elaborate and Details? I'm listening."

Tilting his chin up his smiled betrayed only a slight shy embarrassment, "I have *already* bought Josh something nice to let him know there is nothing left for us to settle. Your people made sure he doesn't know that I asked for his head. *If* someone else does? You have a way of showing everything with Josh is fine."

We can add it to the pile of unsaid notions, "the things we have refrained from telling people."

"Indeed. Further? I *do* want to speak with Sasha, but *not* about what she thinks it is. I want to make sure I can welcome her into the family. I have a few questions, but nothing fatal. I *don't think.* Unless she has murder on her mind for me?"

Why would he ask that? "Not to my knowledge."

Nodding quickly with a big grin, "as for Amaranth? I never *dis*liked her. I too had to play a *very* careful gambit when it came to helping her. If *you* saw it? Then *he* would have seen it. *That* is why you do not know that I care for her as I do. I had to hide it from him. I was *never* against her, but I *need* you to know. I can have Stanley send you the details."

That is more like the brother I used to know. "That is heartening to know. Also, you know how much I love details. Do it."

"I will." Touching her shoulder with a familial softness to the gesture, "are you taking her home?"

"I am, *if* she'll come with me."

Withdrawing his hand with his words, "I understand."

"You don't like it."

Rolling his eyes with a sarcastic frown, "of course not, it puts both of you together. I would prefer to keep her safer than you'd let me keep you. The upside is that you're not going to let another one of our enemies touch her again. Which is why," resuming his smile, "I'm not going to file anything against it. This is your moment and I will not challenge your Dominion."

"Understood." Stopping she hugged him again, "I appreciate it."

Speaking with a warm conviction she had not heard from him in too long, "I am not your *Master*. I am the Commander of *your* forces. Those who are loyal to you. I am your brother. I am your family. Never forget that I answer *to* you."

Feeling his embrace reaffirm she broached the words carefully, "say the rest."

"Sis, if you don't feel well for any reason –"

"I will seek aid." Stepping back she left her left hand on his bicep, "Yuri doesn't trigger Echoes of Abuse. I don't find myself diminished by him, his presence, or his closeness. When I embrace him, I don't feel *less.*" Meeting his gaze, "is that what you needed to know?"

Without looking away he set to touching her hand gently, "yes."

Noting the happiness in the wake of the words, "I'm happy to hear myself speak those words."

"Good."

Watching his hands fall away, "do you need to go?"

Placing his thumbs into his duty coat pockets, "I do. I cannot be here. There is no place for me in *this* moment."

I have to seek assurances, "will you leave the rest of those who had no part of this alone?"

"For you?" Brushing the idea off with a single chuckle, "I will trust in the skills of your people."

"Be good brother."

Stepping away from her with a strangely slow and forced speed, "I will endeavor to be myself."

Speaking the blessing with love, "may the Winds of Provence always favor you."

Stopping at the rear exit of the house he looked back to her with a somber air to him as his tone rang with praise, "to you as well."

Watching him leave she leaned against the wall as the unexpected nature of the moment left her lightened. *That went well.*

650

6.2.2 - 12:22

207 Journey's End – Hidden Bedroom

† Sasha Herb

It's kind of dark in here. Rolling the low light LED sphere into the room she smiled as the chamber was illuminated with a comforting glow.

What is that smell?

Sniffing again she felt a queasy feeling at the exotic scent in the air. *That's not aromatherapy. That's a Musk. Looking around the corner of the room she spotted the aroma dispenser on a high shelf. Smells like Passion Play.*

Thanks Badger.

Moving fully around the corner into the sparsely furnished room she took note of the figure laying on her right side in the bed, the light from the charger the tablet was sitting on, and the sound of the Sleepers Noise Generator.

Moving closer she watched the breathing of the sleeper to confirm a Sleeper's Cadence. *That looks like Amaranth.*

I need to mitigate the trauma if I can.

Signaling to Sevilan she smiled at his face of humored annoyance as he held his hand out to her. Taking her rifle off she passed it to him. Nodding she moved toward the far side of the bed and had a seat at the edge of the bed.

She's been through enough. Removing her right glove and moving her goggles up she took a moment to compose herself. Reaching out she touched Amaranth on the cheek as gently as she could.

The questioning noise which came from her half-awake form left Sasha still smiling. *And now to finish waking her gently.* Running her outstretched finger over her cheek she was rewarded with words.

With a slow cadence of forced composure, "you're not Arlo."

"You don't sound worried."

"You're not Kunlow, and I'm still alive. Why should I be worried?" Giggling for a moment she looked up at her, "Dagger Herb, what do I –" losing the moment she weakly pounced on her with a muffled cry.

Running her bare hand into Amaranth's hair and trying to be soothing she waited a moment before trying words, "we're here."

Nodding she relaxed a moment before moving to Sasha's leg. Resting her head just behind the knee she sighed, "I'm here. Present. Accounted for."

This poor girl. Cradling the back of her head she nodded once, "I have only insufficient questions."

"Not going to use the Mission Checklist?"

The sad truth, "one was not written by those of us present."

Asking quickly with the voice of conspiracy, "who is, *us?*"

Keeping it simple, "myself, Cloak Sevilan, and Miss Bachman. She's out in the living room."

With a wide eyed shock, "she's *here?*"

I thought they told you. "I was under the impression you had been informed."

Hugging her leg she giggled, "I was, but I didn't grasp it."

Setting her hand down next to her face on her leg she smiled with encouragement, "no small amount of people worked very hard to get you back."

Taking her hand with a pixie grin she giggled, "I don't know what to feel." Looking past them, "the light is calm though."

"It's a Guild Approved Darkness Illumination Sphere. Engineered to not hurt the eyes but to provide enough illumination of a soft spectrum to get the job done. I used that and not the Dagger Brightness Bomb."

Nodding with a calming state she looked over at Frank, "Captain Sevilan?"

Nodding at her, "yes Miss Dinclair?"

Pulling the blanket over her head she asked with enough volume to be heard, "do you have questions?"

Moving to the edge of the bed his voice took on his paternal air, "confirmation of length of captivity?"

"Five days. The tablet kept me from losing track of time or days."

"Physical state?"

"I do not need, require, or would be served by having Medical check me."

"Thank you for the officious responses."

"I learned from," stopping short she pulled the blanket down and looked up to her with a questioning look.

Speaking to her questioning look, "your father?"

Closing her eyes she spoke the confession, "yes."

Petting her hair gently again, "Complications?"

"My clothes are in that locked cabinet over there. I had access to a shower stall and a Necessarium."

Chiming in Frank was supportive, "noted. Sasha will get the cabinet open and we'll get your things."

"Noted." Piping up with hope, "could you go get Susan?"

Speaking the acknowledgment with his military timbre, "on it."

Looking back up at her Amaranth's thankful timbre was clear, "I got the presents."

I thought we had figured out a bypass for the cameras. "I did my best to not be seen."

Reassuring her with a voice of condolence, "there are extra cameras."

Wait a rusted moment, "then he knew the whole time."

"He asked me if I liked the things you dropped off. He knew, the whole time."

Shoved into an emotional wall she hung her head at the gravity of the moment, "I don't have words for you."

Rising up she hugged her, "I was given strength. I did *nothing* he wanted, I gave him *nothing.* I did my best to keep my faith."

Putting the foot in front of the other foot internally she soldiered on, "you don't have to worry about him now."

Clutching at her the shameful hope was clear, "he was caught?"

"It's how we have the combination."

Pressing her with a tremble, "he will no longer exist?"

"From what I understand? He'll be compost before the week is out."

"I approve." Lowering herself she trembled again, "I shouldn't, should I?"

"Grief is a scary force. As is the mind. If you tell yourself you're not a good person for approving, then you advocate for him being alive. If you tell yourself you're not a good person for wanting him dead? That doesn't take into account that this isn't your call. Someone *else* is making the call. You are not the one who makes the call, just the one who has to feel the emotions in the wake of being here to feel them."

Hugging her with a heartfelt relief, "thank you. I approve."

"Noted." Touching her shoulder gently, "did Arlo cross any lines we don't know about?"

"He did not cross the line you fear the most. He did cross a line though. He left me different clothes to dress myself. The changing screen over there is what I stayed behind when I surrendered my clothes. I had to change into something."

"Do you need to share something?"

"I know what question you want answered. Failed Expression of Supportive and Loving Husband with Devoted Wife. Obsession with Forced Compatibility."

I feel a little ill. "Do you feel damaged?"

"A little. Don't call The Guild yet."

Not my call. "I won't be the one to make that call."

"Thank you."

"Noted."

I think I hear Susan. She can fix this, the power of miracles will be seen one more time.

6.2.4 - 12:26

207 Journey's End - Interior

:.:..Susan Bachman

Standing in the doorway to the kitchen with a distracting reminder from her nose that Arlo had not done the dishes before he left, she moved into the living room to escape the smell.

Cocking his head with his quiet question Yuri appeared supportive, "what did he want?"

"More than I imagined. He wanted to give me Dominion and clear up the questions I had."

Posing the question with an attempt at jovial conversation, "good visit?"

Nodding with a smile, "good visit."

Standing in silence with Yuri she heard the sound of Frank coming back as Yuri spoke the heralding words, "I hear Frank coming."

Turning to the doorway she watched Frank stop. "It's a short hallway. High Consul, you are requested. This is your moment now."

Time to be strong. "SitRep?"

With a brisk professionalism, "she is not weeping, bruised, or shying away from a hug. I am ready to hope for more than I would normally."

Nodding she turned to Yuri, "she doesn't know you yet. Wait here."

"I can do that."

Following Frank into the darkness she rolled her small pocket LED light into her hand to help illuminate her way. Stepping into the room proper she kept it pointed at the floor as her eyes adjusted to the glow from the sphere on the floor. "Amaranth?"

Waving a hand from the other side of Sasha, her quiet voice, fighting with giggles, spoke, "hello Miss Bachman."

She sounds well enough I am going to cry. "Mea culpa."

Letting out a short, sad, and oddly soft noise her words came out, "I accept it, I *do*, please don't shoulder me like that though. Please don't ask me to take the debt with it."

Trying to keep the tears from starting, "can I shoulder you at all?"

With a loud sniffle, "I have no one else I would want to hear that from."

"I should have –"

Rising from the bed with an alacrity she wasn't expecting Amaranth threw herself onto her. Reeling from the collision she wrapped her arms around her and held her tightly.

Adjusting her grip she became aware of how perfumed the moment was. *These are not her smells.*

Roaring to life, "*I said,*" pausing before her voice resumed with less volume, "I said, I said I accepted it. *No* more. I beg you."

Petting her hair firmly, "I'm taking you home, to my home."

Clutching her with a forceful hug, "I will go with you."

"Thank you."

Asking as the conspirator, "answer me this though, were you the one with the lower jaw face covering at my party?"

I can finally tell her. "I was. Guards Kipper and Holden were the goblin and ghost respectively."

"You were there, but you didn't disobey Protocol."

Adding with a smile of triumph, "also I did not reveal myself to you, so I was obeying his wishes."

Without letting go of her, "I am pleased to meet you finally."

"Likewise." Looking down her backside she felt an embarrassed flare of revelation, "where are your usual clothes?"

Speaking with a forced neutrality, "in the locked cabinet over there."

Turning her attention to Sasha, "get it open."

Replying with a nod of her head she moved quickly to the cabinet. Turning her gaze away from Sasha she touched the top of Amaranth's head gently, "you can change soon. Use the pillow cases as bags."

"I can do that."

"We can talk more when we get home."

Giggling with a joyful timbre, "I am certain I'll like that."

Watching her startle at the sudden sound of the lock giving way and the cabinet opening she hugged her once more, "we'll go now."

Stepping back she accepted the light blanket from the bed from Frank. Wrapping herself up she hid the outfit that appeared tailor made for her but nothing like what she had ever seen her in.

I don't know what to say.

Giggling at her from under the blanket, "awkward."

The combination of stranger and sibling, and she's dressed like a lover. Agreeing wholeheartedly, "yes."

Waving her off as she moved to the cabinet, "I will be out in a minute!"

Nodding to Sasha and Frank she gestured for the 'tactical retreat.' "I don't have words."

Giggling again, "I don't either! We can discuss it later!"

"We can even try to make sure the conversation is healthy by Guild Standards. I'll be down the hall."

Moving briskly down the hall she felt a lightness in her chest that she didn't want to let go of. Stepping into the light of the house proper she turned off her LED light with a chuckle, "awkward."

Echoing her Sasha sighed with a humored lilt, "awkward."

Shaking his head as he moved past them Frank seemed less humored, "the fear of any father."

Looking between the three of them with an 'at a loss' grin Yuri gestured something she was not sure of the exact meaning of, "what happened?"

"Yuri," taking a breath she settled herself against the needless anger, "Arlo, dressed her in Lover's Attire. I don't know where he found it in her size. Odds are he had it custom made. I am not going to question further. Not today at least."

Asking with a quizzical horror, "did he make her his –"

Jumping in with a friendly rush Sasha spoke, "not that we can tell. She says that it was not what happened. I'm more than happy to accept that outcome."

Shaking his head sadly Frank spoke with a gruff candor, "her words to Sasha were that Arlo was a Failed Expression of Supportive. He would have wanted her to change her heart for him. He would have to wait so he could have his *victory* over her."

"Is this a thing in these lands?"

Turning to face Yuri directly Frank seemed disappointed, "I can tell you this Yuri, men in these lands? We try to grow up *right.* Sometimes though, a man gets a bad set of ideas in his head. He questions the lessons. And in those questions? He dooms himself. We are fortunate in that Arlo's failure he ended up the most docile version of failure."

"The most docile?"

"The Failed Supportive is the most passive and docile. They don't take direct action that can be seen as charming, so even as conversation and company they are failures." Finding a place to sit, on the edge of a tall armed chair, Frank nodded once, "they are not brave, they are not charming, they aren't even smart enough to see the fallacy of their emotions, they are a broad spectrum failure."

Posing the question with an audible trepidation, "in all these notions, what would I be?"

My turn to answer. Turning to Yuri she smiled, "the Wounded Warrior, who *is* Supportive and Kind. Wounds of the heart and mind do not a failure make. It is the acceptance of a Failed Belief. If you were a Failure? You would not have passed the seven times I questioned this."

Closing his eyes for a moment with a hushed awe about him, "thank you."

"Noted."

6.2.5 - 12:33

207 Journey's End - Interior

† Sasha Herb

She makes me feel safe despite this stripe to her true colors.

Watching quietly she fidgeted a moment in the wake of the declaration she had just heard. Looking within she felt a certain sadness in her frozen tongue. *Knowing what I know from Frank I want to hold her and tell her I'm with her, no matter what.*

Watching Susan wander around the room with her typical methodical grace she felt her mind reflecting on the sight. *I will never forget the world I came back to after Guthrie. What she just said, she put Yuri to the Seven Questions and he passed. That she could see a person pass after everything? We did good.*

Trying to change her train of thought she thought over the logistics of her life. *I have to stay away from the dark place of false hindsight. The lure of the thought of having paid the price with her Guard, knowing that she would live safely after, it's tempting to wallow in.*

Hearing footfalls coming up the hall, *then I wouldn't be at her side. I wouldn't have the chance to repay her with my lifetime in exchange for having it to use on time in her world. Sometimes it's just better to be a lifetime in another's debt.*

6.2.6 - 12:35

207 Journey's End - Interior

☼ Yuri

Tilting his head gently to the side he took in the face which carried the Bachman features with the strong familial resemblance. *This is Amaranth.*

Passing a sphere back to Sasha without a word Amaranth turned to face him. *She looks at me with wonder.*

"Dobriy den. Ochen priyatno."

I have not heard even the attempt at those words in so long. Feeling the ache slam into him full force he closed his eyes with a nod, "we are in these lands, so I greet you with, good afternoon Amaranth. It is a pleasure to meet you."

"You are the Winter Wolf. Ally of my family?"

Opening his eyes he smiled as the wash of melancholy started to flow away, *be present and mindful.* "I am the Winter Wolf. I am glad that the two titles I hold, Gingerbread Son and Winter Wolf did not get smooshed together. Else I would be the Gingerbread Wolf. The most fearsome dessert of all time!"

Regarding him with a renewed wonder she giggled, "I get to meet you."

Signaling with her words Susan spoke with candor, "he has passed the Seven Questions."

Echoing the candor Sasha followed up, "he is not here to come between Susan and myself. He is not that man."

Glancing at Susan and Sasha, with a look of inquiry, Frank laughed, "my turn? He kept up, and then moved faster than me."

Moving her gaze between the three of them Amaranth giggled again, "I know who he is! I read all of the words I could find on The Network that I could. It's not as if he is a stranger. He's Yuri, the Winter Wolf, the Gingerbread Son, and the one who has been next to The Derecho since the moment she blew out of Central on a wing and a prayer. I have no doubts of his credentials." Turning to him she held out two of her three pillowcase bundles, "I do appreciate their vote of confidence in you though."

"I will carry these." Taking them he nodded with an appraisal of the weight, "no small amount of clothes. Did I hear glass clink?"

"You did. The one is the contents of the refrigerator. The other is some of my clothes. He didn't know what I would want, so he took no small amount with me." Flexing her free arm, "I'm not the weight training type, and I'm tired. Those," pointing to the pillow cases, "are heavy."

I remember feeling weak. "We will get you home and get you fed. You took the food?"

Setting her burdens down on the couch she smiled with a morose humor, "it's good food. He had top tier intel on me. I wouldn't want to waste the food."

"Noted."

Their father had an unforgettable face. I can see the softer aspects of it in her face.

"You are more handsome in person. They did not speak as favorably as they could have when they spoke of you."

The King Making. "Noted, and I accept your King Making."

"Noted." Opening her arms, "will you accept a hug?"

"I would." Moving in he moved to one knee to compensate for their height difference. Moving her in to the outside of his kneel he moved his arm around her. Holding her there he heard her sniffle as she leaned on his shoulder. *The emotive sadness of the Bachman. She has it too.*

Moving over to them Frank spoke with a soft gruffness, "my complaints about feeling old I could make aside? I wish to lay an offer of a Pledge before the two of you. If you have need of me? I would be only a comm call away." Feeling Frank's hand touch his other shoulder as he moved around them, "I have seen such *good* from you. I would welcome you to my life as a son if you would need an old man such as myself to ask for help."

I am humbled. "I am humbled, and honored, by the notion you would have me as part of your family."

"You have taken such care with my family already Yuri, it would be my honor to know we would be as family."

I have only one answer, "I Pact this Pledge."

Answering with a somber strength, "this Pledge I Pact with you." Letting out a long exhale, "as soon as you have a comm unit I'll make sure you know how to reach me."

I feel the end of my feelings of hiraeth. "Noted. Thank you."

Turning his attention Frank continued with addressing Amaranth directly, "you know me."

Appraising him with a positive tone, "you are Frank Sevilan, Ally of House Bachman, the closest thing my father had to a brother as he would not want to curse another man with that honorific."

Stopping short he smiled, "you do know me."

"The Codex states in the Primer on Family," stopping herself she smiled with a shyness, "you know that. You know that if I Pact the Pledge with you, I can have an easier time of leaving with Susan."

"Yes." Tapping her nose gently with a curled up finger, "I really would be just one comm call away though."

"Of that I have no doubt. I Pact the Pledge."

"This Pledge I Pact with you."

Susan appears to be on the verge of tears. Chiding himself as the revelation hit him, *the man needs anchors to this reality. Share the anchors, share the brace, keep the salvation mutual.*

Speaking to her back Susan offered a Pledge with her intonation, "the empty chasm between us will be gone soon enough."

Stepping away from his hug Amaranth stepped back and turned to face Susan. Getting to his feet he listened as her words tumbled out with an emotional turmoil to them.

"Ten years. I have memories of you stretching back for ten years. You could never stay near. You brought me a present when it was just me and mom out of the house, at the strangest of times in the year. You *celebrated* me." Talking with her hands she continued, "I grew up outside of your shadow, the *only* bright idea that father had in keeping us apart. Not risking me failing to grow in the shadow cast by your presence on our world. I would be me, you would be you, and I would just try so hard to understand how you would celebrate me. How could *you,* care for *me?* Your mother, she had to leave us, for my mother to know dad. I used to believe that I could only exist because of that shared pain."

Taking the offered handkerchief from Frank she continued, "I have rehearsed these lines so many times and they change each time. To not want to waste this moment on the wrong thing, or missing something." Blowing her nose with unapologetic energy to the gesture she trembled for a moment. Raising her forearm she blotted her eyes with her sleeve. "You wrote me such kind things on those cards. I went from the thing that only existed because of pain to the idea of salvation. I *forgave him,* because I didn't want to see him hurt like that anymore. He *rests.* My father *rests,* and all I can be is glad because he no longer suffers."

Moving in and taking her in her arms Susan fell to one knee with a reckless disregard for appearances. Wrapping her up she spoke firmly, "we are family now. I can take you home now. We can be *sisters,* as we have always been."

Watching the moment of shared pain he sat down on a nearby chair. *I was not ready.* Looking up through the blur of his own tears he took the offered handkerchief from Sasha. *I am still me.* Covering his eyes he took inventory of himself. *I did not lose my heart in the desert. I didn't leave it in the plane when I crash landed. I didn't leave it on the luggage rack of the boat. Have it taken from me in that dungeon in Kyoto. Or drop it in the ocean. I still have it. This still hurts.*

Lowering the handkerchief he opened his eyes to assess the moment.

With her chin raised high Amaranth spoke firmly, "you are my sister."

Moving her chin up Susan smiled back at her, "if you would have me."

Widening her eyes she bared her teeth, "don't you dare self diminish on me."

Responding with a gentle tap on the nose with a forefinger, "I forget myself sometimes."

Moving to the side of them Frank spoke with an encouraging and consoling tone, "I was there for her Amaranth, she didn't go without a father."

"I know. I am honored that you accept me."

"If I could have been in two places at once, I would have."

Looking up with wide eyes she giggled after a moment of silence, "I don't know how much more I can take."

Stepping over Sasha placed a hand on her shoulder, "as we stand together, know that I stand in this union too."

Resuming a wide eyed wonder, *"you too?* Are you going to marry Susan? Are you going to be the Consort?"

"Yes."

Looking at the scene before him with a lightening in his chest and spirit he saw his vision starting to blur again. *I can feel the tears on my left eye. And if I can feel it, I know if I blink it will escape as a teardrop.* Blinking twice Yuri felt the droplet roll down his face. *I am still me.*

Speaking with the gravel of his years Frank seemed satisfied with the moment, "we should finish this, you can get home, and get something to eat."

"What of you Sasha?"

Volunteering quickly, "I need to stay here and cleanse the scene. I'll be working with Cloak and Dagger to erase the idea that these days ever happened to this place."

"Noted. And you Frank?"

Keeping it professional, "with Sasha staying? I have to get back to Consul Kunlow. Octavia wants to tell me more about her Faith, and as I do not know it? I would like to."

"Noted."

Appearing pleased Frank moved to the side of the proceedings, "and now for the last piece of the equation." Looking toward Yuri, "do your best Yuri. You are the first man to get past everything that has kept my girls from having each other much less anyone else. Be careful, but not because I fear your character. Be careful because for them this is a new life that they can live. Do you honor the union between my girls?"

I do. Funny I would think these words to use as I feel this affirmation is no less a bonding reply. "I do."

"Will you do your best?"

"I will."

"Then good journey to you, be a good son."

Looking back to the trio of women which he had just bound himself to he spotted the motion of Amaranth offering him a handkerchief. *This is the one she used. I am sure they have a meaning for this.* Reaching out he took the fabric and cleaned up the tears which had joined the first. *I am still me. I did not forget my heart with the shell casings either. It still beats strongly in my chest.*

Speaking his name as a loving question Susan's tone carried the weight of the moment, "Yuri?"

I am still here. "Yes Susan?"

"Can you drive?"

Such a simple question after everything, "I can."

Turning her attention to Sasha, "when you are done with your toil, I will call on you Dagger Herb. I might get to call on Sasha too."

"I am as always your faithful Dagger. And your Aardvark."

"Thank you both." Walking with a slight shake to her gait toward the door, "time to go home."

Oh, good question time, "which path do I select?"

"Path three. I would like to sit in the back with Amaranth and," cursing under her breath at the soft sound of her comm chirping, "have to ignore her because my thrice forsaken comm is receiving messages."

Finding the face saving words for her, "it is something she will have to get used to in your house, you are needed."

"I know." Putting her arm around Amaranth's shoulder, "you can ride in the back with me."

Time to go home. "Let's go."

THE AFTERWORD / PARATEXT

Hi.

It's me, the Author.

If you have a moment I'm having a one sided Q/A just in case I think or thought of something that is pertinent to you. I hope this is worth the time for you.

Q: This is a Book One?
A: Yes. This is a Book One.

Q: This is the beginning of a Saga/Series/Setting then?
A: Yes. I am going to attempt to join the great writers of our time and past times in creating a place and then populating it with stories and tales to entertain you, the reader.

Q: Is there a Book Two yet?
A: It is being 'Edited' at the time of this writing.

Q: Is this a metaphor?
A: No. It is a story.

Q: Is this Allegory?
A: I tried to avoid 'hidden meanings' and create a story which would present itself at 'face value'

Q: This is entertainment then?
A: Yes. The objective is to entertain you. The depth and complexity I attempted was solely to enrich the work.

Q: Are 'The Last Spoonful' and 'Indian Runner Ducks' both real pieces of art?
A: Yes. Maggie loved ducks and I used two examples that are available right now to illustrate what the art in the home looked like. I do not know or am affiliated in any way with either painting or artists.

Q: Are you an advocate of (Insert Idea)?
A: I am only using ideas and set pieces of ideas and philosophies to tell a story of a people who are not us or a metaphor of us. This is a "Future Speculation" of an Earth after technology, tragedy, and apocalypse.

Q: What if I do not believe you and want to state that your work means something deeper and you are an advocate of it?

A: Then you will do such a thing and call me a liar. I am stating here that this is meant solely for entertainment purposes. If you wish to slay the Author then I cannot stop you from the demise of the idea of me in your own mind. You are the final say over your subjective truth. I am only giving mine.

Q: What if I really liked the work and want to write fan-fiction or create other forms of fan-work?

A: Before I say Yes, I want to point out something from Wikipedia.

Fan writers who argue that their work is legal through the fair use doctrine use specific fair use arguments in the context of fan works, such as:

1. Fan works do not deprive the owner of the source material of income
2. Fan works may work as free advertisement and promotion of the original source material
3. Fan works are usually non-profit.
4. Fan works do not copy, or attempt to substitute for, the original work.

Wikipedia contributors, "Legal issues with fan fiction," *Wikipedia, The Free Encyclopedia,* https://en.wikipedia.org/w/index.php?title=Legal_issues_with_fan_fiction&oldid=876659772 (accessed January 10, 2019).

To answer your question I would say that the above is a wonderful Guideline for making your Fan-Work. I honestly do not want to feel behooved to hunt anyone down with a Copyright Claim over this. I don't want to be the Author who intimidates a website into taking down illegal dreams and ponderances because they are offended that someone would write them.

Which means that odds are I will not be reading your fan-works.

Q: Can your advise me on how to be an Author/Writer?

A: Can you advise me? I'm still learning.

Q: What is 'Canon' ?

A: If it shows up within the published Text it is Canon. I will not be sitting on social media answering questions of Canon. I would sooner work the answers into a future story and state it there than short hand it in a missive from on high.

A Extended: Not that I couldn't talk someone's ear right off with the World Building but I don't want to do that here. Or via Social Media. I would rather address it in the text. Knowing the questions that are pending to be answered and weaving them into the story.

Q: If I am offended you wrote something?

A: Then I would advise you to sort out the nature of the offense and what it means to you. As I said, entertainment.

Q: Are the people of the Provinces "The Bad Guys?"
A: Your subjective answer is your own ParaTextual Agreement with yourself. The work changes color and meaning when the definitions such as that are applied to the work. My intention was to write 'people' who behaved remotely like 'people' and not so much 'characters.'
A Extended: If I told you this was Speculative Fiction? Alternate History of a Future People? A Christian Romance Novel? A Political Drama? Each term is a lens and check-list of criteria for what makes a work into a genre piece. You, the reader, have the unique joy and task of deciding what you just read is.

Q: Can I find you on Social Media?
A: I'll be out there. I don't know *if* you want to find me but I'll be out there. And if you do find me, hopefully, it won't be to just quote me something I missed in my editing. I edited this myself. Mistakes were made. Hopefully I found them all.

Q: Tell me a funny anecdote from the experience of writing your novel?
A: The amount of times I wanted to give up and just write Urban Fantasy/Romance/Smut instead was perhaps enough times I lost count. It felt like an 'easier road' to walk. Grass Greener / Other side sort of thing. Also the line for the morning blessing Octavia says and understanding enough of the Faith behind those moments of dialogue was four hours for the opening blessing and another bit of reading for the rest.

Q: Can you tell me about the Cover?
A: Local artist. Shelby Thomas. It's an Oil Painting and it's hanging up on my wall. The Front Cover was photographed and lettered by Lemonwing Photography (Also Local). I wanted something distinct and eye catching. And I wanted it to make sense.
The Winter Wolf, there he is. And behind him? The lush landscape of the heart of the High Consul. I explained the situation to Shelby, the characters, and I was delighted in the final creation. (I told Shelby "You are the Artist. Be inspired and create.")
The cover is not a lie. It is not a scene that did not happen. It is not representative of something that is not shown within the work. Also with the Art within the world it can be seen as an In-Universe creation for the cover of the Introduction to the place.
The Winter Wolf lost his snow and ice in a place of warmth and light and bright colors.

Q: What is it like to have created this alternate future?
A: When I wake up in the morning, the world you just read about wakes up with me. They are not so much flies trapped in amber as a rolling story from the time of William onward.
(With the occasional flashback to Elianna or Rolf and those stories)
There are scenes and plot points and understanding that goes into the tapestry of their world that I cannot cram into this one work.

Or the next one.

Thus it will be many works to show and entertain with the whole story.

Going back to the Fan-Work idea? It is my role in this to take the world I see and understand and translate it into English, place it on these pages, and entertain you with it.

When you write the Fan-Work, you get to put this stuff down when it's over. It's a set of dolls and a playset for you. It's your reaction to what you saw, your imagination ignited, and then you run off with it and see where you go. Then maybe others join in and you trade your subjective understanding of the work with each other and have fun with it.

I do not begrudge you this.

You might even write erotica. Oh noes.

I am not against erotica. I know 'Rule 34' (Not advocating it. I am just aware it exists) and I will be in a strange way validated as a presence when my work joins that which has been touched by the idea.

I have my take on what happens / happened.

I won't begrudge you yours.

You're not a thought criminal.

Just don't expect me to read it.

Q: What is your Blackheart's Motive for writing this book?

A: If you are entertained? You will give me money. If you give me your money to be entertained I can write the next one and entertain you again. And we can do this again and again as you get what you paid for and I get to make this my Calling / Vocation / Career.

I hope you will be seeing me again in the Afterword for Book Two. As I am not technically author inserted anywhere in these books. No single character is me. I can't point and snicker and say "there I am!"

Which means you only see me here. Until next time.

A Blue Sky to you! And even if the sky turns, may it turn back.

Blessings of Peace to you.

- S. M. Gilbert